American Empire: The Centre Cannot Hold

'Exciting action, well-drawn characters who draw you into their lives and joys and sorrows, a tightly logical and engrossing plot and an encyclopaedic knowledge of history that enriches the narrative without slowing it – what's not to like?' *S. M. Stirling*

American Empire: Blood and Iron

'A masterpiece . . . Sure to please and terrify.' *Sci Fi Weekly*

Harry Turtledove:

'The wizard of If' *Chicago Sun-Times*

'Harry Turtledove has established himself as a grand master of the alternative history form' *Poul Anderson*

'Turtledove [is] the standard-bearer for alternate history' *USA Today*

'Authentic speculative quality, energy and dash' *Time Out* on *A World of Difference*

'Nobody plays the what-if game of alternative history better than Turtledove' *Publishers Weekly*

About the author

Harry Turtledove is a Hugo-award-winning writer of
alternate history and science fiction. He has lived in
Southern California all his life. He has a PhD in history
from the University of California at Los Angeles and has
taught at UCLA, California State Fullerton and California
State University, Los Angeles. He is married to the novelist
Laura Frankos and they have three daughters.

AMERICAN EMPIRE:

The Centre Cannot Hold

Harry Turtledove

NEW ENGLISH LIBRARY
Hodder & Stoughton

First published in Great Britain in 2002
by Hodder and Stoughton
First published in paperback in Great Britain in 2003
by Hodder and Stoughton
A division of Hodder Headline
A New English Library paperback

A CIP catalogue record for this title is available
from the British Library

ISBN 0 340 82012 8

Typeset in Sabon by Palimpsest Book Production Limited,
Polmont, Stirlingshire
Printed and bound in Great Britain by
Mackays of Chatham plc, Chatham, Kent

Hodder and Stoughton
A division of Hodder Headline
338 Euston Road
London NW1 3BH

AMERICAN EMPIRE:

The Centre Cannot Hold

REPUBLIC OF QUÉBEC

OCCUPIED CANADA

CANADA

ONTARIO

Rivière-du-Loup

Québec ✪

Montréal

NEW BRUNSWICK

P.E.I.

NOVA SCOTIA

MAINE

WISCONSIN

MICHIGAN

VT.

N.H.

Guelph
Arthur
Berlin

Toronto

NEW YORK

Boston
MASSACHUSETTS

RHODE ISLAND
CONNECTICUT

Pontiac

Chicago

Toledo

PENNSYLVANIA

NEW JERSEY

New York City

ILLINOIS

OHIO

INDIANA

Philadelphia

Cincinnati

Ohio R.

MD

DEL.

WA

es Moines

Mississippi River

Covington

W. VA

Washington, D.C. ✪

KENTUCKY

Richmond ✪

SOURI

Nashville

VIRGINIA

ARKANSAS

TENN.

NORTH CAROLINA

AMERICA

Columbia

S.C.

St. Matthews

Atlanta

Charleston

Birmingham

Augusta

ALABAMA

MISSISSIPPI

GEORGIA

LOUISIANA

FLORIDA

Mobile

New Orleans

ATLANTIC OCEAN

N
W   E
S

Gulf of Mexico

Habana   CUBA (C.S.A.)

I

Lieutenant Colonel Abner Dowling strode into the offices of the U.S. Army General Staff in Philadelphia, escaping the January snow outside. He was a big, beefy man—unkind people, of whom he'd met altogether too many, would have called him fat—and walked with a determination that made other, younger officers get out of his way, even though his green-gray uniform bore not a trace of the gold-and-black ribbon that marked a General Staff man.

He looked around with more than a little curiosity. He hadn't been in General Staff headquarters for many years—not since before the Great War, in fact. He'd spent the past ten years as adjutant to General George Armstrong Custer, and Custer's relationship with the General Staff had always been . . . *combustible* was the first word that came to mind. The first printable word, anyhow.

But Custer was retired now—retired at last, after more than sixty years of service in the Army—and Dowling needed a new assignment. *I wonder what they'll give me. What ever it is, it's bound to be a walk in the park after what I've gone through with Custer.* Anything this side of standing sentry on the battlements of hell would have seemed a walk in the park after ten years with Custer. The man was unquestionably a hero. Dowling would have been the first to admit it. Nevertheless . . .

He tried not to think of Custer, which was like trying

1

not to think of a red fish. Then he got lost—General Staff headquarters had expanded a great deal since his last visit. Having to ask his way did take his mind off his former superior. At last, by turning left down a corridor where he had turned right, he made his way to the office of General Hunter Liggett, chief of the General Staff.

Liggett's adjutant was a sharp-looking lieutenant colonel named John Abell. When Dowling walked into the office, the fellow was talking on the telephone: "—the best we can, with the budget the Socialists are willing to let us have." He looked up and put his hand over the mouthpiece. "Yes, Lieutenant Colonel? May I help you?"

"I'm Abner Dowling. I have a ten o'clock appointment with General Liggett." By the clock on the wall, it was still a couple of minutes before ten. Dowling had built in time for things to go wrong. *Custer never did anything like that. Custer never figured anything would go wrong.* Dowling shook his head. *Don't think about Custer.*

Lieutenant Colonel Abell nodded. "Go right in. He's expecting you." He returned to his interrupted telephone conversation: "I know what we should be doing, and I know what we are doing. There will be trouble one day, but they're too sure of themselves to believe it."

However much Dowling wanted to linger and eavesdrop, he went on into General Liggett's inner office and closed the door behind him. Saluting, he said, "Reporting as ordered, sir."

Hunter Liggett returned the salute. He was a jowly man in his mid-sixties, with a penetrating stare and a white Kaiser Bill mustache waxed to pointed perfection. "At ease, Lieutenant Colonel. Sit down. Make yourself comfortable."

"Thank you, sir." Dowling eased his bulk down into a chair.

"What are we going to do with you?" Liggett said. It had to be a rhetorical question; the answer surely already lay there on his desk. He went on, "You've seen a lot these past few years, haven't you? By now, I suspect, you could handle just about anything. Couldn't you, Lieutenant Colonel?"

Dowling didn't like the sound of that. "I hope so, sir,"

he answered cautiously. Maybe he wouldn't get a walk in the park after all. "Ahh . . . What have you got in mind?"

"Everyone is very pleased with your performance in Canada," General Liggett said. "The assistant secretary of war, Mr. Thomas, spoke highly of you in his report to President Sinclair. He wrote that you did your best to make a difficult and unpleasant situation go more smoothly. Any time a soldier wins praise from the present administration, he must have done very well indeed."

"Thank you, sir." Dowling remembered that Liggett had become chief of the General Staff during the present Socialist administration, replacing General Leonard Wood. That made him watch his tongue. "I'm glad Mr. Thomas was pleased. I didn't really do that much. Mostly, I just sat there and kept my mouth shut." N. Mattoon Thomas had come up to Winnipeg to force General Custer into retirement. Custer hadn't wanted to go; Custer never wanted to do anything anyone told him to do, and he thoroughly despised the Socialists. But they'd held the high cards, and he hadn't.

"Well, whatever you did say, Mr. Thomas liked it," Liggett said. "He wrote of your tact and your discretion and your good sense—said if you were a diplomat instead of a soldier, you'd make a splendid ambassador." Liggett chuckled. "Damn me to hell if you're not blushing."

"I'm flattered, sir." Dowling was also embarrassed. Like a lot of fat men, he flushed easily, and he knew it.

General Liggett went on, "And it just so happens that we have a post where a man with such talents would be very useful, very useful indeed."

"Does it? Do you?" Dowling said, and Liggett gave him a genial nod. Dowling had a fair notion of where such a post might be. Hoping he was wrong, he asked, "What have you got in mind, sir?"

Sure enough, Liggett said, "I've had to relieve Colonel Sorenson as military governor of Salt Lake City. He's an able officer, Sorenson is; don't get me wrong. But he turned out to be a little too . . . unbending for the position. By President Sinclair's orders, we are *trying* to bring Utah back towards being a normal state in the Union once more. A tactful, diplomatic officer running things in Salt Lake could do us a lot of good there."

"I . . . see," Dowling said slowly. "The only trouble is, sir, I'm not sure I think Utah *ought* to be a normal state in the Union once more." The Mormons in Utah had caused trouble during the Second Mexican War, back at the start of the 1880s—as a result of which, the U.S. Army had landed on them with both feet. Then, in 1915, perhaps aided and abetted by the Confederates and the British from Canada, they'd risen in open rebellion. The Army had had to crush them one town at a time, and had made a peace only in the Tacitean sense of the word, leaving desert behind it.

"Between you and me and the four walls of my office, Lieutenant Colonel, I'm not sure I think so, either," Liggett answered. "But the Army doesn't make policy. That's the president's job. All we do is carry it out. And so . . . would you like to be the next military governor of Salt Lake City?"

Maybe I should have been a nasty son of a bitch when I was working for Custer, Dowling thought. But he said what he had to say: "Yes, sir." After a moment, he added, "If I'm being diplomatic . . ."

"Yes?" Liggett asked.

"Well, sir, wouldn't you say the good people of Salt Lake City might see it as an insult to them if a full colonel were replaced by a lieutenant colonel?" Dowling said. "Couldn't it lead them to believe the United States Army finds them less important than it once did?"

Amusement glinted in Liggett's eyes. "And how do you propose to make sure the good people of Salt Lake City— if there are any—don't find themselves insulted?"

"I can think of a couple of ways, sir," Dowling replied. "One would be to appoint somebody who's already a bird colonel as military governor there."

"Yes, that stands to reason," Liggett agreed. "And the other?" He leaned back in his swivel chair, which squeaked. He seemed to be enjoying himself, waiting to hear what Dowling would say.

Dowling had hoped the chief of the General Staff

would come out and say it for him. When Liggett didn't, he had to speak for himself: "The other way, sir, would be to promote me to the appropriate rank."

"And you think you deserve such a promotion, eh?" Liggett rumbled.

"Yes, sir," Dowling said boldly. *After ten years with Custer, I deserve to be a major general, by God.* And if he said no, he knew he'd never be promoted again.

General Liggett shuffled through papers on his desk. Finding the one he wanted, he shoved it, face down, across the polished expanse of mahogany to Dowling. "This may be of some interest to you, then."

"Thank you," Dowling said, wondering if he ought to thank Liggett. He turned the paper over, glanced at it—and stared at his superior. "Thank you very much, sir!" he exclaimed.

"You're welcome, Colonel Dowling," Liggett replied. "Congratulations!"

"Thank you very much," Dowling repeated. "Uh, sir . . . Would you have given me this if I hadn't asked for it?"

Liggett's smile was as mysterious as the Mona Lisa's, though a good deal less benign. "You'll never know, will you?" His chuckle was not a pleasant sound. He found another sheet of paper, and passed it to Dowling, too. "Here are your orders, Colonel. Your train goes out of Broad Street Station tomorrow morning. I'm sure you'll do a fine job, and I know for a fact that General Pershing is looking forward to having you under his command."

"*Do* you?" All of a sudden, Dowling's world seemed less rosy. During the war, Pershing's Second Army had fought side by side with Custer's First in Kentucky and Tennessee. The two armies had been rivals, as neighbors often are, and their two commanders had been rivals, too. Custer was suspicious of his younger colleague, as he was suspicious of any other officer who might steal his glory. Dowling had forgotten Pershing was military governor of Utah these days.

"I think I know what's bothering you, Colonel," Liggett said. If anyone knew about rivalries, the chief of

5

the General Staff would be the man. He went on, "You don't have to worry, not on that score. I meant what I said: General Pershing is eager to have you."

But what will he do with me—to me—once he's got me? Dowling wondered. He couldn't say that. All he could say was, "That's good to hear, sir."

"Which means you don't believe me," Liggett said. "Well, that's your privilege. You may even be right. I don't think you are, but you may be."

Dowling was by nature a pessimist. If he hadn't been before, ten years under General Custer would have made him one. "I'll do the best I can, sir, that's all," he said. *And what ever Pershing does to me, by God, I'll have eagles on my shoulder straps. That makes up for a lot.*

General Liggett nodded. "As long as you do that, no one can ask any more of you."

"All right, sir." Dowling started to rise, then checked himself. "May I ask you one more thing, sir? It's got nothing to do with Mormons."

"Go ahead and ask," Liggett told him. "I don't promise to answer, not till I've heard the question."

"I understand. What I want to know is, are we really cutting back on building new and better barrels? I've heard that, but it strikes me as foolish." Like most professional soldiers, Dowling had no use for the Socialist Party. There as in few other places, he agreed with the man under whom he'd served for so long. He would have expressed himself a lot more strongly had he been talking with General Leonard Wood, a lifelong Democrat and a friend of ex–President Theodore Roosevelt.

But Liggett nodded again, and didn't sound happy as he answered, "We aren't just cutting back, as a matter of fact. We're gutting the program. No money in the budget any more. That outfit at Fort Leavenworth called the Barrel Works . . ." He slashed a thumb across his throat. "As our German friends would say, *kaputt.*"

"That's—unfortunate, sir." Dowling used the politest word he could. "Barrels won us the last war. They won't count less in the next one."

"Don't be silly, Colonel. There'll never, ever be another

6

war. Just ask President Sinclair." *He's still a soldier first, then,* Dowling thought. *Good.* Both men laughed. But for the bitter undertone in each one's voice, the joke might have been funny.

Anne Colleton was studying the *Wall Street Journal* when the telephone rang. She muttered something under her breath, put down the five-day-old newspaper, and went to answer the phone. Back in the days when she'd lived on the Marshlands plantation, her butler, Scipio, or one of the other Negro servants would have done that for her and spared her the interruption. These days, though, the Marshlands mansion was a burnt-out ruin, the cotton fields around it going back to grass and bushes. Anne lived in town, not that St. Matthews, South Carolina, was much of a town.

"This is Anne Colleton," she said crisply. She was in her mid-thirties. With her sleek blond good looks, she could have lied ten years off her age with no one the wiser—till she spoke. Few people younger than she—few her own age, for that matter, but even fewer younger—could have so quickly made plain they put up with no nonsense at all.

"And a good day to you, Miss Colleton," replied the man on the other end of the line. By the hisses and pops accompanying his voice, he was calling from some distance away. He went on, "My name is Edward C.L. Wiggins, ma'am, and I'm in Richmond."

Long distance, sure enough, Anne thought—he sounded as if he were shouting down a rain barrel. "What is it, Mr. Wiggins?" she said. "I don't think we've met."

"No, ma'am, I haven't had the pleasure," he agreed, "but the Colleton name is famous all over the Confederate States."

He doubtless meant that as pleasant flattery. Anne Colleton had heard enough pleasant flattery to last the rest of her life by the time she was sixteen—one consequence of her looks men seldom thought about. "You can come to the point, Mr. Wiggins," she said pleasantly, "or I'll hang up on you no matter where you are."

"Once upon a time, President Semmes sent me up to Philadelphia to see if I could dicker a peace with the Yankees, but they wouldn't do it," Wiggins said.

That wasn't coming to the point, or Anne didn't think it was, but it did get her attention. "This would have been fairly early on, before we finally had to quit?" she asked.

"That's right, ma'am," he said.

"I heard rumors about that," she said. "With all the money I gave the Whigs in those days, I would have thought I deserved to hear something more than rumors, but evidently not. So you were representing President Semmes, were you?"

"Yes, ma'am, in an unofficial sort of way."

"And whose representative are you now, in an unofficial sort of way? I'm sure you're somebody's."

Edward C.L. Wiggins chuckled. "I heard you were one clever lady. I guess I heard right."

"Who told you so?" Anne asked sharply.

"Well, now, I was just getting to that. I—"

Anne did hang up then. She wasted not a minute getting back to work. With her finances in the state they were, they needed all the time she could give them. They needed more than that, too: they needed something close to a miracle. She wasn't a pauper, as so many prewar planters were these days. But she wasn't rich enough not to have to worry, either, and she didn't know if she ever would be.

A few minutes later, the phone rang again. Anne picked it up. "Why, Mr. Wiggins. What a pleasant surprise," she said before whoever was on the other end of the line could speak. If it wasn't Wiggins, she would have to apologize to someone, but she thought the odds were good enough to take the chance.

And it was. "Miss Colleton, if you would let me explain myself—"

She cut him off, though she didn't—quite—hang up on him once more. "I gave you two chances to do that. You didn't. If you think I'm in the habit of wasting my time on strange men who call me out of the blue, you're mistaken—and whoever told you what you think you know

8

about me hasn't got the faintest notion of what he's talking about."

"Oh, I don't know." Wiggins' voice was dry. "He told me you were sharp as a tack but a first-class bitch, and that doesn't seem so far out to me."

"I'm sure he meant it as an insult, but I'll take it for a compliment," Anne said. "Last chance, Mr. Wiggins—who told you that?"

"Jake Featherston."

Anne had expected almost any other name than that of the Freedom Party leader. Something she didn't want to call alarm shot through her. She took Jake Featherston very seriously. That didn't mean she wanted anything to do with him. She'd backed him for a while, yes, but she backed winners, and he didn't look like one any more. Trying to gain time to recover her composure, she asked, "If you used to work for the Whigs, why are you calling me for Featherston now?"

"On account of what I saw when I went to Philadelphia, ma'am," he replied. "The United States don't respect you when you're weak. If you're down, they'll kick you. But if you're strong, they have got to sit up and take notice. That's a fact."

"I agree with that. I think everyone in the Confederate States agrees with that," Anne said.

"Well, there you are," Wiggins said cheerily. "If you agree with that, the Freedom Party is really and truly the only place for you, because—"

"Nonsense." Anne didn't care about his reasons. She had reasons of her own: "The Freedom Party has about as much chance of electing the next president as I do of getting elected myself. I have no intention of giving Jake Featherston one more dime. Ever since that madman of a Grady Calkins murdered President Hampton, it'd take a special miracle for anyone from the Freedom Party to get himself elected dog catcher, let alone anything more. I don't spend my money where it does me no good."

"I don't think the clouds are as black as you say, ma'am," Wiggins replied. "Yes, we lost a couple of seats in the election last November, but not as many as people said we would. We'll be back—you wait and see if we aren't. Folks don't have much in the way of memory—and besides, ma'am, we're *right*."

"If you can't win an election, whether you're right or not doesn't matter," Anne pointed out.

"We will." Wiggins sounded confident. She got the idea he sounded confident all the time. He went on, "I want to say a couple of other things, and then I'm through. First one is, Mr. Featherston, he knows who's for him, and he knows who's against him, and he never, ever, forgets the one or the other."

He was, without question, right about that. Featherston was as relentless as a barrel smashing through one line of trenches after another. Anne didn't intimidate easily, but Jake Featherston had done the job. That just gave her more reason to harden her voice and say, "I'll take my chances."

Edward C.L. Wiggins chuckled. "He told me you were near as stubborn as he is himself, and I see he's right. One more thing, and then I'm through, and I won't trouble you any more."

"Go ahead," Anne said. "Make it short." *I've already wasted more than enough time on you.*

"Yes, ma'am. Here's what I've got to say: there's only one party in the CSA that's got any notion at all about what the devil to do about the nigger problem in this country, and that's the Freedom Party. And now I'm done. Good-bye." He surprised her by hanging up.

Slowly, she put the mouthpiece back on its hook and set down the telephone. She said a word she was unlikely to use in public, one that would have made strong men gasp and women of delicate sensibilities blush and faint. Wiggins had known how to get through to her, after all. No one was likely to forget the Red Negro uprising that had tied the Confederacy in knots late in 1915 and early in 1916. No one knew how much it had helped the USA win the war, but it couldn't have hurt. The Freedom Party stood foursquare for vengeance, and so did Anne Colleton.

And why not? she thought. *One brother dead, my plantation wrecked, me almost murdered . . . Oh, yes, I owe those black bastards just a little. The whole country owes them just a little, whether the Whigs and the Radical Liberals want to admit it or not.*

She repeated that word, louder this time. Behind her, her surviving brother burst out laughing. She whirled around. "Confound it, Tom," she said angrily, "I didn't know you were there."

Tom Colleton laughed harder than ever. "I'll bet you didn't," he answered. "If you had, you would have said something like, 'Confound it,' instead." He was a couple of years younger than Anne, and a little darker, with hair light brown rather than gold. He'd gone into the war an irresponsible boy and come out of it a lieutenant-colonel and a man, something of which Anne still had to remind herself now and again.

She shrugged now. "I probably would have. But I meant what I did say."

"Who was on the telephone?" he asked.

"A man named Edward C.L. Wiggins," Anne replied. "He wanted money from us for the Freedom Party."

Tom frowned. "Those people don't take no for an answer, do they?"

"They never have," Anne said. "It's their greatest strength—and their greatest weakness."

"Did you find out why he travels with a herd of initials?" her brother asked. She shook her head. Tom went on, "What did you tell him?"

"No, of course," Anne answered. "The way things are now, I'd sooner cozy up to a cottonmouth than to Jake Featherston."

"Don't blame you a bit," Tom Colleton said. "He's an impressive man in a lot of ways, but. . . ." He shook his head. "He puts me in mind of a time bomb, wound up and waiting to go off. And when he does, I don't think it'll be pretty."

"There were times when I thought he had all the answers," Anne said. "And there were times when I thought he was a little bit crazy. And there were times when I thought both those things at once. Those were the ones that scared me."

11

"Scared me, too," Tom agreed, "and we don't scare easy."

"No. We'd be dead by now if we did," Anne said, and Tom nodded. She eyed him. "And speaking of looking pretty, you're fancier than you need to be for staying around here. Is that a necktie?" She thought its gaudy stripes of crimson and gold excessive, but declined to criticize.

Her brother nodded again. "Sure is. Bought it from what's-his-name, the Jew tailor. And I'm going to pay a call on Bertha Talmadge in a little while."

Before the war, Anne would have discouraged such a call—with a bludgeon, if necessary. The Muncies, Bertha's parents, were grocers, and their daughter no fit match for a planter's son. These days . . . Well, grocers never starved. And Bertha Talmadge, though a widow whose husband, like so many others, had died in the trenches, was reasonably young, reasonably pretty, reasonably bright.

Anne nodded approval. "Have a nice time. You should find yourself a wife, settle down, have yourself some children."

He didn't get angry at her, as he would have before the war. In fact, he nodded again himself. "You're right. I should. And, as a matter of fact, so should you."

"That's different," Anne said quickly.

"How?"

Because he was her brother, she told him: "Because my husband would want to try to run everything, because that's what men do. And odds are he wouldn't be as good at it as I am. That's why."

"And even if he was, you wouldn't admit it," Tom said.

That was also true. Anne Colleton, however, had not the slightest intention of admitting it. Giving her brother her most enigmatic smile, she went back to the *Wall Street Journal*.

Mary McGregor was only thirteen years old, but her course in life was already set. So she told herself, anyhow, and also told her mother and her older sister as they sat down

12

to supper on their farm outside Rosenfeld, Manitoba: "The Yankees killed my brother. They killed my father, too. But I'm going to get even—you see if I don't."

Fright showed on her mother's careworn face. Maude McGregor touched the sleeve of her woolen blouse to show Mary she still wore mourning black. "You be careful," she said. "If anything happened to you after Alexander and Arthur, I don't think I could bear it."

She didn't tell Mary not to pursue vengeance against the Americans occupying Canada. Plainly, she knew better. That would have been telling the sun not to rise, the snow not to fall. Ever since the Americans arrested her older brother during the war on a charge of sabotage, lined him up against a wall, and shot him, she'd hated them with an altogether unchildlike ferocity.

"Of course I'll be careful," she said now, as if she were the adult and her mother the worried, fussy child. "Pa was careful. He just . . . wasn't lucky at the end. He should have got that . . . blamed General Custer." However much she hated Americans, she wasn't allowed to curse at the supper table.

Her older sister nodded. "Who would have thought Custer would be waiting for Father to throw that bomb and ready to throw it back?" Julia said. "That *was* bad luck, nothing else but." She sighed. She hadn't only lost her father. Arthur McGregor's failure had also cost her an engagement; the Culligans had decided it just wasn't safe to join their son, Ted, to a bomber's family.

"Part of it was," their mother said. "Mary, would you please pass the butter?" Mayhem and manners lived together under the McGregors' roof.

"Here you are, Ma," Mary said, and her mother buttered her mashed potatoes. Mary went on, "What do you mean, part of it was bad luck? It *all* was!"

Her mother shook her head. "No, only part. The Americans suspected your father. They came sniffing around here all the time, remember. If they hadn't suspected, Custer wouldn't have been ready to . . . to do what he did."

What he'd done by throwing the bomb back had blown

13

Arthur McGregor to red rags; the family could have buried him in a jam tin. No one still alive wanted to think about that. "I'll be careful," Mary said again. She brushed a wisp of auburn hair back from her face in a gesture her mother might have made. Maude McGregor had reddish hair, too. Julia was darker, as her father had been.

Maude McGregor said, "I just thank God you're only thirteen, and not likely to get into too much mischief for a while. You know the Yankees will keep an eye on us forever, on account of what the menfolks in our family did."

"Alexander never did anything!" Mary said hotly.

"They thought he did, and that was all that mattered to them," her mother answered. "Your father never would have done any of the things *he* did if that hadn't happened—and we'd all be here together." She stared down at the heavy white earthenware plate in front of her.

"I'm sorry, Mother." Seeing her mother unhappy could still tear Mary to pieces inside. But she wasted little time amending that: "I'm sorry I made you unhappy." She wasn't sorry she wanted revenge on the Americans. Nothing could make her sorry about that.

"We've been through too much. I don't want us to have to go through any more," her mother said. Maude McGregor quickly brought her napkin up to her face. Pretending to wipe her mouth, she dabbed at her eyes instead. She tried not to let her children catch her crying. Sometimes, try as she would, she failed.

Mary said, "Canada's been through too much. There isn't even a Canada any more. That's what the Americans say, anyhow. If they say it loud enough and often enough, lots of people will start believing it. But I won't."

"I won't, either," Julia said. "I quit the schools when they started teaching American lies. But you're right—plenty of people are still going, and plenty of them will believe what ever they hear. What can we do about it?"

"We've got to do something!" Mary exclaimed, though she didn't know what.

Her mother got up from the table. "What ever we do, we won't do it now. What we will do now is wash the dishes and get ready for bed. We'll have a lot of work tomorrow, and it's not any easier because. . . ." She shook her head. "It's not any easier, that's all."

It's not any easier because we haven't got any menfolk left alive to help us. That was what she'd started to say, that or something like it. And things would only get harder when winter of 1924 turned to spring and they would have to try to put a crop in the ground by themselves. Like any farm daughter, Mary had worked since she could stand on her own two feet. The idea didn't worry her. Having to do men's work as well as women's . . . How could the three of them manage without wearing down to nubs?

She didn't know that, either. She only knew they had to try. *My father kept trying, and he made the Yankees pay. I will, too, somehow.*

Julia washed dishes and silverware and scrubbed pots till her hands turned red. Mary dried things and put them away. Yesterday, they'd done it the other way round. Tomorrow, they would again.

After the last plate went where it belonged, Mary took a candle upstairs. She used it to light the kerosene lamp in her room. The Americans had started talking about bringing electricity out from the towns to the countryside, but all they'd done so far was talk. *More lies,* she thought.

She changed out of her shirtwaist and sweater and skirt into a long wool flannel nightgown. With thick wool blankets and a down comforter on the bed, she didn't fear even a Manitoba winter—and if that wasn't courage, what was? Before she lay down, she knelt beside the bed and prayed.

"And keep Mother safe and healthy, and keep Julia safe and healthy, and help me pay the Americans back," she whispered, as she did every night. "Please, God. I know You can do it if You try." God *could* do anything. She believed that with all her heart. Getting Him to do it— that was a different, and harder, business.

When Mary's head did hit the pillow, she fell asleep as if clubbed. She woke the next morning in exactly the same position as when she'd gone to sleep. Maybe she'd shifted back into it during the night. Maybe she hadn't had the energy to roll over.

Once she crawled out of bed, the aromas of tea and frying eggs and potatoes floating up to the bedroom from the kitchen helped get her moving. She put on the same skirt and sweater with a different shirtwaist and hurried downstairs. "Good," her mother said when she made her appearance. "Another five minutes and I'd've sent Julia after you. Here you are." She used a spatula to lift a couple of eggs from the skillet and set them on Mary's plate. Potatoes fried in lard went alongside them.

"Thanks, Ma." Mary put salt on the eggs and potatoes and pepper on the eggs. She ate like a wolf. Her mother gave her a thick china mug full of tea. Mary poured in milk from a pitcher and added a couple of spoonsful of sugar. She drank the tea as hot as she could bear it.

Julia was already on her second cup. "How do the Americans stand drinking coffee all the time?" she wondered aloud. "It's so nasty."

"It's disgusting," Mary said. She honestly believed she would have thought that even if the Yankees hadn't done what they'd done. She'd tried coffee a couple of times, and found it astonishingly bitter.

To her surprise, her mother said, "Coffee's not so bad. Oh, I like tea better, but coffee's not so bad. It'll pry your eyes open even better than tea will, and that's nice of a morning."

Hearing Maude McGregor defending something Mary thought of as American and therefore automatically corrupt rocked her. She didn't quarrel, though; she had no time to quarrel. As soon as she finished breakfast, she put on rubbers and an overcoat that had belonged to Alexander. It was much too big for her, even though she'd nearly matched her mother's height, but that didn't matter. Along with earmuffs and mittens, it would keep her warm while she did the chores.

"I'm going out to the barn," she said. Her older sister shut the door behind her.

Instead of heading straight to the barn, Mary paused at the outhouse first. It didn't stink the way it did in warmer weather, but she would almost rather have sat down on a pincushion than on those cold planks. She got out of there as fast as she could.

Several motorcars were coming up the road from the U.S. border toward Rosenfeld. The snow that scrunched under Mary's rubbers sprayed up from their tires. They were all painted green-gray, which marked them as U.S. Army machines. *I hope something horrible happens to you,* Mary thought. But the motorcars cared nothing for her curses. They just kept rolling north.

The railroad line ran to the west of the farm. Coal smoke spewing from the stack, a train rumbled past. The shriek of the whistle, far off in the distance, seemed the loneliest sound in the world. The train was probably full of Yankees, too. More and more these days, the Yankees were tying the Canadian railroads to their own.

"Damn them," Mary mouthed, and went into the barn. It was warmer there; the body heat of the horse and the cow and the sheep and the pigs and, she supposed, even the chickens helped keep it that way. And the work she had to do certainly kept her warm. She gathered eggs and fed the animals and shoveled manure that would go on the fields and the vegetable plots when warmer weather came again.

As she worked, she looked around. Somewhere in here, her father had made the bombs that did the Americans so much harm before one of them killed him. U.S. soldiers had torn the farmhouse and the barn to pieces, looking for his tools and fuses and explosives. They hadn't found them.

Of course they didn't find them, Mary thought. *My father was cleverer than a hundred Yankees put together. He just . . . wasn't lucky with General Custer, that's all.*

She picked up the basket of eggs, which she'd set on an old broken wagon wheel that had been sitting in the barn as long as she could remember— and probably a lot longer than that. She sighed. She didn't want to go back out into the cold, even to take the eggs back to the farmhouse. Idly, she wondered why her father had never repaired and used the wheel—either that or got a few cents for the iron on the tire and the hub. He hadn't been a man to waste much.

17

If I had the tools, if I knew how, would I make bombs and keep fighting the Americans? Mary nodded without a moment's hesitation, despite the thought that followed hard on the heels of the other: *if they caught you, they'd shoot you.* More than most children her age, she knew and understood how very permanent death was. Losing Alexander and her father had agonizingly driven home that lesson.

"I don't care," she said, as if someone had said she did. "It would be worth it. We have to hit back. We *have* to." *One of these days, I'll learn how. It won't take so long, either. I promise it won't, Father.* She picked up the basket of eggs from the old wagon wheel and, however little she wanted to, went back out into winter.

Flags flying, horns blaring, rails decked in bunting of red, white, and blue, the USS *O'Brien* came into Cork harbor. The Irish had laid on a spectacular welcome for the destroyer with the fortunately Hibernian name, with fireboats shooting streams of water high into the air. On the shore, a brass band in fancy green uniforms blared away. Schoolchildren had the day off. Some of them waved American flags, others the orange, white, and green banner of the Republic of Ireland—which, with U.S. help, had finally gained control over the whole island.

From his station at the forward four-inch gun, Ensign Sam Carsten grinned at the celebration. He'd seen the like before, in Dublin. He was a tall, muscular, very blond man who burned whenever the sun came out, no matter how feebly. A cloudy day in Irish late winter suited him down to the ground. He didn't have to worry about smearing zinc-oxide ointment and other things that didn't work onto his poor, abused hide, not for a while he didn't.

He turned to the petty officer who was his number two at the gun. "They wouldn't have been so friendly if we'd come in while the limeys were still running this place, eh, Hirskowitz?"

"You're right about that, sir." Nathan Hirskowitz was a dour Jew from New York City, as dark as Carsten was fair. He had swarthy skin, brown eyes, and a blue-black stubble he had to shave twice a day.

18

Getting called *sir* still bemused Carsten. He was a mustang, up through the ranks; he'd spent going on twenty years working his way up from ordinary seaman. If the officer in charge of the gun he'd served on an aeroplane carrier hadn't encouraged him, he didn't think he would ever have had the nerve to take the qualifying examination. He wished he were still aboard the *Remembrance*; naval aviation fascinated him, even if he was a gunnery man first. But the carrier hadn't had any slots for a new-minted ensign, and so. . . .

"Matter of fact, they'd've tried to blow our heads off," Sam said. Hirskowitz nodded. Carsten scanned the harbor. Lots of fishing boats, some merchant steamers, a couple of old U.S. destroyers now flying the Irish flag, and . . . He stiffened, then pointed. "We've got company. Nobody told me we were going to have company."

Hirskowitz let out a disdainful sniff. "You think they're going to tell you things you need to know just because you need to know them?"

The *S135* was a German destroyer, a little smaller than the *O'Brien*, mounting three guns rather than four. The German naval ensign fluttered from her stern: a busy banner, with the black Hohenzollern eagle in a white circle at the center of a black cross on a white field. In the canton, where the stars went on an American flag, was a small version of the German national banner: a black Maltese cross on horizontal stripes of black, white, and red. As the *O'Brien* edged toward a quay, the *S135* dipped her flag in salute. A moment later, the American ship returned the compliment.

"You see? They're allies," Nathan Hirskowitz said.

In a different tone of voice, that would have sounded light, cheery, optimistic—all words noticeably not suited to the petty officer's temper. As things were, Hirskowitz packed a world of doubt and menace into four words.

"Yeah." Carsten did his best to match him in one. Without a doubt, the United States and the German Empire were the two strongest nations in the world these days. What was in doubt was which of them was stronger. Officially, everything remained as it had been when they joined together to put Britain and France and the CSA in the shade. Unofficially . . .

"If our boys go drinking and their boys go drinking, there's liable to be trouble," Carsten said.

"Probably." Hirskowitz sounded as if he looked forward to it. After making a fist and looking at it in surprise—what was such a thing doing on the end of his arm?—he went on, "If there is trouble, they'll be sorry for it."

"Yeah," Sam Carsten said again. For one thing, the *O'Brien* had a bigger crew than the German destroyer. For another, winning the Great War had made him certain the USA could win any fight. He shook his head in bemusement. That was certainly a new attitude for an American to take. After losing the War of Secession and getting humiliated in the Second Mexican War, Americans had come to have a lot of self-doubt in their character. *Amazing what victory can do,* he thought.

He peered toward the *S135*. By the polished way the sailors over there went about their business, they'd never heard of self-doubt. And why should they have? Under Bismarck and under Kaiser Bill, Germany had gone from triumph to triumph. Victories over Denmark and Austria and France let her unite as a single kingdom. And victory in the Great War left her a colossus bestriding Europe in almost the same way the USA bestrode North America.

Sailors aboard the *O'Brien* threw lines to waiting longshoremen, who made the destroyer fast to the quay. "Welcome!" one of the longshoremen called in a musical brogue. "I'll be glad to buy some of you boys a pint of Guinness, that I will."

"What's Guinness?" Hirskowitz asked Carsten.

"It's what they make in Ireland instead of beer," Sam said helpfully. "It's black as fuel oil, and almost as thick. Tastes kind of burnt till you get used to it. After that, it's not so bad."

"Oh." Hirskowitz weighed that. "Well, I'll see. They make real beer, too?"

"Some. And whiskey. Got some good whiskey the last couple of times I was here."

"When was that, sir?"

"Once during the war," Carsten answered. "We were running guns to the micks to help 'em give the limeys hell. They paid us back in booze." He smacked his lips at the memory. "And then again in *Remembrance* afterwards, when we were helping the Republic put down the limeys and their pals up in the north."

The captain of the *O'Brien*, an improbably young lieutenant commander named Marsden, assembled the crew on the foredeck and said, "I'm pleased to grant you men liberty—this is a friendly port, and everybody has gone out of his way to make sure we're welcome. I know you'll want to drink a little and have a good time."

Sailors nudged one another and grinned. Somebody behind Sam said, "Skipper's all right, ain't he?" Carsten frowned. He knew boys would be boys, too, but that didn't mean an officer was supposed to encourage them. He wouldn't have done that as a petty officer, and he wouldn't do it now.

But then Marsden stiffened and seemed to grow taller. His voice went hard as armor plate as he continued, "Having a good time doesn't mean brawling. It especially doesn't mean brawling with the Kaiser's sailors. We're on the same side, us and the Germans. Anybody who's stupid enough to quarrel with them will have the book thrown at him, and that's a promise. Everybody understand?"

"Yes, sir!" the sailors chorused.

"What do you say, then?"

"Aye aye, sir!"

"Good." Lieutenant Commander Marsden's smile showed sharp teeth. "Because you'd better. Dismissed!"

Sam Carsten didn't get to go into Cork for a couple of days. He was less than impressed when he did. It wasn't a very big city, and it was grimy with coal smoke. And he almost got killed the first two or three times he tried to cross the street. Like their former English overlords, the Irish drove on the wrong side of the road. Looking right didn't help if a wagon was bearing down on you from the left.

Before long, Carsten discovered he'd given Nathan

Hirskowitz at least half a bum steer. Along with the swarms of GUINNESS IS GOOD FOR YOU! signs, pubs hereabouts also extolled the virtues of a local stout called Murphy's. Sam strolled into one and, in the spirit of experiment, ordered a pint of the local stuff. He'd changed a little money, but the tapman shoved his sixpence back across the bar at him. "You're one o' them Yanks," he said. "Your money's no good here."

"Thanks very much," Carsten said.

"My pleasure, sir, that it is." The fellow left a little more than an inch of creamy head on the pint, and drew a shamrock in the thick froth with the drippings from the tap. Catching Sam's eye on him, he smiled sheepishly. "Just showing off a bit." Sam smiled back; he'd seen the same stunt and heard the same line in Dublin. Every tapman in the country probably used it on strangers. This one slid Sam the glass. "Enjoy it, now."

"I bet I will." Carsten took a sip. The tapman waited expectantly. Sam smiled and said, "That's mighty good." But in truth, he couldn't have told Murphy's from Guinness to save his life.

A couple of American sailors came in not long after he did. He nodded to them. They sat down well away from him—he was an officer, after all, even if he sometimes had trouble remembering it—and ordered drinks of their own. Then a couple of more sailors came in. An Irishman stuck his nose in the door, saw all the blue uniforms, and decided to do his drinking somewhere else.

Carsten raised his finger to order another Murphy's. The tapman was pouring it for him when half a dozen more sailors walked into the pub. They too wore navy blue uniforms, but theirs were of a different cut, and their hats struck Sam's eye as odd. They were off the *S135*, not the *O'Brien*.

They eyed the Americans already there with the same wariness those Americans were showing them. Sam didn't know German rank markings any too well, but one grizzled German sure had the look of a senior petty officer. The man spoke English, of a sort: "Friends, *ja*?"

"Yes, friends," Carsten said, before any of the

O'Brien's men could say anything like, *No, not friends*.

"*Gut, gut,*" the German said. "England, *Frankreich*—" He shook his head. "No, France . . ." He made it sound more like a man's name—Franz—than a country's, but Carsten nodded to show he got it. "England, France—so." The squarehead made a thumbs-down gesture that might have come from a Roman amphitheater.

All the Americans got that. "Yeah," one of the sailors said. "To hell with England and France, and the horse they rode in on."

The German plainly didn't know about the horse they rode in on, but the smiles from the Americans encouraged his pals and him to come in and order beers for themselves. Sam noticed the tapman took their money, where he hadn't for any of the Americans. If the Germans noticed that, too, it might cause trouble.

Picking up his pint of Murphy's, he went over and sat down by the German who knew a little English. "Hello," he said.

"Good day, sir," the veteran said. He didn't come to ramrod attention, the way he would have for one of his own officers—the Germans were devils for discipline, even by the tough standards of the U.S. Navy—but he wasn't far from it. One of his own officers probably wouldn't have deigned to talk with him at all.

"We should stay friends, your country and mine, eh?" Sam said.

"*Jawohl, mein Herr!*" the petty officer said. He translated that for his pals. They all nodded. Sam got out a pack of cigarettes. He offered them to the Germans. The tobacco was as good as prewar, imported from the CSA. All the Germans took a cigarette or two except one man who apologetically showed him a clay pipe to explain why he didn't. "*Danke,*" the petty officer said. "Thank you."

"You're welcome." Carsten raised his mug. "Let's stay friends."

Again, the petty officer translated. Again, his men solemnly nodded. They all drank with Sam. A couple of the Americans came over. One spoke a little German, about as much as the petty officer spoke English. A couple of hours passed in a friendly enough way—especially since the tapman had the sense to stop charging the Germans. But Sam knew he would have to draft a report when he got back to the *O'Brien*. He suspected the German petty officer would be doing the same thing on the *S135*.

Friends? he thought. *Well, maybe.* He eyed the capable-looking German sailors. The fellow with the clay pipe sent up a cloud of smoke. *Maybe friends, yeah. But rivals? Oh, you bet. Rivals for sure.*

Winter, spring, summer, fall—they didn't matter much in the Sloss Works. It could be snowing outside—not that it snowed very often in Birmingham, Alabama—but it would still be hell on earth on the pouring floor in the steel mill.

Jefferson Pinkard shook his head. Sweat ran down his face. It was hot as hell in here, no doubt about that. But he'd seen hell on earth fighting the Red Negro rebels in Georgia, and again, worse, fighting the damnyankees in the trenches in west Texas. You could hurt yourself—you could kill yourself—right here, but nobody was trying to do it for you.

When the shift-change whistle screamed—a sound that pierced the din of the mill like an armor-tipped shell plowing through shoddy concrete—he nodded to his partner and to the men who'd come to take his crew's place. "'Night, Fred. 'Night, Calvin. 'Night, Luke. See y'all tomorrow."

He clocked out by himself. Once upon a time, he'd worked side by side with his best friend and next-door neighbor, Bedford Cunningham. But Bedford had got conscripted before he did, and had come back to Birmingham without most of his right arm. Pinkard had stayed at the Sloss Works a while longer, working side by side with black men till he got conscripted, too.

But after he'd put on butternut . . . After he'd put on butternut, Emily had got lonely. She'd been used to getting it regular from him, and she wanted to keep getting it regular regardless of whether he was there or not. He'd come home on leave one night to find her on her knees in

24

front of Bedford Cunningham, neither of them wearing any more than they'd been born with.

Pinkard growled, deep in his throat. "Stinking tramp," he muttered. "It was the war, it was the goddamn war, nothin' else but." Even after he'd come back when the fighting stopped, their marriage hadn't survived. Now he lived in the yellow-painted cottage—company housing— all by himself. It was none too clean these days—nothing like the way it had looked when Emily took care of things— but he didn't care. He had only himself to please, and he wasn't what anybody would call a tough audience.

He headed back toward the cottage, part of the stream of big, weary men in overalls and dungarees heading home. He walked by himself, as he always did these days. Another, similar, stream was coming in: the swing shift. It had a few more blacks mixed in than the outgoing day shift, but only a few. Blacks had taken a lot of better jobs during the war; now whites had almost all of them back.

"Hey, Jeff!" One of the whites waved to him. "Freedom!"

"Freedom!" Pinkard echoed. "When you gonna get your ass to another Party meeting, Travis?"

"I be go to hell if I know," the other steel worker answered. "When they take me off swing, I reckon, but God only knows when that is. Remember me to the boys tonight, will you?"

"Sure will," Pinkard said. "That's a promise." He walked on. When he got to the cottage, he lit a kerosene lamp (there was talk about putting electricity into the company housing, but so far it was nothing but talk), got a fire going in the coal-burning stove, and took a ham out of the icebox. He cut off a big slice and fried it in lard, then did up some potatoes in the same iron frying pan. The beer in the icebox was homebrew—Alabama had been formally dry since before the war—but it washed down supper as well as anything storebought could have.

He put the plate and the frying pan in the sink, atop a teetering mountain of dirty dishes. One day soon he'd have to wash them, because he was running out of clean ones. "Not tonight, Josephine," he muttered; he'd started talking to himself now that he was the only one in the house. "I got important things to do tonight, by God."

He scraped stubble from his chin with a straight razor, splashed on water, and then shed his overalls and work shirt for a clean white shirt and a pair of butternut wool trousers. He wished he had time to shine his shoes, but a glance at the wind-up alarm clock ticking on his nightstand told him he didn't, not if he wanted to get to the meeting on time. And there was nothing in the world he wanted more.

The trolley stopped at the edge of the company housing. Looking back over his shoulder, Jeff saw the mills throwing sparks into the night sky, almost as if it were the Fourth of July. A couple of other men came up to wait for the trolley. They too wore white shirts and khaki trousers. "Freedom!" Jefferson Pinkard said.

"Freedom!" they echoed.

Jeff sighed. Back in the days before Grady Calkins had shot down President Hampton when he came to Birmingham, a lot more men would have come to Party meetings. The Freedom Party had looked like the wave of the future then. Now . . . Only the dedicated, the men who really saw something wrong with the CSA and saw that Jake Featherston knew how to fix it, went to Freedom Party meetings these days. And even now . . . "Where's Virgil?" Jeff asked.

Both other men shrugged. "Don't rightly know," one of them said. "He was at the foundry, so I don't reckon he's feelin' poorly."

Bell clanging, the trolley came up. Jeff was glad to climb aboard and drop five cents in the fare box so he wouldn't have to think about what Virgil's absence might mean. He was also glad to pay a fare measured in cents and not in thousands or millions of dollars. After the war, inflation had ripped the guts out of the Confederate States. Its easing had hurt the Freedom Party, too, but that was one bargain Pinkard was willing to make.

Several more men in white shirts and butternut trousers got on the trolley at its next few stops. Jeff liked the uniform look they had. It reminded him of the days when he and a lot of others who were now Freedom Party members had worn Confederate butternut together. They'd been fighting for something important then, just as they were now. They'd lost then. *This time, by Jesus, we won't!*

The Freedom Party men all got out at the same stop. Not far away stood the old livery stable where the Party met in Birmingham. As a livery stable, the place was a failure, with motorcars and trucks driving more horses off the road every year. As a meeting hall, it was . . . *Tolerable,* Jeff thought.

But he was smiling as he went inside. This was where he belonged. Emily was gone. She was gone, at least in part, because the Freedom Party had come to mean so much to him. Whatever the reason, though, she *was* gone. The Party remained. This *was* such family as he had left.

Party members crowded the floor. The hay bales on which men had once sat weren't there any more. Folding chairs replaced them. Their odor, though, and that of horses, still lingered in the building. The smells had probably soaked into the pine boards of the wall.

Jeff found a seat near the rostrum at the front. He shook hands with several men sitting close by. "Freedom!" they said. Pinkard had to be careful to whom he used the Party greeting at the Sloss Works. Whigs and especially Radical Liberals had no use for it.

Caleb Briggs, the Freedom Party leader in Birmingham, ascended to the rostrum and stood behind the podium, waiting for everyone's attention. The short, scrawny dentist looked very crisp, the next thing to military, even if he'd never be handsome. Party men who'd been standing around chatting slipped into their seats like schoolboys fearing the paddle.

"Freedom!" Briggs said.

"Freedom!" the members chorused, Jefferson Pinkard's shout one among many.

"I can't hear you." Briggs might have been a preacher heating up his congregation.

"Freedom!" they shouted again, louder—but not loud enough to suit Caleb Briggs, who cupped a hand behind

27

his ear to show he still couldn't hear. *"FREEDOM!"* they roared. Pinkard's throat felt raw after that.

"Better," the leader allowed. Jeff heard him through ringing ears, almost as if after an artillery bombardment. Briggs took a sheet of paper from the breast pocket of his white shirt. "I have a couple of important announcements tonight," he said. "First one is, we'll be looking for an assault squad to hit a Whig rally Saturday afternoon." A host of hands shot into the air. Briggs grinned. "See me after the meeting. You need to know there'll be cops there, and they're taking a nastier line with us after the unfortunate incident." That was what the Party called President Hampton's assassination.

"I'll go," Pinkard muttered. "By God, I want to go." He hadn't been a brawler before he got conscripted, but he was now.

"Second thing," Briggs said briskly. "The damnyankees are backing the Popular Revolutionaries in the civil war down in the Empire of Mexico. Goddamn lickspittle Richmond government isn't doing anything about that but fussing. We need to do more. The Party's looking to raise a regiment of volunteers for the Emperor, to show the greasers how it's supposed to be done. If you're interested in *that*, see me after the meeting, too."

Jeff kept fidgeting in his seat through the rest of Briggs' presentation, and the rest of the meeting, too. Not even the patriotic songs and the ones from the trenches held his interest. He swarmed forward as soon as he got the chance. "I want to volunteer for both," he said.

"All right, Pinkard," Caleb Briggs replied. "Can't say I'm surprised." He knew about Emily. "I don't make any promises on the filibuster into the Mexican Empire, but the other . . . we'll find a way to get you over by city hall."

And they did. Pinkard worked a half day on Saturday. As soon as he got off, he hurried to the trolley and went downtown. He gathered with the other Freedom Party men at a little diner one of them owned. There he changed from his overalls into the white shirt and butternut trousers he carried in a denim duffel bag. There, too, he picked up a stout wooden bludgeon— two and a half feet of ash wood, so newly turned on the lathe it smelled of sawdust.

Along with the other Freedom Party men, he hurried up Seventh Avenue North toward the city hall. They naturally fell into column and fell into step. People scrambled off the sidewalk to get out of their way. Jeff made a horrible face at a little pickaninny. The boy wailed in fright and clung to his mother's skirts. She looked as if she might have wanted to say something, but she didn't dare. *You better not,* he thought.

In front of city hall, a Whig speaker with a megaphone was exhorting a crowd that didn't look to be paying too much attention to him. Eight or ten policemen stood around looking bored. "Outstanding!" Briggs exclaimed. "Nobody gave us away. They'd be a lot readier if they reckoned we were gonna hit 'em." His voice rose to a great roar: "Freedom!"

"Freedom!" Jefferson Pinkard bawled, along with his comrades. They charged forward, tough and disciplined as they'd been during the war. Whistles shrilling, the Birmingham policemen tried to get between them and the suddenly shouting and screaming Whigs. If the cops had opened fire, they might have done it. As things were, their billy clubs were no improvement on the Freedom Party bludgeons. Jeff got one of the men in gray in the side of the head.

Then he was in among the Whigs, yelling, "Freedom!" and "Damnyankee puppets!" at the top of his lungs. His bludgeon rose and fell, rose and fell. Sometimes he hit men, sometimes women. He wasn't fussy. Why fuss? They were all traitors, anyway. A few of them tried to fight back, but they didn't have much luck. The Whig rally smashed, their enemies bloodied, the Freedom Party men withdrew in good order. Jeff had a hard-on all the way back to the diner. *Those bastards,* he thought. *They got just what they deserved.*

Sylvia Enos wasn't used to being a celebrity. She wished people wouldn't stop her on the streets of Boston and tell her she was a hero. She didn't want to be a hero. She'd never wanted to be one. *All I wanted was to have George back again,* she thought as she hurried back toward her block of flats.

But she'd never see her husband again. George Enos had been aboard the USS *Ericsson* when the CSS *Bonefish* torpedoed her—after the Confederate States yielded to the USA. Roger Kimball, the captain of the *Bonefish*, had known the war was over, too. He'd known, but he hadn't cared. He'd sunk the destroyer that carried George and more than a hundred other sailors, and then he'd sailed away.

He'd tried to cover it up, too. No one could prove a British boat hadn't done the deed—till the *Bonefish*'s executive officer, in a political fight with Roger Kimball, broke the story in the papers to discredit him. The story said Kimball was living in Charleston, South Carolina.

And so Sylvia had taken a train down to Charleston. Customs at the border hadn't searched her luggage. Why should the Confederates have bothered? She looked like what she was: a widow in her thirties. That she also happened to be a widow in her thirties with a pistol in her suitcase had never crossed the Confederates' minds.

But she was. And when she got to Charleston and found out where Kimball lived, she'd knocked on his door and then fired several shots into him. She'd expected to spend the rest of her life in jail, or to hang, or to cook in an electric chair—she hadn't known how South Carolina disposed of murderers.

Instead, thanks to politics and thanks to an extraordinary woman named Anne Colleton, she found herself free and back in Boston. *The CSA couldn't afford to be too hard on someone who killed a war criminal,* she thought. *And why? Because the United States are stronger than they are.* That was heady as whiskey. Till the Great War, the CSA and England and France had called the tune. No more.

But, no matter how strong the United States were, they weren't strong enough to give her back her husband. The hole in her life, the hole in her family, would never heal. She had no choice but to go on from there.

30

A tall, skinny man in an expensive suit and homburg stopped in front of her, so that she either had to stop, too, or to run into him. "You're Sylvia Enos," he exclaimed. "I've been looking for you. Give me a moment of your time."

He didn't even say please. Sylvia's patience had worn thin. "Why should I?" she asked, and got ready to push past him. She reached up to fiddle with her hat. She had a hat pin with an artificial pearl at one end and a very sharp point at the other. Some men were interested in her for the sake of politics, others for other, murkier, reasons.

But this fellow proved one of the former sort. "Why? For the sake of your country, that's why." He had the map of Ireland on his face; the slightest hint of a brogue lay under his flat New England vowels.

"Look, whoever you are, I haven't got time for anything except my children, so if you'll excuse me—" She started forward. If he didn't get out of the way, maybe she'd use the hat pin whether he had designs on her person or not.

"My name is Kennedy, Mrs. Enos, Joe Kennedy," he said. "I'm the head of the Democratic Party in your ward."

No hat pin, then, except in an emergency. If she got on the wrong side of a politician, he could make life hard for her, and life was hard enough already. With a sigh, she said, "Speak your piece, then, Mr. Kennedy—though I don't know why you're bothering with me. After all, women can't vote in Massachusetts."

His answering smile was forced. The Democrats had always been less eager for women's suffrage than either the Socialists or what was left of the Republican Party. But he quickly rallied: "Do you want us weak, too weak to take our proper place in the world? If you do, the Socialist Party's the perfect place for you. They're trying to throw away everything we won in the war."

That did hit home. "What do you want from me, Mr. Kennedy? Tell me quickly, and I'll give you my answer, but I have to get home to my son and daughter."

Something glinted in his eyes. It made Sylvia half reach for the pin again. Kennedy wore a wedding ring, but Sylvia had long since seen how little that meant. Men got it where they could. George, she made herself remember, had been the same way. But all the ward leader said was, "An hour of your time at our next meeting would be very fine, to show you stand with us on the issues of the day."

He acted as if it were a small request, something where she wouldn't need to think twice before she said yes. But she shook her head. "You must be rich, to have hours you can throw around. When I'm not working, I'm cooking or minding the children. I'm sorry, but I've got no time to spare."

Kennedy's mouth tightened. He drummed the fingers of his right hand against his trouser leg. Sylvia got the feeling he wasn't used to hearing people tell him no. The vapor that steamed from his nostrils as he exhaled added to the impression. It also made him look a little like a demon.

But then, as suddenly as if he'd flipped the switch to an electric light, he gave Sylvia a bright smile. "If you like, my own wife will watch your children while you come. Rose would be glad to do it. She knows how important to the country winning the next election is."

That couldn't mean anything but, *My wife will watch your children if I tell her to.* Whatever it meant, it did put Sylvia in an awkward position. She said, "You know how to get what you want, don't you?"

"I try," Joe Kennedy said. This time, the smile he gave her had nothing to do with the automatic politician's version he'd used a moment before. This one was genuine: a little hard, a little predatory, and a little smug, too.

How could anyone marry a man with a smile like that? But that, thank heaven, wasn't Sylvia's worry. Kennedy stood there with that hot, fierce smile, waiting for her answer. Now he'd gone out of his way to give her what she'd said she wanted. How could she tell him no? She saw no way, though she still would have liked to.

With a sigh of her own, she told him, "I'll come to your meeting, if it's not at a time when I'm working."

"I hope it isn't," he said. The smile got broader—she'd given in. She might almost have let him take her to bed.

He went on, "We hold them Saturday afternoons, so most people can use the half-holiday."

Sylvia sighed again. "All right, though heaven only knows how I'll get my shopping done—or why you think your people want to listen to me."

"Don't worry about your shopping," Kennedy said, which had to prove he didn't do much for himself. "And people want to hear you because you took action. You saw a wrong and you fixed it. Teddy Roosevelt would be proud of you. Even the Socialists had to take notice of the justice in what you did. And I'll be by to pick you up Saturday afternoon at one o'clock, if that's all right."

"I suppose so," Sylvia said, still more than a little dazed. Joe Kennedy tipped his homburg and went on his way. Sylvia checked the mailbox in the lobby of her block of flats, found nothing but advertising circulars, and walked up three flights of stairs to her apartment.

"What took you so long, Mother?" George, Jr., asked. He was thirteen now, which seemed incredible to her, and looked more like his dead father every day. Mary Jane, who was ten, was frying potatoes on the coal stove.

"I ran into a man," Sylvia answered. "He wants me to talk at the Democratic club's ward meeting. His wife will keep an eye on you two while I'm gone." She went to the icebox and got out the halibut steaks she'd fry along with the potatoes. Mary Jane still wasn't up to main courses.

"Saturday afternoon? I won't be here anyway," George, Jr., said.

"What? Why not?" Sylvia asked.

"Because I got a job carrying fish and ice down on T Wharf, that's why." Her son looked ready to burst with pride. "Thirty-five cents an hour, and it lets me get started, Ma."

Slowly, Sylvia nodded. "Your father started on T Wharf right about your age, too," she said. People who caught fish in Boston almost always started young. But George, Jr., suddenly didn't seem so young as all that. He was old enough to have convinced someone to hire him, anyhow.

He said, "I'll bring all my money home to you, Ma, every penny. Cross my heart and hope to die if I don't. I won't spend a bit on candy or pop or anything, honest I won't. I know we need it. So did the fellow who hired me. He asked if I was Pa's boy, and when I said yes he gave me the job right there. His name's Fred Butcher."

"Oh, yes. I know him—you've met him, too, you know." Sylvia nodded again. "He used to go out with your father on the *Ripple*. He was first mate in those days, and he's done well for himself since."

"As soon as I can, Ma, *I'll* go out and make money," Mary Jane promised, adding, "I don't much like school anyway."

"You need to keep going a while longer," Sylvia said sternly. She rounded on her son. "And so do you. If you study hard, maybe you can get a good job, and you won't stay down on T Wharf your whole life."

She might as well have spoken Chinese. Staring at her in perfect incomprehension, George, Jr., said, "But I *like* it down on T Wharf, Ma."

Sylvia flipped the halibut steaks with a spatula. She thought about explaining why all the backbreaking jobs associated with the fishing weren't necessarily good choices, but she could tell he wouldn't listen. His father wouldn't have, either. She didn't start a fight she had no hope of winning. Instead, she just said, "Supper will be ready in a couple of minutes. Go wash your hands, both of you."

Joe Kennedy and his wife knocked on the door that Saturday afternoon a few minutes after Sylvia got home. Rose Kennedy was pretty in a bony way, and more refined than Sylvia had expected. She did warm up, a little, to Mary Jane. "You're sweet, dear. Will we be friends?"

Mary Jane considered, then shrugged. Joe Kennedy said, "Come on, Mrs. Enos. My motorcar's out in front of the building. People are looking forward to hearing you; they really are."

That still astonished Sylvia. So did Kennedy's motorcar. She'd expected a plain black Ford, the kind most people drove. But he had an enormous Oldsmobile roadster,

34

painted fire-engine red. He drove as if he owned the only car on the street, too, which in Boston was an invitation to suicide. Somehow, he reached the Democratic Party hall unscathed. Sylvia discovered a belief in miracles.

"Here she is, ladies and gentlemen!" Kennedy introduced her as if she were a vaudeville star. "The brave lady you've been waiting for, Sylvia Enos!"

Looking out at that sea of faces frightened Sylvia. The wave of applause frightened and warmed her at the same time. She stammered a little at first, but gained fluency as she explained what she'd done in South Carolina, and why. She'd told the story before; it got easier each time. She finished, "If we forget about the war, try to pretend it never happened, what did we really win? Nothing!" The applause that came then rang louder still.

II

Jake Featherston drummed his fingers on his desk. Spring was in the air in Richmond; the trees were putting on new leaves, while birdsong gladdened every ear. Or almost every ear—it did very little for Featherston. He'd led a battery of three-inch guns during the war, and much preferred their bellowing to the sweet notes of catbird and sparrow. When the guns roared, at least a man knew he was in a fight.

"And we are, God damn it," Featherston muttered. The leader of the Freedom Party was a lanky man in his mid-thirties, with cheekbones and chin thrusting up under the flesh of his face like rocks under a thin coat of soil on some farm that would always yield more trouble than crops. His eyes . . . Some people were drawn to them, while others flinched away. He knew that. He didn't quite understand it, but he knew it and used it. *I always mean what I say,* he told himself. *And that shows. With all the lying sons of bitches running around loose, you'd better believe it shows.*

If he looked out his window, he could see Capitol Square, and the Confederate Capitol in it. His lip curled in fine contempt. If that wasn't the home of some of the biggest, lyingest sons of bitches in the whole wide world . . . "If it isn't, then I'm a nigger," Featherston declared. He talked to himself a fair amount, hardly noticing he was doing it. More than three years of serving a gun had taken a good deal of his hearing. People who didn't care for him claimed he was selectively deaf. They had a point, too, though he wasn't about to admit it.

The Capitol shared the square with a large equestrian statue of George Washington—who, being a Virginian, was much more revered in the CSA than in the USA these days—and an even larger one of Albert Sidney Johnston, hero and martyr during the War of Secession. Somewhere between one of those statues and the other, Woodrow Wilson had declared war on the USA almost ten years before.

"We should've licked those Yankee bastards," Featherston said, as if somebody'd claimed otherwise. "If the niggers hadn't risen up and stabbed us in the back, we *would've* licked those Yankee bastards." He believed it with every fiber of his being.

And if that jackass down in Birmingham hadn't blown out President Hampton's stinking brains, what there were of them, the Party'd be well on its way towards putting this country back on its feet again. Jake slammed a scarred, callused fist down on the desk. Papers jumped. *I was so close, dammit.* He'd come within a whisker—well, two whiskers—of winning the presidential election in 1921. Looking toward 1927, he'd seen nothing but smooth sailing ahead.

Of course, one of the reasons the Freedom Party had almost won in 1921 was that its members went out there and brawled with anybody rash enough to have a different opinion. If you looked at things from one angle, President Hampton's assassination followed from the Freedom Party's nature almost as inexorably as night followed day.

Jake Featherston was not, had never been, and never would be a man to look at things that way.

He'd watched the Party lose seats in the 1923 Congressional elections. He'd been glad the losses weren't worse. Other people celebrated because they were as large as they were. Up till that damned unfortunate incident, the Freedom Party had gone from success to success, each building momentum for the next. Unfortunately, he was finding the process worked the same way for failure.

What do we do if the money doesn't keep coming in?

What can *we do if the money doesn't keep coming in?* he wondered. Only one answer occurred to him. *We go under, that's what.* When he'd first joined the Freedom Party in the dark days right after the war, it had been nothing to speak of: a handful of angry men meeting in a saloon, with the membership list and everything else in a cigar box. It could end up that way again, too; he knew as much. Plenty of groups of disgruntled veterans had never got any bigger, and the Party had swallowed up a lot of the ones that had. Some other group could swallow it the same way.

"No, goddammit," Jake snarled. For one thing, he remained convinced he was right. If the rest of the world didn't think so, the rest of the world was wrong. And, for another, he'd got used to leading an important political party. He liked it. Without false modesty—and he was singularly free of modesty, false and otherwise—he knew he was good at it. He didn't want to play second fiddle to anybody else, and he didn't want to go back to being a big fish in a tiny pond.

The telephone on his desk jangled. He picked it up. "Featherston," he barked into the mouthpiece.

"Yes, Mr. Featherston," his secretary said. "I just wanted to remind you that you've got that talk on the wireless coming up in a little more than an hour. You'll want to make sure you're at the studio on time."

"Thank you kindly, Lulu," Featherston answered. He was more polite to Lulu Mattox than to practically anybody else he could think of. Unlike most people, his secretary deserved it. She was a maiden lady, somewhere between forty and seventy. Once upon a time, he'd read or heard— he couldn't remember where or when—that Roman Catholic nuns were the brides of Christ. What he really knew about Catholicism would fit on the head of a pin; he'd been raised a hardshell Baptist, and he didn't get to any church very often these days. But Lulu Mattox, without a doubt, was married to the Freedom Party. She gave it a single-minded devotion that put the enthusiasm of any mere Party man to shame. She had all the files at her fingertips, too, for she was the best-organized person Jake had ever met. He didn't know what he would do without her.

A few minutes later, he went downstairs. Guards outside the building came to attention and saluted. "Freedom!" they said. The uniforms they wore were similar but not quite identical to those of the Confederate Army. The bayoneted Tredegar rifles they carried were Army issue. Someone might have asked questions about that, but the Freedom Party had gone out of its way to show the world that asking questions about it wasn't a good idea.

"Freedom!" Jake echoed, returning those salutes as if he were a general himself. Part of him loathed the fat fools with the wreathed stars on their collar tabs who'd done so much to help the CSA lose the war. The rest of him wished he had that kind of power himself. *I'd do a better job with it than those bastards ever could have.*

A motorcar driven by another uniformed Freedom Party man stopped in front of the building. It was a boxy Birmingham, built in the CSA. Jake Featherston was damned if he'd go around Richmond in a Yankee automobile. "That wireless place," he told the driver.

"Sure, Sarge," the man replied. He was a large, burly fellow named Virgil Joyner. He'd been with the Freedom Party almost as long as Featherston had, and he'd been through all of the faction fights and the brawls with the Whigs and the Radical Liberals. Not many people could get away with calling Jake anything but "boss," but he'd earned the right.

The broadcasting studio was in a new brick building on Franklin near Seventh, not far from the house in Richmond where Robert E. Lee and his family had lived for a time after the War of Secession. Featherston knew that only because he'd grown up in and around Richmond. Nothing remained of the house these days; Yankee bombs and the fires that so often followed them had leveled it.

"Hello, Mr. Featherston!" exclaimed the bright little man who ran the studio and the wireless station of which it was a part. His name was Saul Goldman. Since he was a Jew, Featherston assumed he sounded so cheerful, so friendly, because he was getting paid. He was bound to be a Radical Liberal himself, if not an out-and-out Red. *Long as we give 'em the money, these bastards'll sell us the rope we use to hang 'em,* Featherston thought scornfully.

But if Goldman acted friendly, he'd play along—for now. "Good to see you," he said, and shook hands polite as a banker. "Everything ready for me?"

"Yes, sir. You're in Studio B this time. Follow me. You have your script?"

"Oh, yeah. You bet I do." Featherston followed Goldman down a narrow, dingy hall to a cramped little studio whose walls and ceiling were covered by what looked like the cardboard bottoms of egg cartons. The stuff looked funny, but it helped kill echoes. The studio held a table with a microphone on it and a rickety chair. That was all. Jake pointed to the engineer in the next room, whom he could see through a window. "He'll give me the signal when it's time?"

Saul Goldman smiled. "That's right. You know the routine almost like you work here."

"I'd better by now, don't you think?" Featherston sat down in front of the microphone and set his script on the table. He went through it quickly to make sure he had all the pages. Once he'd lost one, and had to ad-lib a bridge to the next one he had. Goldman slid out of the studio, closing the door behind him. The back of the door had more of those egg-carton sound deadeners glued to it.

After a bit, the engineer flashed two fingers—two minutes to go. Jake nodded to show he got it. The engineer was a professional, a man whose competence Jake respected. One finger—one minute. Then the fellow pointed straight at him at the same time as a red light went on. For half an hour, the airwaves were his.

"Confederates, wake up!" he said harshly. "This is Jake Featherston of the Freedom Party, and I'm here to tell you the truth." He used that phrase to introduce every wireless talk.

He leaned toward the microphone, as he would have leaned toward a crowd. The first few times he'd done this, not having an audience in front of him had thrown him off stride. Now, though, he could imagine the crowd, hear it in his mind shouting for more. And he had more to give it.

"We can be a great country again," he said. "We can, but will we? Not likely, not with the cowards and idiots we've got running things in Richmond these days. All they want to do is lick the Yankees' ... boots." You couldn't say some things on the air. No, you couldn't say them, but sometimes implication worked better anyhow.

"They want to lick the Yankees' boots," Jake repeated. "They're great ones for sucking up to people, the Whigs are. They even suck up to our Negroes, our own Negroes, if you can believe it. And do you know what, folks? They've got reason to do it, may I go to the Devil if I lie." He couldn't say *hell* on the air, either, but he got his message across. "I'll tell you what the reason is. Thanks to the Whigs, some of those niggers are citizens of the Confederate States, just like you and me.

"That's right, friends. This here was supposed to be a white man's country, but do the Whigs care about that? Not likely! Thanks to them, we've got niggers who can vote, niggers who can serve on juries, niggers who don't have to show passbooks to anybody. That'd be bad enough if they'd put the coons in the Army so we could win the war. But they put 'em in, *and we lost anyways*. And then the Whigs went out and won the next election even so. Maybe some of you all see the sense in that. I tell you frankly, I don't."

He went on till the engineer signaled it was time to wind down, and ended as the man drew a finger across his throat. When he walked out of the studio, his shirt was as sweaty as if he'd spoken before a crowd of thousands. Saul Goldman came up and shook his hand. "Very good speech," the Jew said. "Very good indeed."

"I will be damned," Featherston said. "I think you really mean it. You're not making fun of me." Goldman nodded. Jake asked the obvious question: "How come?"

"I'll tell you." Goldman had ... not an accent, but the ghost of one, barely enough to suggest his parents would have spoken differently. "Anywhere else, when things go wrong, what do they do? They blame the Jews. Here, you blame the colored people. I am a Jew, a Jew in a country where things went wrong, and no one wants to kill me on account of it. Shouldn't I be grateful?"

41

Jake had never been much for seeing the other fellow's point of view, but he did this time. "Well, well," he said. "Isn't that interesting?"

Part of Colonel Irving Morrell—and the bigger part, at that—wanted to be back at Fort Leavenworth, making barrels larger and stronger and better. Part of him, but not all. The rest, the part that was a student of war rather than a combat soldier, found a lot to interest it back at the General Staff. Quite a few things crossed his desk that never made it into the newspapers.

He showed one of them to Lieutenant Colonel John Abell, asking, "Is this true?"

"Let me read through it first," Abell said. General Liggett's adjutant was thin and pale and almost sweatless, a pure student of war. Though probably brave enough, he would have been out of place on anything so untidy as a real battlefield. He and Morrell didn't much like each other, but over the years they'd developed a wary respect for each other's abilities. He took his own sweet time reading the report, then gave a judicious nod. "Yes, this ties in with some other things I've seen. I believe it's credible."

"The Turks really are massacring every Armenian they can get their hands on?" Morrell asked. Abell nodded again. Morrell took back the typewritten report, saying, "That's terrible! What can we do about it?"

"We, as in the United States?" Abell asked, precise as usual. Morrell gave him an impatient nod. He said, "As best I can see, Colonel, nothing. What influence can we bring to bear in that part of the world?"

Morrell grimaced and grunted. His colleague was all too likely to be right. He'd had to find Armenia on a map before fully understanding the report he'd received. How many Americans would even have known where to look? The distant land at the edge of the Caucasus might have been lost among the mountains of the moon, as far as most people were concerned. With the best will in the world, the Navy couldn't do a thing. And as for sending soldiers across a Russia whose civil strife looked eternal ... The idea was absurd, and he knew it.

42

He tried a different tack: "Can Kaiser Bill do anything? When Germany spits, the Turks start swimming. And the Armenians are Christians, after all."

Lieutenant Colonel Abell started to say something, then let out his breath without a word. A moment later, after sending Morrell a thoughtful look, he said, "May I speak frankly, Colonel?"

"When have I ever stopped you?" Morrell asked in turn.

"A point," Abell admitted. "All right, then. There are times when you give the impression of being a man whose only solution to a problem is to hit something, and to keep hitting it till it falls over."

"Teddy Roosevelt spent a lot of time talking about the big stick, Lieutenant Colonel," Morrell said. "As far as I can see, he had a pretty good point."

John Abell looked distinctly pained. Sniffing, he said, "Our former president, however gifted, was *not* a General Staff officer, nor did he think like one. Which brings me back to what I was saying—you often give that same bull-moose impression, and then you turn around and come up with something not only clever but subtle. That might be worth pursuing. It would have to go through the State Department, of course."

Morrell grunted again. "And why should the boys in the cutaways and the striped trousers pay any attention to us green-gray types?"

For once, Abell's answering smile was sympathetic. The United States were one of the two most powerful countries in the world these days, sure enough. Very often, the American diplomatic corps behaved as if the U.S. Army had had nothing to do with that. Such a supercilious attitude infuriated Morrell. Of course, his fury mattered not at all; had people in the State Department known of it, it would more likely have amused them than anything else.

Abell said, "May I make a suggestion?"

"Please."

"If it were I," the brainy lieutenant colonel said, flaunting his grammatical accuracy, "I would draft a memorandum on the subject, send it to General Liggett,

43

and hope he could get it to the secretary of war or one of his assistants. Being civilians, they have a better chance than we of getting the diplomats to notice the paper."

"That's . . . not bad, Lieutenant Colonel," Morrell said. Abell hadn't even tried to steal the idea for himself, and he had Liggett's ear. Though it wasn't obvious at first glance, he could be useful. Morrell chuckled. *He probably thinks the same about me.* He went on, "I'll take care of it right away. Thanks."

"Always glad to be of service, sir." Now Abell sounded as coolly ironic as usual.

When Morrell spoke that evening of what he'd done during the day, his wife nodded vigorous approval. "I hope something comes of it, Irv," Agnes Morrell said. "Hasn't this poor, sorry world seen enough killing these past few years?"

"Well, I think so," Morrell answered. "You won't find many soldiers singing the praises of murder, you know."

"Of course I know that," Agnes told him, more than a little indignantly. She was in her early thirties, not far from his own age, and had been another soldier's widow before meeting him at a dance back in Leavenworth. She had brown eyes; her black hair, these days, was cut short in what the fashion magazines called a shingle bob. It was all the rage at the moment. Morrell didn't think it quite suited his wife, but didn't intend to tell her so. As far as he could see, such things were her business, not his. She went on, "Supper will be ready in a few minutes."

"Smells good." Morrell's nostrils flared. Compared to some of the things he'd eaten in Sonora and the Canadian Rockies and Kentucky and Tennessee, it smelled very good indeed. "What is it?" Back on the battlefield, there'd been plenty of times he hadn't wanted to know. Horse? Donkey? Cat? Buzzard? He couldn't prove it, which meant he didn't have to think about it . . . too often.

"Chicken stew with dumplings and carrots," Agnes said. "That's the way you like it, isn't it?"

Spit flooded his mouth as he nodded. "I knew I married you for a couple of reasons," he said.

"A couple of reasons?" Her eyebrows, plucked thin,

flew up in mock surprise. "What on earth could the other one be?"

He walked over to her and let his hand rest lightly on her belly for a moment. "We'll find out if it's a boy or a girl sooner than we think."

"It won't be tomorrow," Agnes reminded him. She'd been sure she was in a family way for only a few weeks. There wasn't much doubt any more; not only had her time of the month twice failed to come, but she was perpetually sleepy. And she had trouble keeping food down. She gave Irving Morrell a much bigger helping than she took for herself, and she ate warily.

When they undressed for bed that night, he used a forefinger to follow the new tracery of blue veins that had sprung out on Agnes' breasts. She gave him a mischievous smile. "All those veins probably remind you of the rivers on a campaign map."

"Well, I wouldn't have thought of it just that way," Morrell answered, cupping her breast in the palm of his hand. "What sort of campaign did you have in mind, honey?"

"Oh, I expect you'll think of something," she answered. He squeezed, gently—but not quite gently enough. The corners of her mouth turned down. "They're sore. People say you get over that, but I haven't yet."

He tried to be more careful, and evidently succeeded, for things went on from there. When they'd progressed a good deal further, Agnes climbed on top of him. The idea had startled him when she first proposed it; he'd always thought a man belonged in the saddle. But she didn't have his weight on her tender breasts this way—and, he'd discovered, it was fine no matter who went where.

A couple of days later, he got called to General Hunter Liggett's office. With General Liggett was a tall, long-faced man five or ten years older than Morrell. "Colonel, I'd like to introduce you to Mr. N. Mattoon Thomas, the assistant secretary of war."

"Pleased to meet you, sir." Morrell lied without hesitation. Thomas was the man who'd gone up to Canada to put General Custer out to pasture. Morrell still didn't know if Custer was a good general. He had his doubts, in fact. But Custer had turned a whole great assault column of barrels loose against the CSA, and Morrell had ridden a barrel at the head of that column. Without the break-throughs they'd won, the Great War might still be going on.

"Likewise, Colonel. I'm very glad to meet you." N. Mattoon Thomas was probably lying, too. In the Army, it was an axiom of faith that the Socialists wanted to get rid of everything that had let the USA win the war. That Thomas had forced George Custer into retirement didn't speak well for him, not in Morrell's eyes.

Hunter Liggett said, "Colonel, I passed your memorandum on the unfortunate situation in Armenia to the assistant secretary here, in the hope that he might send it on to the Department of State."

"A very perceptive document," Thomas said. "I dare hope it will do some good, although one never knows. Very perceptive indeed." He studied Morrell as an entomologist might study a new species of beetle. "I should hardly have expected such a thing from a soldier."

Morrell gave him a smile that was all sharp teeth. "Sorry, sir. We don't gas grandmothers and burn babies all the time."

Silence slammed down in General Liggett's office. The head of the General Staff broke it, saying, "What Colonel Morrell meant, sir, was—"

"I know perfectly well what Colonel Morrell meant," Thomas said, his voice cold as the middle of a meat locker. "He resents my party for telling him he may not play with big iron toys forever and tell the American people, 'Hang the expense! We may need these one day.' I wear his resentment as a badge of honor." He gave Morrell a nod that was almost a bow. "And what have you got to say about that, Colonel? You seem in an outspoken mood today."

"I've never said, 'Hang the expense,' sir," Morrell answered. "But we *may* need better barrels one day, and they *aren't* toys. If your party thinks what we do is play, why not get rid of the Army altogether, and the Navy, too?"

Before Thomas could reply, the telephone on General Liggett's desk rang. He snatched it up. "Confound it, you know what sort of meeting I'm in," he snapped, from which Morrell concluded he was talking to Lieutenant Colonel Abell in the outer office. But then Liggett said, "What? What's that?" Color drained from his face, leaving it corpse-yellow. "Dear God in heaven," he whispered, and hung up.

"What is it?" Morrell and N. Mattoon Thomas said the same thing at the same time.

General Liggett stared blindly from one of them to the other. Tears glistened in his eyes. All at once, he looked like an old, old man. "Teddy Roosevelt is dead," he said, sounding as stunned and disbelieving as a shell-shocked soldier. "He was playing a round of golf outside Syracuse, and he fell over, and he didn't get up. Cerebral hemorrhage, they think."

"Oh, my God." Again, Morrell and Thomas spoke together. Thomas might be a Socialist, but Theodore Roosevelt had been a mighty force in the United States for more than forty years. No one, regardless of party, could be indifferent to that.

So far Morrell thought, and no further. Then what he'd just heard really hit him. To his amazement and shame and dismay, he began to weep. A moment later, blurrily, he saw tears running down the faces of Hunter Liggett and N. Mattoon Thomas, too.

Congresswoman Flora Blackford should have been packing for the trip from Philadelphia to Chicago, for the Socialist Party's nominating convention. President Upton Sinclair would surely get his party's nod for a second term: the Socialists' first president, elected almost forty years after the modern Socialist Party began in Chicago, when in the aftermath of the Second Mexican War Abraham Lincoln led the Republican left wing out of one organization and into another.

Yes, the presidential nomination was a foregone conclusion. The vice presidency? Flora smiled to herself. The vice presidency was a forgone conclusion, too. Nothing in the world, as far as she could see, would keep Hosea Blackford, her husband, from getting the nomination again. And then, in 1928 . . . He'd once said he didn't expect to get the nod for the top of the ticket then. Maybe, though, maybe he was wrong.

Such things were what she should have been thinking about—what she had been thinking about up till a few days before. Now she put her most somber clothes into a suitcase. She wouldn't be going to Chicago, not yet, and neither would her husband. She'd always wanted to visit the city where the modern Party was born, and she would—but not yet. Instead, she packed for the short trip down to Washington, D.C., for the funeral of Theodore Roosevelt.

Hosea Blackford came into the bedroom carrying black trousers and a white shirt. As he put them in the suitcase, he shook his head. "I'm almost as old as Teddy Roosevelt, and I still feel as though my father just died."

Both of Flora's parents were still alive, but she nodded. "Everybody in the whole country feels that way, near enough," she answered. "We didn't always like him—"

"If we were Socialists, we practically never liked him," Hosea Blackford said.

Nodding, Flora went on, "But whether we liked him or not, he made us what we are. He raised us. He raised this whole country. It's no wonder we feel lost without him."

"No wonder at all," her husband said over his shoulder as he went back to the hall closet for a black jacket and a black homburg. "He was always sure he knew what was best for us. He wasn't always right, but he was always sure." He chuckled. "Sounds like my pa, I'll tell you that." His flat Great Plains accent was a world away from her Yiddish-flavored New York City speech.

He went back for a black cravat. Flora closed the suitcase. "Are we ready to go?" she asked.

"I expect so." He looked out the window of the flat that had been his alone—across the hall from hers—which they now shared. A motorcar waited in front of the building. Grunting, he picked up the suitcase.

When they went outside, the driver saw him carrying

48

it and rushed to take it from him. Grudgingly, Blackford surrendered it. He gave Flora a wry grin. Ever since she was elected to Congress, she'd wrestled with the problem of the privileges members of government—even Socialist members of government—enjoyed. For all her wrestling, for all her commitment to class struggle, she had yet to come to a conclusion that satisfied her.

She and her husband enjoyed even more privilege on the southbound train: a fancy Pullman car all to themselves, and food brought to them from the diner. When they got to Washington, another motorcar whisked them to the White House.

The flag in front of the famous building flew at half staff. The White House itself looked much as it had before the Great War. Repairs there had been finished almost a year before. The Washington Monument off to the south, however, remained a truncated stub of its former self. Scaffolding surrounded it; it would rise again to its full majestic height.

"If there's ever another war, all this work will go to waste," Flora said.

"One more reason there'd better not be another war," her husband answered, and she nodded.

President Upton Sinclair met them in the downstairs entry hall. After shaking hands with his vice president and kissing Flora on the cheek, he said, "I would sooner have done this in Philadelphia, but Roosevelt left word he wanted the ceremony here, and I couldn't very well say no."

"Hardly," Hosea Blackford agreed. "What does it feel like?—staying in the White House, I mean."

"Well, look at the place. I feel as though I were living in a museum." Sinclair waved. He was a tall, slim man in his mid-forties: the youngest man ever elected president. His youthful vigor had served him well in 1920, when Teddy Roosevelt, even then past sixty, could be seen as a man whose time, however great, had passed him by. The president shook his head. "It's even worse than living in a museum. It's the *reproduction* of a museum. They didn't get a whole lot out of here before the Confederates

49

bombarded the place in 1914. Frankly, I'd rather be in Philadelphia. The Powel House doesn't make me think I'll get thrown out if I speak above a whisper."

Flora found herself nodding. "It is more like the American Museum of Natural History than any place where you'd want to stay, isn't it?"

"That's right." President Sinclair nodded emphatically.

"Strange that *we* should be doing the honors for Roosevelt," Hosea Blackford observed.

"He was a great man," Flora said. "A class enemy, but a great man."

"Easier to admire a foe, especially an able one, after he's gone," Sinclair said.

Like a lot of men largely self-taught—Abraham Lincoln had been the same—her husband was fond of quoting Shakespeare: " 'Why, man, he doth bestride the narrow world like a Colossus; and we petty men walk under his huge legs, and peep about to find ourselves dishonorable graves.' "

"An American Caesar." President Sinclair nodded. "That fits."

But Flora shook her head. "No. If he'd been Caesar, he never would have given up the presidency when he lost four years ago. He would have called out the troops instead. And if Teddy Roosevelt had called them, they might have marched, too."

No one cared to contemplate that. Hosea Blackford said, "Well, he's gone now, and . . . 'I come to bury Caesar, not to praise him.' "

"And we'll give him a grand funeral, too," the president added. "We can afford to do that. He's a lot easier to deal with dead than he was alive."

Sleeping in the Mahan Bedroom felt strange to Flora; it was as big as the flat in which she and her whole family had lived in New York. The next morning, a colored servant—a reminder that Washington had once been closely aligned with the states now forming the Confederacy—brought her and her husband bacon and eggs and fried potatoes. She ate the eggs and potatoes; her husband demolished her bacon along with his own. "I shouldn't, I suppose," he said.

"Don't worry about it. I don't," she answered, which was true most of the time. Only later did she wonder in what the eggs and potatoes had been cooked. Bacon grease? Lard? She was Socialist and secular and very Jewish, all at the same time, and every so often one piece bounced off another and left her unsure of what she ought to feel.

Tens—hundreds—of thousands of people lined the route from the Capitol to the remains of the Washington Monument and then south. She and Hosea Blackford took their places on a reviewing stand near the Monument to watch Theodore Roosevelt's funeral procession, along with members of Congress and some foreign dignitaries: she recognized the ambassador from the Confederate States, who stood close by his colleagues from Britain, France, and the Empire of Mexico in a glum knot. No one else came very close to them.

Down among the ordinary spectators near the stand were a middle-aged woman wearing a gaudy medal—the Order of Remembrance, First Class—and a younger one who looked like her with the slightly less flamboyant Order of Remembrance, Second Class, hanging around her neck. They both held young children. The gray-haired man with them, who had a Distinguished Service Medal on his black jacket, said, "If she gets fussy, Nellie, give her to me."

"I will, Hal," the older woman answered. Flora wondered what she'd done during the war to earn such an important decoration.

She never found out. Indeed, a moment later, she forgot all about the people in the crowd, for flourishes of muffled drums announced that the procession was approaching. Behind the drummers—one each from the Army, Navy, Marines, and Coast Guard—came a riderless black horse led by a soldier. As the animal slowly walked past, Flora saw that it had reversed boots thrust into the stirrups and a sheathed sword lashed to the saddle.

Six white horses, teamed in twos, drew the black caisson carrying Roosevelt's body in a flag-draped coffin. All six of the horses were saddled. The saddles of the three on the right were empty; a soldier, a sailor, and a Marine rode the three on the left.

President Upton Sinclair, in somber black, marched bareheaded behind the caisson, along with some of Roosevelt's relatives—including one man of about Flora's age who had to be pushed along in a wheelchair. She wondered what sort of injury he'd taken in the war that had crippled him so.

The premier of the Republic of Quebec strode along a few paces after Sinclair and the Roosevelt family, accompanied by a couple of Central American heads of state who'd taken a fast liner to reach the USA in time for the funeral. After them came the ambassadors from the German Empire, Austria-Hungary, and the Ottoman Empire: the great wartime allies, given pride of place. Envoys from Chile and Paraguay and the Empire of Brazil came next, followed by other emissaries from Europe and the Americas—and the ambassador from the Empire of Japan, elegant in a black cutaway. Alone of all the Entente nations, Japan hadn't yielded to the Central Powers. She'd just stopped fighting. It wasn't the same thing, and everyone knew it.

After the foreign dignitaries marched a band playing soft, somber music. Another riderless horse brought up the rear of the procession. Flora found that excessive, but nobody'd asked her opinion. And the Socialist Party, being in power, did have an obligation to send the departed Roosevelt to his final rest with as much grandeur as possible, to keep the Democrats from screaming about indifference or worse.

Once the procession had passed the reviewing stand, it turned south, toward the Potomac. The crowds there were just as thick as they had been between the Capitol and the Washington Monument. The sounds of weeping rose above the music of the band. "Say what you will, the people loved him," Hosea Blackford remarked.

"I know." Flora shook her head in wonder. "In spite of the war he led them into, they loved him." That war had cost her brother-in-law his life and her brother a leg. And David voted Democratic despite—or maybe because of—that missing leg, though he'd been a Socialist before.

Her husband said, "Well, he won it, no matter how

52

much it cost. And now he gets his last revenge on the Confederate States." He chuckled in reluctant admiration.

Flora didn't know whether to admire Teddy Roosevelt's final gesture or to be appalled by it. On the southern bank of the Potomac, in what had been Virginia but was now annexed to U.S. West Virginia, Robert E. Lee had had an estate. Since the Great War rolled over it, it had lain in ruins. That hadn't bothered Roosevelt at all. He'd left instructions—and President Sinclair had agreed—that his last resting place should be in the grounds of Arlington.

Clarence Potter paid two cents for a copy of the *Charleston Mercury*. "Thanks very much," he told the boy from whom he bought it.

"You're welcome, sir," the boy said, the thick drawl of the old South Carolina coastal city flavoring his speech. He cocked his head to one side. "You a Yankee, sir? You sure don't talk like you're from hereabouts."

"Not me, son." Potter shook his head. The motion threatened to dislodge his steel-framed spectacles. He set them more firmly on the bridge of his long, thin nose. "I came to Charleston after the war, though. I grew up in Virginia."

"Oh." The newsboy relaxed. He probably hadn't gone more than ten miles outside of Charleston in his whole life, and wouldn't have known a Virginia accent from one from Massachusetts or Minnesota.

Holding his newspaper so he could read as he walked, Potter hurried down Queen Street toward the harbor. He moved like an ex-soldier, head up, shoulders back. And he had been a soldier—he'd served as a major in intelligence in the Army of Northern Virginia during the war. His accent had aroused some talk, and some suspicion, there, too. Even men who knew accents thought he sounded too much like a Yankee for comfort. And so he did; not long before the war, he'd gone to Yale, and the way people spoke in New Haven had rubbed off on him.

Below the fold on the front page was an account of a speech by Jake Featherston, raising holy hell because Teddy

Roosevelt's bones were resting in the sacred soil of Virginia. Potter clucked and rolled his eyes and made as if to chuck the paper into the first trash can he saw. He would have bet Featherston would make a speech like that. But in the end, he didn't throw away the *Mercury*. He opened it and read till he'd seen as much of the speech as it reprinted.

He clicked his tongue between his teeth as he refolded the newspaper. Featherston would pick up points for what he'd said. *Damn Teddy Roosevelt and his arrogance,* Potter thought. As far as he was concerned, anything that helped the Freedom Party was bad for the Confederate States of America.

He'd got to know Jake Featherston pretty well during the war. Featherston had made the fatal mistake of being right when he said Jeb Stuart III's Negro servant, Pompey, was in fact a Red rebel. Young Captain Stuart, not believing it, had got Pompey off the hook, only to have his treason proved when the Negro uprising broke out a little while later. Stuart had gone into action seeking death after that, and, on a Great War battlefield, death was never hard to find.

General Jeb Stuart, Jr., a hero of the Second Mexican War, was a power in the War Department in Richmond. He'd made sure Jake Featherston, who'd been right about his son's error in judgment, never got promoted above the rank of sergeant no matter how well he fought—and Jake fought very well indeed. For that matter, Potter himself had also been involved in uncovering Jeb Stuart III's mistake, and he'd advanced only one grade in three years himself.

But his failure to get promoted affected only him. Had Jeb Stuart, Jr., relented and given Featherston the officer's rank he deserved, the CSA would have been saved endless grief. Clarence Potter was sure of that. Featherston had been taking out his rage and frustration against Confederate authorities ever since.

I knew even then he was monstrous good at hating, Potter thought. *Did I ever imagine, while the fighting was going on, that he'd turn out to be as good at it as he has?* He shook his head. He was honest enough to admit to himself that he hadn't. He'd thought Jake Featherston would disappear into obscurity once the war ended. Most men—almost all men—would have. The exceptions were the ones who had to be dealt with.

For the time being, it looked as if Featherston *had* been dealt with. Not so long before, his speech would have stood at the top of the front page, not below the fold. He was a falling star these days. With luck, he wouldn't rise again.

When Potter got to the harbor, he stiffened. A U.S. Navy gunboat was tied up at one of the quays. Seeing the Stars and Stripes here, where the Confederacy was born and the War of Secession began, raised his hackles. The flag stood out; the C.S. Navy used the Confederate battle flag as its ensign, not the Stars and Bars that so closely resembled the U.S. banner. And the U.S. Navy men's dark blue uniforms also contrasted with the dark gray their Confederate counterparts wore.

These days, Clarence Potter made his living as an investigator. He'd been looking into smuggling going through the harbor, and had headed there to report his findings to the harbormaster. But that warship flying the hated Northern flag drew him as a magnet drew iron.

He wasn't the only one, either. Men in both C.S. naval uniform and in civilian clothes converged on the U.S. gunboat. "Yankees, go home!" somebody yelled. Scores of throats roared agreement, Potter's among them.

"Avast that shouting!" a U.S. officer on the deck of the gunboat bawled through a megaphone. "We've got every right to be here under the armistice agreement, and you know it damned well. We're inspecting to make sure you Confederates aren't building submersibles in these parts. If you interfere with us while we're doing our duty, you'll be sorry, and so will your whole stinking country."

They love us no better than we love them, Clarence Potter reminded himself. And that lieutenant commander had a point. If he and his men couldn't make their inspection, the CSA would pay, in humiliation and maybe in gold as well. The Yankees had learned their lessons well; as victors, they were even more intolerable than the Confederates had been.

"Yankees, go home!" the crowd on the quay shouted, over and over.

At a barked order, the sailors on the gunboat swung their forward cannon to bear on the crowd. The gun was only a three-incher—a popgun by naval standards—but it could work a fearful slaughter if turned on soft flesh rather than steel armor. Sudden silence descended.

"That's better," the U.S. officer said. "If you think we won't open fire, you'd goddamn well better think again."

"You'll never get out of this harbor if you do," somebody called.

The U.S. lieutenant commander had spunk. He shrugged. "Maybe we will, maybe we won't. But if you want to start a brand new war against the United States of America, go right ahead. If you start it, we'll finish it."

No one from the United States would have talked like that before the Great War. The Confederate States had been on top of the world then. No more. The Yankees had the whip hand nowadays. And people in Charleston knew it. The crowd in front of the U.S. gunboat dispersed sullenly, but it dispersed. Some of the men who walked away knuckled their eyes to hold back tears. The Confederates were a proud folk, and choking on that pride came hard.

Potter made his way to the harbormaster's office. That worthy, a plump man named Ambrose Spawforth, fumed about Yankee arrogance. "Those sons of bitches don't own the world, no matter what they think," he said.

"You know that, and I know that, but do the damnyankees know it?" Potter answered. "I'll tell you something else I know: the way that bastard in a blue jacket acted, he just handed the Freedom Party a raft of new votes."

Spawforth was normally a man with a good deal of common sense. When he said, "Well, good," a chill ran through Clarence Potter. The harbormaster went on, "Isn't it about time we start standing up to the USA again?"

"That depends," Potter said judiciously. "Standing up to them isn't such a good idea if they go and knock us down again. Right now, they can do that, you know."

"Don't I just!" Spawforth said. "We're weaklings now.

We need to get strong again. We can do it. We *will* do it, too."

"Not behind Jake Featherston." Potter spoke with absolute conviction.

But he didn't impress Spawforth, no matter how certain he sounded. The fat man said, "He'll tell the Yankees off. He'll tell the niggers off. He'll tell the fools in Richmond off, too. That all needs doing, every bit of it."

One of Potter's eyebrows rose. "Splendid," he said. "And what happens after he tells the Yankees off?"

"Huh?" Plainly, that hadn't occurred to Spawforth.

"The likeliest thing is, they take some more of our land or they make us start paying them reparations again," Potter said. "We aren't strong enough to stop them, you know. Do you want *another* round of inflation to wipe out the currency?"

He was—he always had been—a coldly logical man. That made it easy for him to resist, even to laugh at, Jake Featherston's fervent speechmaking. It also made him have trouble understanding why so many people took Featherston seriously. Ambrose Spawforth was one of those people. "Well, what we need to do is get strong enough so the USA can't kick us around any more," he said. "The Freedom Party's for that, too."

"Splendid," Potter said again, even more sardonically than before. "We tell the United States we aim to kick them in the teeth as soon as we get the chance. I'm sure they'll just go right ahead and let us."

"You've got the wrong attitude, you know that?" the harbormaster said. "You don't understand the way things work."

What Potter understood was that you couldn't have whatever you wanted just because you wanted it. Even if you held your breath till you turned blue, that didn't mean you were entitled to it. As far as he could see, the Freedom Party hadn't figured that out and didn't want to.

He also understood getting deeper into an argument with Spawforth would do him no good at all. The man didn't have to hire him to snoop around the harbor. Yes, he'd been in intelligence during the war. But plenty of beady-eyed, needle-nosed men were at liberty in Charleston these days. A lot of them could do his job, and do it about as well as he did.

And so, however much he wanted to prove to the world at large—and to Ambrose Spawforth in particular—that Spawforth was an ass, an imbecile, an idiot, he restrained himself. Instead of laying into the man, he said only, "Well, I didn't come here to fight about politics with you, Mr. Spawforth. I came to tell you about the fellows who're sneaking dirty moving pictures into the CSA and taking tobacco out."

"Tobacco? So that's what they're getting for that filthy stuff, is it?" Spawforth said, and Potter nodded. The harbormaster looked shrewd. "If it's tobacco, they're likely Yankees. I would've reckoned 'em some other kind of foreigners—goddamn Germans, maybe—from the girls on the films, but they don't talk or nothin', so I couldn't prove it."

"Yes, the films are coming in from the USA. I'm sure of that." Potter looked at Ambrose Spawforth over the tops of his spectacles. "So you've seen some of these moving pictures, have you?"

The harbormaster turned red. "It was in the line of duty, damn it. Have to know what's going on, don't I? I'd look like a right chucklehead if I didn't know what all was coming through Charleston harbor."

He had enough of a point to keep Potter from pressing him. And the veteran, in the course of his own duties, had seen some of the films himself. He didn't think the girls looked German. They were certainly limber, though. He took some papers from his briefcase. "Here's my report—and my bill."

Jonathan Moss hadn't taken up the law to help Canadians gain justice from the U.S. occupying authorities. Such thoughts, in fact, had been as distant from his mind as the far side of the moon before the Great War started. He'd spent the whole war as an American pilot in Ontario, beginning in observation aircraft and ending in fighting scouts. He'd come through without a scratch and as an

58

ace. Not many of the men who'd started the war with him were still there at the end. He knew exactly how lucky he was to be here these days, and not to need a cane or a hook or a patch over one eye.

U.S. forces had planned to take Toronto within a few weeks of the war's beginning. But the Canadians and the English had had plans of their own. The U.S. Army had taken three years to get there. Almost every inch of ground around Lake Erie from Niagara Falls to Toronto had seen shells land on it. The city itself . . .

Having spent a lot of time shooting it up from the air, Moss knew what sort of shape Toronto had been in when the fighting finally stopped. It was far from the only Canadian place in such condition, either. Towns came back to life only little by little. Wrecked buildings got demolished, new ones went up to take their places. But the key words were *little by little*. Canadians, these days, didn't have much money, and the American government was anything but interested in helping them with their troubles.

That meant a lot of people doing the wrecking and the rebuilding weren't Canadians at all, but fast-buck artists up from the States. That was certainly true in Berlin, where Moss had his practice. (The town had briefly been known as Empire during the war, but had reverted to its original name after the Americans finally drove out stubborn Canadian and British defenders.) Americans in conquered Canada often behaved as if the law were for other people, not for them. Sometimes the military government looked the other way or encouraged them to act like that.

Moss had defended one Canadian's right to reclaim a building he incontrovertibly owned—that it was the building where he'd had his office made the case especially interesting for him. Not only had he taken the case, he'd won it. That got him more such business. These days, most of his clients were Canucks. Some of his own countrymen accused him of being more Canadian than the Canadians. He took it as praise, though doubting they meant it that way.

And, when Saturday rolled around and the courts

closed till the following Monday, he got into his powerful Bucephalus and roared off to the west. The motorcar did more to prove his family had money than to prove he did. The road to the little town of Arthur proved nobody in the province of Ontario had much money to set things to rights.

What had been shell holes in ground torn down to the bone were now ponds or simply grassy dimples in fertile soil. Rain and ice and grass and bushes softened the outlines of the trenches that had furrowed the countryside like scourge marks on a bare back. Even the ugly lumps of concrete that marked machine-gun nests and larger fortifications were beginning to soften with the passage of time, weathering and getting a coating of moss. Though cities were slow in recovering, the farmland in the countryside was back in business. Several trucks hauling broken concrete and rusted barbed wire back toward scrap dealers in Berlin or Toronto passed Moss on the opposite side of the road.

Here and there, fresh barbed wire stayed up: not in the thickets of the stuff used during the war, but single, sometimes double, strands. Signboards showed a skull and crossbones and a two-word warning in big red letters: DANGER! MINES! *How long will those mines stay in the ground?* Moss wondered.

From Berlin over to Arthur was about thirty miles. Even with his powerful automobile, Moss needed almost an hour and a half to get to the little farm outside of Arthur. That wasn't the Bucephalus' fault, but the road's—especially after rains like the ones they'd had a couple of days earlier, it was truly appalling.

His squadron had been stationed at an aerodrome only a mile or so from this little farm. It had been stationed here for a long time; the front hadn't moved fast enough to make frequent relocations necessary. And so Jonathan Moss, wandering the countryside in search of whatever—and whomever—he might find, had got to know a woman whose maiden name, she'd bragged, was Laura Secord.

She was named for a relative who'd made herself famous during the War of 1812, warning that the

Americans were coming in much the same way as Paul Revere had warned that the British were coming during the Revolution. If that hadn't been enough to make her a Canadian patriot, she'd been married to a soldier who was either missing or captured.

She hadn't wanted to look at Jonathan. He'd certainly wanted to look at her. She was tall and blond and shapely and pretty—and she was more of a man than most of the men he knew. She could take care of herself. In fact, she insisted on taking care of herself. He'd come back right after the war ended. Her husband hadn't. She sent him off with a flea in his ear anyhow.

But, when she was desperate for money to keep from being taxed off the farm, she'd written to him while he was in law school. He'd lent it to her. That had helped ease him into her good graces, though she'd paid back every dime. Helping that fellow over in Berlin regain his building had done far more. Any practical-minded American would say what happened mattered more than how it happened. Now . . .

Now, when Moss pulled onto the track that led from the road to her farmhouse and barn, he squeezed the bulb on the motorcar's horn. The raucous noise made a cow look up from the long, green grass it was cropping. The cow didn't act too startled. It had heard that noise before.

So had Laura Secord. Moss stopped the automobile just in front of her house. She came toward him, nodding a greeting. She carried a headless chicken, still dripping blood, by the feet. A hatchet was buried in a red-stained stump that did duty for a chopping block.

"Hello, Yank," she said, and held up the chicken. "Once I settle her, she'll make us a fine stew. Her laying's down, so I don't care about culling her."

"Suits me," Moss said. "How have you been?"

"Not bad," she replied.

By a year's custom, they were decorous with each other as long as they stayed outside, which made Moss want to hurry into the farmhouse. But this . . . Moss frowned. She sounded more—or rather, less—than merely decorous. He asked, "Is something wrong?"

She didn't answer right away. When she did, all she said was, "We can talk about it a little later, if that's all right."

"Sure. Whatever you want." Moss didn't see what else he could say. He wondered if he'd done something to put her nose out of joint. He didn't think so, but how could a mere male—worse, an American male—know for sure?

When they went inside, she gutted the chicken and threw the offal out for the farm cats, which were the wildest beasts Moss had ever known. She plucked the carcass with automatic competence, hardly looking at what her hands were doing. Then she got a fire going in the stove, cut up the bird, threw it in a pot with carrots and onions and potatoes and a cabbage, and put it over the fire to cook.

As soon as she'd got the chicken stew going, he expected her to throw herself into his arms. That was how things had gone since they became lovers. When they got inside the farmhouse, all bets were off. The first time they'd gone to bed together, they hadn't gone to bed. He'd taken her on the kitchen floor. If she hadn't got splinters in her behind, it wasn't because he hadn't rammed her against the floorboards.

Today, though, she shook her head when he took a step toward her. "We need to talk," she said.

"What about?" Moss asked with a sinking feeling worse than any he'd known while diving to escape an enemy pilot. Whenever a woman said something like that, the first careless joy of two people as a couple was over.

"Come into the parlor," Laura Secord told him. That surprised him, too; she hardly ever used the impressive-looking room. He'd walked past it on the way to the stairs that led to her bedroom, but he wasn't sure he'd ever actually been inside it. What could he do now, though, but nod and let her lead the way?

At her gesture, he sat down on the sofa. The upholstery crackled under his weight; the sofa wasn't used to working. On the table in front of the sofa stood a framed photograph of her late husband in Canadian uniform. Moss had resolutely forgotten his surname; thinking of Laura by her maiden name made it easier for him to forget the dead man altogether. But how could you forget someone whose image stared at you out of eyes that looked hard and dangerous?

The chair in which Laura Secord sat also made noises that suggested it wasn't used to having anyone actually sit in it. She looked at Moss, but didn't say anything. "You were the one who wanted to talk," he reminded her. "I asked you once, what about?"

She bit her lip and looked away. Something close to a sob burst from her. *She's going to send me packing,* Moss thought with sudden sick certainty. *She can't stand a damn Yank rumpling her drawers any more, no matter how much she likes it. What do I do then?* he wondered, panic somewhere not far under the surface of his mind. He'd spent years alternately chasing her and trying—always without much luck—to get her out of his mind. Now that he'd finally got her, finally found out just how much woman she was, losing her was the last thing he wanted. But two had to say yes. One was plenty for no.

"What is it?" he said again, like a man bracing himself for the dentist's drill. "After this buildup, don't you think you'd better tell me?"

Laura nodded jerkily. But then, instead of talking, she sprang up to light a kerosene lamp. The yellow glow added enough light to the parlor for him to see how pale she was. Another thought intruded on him—*she's going to have a baby.* He gave a tiny shrug. *We'll deal with that, dammit. Shakespeare's first kid came along seven months after he got married. The world won't end.*

She sat down again, biting her lip. Moss' nostrils twitched—not at the way she was behaving, but because he'd just got the first whiff of the stew. At last she said, so low he had to lean forward to hear her (which made the couch rustle again), "There's going to be . . . an uprising. Here. In Canada. Against . . . against the United . . ." She didn't get *States* out. Instead, she buried her face in her hands and wept as if her heart were breaking.

It probably is, Moss realized. "Why are you telling me? I thought you'd be . . ."

"Cheering them on?" Laura asked. He nodded, though

leading them on was more what he'd had in mind. She said, "Because I don't want you to get hurt. Because I—" She stopped again.

"Well!" he said, quite taken aback. He didn't say anything else for close to a minute; what man wouldn't savor such a compliment? *She cares for me,* he thought dizzily, *and not just for my* ... He shook his head and asked the other question that needed asking: "How do you know about this?"

Laura looked at him as if he'd been foolish. *And so I have,* he decided. She answered as she might have to a child: "I am who I am—I am what I am—after all."

"They thought you'd be cheering them on, too," Moss said. "Cheering them on or helping them, I mean."

"Yes." In the one word, Laura Secord unwittingly spoke volumes on how close they'd come to being right. Then she burst into tears. When Moss tried to comfort her, she pushed him away as fiercely as if he were still the enemy she'd thought him for so long.

Lucien Galtier took life a day at a time. As far as he could see, that was a good idea for any man, and an especially good idea for a farmer like himself. Sometimes you got sunshine, sometimes rain or snow or just clouds. Sometimes you got peace. Sometimes, he'd seen, you got war.

Sometimes you got a whole new country. He still had trouble remembering he lived in the Republic of Quebec. The USA had invaded the Canadian province of Quebec and found enough men willing to detach it from its long-time home to make a new nation. *Without the United States, my country would not be,* Galtier thought.

That had been a very strange notion, the first time it crossed his mind. By now, though, he'd realized the United States did as they pleased all through North America. *When they point at this one and say Come! he cometh, and when they point at that one and say Go! he goeth.*

"That's from the Bible, isn't it?" his wife asked when he spoke the thought aloud to her.

"I think so, Marie," he answered, scratching his head as he tried to remember where he'd found the language in which he robed his thought. He wasn't a tall man, or broad through the shoulders; his strength was of the wiry sort that didn't show. It was also of the wiry sort that endured after a bigger man's youthful power faded with the passing years. He'd seen his fiftieth birthday. The only real difference between it and his fortieth was that he'd gone gray over the past ten years. He'd had only a few silver strands among the midnight at forty. Now the black hairs were the ones that were few and far between.

Marie, as far as he could tell, hadn't aged a day. He marveled at how she'd managed that. She'd lived with him for thirty years now. If that wasn't enough to give her gray hair, nothing ever would.

She said, "The Romans in our Lord's day didn't use their power for good, did they?"

"I don't know these things," Lucien exclaimed. "If you wanted someone who knows about Romans, you shouldn't have married a farmer." He raised a sly eyebrow. "Maybe you should have married Bishop Pascal."

"You're trying to make me angry," Marie said. "You're doing a good job of it, too. It's not so much that Bishop Pascal can't marry. It's thinking I might want to marry him if he could. You could squeeze enough oil out of that man to light a house for a year."

"But it would be sweet oil," Galtier said. His wife made a face at him.

Before they could start up again, Georges, their younger son, came into the farmhouse with a newspaper from Rivière-du-Loup in his hand. "They've gone and done it!" he said, waving the paper at Lucien and Marie.

"Who has gone and done what?" Lucien Galtier asked. With Georges with newspaper in hand, he might settle on anything. Charles, his older brother, was much more like the elder Galtier, both in looks and character. Georges towered over his father—and also, as he had since he was a boy, delighted in whimsy for its own sake. Had someone gone and hauled a cow onto a roof? Georges might well make a story like that out to be the end of the world.

Not this time, though. "The Canadians have risen against the United States!" he said, and held the paper still long enough to let his father and mother see the big black headline.

"*Calisse!*" Galtier muttered. "*Mauvais tabernac!*" Marie clucked at his swearing, but he didn't care. He reached for the newspaper. "Oh, the fools! The stupid fools!" He crossed himself.

"They'll get what's coming to them," Georges said. He took the Republic of Quebec for granted. He'd lived the last third of his life in it. To him, as his words showed, Canada was a foreign country.

Things were different for Lucien. Back in the 1890s, he'd been conscripted into the Canadian Army. He'd soldiered side by side with men who spoke English. He'd learned some himself; its remembered fragments had come in handy in ways he hadn't expected. He'd also been told, "Talk white!" when he spouted French at the wrong time. Despite that, though, he'd seen that English-speaking Canadians weren't so very different from their Quebecois counterparts. And memories of when Quebec had been part of something stretching from Atlantic to Pacific remained strong in him.

"Give me the paper," he said. "I want to see what they say about this."

Something in his tone warned Georges this would not be a good time to argue or joke. "Here, Papa," he said, and handed him the newspaper without another word.

Galtier had to hold it out at arm's length to read it. His sight had lengthened over the past ten years, too. "Shall I get your reading glasses?" Marie asked. "I know where you left them—on the nightstand by the bed."

"Never mind," he answered. "I can manage well enough. . . . Uprisings in Toronto and Ottawa and Winnipeg, in Calgary and Edmonton and Vancouver."

"The Americans say they are putting them down," Georges said.

"Of course they say that. What else would you expect them to say?" Galtier replied. "During the war, both sides told lies as fast as they could. The Americans must have captured Quebec City and Montreal and Toronto half a dozen times each—and they must have been chased south over the border just as often."

66

Georges pointed to a paragraph Lucien was about to read on his own. "The premier of the Republic is sending soldiers to help his American allies—that's what he calls it, anyhow."

" '*Osti,*" Galtier muttered. He wasn't surprised so much as disgusted. He'd been thinking of the Bible. The Americans were saying *Come!*—and the Quebecois were duly coming. Or was that fair? Didn't allies help allies? Weren't Quebec and the USA allies? Why wouldn't French-speaking troops in blue-gray help Americans in green-gray?

"Can the Canadians win, do you think?" Georges asked. He certainly thought of his former countrymen as foreigners.

"No." Galtier shook his head. "The Americans are soft in certain things—they have certainly been softer here in Quebec than they might have been." Yes, he had to admit that. "But think even of your brother-in-law. Remember what he thinks of the British. The United States will not be kind in Canada. They will crucify the whole country, and they will laugh while they are doing it."

"The Canadians are brave," his son said.

"They're foolish," Galtier replied.

"Haven't we seen enough war? Haven't we seen too much war?" Marie said. Actually, this part of Quebec had fallen to the Americans fairly fast. It had seen occupation, but not too much true combat. Near Montreal, near Quebec City, the story was different.

"*They* don't think so." Georges sounded excited. *He knows no better,* Galtier thought. War around here hadn't seemed too bad.

"Listen to this, son," Galtier said after turning the paper to an inside page so he could see the rest of the story. "Listen carefully. 'American occupying authorities vow that these uprisings will be put down, and all rebels punished under martial law. This is a rebellion against duly constituted authority, not a war; captured rebels do not have the privileges granted to legitimate prisoners of war.' Do you know what that means? Do you understand it?"

"I think so, Father." Georges, for once, sounded serious. He didn't try to make a joke of it.

Lucien Galtier spelled things out anyhow: "It means the Americans will hang or shoot anyone they catch who rose up against them. They won't waste time with a lot of questions before they do it, either."

"And we take money from the Americans for the hospital they built on our patrimony," Georges said. "We even have an American in our family."

"You have a half-American nephew," Galtier replied. "You have an American brother-in-law, as I have an American son-in-law. And Leonard O'Doull is a good fellow and a good doctor, and you cannot say otherwise."

"Nooo," Georges admitted reluctantly. "But if they're doing these things in Canada—"

"They're doing them because the Canadians have risen up," Galtier said. "If the Canadians had stayed quiet, none of this would have happened. None of it has happened here in Quebec, *n'est-ce pas?*"

"*Oui, tu as raison, Papa,*" Georges said. "But even if you are right, is it not that we have made a deal with the Devil, you might say?"

That same thought had crossed Galtier's mind, too. He did his best to fight it down whenever it did. Now he said, "No. We are a small man. The United States, they are a large, strong man who carries a gun. Are we foolish because we do not go out of our way to step on his toes? I think not."

"Maybe," his son said, more reluctantly still. Then he asked, "What time is it?"

"Am I a clock?" Galtier said. "You can look at one as easily as I."

Georges did, and then exclaimed in dismay. "Is it half past four already? *Tabernac!* I thought it was earlier."

"And why does the hour matter so much?" Galtier inquired with a certain ironic curiosity, part of which was about whether his guess was right.

Sure enough, his younger son shuffled his feet a couple of times before answering, "When I was in town, I heard there would be a dance tonight. I thought I might go."

"Did you?"

"Yes, I did." Georges attempted defiance. He didn't

do a good job of it. His older brother, Charles, or any of his four sisters could have given him lessons.

Lucien and Marie shared amused looks. They'd met at a dance, somewhere a little more than thirty years before. Nor were they the only couple in the neighborhood who had—far from it. Galtier said, "All right, son. Have a good time."

Georges started to argue, to protest. Then he really heard what his father had said. He blinked. "It's all right?" he asked suspiciously.

"I said so, didn't I?"

Marie added, "There's plenty of hot water on the stove, if you have time to bathe and shave before you go."

"*Merci, chère Maman.* I'll do that quick as a wink." Georges still looked as if he didn't trust his ears. He went off to the kitchen to take the hot water to the bathroom, still scratching his head.

When he was, or at least might have been, out of earshot, Marie said, "High time he got married. I began to worry about Charles when he waited so long."

"Madeleine Boileau is a nice girl, and she made him a good match this past winter," Galtier said. His wife nodded. He went on, "She is a better match than we could have got without our American doctor son-in-law, or without the money from the Americans for the property on which the hospital stands."

"I know that," Marie said. "You must know it, too. Why bring it up now? We've had these things for some time."

"Why bring it up now?" Galtier echoed. "To convince myself what we've done is worthwhile, that's why. Because there are times when I feel our money is like Judas' thirty pieces of silver, that's why. Because I almost envy the Canadians for rising, *that's* why."

Marie eyed him. "Would you disown your grandson?"

"No. Never." Lucien didn't hesitate. He did laugh. "All right. You have me."

"I should hope so," Marie said.

III

A cold, nasty rain poured down on Augusta, Georgia. Had the town been up in the USA, Scipio suspected it would have got snow, even though this was only the end of October. He'd seen snow a few times, here and in South Carolina, where he'd lived most of his life. He didn't like it a bit.

The rain drummed on his cheap black umbrella. Some of the Negroes in the Terry, Augusta's black quarter, had no umbrellas. They dashed through the streets on the way to work, water splashing up under their galoshes—when they had galoshes. Scipio did. He was fastidious about his person. Part of that was personal inclination, part habit ingrained in him by more than half a lifetime spent as Anne Colleton's butler. She'd always insisted on perfection in everything, and she'd known how to get what she wanted.

His foot slipped out from under him. He had to make a mad grab for a lamppost with his free hand. That kept him from falling on his backside, but the desperate embrace left his arm and one side of his chest almost as wet as if he had fallen.

He muttered under his breath all the way to Erasmus' fish market and restaurant. YOU BUY—WE FRY! was painted on the window in big letters. The front door was unlocked. Scipio gladly ducked inside, closing the umbrella as he did so.

Erasmus, as always, had got there before him. The gray-haired black man was sipping on a steaming cup of coffee almost white with cream—he'd already been to the fish market alongside the Savannah River to get the best of the day's catch and put it on ice here.

"Mornin'," he said to Scipio, and then, "Wet out." He got the most mileage from every word he used.

"Do Jesus, sho' is!" Scipio exclaimed. "I's soaked clean through." His accent was that of the Congaree, thicker and more ignorant-sounding than Erasmus'. He could also use the English of an educated white man—again, Anne Colleton's doing—but he had nothing between the one and the other.

"Can't be helped." Erasmus took another sip of coffee. He pointed to the pot. "Pour yourself some if you got a mind to, Xerxes."

"I do dat," Scipio said. No one in Augusta, not even Bathsheba, his wife, knew his rightful name. He'd used several aliases since escaping from the wreckage of the Congaree Socialist Republic. His passbook said he was Xerxes, and he wasn't about to argue with it. Xerxes was as free as a black man in the Confederate States could be. Scipio still had a large price on his head back in South Carolina.

He poured less cream—the pitcher sat on ice next to some catfish—into his coffee than Erasmus used, but added a couple of teaspoons of sugar. His boss' eyes were on him. Erasmus didn't approve of anyone standing around idle, especially not someone he was paying. Getting a cup of coffee didn't mean lollygagging around for half an hour till Scipio finished it. He took the cup out in front of the display full of ice and fish, grabbed a push broom, and started sweeping up under and around the restaurant tables.

Erasmus said, "You's a pretty good fellow, Xerxes."

"I thanks you," Scipio answered, chivvying small specks of dust to destruction.

"Yes, suh, you's a pretty good fellow," Erasmus said again. "You works." By the way he spoke, those two traits were intimately connected. He watched Scipio sweep a little

71

longer, then added, "You know what I say? I say you ought to git your own place, work for your own self. I hates to lose you, but you smart if you go."

Scipio stopped sweeping. Erasmus must have been serious, for he didn't give his employee a put-upon stare. Slowly, Scipio said, "Ain't never thought about that none."

He told the truth. Never in his life had he contemplated being his own master. He'd been born a slave, before the Confederate States manumitted their Negroes in the aftermath of the Second Mexican War. Even after manumission, he'd always been a house nigger, first in the kitchens at Marshlands, then as butler there. He'd done factory labor and worked as a waiter since. Every single place, he'd had somebody telling him what to do. (Whenever he thought of Anne Colleton, he shivered, even now. Getting out of South Carolina had put some distance between them, the state border being more important than the miles. Was it enough? He hoped so.)

"Ought to do some thinkin', then, I reckon," Erasmus said. "You ain't stupid. You kin read'n write'n cipher— more'n I kin do my ownself. You works hard, an' you saves your money. What else you need?"

Maybe he didn't expect an answer, but Scipio gave him one: "Dunno dat I wants to boss other niggers around. You hear what I sayin'?"

"Yeah, I hears it. But you ain't real likely to hire no white folks." Erasmus bared his teeth to show that was meant for a joke. Scipio dutifully smiled back. His boss went on, "I hear what you say. But you gots to have people workin' fo' you. Job gits too big fo' one man to do it all by hisself."

"Don' want to play de buckra." Scipio made as if to crack a whip. He might have been driving along a slave coffle in the days before manumission.

"I hear black folks say that every now and again," Erasmus admitted. "But you tell me true, now—I treat you like white folks treats niggers?"

"No," Scipio admitted. "Had one fella, he weren't too bad, but de rest—" He shook his head.

"Oglethorpe," Erasmus said. Scipio nodded in

surprise; he hadn't mentioned his earlier boss for quite a while. Erasmus owned a stubborn memory. He continued, "I knows Aurelius a bit. He been waitin' tables for John Oglethorpe since dirt. He says that there buckra a lot like me, you work for him, he don't give you no trouble. He could do that, too."

"Could," Scipio said. "Mebbe could. Dunno dat I gots it in me to give no orders, though, not no way." He hadn't even liked giving orders as a butler, when Anne Colleton was the ultimate authority behind them. Doing it on his own hook? No, he wasn't sure about that at all.

"Well, you don't want to do what you *kin* do, that's your business," Erasmus said. "Like I told you, I ain't sorry you works for me. But you is wastin' yourself, you wants to know what I think."

How many Negroes in the Confederate States aren't *wasting themselves?* Scipio wondered. He'd got himself an education as good as any white man's. What could he do with it? Sound impressive as the butler at Marshlands during the war. Now, wait tables. If he'd tried to set up as a businessman— not in the sense Erasmus meant, but as an investor, a capitalist—he would have been lucky if whites here only laughed at him. More likely, they would have lynched him.

And most blacks? Besides having whites hate them, most blacks never got the education that would have let them make the most of their abilities—that would have let them discover what abilities they had. And then whites called them stupid and inferior because they didn't succeed.

"Sometimes I reckons dem Red niggers, dey knew what dey was doin'," he said. He'd never dared say anything like that to Erasmus before.

The older man studied him, then slowly shook his head. "Them Reds, they was about tearin' down, not buildin' up. Tearin' down don't do no good. Never has, never will." He sounded very certain.

Before Scipio could answer, the day's first customer came in: a fat black man dripping rain from the brim of his homburg and from the hem of his rubberized-cotton raincoat. "Bacon an' a couple eggs over medium an' grits an' coffee," he called to Erasmus.

Erasmus already had the eggs and bacon on the stove. "Like I don't know what you has for breakfast, Sophocles," he said reproachfully.

Scipio poured coffee for Sophocles and brought it to him. As soon as Erasmus had the rest of the man's breakfast ready, he carried that over, too. "Half a dollar, all told," he said.

"Here y'are." Sophocles slapped down sixty cents. "Things is up a little from last year," he remarked.

"But only a little," Scipio said. "Do Jesus, when dey was playin' games wid de money, breakfas' cost you fifty million dollars, maybe fifty billion dollars. I's powerful glad dey fix it—dey pretty much fix it, anyways."

Sophocles and Erasmus both nodded. Inflation had almost destroyed the CSA. How could anybody do business when money might lose half its value between the morning when you got it and the afternoon when you found a chance to spend it? Prices *were* higher now than they had been when the currency was restored; the C.S. dollar didn't trade at par with its U.S. counterpart. But it was still close, and didn't seem to be sinking very fast.

Erasmus said, "The white folks don't go runnin' to the Freedom Party fast as their legs can take 'em when their money worth somethin'."

Sophocles nodded again, chewing a mouthful of bacon. So did Scipio. "De Freedom Party buckra, dey scares me plenty," he said. "Dey wish we was all dead. Dey he'ps we along, too, case we don' feel like dyin'." More nods.

More customers came in. On such a miserable morning, business was slower than usual. Scipio kept hopping even so. When he wasn't carrying food out to hungry men and women, he was washing dirty dishes or making fresh coffee or stirring the big pot of grits. Erasmus didn't let him do much real cooking, but did give him jobs like that. He also wrapped fish for people who didn't come in to eat there.

However much he did, he would have felt like a fool complaining about it, for Erasmus did more. Erasmus worked harder than anybody he'd ever seen, save possibly John Oglethorpe. Maybe their both owning their businesses had something to do with that.

Erasmus certainly worked harder than any other black man Scipio had ever seen. And he'd been born a slave; he'd spent more time in bondage than Scipio had. A lot of Negroes still held to the slave's pace of labor, doing just enough to satisfy an overseer, even though they were free now. Erasmus worked to satisfy an overseer, too, but his lived inside his head. He had a harsher straw boss than any cursing, whip-wielding, tobacco-chewing white man. His boss whipped him on from within.

Could I do that? Scipio wondered. He had his doubts. He *wanted* things done properly, yes; Anne Colleton had made sure to instill that into him. But did he have the driving *need* to get things done, even when he was the only one urging himself on? He'd rarely seen it in himself. He'd rarely had to look for it, either. If he ever got his own place, he'd have to.

After the breakfast rush, such as it was, eased, Erasmus put on a wide-brimmed hat of no known make and a rain slicker. "Mind the store a spell, Xerxes," he said. "I gwine buy some more fish. One of the boats was late, and I reckon I kin git some prime deals, on account of most folks ain't comin' back."

"I do dat," Scipio said. Erasmus hurried out into the rain. *Would I do the same?* Scipio wondered. He was honest enough to admit to himself he didn't know.

The closing whistle shrilled in the Toledo steel mill. Chester Martin pushed his helmet up onto the top of his head. He blinked against the glare as he hurried to clock out. He'd been looking at molten steel through smoked-glass rectangles all day. Now he saw all the light there was to see. It was almost too much to bear.

As he stuck his card in the time clock, he spoke up to anyone who'd listen: "Election day today. Don't forget to vote, dammit. Only way you should forget to vote is if you want the Democrats back in Powel House."

That made most of the men around him grin and wave

and call out agreement. Socialists filled the Toledo steel mills, as they filled so many factories. After the postwar strikes, the Socialist Party had gained more ground than at any time since the 1880s.

Funny, Martin thought as he hurried out of the big building to catch a streetcar to his polling place and his home. *I saved Teddy Roosevelt's life when he came into the trenches to see what the war was like. Well, maybe I did—I sure made him get down when the Confederates started shelling us.* He had a letter from Roosevelt, written after he got wounded. He intended to keep that letter forever. But he was a Socialist all the same.

A streetcar clanged to a stop. That wasn't his route. Then the right one came. He climbed aboard, throwing five cents in the fare box. A lot of the passengers looked like him: tired, grubby men in overalls and heavy shoes and collarless shirts and cloth caps. He had sandy hair and a pointed nose to distinguish himself from most of the rest. The odor of perspiration filled the streetcar. Even in November, Toledo factory workers had no trouble breaking a sweat.

The American flag flew in front of the elementary school that housed his polling place. The new stars in the canton that represented Kentucky and Houston gave it a pattern he still hadn't got used to. The polling place itself was in the school auditorium, which was full of seats too small for grown-up backsides. Martin smiled, remembering the days when he'd sat in chairs like that. *I'd never killed anybody then,* he thought, and the smile slipped.

He had to wait in line to get his ballot. Lots of men—and women, who could vote in presidential elections in Ohio—lined up to get their ballots. "Here you are," the clerk said when he came to the front of the line. "Take the first available voting booth." He sounded bored. How many times had he said those identical words since the polls opened this morning? Too many, by all the signs.

A pretty woman a few years younger than Chester Martin pushed aside the curtain that kept her ballot secret and came out with the folded paper in her hand. They did a little accidental dance, each trying to get around the other, and were laughing by the time she went past him and he made his way into the booth.

He voted quickly. He put an X by the names of Upton Sinclair and Hosea Blackford, then went on to vote for the other Socialist candidates. He wasn't altogether happy with the way the Party had handled the Canadian uprising; had he been in charge of things, he would have taken an even stronger line than President Sinclair had. *Why did we fight the war, if we coddle the Canucks once it's done?* But the Socialists were his party, he was making good money, and there were plenty of jobs. He wasn't about to abandon the Party over foreign policy. He went down the line, from Congressman to state officials, voting the straight ticket.

After he'd finished, he handed the clerk the ballot. The fellow ceremoniously stuck it in the locked ballot box, declaring, "Chester Martin has voted." Martin felt proud, as if his vote had singlehandedly saved the country. He knew how silly that was, but couldn't help it.

He hurried out of the auditorium, out of the school. His family's flat was only four blocks away. He'd intended to walk it and save himself five cents, but seeing the pretty woman at the streetcar stop made him change his mind. "Did you vote for President Sinclair?" he asked, fumbling in his pocket for a nickel.

"As a matter of fact, I did," she said. That made him grin with relief; he wouldn't have wanted much to do with a staunch Democrat. He didn't think he would, anyhow. She added, "He's the only one I could vote for, of course. I don't think that's right."

"I don't, either," Martin said, more sincerely than otherwise. "My sister gets to vote for the first time today, and that's all she gets to mark: one square. It really doesn't seem fair."

They chatted, waiting for the streetcar. He found out her name was Rita Habicht, and that she was a typist for a company that made galvanized pipe. He gave her his own name just when the trolley clattered up. *Slow down,* he thought as it rattled along the tracks. *Slow down, dammit*. But it didn't. In no time at all, the streetcar got to his stop.

He let it start up again without getting off. "Have you got a telephone?" he asked.

She hesitated. Then she took a scrap of paper from her handbag, wrote on it, and gave it to him. "Here."

He tucked it into the front pocket of his overalls. "Thanks," he said. "I'll call you." He did leave at the next stop, and had to walk most of a mile back in the direction from which he'd come.

"What took you so long?" his younger sister asked when he finally came through the door. Sue had a sharp nose much like his, but her hair was brown, not sandy. Without waiting for an answer, she went on, "I got to vote. It took forever, but I got to vote." She'd been just too young at the last presidential election.

"Good for you, Sis." Chester gave her a hug. "I remember how that felt—the first time, I mean."

"What took you so long coming home?" Sue asked again.

"Trolley went past the stop, and I had to walk back," he answered.

She looked at him. "It must have gone a long way past the stop, for you to be as late as you are." He could feel himself turning red. His sister started to laugh. "You're blushing!" she exclaimed, as she might have done when they were both children. She wagged a saucy finger at him. "Was she pretty?"

He looked down at the carpet, and at the woven flowers and birds he'd seen every day for years without really looking at them. "Well . . . yeah," he mumbled.

Now Sue stared. "You're not doing that just to drive me crazy," she said. "You really did meet somebody."

"I met her at the polling place, matter of fact," Martin said. "We got to talking, and we seemed to like each other all right, and I got a telephone number from her."

"Will you call her?" Sue asked.

"I'd be a fool not to, don't you think?" he answered.

The door opened behind him. His father came into the flat. "What would you be a fool about this time,

Chester?" Stephen Douglas Martin asked. He was an older version of his son, also a steelworker, and a man who'd stubbornly remained a Democrat.

"I'd be a fool to think I could say anything without you making a crack about it," Chester replied.

His sister said, "He met a girl."

"Happens to a lot of people," his father observed. "Well, to a lot of fellows, anyhow." He turned to Chester. "Come on, boy, tell me more. Who is she? What does she do? How did you meet her? Why didn't you tell me about it sooner?"

"How could I tell you about it sooner when it only just now happened?" Martin asked in some irritation. "Her name's Rita. She's a typist. I met her at the polling place. There. Are you happy now?"

"I don't know." His father looked as surprised as his sister had. "This all sounds pretty sudden."

"Oh, for heaven's sake," Chester said. "I didn't propose to her. All I did was ask for her telephone number."

"Ask for whose telephone number?" his mother asked. Louisa Martin had heard her husband come in, where she hadn't heard her son. She hurried out from the kitchen to give them both a peck on the cheek.

Chester told the whole story over again for the third time. By then, he'd started to feel as if it had happened to somebody else. His mother exclaimed. So did his father, in chorus with her. They sounded pleased and dubious at the same time.

At the supper table, over a pork roast stuffed with cabbage, his mother said, "It really is about time you settled down, son, and started raising a family of your own."

He rolled his eyes. "I haven't even asked if she wants to go to a picture show with me, and you've already got me married off."

"You shouldn't rush into things with a girl you just met," his father said.

He could have pointed out that he *wasn't* rushing into anything. He could have, but he didn't. What point? Neither his father nor his mother would pay the least attention. He was sure of that. He changed the subject: "I wish we had one of those wireless machines. Then we could find out who's winning the election tonight without waiting for the morning paper."

"They're so expensive," his mother said.

"They're less than they were last year," Chester said.

"Maybe they'll be still less next year, or the year after that," his mother said. "If they are, maybe I'll think about getting one. But I've got better things to do with a few hundred dollars right now than to put them into a cabinet that sits there and makes noise all the time."

"It's not just noise, Mother," Sue said. "It's music and people talking and all sorts of exciting things."

"I think it's nothing but a fad, myself," Stephen Douglas Martin said. "After all, once you've heard a band playing John Philip Sousa marches once, how many more times are you going to want to?"

"You could hear something different the next time," Chester said.

"Yes, but are there enough different new things to put on the wireless every hour of the day, every day of the week, every week of the year?" His father shook his head. "I don't think so."

Since Chester had no idea whether there would be or not—and since he didn't think his father had any idea, either—he didn't argue. He said, "I could go over to the Socialists' hall and find out."

"Well, if you want to," his mother said, her tone suggesting she would sooner he stayed.

In the end, he did stay. He'd already put in a long, hard day, one made longer and harder by voting and by walking back to the flat after he'd met Rita Habicht. He went to sleep in his cramped little bedroom. Whenever he thought about how crowded things were, he remembered three years of sleeping in the trenches, sometimes under rain or snow. Compared to that, this didn't look so bad.

In the morning, newsboys hawked papers with big, black headlines: SINCLAIR REELECTED! They shouted out the same thing. Chester felt like cheering; his father, no doubt, would be irate. His father could lump it, for all of him. *Four more years to show the country what we can do,* he thought, and went off to his own dangerous, back-breaking job whistling a cheery tune.

Cincinnatus Driver was sure he was the happiest black man in Des Moines, Iowa. Des Moines didn't have a whole lot of black men in it, happy or otherwise, but he would have bet he led the parade. The reason he was a man with a song in his heart was simple: he'd just found the perfect Christmas present for his son, Achilles.

The tin fire engine was a foot and a half long, with rubber tires, a ladder that went up almost a yard, a bell that made a godawful racket, and half a dozen lead firemen. He was sure Achilles, who was nine, would play with it not just for hours but for weeks. Grinning, he carried it over to the clerk behind the cash register.

"That'll be a dollar and ninety-nine cents," the woman said briskly.

"Here y'are, ma'am." Cincinnatus gave her two dollar bills. His accent was softer than the sharp local English; along with his family, he'd left Covington, Kentucky, not long after the war ended. He'd hoped he'd left his troubles behind him. So far, his hopes looked like coming true.

"Here's your change." The clerk handed him a penny. She smiled. "I hope your little boy enjoys it."

"Thank you kindly, ma'am." Cincinnatus smiled, too. He wouldn't have got so much politeness from a white woman in Covington. He might not have got it here, either. He'd seen that—some places, they wouldn't sell him things till they saw his money. But, on the whole, Negroes didn't have too hard a time in Des Moines. They were thin enough on the ground here to be reckoned a novelty, not a menace.

Still smiling, Cincinnatus took the fire engine out to his truck. The machine was a beat-up White of Great War vintage. Cincinnatus had driven such snorting beasts all through Kentucky and down into Tennessee during the war, in the service of the U.S. Army. Now he worked on his own behalf—and a White made in 1916 or 1917 was, by the end of 1924, something less than it had been.

He didn't care. The truck was a lot better than the spavined Duryea he'd driven from Covington to Des

Moines. It held a lot. He was able to make a good many repairs on it himself; he'd had practice. And, when he couldn't fix the truck, he'd found a mechanic who was both cheap and competent: an immigrant from Italy for whom a black man was but one wonder of a wonder-filled America.

He cranked the engine to get it to turn over. *One of these days, I'm going to put a self-starter in this machine.* He'd had that thought before, too. But the motor hadn't had a chance to cool down, so cranking it was easy. He got behind the wheel, trod on the clutch, put the truck in gear, and drove off. Night fell as he made his way to the northwestern side of town. The White was of recent enough vintage to have electric headlights and not acetylene lamps; he could turn them on from the cabin, and didn't have to get out and fiddle with matches.

The truck wheezed to a stop in front of the apartment building where his family lived. The motor shook and coughed a couple of times after he took out the ignition key, then fell silent. He got out. Wrapping the toy fire engine in some burlap, he carried it into the building.

In the lobby, Joey Chang, who ran a laundry and whose family lived on the floor above Cincinnatus, nodded to him and said, "Hello."

"Hello, Joey," he answered, doing his best to hide a smile. The Chinaman seemed as exotic to him as a mere Negro did to an Italian immigrant. There might have been a couple of Chinese in Covington back when it was part of the CSA. On the other hand, there might not have, too. He'd never eaten chop suey before coming to Des Moines. He liked Chinese food. It was cheap and good and something out of the ordinary.

As soon as he walked into his own flat, Cincinnatus was glad he'd camouflaged the fire engine, because Achilles sat at the kitchen table doing homework. The boy pointed. "What you got, Pa?"

"None o' your business. Get back to work," Cincinnatus answered. Back in Covington, before the war, there'd been no public schools for Negroes. Finding school not only present but required in Des Moines had made a lot of the hardships in uprooting his family worthwhile. Wagging a finger at Achilles, he went on, "I had to sneak around to learn my letters. You got help. I expect you to take advantage of it."

"I am, Pa," his son said. "But you still haven't told me what you got there." Achilles' accent was an odd mix of Kentucky and Iowa. Cincinnatus knew he would have said *ain't told me* himself. He also knew that was wrong, but it seemed natural to him in a way it didn't to the boy.

He went into the kitchen, where Elizabeth had a beef tongue boiling in a pot with potatoes and carrots, and with some cloves that gave the air a spicy smell. She too pointed to the burlap-wrapped toy. "What's that?"

Cincinnatus showed her—the fire engine wasn't for her, after all. Her eyes widened. She nodded. He said, "You got a place in here where we can hide this till the day?"

"Right here." She opened a cabinet and pointed to a top shelf. He stood on tiptoe to push the fire engine back as far as he could. That done, he gave her a kiss. She smiled, as if to say something might come of that later on.

Then Amanda toddled into the kitchen and wrapped her arms around his shins. "Dada!" she said. Hard to believe she was a year and a half old now. Above her head, Cincinnatus and Elizabeth exchanged wry, tired grins. Something might not come of Elizabeth's inviting smile, too. Before Amanda was born, Cincinnatus had forgotten, perhaps mercifully, how much of a handful a baby in the house was. She'd reminded him, though.

"Oh, I almost forgot," Elizabeth said. "We got us a letter today."

"A letter?" Cincinnatus said in surprise. "Who from?" Most—almost all—the mail they got was either bills or advertising circulars. Only a few people they knew, either friends or relatives, could read and write.

For that matter, Elizabeth could hardly read and write herself. Till Achilles started going to school, she hadn't even known the ABCs. But he'd taught her some of what he'd learned. Now she said, "It came from Covington, I know that. But I can't make out who sent it, and I didn't open it up. Didn't reckon I could cipher it out myself, and

I didn't know if it was anything Achilles ought to see, you know what I mean?"

"Sure do." Cincinnatus looked in the icebox and took out a bottle of beer. Iowa was a dry state that took being dry seriously. The beer was unofficial, illegal homebrew, made by Mr. Chang upstairs. Till he came to Des Moines, Cincinnatus hadn't know that Chinamen drank beer, let alone made it themselves. As he yanked the cork out of the bottle, he said, "Why don't you let me have a look at it now?"

"I do that," she said. When she left the kitchen, her skirt swirled, showing off her ankles and several inches of shapely calf. She'd finally given in to what everyone else was wearing these days. Cincinnatus thought the new styles risqué, but that didn't keep him from looking. On the contrary. She brought back the envelope. "Here."

Sure enough, it bore a Covington postmark. Cincinnatus tried to puzzle out the return address, but couldn't. He took a clasp knife from his pocket and opened the envelope. Looking up from the letter, he asked Elizabeth, "You recollect a fellow name of Hadrian, moved next door to my folks a little after the war ended?"

She thought, then nodded. "Believe I do. Never had nothin' much to do with him, though. How come? What's he say?"

"Says Pa's sick, mighty sick, maybe fixin'-to-die sick." Cincinnatus wished he'd never got the letter. He went on, "Says Ma asked him to write me, get me to come back down there 'fore Pa goes." Tears blurred his vision. His father wasn't an old man, but anybody could take sick.

"Mama Livia, she can't very well write you her own self," Elizabeth said. That was true; Cincinnatus' mother and his father, Seneca, were both illiterate. They'd grown up as slaves, back in the days when teaching a Negro his letters was against the law.

"I know." Cincinnatus took a long pull at the beer bottle, wishing it were something stronger. He read the letter again, as if expecting it to say something different the second time around. That was foolish, but who wasn't foolish sometimes?

"What you gwine do?" Elizabeth asked.

"I got to go," Cincinnatus said. "We got enough money to pull through if I'm gone a week or two." They had more money than that, even after he'd bought the bigger truck. He'd always salted away as much as he could. Even when Kentucky was still a Confederate state, he'd done his best to get ahead, and his best had been about as good as a Negro's could be in the CSA.

Elizabeth nodded. "All right. You take the truck or you ride a train?"

"Train," he answered. "Hadrian, he say to wire him when I come, an' he'll meet me at the station." He finished his beer in a couple of big gulps. "Wish he would've wired me. I be there by now." He sighed. "Letter's cheaper, I reckon. What can you do?"

"I say prayers Sunday an' every night for your father," Elizabeth said. "Papa Seneca, he's a nice man."

"Yeah," Cincinnatus said tonelessly. As people will, he'd come to take his father for granted. The idea that the older man might not be there forever—might not be there for very much longer—hit him hard, and all the harder because it caught him by surprise. Everything had been going so well. Everything still was—for him. But with his father sick, that didn't matter any more.

There was a Western Union office in the Des Moines train station. Cincinnatus sent Hadrian a telegram from there. A couple of hours later, he boarded an eastbound train. A crow flying from Des Moines to Covington would have gone about six hundred miles. The train took a longer route, and took its own sweet time getting there. It seemed to stop at every worthless little town along the way, too. Cincinnatus stared out the window, now and then drumming his fingers on his trouser leg in impatience.

On a train in the CSA, the attendants would have been black men. Here, they were almost all foreigners of one sort or another. They muttered things about Cincinnatus that he couldn't understand, but he didn't think any of them were compliments.

The Confederates had dropped the old railroad bridge from Cincinnati to Covington into the Ohio when the

Great War broke out. The train rattled over its replacement in the wee small hours. Cincinnatus yawned and knuckled his eyes. He hadn't slept a wink. He hoped his father was still breathing.

He had no trouble spotting Hadrian: his family's neighbor was the only Negro waiting on the platform. He didn't look to have slept much, either. "C-come along with me," he said. Cincinnatus didn't remember him stammering. He had a nervous tic under one eye, too.

No sooner had they got off the platform than four big, tough-looking white men in plain clothes surrounded them. "You fuckin' *bastard*!" Cincinnatus exclaimed. He knew he'd been betrayed—he just didn't know to whom yet. Hadrian miserably hung his head. What had these people done or threatened to get him to write that letter?

They all piled into a big Oldsmobile. When it stopped in front of the city hall, Cincinnatus knew who had him. It didn't make him feel any better—worse, in fact. "Come along, boy," one of the whites snapped. He'd probably been a cop in the days when Covington belonged to the CSA.

However unwillingly, Cincinnatus went. The man waiting for him inside gave him a smile that might have come from a hunting hound. His luminous, yellow-brown eyes strengthened the resemblance. "Howdy, Cincinnatus," Luther Bliss said. "Been a while, hasn't it?" The head of the Kentucky State Police—the Kentucky secret police—didn't wait for an answer. He turned to Cincinnatus' hard-faced escorts and spoke three words: "Lock him up."

Every once in a while, Nellie Jacobs would take her Order of Remembrance out of its velvet box and look at it. She didn't wear it much—where would a woman who ran a coffee shop in Washington, D.C., have occasion to wear the USA's highest civilian decoration? The last time she'd put it on was for Teddy Roosevelt's funeral. Roosevelt had presented the medal to her with his own hands. He'd given Nellie's daughter, Edna, a medal, too, but hers was only second class, not first.

She didn't know she was being a spy, Nellie thought.

Lord, she wouldn't have cared if the Confederates held Washington forever. It was funny, if you looked at it the right way.

The eagle on the Order of Remembrance stared fiercely back at her. Of course, Roosevelt hadn't known the whole story, any more than Edna had. Roosevelt hadn't known she'd stuck a knife into Bill Reach, the U.S. spymaster in Washington. Nobody knew that, nobody but Nellie. Not even her husband knew, and Hal Jacobs had reported directly to Reach.

"He had it coming, the filthy son of a bitch," Nellie muttered. It wasn't that Bill Reach had been a drunkard, though he had. But he'd also been a lecher and, in his younger days, a man who'd had—and paid for—assignations with Nellie. He'd thought he could keep on having them, too, if he just slapped down the cash.

Nellie's long oval face settled into the lines of disapproval it had worn so often since she'd escaped the demi-monde. *Shows how much he knew,* she thought. She'd fought hard for respectability. She hadn't been about to throw it away for a drunken bastard and his red, throbbing prick. One of the things she liked about her husband was that he didn't trouble her in the bedroom very often. *Old men have their advantages.*

Her mouth twisted. *You're no spring chicken yourself,* she thought. She'd turned fifty earlier in the year. She felt every year of her age, too. It wasn't so much that she was going gray, though she was. That aside, she looked a good deal younger than her years. But keeping up with a four-year-old would have made anybody feel her years.

As if the thought of Clara were enough to make her get into mischief, she called, "Ma! Help me tie my shoe!"

"I'm coming," Nellie said. Her back twinged when she got off her bed. Clara couldn't tie her shoes yet. Sometimes she insisted on trying anyhow. Four-year-olds were nothing if not independent. That they drove their parents mad never once crossed their minds, of course. That was part of their . . . charm.

"I'm going to go out and play," Clara declared when Nellie hurried into her bedroom.

"Not yet, you're not." Nellie surveyed the damage. "Oh, child, what *have* you gone and done?"

Actually, the damage itself left little room for doubt. Clara had put her shoes on the wrong feet and then tied as many knots as she could in the shoelaces. She couldn't manage a bow, but knots she had no trouble with. The shoes came up well over her ankles; they were almost boots, and fit snugly even before Clara created her knotty problem.

Nellie couldn't even get the shoes off her daughter till she untied some—several—of the knots. Clara didn't want to hold still for the process. Four-year-olds didn't hold still unless they were asleep or coming down with something. Nellie asked her twice not to squirm. That failing, she swatted Clara's bottom. Her daughter squalled, but then did hold still . . . for a little while.

It was, Nellie decided, long enough. It was, at any rate, long enough for her to get the shoes on their proper feet and tie a couple of bows. "Play on the sidewalk in front of the shop here," Nellie warned. "Don't you go out in the street. I'm going to come downstairs and keep an eye on you. If you even go *near* the street, you'll get a spanking like you'll never forget. No, you'll get two—one from me, and one from your pa."

"I promise, Ma." Clara solemnly crossed her heart. "Hope to die."

No, it's so you don't die, Nellie thought, but Clara wouldn't have had the faintest idea what she was talking about. "Let's go downstairs," Nellie said. Clara took her favorite toy, a rag doll named Louise, and went down to the ground floor at what Nellie would have reckoned a suicidal pace. Nellie followed more sedately.

Nellie turned away for a moment to get a whisk broom and a dust pan. The coffee shop was closed on Sundays, of course; Washington's blue laws were as strict as any in the USA. But the more cleaning she did now, the less she would have to worry about come Monday morning, when she'd also be busy brewing coffee, frying eggs and ham and bacon and potatoes, toasting bread, and serving her customers. Her door might be shut, but she didn't reckon Sunday a day of rest.

Before Nellie had taken more than three steps, brakes screeched out in the street. Metal crumpled. Glass tinkled musically. It reminded her of artillery bombardments during the war, but wasn't so dramatic.

Or it wouldn't have been . . . . "Oh, God in heaven!" Nellie said, and dashed outside. "Clara!" she shouted. "Where are you, Clara?"

No answer. Fear rising in her like the tide, Nellie stared at the accident. A Ford and a Packard had locked horns. The Ford, predictably, was the loser. Steam gushed from its ruptured radiator. Its driver descended to the street holding a handkerchief to his head, which he'd bloodied when he greeted his windshield face first.

"Clara!" Nellie called again. "Dear God, please . . ." The last time she'd prayed had been during the U.S. artillery barrage that nearly leveled Washington before the Confederates finally, sullenly, drew back into Virginia. God must have heard that prayer—she'd come through alive. But everything back then seemed small and unimportant when set against her daughter's safety. *"Clara!"*

The gray-haired man who'd been driving the Packard had to kick at his door before it would open. He didn't seem badly hurt, and started shouting at the other man: "You idiot! You moron! You thumb-fingered baboon!"

"Fuck you, Grandpa," the man with the bloodied face replied. "You drove right into me."

"Liar!"

"Liar yourself!"

Neither one of them said anything about a little girl, and neither one of them paid any attention to Nellie. "Clara!" she called once more. She didn't want to look closely at the accident, for fear she would see little legs sticking out from under a wheel. *"Clara!"*

"Boo!"

Nellie sprang a foot in the air. There stood her daughter, coming out from behind the stout iron base of a street lamp. "Thank you, Jesus," Nellie whispered. She ran to her little girl and held her tight.

"Fooled you, Mama!" Clara said happily. "I got down there and— *Ow!*" Nellie applied her hand to the part on which her daughter was in the habit of sitting, much harder than she had before they went outside. Clara started to howl. "What's that for, Mama? I didn't do nothing!"

"Oh, yes, you did," Nellie said, and spanked her again. "You scared me out of a year's growth, that's what you did. I was afraid one of those cars ran over you, do you know that?"

Clara, at the moment, knew nothing except that her fanny hurt. She tried to get away, and had no luck whatsoever. Nellie dragged her back into the coffee shop. "Louise!" Clara wailed.

Although Nellie was tempted to leave the doll out on the sidewalk, that would have cost more tears and hysterics than it was worth. She snarled, "You stay here. Don't move a muscle!" at Clara, and then went back to retrieve Louise. She all but threw the rag doll at her daughter. "Here!"

"Thank you, Mama," Clara said in an unwontedly small voice. She *hadn't* moved a muscle, and evidently had figured out this was no time to say or do anything that might land her in more trouble.

When Nellie's husband came back from a friend's later that morning, Nellie told him the whole story. Clara looked at him in silent appeal; he was often softer than her mother. But not this time. Hal Jacobs sighed, wuffling out his white mustache. "Clara, you must not play games like that," he said. "Your mother thought you were hurt, maybe even killed."

"I'm sorry, Pa," Clara said. Maybe she even meant it. She seemed more inclined to be good for Hal than she was for Nellie. *She takes after her half sister,* Nellie thought sourly. Edna had always done what she wanted, not what Nellie wanted. She'd taken great pleasure in flaunting it, too.

And she'd married well in spite of everything. When she came to visit as the sun was setting, she wore a maroon silk dress that daringly showed her legs halfway to her knees. Nellie, who'd had a really gamy past, had spent more than thirty years trying to live it down. Edna, in keeping with young people everywhere these days—or so it seemed to Nellie—flaunted her fast life.

"Be good, Armstrong," she told her son. Armstrong Grimes—Edna's husband, Merle, came from the same town in Michigan as General Custer—was two, only a couple of years younger than Clara, his aunt. Having told him to be good, Edna let him run wild—that seemed to be her idea of how to raise children.

"How are you, dear?" Nellie asked, pouring Edna a cup of coffee.

"Couldn't be better, Ma," Edna answered expansively. She looked like a twenty years' younger version of her mother, but without the pinched, anxious expression Nellie so often wore. She still thought she could beat the game of life. Nellie was convinced nobody could. But Edna had her reasons. She went on, "Merle just got himself promoted in the Reconstruction Agency. That's another forty dollars a month, and you'd best believe it'll come in handy."

"Bully," Nellie said, meaning perhaps a third of it. She'd had to fret and scrape for every dime she ever made— she'd had to do worse things than fret and scrape for some of the dimes she'd made before Edna was born. As far as she could see, her daughter had things easy but didn't begin to guess how lucky she was.

Before Edna could go on bragging, a shriek rose from the direction of the kitchen. "Ma!" Clara squealed. "Armstrong just pulled my hair, Ma!"

Edna laughed. Nellie didn't. "Well, pull his back," she said.

Her older daughter bristled. A moment later, Armstrong Grimes started to cry. Then Clara shrieked again. "Ma! He *bit* me!"

"You going to tell her to bite him back, too?" Edna asked. Nellie glared. Children, whether four or thirty, could drive you right out of your mind.

Reggie Bartlett was a first-rate weather prophet. He looked at his boss and said, "Reckon it'll rain tomorrow."

Jeremiah Harmon looked up from the pills he was compounding. "Shoulder kicking up again?" the druggist asked.

"Sure is," Bartlett answered. "Leg, too, matter of fact.

I took me a couple of aspirins, but they don't shift the ache." He'd spent the end of the war in a U.S. military hospital after catching two bullets from a machine-gun burst and getting captured down in Sequoyah. The wounds had finally healed, but their memory lingered on.

"Wouldn't surprise me if you were right." Harmon added a little water to his mix and put it in a twenty-pill mold. He swung the hinged top of the mold into place. "There we go. These'll make somebody piss like a race-horse."

"I've heard that one a million times. How do race-horses piss?" Reggie asked, and then, before his boss could, he answered his own question: "Pretty damn quick, I bet."

Jeremiah Harmon snorted. "You've always got a snappy comeback, don't you?"

"I do my best," Bartlett answered. He had an engaging grin, one that let him say things a dour man could never have got away with.

The bell over the front door jangled. A customer came in. "Help you with something, sir?" Reggie asked.

"Yes. Thanks. Chilly out there." The man came up to the counter. Bartlett wished he hadn't. His breath was so dreadful, he might not have used a toothbrush since before the Great War. Maybe, if God were kind, he'd ask about one now, or about mouthwash. But no such luck; he said, "What have you got in the way of rat poison?"

You could breathe on them, Reggie thought. *That'd do the job, the way the Yankees' chlorine killed the rats in the trenches on the Roanoke front.* No matter how engaging his grin, though, he knew he couldn't get away with that. Life in Richmond was too civilized for such blunt truths. "Here, let me look," he said, and pulled up a bright yellow box with an upside-down rat with X's for eyes on the front of it. "This ought to do the job."

"It'll shift 'em, will it?" the man asked, breathing decay into Reggie's face.

"Sure will, sir." Reggie drew back as far as he could, which wasn't nearly far enough. "Rats, mice, even cock-roaches. You put it down, they eat it, and they die."

"Reckon I can manage that." The customer dug a hand in his pocket. Coins jingled. "How much?"

"Twenty-two cents," Bartlett said. The man gave him a quarter. He solemnly returned three pennies.

"Thanks." The fellow put them in his pocket. He took the box of rat poison and headed out the door. "Freedom!" Without waiting for an answer, he left the drugstore.

Reggie's boss looked up from the pills, which he was removing from the mold. "You showed fine patience there," he said. "I don't know if I could have done the same. I could smell him all the way over here."

"You could give a man like that a straight flush in a poker game, and he'd still find a way to lose," Bartlett said. "No wonder he's a Freedom Party man."

"His money is as good as anyone else's," Harmon said. "In fact, you can gloat if you like, because his money's going into my pocket, and into yours, and neither one of us can stand Jake Featherston."

"We're not fools. I hope to God we're not fools, anyway," Reggie answered. "The only thing Featherston can do is make a speech that sounds good if you're a sorry so-and-so who can't add six and five without taking off your shoes."

"I'm not going to try to tell you you're wrong—you ought to know that." Harmon looked at the clock on the wall. "Just about quitting time. Why don't you knock off a couple of minutes early? Call it a bonus for the way you dealt with that fellow."

"Thank you kindly. I don't mind if I do." Bartlett put on his coat and his fedora. "I'll see you in the morning."

"See you then." Jeremiah Harmon was busy making more pills. Reggie sometimes wondered if he ever went home at night.

The man with slit-trench breath had been right: it was chilly outside. Bartlett wished he'd brought along a pair of earmuffs. As he hurried toward the trolley stop a couple of blocks away, he went past some posters that hadn't been pasted to a half ruinous wall when he walked by it on the way to work that morning.

VOTE FREEDOM IN 1925! they shouted in red letters

on a white background. Below that, in smaller type, they added, *Jake Featherston talks straight. Every Wednesday on the wireless. The truth shall set you free.*

"And when will you ever hear the truth from that son of a bitch?" Reggie muttered. He'd heard Jake Featherston on the stump in the very earliest days of the Freedom Party. He hadn't liked what he heard then, and he hadn't liked anything he'd heard from Featherston or the Freedom Party since.

Only difference is, Featherston was a little snake then, and he's a big snake now, Bartlett thought. But even a big snake could lose some hide now and then. Reggie hooked his fingernails under the top of one of those posters and yanked. As he'd hoped, most of it tore away. The fellows who'd hung the posters had done a fast job, a cheap job, but not a good one. They hadn't used enough paste to stick them down tight. Whistling "Dixie," he ripped down one poster after another.

He hadn't got all of them, though, before a raucous voice shouted, "Hey, you bastard, what the hell you think you're doing?"

"Taking down lies," Reggie answered calmly.

"Them ain't lies!" the man said. He was about Reggie's age, but shabby, scrawny, still wearing a thread-bare butternut uniform tunic that had seen a lot of better years. Veterans down on their luck swelled the ranks of the Freedom Party. This one snarled, "You touch another one o' them posters, and I'll beat the living shit out of you."

"You don't want to try that, buddy," Bartlett said. Down came another poster. The shabby veteran howled with rage and trotted toward him. Thanks to the wounds Reggie had taken in Sequoyah, he wasn't much good either at fisticuffs or running away. He'd had run-ins with Freedom Party men before, too.

During the war, a .45 had been an officer's weapon, nothing to speak of when set against the Tredegar rifles most ordinary soldiers carried. These days, the .45 in a hidden holster on Reggie's belt put him in mind of an extra ace up his sleeve. He took it out and pointed it at the onrushing would-be tough guy. His two-handed grip said he knew exactly what to do with it, too.

The Freedom Party man skidded to a stop in the middle of the street, so abruptly that he flailed his arms and rocked back on his heels. The barrel of the .45 had to look the size of a railroad tunnel as Reggie aimed it at his midriff. "I told you, you don't want to try that," Reggie said.

"You'll pay for this," the scruffy veteran said. "Everybody's gonna pay for fucking with us. You're going on a list, you—" He decided not to do any more cussing. Running your mouth at a man with a pistol when you didn't have one of your own wasn't the smartest thing you could do. Even a Freedom Party muscle man could figure that out.

"Get lost," Bartlett told him. He gestured with the .45 to emphasize the words. "Go on down to the corner there, turn it, and keep walking. You do anything else, you'll be holding up a lily."

Face working with all the things he dared not say, the other man did as he was told. Bartlett finished tearing down the posters, then went on to the trolley stop. His only worry was that the Freedom Party man had a weapon of his own, one he hadn't had a chance to use. But the fellow had talked about beating him up, not shooting him. And he didn't reappear.

Up came the trolley, bell clanging. Reggie tossed a dime into the fare box and took a seat. The dime should have been five cents; prices weren't quite what they had been before the war. But they weren't what they had been afterwards, either—he wasn't paying a million dollars, or a billion, for the privilege of riding across town to his flat.

Nobody on the trolley car had the slightest idea who he was or what he'd just done. That suited him fine, too. He had a chance to relax a little and look out the window. Before long, the trolley passed more of those VOTE FREEDOM IN 1925! posters. Reggie's lip curled. He couldn't rip them all down, however much he wished he could.

Seven and a half years after the Great War ended, not all the destruction U.S. aeroplanes had visited on Richmond was yet repaired. Plenty of burnt-out and bombed building fronts stared at the street through window frames naked of glass; they might have been so many skulls peering out through empty eye sockets. *The damnyankees made my home town into Golgotha,* Bartlett thought. *One of these days, we'll have to pay them back. But how?*

He shivered, though the crowded trolley was warm with humanity. That was how the Freedom Party thought, and how it got its members. *Haven't you had enough of war?* he asked himself. Asked that way, he could hardly say no.

He got off at the shop nearest his flat. For supper, he fried up a ham steak and some potatoes. After he did the dishes—he was a fussy, neat bachelor—he read for a while and went to bed. He wouldn't have minded a wireless set, so he could listen to music or a football game, but not on the salary of a druggist's assistant.

The next day did bring a chilly drizzle. Work at the drugstore went much as the previous day had. He didn't bother telling his boss about the fuss over the posters. Jeremiah Harmon had no use for the Freedom Party, no, but Reggie didn't want him fussing like a mother hen, which was just what he would have done.

"Hey, you!" somebody called to Reggie when he walked to the trolley stop that evening. It was the veteran he'd quarreled with. He wore a disreputable hat to keep the rain off his face.

His hand went to the .45. "Told you I didn't want you bothering me," he said.

"No bother, pal," the fellow said. He pasted on a smile as he came up to Bartlett, and he made sure he kept his hands in plain sight. "We've all got to live and let live, ain't that right?"

Reggie stared. "That's not how you talked yesterday," he said, his voice hard with suspicion. "What's wrong with you now?"

"Not a thing," the Freedom Party man said. "I just got a little hasty, is all. You went through some of the things I did, you'd get hasty, too."

"I went through plenty myself," Bartlett said. "You want to go through it again? That's what that damn Featherston's got in mind."

"No, pal. You don't understand at all," the veteran said. He still had on the same ancient tunic he'd worn the evening before.

Noticing that, Reggie didn't notice the footsteps coming up behind him till they stopped. That made him notice, and made him start to turn, his pistol coming out of the holster. Too late. He heard three shots. Two slugs hammered him in the chest. The next thing he knew, he was on the ground, reaching for the .45 that had fallen from his fingers.

The veteran scooped it up. "Nice piece," he said, and then, grinning, "Freedom!" Reggie heard him as if from far away, and further every moment. He didn't hear the man and his friend running away at all, or anything else ever again.

Three guards came up to Cincinnatus Driver's cell. Two of them stood in the corridor, their pistols aimed at his midsection. The third opened the cell door. "Come along," he said.

"Where you takin' me?" Cincinnatus asked.

"That ain't none o' your business, boy," the guard snapped, for all the world as if Kentucky were still part of the CSA, not the USA. "Come along, you hear?"

"Yes, suh." Cincinnatus got up off his cot and came. He'd quickly learned how far he could go with these guards before they stopped talking and started persuading him by other means. One beating had been plenty to drive the lesson home: not just the beating itself, but how much they enjoyed giving it to him. If they ever decided to beat him to death, they would do it with smiles on their faces.

"Hands behind your back," the guard told him. He obeyed. The guard clicked handcuffs onto his wrists. They were cruelly tight, but Cincinnatus kept his mouth shut about that, too. Complaining just got them tightened more.

The guards marched him along the corridor. He recognized some of the men sitting or lying in their cells. Some, black like him, were Reds. Others, whites, were men who'd been Confederate diehards during the war and probably belonged to the Freedom Party nowadays. Maybe some of the other prisoners recognized him, too. If so, no one gave a sign.

"This way," one of the guards told him. They led him across the exercise yard he normally saw for an hour a week, down another corridor, and into an office. A tall, backless stool sat in front of the desk. Luther Bliss sat behind it. The guards slammed Cincinnatus down on the stool, hard.

"Here we are again," the head of the Kentucky State Police said.

"Yes, suh," Cincinnatus said. "I want a lawyer, suh." He hadn't tried that one in a while. The worst the other man could tell him was no.

Bliss' smile never touched his hunting-dog eyes. "If you was still in Des Moines, maybe you could have one," he answered. "But this here's Kentucky, and the rules are different here. This is one of the reclaimed states, and we aren't about to put up with treason or rebellion. You mess around with that stuff and you get caught, we take care of you our own way."

"I wasn't messin' around with nothin' here," Cincinnatus said bitterly. "I was just livin' my life up in Iowa till you got that sorry Hadrian nigger to write that lyin' letter to get me down here in the first place. You call that fair . . . suh?"

"I had you once before," Luther Bliss replied in meditative tones. "I had you, and I was going to squeeze you, and Teddy Roosevelt made me turn you loose. He made me pay you a hundred dollars out of my own pocket, too. I have . . . a long memory for these things, Cincinnatus."

Cincinnatus hadn't forgotten that, either, though Bliss hadn't mentioned it till now. "Do Jesus, Mr. Bliss, you want your hundred dollars back, I'll pay it to you. Just let me wire my wife an'—"

Bliss shook his head. "I get paid back with interest."

"I'll pay you interest. I got the money. I done pretty good for myself up there."

"I don't want your money. I get paid back *my* kind of interest."

He was what he was. His kind of interest involved

pain and misery. That was what he dished out. That was what the people who told him what to do wanted him to dish out. If, every once in a while, he dished them out to people who didn't really deserve them, the people who told him what to do probably didn't mind. They might even figure he deserved a little fun on the job.

Like a hunting dog taking a scent, Luther Bliss leaned forward. "Enough chitchat. About time we get down to business, I reckon."

Before Cincinnatus could brace himself, one of the guards slapped him in the face. He tumbled off the stool and also banged his funny bone on the floor as he fell. "Why'd he do that, Mr. Bliss?" he said, slowly climbing to his feet. "I ain't done nothin' to nobody."

"You lie. Everyone lies." Luther Bliss sounded sad but certain. Policemen got used to people lying to them. Maybe they even got to where they expected it. Secret policemen probably heard and expected even more lies than any other kind. Bliss pointed to the stool. "Sit your nigger ass back down, Cincinnatus. You got to tell the truth when I ask my questions."

"You didn't ask me no questions," Cincinnatus said reproachfully. "Joe there, he jus' hauled off an' hit me."

"That's for all the lies you've already told me, and to remind you not to tell me any more," Luther Bliss answered. Again, his smile never reached his eyes. "You ought to be thankful we've gone easy on you so far."

"Easy!" Cincinnatus exclaimed. "He damn near knocked my head off." A few months in jail—and years of sparring before then—had given him and the secret policeman an odd sort of camaraderie. He could, up to a point, speak his mind without making Luther Bliss any more likely to do something dreadful to him.

Bliss nodded now. "He just thumped you a bit. Worse we've done, we've beaten you up. That ain't so much of a much, Cincinnatus, believe you me it ain't. It's a new age we're livin' in. Electricity's everywhere. You take an ordinary car battery and some wires, and you clip 'em to a man's ears, or to the skin of his belly, or maybe to his privates. . . ."

Cincinnatus didn't want to show fear. But his mouth went dry at the thought of electricity trickling through his balls. Would he ever be able to get it up again after something like that? *Please, Jesus, don't let me find out!*

Meditatively, Bliss went on, "Other nice thing about that is, it doesn't leave any marks. You niggers don't show bruises as much as a white man would, but even so. . . ." He leaned forward. "I reckon you already told me everything you know about Kennedy and Conroy and the rest of those goddamn diehards."

"Mr. Bliss, I done sung like a canary 'bout them bastards." There Cincinnatus spoke the truth. He owed no loyalty to the white men who'd done all they could to help the Confederate cause in Kentucky. They might have killed him or betrayed him to U.S. authorities, but they'd had no great hold on his loyalty. As far as he could see, any Negro who backed the Confederates from anything but compulsion was some kind of idiot.

The secret policeman pointed to him. "You're still holding out, though, when it comes to Apicius and the rest of the Reds. Like calls to like. Just like the diehards, you coons stick together."

"Do Jesus, how can I know what they're up to when I moved away years ag—" Cincinnatus got that far before the guard belted him again. This time, he was braced for it, and didn't fall off the stool. He tasted blood in his mouth.

"You don't expect me to believe anything like that, do you?" Luther Bliss sounded sad, like a preacher contemplating sinful mankind. "I ain't stupid, Cincinnatus, no matter what you think."

"I never reckoned you was." Again, Cincinnatus told the exact truth. Fear of Bliss had helped him decide to leave Kentucky, but he'd never thought the other man was dumb. Just the opposite: he didn't care to live under Bliss' magnifying glass for the rest of this days. Living under his thumb, though, was even worse.

"You get letters. You know what's going on here," the secret policeman said.

"Not hardly," Cincinnatus told him. "Don't hardly

100

know that many folks what can read an' write. You keepin' tabs on me all the time like I reckon you been doin', you know that's true."

For a moment, he thought he'd got through to Bliss. The man's eyes narrowed. He looked thoughtful. But then, a moment before he spoke, Cincinnatus realized he was playing a part. He was building up hope in his captive only to dash it: "Well, sonny, so what? Long as you're here, you'll pay for everything you done anyways."

Cincinnatus would have been more devastated if he'd had more hope to lose. He wanted to tell Bliss where to head in. A couple of times, back in the days when he was still free, he *had* told Bliss where to head in. He'd enjoyed it mightily then, too. But he was paying for it now.

"What you got to tell me about them Reds?" Luther Bliss asked now.

"I done told you everything I ever knew," Cincinnatus answered. It wasn't quite true, but he didn't think Bliss knew that.

He did know what was coming next. It came. Joe and the other guards got to work on him. They enjoyed what they did, yes, but not to the point of getting carried away and doing him permanent harm: they were, in their way, professionals. It went on for a very long, painful time.

What hurt most of all, though, was a casual remark Bliss made halfway through the torment: "You might as well sing, by God. It isn't like anybody on the outside gives a damn about what happens to one miserable nigger in a Kentucky jail."

At last, the beating stopped. The guards dragged Cincinnatus back to his cell. He probably could have walked. He made himself out to be weaker and hurt worse than he really was. Maybe that made them go a little easier on him than they would have otherwise. On the other hand, maybe it didn't do a single goddamn thing.

"See you next time, boy," Joe said as his pal undid the manacles from Cincinnatus' wrists.

Cincinnatus lay on his cot like a dead man. Had Luther Bliss sent for him more often, he *would* have been a dead man in short order. Maybe Bliss didn't want to kill him right away. Maybe, on the other hand, the secret policeman was taking so many different vengeances, he wasn't in a hurry about finishing off any one of them.

It isn't like anybody on the outside gives a damn about what happens to one miserable nigger in a Kentucky jail. In a way, that was a lie. Cincinnatus knew as much. Elizabeth cared. Achilles cared. Amanda cared. But what could they do? They were black, too, black in a white man's country. Nobody who could do anything cared about Cincinnatus. That burned like acid. It would keep on burning long after the pain of this latest beating eased, too.

He ran his tongue over his teeth. So far, the goons had broken only one. He'd taken no new damage there today. They hadn't done anything to him this time that wouldn't fade in a couple of weeks. In the meantime ... *In the meantime, it's gonna hurt, and ain't nothin' you can do about it.*

A cart squeaked up the corridor: supper trays. Cincinnatus wondered if he'd be able to eat. *You better. You got to stay strong.* A redheaded white man shoved a tray of something that smelled greasy into Cincinnatus' cell. The fellow wore the same sort of uniform as the guards who'd beaten him.

In a low voice, the redhead said, "Freedom." Cincinnatus suppressed a groan. Just what he needed— somebody with diehard sympathies mocking him. *I ought to report you, you bastard. Luther Bliss'd make you pay.* But then the fellow went on, "We'll get you out." He pushed the cart away. Cincinnatus stared after him. Did he mean that? And, if he did, whose side was he really on?

IV

Another trip down to Washington. Flora Blackford preferred Philadelphia, and didn't care who knew it. But she was willing to excuse the trip to the formal capital of the USA for one reason: so her husband could for the second time take the oath of office as vice president of the United States.

"Now we think about 1928," she told him as the Pullman car rattled south from Philadelphia. Then she shook her head. "No. That's not right. We should have been thinking about 1928 since the minute we won last November."

Hosea Blackford's smile showed amusement—and, she was glad to see, ambition, too. "I don't know about you, Flora," he said, "but I *have* been thinking about it since the minute we won last November, and a while before that, too. When I first saw what the office was, I didn't think I could do much with it or go any further. I've changed my mind, though."

"Good," Flora said. "You should have, and you'd better think about it. You can be president of the United States. You really can."

"That wouldn't be too bad for a boy off a Dakota farm, would it?" he said. "You always hear talk about such things. 'Any mother's son can grow up to be president.' That's what people say. Having the chance to make it come true, though . . ."

"Of course, if you thought being president was the most important thing in the world, you never should have married me." Flora tried to keep her tone light. Other people would be saying the same thing much more pointedly in the years to come. She was as sure of that as she was of her own name. A presidential candidate with a Jew for a wife? Unheard of! How many votes would it cost him?

"That *has* occurred to me," Hosea Blackford said slowly. "It couldn't very well *not* have occurred to me. But then I decided that, if I had to choose between the two, I would rather spend the rest of my life with you than be president. So I'll take my chances, and the country can take its."

Flora stared at him. Then she kissed him. One thing led to another. The run from Philadelphia down to Washington wasn't a very long one, especially not when traveling on President Sinclair's express. They barely had time to get dressed again and set their clothes to rights before the train came in to Union Station.

"It's a good thing you don't have to wrestle with a corset, the way you would have before the war," Hosea said, adjusting his necktie in the mirror.

"Don't speak of such things—you don't know what you're talking about," Flora answered. "The only thing I can think of is, whoever put women in corsets must have hated us. Especially in summertime. A corset on a hot summer day . . ." She shuddered.

"Well, you wouldn't have had to worry about the heat today." Her husband looked out the window. "The snow's still coming down."

"March is late in the year for a snowstorm," Flora said. "I wonder if what people say is true: that the weather's been peculiar since the Great War, and that it made the weather peculiar."

Hosea Blackford laughed. "Back in Dakota, I would have said *May* was late for a snowstorm, but nothing sooner than that. If you ask me, the weather's always peculiar. I have a suspicion it's peculiar because it's peculiar, too, and not because we made it that way. I can't prove that, but it's what I think. The weather's bigger than anything we can do, even the Great War."

"I hope you're right," she said.

On the platform, a military band blared away. Flora didn't care for that. It wasn't a proper Socialist symbol, even if it was a symbol of the presidency. But if President Sinclair wanted it—and he did—she could hardly complain. People called her the conscience of the Congress, but this wasn't a question of conscience—only one of taste.

A limousine whisked the president and his wife to the White House. Another one brought the Blackfords there. The journey took only a few minutes. When Flora saw the Washington Monument, she pointed. "It's taller than it was when we came down here for Roosevelt's funeral. You can really tell."

Her husband nodded. "Before President Sinclair's term is up, it'll be back to its full height. No mark on the sides to show how much of it the Confederates knocked down, either. I think that's good."

"So do I," Flora agreed. "No matter what the Democrats say, there can be such a thing as too much remembrance."

"Yes." Hosea sighed. "Some people just can't see that. Why anyone would want to remember all the horror we went through during the Great War . . . Well, it's beyond me."

"Beyond me, too," Flora said. "Try not to get into an argument with my brother tomorrow."

"I won't argue if David doesn't," her husband said. "I'll try not to argue even if he does." David Hamburger had lost a leg in the last year of the war. In spite of that—or maybe because of it—he'd gone from Socialist to conservative Democrat since. Having paid so much, he couldn't, wouldn't, believe that payment hadn't been worthwhile.

During President Sinclair's—and Vice President Blackford's—first inauguration, Flora had been a Congresswoman, yes. But she hadn't been Blackford's wife, and hadn't been fully swept up into the social whirl surrounding the occasion. Now she went from one reception to another. She found it more wearing than enjoyable.

When she said as much, Hosea Blackford laughed. "Are you sure you're a New York Jew, and not one of those gloomy Protestants from New England? No matter what they say, there's nothing in the Bible against having a good time."

"I didn't say there was," Flora answered. "But it all seems so—excessive."

"Oh, is that all you're worrying about?" Hosea laughed again. "Of course it's excessive. That's the point of it."

She gave him a disapproving look. "I'm sure Louis XVI said the same thing just before the French Revolution."

"Not fair," Hosea said.

"Maybe not." Flora didn't want to argue with her husband, any more than she wanted him quarreling with her brother. But she wasn't altogether convinced, either.

She found believing him easier when Inauguration Day came. When the Socialists won the election in 1920, electricity had filled the air. The Democrats had dominated U.S. politics since the election of 1884. Some people had feared proletarian revolution. Some had looked for it.

It hadn't come. Politics had gone on as usual—the same song, but in a different key. Flora supposed that was a good thing. She still sometimes had a sense of opportunity missed, though.

This second Socialist inauguration seemed different. Now no one acted astonished the day had ever come. People took it for granted, in fact. Flora didn't know whether that was good or bad, either. She did know that, up on the reviewing stand in front of the White House, she wondered if she'd freeze to death before her husband and President Sinclair took the oaths of office for their second terms.

But having her family up on the stand with her made up for a lot. Her older sister Sophie's son Yossel was very big now—he was almost ten. He'd never seen his father, who'd been killed in action before he was born. Flora had hardly seen her younger sister Esther's new husband, a clerk named Meyer Katz. She was also startled at how gray her parents were getting.

She wished her brother David hadn't worn his Soldiers' Circle pin, with a sword through the year of his conscription class. Only reactionaries did. But he wore his Purple Heart next to it. That and the stick he used and the slow, rolling gait of a man who made do with an artificial leg after an above-the-knee amputation meant no one near him said a word about it. His younger brother, Isaac, had gone through his turn in the Army after the Great War. His tour had been quiet, uneventful. He didn't wear a pin on his lapel.

In President Sinclair's second inaugural address, he talked about justice for the working man, old-age pensions, and "getting along with our neighbors on this great continent." The first two drew fierce applause from the crowd, the third rather less.

"Memories of the war are still too fresh," Hosea Blackford said when all the speeches and parades were over. "In another ten years, people will look more kindly on the Confederate States."

"Not everyone will," David Hamburger said. He was only a tailor talking to the vice president of the United States, but he spoke his mind.

His brother-in-law frowned. They were going to argue after all. "Would you want your children to go through what you did? Do you think the Confederates are mad enough to want their children to go through it again?"

"I hope there's never a war again," Flora said.

"I hope the same thing," David answered. "But hoping there won't be and staying ready in case there is are two different animals."

"We'd do better if we'd made a just peace, not the harsh one Teddy Roosevelt forced the CSA to swallow," Hosea Blackford said. "And we're still trying to figure out what to do with Canada."

"You try giving away anything Roosevelt won and you'll lose the next election quicker than you ever thought you could," David said.

"I don't think so," Flora said. "If we aren't a just nation, what are we?"

"A strong one, I hope," her brother answered. They

eyed each other. They both used English, but they didn't speak the same language.

No one questioned the Socialist Party's agenda at any of the inaugural banquets and balls that night. Even the Democratic Congressmen and Senators who made their appearance were smiling and polite. They wouldn't show their teeth till Congress went back into session up in Philadelphia.

Flora was just as well pleased to return to the *de facto* capital. Over the past eight years, it had become home to her. Her husband teased her as the train pulled into Broad Street Station: "You'll be busier than I will. The vice president's main job is growing moss on his north side."

"You knew that when you accepted the nomination the first time," Flora said.

He nodded. "Well, yes. Even so, these past four years have really rammed it home."

But Flora had trouble charging into the new session as she was used to doing. She found herself sleepy all the time, without the energy she usually took for granted. Before long, she was pretty sure she knew why. When she no longer had room for doubt, she said, "Hosea, I'm going to have a baby."

His eyes grew very wide. After a moment, he started to laugh. "So much for prophylactics!" he blurted. Then he gave her a kiss and said, "That's wonderful news!"

Flora wished he'd said that before the other. "I think so, too," she said. "The world he'll see . . ."

"I know. That's astonishing to think about." Hosea Blackford ran a hand through his hair. It was thick, but gray. "I only hope I'll see enough of it with him for him to remember me. This is one of those times that reminds me I'm not so young as I wish I were."

"You're not *too* old," Flora said slyly. Her husband laughed again. Even so, the moment didn't quite turn out the way she wished it would have.

The McGregors' wagon plodded toward Rosenfeld. The horse's tail switched back and forth, back and forth, flicking at the flies that came to life in the springtime.

Mary McGregor felt like a turtle poking its head out of its shell. All through the harsh Manitoba winter, she'd stayed on the farm. Going into town then wasn't for the fainthearted. Her mother had done it, for kerosene and other things they couldn't make for themselves, but she hadn't wanted to take Mary or Julia along.

A Ford whizzed past them. The horse snorted at the dust the motorcar kicked up. Mary coughed, too. "Those things are ugly and noisy," she said. This one had been particularly ugly—it was painted barn red, so anyone could see it coming, or going, for miles.

"They go so fast, though," Julia said wistfully. "You can get from here to there in nothing flat. And more and more people have 'em nowadays."

"People who suck up to the Yankees," Mary said.

Her older sister shook her head. "Not all of them. Not any more."

From the seat in front of them, their mother looked back over her shoulder. "We're not getting one any time soon," Maude McGregor said, and brushed a wisp of hair back from her face. Her voice was harsh and flat, as it so often was these days. "Hasn't got anything to do with politics, either. They're expensive, is what they are."

That silenced both Mary and Julia. The farm kept them all fed, but it could do no more than that—or rather, they could make it do no more than that. *If Pa were alive, and Alexander, we'd be fine,* Mary thought. But there was always too much work and not enough time. She didn't know what to do about that. She didn't think anybody could do anything about it.

"We ought to be coming up to the checkpoint outside of town pretty soon," Julia said.

"We've passed it by now," Maude McGregor said, even more flatly than before. "It's not up any more."

Mary felt like bursting into tears. Two or three years before, she would have. Now she faced life with a thoroughly adult bleakness. "The rebellion's all over, then," she said, and nothing more lived in her voice than had in her mother's.

"It never had a chance," Julia said.

That was enough to rouse Mary, whose red hair did advertise her temper. "It *would* have," she said, "if so many people hadn't sat on their hands. And if there hadn't been so many traitors."

For some little while, the clopping of the horse's hooves, the squeak of an axle that was getting on toward needing grease, and the occasional clank as an iron tire ran over a rock in the roadway were the only sounds. *"Traitors" is an ugly word,* Mary thought. But it was the only one that fit. The Americans had known the uprising was coming before it really got started. The *Rosenfeld Register*—the weekly newspaper—had even said a Canadian woman with a name famous for patriotism helped with information about it because she was in love with a Yank. The only famous woman patriot Mary could think of offhand was Laura Secord. Did she have descendants? Mary wouldn't have been surprised. She didn't think the uprising would have had much of a chance anyhow. With such handicaps, it had had none. All that was left now was punishing those who'd done their best for their country.

Maude McGregor drove around a muddy crater in the road. This one was new; it didn't date back to the days of the Great War. Mary hoped it had blown up something large and American.

Before long, Julia pointed ahead and said, "There it is! I see it."

Mary McGregor saw Rosenfeld, too. Like her sister, she couldn't help getting excited. Rosenfeld had perhaps a thousand souls. If two railroads hadn't come together there, the town would have had no reason for existing. But there it was. It boasted a post office, a general store, the weekly newspaper, a doctor's office, and an allegedly painless dentist. He'd filled a couple of Mary's teeth. It hadn't hurt him a bit. She wished she could say the same.

"I suppose Winnipeg's bigger," Mary said, "but it can't be *much* bigger."

"I wouldn't think so," Julia agreed. Neither of them had ever seen a town bigger than Rosenfeld. Up in front of them, Maude McGregor chuckled quietly. Mary wondered why.

Regardless of whether there were towns bigger than Rosenfeld, it was quite crowded and bustling enough. Wagons and motorcars clogged its main street. Locals in city clothes—white shirts, neckties, jackets with lapels—and U.S. Army men in green-gray shared the sidewalk. Women wore city clothes, too. Julia pointed again. "Will you look at that?" she said, deliciously scandalized. Mary looked—and gaped.

"Disgraceful," her mother said grimly. Maude McGregor's skirt came down to her ankle, as her skirts had done for as long as Mary could remember. But this woman showed off half her legs, or so it seemed.

"If it's the style, Ma—" Julia began, her voice hesitant.

"No." Her mother hesitated not at all. "I don't care what the style is. No decent woman would wear anything like that. No daughter of mine will." Several women in Rosenfeld wore dresses and skirts that short. Were they all scarlet? Mary didn't know, but she wouldn't have been surprised.

Her mother had to pull off the main street to find a place to hitch the wagon. As Maude McGregor got down to give the horse the feed bag, Mary pointed to a sign-board plastered to a wall. "Ma, what's a Bijou?" She knew she was probably mispronouncing the unfamiliar word.

"It's a motion-picture house," her mother answered after reading some of the small print under the big name.

"A motion-picture house? In Rosenfeld?" Mary and Julia exclaimed together. Julia went on, "This *is* the big city," while Mary asked, "Can we go see something, Ma? Can we, please?" She knew she sounded like a wheedling little girl, but she couldn't help it.

"I don't know." Here her mother wavered, where she'd been very sure about skirts. "The flyer says it costs a quarter each to get in, and seventy-five cents is a lot of money."

"We'd only do it once, Ma. It's not like we come here every day," Mary said, wheedling harder than ever.

Julia added, "It's a new business in town. It's not like those start up every day, either."

111

"Well—all right," Maude McGregor said. Mary clapped her hands. "But only this once, understand? You pester me about it every time we come to town and you'll find out your backsides aren't too big to switch."

"We promise, Ma," Mary and Julia chorused. They looked at each other and winked. They'd won! That didn't happen very often.

A line snaked toward the Bijou's box office. A lot of the people in the line were American soldiers. Mary ignored them. The soldiers ignored her, too, though they plainly noticed her older sister and her mother. Julia and Maude McGregor paid no attention to the men in green-gray.

Three quarters slapped down on the counter. Mary heard her mother sigh. The fellow behind the counter peeled three tickets off an enormous roll and handed them to her mother. Another young man at the door importantly tore the tickets in two. Inside the theater, the smell of buttered popcorn almost drove Mary mad. Along with the popcorn, the girl behind the counter sold lemonade and more different kinds of candy than Henry Gibbon carried in his general store.

Maude McGregor led Mary and Julia past such temptations and into the theater itself. Both her daughters let out pitiful, piteous sighs. She took no notice of them. She was made of stern stuff.

The maroon velvet chairs inside the theater swung down when you put your weight on them. That proved entertaining enough to take Mary's mind off candy, at least for a little while. A couple of rows in front of her, a little boy bounced up and down, up and down, up and down. She wanted to spank him. Before too long, his father did.

Without warning, the lights went dim. A man at a piano—a man Mary hadn't noticed up till then—began to play melodramatic music. The curtains slid back from an enormous screen. Some sort of machine behind her began making noise: the projector. Then the screen filled with light, and she forgot everything else.

"It's . . . photographs come to life," she whispered to Julia. Her sister nodded, but never took her eyes away from

112

the screen. Mary didn't, either. Those enormous, moving black-and-white people up there held her mesmerized.

NEWS OF THE WORLD, a headline read, briefly interrupting the motion. Then she saw a man in a silly uniform and an even sillier hat waving to soldiers marching past. KAISER WILHELM REVIEWS TROOPS RETURNING FROM OCCUPIED PARTS OF FRANCE, another headline explained.

Swarthy men, many of them wearing big black mustaches, fired rifles and machine guns at one another in a country that looked dry and hot. SCENES FROM THE CIVIL WAR IN THE EMPIRE OF MEXICO, the caption said. Mary stared, entranced. She'd never been farther from the farm than Rosenfeld, but here was the whole world in front of her eyes.

Two men in suits crossed a bridge from opposite sides and shook hands. That was labeled, PRESIDENT OF USA, PREMIER OF QUEBEC MEET IN FRIENDSHIP. All of a sudden, Mary wasn't so sure she wanted the whole world in front of her eyes.

And then she saw ruined city blocks, explosions, diving aeroplanes with machine guns blazing, glum survivors, grim prisoners with hands in the air, overturned motorcars and dead bodies lying in the street, and other bodies swinging from a gallows. SCENES FROM THE REBELLION IN CANADA, the explanatory sign said. She hadn't seen much war. It had swept through Rosenfeld and stayed to the north. And she'd only been a little girl then. She gulped. This was what she wanted, was it?

Not even the main feature, a melodrama with a car chase, a chase through and on top of the cars of a train, and an astonishingly handsome leading man who wed the astonishingly beautiful leading lady and gave her a tender kiss just before the lights came back up, could take all those images of devastation out of her mind.

"That's what they're doing to our country," she said as she and her mother and sister filed out of the theater. "They want us to know it, too."

"They want us to be afraid," Julia said.

"They know how to get what they want, too," Maude

113

McGregor said grimly. "Come on. Let's buy what we need and get back to the farm."

They were on their way to Henry Gibbon's general store when Mary saw a SCENE FROM THE REBELLION IN CANADA that wasn't what the Americans who'd made and approved the moving picture had in mind. Through the streets of Rosenfeld came a column of prisoners, on their way to the train station from God only knew where. They were scrawny and hollow-eyed and wore only rags. They must have been some of the last men captured, for most of the rebels had given up weeks, even a couple of months, before. The McGregors bathed once a week or so, like most farm families; Mary was used to strong odors. The stench that came from the prisoners made her stomach want to turn over.

One of the men started to sing "God Save the King." An American guard in green-gray hit him in the head with a rifle butt. Blood streamed down his face. The guard laughed. The prisoner stumbled on. Tears stung Mary's eyes. She didn't let them fall. She kept her face still and vowed . . . remembrance.

Abner Dowling looked down at what had been a plate of ham and fried potatoes. "By God, that was good," he said.

"Yes, sir," said his adjutant, a dapper young captain named Angelo Toricelli. He had only about half of Dowling's girth, but he'd worked similar execution on a beefsteak and a couple of baked spuds.

"Nothing wrong with the way the Mormons cook," Dowling said, blotting his lips on his napkin.

"No, sir," Captain Toricelli agreed.

Having spent a lot of time as an adjutant, Dowling recognized the younger man's resigned tone, though he was resolved not to do so much to deserve resigned agreement as his own cross, General Custer, had done. Thinking of a cross made him suspect he knew what was bothering Toricelli. "Does it bother you that I eat so much, Captain?"

One of Toricelli's eyebrows twitched in surprise. "Not . . . really, sir," he said after a moment. "It's none of my business. I would never ask anyone to be anything he's not."

114

"Interesting way to put it," Dowling remarked. Then he laughed, which set several of his chins jiggling. Laugh or not, though, he changed the subject: "How do you like being a gentile in Utah? Me, I think it's pretty funny."

"The Mormons can say we're gentiles," Toricelli answered. "You can go around saying all sorts of things. That doesn't mean they're true."

"I suppose not." Dowling left a silver dollar on the table to cover their meals. He got to his feet. So did Toricelli, who hurried to open the restaurant's front door for him. That was one of the things adjutants were for, as Dowling knew only too well.

"Pretty day," Toricelli remarked as they came out onto the street.

"It is, isn't it?" Dowling said. Spring was in the air. Snow had retreated up the slopes of the Wasatch Mountains to the east. Sea gulls wheeled overhead, which Dowling never failed to find strange so far inland. And, as always, sounds of building filled the air.

Salt Lake City had surrendered to U.S. forces nine years before. Dowling had seen photographs of it just after the Mormon rebels finally yielded to superior force. They'd fought till they couldn't fight any more. The city had looked more like the mountains of the moon than anything that sprang from human hands and minds. Hardly one stone remained atop another. The Mormons had simmered resentfully under the harsh treatment they'd got from U.S. authorities ever since the Second Mexican War. When they rose during the Great War, they'd done a lot more than simmer.

Now . . . Now, on the outside, everything here seemed calm. Salt Lake City—and Provo to the south and Ogden to the north—were three of the newest, shiniest towns in the USA. Most of the rubble had been cleared away. Most of the Mormons who'd survived the uprising were getting on with their lives. On the surface, Utah seemed much like any other state. When Dowling's train first brought him to Salt Lake City, he'd wondered if his presence, if the U.S. Army's presence, was necessary.

He'd been here more than a year now. He no longer

wondered. As he and Toricelli walked east along South Temple Street towards Army headquarters, no fewer than three people—two men and a woman—shouted "Murderer!" at them: one from a second-story window, one from behind them, and one from a passing Ford.

Toricelli eyed the motorcar as it sped away, then muttered something pungent that might not have been English under his breath. "I wasn't able to read the license plate," he said. "If I had, we could have tracked that son of a bitch down."

"What difference does it make?" Dowling said. "They all feel that way about us. One more, one less—so what?"

"It makes a lot of difference, sir," his adjutant said earnestly. "Yes, they're going to hate us, but they need to fear us, too. Otherwise, they start up again, and we did all that for nothing." To show what he meant by *that*, he waved across South Temple Street to Temple Square.

No rebuilding there. By order of the military administration, the Mormon Tabernacle and the Temple and the other great buildings of the Church of Jesus Christ of the Latter-Day Saints remained as they had fallen during the Federal conquest of Salt Lake City: another reminder to the locals of the cost of rising against the United States. Rattlesnakes dwelt among the tumbled stones. They were the least the occupiers had to worry about.

Colonel Dowling murmured a few lines from Shelley:

" 'My name is Ozymandias, king of kings.
Look on my works, ye Mighty, and despair!'
Nothing besides remains. Round the decay
Of that colossal wreck, boundless and bare,
The lone and level sands stretch far away."

Angelo Toricelli gave him a quizzical look. "I've heard other officers recite that poem, sir."

"Have you? Well, I'm not surprised," Dowling said. Even fallen, the gray granite Temple inspired awe. A gilded copper statue of the angel Moroni had topped the tallest spire, which the Mormons had used as an observation post till U.S. artillery knocked it down. No American soldiers had ever found a trace of that statue. Persistent rumor said the Mormons had spirited away its wreckage and venerated it as a holy relic, as the Crusaders had venerated pieces of the True Cross. Dowling didn't know about that. He did know there was an enormous reward for information leading to the capture of the statue, or of any significant part of it. No one had ever collected. No one had ever tried to collect.

At the corner of Temple and Main, Captain Toricelli said, "You want to be careful crossing, sir. For some reason or other, Mormons in motorcars have a devil of a time seeing soldiers."

"Yes, I've noticed that," Dowling agreed. His hand fell to the grip of the .45 on his hip. Most places, an officer's pistol was a formality almost as archaic as a sword. Even more than in occupied Canada, Dowling felt the need for a weapon here.

Soldiers in machine-gun emplacements protected by reinforced concrete and barbed wire surrounded U.S. Army headquarters in Salt Lake City. Sentries carefully checked Dowling and Toricelli's identification cards. They'd discovered the unfortunate consequences of not checking such things. The Mormons had Army uniforms they'd taken during the Great War, and some of them would kill even at the cost of their own lives. Not much news of such assassinations had got out of Utah, but that made them no less real.

"Oh—Colonel Dowling," a soldier said as Dowling walked down the hall to his office. "General Pershing is looking for you, sir."

"Is he? Well, he's just about to find me, then." Dowling turned to his adjutant. "I'll see you in a while, Captain."

"Of course, sir," Angelo Toricelli said. "I have a couple of reports to keep me busy."

"If you can't stay busy in Utah, something's wrong with you," Dowling agreed. And off he went to see the commanding general.

John J. Pershing was in his mid-sixties. He didn't look younger than his years so much as tough and well-preserved for them. His jaw jutted. His gray Kaiser Bill mustache—the style was now falling out of favor with younger men—added to his bulldog appearance. His icy blue eyes seized and held Dowling. "Hello, Colonel. Take a seat. There's coffee in the pot, if you care for some."

"No, thank you, sir. I'm just back from lunch," Dowling answered.

General Custer would have been even money or better to make some snide crack about his weight. Pershing simply nodded and got down to business: "I'm worried, Colonel Dowling. This place is like a powder keg, and I'm afraid the fuse is lit."

"Really, sir?" Dowling said in surprise. "I know Utah's been a powder keg for more than forty years, but why do you think it'll go off now? If the Mormons were going to rise against us, wouldn't they have tried it when the Canucks did?"

"Strategically, that makes good sense," Pershing agreed. "But the trouble that may come here hasn't got anything to do with what happened up in Canada. You are of course aware how we hold this state?"

"Yes, sir: by the railroads, and by the fertile belt from Provo up to Ogden," Dowling answered. "Past that, there's a lot of land and not a lot of people, so we don't worry very much."

"Exactly." Pershing nodded. "We just send patrols through the desert now and again to make sure people aren't plotting too openly." He sighed. "Out in the desert, maybe a hundred and seventy-five miles south of here, there's a little no-account village called Teasdale. A troop of cavalry rode through it a couple of weeks ago. The captain in command discovered several families that were pretty obviously polygamous."

"Uh-oh," Dowling said.

"I couldn't have put it better myself," Pershing replied.

Polygamy had been formally illegal in Utah since the Army occupation during the Second Mexican War. It hadn't disappeared, though. Dowling wished it had, because, more than anything else, it got people exercised. Fearing he already knew the answer, he asked, "What did the cavalry captain do, sir?"

"He applied the law," Pershing said. "He arrested

everyone he could catch, and he burned the offending houses to the ground."

"And he came out of this place alive? I'm impressed."

"Teasdale's a very small town—smaller still, after he seized the polygamists," Pershing replied. "And he is an able young man. Or he would be, if he had any sense to go with his tactical expertise. Naturally, even though this happened in the middle of nowhere, news got out right away. And, just as naturally, even a lot of Mormons who aren't ardent polygamists are up in arms about it."

"Not literally, I hope," Dowling said.

"So do I, Colonel. But we must be ready, just in case," Pershing said. "I've asked Philadelphia to send us some barrels to use against them at need. If the War Department decides to do it instead of reprimanding me for asking for something that costs money, I'm going to put you in charge of them. You became something of an expert on barrels, didn't you, serving under General Custer and with Colonel Morrell during the war?"

I became an expert on not getting myself court-martialed on account of barrels, is what I became, Dowling thought. *Custer wanted to use them against War Department doctrine, and I had to cover for him. Does that make me an expert?* Aloud, he answered, "I'll do whatever I can, sir."

"I'm sure of it," Pershing said. "This may all turn out to be so much moonshine, you understand. The War Department may need a real rising from the Mormons before they send in the weapons that would have over-awed them and stopped the rising in its tracks. And the powers that be may not send us anything even in case of rebellion. They're in a cheese-paring mood back there, sure enough. They've stopped spending *any* money on improving barrels, you know."

"Yes, I do know that," Dowling replied. "I don't like it."

"Who would, with a brain in his head?" Pershing said. "But soldiers don't make policy. We only carry it out, and get blamed when it goes wrong. I wonder how fast and how well the Confederate States are rearming."

"They aren't supposed to be doing anything of the sort, sir," Dowling said.

Pershing tossed his head, like a horse bedeviled by flies. "I know that, Colonel. I wonder anyway."

A bullet cracked past Jefferson Pinkard's head. He ducked, not that that would do him any good if the bullet had his name on it. Somewhere not far off, rebel Mexican machine gunners started firing at something they imagined they saw. A field gun banged away, flinging shells into the uplands town of San Luis Potosí.

Like most Confederates, Pinkard had thought of the Empire of Mexico as his country's feebleminded little brother—when he'd bothered thinking of it at all, which wasn't very often. In the comfortable days before the war, the Empire did as the Confederacy asked. The Confederates, after all, shielded Mexico from the wrath of the USA, which had hated the Empire since its creation during the War of Secession.

The truth, nowadays, was more complicated. The USA backed the rebels against the Empire. The CSA couldn't officially back Maximilian III, but Freedom Party volunteers like Pinkard numbered in the thousands—and the Freedom Party wasn't the only outfit sending volunteers south to fight the Yankees and their proxies.

That all seemed straightforward enough. What Jeff hadn't counted on was that there would have been—hell, there had been—rebels even without U.S. backing. Maximilian III would never land on anybody's list for sainthood.

Pinkard shrugged. "He may be a son of a bitch, but he's *our* son of a bitch, by God," he muttered. Behind him, another field gun, this one on his side, started answering the rebels' piece. It seemed to be firing as much at random as the enemy gun.

Stupid bastards, he thought, not sure whether he meant the enemy or his own side. None of them would have lasted long during the Great War; he was sure of that. Both sides were brave enough, but neither seemed to know just what it was supposed to do. They lacked the experience C.S. and U.S. forces had so painfully accumulated.

Another machine gun started rattling. Ammunition was tight. Both sides imported most of it. That didn't keep gunners from shooting it off for the hell of it. Who was going to tell 'em they couldn't? They had the weapons, after all.

A Mexican private came up to Jeff. Like Pinkard's, his cotton uniform was dyed a particularly nasty shade of yellow-brown. It looked more like something from a dog with bad digestion than a proper butternut, but all the greasers and the Confederate volunteers wore it, so Jeff could only grouse when he got the chance. He couldn't change a thing. The Mexican said, "*Buenos días*, Sergeant Jeff." It came out of his mouth sounding like *Heff*. "The *teniente*, he wants to see you."

"All right, Manuel. I'm coming." Pinkard pronounced the Spanish name *Man-you-well*. He took that for granted, though what the locals did to his never ceased to annoy him. He walked bent over. The Mexicans built trenches for men of their size, and he overtopped most of them by half a head. The rebel snipers weren't nearly so good as the damnyankees had been up in Texas, but he didn't want to give 'em a target. He nodded to Lieutenant Hernando Guitierrez. "What can I do for you, sir? *En qué puedo servirle?*" Again, he made a hash of the Spanish.

It didn't matter, not here. Lieutenant Guitierrez probably spoke better English than Pinkard did. He was every bit as tall, too, though not much more than half as wide through the shoulders. By his looks, he had a lot more Spaniard and a lot less Indian in him than did most of the men he commanded. He said, "I have a job for you, Sergeant."

"That's what I'm here for," Pinkard agreed.

"Er—yes." The Mexican lieutenant drummed his fingers on his thigh. Jeff had a pretty good idea what was eating the fellow. He was only a sergeant himself (and he'd never risen higher than PFC in the C.S. Army), but he got more money every month than Guitierrez did. And, although he was only a sergeant, it wasn't always obvious

121

that his rank was inferior to the other man's. Why else were Confederate volunteers down here, if not to show the greasers the way real soldiers did things?

"What can I do for you, Lieutenant?" Jeff asked again, not feeling like pushing things today.

Guitierrez gave him what might have been a grateful look. "You are familiar, Sergeant, with the machines called barrels?"

"Uh . . . yeah." Pinkard was familiar enough to start worrying, even though the clanking monsters had been few and far between in Texas during the Great War—especially on the Confederate side. "What's the matter? The rebels going to start throwing 'em at us? That's real bad news, if they are."

"No, no, no." The Mexican officer shook his head. He had a sort of melancholy pride different from anything Pinkard had known in his own countrymen. "*We* have three, built in Tampico by the sea and coming up here to the highlands by railroad. I want you to lead the infantry when we move forward with them against the peasant rabble who dare to oppose Emperor Maximilian."

"*You people* built barrels?" Once he'd said it, Jeff wished he hadn't sounded quite so astonished. But that was too late, of course.

Lieutenant Guitierrez's lips thinned. "Yes, we did." But then he coughed. He was a proud man, but also an honest man. "I understand the design may have come from the Confederate States—unofficially, of course."

"Ah. I get you." Jeff laid a finger by the side of his nose and winked. The Confederates couldn't build barrels on their own. The Yankees would land on them with both feet if they tried. But what happened south of the border was a different story. "When does the attack go in, and what are we aiming for?"

"We want to drive them from those little hills where they can observe our movements. They are shelling San Luis Potosí from that forward position, too," Guitierrez replied. "If all goes well, this will be a heavy blow against them. As for when, the attack begins the morning after the barrels come into place."

He didn't say when that morning would be. He was probably wise not to. For one thing, Pinkard had already discovered what *mañana* meant. For another, barrels, no matter who built them, broke down if you looked at them sideways. Pinkard grunted. "All right, Lieutenant. Soon as they get here, I'll lead your infantry against the rebels. You'll follow along yourself to see how it's done, right?"

He wasn't calling Guitierrez a coward. He'd seen the other man had courage and to spare. And Guitierrez nodded now. "*Claro que sí*, Sergeant. Of course. That is why you are here: to show us how it is done."

Jeff grunted again. In one sense, the Mexican lieutenant was right. In another . . . Pinkard was here because his marriage was as much a casualty of the Great War as a fellow with a hook for a hand. He was here because he had a fierce, restless energy and an urgent desire to kill something, almost anything. He couldn't satisfy that desire back in Birmingham, not unless he wanted to fry in the electric chair shortly thereafter.

Three days later—not a bad case of *mañana*, all things considered—the barrels came into position, clanking and rattling and belching and farting every inch of the way. Pinkard wasn't surprised to find more than half their crewmen were Confederate volunteers. He *was* surprised when he got a look at the barrels themselves. They weren't the rhomboids with tracks all around that the CSA, following the British lead, had used during the Great War. And they weren't quite the squat, hulking monsters with a cannon in the nose and machine guns bristling on flanks and rear the USA had thrown at the Confederacy.

They did have a conning tower like that of a U.S. barrel—their crewmen called it a turret. It revolved through some sort of gear mechanism, and carried a cannon and a machine gun mounted alongside it. Two more bow-mounted machine guns completed their armament. "Since the turret spins, we don't need nothin' else," a crewman said. "Means we don't have to try and shoehorn so many men inside, neither."

"Sounds like somebody's been doing a lot of thinking about this business," Pinkard said.

"Reckon so," the other man agreed. "Now if the same somebody would've thunk about the engine, too, we'd all be better off. A good horse can still outrun these miserable iron sons of bitches without breathing hard."

During the Great War—even the attenuated version of it fought out in Texas—a big artillery barrage would have preceded the barrels' advance. Neither side in this fight had enough artillery to lay down a big barrage. It didn't seem to matter. The barrels rolled forward, crushing the enemy's barbed wire and shooting up his machine-gun nests. "Come on!" Pinkard shouted to the foot soldiers loyal to Maximilian III. "Keep up with 'em! They make the hole, an' we go through it. Stick tight, and the enemy'll shoot at the barrels and not at you so much."

That was how things had worked during the Great War. In English and horrible Spanish, Jeff urged his men forward. Forward they went, too. The only thing he hadn't counted on was the effect barrels, even a ragged handful of barrels, had on troops who'd never faced them before. The rebels, or the braver men among them, tried shooting at the great machines. When their rifle and machine-gun bullets bounced off the barrels' armor, they seemed to decide the end of the world was at hand. Some ran away. The barrels' machine guns scythed them down like wheat at harvest time. Others threw down their rifles, threw up their hands, and surrendered. *"Amigo!"* they shouted hopefully.

Jefferson Pinkard had never had so many strangers call him *friend* in all his born days. In Texas, the Confederates had gone raiding to catch a handful of Yankee prisoners. Here, prisoners were coming out of his ears. "What do we do with 'em, Sergeant?" asked a soldier who spoke English—maybe he'd worked in the CSA once upon a time. "We go—?" The gesture he made wasn't the throat-cutting one Pinkard would have used, but it meant the same thing.

For once, Jeff's blood lust was sated. Slaughter in the heat of battle was as fine as taking a woman, maybe finer. Killing prisoners felt like murder. *Maybe I'm still a Christian, after all.* "Nah, they've surrendered," he answered. "We'll take 'em back with us. We'd better. Till those barrels break down, they're gonna keep bringin' in plenty more."

"*Sí, es verdad,*" the soldier said, and translated Pinkard's words for the other Mexicans. They all assumed he knew how to handle a flood of prisoners of war, too—including the prisoners themselves, who swarmed up to him to kiss his hands and even try to kiss his cheeks in gratitude for being spared.

"Cut that out!" he roared. It made him wish he had ordered a massacre. Instead, he led the captured rebels—who were even more ragged and sorry-looking than the Mexican imperialists—back out of the fighting. Once he got them behind the line, he had to figure out what to do with them next. Nobody else seemed to want to do anything that looked like thinking.

He commandeered some barbed wire and some posts to string it from. After he herded the prisoners into the big square he'd made, he told off guards to make sure they didn't head for the high country. Then he had to yell to make sure they got something—not much, but something—to eat and drink. And he had to go on yelling, to make sure *mañana* didn't foul things up. By the time three or four days went by, all the Mexicans assumed he was in charge of the prisoner-of-war camp. Before very much longer, he started thinking the same thing himself.

Colonel Irving Morrell hated soldiering from behind a desk. He always had. As best he could tell, he always would. And he especially hated it when there was fighting going on and he found himself a thousand miles away. The reports filtering north from the civil war in the Empire of Mexico struck him as particularly maddening—and all the more so because he couldn't get anybody else in the War Department to take them seriously.

"God damn it, the imperialists are cleaning up with these new barrels of theirs," he raged to his superior, a stolid senior colonel named Virgil Donaldson. He waved papers in Donaldson's face. "Has anybody besides me read this material? By what it's saying, they've got just about all the features we put on our fancy prototype at Fort

Leavenworth. But we built our prototype and said to hell with it. Those bastards have got a production line going in Tampico."

Colonel Donaldson puffed on his pipe. He had a big red face and a big gray mustache. He looked more like somebody's kindly uncle than a General Staff officer. He sounded like somebody's kindly uncle, too, when he said, "Take an even strain, Colonel Morrell. You'll burst a blood vessel if you don't, and then where will you be?"

"But, sir—!" Morrell waved the papers again.

"Take an even strain," Donaldson repeated. He liked the phrase. Before Morrell could explode, Donaldson went on, "Who cares what a bunch of goddamn greasers are up to, anyway?"

"But it's not just greasers, sir," Morrell said desperately. "These barrels have Confederate mercenaries as crew. They've got to have Confederates designing them, too. And the Confederate States aren't allowed to build barrels. The armistice agreement makes that as plain as the nose on my face."

A ceiling fan spun lazily. A fly buzzed. Outside Donaldson's window, summer heat made the air shimmer. The government building across the street from General Staff headquarters might have belonged to some other world, some other universe. Morrell laughed softly. He'd had that feeling about the General Staff before, with no tricks of the eye to start it going.

Trying to come back to what he was sure was reality, he said, "We ought to protest to Richmond. The Confederate government is turning a blind eye toward what has to be several regiments' worth of their veterans going south to fight on Maximilian's side. That may not be against the letter of their agreements with us, but it's dead against the spirit."

After another puff on that pipe, Colonel Donaldson said, "Nice idea, but don't hold your breath. President Sinclair is looking for good relations with the CSA. He doesn't want to bother Richmond with trifles, and he thinks anything this side of a Confederate invasion of Kentucky is a trifle."

Morrell muttered something under his breath. It wasn't

that he thought Donaldson was wrong. No, he feared his superior was right. "Why did we bother to win the war, if we won't make it count?"

"You'd have to talk to President Sinclair about that, Colonel Morrell," Donaldson answered. "*Why* isn't my job, or yours, either. It's for the civilians. They decide what to do, and they tell us. Doing it is our department."

"I know, sir." The lesson had been drilled into Morrell since his West Point days. During the War of Secession, U.S. generals had spoken of overthrowing the republic and becoming military dictators. Then they'd gone out and lost the war, so they'd never had the chance to do more than talk about it. No one had wanted to take the risk of such things since, though it was only now, a lifetime later, that the United States had to deal with the consequences of victory rather than defeat.

"In fairness, we could use some peace and quiet with Richmond right about now," Donaldson said. "After all, we've got Germany to worry about, too."

"Well, yes," Morrell admitted reluctantly. He knew why he was reluctant to admit any such thing, too: "But if we ever do fight the Kaiser, that'll be the Navy's worry, not the Army's. At least, I have a devil of a time seeing how the Germans could invade us, or how we could land troops in Europe."

"It wouldn't be easy, would it?" Donaldson said. "But, of course, a lot depends on who's friends with whom. The Germans have the same worries about France and England as we do about the CSA. And God only knows what's going to happen to the Russians, even now. They're having more trouble putting down their Reds than the Confederates ever did during the war."

"Not our worry, thank God." Morrell chuckled. The puff of smoke Donaldson sent up might have been a fragrant question mark. Morrell explained: "The Russian Reds make up the best names for themselves. I especially like the two who are operating in that town on the Volga— Tsaritsin, that's the name of the place. The Red general is the Man of Steel, and his second-in-command goes by the Hammer. The Reds in the CSA weren't so fancy."

"They were nothing but a bunch of coons," Donaldson said. "You can't expect much from them."

That made Morrell thoughtful. "I wonder," he said. "I do wonder, sir. When I was in the field, I ran up against Negro regiments a few times. Far as I could tell, they didn't fight any worse than raw regiments of white Confederate troops."

"Huh." The older man sounded deeply skeptical. But then he shrugged. "*That's* not our worry, either, thank God."

"No, sir," Morrell agreed. "Are you sure there's no point to writing that report about the barrels down in Mexico, sir? I really do think that's alarming."

Donaldson sighed the sigh of a man who'd been a cog in a bureaucratic machine for a long time. "You can write the report, Colonel, if it makes you happy. I'll even endorse it and send it on. But I can tell you what will happen. The most likely thing is, nothing. It'll go into a file here along with a million other reports. That's what happens if you're lucky."

"I don't call that luck," Morrell said.

"Compared to the other thing that could happen, it's luck," Donaldson told him. "Believe you me, it's luck. Because the other thing that could happen is, somebody reads the report and passes it on to somebody else, somebody outside the General Staff, and it gets into the hands of one of those precious civilians—say, somebody like N. Mattoon Thomas, the assistant secretary of war."

"But he's just the man—just the sort of man—who ought to see a report like this one," Morrell said. "He thought well of the one I did on the mess in Armenia."

"Well, maybe. But maybe not, too. Armenia's a long ways off, you see. The Confederate States are right next door," Colonel Donaldson said. "If you're lucky, *he* reads it and then he throws it into a file in the War Department offices. Different file, but that's all right." He held up a hand to silence Morrell, then went on, "If you're not so lucky, he reads it and he thinks, *Who's this smart-aleck soldier trying to tell me how to do my job?* And if that's what somebody like N. Mattoon Thomas thinks, pretty soon you're not here in Philadelphia any more. You're commanding a garrison in the middle of nowhere: Alberta or Utah or New Mexico, somewhere like that."

He spoke as if of a fate worse than death. That was probably how he saw it. That was how any soldier who was first of all a cog in a bureaucratic machine and only afterwards a fighting man would have seen it. But Morrell didn't want to be here in the first place. Getting back out into the field, even somewhere in the back of beyond, sounded pretty good to him.

Yes, it does—to you, he thought then, several beats later than he should have. *What will Agnes think about it? You've got a little girl now, Morrell. Do you want to haul Mildred off to God knows where, just because you couldn't stand to keep your big mouth shut?*

He muttered unhappily. Colonel Donaldson thought he was contemplating the horrors of life outside Philadelphia. "Dismissed," Donaldson said.

Unhappily, Morrell left his superior's office. Even more unhappily, he went back to his own. *Where does your first loyalty lie? To your wife and daughter, or to the United States of America?*

He cursed softly. But he didn't need long to make up his mind. Agnes had been a soldier's widow before she met him, dammit. She knew what the price of duty could be. If they had to go off to Lethbridge or Nehi or Flagstaff, she'd take that in stride. It might even end up better for Mildred.

Morrell nodded to himself. He fed a sheet of paper into the typewriter that squatted on his desk like some heathen god. He typed with his two index fingers—a slower way of doing things than proper touch-typing, but it got the job done well enough. If the powers that be chose to ignore his report, that was their business. But he was going to make sure they saw what he saw.

He did warn his wife what he'd done, and what might happen as a result. To his relief, she only shrugged. "Philadelphia's a nice town," she said. "But I got along well enough in Leavenworth, too."

He kissed her. "I like the way you think."

129

"It isn't a question of thinking," Agnes said. "It's a question of doing what you have to do." Mildred Morrell didn't say anything. She just kicked her legs and grinned up at her father from her cradle, showing off her first two brand new baby teeth. Some of her babbles and gurgles had *dada* in them, but she didn't yet associate the sound with him.

"What will you think, if you grow up in Lethbridge or Nehi instead of Philadelphia?" Morrell asked her. Mildred only laughed. She didn't care one way or the other. "Maybe, just maybe," her father said, "I'm fixing things so you don't have to go through a war when you grow up. I hope I am, anyway."

He was eating lunch the next day when Lieutenant Colonel John Abell came up to him. Without preamble, General Liggett's adjutant said, "You do believe in cooking your own goose, don't you, Colonel?"

"Ah." Morrell smiled. "You've read it, then?"

"Yes, I've read it." The astringently intellectual General Staff officer shook his head in slow wonder. "Amazing how a man can analyze so brilliantly and be so blind to politics, all at the same time."

After another bite of meat loaf, Morrell said, "You've told me as much before. What am I being blind to today?"

"One and a half million dead men, Colonel, and I'd think even you should notice them," Lieutenant Colonel Abell answered with a certain somber relish. "One and a half million dead men, or a few more than that—all the reasons why there's no stomach in the USA for another war against the Confederate States."

Morrell winced. His smile faded. John Abell was a snob. That didn't mean he was a fool—anything but. "Don't you believe most people would rather fight a small war now if the Confederates don't back down—which I think they would—than fight a big one ten or twenty years down the road?"

"Some people would. A few people would. But most?" Abell shook his head. "No, sir. Most people don't want to fight any war at all, and they'll do almost anything to keep from fighting. Meaning no offense, sir, but I think you've just cooked your own goose."

With a shrug, Morrell said, "Well, even if I have, I won't mind getting back in the field again." Lieutenant Colonel Abell looked at him as if he'd spoken in Hindustani, or maybe Choctaw. Like Colonel Donaldson, Abell was a creature of the General Staff, and didn't care to contemplate life outside it. Morrell did, which gave him a certain moral advantage. *And how much good will that do you in Lethbridge when the blizzards come?* he wondered, and wished he hadn't.

Tom Colleton held out a package too well wrapped for him to have done it himself. "Happy birthday, Sis!" he told Anne.

"Oh, for heaven's sake," she said in fond exasperation. "You shouldn't have." She kissed him on the cheek, but at least half of her meant every word of that. The birthday in question was her thirty-ninth, and the only one she would have felt less like celebrating was her fortieth.

"Well, whether I should have or not, I damn well did," her younger brother answered. Tom still had a few years to go before facing middle age—and forty meant less to a man than it did to a woman, anyhow. From forty, a woman could see all too well the approaching end of too many things, beauty among them. *From thirty-nine, too,* Anne thought gloomily. But Tom was grinning at her. "Go on— open it."

"I will," she said, and she did, tearing into the wrapping paper as she would have liked to tear into Father Time. "What on earth have you got here?"

"I found it the last time I was in Columbia," he said. "There. Now you've got it. See? It's—"

"A book of photographs of Marcel Duchamp's paintings!" Anne exclaimed.

"Seeing as he exhibited at Marshlands, I thought you'd like it," her brother said. "And take a look at page one seventy-three."

"Why? What's he done there?" Anne asked suspiciously. Tom's grin only got wider and more annoying. She flipped through the book till she got to page 173. The painting, especially in a black-and-white reproduction, resembled nothing so much as an explosion in a prism factory. That didn't surprise Anne. When Duchamp displayed his *Nude Descending a Staircase* at Marshlands just before the Great War broke out, the work had hung upside down for several days before anyone, including the artist, noticed. But here . . .

Tom looked over her shoulder to make sure she'd got to the right page. "You see?" he said. "You see?" He pointed to the title below the photograph.

"'Mademoiselle Anne Colleton of North Carolina, Confederate States of America,'" Anne read. She said something most unladylike, and then, "For God's sake, he doesn't even remember what state he was in! I'm not surprised, I suppose—all he cared about while he was here was getting drunk and laying the nigger serving girls."

"What do you think of the likeness?" her brother asked.

Before the war, Anne had been a champion of everything modern. Life was harder now. She had little time for such fripperies. *And I'm older than I was then,* she thought bleakly. *It's harder to stay up to date, and to stay excited about being up to date.*

She took a longer look at "Mlle. Anne Colleton." It still seemed made up of squares and triangles and rectangles flying in all directions. But lurking among them, cunningly hidden, were features that might have been her own. Slowly, she said, "It's not as bad as you make it out to be."

"No, it's worse," Tom said. "When I was in the trenches, I saw men who got hit by shells and didn't look this bad afterwards." He brought his experience to the abstract painting, just as Anne brought hers. That was bound to be what Marcel Duchamp had had in mind. Anne might have cared more if he hadn't made such a nuisance of himself while at Marshlands, and if he hadn't been such a coward about recrossing the Atlantic after the war began and both sides' submersibles started prowling.

As things were, she only shrugged and said, "It *is* a compliment of sorts. Whatever he thought of me, he didn't forget me once he got back to France."

"Nobody ever forgets you, Sis," Tom Colleton said. Then he added something he never would have dared say before the war. Going into the Army had made a man of him; he'd been a boy, a comfortable boy, till then. He asked, "How come you never married any of the fellows who sniffed around after you? There were always enough of 'em."

Had he presumed to ask such a question before the Great War, she would have slapped him down, hard. Now, though she didn't like it, she gave it a serious answer: "Some of them wanted to run me and to run my money. Nobody runs me, and I run the money better than most men could. I've said that before. And the others, the ones who didn't care so much about the money . . ." She laughed a hard and bitter laugh. "They were sons of bitches, just about all of them. I recognize the breed. I'd better—takes one to know one, people say."

Almost fondly, she remembered Roger Kimball. The submarine officer had been a thoroughgoing son of a bitch. He'd also been far and away the best lover she ever had. She didn't know what that said. (Actually, she did know, but she didn't care to dwell on it.) But, in the end, Kimball had chosen the Freedom Party over her. And he was dead now, shot by the widow of a U.S. seaman whose destroyer he'd sunk after the CSA had asked for and been granted an armistice.

She waited for Tom to give her a lecture. But he only asked another question: "Can you go on by yourself for the rest of your days?"

"I don't know," Anne admitted. To keep from having to think about it, she tried to change the subject: "What about you, Tom? You're as single as I am."

"Yeah, I know," he said with a calm that surprised her. "But there are a couple of differences between us. For one thing, I'm a few years younger than you are. For another, I'm starting to look hard, and you're not."

"Are you?" she said, surprised. "You didn't tell me anything about that."

Tom nodded, almost defiantly. "Well, I am, and yes, I know I haven't told you anything. No offense, Sis, but you like running people's lives so much, you don't like it when they try and run their own." That held enough truth to make Anne give him a wry nod in return. He dipped his head, acknowledging it, and continued, "There's one more thing, no offense. A lot of ways, when a man gets married matters a lot less than when a woman does."

And that was all too true, as well. In a fair, just world it wouldn't have been, but Anne had never been naive enough to imagine the world either fair or just. Looks weren't what kept a man, but they were what lured him. She'd used her own blond beauty to advantage more times than she could count. Again, turning thirty-nine reminded her she wouldn't be able to do that forever. If she wanted to have a baby or two, she wouldn't be able to do that forever, either.

She sighed. "Well, Tom, when you're right, you're right, and you're right, dammit. I'm going to have to do something about it."

Her brother blinked. He'd probably been expecting a shouting match, not agreement. "Just like that?" he asked.

Anne nodded briskly. "Yes, just like that, or as close to just like that as I can make it. Or don't you think I can do what I set my mind to doing?" If he said he didn't, he *would* have a shouting match on his hands.

But he only laughed. "Anybody who thinks that about you is a damn fool, Sis. Now, I may be a damn fool—plenty of people have called me one, and they've had their reasons—but I'm not that particular kind of a damn fool, thank you kindly."

Although Anne laughed, too, she also gave him another nod. "Good. You'd better not be."

She meant what she said. As if to prove it, she drove up to Columbia a couple of days later. She knew the eligible bachelors in little St. Matthews, South Carolina, much too well to have the slightest interest in marrying any of them. He was too old; *he* was too dull; he was too grouchy; *he* couldn't count to twenty-one without dropping his pants. The pickings had to be better, or at least wider, in the state capital.

They would be better still down in Charleston, but

Columbia was a lot closer. That made it more convenient both for her and for the battered Ford she drove. Keeping the motorcar alive would probably let the local mechanic send his children to college, but she had to let it keep nibbling her to death a bit at a time. She couldn't afford a new one, however much she wanted one.

Before the war—that phrase again!—and even into it, she'd driven a powerful, comfortable Vauxhall, imported from England. Confederate soldiers had confiscated it at gunpoint during the Red uprising of 1915. *Almost ten years ago now,* she thought with slow wonder. The Ford, now, the Ford was a boneshaker that couldn't get past thirty-five miles an hour unless it went over a cliff. And it was a Yankee machine. But it was what she had, and it ran . . . after a fashion.

She did like driving into Columbia. The town's gracious architecture spoke of the better days of the last century. When the Negroes rebelled here, some houses, some blocks, had gone up in flames, but most of the city remained intact—and the damage, at last, was largely repaired. She couldn't imagine a conflagration big enough to destroy the whole town. Columbia was too big for such disasters.

Charleston had better hotels than Columbia, but the Essex House, only a few blocks from the green bronze dome of the State Capitol, would do. The Essex House also boasted a first-rate switchboard. She had no trouble keeping up with her investments while away from home. And she could even study day-old copies of the *New Orleans Financial Mercury* and three-day-old editions of the *Wall Street Journal.* Since she kept most of her money in U.S. rather than C.S. markets, the latter did her more good.

But here she was more interested in men who might have investments of their own than in investments themselves. Dinner at the hotel restaurant the first night she got into town made her wonder if she'd waited several years too long to make this particular hunting expedition. Before the war, she couldn't possibly have eaten without shooing away anywhere from two to half a dozen men more interested in other pleasures than in those of the table. Here, she enjoyed—or didn't so much enjoy—some very tasty fried chicken without drawing so much as a single eye.

I might as well be eating crow, she thought as she rose, unhappy, from the table.

A visit to her assemblyman the next day was no more reassuring. Edgar Stow was younger than she was. He wore the ribbon for the Purple Heart in his lapel; the three missing fingers on his left hand explained why. Because of those missing digits, he had what she took to be a wedding band on the surviving index finger. He was polite to Anne, but polite to Anne as if she was an influential constituent (true) rather than a good-looking woman (false?). He also seemed maddeningly unaware of what she was trying to tell him.

"Parties? Banquets?" He shook his head. "It's pretty quiet here these days, ma'am. The old-timers, the men who've held their seats since before the war, they complain all the time about how dead it is. But we get a lot more business done nowadays than they ever did."

Stow sounded pleased with himself. He had an ashtray on his desk made from the brass base of a shell casing, with a couple of dimes bent into semicircles and welded to it to hold cigarettes. He'd surely made it, or had it made, while he was in the Army. Anne wanted to pick it up and brain him with it. His blindness stung. But that *ma'am* hurt worse. By the way he said it, he might have been talking to his grandmother.

"So what exactly can I help you with today, ma'am?" he asked, polite, efficient—and stupid.

Anne didn't tell him. *Why waste my time?* she thought as she left his office. But she had to wonder if she'd already wasted too much time.

V

Sam Carsten smeared zinc-oxide ointment on the bridge of his nose. It wouldn't do him any good. He was dolefully certain of that. When summer came, he got a sunburn. He'd got sunburned in San Francisco, which wasn't easy. Hell, he'd got sunburned in Seattle, which was damn near impossible.

The port of Brest, France, toward which the USS *O'Brien* was steaming, lay on the same parallel of latitude as Seattle. Somebody'd told that to Carsten, but he'd had to look it up for himself in an atlas before he would believe it. The bright sunshine dancing off the ocean—and off the green land ahead—seemed almost tropical in comparison to what Seattle usually got.

He patted the breech of the destroyer's forward four-inch gun. "This here is one more place I figured I'd have to fight my way into," he remarked.

"Yes, sir," Nathan Hirskowitz agreed. The petty officer shrugged. "But we've got one thing going for us, even on a little courtesy call like this."

"You bet we do," Sam said. "We aren't Germans."

Hirskowitz nodded. He scratched his chin. Whiskers rasped under his nails, though he'd shaved that morning. "Yes, sir," he said. "That's what I was thinking, all right."

"They just don't like Germans here in France, same as they just don't like Englishmen in Ireland." Carsten thought for a moment, then went on, "And same as they just don't like *us* in the CSA—what do you want to bet a ship from the Kaiser's High Seas Fleet gets the same sort of big hello in Charleston as we do here?"

"I won't touch that one. You got to be right," Hirskowitz said.

"Damn funny business, though," Sam said. "We were at war with the froggies, too, same as Kaiser Bill was at war with the Confederates."

"But we didn't lick France, same as the Germans didn't lick the Confederate States. That makes all the difference." Hirskowitz added something in French.

"What the hell's that mean?" Sam asked in surprise.

"Something like, the better you know somebody, the more reasons you can find to despise him," the gunner's mate answered.

"Well, I've known you for a while, and this is the first I knew you spoke any French."

Nathan Hirskowitz surprised Sam again, this time by looking and sounding faintly embarrassed: "It's my old man's fault, sir. He came to the United States out of this little Romanian village in the middle of nowhere—that's what he has to say about it, anyway. But he'd taught himself French and German and English while he was still there."

"That's pretty good," Sam said. "He taught you, too, eh?"

"Yeah, me and my brothers and my sister. German was easy, of course, because we already used Yiddish around the house, and they're pretty close. But he made us learn French, too."

"So what does he do in New York City?" Sam asked. "How come you aren't too rich to think about joining the Navy?"

"How come?" Hirskowitz snorted. "I'll tell you how come, sir. Pop had a storing and hauling business. But he liked horses better than trucks, and so that went under. He's smart, but he's a stubborn bastard, my old man is. And since his business went under, he hasn't done much of anything. He sponges off the rest of my relatives, that's all. You listen to him talk, he's too smart to work."

"Oh. One of those." Carsten nodded; he'd met the type. "Too bad. Any which way, though, I expect I'll stick with you when we get shore leave. Always handy to have somebody along who knows the lingo."

"Sir, you're an officer, remember? You got to find one of your own who speaks French. You can't go drinking with a no-account gunner's mate."

Sam cursed under his breath. Hirskowitz was right, no doubt about it. The trouble was, Carsten didn't like drinking with officers. That was the bad news about being a mustang. He'd spent close to twenty years as an able seaman and petty officer himself. His rank had changed, but his taste in companions hadn't. Officers still struck him as a snooty lot. But he would hear about it, and in great detail, if he fraternized—that was the word they'd use—with men of lower rank.

Up to the wharf came the *O'Brien*. The skipper handled that himself, disdaining the help of the tugboats hovering in the harbor. If he made a hash of it, he'd have nobody but himself to blame. But he didn't. With all the Frenchmen watching—and, no doubt, with some Germans keeping an eye on the destroyer, too—he came alongside as smoothly as if parking a car.

A French naval officer whose uniform, save for his kepi, didn't look a whole lot different from American styles, came aboard the *O'Brien*. "Welcome to *la belle France*," he said in accented English. "We have been allies before, your country and mine. We are not enemies now. It could be, one day, we shall ally again."

He didn't say against whom he had in mind. He didn't say—and he didn't need to say. The *O'Brien*'s executive officer said something in French. Sam didn't want to go drinking with the exec. The Frenchman saluted. The executive officer returned the salute. He said, "We come to France on a peaceful visit, and hope that peace will last forever."

With a very Gallic shrug, the French officer replied, "What lasts forever? Nothing in this world, *monsieur*. I need to say one thing to you, a word of—*comment dit-on?*—a word of warning, yes. Your men are welcome to go ashore, but they should use a certain ... a certain caution, *oui*?"

Since the Frenchman plainly wanted the *O'Brien*'s crew to hear that, the exec carried on in English: "What sort of caution, sir?"

"Political caution," the local said. "The *Action Française* has no small power here in Brest. You know the *Action Française*?"

"*Mais un petit peu,*" the executive officer said, and then, "Only a little."

"Even a little is too much," the Frenchman told him. "They are royalist, they are Catholic—very, very Catholic, in a political way—and (forgive me) they oppose those who were the allies of the United States during the ... the unpleasantness not so long past."

They hate the Germans' guts, Carsten thought. *That's what he means, but he's too polite to say so.* The *O'Brien*'s executive officer nodded and said, "Thanks for the warning. We will be careful."

"I have done my duty," the French officer answered. *I wash my hands of the lot of you,* he might have said. With another salute, he went back over the gangplank, up onto the pier, and into Brest.

Carsten wondered if the skipper would keep his crew aboard the ship after a greeting like that, but he didn't. He did warn the men who got liberty to stick together and not to cause trouble. Sam hoped they would listen, but sailors in port weren't always inclined to.

He went ashore himself, as much from simple curiosity as from any great desire to paint the town red. Brest wasn't the sort of place to which tourists thronged. It was, first and foremost, a navy town. That didn't faze Sam. The steep, slippery streets were another matter. Brest sat on a ridge above the Penfeld River, and seemed more suited to mountain goats than to men.

Mountain goats, though, didn't go into bars. Carsten did, the first chance he got. "Whiskey," he told the bartender, figuring that word didn't change much from one language to another.

But the fellow surprised him by speaking English: "The

apple brandy is better." Seeing Sam's look of surprise, he explained, "Many times during the Great War—and since—sailors from *Angleterre* come here."

"All right. Thanks. I'll try the stuff." When Sam did, he found he liked it—Calvados was the name on the bottle. He drank some more. Warmth spread through him. A navy town had to have friendly women somewhere not too far from the sea. *After I drink some more, I'll find out about that,* he thought.

Before he could, though, three or four French officers came in. One of them noticed his unfamiliar uniform. "You are—American?" he asked in halting English. "You are from the *contre-torpilleur* new in the harbor?"

"Yes, from the destroyer," Sam agreed.

"And what think you of Brest?" the fellow asked.

"Nice town," Carsten said; his mother had raised him to be polite. "And this Calvados stuff—this is the cat's meow." The Frenchman looked puzzled. Sam simplified: "It's good. I like it."

"Ah. 'The cat's meow.'" The French officer—a tough-looking fellow in his forties, a few years older than Sam—filed away the phrase. "Would it please you, *monsieur*, to see more of Brest?"

"Thank you, friend. I wouldn't mind that at all," Sam answered, thinking, among other things, that an officer ought to know where the officers' brothels were, and which of them had the liveliest girls. But the Frenchman—his name turned out to be Henri Dimier—took him to the maritime museum housed in a chateau down by the harbor, and then to the cathedral of St. Louis closer to the center of town. Maybe he was an innocent, maybe he thought Sam was, or maybe he was subtly trying to annoy him. If so, he failed; Carsten found both buildings interesting, even if neither was exactly what he'd had in mind.

When they came out of the cathedral, a whole company of blue-uniformed policemen rushed up the street past them. "What's going on there?" Sam asked.

"I think it is the *Action Française*," Dimier answered, his face hard and grim. "They are to have a—how do you

141

say?—a meeting in the *Place de la Liberté*. It is not far. Would you care to see?"

"Well . . . all right." It wasn't what Sam had had in mind. It wouldn't be much fun. But it might be useful, and that counted, too. *I suppose that counts, too,* he thought mournfully.

The *Place de la Liberté* wasn't far from the cathedral: only two or three blocks. Even before Carsten and Henri Dimier got there, the sound of singing filled the air. A forest of flags sprouted inside the park. Some were the familiar French tricolor, others covered with fleurs-de-lys. Pointing, Sam asked, "What are those?"

"That is the old flag, the royal flag, of France," Dimier replied. "They want to, ah, return to his throne the king."

"Oh." Carsten wasn't sure what to make of that. The mere idea struck him as pretty strange. He tried another question: "What are they singing?"

"I translate for you." The French officer cocked his head to one side, listening. "Here. Like this:

> "The German who has taken all,
> Who has robbed Paris of all she owns,
> Now says to France:
> 'You belong to us alone:
> Obey! Down on your knees, all of you!'

"And here is the—the refrain—is that the word?

> "No, no, France is astir,
> Her eyes flash fire,
> No, no,
> Enough of treason now.

"Would you hear more, *monsieur*?"

"Uh—yeah. If you don't mind." *I do need to know this. We all need to know it.*

Dimier picked up the song again:

> "Insolent German, hold your tongue,
> Behold our king approaches,

142

And our race
Runs ahead of him.
Back to where you belong, German,
Our king will lead us!"

And the refrain:

"One, two, France is astir,
Her eyes flash fire,
One, two,
The French are at home."

And once more:

"Tomorrow, on our graves,
The wheat will be more beautiful,
Let us close our ranks!
This summer we shall have
Wine from the grapevines
With royalty.

"Do you understand, being an American, what all this means?"

"I doubt it," Sam answered. "Do *you*?"

Before Henri Dimier could answer, the men of the *Action Française* charged the police who were trying to hold them in the square. For a moment, clubs flailing, the police did hold. But then the ralliers—the rioters, now—broke through. With shouts of triumph, they swarmed into the streets of Brest. Sam had a devil of a time getting back to the *O'Brien*. After that, though, he understood, or thought he understood, a good deal that he hadn't before.

Clarence Potter was a meticulous man. If he hadn't been, he couldn't very well have had a successful career in intelligence work during the war. That habit of precision was one reason why he had no use for the Freedom Party. To his way of thinking, Jake Featherston and his followers only wanted to smash things up, with no idea what would replace them.

He stood in Marion Square in Charleston, listening to

143

a Freedom Party Congressional candidate. The fellow's name was Ezra Hutchinson. He was a rotund man who put Potter in mind of a hand grenade in a white summer suit. He exploded like a hand grenade, too. Unlike a hand grenade, though, he kept doing it over and over.

"Now hear me, friends!" he thundered, pumping a fist in the air atop the portable platform on which he stood. "Hear me! We've turned the other cheek to the USA for too long! It's high time we took our place in the sun again our own selves. We're a great country. We ought to start acting like it, by God!"

Some of the people in the little crowd in front of the platform clapped their hands. Ezra Hutchinson didn't stand up there alone. A dozen Freedom Party hardnoses in white shirts and butternut trousers backed him. They all applauded like machines. Whenever he paused a little longer than usual, they barked out, "Freedom!" in sharp unison.

"Freedom!" echoed several voices from the crowd.

"We're a great country!" Hutchinson repeated. "But who remembers that, here in the CSA? The Radical Liberals? Hell, no—they'd rather be Yankees. The Whigs? Oh, they say they do, but they'd rather suck up to the Yankees. I tell you the truth, friends: the only party that remembers when the Confederate States had *men* in them is the Freedom Party."

That gave Clarence Potter the opening he'd been waiting for. He shouted, "The only party that shoots presidents is the Freedom Party!"

People stirred and muttered. Wade Hampton V was only a couple of years dead, but a lot of folks didn't seem to want to remember how he'd died. The Freedom Party sure as hell didn't want people to remember how he'd died. It was doing its best to act respectable. As far as Potter was concerned, its best could never be good enough.

Some of the goons on the platform turned their heads his way. More goons were sprinkled through the crowd, some in the Party's near-uniform, others wearing their ordinary clothes. But Ezra Hutchinson only smiled. "Where were you during the war, pal?" he asked; Freedom Party men often believed they were the only ones who'd done any fighting.

"I was in the Army of Northern Virginia," Potter answered, loudly and distinctly. "Where were *you*, you fat tub of goo?"

Hutchinson's smile disappeared. He'd been a railroad scheduler during the Great War, and never come within a hundred miles of a fighting front. But then he stuck out his chins and tried to make the best of it: "I served my country! Nobody can say I didn't serve my country."

He waited for Potter to make some other gibe so he could give a sharper comeback. But Potter said nothing more. He just let the candidate's words hang in the air. When Hutchinson did try to go back to his speech, he seemed flat, uninspired.

Several Freedom Party men started working their way back through the crowd toward Potter. He was there by himself. He carried a pistol—he always carried a pistol—but he didn't want to use it unless he had to. He slipped away and around the corner before any of the goons got a good look at him. He'd done what he'd set out to do.

But, in a way, the Freedom Party men had done what they'd set out to do, too: they'd made him retreat. And they would make it hard for other candidates to speak; they weren't shy about attacking their rivals' gatherings. Jake Featherston, damn him, had turned Confederate politics into war.

Who knows where Featherston would be now if that Grady Calkins hadn't gone and shot President Hampton? Potter thought. But snipers were part of war, too: a part that had upped and bit the Freedom Party.

Potter discovered the real problem at a Whig meeting a few days later. Everything there was stable, orderly, democratic. Speaker yielded politely to speaker. No one raised his voice. No one got excited. And, Potter was convinced, no one could possibly have hoped to influence the voters or make them give a damn about keeping the Whigs in power in Richmond.

He threw his hand in the air and was, in due course, recognized. "I have a simple question for you, Mr.

145

Chairman," he said. "Where are our hooligans, to break up Freedom Party rallies the way Featherston's bastards work so hard to break up ours?"

People started buzzing. You didn't often hear such questions at a gathering like this. The chairman's gavel came down, once, twice, three times. Robert E. Washburn was a veteran of the Second Mexican War. He wore a big, bushy white mustache, and both looked and acted as if the nineteenth century had yet to give way to the twentieth. "You are out of order, Mr. Potter," he said now. "I regret to state that I have had to point this out to you at previous gatherings as well."

Heads bobbed up and down in polite agreement with Washburn's ruling. Too many of those heads were gray or balding. The Whigs had dominated Confederate politics for a long time, as the Democrats had in the USA. The Democrats had got themselves a rude awakening. Potter feared the Freedom Party would give the CSA a worse shock than the Socialists had given the United States.

He said, "I am not out of order, Mr. Chairman, and it's a legitimate question. When the damnyankees started using gas during the war, we had to do the same, or else leave the advantage with them. If we don't fight Featherston's fire with fire, what becomes of us now?"

Down came the gavel again. "You *are* out of order, Mr. Potter," Washburn repeated. "Your zeal for the cause has outrun your respect for the institutions of the Confederate States of America."

He seemed to think that was plenty to quell Potter, if not to make him hang his head in shame. But Clarence Potter remained unquelled. "Featherston's got no respect for our institutions," he pointed out. "If we keep too much, we're liable not to have any institutions left to respect after a while."

Now heads went back and forth. People didn't agree with him. He'd run into that before. It drove him wild. He'd seen a plain truth, and he couldn't get anyone else to see it. Jake Featherston had come much too close to smashing his way to a victory in 1921, and he would be even more dangerous now if that Calkins maniac hadn't

146

shown up the Freedom Party for what it was. Potter felt like knocking these placidly disagreeing heads together. That brought him up short. *I'm not so different from Featherston after all, am I?*

Robert E. Washburn said, "We rely upon the power of the police to protect us against any further, uh, unfortunate outbursts."

That was an answer of sorts, but only of sorts. "And how many coppers start yelling, 'Freedom!' the minute they take off their gray suits?" Potter asked. "How well do you think they'll do their job?"

He did make the buzz in the room change tone. A great many policemen favored the Freedom Party. That was too notorious a truth to need retelling. It had caused problems in 1921 and again in 1923, though the Freedom Party men had been on their best behavior then. How could anybody think it wouldn't cause problems in the upcoming Congressional election?

The local chairman was evidently of that opinion. "Thank you for expressing your views with your usual vigor, Mr. Potter," Washburn said. "If we may now proceed to further items of business. . . ?"

And that was that. They didn't want to listen to him. And what the Whigs didn't want to do, they didn't have to do. More than sixty years of Confederate independence had taught them as much, and confirmed the lesson again and again. *What would teach them otherwise?* he wondered. The answer to that seemed obvious enough: *losing to the Freedom Party.*

As the Charleston Whigs droned on, Potter got to his feet and slipped out of their meeting. Nobody tried to call him back. Everybody seemed glad he was going. They didn't want to hear their grip on things was endangered. *They deserve to lose, by God,* he thought as he went out into the heat and humidity of a Charleston summer. But then, remembering Jake Featherston's burning eyes as he'd seen them again and again during the Great War, Potter shook his head. *They almost deserve to lose. No one deserves what those "Freedom!"-shouting yahoos would give us if they won.*

Pigeons strutted along the street, cooing gently. They were slow and stupid and ever so confident nobody would bother them. Why not? They'd proved right again and again and again. This one stranger in their midst wouldn't prove any different . . . would he?

Clarence Potter laughed. He threw his arms wide. Some of the pigeons scurried back from him. One or two even spread their wings and fluttered away a few feet. Most? Most kept right on strutting and pecking, and paid him no attention whatsoever. "You goddamn dumb sons of bitches," he told them, laughing though it wasn't really funny. "You might as well be Whigs." The birds went right on ignoring him, which proved his point.

He wondered whether the Radical Liberals would take him seriously. Odds were, they would. The Freedom Party, after all, was replacing them as the Whigs' principal opposition. But then he wondered if it mattered whether the Rad Libs took him seriously. It probably didn't. No one except a few dreamers had ever thought the Radical Liberals could govern the CSA. They gave the states of the West and Southwest a safety valve through which they could blow off steam when Richmond ignored them, as it usually did. Closer to the heart of the CSA, the Radical Liberals let people pretend the country really was a democratic republic—without the risks and complications a real change of power would have entailed.

Why do I bother? Potter wondered as he strode past the pigeons that, fat and happy and brainless, went on pretending he wasn't there—or, if he was, that he couldn't possibly be dangerous. *Easier just to sit back and let nature take its course.*

But he knew the answer to that. It was simple enough: he knew Jake Featherston. *Ten years now since I walked into the First Richmond Howitzers' encampment. Ten years since he told me Jeb Stuart III's body servant might be a Red, and since Jeb Stuart III, being III of an important family, made sure nothing would happen to the nigger.* Jeb Stuart III was dead, of course. He'd looked for death when he realized he'd made a bad mistake. He'd had plenty of old-fashioned Confederate courage and honor. But he'd taken however many Yankee bullets he took without having the faintest conception of just how bad a mistake he'd made.

"The whole Confederacy is still finding out just how bad a mistake you made, Captain Stuart," Clarence Potter muttered. A young woman coming the other way—a young woman in a shockingly short skirt, one that reached so high, it let him see the bottom of her kneecap—gave him a curious glance as she went by.

Potter was by now used to garnering curious glances. He wasn't nearly so used to women showing that much leg. He looked back over his shoulder at her. For a little while, at least, he forgot all about the Freedom Party.

When the steam whistle announcing shift change blew, Chester Martin let out a sigh of relief. It had been a good day on the steel-mill floor. Everything had gone the way it was supposed to. Nobody'd got hurt. You couldn't ask for more than that, not in this business.

Instead of heading straight home, he stopped at the Socialist Party hall not far from the mill. A good many men from his mill and others nearby sat and stood there, talking steel and talking politics and winding down from the long, hard weeks they'd just put in. "How's it going, Chester?" somebody called. Martin mimed falling over in exhaustion, which got a laugh.

Somebody else said, "They don't work us as hard as they worked our fathers."

"Only goes to show what you know, Albert," Chester retorted. "My old man's got one of those soft foreman's jobs. He hardly even has calluses on his hands any more, except from pushing a pencil. They work me a hell of a lot harder than they work him."

"Sold out to the people who own the means of production, has he?" Albert Bauer said—he was and always had been a Socialist of the old school.

Before Chester could answer that, someone else did it for him: "Oh, put a sock in it, for Christ's sake. *We're* starting to own the means of production. At least, I've bought some shares of stock, and I'll bet you have, too. Go on, tell me I'm a liar."

Bauer said not a word. In fact, so many people said not a word that something close to silence fell for a moment. *Have that many of us bought stocks?* Chester wondered. He had a few shares himself, and knew his father had more than a few: Stephen Douglas Martin had been picking up a share here, a share there, ever since he started making good money when he wasn't conscripted into the Great War.

"Funny," Martin said. "The Party talks about government owning the means of production, but it never says much about the proletariat buying 'em up one piece at a time."

"Marx never figured anything like that would happen," someone said. "Neither did Lincoln. Back when they lived, you couldn't make enough money to have any left over to invest."

"As long as Wall Street keeps going up and up, though, you'd have to be a damn fool *not* to throw your money that way," somebody else said. "It's like stealing, only it's legal. And buying on margin makes it even easier."

Nobody argued with him. Even now, most of the men who left their jobs at the steel mills left only because they were too old or too physically worn or too badly hurt to do them any more. Those were the people for whom the Socialists were trying to push their old-age insurance policy through Congress. But if you could quit your work at sixty-five, or even sixty, and be sure you had enough left to live on for the rest of your days thanks to what you'd done for yourself while you were working . . . If you could manage that, the whole country would start looking different in twenty or thirty years.

I'll turn sixty-five in 1957, Martin thought. It didn't seem so impossibly far away—but then, he had just put in that long, long day at the mill.

He rode the trolley home, ate supper with his parents and his sister, and went to bed. When the wind-up alarm clock next to his head clattered the next morning, he just turned it off. He didn't have a moment's sleepy panic, thinking it was some infernal device falling on his trench. *I've been home from the Great War for a while now,* he thought as he put on a clean work shirt and overalls. But he would take a couple of puckered scars on his left arm to the grave. As it had on so many, the war had left its mark on him.

When he went into the kitchen, his father was already there, smoking his first cigar of the day. His mother fried eggs and potatoes in lard. She used a wood-handled iron spatula to flip some onto a plate for him. "Here's your breakfast, dear," she said. "Do you want some coffee?"

"Please," he said, and she poured him a cup.

His father said, "Saturday today—only a half day."

Chester nodded as he doctored the coffee with cream and sugar. "That's right. You know I won't be home very long, though—I'm going out with Rita."

Stephen Douglas Martin nodded. "You already told us, yeah."

His mother gave him an approving smile. "Have a good time, son."

"I think I will." Chester dug into the hash browns and eggs so he wouldn't have to show his amusement. His folks had decided they approved of Rita Habicht, or at least of his seeing her. They must have started to wonder if he would ever see anybody seriously. But he wasn't the only Great War veteran in no hurry to get on with that particular part of his life. Plenty of men he knew who'd been through the mill (and, as a steelworker, he understood exactly what that phrase meant) were still single, even though they'd climbed into their thirties. It was as if they'd given so much in the trenches, they had little left for the rest of their lives.

He took the trolley past the half-scale statue of Remembrance—who would have looked fiercer without half a dozen pigeons perched on her sword arm—to the mill, where he put in his four hours. Then he hurried back home, washed up, shaved, and changed from overalls, work shirt, and cloth cap to trousers, white shirt, and straw hat. "I'm off," he told his mother.

"You look very nice," Louisa Martin said. He would have been happier if she hadn't said that every time he went anywhere, but still—you took what you could get.

He rode the trolley again, this time to the block of

flats where Rita lived. She had one of her own. She'd got married just before the war started. Her husband had stopped a bullet or a shell in one of the endless battles on the Roanoke front. Martin had fought there, too, till he got wounded. He'd never met Joe Habicht, but that proved exactly nothing. Rita had had a baby, too, and lost it to diphtheria the day after its second birthday. Women fought their own battles, even if not with guns. Through everything, though, she'd managed to hang on to the apartment.

She didn't keep Chester waiting when he knocked on the door. His heart beat faster as she opened it. "Hi," he said, a big, silly grin on his face. "How are you?"

"Fine, thanks." She patted at her dark blond hair. It was a little damp; she must have washed after getting back from her Saturday half day, too. "It's good to see you."

"It's good to be here," he said, and leaned forward to kiss her on the cheek. "You look real pretty."

Rita smiled. "You always tell me that."

"I always mean it, too." But Martin started to laugh. When she asked him what was funny, he wouldn't tell her. *I'll be damned if I want to admit I sound just like my mother,* he thought. Instead, he said, "Shall we go on over to the Orpheum?"

"Sure," she said. "Who's playing there today?"

"Those four crazy brothers from New York are heading the bill," he answered.

"Oh, good. They *are* funny," Rita said. "I was in stitches the last time they came through Toledo." That had been a couple of years before; she and Chester hadn't known each other then. He wondered with whom she'd seen the comics. That she had a past independent of him occasionally bothered him, though he'd never stopped to wonder if his independent past bothered her. But neither of them had seen anybody else for several months now. That suited Chester fine, and seemed to suit Rita pretty well, too.

They held hands at the trolley stop. An old lady clucked disapprovingly, but they paid no attention to her. Things were looser now than they had been when she was a young woman. As far as Chester Martin was concerned, that was all to the good, too. He was sorry when the trolley car came clanging up so soon.

He slid a silver dollar to the ticket-taker at the Orpheum, and got back a half dollar and two yellow tickets. He and Rita went up to the first balcony and found some seats. He took her hand there, too. She leaned her head on his shoulder. When the house lights went down, he gave her a quick kiss.

A girl singer and a magician led off the show. As far as Martin was concerned, the magician couldn't have disappeared fast enough. A trained-dog act ended abruptly when the dog, which could jump and fetch and even climb ladders to ring a bell at the top, proved not to be trained in a much more basic way. He got an enormous laugh, but not one of a sort the fellow in black tie who worked with him had in mind. The dancer who came on next got another laugh by soft-shoeing out holding his nose.

"I wouldn't have done that," Rita said, even though she'd laughed, too. "Now he'll squabble with the man with the dog all the way to the end of the tour." Chester wouldn't have thought of that for himself. Once she said it, he realized she was bound to be right.

At last, after a couple of other acts Martin knew he wouldn't remember ten minutes after he left the Orpheum, the Engels Brothers came out, along with the tall, skinny, dreadfully dignified woman who served as their comic foil. They were all young men, not far from Chester's age, but got their name from the enormous, fuzzy beards they wore. One of the beards was dyed red, one yellow, one blue, and the fourth left black. From the balcony, Martin couldn't tell if the beards were real or fakes. For the comics' sake, he hoped they were phony.

The Brother with the undyed beard talked enough for any three men. The one with the yellow beard didn't talk at all, but was so limber, he seemed to have no bones. The one with the blue beard tried to slap everybody else into line. The one with the red beard spent all his time chasing the tall, skinny woman, who seemed more bewildered than flattered by his attentions.

At one point, they all started pelting one another with oranges. It might have been trench warfare up there—by the way the Engels Brothers dodged around the prop furniture, they'd been in the trenches—except that the woman kept standing up and getting nailed. By the time they'd finished, the stage was a worse mess, much worse, than it had been after the dog act. But this was a lot funnier, too.

The Engels Brother with the black beard proved the sole survivor. He looked out at the audience and said, "Orange you glad you aren't up here?" The curtain came down.

"That was ... I don't know exactly what that was, but I don't know when I've laughed so hard, either," Rita said as she got up and made her way toward the exit. Since Chester Martin was rubbing at his streaming eyes with his handkerchief, he couldn't very well argue with her.

They had supper at a diner across the street from the Orpheum, then took the trolley back to Rita's block of flats. "I had a wonderful time," she said as she fumbled in her handbag for the key.

"I always have a terrific time with you, Rita." Chester hesitated, then asked, "Can I come in for a minute, please?"

She hesitated, too. She was careful of her reputation. He'd seen that from the first time he took her out. He liked it. She said, "You're not going to be—you know—difficult, are you?"

He would have liked nothing better than to be difficult, but he solemnly shook his head. "Cross my heart," he answered, and did.

"All right." Rita opened the door and flipped on a light. "The place is a mess." It was, to Martin's eye, perfectly neat. Rita sat down on the overstuffed sofa. She patted the upholstery next to her, asking, "What have you got in mind?"

Instead of sitting there, Chester awkwardly went to one knee in front of her. Her eyes got very big. Tongue stumbling, heart pounding, he repeated, "I always have a terrific time with you. I don't think I'd ever want to be with anybody else. Will you—will you marry me, Rita?" He took a velvet jewelry box from his pocket and flipped it open to show her a ring set with a tiny chip of diamond.

She stared at him. "I wondered if you were going to ask me that tonight," she whispered, and then, "The ring is beautiful."

"You're beautiful," he said. "Will you?"

"Of course I will," she answered.

Afterwards, he wasn't quite sure who kissed whom first. When he came up for air, he gasped, "You never kissed me like that before."

"Well, you never asked me to marry you before, either," Rita answered.

He laughed. They kissed again. Heart pounding, he asked, "What else don't I know?"

"You'll find out," she said. "After the wedding."

Scipio paid five cents for a copy of the *Augusta Constitutionalist*. In one way, that struck him as a lot of money to shell out for a newspaper. In another, considering that he would have paid millions if not billions of dollars when the currency went crazy a couple of years before, it wasn't so bad.

"Thanks, uncle," said the white man who took his money. He didn't answer. He just opened up the paper and read it as he hurried towards Erasmus' fish market and restaurant.

Had he answered, what would he have said? Angry at himself for even wondering, he shook his head as he walked along. White men never called black men *mister*, not in the Confederate States of America they didn't. If he held his breath till they started to, he'd end up mighty, mighty blue. The fellow with the pile of papers at his feet would just have called him an uppity nigger, or maybe a crazy nigger, if he'd complained.

Maybe the worst of it was, the white man had been trying to be polite. *I can't win,* Scipio thought. *Why do I bother imagining I could?*

Even more to the point, he wondered why he'd wasted any money on the paper. The headline screamed about a lurid love triangle that had ended in an axe murder. It would have been made to seem a lot more lurid had the parties involved been colored. Or, on the other hand, it

155

might not have made the paper at all in that case. A lot of whites expected Negroes to act that way, and took it for granted when they did.

Much smaller stories talked about Congressional candidates' latest promises. Scipio wondered why he bothered even glancing at those. It wasn't as if he could vote. But the remarks of Eldridge P. Dinwiddie, the Freedom Party candidate in Augusta, did make his eyes widen as if he'd just poured down a couple of cups of Erasmus' strong, chicory-laced coffee.

"Too many Red rebels are still hiding in plain sight," Dinwiddie was quoted as saying. "The Whigs have forgotten all about them. Going after them would remind people of how badly the party that's in power bungled the war effort. But if you elect me, I'll make sure they aren't forgotten and are brought to justice. I aim to see all those nigger traitors hang."

Mr. Dinwiddie, wrote the reporter who'd listened to him, *received prolonged and vociferous support for his suggestion.*

"Hell wid Mistuh Dinwiddie," Scipio muttered under his breath. Being one of those fugitive Reds himself, he didn't care for the notion of getting hunted down and hanged. Here and there, faded posters still offered a reward for his capture.

But that was in another country; and besides, the wench is dead. Every so often, a phrase from the education Anne Colleton had made him acquire floated up out of his memory. This one fit. South Carolina might have been another country. The name on his passbook here in Georgia was Xerxes. Everyone here, even his wife, knew him by that name and no other.

Anne Colleton, though, wasn't dead. If she ever saw him, he would be, and in short order. Like most late summer days in Augusta, this one was hot and muggy. Scipio shivered even so.

Foreign news got shoved onto page three. There'd been another battle in the endless Mexican civil war. Imperial forces claimed victory. The rebels weren't calling them liars too loudly, so maybe they'd actually won. Venezuela and

Colombia were talking about going to war with each other. The paper said the United States had sent the Kaiser a note warning him against arming or encouraging the Venezuelans, and that he'd denied doing any such thing—and warned the USA against encouraging or arming the Colombians. A party called French Action had caused riots in Paris at the same time as the French government claimed it was two years ahead of schedule in paying reparations in Germany. Japanese aeroplanes had bombed a town somewhere in China.

He was so engrossed in the article about allowing the forward pass in football—some people condemned it as a damnyankee innovation, while others claimed it added excitement to the game—he almost walked past Erasmus' place. "Mornin', Xerxes," his boss said when he came in.

"Mornin'," Scipio answered. "How you is?"

"Tolerable," Erasmus said. "Little better'n tolerable, mebbe. How's your ownself?"

Scipio shrugged. "Not bad. I's gettin' by."

"Can't ask much more'n that, not till Judgment Day, anyways." Erasmus raised a salt-and-pepper eyebrow. "You saved, Xerxes?"

How do I answer that? Scipio wondered. His education had weakened his faith. And, he discovered, so had his time with the Red rebels, all of whom had been as passionate in their disbelief as a lot of Christians were in their belief. He hadn't thought the Marxist ideology had rubbed off on him, but it seemed to have after all. After a moment's thought, he said, "Hope so."

"Should ought to be able to say better'n that," Erasmus said, but then, to Scipio's relief, he let it go. Pointing to the *Constitutionalist*, he asked, "You done with that?"

"Done wid it now, yeah," Scipio answered: the only thing he could have said. Erasmus didn't put up with reading on the job. That wasn't because he couldn't read a newspaper himself, though he couldn't. It was because, when you worked for Erasmus, you *worked* for Erasmus.

"Throw it on the fish-wrappin' pile, then," Erasmus said.

As Scipio did, he asked, "What you think 'bout de for'ard pass, boss?"

"Bunch o' damn foolishness, you ask me," Erasmus answered. "Anybody got the time to git all hot and bothered about it gots *too* goddamn much time, an' dat's the Lord's truth. Devil fill up your time just fine, you bet. Forward pass?" He rolled his eyes. "Might as well worry over that other damnfool damnyankee game—what the hell they call it? Baseball, dat's the name."

Scipio had never seen a baseball game, or even a baseball, in his life. Because he was—or rather, had been—widely read, he knew the sport was played in the northeastern part of the United States. But it had never caught on all across the USA, the way football had. And it certainly hadn't caught on in the Confederate States.

Erasmus eyed him. "You got any more ways o' wastin' time 'fore you starts earnin' what I pays you?"

"Only one," Scipio said with a grin. He grabbed a mug and poured it full of coffee from the big pot on the stove, then added cream and sugar. But he didn't sit down to drink it. He carried it with him as he started sweeping and tidying up. Erasmus had a steaming mug at his side, too. As long as Scipio worked hard, the older man didn't mind coffee or things like that.

The first breakfast customer came in a couple of minutes later. "Mornin', Aristotle," Scipio said. "How you is?" By now, he knew dozens of regulars by name and preferences. "You wants de usual?"

"Sure enough do," Aristotle answered. Scipio turned to Erasmus, who was already doing up a plate of ham and eggs and grits. Erasmus knew his customers even better than Scipio did. They were *his*, after all.

After the breakfast rush petered out, Scipio washed a young mountain of dishes and silverware, then dried them and stacked them neatly to get ready for lunch, which would be even more hectic. Once he'd done that, he helped Erasmus clean catfish and crappie. The proprietor would fry a lot of them during lunch, and even more during dinner. Erasmus was a wizard with a knife. Every cut he made was perfect, and he moved as fast as any slicing machine. Scipio . . .

"You makes me 'shamed," Scipio said, for Erasmus

158

could clean three fish to his one, and do a neater, better job on them to boot. "Watchin' you makes me 'shamed."

"Shouldn't ought to," Erasmus answered. "You is doin' the best you kin. Good Lord don't want no more'n dat from nobody. I been cuttin' up fish for a livin' since I was ten years old. Maybe you went fishin' couple-three times a year, gutted what you cotched. It make a difference, it surely do."

"Mebbe." Scipio would have thought Erasmus was humoring him, but Erasmus had no sense of humor when it came to work, none at all.

And now his boss said, "You's better'n you was, too, an' dat's a good thing. You didn't get no better, don't reckon I'd let you mess around with knives no more."

Scipio looked at his hands. He had a couple of cuts, along with several scars he'd picked up earlier. Seeing what he was doing, Erasmus held out his own hands. He had more scars than Scipio could count, a maze, a spiderweb, of scars, new, old, short, long, and in between. "Do Jesus!" Scipio said softly.

Erasmus only shrugged. "Ain't nobody perfect, Xerxes. Ain't nobody even close to perfect. Yeah, I's pretty damn good. But I been doin' this goin' on fifty years now. Every so often, the knife is gonna slip."

"Uh-huh." Scipio couldn't take his eyes off those battered hands. He'd noticed them, but he hadn't really studied them. They repaid study. Like so many who did something supremely well, Erasmus had suffered for his art. Scipio kept looking at them till a fat woman came in and asked Erasmus for three pounds of crawdads.

What have I got that shows what I've done with my life? Scipio wondered. Only one thing occurred to him: the way he talked, or could talk if doing so wouldn't put him in mortal danger. He *felt* smarter when he talked like an educated white man than he did using the thick Congaree River Negro dialect that was his only other way of putting his thoughts out for the world to know. He didn't suppose he actually *was* smarter, but the illusion was powerful, and it lingered.

Erasmus wrapped the crawdads in the *Augusta*

Constitutionalist Scipio had been reading that morning. The woman paid him, said, "Thank you kindly," and left.

"I been tellin' you and tellin' you," Erasmus said, "you ought to save your money and git yourself your own place. You end up doin' a lot better working for your ownself than you do when you works for me."

"Don't like tellin' folks what they gots to do," Scipio answered, not for the first time. "Reckon I kin"—if he'd run Marshlands for Anne Colleton, he could surely manage a little café for himself—"but I don't like it none."

"You gots to have some fire in your belly to do a proper job," Erasmus agreed. "But you gots to have some fire in your belly to git ahead any which way."

He eyed Scipio speculatively. Scipio concentrated on cleaning a catfish. He was better at doing what others told him than at telling others what to do. Back at Marshlands, he'd had Anne's potent authority behind him. If he started his own business, *he'd* be the authority. No, he didn't care for that. Still feeling Erasmus' eye on him, he said, "I gits by."

He sounded defensive, and he knew it. Erasmus said, "Any damn fool can get by. You could do better, an' you should ought to."

Scipio didn't answer. Before too long, the first dinner customers started coming in. He hurried back and forth from the stove to the tables out front. The sizzle and crackle of fish going into hot oil filled the place. He served and took money and made change and then did endless dishes, getting ready for the next morning. When he finally left, Erasmus stayed behind, still busy.

And when he got back to his flat, Bathsheba was waiting at the door to give him a kiss. Her eyes glowed. Scipio hoped he knew what she had in mind, and hoped that, after a long, hard day, he could perform. He turned out to be wrong—or, at least, not exactly right. She took his hand and set it just above her navel. "We gonna have us a young 'un," she said.

All of a sudden, Scipio discovered he might have fire in his belly after all.

*   *   *

Hipolito Rodriguez knew he should have counted himself a lucky man. For one thing, he'd come through the Great War without a scratch. If that by itself wasn't enough to make him light candles in the church in the little mining town of Baroyeca, he couldn't imagine what would be.

And, for another, Baroyeca lay in the Confederate state of Sonora, not in the Empire of Mexico farther south. It was close enough to the border to hear the echoes of the civil war that convulsed the country of which Sonora had once been a part, but not close enough to have let any of the fighting come near.

Nothing bothered Baroyeca very much. A couple of men hadn't come home from the war in the north. A few others had come home, but maimed. Mostly, though, days went on as they always had. Rodriguez's farm outside of town yielded no better crops than it ever had, but he managed to keep his wife, three sons, and two daughters fed.

And, every so often, he had enough money left in his pocket to go into town and spend some time at *La Culebra Verde*—the Green Snake—the cantina across the street from the church where he lit candles to thank God for his salvation. Having been preserved alive, didn't he have the right to enjoy himself every once in a while?

"Why not?" Carlos Ruiz said when he posed the question out loud one day. Carlos was his age, and had fought in Tennessee, where things had been, by all accounts, much worse than his own experience in Texas. Ruiz asked his counterquestion in English, not Spanish.

"*Sí*, why not?" Rodriguez agreed, the last two words also in English. He dropped back into Spanish to continue, "My children speak as much of the new language as of the old. Ten million devils from hell take me if I know whether to be glad or sorry."

"If you want them to stay here and be farmers or marry farmers, Spanish is good enough," Ruiz said—in Spanish. "If you hope they try to make money, English is better."

He was a farmer himself, and wore the ribbon for a Purple Heart on his baggy cotton shirt. Had he been a rich man, or a townsman, or even someone who hadn't also fought in the north, Hipolito Rodriguez might have got angry, especially since he'd been drinking for a while. As things were, he only shrugged and said, "How much good will English do people who look like us, Carlos?" Like Ruiz, like almost everybody in Baroyeca, he was short, with red-brown skin and hair blacker than moonless midnight. "Even with English, what are we but a couple of damn greasers?" The last five words were in the official language of the Confederacy.

"We may be greasers," Ruiz said, also in English, "but we ain't no niggers. *Mallates*," he added in Spanish, in case Rodriguez didn't understand him. Then back to English: "In the law, we're the same as anybody else."

That was true. The people of Sonora and Chihuahua were Confederate citizens, not merely residents of the CSA. They could vote. They could run for office. They could—if they were rich enough, which some few were—marry whites from the other states in the Confederacy. They could. And yet . . . Rodriguez sighed and took another pull at the beer in front of him. "The law, it means only so much."

That was also true. If it weren't for Negroes, Sonorans and Chihuahuans would have been at the bottom of the pile. Most Confederates who called themselves white looked down their noses at them. Rodriguez had seen as much during the war, the first time he'd ever had much to do with ordinary whites.

"When the election comes, who will you vote for?" Ruiz asked.

Rodriguez shrugged. "My *patrón* is a Radical Liberal." Ever since Sonora and Chihuahua came into the CSA, small farmers like him had voted as the great landowners in the area wanted them to vote. But, like so many things, that wasn't quite as it had been before the Great War. Rodriguez didn't want to say as much out loud, though. What he didn't say couldn't get back to anyone. He lifted his cup, emptied it, and asked the same question of Carlos Ruiz.

Ruiz gave back the same shrug. "Don Joaquin is a Radical Liberal, too." Hipolito Rodriguez nodded. The

Radical Liberals had been strong in the Confederate Southwest for years. Voting for them had always been a way to show Richmond the people here weren't happy with the neglect the Whigs gave them.

"I'd better go home," Rodriguez said, setting his mug on the table in front of him. "If I go now, Magdalena won't yell at me ... so much." He got to his feet. The room swayed slightly, but only slightly. *I'm not drunk,* he thought. *Of course I'm not drunk.*

"*Hasta luego, amigo,*" Ruiz said. By the way he sat, he wasn't going anywhere for quite a while.

"*Luego,*" Rodriguez answered. He walked to the door—steadily enough, all things considered—and left *La Culebra Verde*. The cantina had thick adobe walls that kept out the worst of the heat. When he went out into the street, it smote full force. His broad-brimmed straw hat helped some, but only some. He sighed as he drew in a lungful of bake-oven air. He'd known it would be like this. It always was.

Baroyeca looked a lot like any other little Sonoran town. The main street was unpaved. Dust hung in the air. Horses and a few motorcars stood in front of shops. Like the cantina, most of the rest of the buildings were of adobe. Some had roofs of half-round red tiles, some of thatch, a few of corrugated tin.

A roadrunner trotted down the street as if it owned it. The bird held a still-wriggling lizard in its beak. When a stray dog came towards it, it flapped up into the branches of a cottonwood tree and gulped the lizard down. The dog sent a reproachful stare after it, as if to say, *That's not fair.*

"Life's not fair," Rodriguez muttered. Both dog and road-runner ignored him.

Advertising slogans were painted on the whitewashed fronts of the shops. Here and there, signs and posters added to the urge to sell. Rodriguez remembered his father saying there hadn't been so many of those when he was young.

Posters—well printed in both Spanish and English— extolled the virtues of Horacio Castillo, who was seeking a fourth term in the Confederate Congress. Castillo, his pictures showed, was a plump man with a neat, thin mustache. FOR PROGRESS AND SECURITY, VOTE RADICAL LIBERAL, his posters said.

A few posters also touted the Whig candidate. Vicente Valenzuela wouldn't win, but he'd put up a respectable showing.

And then there were the scrawls on the walls, again in both Spanish and English. ¡LIBERTAD! some said, while others shouted, FREEDOM! Rodriguez eyed them thoughtfully. The Freedom Party had never been strong in Sonora up till this election. It probably wouldn't win now, either. But it was making itself known in ways it hadn't before.

Most of what Rodriguez knew about the Freedom Party was that it wanted another go at the USA and wanted to keep black men in their place. He didn't like the USA, either. And if black men weren't on the bottom in the CSA, he would be, so he wanted them kept down.

But a Freedom Party man had murdered the president of the Confederacy. Rodriguez scowled. That was no way to behave. He sighed. It was too bad. If people could only forget that . . .

He sighed again, and headed for his farm. A horse-drawn wagon coming into town kicked up more dust, a yellow-gray cloud of it. A couple of men with rifles rode atop the wagon. They gave Rodriguez a hard, watchful stare as it rattled past. He sighed yet again. He was no *bandido*. And, even if he were a *bandido*, it wasn't as if the silver mines in the hills outside of Baroyeca yielded enough precious metal to be worth stealing. Fewer than half as many miners as before the war went down into those dark shafts. If the mine ever failed altogether, what would become of Baroyeca? He didn't like to think about that, either.

High up in the sky, several vultures wheeled, riding the columns of hot air that rose from the baking ground. If Baroyeca dried up and blew away, even the vultures might not find enough to eat in this valley.

After not quite half an hour, Rodriguez got back to his farm. He raised corn and beans and squashes and chickens and pigs. A sturdy mule, one of the best for miles

164

around, did the plowing and hauling. He raised almost all his own food. *But if Baroyeca fails, what will I do for salt and nails and cotton cloth and coffee and all the other things I can't make for myself?* He clicked his tongue between his teeth. He had no idea.

A scrawny dog ran toward him, growling and baring its teeth. "*Cállate*, Maximiliano!" Rodriguez shouted. The dog skidded to a stop about ten feet away. It whined and wagged its tail, as if to say, *Well, you might have been someone dangerous, and I was on the job.* Rodriguez wasn't fooled. He'd had Maximiliano for three years now, and had never seen a stupider dog. He'd known exactly what he was doing when he named the beast for the Emperor of Mexico.

On the other side of the border, naming a dog for the Emperor might have got him stood up against a wall and shot for a rebel. All things considered, he was just as glad to be where he was.

His older daughter, Guadalupe, carried a hen by the feet toward the chopping block by the house. Spit flooded into Rodriguez's mouth at the thought of chicken stew or any of the other interesting things Magdalena, his wife, could do with the bird. He waved to Guadalupe. She was eleven now; she'd been born just before he got conscripted. It wouldn't be more than another year or two before she started having a real shape, before boys began sniffing around, and before life began wheeling through a new cycle. The thought made him feel old, though he'd just passed thirty.

In the house, Miguel and Jorge were wrestling. They were less than a year apart, seven and six, and Jorge, the younger, was big for his age, so the match was pretty even. Susana, who was five, watched them with her thumb in her mouth, probably glad they weren't picking on her. Rodriguez didn't see Pedro, the youngest; he was probably taking a nap.

"*Hola*," Rodriguez said to Magdalena, who sat patting tortillas into shape. His mouth watered again. As far as he was concerned, she made the best tortillas in the whole valley.

"Hola," she answered, cocking her head to one side to study him. *"Como estás?"*

He recognized that gesture, and straightened up in indignation. "I'm not drunk," he declared.

Magdalena didn't answer right away. After she'd finished studying him, though, she nodded. "No, you're not," she admitted. "Good. And what's new in town?"

"It's still there," he said, which, given the state of the silver mine, wasn't altogether a joke. He added, "A wagon came into town from the mine while I was walking home."

"Yes, I saw it go by," Magdalena said. "Who was at the cantina? What's the gossip?"

"I was mostly talking with Carlos," he answered. "We were going on about how you hear more and more English these days." He spoke in Spanish; Magdalena was far more comfortable in it than in the other language.

She nodded even so. "The way the older children bring it back from school, I wonder if their children will know any Spanish at all."

"It's good they go to school, in English or Spanish," Rodriguez said. "Maybe then they won't have to break their backs and break their hearts every day, the way a farmer does."

Magdalena raised an eyebrow. Rodriguez felt heat under his swarthy skin. He hadn't broken his back today. He spread his hands, as if to say, *You want too much if you expect me to work hard* every day. His wife didn't say anything. She didn't have to. The eyebrow had already done the job.

Rodriguez said, "And we talked politics."

"Ah." Magdalena perked up. "What will you do?" Here in Sonora, women's suffrage was a distant glow on the horizon, if that. She couldn't vote herself. But that didn't keep her from being interested.

"I don't know yet," Rodriguez answered. "I don't know, but I think I may just vote for the Freedom Party."

Brakes squeaking a little, the Birmingham pulled up in front of the Freedom Party offices in Richmond. Jake Featherston's guards fanned out and formed a perimeter on the sidewalk. They were well armed and alert; they might have been about to clear the damnyankees out of a stretch of trench. Featherston's enemies inside the CSA weren't so obvious as U.S. soldiers in green-gray, but they probably hated him even more than the Yankees had hated their Confederate foes. Soldiering, sometimes, was just a job. Jake had also discovered politics was a serious business.

One of the guards nodded and gestured. As Jake came forward from the building, another guard opened the curbside door for him. "Freedom!" the man said as he got into the motorcar.

"Freedom, Henry," Featherston echoed. He settled himself on the padded seat. This beat the hell out of life as an artillery sergeant, any way you looked at it.

"Freedom!" the driver said, putting the Birmingham in gear.

"Freedom, Virgil," Featherston answered. "Everything ready at the other end?"

"Far as I know, Sarge." Virgil Joyner made that sound as if he were addressing a general, not a noncom. Yes, this was a pretty good life, all right.

They went only a few blocks. When the driver pulled to a stop, Featherston scowled. "What the hell?" he said angrily. A squad of Freedom Party guards were arguing with some Richmond policemen in old-fashioned gray uniforms. Several reporters scribbled in notebooks. A photographer's flash immortalized the moment. Featherston got out of the motorcar in a hurry. "What's going on here?" he demanded.

"This is a polling place," one of the cops said. "No electioneering allowed within a hundred feet. Far as I'm concerned, they sure as hell count as electioneering." He pointed to the armed guards.

"We're just here to protect Mr. Featherston," one of the men in not-quite-Confederate uniform insisted. He sounded ready for business. The policemen looked nervous. Well they might—the Freedom Party guards outgunned them, and had proved to the CSA they weren't shy about mixing it up with the police, or with anyone else they didn't like.

167

Here, though, Jake judged it a good time to walk soft. "It's all right, boys," he said, as genially as he could. "Don't reckon anybody'll take a shot at me while I go and vote." He walked past the policemen and toward the doorway above which the Stars and Bars fluttered.

The guards didn't look happy. Like watchdogs, they wanted to stay with their master all the time. But, once he'd decided, they didn't argue. The cops didn't bother hiding their relief.

"Who you gonna vote for, Mr. Featherston?" a reporter shouted.

"Freedom—the straight ticket," Jake answered with a wave and a grin.

Despite that cocky grin, he remained alert as he went to the polling place. If anybody wanted to take a shot at him, this was a hell of a good place to do it. If a rifle muzzle came out of that building, where would he jump? Or from that one? Or that one? He hadn't fought in the trenches—the First Richmond Howitzers had been in back of them—but he'd had plenty of bullets whip past his head. He knew everything that needed knowing about diving for cover.

No shots rang out. He strode into the polling place with grin intact. A man coming out of a curtained booth recognized him, did a double take, and grinned a grin of his own, a big, delighted one. "Freedom!" the fellow blurted.

"Freedom," Featherston said.

Somber, disapproving coughs from the officials at the polling place, four or five graybeards who might have fought in the Second Mexican War or maybe even the War of Secession, but surely not in the Great War. One of them said, "No electioneering, gentlemen, if you please."

"Right," Jake said; he was doing this by the rules. He scrawled his name and address in their registry book, and went into the booth the fellow who'd recognized him had vacated. As he'd told the reporter he would, he put an X by the name of the Freedom candidates for Congress, for the Virginia Assembly and State Senate, and for the Richmond City Council. The last race was nominally nonpartisan, but everybody knew better. With the Whigs and Radical Liberals pretty evenly split in the district, he thought the Freedom Party man had a decent chance of sneaking home a winner, too.

After finishing the ballot, he went out and presented it to the election officials. One of them folded it and put it into the ballot box. "Jacob Featherston has voted," he intoned solemnly.

"Jacob Featherston is a murdering son of a bitch," said a man who'd come out of his voting booth a moment after Jake emerged from his.

More coughs from the old men. "None of that here," one of them said. Another took the ballot. "Oscar Herbert has voted," he declared.

A few years earlier, when the Freedom Party was just getting off the ground, Jake Featherston would have mixed it up with Herbert right outside the polling place, or maybe here inside it. He was no less angry now, but he was shrewder than he had been. *Some day soon, pal, somebody's gonna pay you a little visit,* he thought. *Your name's Oscar Herbert and you live in this precinct. We'll find you. You bet we will.*

Herbert went one way, Featherston the other. He walked through the cops and out to his guards. With audible sighs of relief, they closed in around him. Photographers took more flash pictures. He waved to them.

"How many seats do you expect to lose this time?" a reporter called.

"What's that?" Jake cupped a hand behind his ear as he got into the Birmingham. "Spent too long in the artillery, and my ears aren't what they ought to be." He slammed the car door before the reporter could finish the question again. He *had* lost some hearing during the war, but not so much as that. Still, artilleryman's ear came in handy for avoiding questions he didn't want to answer.

"Back to headquarters, Sarge?" the driver asked.

"You bet," Featherston answered. The car pulled away from the curb.

On the short ride over to Party headquarters, Jake contemplated the question he'd pretended not to hear. He liked none of the answers he came up with. His best guess was that Freedom *would* lose seats in the House of Representatives. He hoped the Party would hold its own, but he didn't believe it. And if he lost seats—he took everything personally, as he always had—how long would people keep finding him a force to be reckoned with?

"We were so close," he muttered. "So goddamn close."

"What's that?" Virgil Joyner said.

"Nothin'. Not a thing." Jake lied without hesitation.

When he got back to Freedom Party headquarters, he wished he hadn't gone and voted so soon. He had nothing to do but sit around and wait and stare at the banks of telegraph clickers and phones and wireless sets that would bring in the election results when there were election results to bring in. That wouldn't be for a while yet. Polls in Virginia didn't close till seven P.M., and those farther west would stay open a couple of hours longer than that. Meanwhile . . .

Meanwhile, he did some more scribbling in *Over Open Sights*. He'd fiddled with the—maybe journal was the right name for it—now and again in the days since the Great War, but he'd never quite managed to recapture the heat he'd known while writing it in the odd moments when he wasn't throwing three-inch shells at the damnyankees.

One of these days, he told himself. *One of these days, I'll be ready to put it out, and people will be ready to read it. I'll know when. I'm sure I'll know when. But the time isn't ripe yet.* He fiddled with the pile of Gray Eagle scratch-pads in lieu of twiddling his thumbs, and accomplished about as much as he would have twiddling them. He changed a word here, took out a couple of words there, added a phrase somewhere else. It all added up to nothing, and he knew that, too.

His secretary stuck her head into the office. "Can I get you something to eat, Mr. Featherston?" she asked, as if she were his mother.

He wouldn't have taken that from anyone else— certainly not from his real mother, were she still alive. But he nodded now. "Thank you kindly, Lulu," he said. "Some fried chicken'd go down mighty nice about now."

170

"I'll take care of it," she promised, and hurried away. Take care of it she did, as she always did. Jake ate like a wolf. No matter how much he ate, his gaunt form never added an ounce. He ate as much from duty as from hunger. His stomach would pain him no matter what when he watched the returns coming in, but it would pain him less with food in there.

A little before seven, Freedom Party leaders and telegraph operators gathered at the headquarters. Featherston made himself greet them, made himself shake hands and smile and slap backs, the way he'd made himself eat. It needed doing, so he did it. But it was a distraction he could have done without.

"Polls are closing," said somebody—somebody with a gift for the obvious—as church bells all through Richmond chimed seven times. A minute or so later, the very first returns began coming over the wire. They meant as little as the changes Jake had made in *Over Open Sights* earlier in the day, but everybody exclaimed over them even so. Featherston did a little exclaiming himself when a Freedom Party candidate jumped into an early lead in a Virginia district he'd been sure was safely Whig.

"Maybe the people are wising up," he said. "I hope they are, God damn it."

In the first days of the Great War, he'd thought the Confederate Army would drive everything before it, too. He'd taken unholy glee in shelling Washington, and he'd delighted in swarming up into Pennsylvania and toward Philadelphia. If the *de facto* capital of the USA had fallen along with the *de jure* one ... But Philadelphia had held, and, inch by painful inch, the C.S. Army had been driven back through Pennsylvania and Maryland and into Virginia itself.

If the niggers hadn't risen up and stabbed us in the back ... But he knew they had, however much white men nowadays tried to pretend otherwise.

On one of the competing wireless sets, an announcer said, "If this trend holds up, it looks like the third district in South Carolina will be coming back to the Whigs in the next Congress after staying in Freedom Party hands these past two terms."

Curses ran through the headquarters, Featherston's loud among them. The Party had held that seat in the debacle of 1923; he'd counted on holding it again. Maybe the people weren't wising up after all. Maybe they were an even bigger pack of damned idiots than he'd thought.

A colored waiter, hired for the occasion, brought around a tray of drinks. Featherston took a whiskey. The Negro nodded respectfully as he did. Jake tossed back the drink. His mouth tightened. *Where were you in the uprising, you sorry black son of a bitch? You didn't have a penguin suit on then, I bet. Probably just another goddamn Red. If we'd shot a few thousand bastards like you before you got out of line, we wouldn't have had any trouble like we did.* He had some sharp things to say about that in *Over Open Sights*.

Another Freedom Party seat, this one from Arkansas, went down the drain. Amid more curses, somebody said, "Well, we didn't elect any Senators till 1921, so we don't have to worry about them for another couple o' years."

That was exactly the wrong attitude to take, as far as Jake was concerned. "We're playing this game to win, dammit," he snarled. "We don't play not to lose. We don't play safe. We're playing to win, and we're gonna win. Remember it, damn you all!"

Nobody argued with him, not out loud. But nobody seemed anything close to convinced, either. That meant he got to crow extra loud when, out of a clear blue sky, the Freedom candidate won a tight three-way race for governor of Texas, and then, in the wee small hours of the morning, when a new Freedom Congressman came in from, of all places, southern Sonora.

"See, boys?" Featherston said around a yawn. "We ain't dead yet. Not even close." *I hope not even close, anyhow.*

VI

During the Great War, Nellie Jacobs had heard more aeroplane motors above Washington, D.C., than she'd ever wanted to. Aeroplane motors, back in those days, had always meant trouble. Either observers were over the city taking photographs to guide bombers and artillery, or else the bombers themselves paid calls, raining destruction and death down on the Confederate occupiers. Later, Confederate bombers had tried to slaughter U.S. soldiers in Washington. Neither side cared much about civilians. Nellie had needed years after the war to stop wanting to duck whenever motors droned overhead.

Now, though, she and her husband stood in the street on the bright, crisp New Year's Day of 1926, staring into the blue sky, pointing, and exclaiming in excitement like a couple of children. "Look! There it is!" Hal Jacobs said, pointing again.

"I see it!" Nellie answered. "Looks like a big old fat cigar up there in the sky, doesn't it?"

"It certainly does," Hal said. "That is just what it looks like, I think."

Clara tugged at Nellie's skirt. "Ma, I have to go potty," she said.

"Well, go on in and go," Nellie said impatiently. "Your dad and me, we're going to stay right here and watch the zeppelin a while longer." Clara made the beginnings of a whimper. "Go on," Nellie told her. "Go on, or I'll warm your fanny for you. You're going to be six this year. You don't need me to hold your hand any more when you go tinkle."

Her daughter ducked into the coffeehouse. Nellie kept staring up at the *Kronprinz Friedrich Wilhelm* as it neared the mooring station that had been set up at the top of the newly refinished Washington Monument. "Can you believe it?" Hal said. "It flew all the way across the Atlantic. All the way across the ocean, without stopping once. What an age we live in!"

"Paper says the crown prince himself is in there." Nellie tried to point to the little passenger gondola hanging beneath the great cigar-shaped gas bag. "On a state visit to President Sinclair."

As Clara came back, Hal nodded. His voice was troubled. "We fought side by side with Kaiser Bill all through the Great War. Sad we should squabble with Germany now. I hope Friedrich Wilhelm can patch things up."

"That'd be good," Nellie agreed. "Don't want to worry about little Armstrong going off to war one of these days." She doted on her grandson, not least because her daughter Edna had to take care of him most of the time. Edna's half sister Clara, on the other hand, had been a not altogether welcome surprise and was an ungodly amount of work for a woman well into middle age. She would, thank God, be going back to kindergarten in a few more days.

Suddenly, the zeppelin's engines stopped buzzing. "They've got it," Hal said, as if he personally had been the one to moor the *Kronprinz Friedrich Wilhelm* to the white stone tower. He sounded delighted to repeat himself: "What an age we live in! When my father was born, there was no telegraph and hardly any railroads. And now we have these wireless sets and—this." He pointed toward the Washington Monument again.

"It's something, all right," Nellie agreed. But then, perhaps incautiously, she went on, "I don't know that it's all to the good."

"Not all to the good?" Her husband looked indignant. "What do you mean? What could be grander than—that?"

"Oh, it's—swell, the young people say now." Nellie

174

brought out the slang self-consciously; like anyone of her generation, she was much more used to *bully*. "But when your pa was born, Hal, this here was all one country, too, you know. We've spilled an awful lot o' blood since on account of it ain't any more."

"Well, yes, of course," he said. The two of them, in conquered and reconquered Washington, had seen more spilled blood than most civilians. He sighed and breathed out a big, puffy cloud of steam. "I can't imagine how things could have been any different, though. You might as well talk about us losing the Revolution and still belonging to England."

"I suppose you're right." Nellie sighed. Hal was the sensible one in the family. He was, as far as she was concerned, sometimes sensible to a fault. Clara came back out. Nellie absentmindedly ruffled her hair. Then she decided to be sensible, too, and said, "Now we've seen it. Let's go inside. It's cold out here."

"Oh, Ma!" Nobody had ever accused Clara of being sensible.

But Hal said, "Your mother is right. If you stay out here too long, you could catch pneumonia, and then where would you be?"

"I'd be out here, having a good time," Clara answered. Pneumonia was just a word to her, not one of the many diseases that could so easily kill children.

"Come on in," Nellie said. She knew what pneumonia was, all right. "Edna and Uncle Merle and Cousin Armstrong are coming over in a little while."

That did get Clara back inside, at the price of continual questions—"When will they come? Why aren't they here yet?"—till her half sister, Edna's husband, and their son arrived half an hour later. Armstrong pulled Clara's hair. She squalled like a cat that had had its tail stepped on, then stamped on his foot hard enough to make him wail even louder.

He got little sympathy from his mother. "Serves you right," Edna said. "I saw what you did to Clara."

"Happy New Year," Merle Grimes said above the wails of the two irate children. Behind his gold-rimmed spectacles, irony glinted in his eyes.

"Well, I do hope the rest of it'll be happier than this godawful racket," Nellie said. "Maybe the crown prince will bury the hatchet once and for all."

"He'd like to bury it in our backs, I think," Grimes said. "One of these days, we really will have to worry about Germany. The Germans are worrying about us right this minute, and you can bet your bottom dollar on that."

Hal handed him a whiskey. After they clinked glasses and toasted 1926, Nellie's husband said, "We'll have a hard time worrying about Germany when we don't even worry about the CSA."

"I know," Grimes said. "Well, good old Kaiser Bill's got other worries besides us, too, and that's not bad."

Nellie raised her glass for a toast of her own. "Here's to no more war anywhere," she said once she'd caught everybody's eye. "Haven't we had enough?"

"Amen!" her husband said, and drank.

"I know *I've* had enough, enough and then some," her son-in-law said. He drank, too. "Wasn't for those . . . miserable Confederates"—he didn't swear around women, but he'd come close there—"I wouldn't limp for the rest of my days."

Edna also drank. "I hope they never, ever come anywhere near Washington again," she said. Nellie eyed her daughter. Edna looked back defiantly, but couldn't help turning red. She'd nearly married a Confederate officer. In fact, she would have married him if a U.S. shell hadn't killed him on his way to the altar. *Almost ten years ago now,* Nellie thought, amazed, wondering where the time had gone. As far as she knew, Merle Grimes had no idea Nicholas H. Kincaid had ever existed.

That was Edna's worry, not her own. She had secrets in her past, too, secrets she wanted to stay buried till they shoveled dirt over her. Her husband reminded her of those secrets by pouring everyone's glass full and proposing a toast of his own: "Here's to our missing friends, gone but not forgotten."

"Oh, God, yes!" Merle said, and gulped that drink down. His mouth tightened; harsh lines sprang out at its corners. "Too many good fellows dead for no reason: Ernie and Clancy and Bob and Otis and—" Behind his spectacles, tears glinted.

"And Bill Reach, too." Hal Jacobs sounded as maudlin as his stepdaughter's husband. "He was worth a division, maybe more, in getting the Confederates out of Washington. I wish he'd lived to see this day, with an American empire stretching north to south, east to west. . . ." He sighed. "He should have, too. Just bad luck."

Now Edna eyed Nellie. Now Nellie flushed and had trouble meeting her daughter's eye. She didn't reckon Bill Reach a missing friend. Reach had mortified her during the war, drunkenly taking her for the strumpet she'd been a long time before. She'd never been able to tell Edna anything since, not hoping to be taken seriously.

But not even Edna knew how Bill Reach had died. No one but Nellie knew that, which was just how she wanted things. She'd been foraging for supplies when he tried to rape her, counting on a broken bottle to intimidate her into cooperating. But she'd carried a butcher knife, and she'd been sober. Bill Reach's body was one of God knew how many hundreds or thousands from the time of the U.S. bombardment, the time before the Confederate Army finally and sullenly pulled out of the U.S. capital. So far as she knew, nobody'd ever found it.

I hope nobody ever does, either, she thought savagely. *I hope he rots in the ground and burns in hell forever. It'd serve him right, by God.*

Her husband had said something to her, but she had no idea what. "I'm sorry, Hal," she said. "I must've been woolgathering."

"It's all right, sweetheart," Hal said with a tender smile. He did love her. She knew that. She was absently fond of him, too, not least because, being a long way from young, he didn't try to make love to her very often. She'd had more than enough of that. Now he went on, "I said, I know you feel the same way about poor Bill as I do. He always praised the information you got to the skies. He did like the bottle a bit too much, but he was a fine man, a first-class patriot."

Nellie managed a nod and a glassy smile. They sufficed.

Edna made a small noise that might have been the start of a snicker, but did stop at Nellie's glower. And then they all got distracted, for Clara came in shouting, "Ma! Ma! Armstrong went and put somethin' down the potty and then he flushed it, and now there's water all over everything! Come quick!"

"Oh, for God's sake!" Nellie sprang to her feet, as did the other grownups.

Getting out the pair of long johns and mopping up the water didn't take long. For Merle Grimes to wallop Armstrong's backside with a hairbrush didn't take long, either. Armstrong's howls needed some little while to subside. So did Nellie's temper. "He's only a little boy, sweetheart," Hal said.

"Boys!" Nellie snorted, in the tone she usually reserved for, *Men!* "You'd never see a little girl doing something like that."

"You tell 'em, Ma," Edna said. She and Nellie argued whenever they got a chance, but she would back her mother in a quarrel against the other half of the human race.

Except there was no quarrel. Hal Jacobs and Merle Grimes looked at each other, as if wondering who would bell the cat. At last, Hal said, "Well, Nellie, you may be right. If the world held nothing but women, we probably wouldn't have fought the Great War."

Merle chuckled. "Oh, I don't know if I'd go that far. They wouldn't have fought it over Serbia, though—I am sure of that. More likely over which was better, Macy's or Gimbel's."

He laughed. So did Hal. And so did Edna, betraying her sex after all. Nellie glared at her—yes, they would squabble over anything. Defensively, Edna said, "Oh, come on, Ma—it *was* funny."

"Well, maybe," Nellie said with the air of one making an enormous concession. She was so obvious about it, her husband and son-in-law started laughing again.

"Peace," Merle Grimes said when he could speak at last. "Peace. It's 1926, and we've already drunk to peace. Let's keep it for as long as we can." Not even Nellie could find anything to argue with there.

* * *

Jonathan Moss got to his feet in the courtroom. "May it please your Honor," he said wearily, "but I must object to the prosecution's speaking of my client as 'the guilty party.' The purpose of a trial is to find out whether or not he is guilty."

His Honor was a U.S. Army colonel named Augustus Thorgood. Down came the gavel. "Overruled." He nodded to the prosecutor, a U.S. Army major named Sam Lopat. "You may proceed."

"Thank you, your Honor," Lopat replied. "As I was saying, Stubbs there is plainly guilty of insurrection against the military government of the United States in the former province of Ontario, as defined in Occupation Administrative Code, section 521, subsection 17."

Horace Stubbs, Moss' client, leaned toward him and whispered, "Thanks for trying."

"We're not out of it yet," Moss whispered back. But he was whistling in the dark, and he knew it.

Major Lopat went on, "Before witnesses, the defendant said the United States deserved to be booted out of Canada on their backside. His very words, your Honor!" His voice trembled with indignation.

"Objection." Moss got to his feet again. "No witnesses have been produced before the court to show my client said any such thing."

"We have the testimony," Lopat said smugly.

"But no witnesses," Moss persisted. "Testimony can come from a man with a personal grudge, or from one out for a profit. How do we know unless we can cross-examine a witness?"

"This is not an ordinary criminal proceeding, Mr. Moss, as you know perfectly well," Colonel Thorgood said. "Testimony from certified informants may be admitted without their being liable to appear in open court, for fear of reprisal against them from the unreconciled."

"How can you possibly hope for justice under such conditions?" Moss asked.

"We aim to stamp out rebellion," the military judge said. "We will, too."

"Yes, your Honor. No doubt, your Honor." Moss

turned Thorgood's title of respect into one of reproach. "But, sooner or later, ignoring the needs of justice and caring only for the needs of expedience *will* come back to haunt you. As Ben Franklin said, your Honor, 'They that can give up essential liberty to obtain a little temporary safety deserve neither liberty nor safety.'"

He'd pulled that quotation out of his *Bartlett's*, hoping he wouldn't have to use it. If he did, his client would be in trouble. Well, Stubbs *was* in trouble, and Moss, like any lawyer worth his pay, used whatever weapons came to hand. And this one struck home. Colonel Thorgood turned red. Major Lopat jumped to his feet. "Now *I* object, your Honor! Incompetent, irrelevant, and immaterial."

"Sustained." Thorgood thumped the gavel. "The record will be stricken."

"Exception!" Moss said. "If you're going to railroad an innocent man, at least be honest about what you're doing."

Bang! The gavel came down again. "This inflammatory speech will also be stricken," Colonel Thorgood declared. He nodded to Lopat. "Carry on, Major."

Carry on Lopat did, with soldierly precision. The case against Horace Stubbs was strong—was, in fact, airtight—as long as one believed what informants said about him. Moss was convinced the informants were lying through their teeth. But he doubted whether Colonel Thorgood cared one way or the other. Thorgood's job was to keep Canada quiet. If he had to shoot every Canuck in sight to do that job, he would, and go to dinner with a hearty appetite five minutes later.

When Major Lopat finished, the military judge nodded to Moss. "Now, Counselor, you may have your say."

"Thank you, your Honor." Moss fought to keep sarcasm from his voice. He thought he still had some small chance, not of getting his client off—that was plainly hopeless—but of earning him a reduced sentence. Further affronting Colonel Thorgood wouldn't help there. He set forth the evidence as best he could, finishing, "May it please your Honor, the only people who claim Mr. Stubbs was in any way involved with recent unfortunate events in Ontario are those whose testimony is inherently unreliable and who have a vested interest in giving him the appearance of guilt regardless of whether that appearance is in any way justified." He sat down.

From the prosecution's table, Major Lopat muttered something about a "damn Canuck-lover." Moss sent him a hard look. The military prosecutor gave back a stare colder than any Canadian winter. Had he worked in the CSA rather than the USA, he would surely have muttered about a "damn nigger-lover" instead.

But, to Moss' surprise, Colonel Thorgood's gavel came down again. "That will be quite enough of that, Major," the judge said.

"I beg your pardon, your Honor," Lopat said politely. He didn't beg Moss' pardon, though.

"Very well, Major. Do keep your remarks to the business at hand. Having said as much to Mr. Moss, I can hardly fail to say the same to you." Thorgood looked down at the notes on his desk. He picked up a pen and scribbled something, then said, "Horace Stubbs, rise to hear the verdict of this court."

With a sigh, Stubbs got to his feet. He could see the writing on the wall as plainly as could Moss. He was a small, thin, middle-aged man. On looks alone, he made an unlikely insurrectionist.

"Horace Stubbs," Colonel Thorgood said, "I find you guilty of the crime of participating in rebellion against the U.S. occupying authorities in the former province of Ontario." Stubbs' shoulders slumped. The military judge scribbled something else. He continued, "Due to the unusual nature of this case, I sentence you to six months' imprisonment and to a fine of $250: failure to pay the latter will result in a further six months' imprisonment." *Bang!* went the gavel. "This court is adjourned."

A couple of husky U.S. noncoms strode forward to take Horace Stubbs off to jail. "Just a minute," he told them. "Just one damn minute." He grabbed Jonathan Moss' hand, hard enough to hurt. "Thank you, sir," he said. "Everything they told me about you, it was all true, and then some. God bless you."

"You're welcome," Moss said in slightly dazed tones as the noncoms took charge of his client and led him away. He'd hoped Colonel Thorgood would go easy on Stubbs. Never in his wildest dreams had he imagined Thorgood would go this easy. Six months and $250? From a military court? That was hardly even a slap on the wrist.

Major Lopat must have felt the same way. As he put papers back into his military-issue briefcase, he sent Moss a sour stare. "Well, Clarence Darrow, you pulled a rabbit out of the hat this time," he said.

"Oh, come on," Moss said—he was damned if he'd admit surprise to the other side. "You didn't have a case, and you know it."

Lopat didn't even bother arguing with him. All the military prosecutor said was, "Yeah? So what? Look where we are."

"Canadians deserve justice, too," Moss said.

"Oh, yeah? Since when? Says who?" Having fired three clichés like an artillery barrage, Major Lopat added, "And a whole fat lot you'd care, too, if you weren't sleeping with a Canuck gal."

That might even have been true. Even so, to Moss it had only one possible answer, and he used it: "Screw you, Sam." He packed his own papers in his briefcase and left the courtroom, grabbing his overcoat as he went. The calendar said spring had started three days earlier, but Berlin, Ontario, paid little attention to the calendar. Snow whitened streets and sidewalks, with more falling even as Moss walked along the street.

He paused thoughtfully in front of a sign that said, EMPIRE GROCERIES. Below the words, a large, American-looking eagle was painted. Maybe the storekeeper meant the American empire, the one that stretched from the Arctic Ocean to the Gulf of California, from the Atlantic to the Pacific. But maybe, too, it was meant to call to mind the name Berlin had briefly borne during the Great War, when its citizens decided living in a town named for an enemy capital was unpatriotic.

Moss chuckled. Laura Secord still refused to call the town anything but Empire. As far as she was concerned, the occupying authorities had no right to change back the name. There were no Canadian patriots more fiery than Laura.

And yet she'd warned him the uprising was imminent. He still didn't fully understand that, and she refused to talk about it now. His best guess was that she hadn't thought the revolt had any chance to succeed, and so she wasn't committing treason by talking about it. But that was only a guess, and he knew it.

He stopped at a diner a few doors down from Empire Groceries. A waiter brought him a menu. The man walked with a limp; he'd taken a bullet in the leg trying to hold back the U.S. Army. He knew Moss had flown aeroplanes for the USA, but didn't hold it against him—much. "Case over?" he asked as Moss sat down at an empty table.

"That's right," Moss answered. "Let me have the corned beef on wheat, and coffee to go with it."

As the waiter scribbled on a pad, he asked another question: "They going to let Horace live?"

"Six months in jail and $250," Moss said exultantly.

The waiter dropped his pencil. "Be damned," he said, grunting in pain as he bent to pick it up. He called back to the cook, who was also the owner. "Hey, Eddie! This fast-talking Yank got Horace off easy!"

"What's 'easy'?" Eddie called back. "Twenty years? Ten?"

"Six months," the waiter answered, sounding as excited as Moss. "And $250."

"Be damned," Eddie said, as the waiter had. That impressed him enough to make him come out front. He had on a cloth cap in lieu of the toque a cook at a fancier place might have worn. He tipped it to Moss. "Lunch on the house, pal."

"Thanks," Moss told him.

"You did it," Eddie said. "Seems like our own barristers haven't had much luck in Yankee courts. Maybe it takes one to know one."

That wasn't exactly praise, though the cook no doubt meant it as such. It also wasn't so, or not necessarily. With a sigh, Moss said, "That fellow they said was a bomber, they threw the book at him no matter what I did."

"Enoch Dupree, you mean?" the waiter said.

Moss nodded. "That's right."

The waiter and Eddie looked at each other. After a long pause, Eddie said, "Hate to tell you, but Enoch, he *was* a bomber. I happen to know it for a fact, on account of his brother-in-law's married to my cousin. I—"

"I don't want to hear about it." Moss held up a hand to show he really meant it. "My job is to give people the best defense they can get, regardless of whether they're guilty or not."

"Don't know I much fancy that," the waiter said. "Shouldn't be guilty people running around loose just 'cause they've got smart lawyers."

"Well, your other choice is to send innocent people to jail," Moss answered. "How do you like that?"

"I don't, much," the Canadian answered. "But I thought it was what you Yanks call justice. Sure has looked like that since you came."

"You shouldn't blame him," Eddie said. "He's done everything he could for us, ever since he hung out his shingle here."

"That's so," the waiter admitted, and Moss felt good till the fellow added, "Sure as hell wish he could do a lot more, though."

Lucien Galtier sighed as he and Marie and Georges and Jeanne—the last two children left at home—got into his Chevrolet for the Sunday trip to Rivière-du-Loup. "I'd sooner go to Mass in St.-Antonin or St.-Modèste," he said, "but sometimes there's no help for it."

"Doing this is wise," his wife said. "As long as we come to church every so often and let Bishop Pascal see us, everything should be fine."

"We don't want to give him any reason to complain about us to the Americans, no," Lucien agreed.

"But the Republic of Quebec is free and independent," Georges said. "And if you don't believe me, just ask the first American soldier you see."

Georges always liked to sound as if he were joking.

Sometimes he was. Sometimes ... Lucien had learned an English expression: *kidding on the square*. That summed things up better than anything in Quebecois French.

"You're getting pretty good at this driving business," Georges went on as they rolled up the paved road past the hospital and toward the town on the southern bank of the St. Lawrence. "Anyone would think you'd been doing it all your life." He chuckled. "They'd hardly even invented horses when you were a boy, eh, Papa, let alone motor-cars?"

"They hadn't invented such smart alecks, I'll tell you that," Lucien said. His younger son preened, as if at praise.

The Église Saint-Patrice in Rivière-du-Loup was called a cathedral these days, though it was the same building it had always been. Quite a few motorcars parked nearby. Times were ... Lucien wouldn't say they were good, but he thought it now and again.

As people filed into the church (being the stubborn Quebecois farmer he was, Galtier refused to think of it as a cathedral, no matter what Bishop Pascal declared), some of them talked about the stocks they'd bought, and about how much money they'd made from them. Lucien felt Marie's eyes on him. Ever so slightly, he shook his head. He'd stayed away from the *bourse*, and intended to go right on staying away from it. It struck him as being much more like gambling than any legitimate way to make money. Gambling, now, gambling was all very well—so long as you knew you could lose as easily as you could win.

He was almost to the door when he heard the word *scandal* for the first time. Now he and his wife looked at each other. He shrugged. Marie did the same. A moment later, he heard the word again. Something juicy had happened. *And I've been on the farm minding my own business, and so I haven't the faintest idea what it is,* he thought regretfully.

"Tabernac," he muttered. The look Marie sent him this time was definitely reproachful. He pretended not to notice. It wasn't—quite—as if he'd cursed on holy ground. The other side of the door, it would have been a different business.

185

No sooner had he gone inside than someone else—a woman—said *scandal*, and immediately started giggling. "What's going on, *mon père*?" Georges asked. Scandal—especially scandal that might be funny—drew him the way maple syrup drew ants.

A young priest named Father Guillaume stood by the altar in Bishop Pascal's place. As Lucien took his seat in the pews, he asked the fellow next to him, a townsman, "Where's the bishop?"

"Why, with the children, of course," the man answered, and started to laugh. Lucien fumed. He didn't want to admit he didn't know what was going on. That would make him look like a farmer who came to town only to sell things and to hear Mass. Of course, he *was* a farmer who came to town only to sell things and to hear Mass, but he didn't want to remind the world of it.

His eldest daughter, Nicole; her husband, the American doctor named Leonard O'Doull; and their son, Lucien, sat down behind his family. He started to lean back and ask them what was so delicious, but Father Guillaume began speaking in Latin just then, so he had to compose himself in patience.

He dared hope the priest's sermon would enlighten him, but it only left him more tantalized and titillated than ever. Father Guillaume talked about those without sin casting the first stone. He praised Pascal, and wished him good fortune in whatever he chose to do with the rest of his life.

Lucien wiggled like a man with a dreadful and embarrassing itch. What ever the scandal was, it must have got Bishop Pascal! He'd never cared for Pascal; the man was too pink, too clever, too . . . too expedient, to suit him. But Pascal had always come up smelling like a rose—till now. *And I don't even know what he did!* Galtier thought in an agony of frustration.

He went up and took communion from Father Guillaume. He swallowed the wafer as fast as he could; he didn't want to speak of scandal with the Body of Christ still on his tongue. But then he made a beeline for his son-in-law.

186

"What? You don't know? Oh, for heaven's sake?" Dr. O'Doull exclaimed. He'd come to Quebec during the war, speaking tolerably good Parisian French. After ten years here, his accent remained noticeable, but only a little. He sounded more as if he'd been born in *la belle province—la belle république,* now—every day.

"No, I don't know," Galtier ground out. "Since you are such a font of knowledge, suppose you enlighten me."

"Mais certainement, mon beau-père," O'Doull said, grinning. "Bishop Pascal's lady friend just had twins."

"Twins!" Lucien said. *"Le bon Dieu!"*

"God was indeed good to Bishop Pascal, wouldn't you agree?" his son-in-law said, and laughed out loud. "I should say, to former Bishop Pascal, for he has resigned his see in light of this . . . interesting development. Father Guillaume will serve the spiritual needs of Rivière-du-Loup until the see has a new bishop."

"Twins," Galtier repeated, as if he'd never heard the word before. "Yes, I can see how he would have to resign after that."

No one was surprised when priests had lady friends. They were men of the cloth, yes, but they were also men. A lot of women, down through the years, had sighed over Father, later Bishop, Pascal. Lucien didn't understand it, but he'd never been a woman, either. And few people were astonished if the lady friends of priests sometimes presented them with offspring. That, too, was just one of those things. Life went on, people looked the other way, and the little bastards were often very well brought up.

"But twins!" Lucien said. "You can't look the other way at twins. By the nature of things, a bishop's twins are a scandal."

"Exactly so, *mon beau-père,*" Leonard O'Doull said. "And that is why Bishop Pascal is Bishop Pascal no more, but plain old Pascal Talon."

"Pascal Talon!" Galtier exclaimed. "That's right—that is his family. I hadn't thought of his family name in years, though. No one has, I'm sure."

"Of course not, not when he belonged to the Church for all those years," Dr. O'Doull said. "That's what belonging to the Church means. That's what it does. It takes you away from your family and puts you in God's family." He laughed again. "But, now that he's gone and made God's family bigger . . ."

Galtier laughed, too. He asked, "Since you are in town and hear all these things the moment they happen—and since you don't bother telling your poor country cousins about them—could you tell me what M. Pascal Talon plans to do now that he is Bishop Pascal no more?" Whatever it was, he had the nasty feeling the man would make a great success of it.

And, sure enough, his son-in-law said, "I understand he's decided Rivière-du-Loup is too small a place for a man of his many talents. He will be moving to Quebec City, they say, where he can be appreciated for everything he is."

A snake, a sneak, a worm, a collaborator, a philanderer—yes, in the capital of the Republic he should do well for himself, Galtier thought. He found some more questions: "And what of the twins? Are they boys or girls, by the way? And what of their mother? Is Pascal now a married man?"

"They're a boy and a girl. Very pretty babies—I've seen them," O'Doull replied. Being a doctor, he'd seen a lot of babies. If he said they were pretty, Lucien was prepared to believe him. He went on, "I am given to understand that Suzette is now Mme. Talon, yes, but I don't think she'll be going to Quebec City with her new husband."

Marie heard that and let out a loud sniff. "He made himself a member of God's family. If he cheated on his vows to the Lord, how can anyone think he won't cheat on his vows to a woman? Poor Suzette."

"Yes, very likely Pascal will cheat on her, but she must have known he cheated when she first started her games with him," Lucien said.

"Why do you always blame the woman?" his wife demanded.

"Why do you always blame the man?" he returned, also heatedly.

"Excuse me." Dr. O'Doull made as if to duck. "I'm going somewhere safer—the trenches during the war were probably safer."

"It will be all right," Galtier said. "We've been married this long. We can probably last a little longer."

Marie didn't argue, but her expression was mutinously eloquent. And, as a matter of fact, Galtier wondered why he did take the former Bishop Pascal's side. It wasn't as if he liked the man. He never had. He'd never trusted him, either. Pascal had always been too smooth, too rosy, to be reliable. That was what Lucien had thought, at any rate. Plainly, a lot of people had had a different opinion.

But was Suzette, the new Mme. Talon, such a bargain? Galtier also had his doubts about that. After all, if she'd let Pascal into her bed, what did that say about her taste? Nothing good, certainly.

"Let's go home," he said.

"All right," Marie answered. Her voice had no, *We'll come back to this later*, in it, so he supposed this wouldn't be a fight that clouded things between them for days at a time. They'd had a few of those, but only a few: one reason they still got on so well after thirty years and a bit more besides.

"Why do you dislike Bishop Pascal so much?" Jeanne asked on the way back to the farm.

"Well, just for starters, because he tried to get us to collaborate with the Americans during the war. And when we wouldn't do it, he got them to take away our land and build the hospital on it," Galtier replied. "You were just a little girl then, so you wouldn't remember very well, but he alienated our patrimony."

"But . . ." His youngest daughter seemed to have trouble putting her thoughts into words. At last, she said, "But my sister married an American. We're paid rent, and a good one, for the land the hospital sits on."

Georges laughed. "How do you answer that one, Papa?"

That was a good question. Galtier did the best he could, saying, "At the time, what Father Pascal did seemed wrong. It worked out for the best. I can't quarrel with that. But just because it worked out for the best doesn't mean Pascal did what he did for good reasons. He did what he did to grab with both hands."

"Suppose the Americans had lost the war," Marie added. "What would have happened to Pascal then?"

"He would have come out ahead of the game, and convinced everyone everything was somebody else's fault," Georges replied at once.

He was probably right, even if that wasn't the answer his mother had been looking for. Lucien sighed. The farmhouse wasn't far now. "Quebec City had better watch out," he said, and drove on.

Sylvia Enos stood in the kitchen of her flat, glaring at her only son. She had to look up to glare at him. When had George, Jr., become taller than she? Some time when she wasn't watching, surely. He looked unhappy now, twisting his cloth cap in his hands. "But, Ma," he said, "it's the best chance I'll ever have!"

"Nonsense," Sylvia told him. "The best chance you'll ever have is to stay in school and get as much learning as you can."

His face—achingly like his dead father's, though he couldn't raise a mustache and they were falling out of style anyhow—went closed and hard, suddenly a man's face, and a stubborn man's at that, not a boy's. "I don't care anything about school. I hate it. And I'm no . . . good in it anyhow." He wouldn't say *damn*, not in front of his mother. Sylvia had done her best to raise him right.

"You don't want to go to sea at sixteen," Sylvia said.

"Oh, yes, I do," he said. "There's nothing I want more."

Till you meet a girl. Then you'll find something you want more. But Sylvia didn't say that. It wouldn't have helped. What she did say was, "If you go to sea at sixteen, you'll be doing it the rest of your life."

"What's wrong with that?" he asked. "What else am I going to be doing the rest of my life?"

"That's why you go to school," Sylvia said. "To find out what else you could be doing."

"But I don't want to do anything else," George, Jr., said, exactly as his father might have. "I just want to go down to T Wharf and out to sea, the way Pop did."

All the reasons he wanted to go to sea were all the reasons Sylvia wanted him to stay home. "Look what going to sea got your father in the end," she said, fighting to hold back tears.

"That was the Navy, Ma." Now George, Jr., just sounded impatient. "I'm not going into the Navy. I just want to catch fish."

"Do you think nothing can go wrong when you're out there in a fishing boat? If you do, you'd better think again, son. Plenty of boats go out from T Wharf and then don't come home again. Storms, fog, who knows why? But they don't. Even if they do come home, they don't always bring back everybody who set out. If you're tending a line or hauling in a net and a big wave comes by ... Do you really want the crabs and the lobsters and the flatfish fighting over who gets a taste of you?"

Most fishermen had a horror of a watery death, and of the creatures they caught catching them. But her son only shrugged and answered, "If I'm dead, what difference does it make?" He was sixteen. He didn't really think he could die. So many sailors had, but *he* wouldn't. Just listening to him, Sylvia could tell he was sure of it.

With a sigh, she asked, "Well, what is this big chance you're talking about, son?"

"I ran into Fred Butcher again the other day, Ma," George, Jr., said.

"He's got fat the last few years, hasn't he?" Sylvia said.

George Jr., grinned. "He sure has. But he's got rich the last few years, too. He doesn't put to sea any more, you know. He hires the men who do."

"I know that." Sylvia nodded. "He's one of the lucky ones. There aren't very many, you know." Butcher wasn't just lucky. He'd always driven himself like a dray horse, and he had a head for figures. Sylvia wished she could have said the same about her son. But, as he'd said himself, he didn't like school, and he'd never been an outstanding scholar.

"I don't care. I *want* to go to sea," he said now. "And Mr. Butcher, he said he'd take me on for the *Cuttlefish*. She's one of the new ones, Ma, one of the good ones. Diesel engine, electricity on board, a wireless set. A fishing run on a boat like that, it's almost like staying ashore, it's so comfy."

Sylvia laughed in his face. He looked very offended. She didn't care. "You tell me that after you've put to sea, and I'll take you seriously. Till then . . ." She shook her head and laughed some more.

But she'd yielded ground, and her son took advantage of it. "Let me find out, then. I'll tell you everything once I get back. Mr. Butcher, he says he'll pay me like a regular sailor, not a first-timer, on account of he was friends with Pop."

That *was* generous. Sylvia couldn't deny it. She wished she could have, for she would. Tears came to her eyes again. She was losing her little boy, and saw no way to escape it. There before her stood someone who wanted to be a man, and who was ever so close to getting what he wanted. She sighed. "All right, George. If that's what you care to do, I don't suppose I can stop you."

His jaw dropped. Enough boy lingered in him to make him take his mother's word very seriously. "Thank you! Oh, thank you!" he exclaimed, and gave Sylvia a hug that made her feel tiny and short. "I'll work as hard as Pop did, I promise, and save my money, and . . . everything." He ran out of promises and imagination at the same time.

"I hope it works out, George. I pray it works out." When a tear slid down Sylvia's face, her son looked alarmed. She waved him away. "You're not going to get me not to worry, so don't even try. I worried about your father every day he was at sea, and I'll worry about you, too."

"Everything will be fine, Ma." George, Jr., spoke with the certainty inherent in sixteen. Sylvia remembered how she'd been when she was that age. And it was worse with boys. They thought they were stallions, and had to paw the ground with their hooves and neigh and rear and show the world how tough they were.

The world didn't care. Most of them needed years to

figure that out. Some never did figure it out. The world rolled over them either way: it ground them down and made them fit into their slots. If they wouldn't grind down and wouldn't fit, it broke them. Sylvia didn't think it intended to. But what it intended and what happened were two different beasts.

It had rammed her into a slot, all right. Here she was, coming up on middle age, living from day to day, wondering how she'd get by, worrying because her only son was quitting school and taking up a dangerous trade. If there weren't ten thousand others just like her in Boston, she'd have been astonished.

But then savage anger and pride shot through her. *I killed the son of a bitch who sank the* Ericsson. *I shot him dead, and I'm walking around free. How many others can say the like? Not a one.*

She'd take that to the grave with her. Most of the time, it wouldn't do her one damn bit of good, not when it came to things like catching a streetcar or dealing with the Coal Board or going to the dentist. But it was hers. Nobody could rob her of it. For one brief moment in her life, she'd stepped out of the ordinary.

George, Jr., brought her back into it, saying, "I'll go right on giving you one dollar out of every three I make, too, Ma. I promise. It'll be the same with this as it's always been with the odd jobs I've been doing. I'll pay my way, honest."

"All right, George," she said. He was a good boy. (She didn't think of him as a man. She wondered if she ever would, down deep where it counted. She had her doubts.)

He asked, "What do you think Pop would say about what I'm doing?"

That was a good question. After some thought, Sylvia answered, "Well, he always did like going to sea." God only knew, that was the truth. Whenever the *Ripple* went out, she'd felt as if she were giving him up to the arms of another woman—the Atlantic had that kind of hold on him. She went on, "I think he'd have wanted you to stay in school, too. But if you got this kind of chance, I don't think he'd have stood in your way."

His face lit up. "Thanks!" Almost as fast as it had

appeared, that light faded. "I wish I would have known him better. I wish I could have known him longer."

"I know, sweetheart. I wish you could have, too. And I wish *I* could have." On the whole, Sylvia meant that. She'd never quite forgiven her husband for having been about to go to a Tennessee brothel with a colored whore, even if he hadn't slept with the woman and even if being about to had saved his life. If he hadn't been on his way to the whorehouse, if he'd gone back aboard his river monitor instead, he would have been on it when Confederate artillery blew it out of the water. But if he'd come home from the war, if he'd been around every day—or half the time, as fishermen usually were—and if he'd kept his nose clean, she supposed she would have.

George, Jr., started for the door. "I'd better go find Mr. Butcher and tell him. I don't know how long he'll hold the job for me."

"Go on, then, dear," Sylvia said, half of her hoping Fred Butcher *wouldn't* hold the job. The door opened. It closed. Her son's footsteps receded in the hallway. Then they were gone.

Sylvia sighed. She muttered something she never would have let anyone else hear. That helped, but not enough. She pulled a whiskey bottle out of a kitchen cabinet. A fair number of states had made alcohol illegal, but Massachusetts wasn't one of them. She poured some whiskey into a glass, then added water and took a drink. Whiskey had always tasted like medicine to her. She didn't care, not now. She was using it for medicine.

She'd medicated herself quite thoroughly when the front door to the flat opened. She hoped it would be George, Jr., coming back all crestfallen to tell her Fred Butcher had given someone else the berth. But it wasn't her son; it was Mary Jane, back from helping her teacher grade younger students' papers. Sylvia's daughter even got paid a little for doing it. She made a better scholar than her brother. That would have been funny if it hadn't been sad. A boy could do so many more things with an education than a girl could, but Mary Jane seemed to want to learn, while George, Jr., couldn't have cared less.

"Hello, Ma," Mary Jane said now, and then, as she got a better look at Sylvia's face, "Ma, what's wrong?"

"Your brother's going to sea, that's what." Without the whiskey in her, Sylvia might not have been so blunt, but that was the long and short of it.

Mary Jane's eyes got wide. "But that's good news, not bad. It's what he's always wanted to do."

"If he'd always wanted to jump off a cliff, would it be good news that he'd finally gone and done it?" Sylvia asked.

"But it's not like that, Ma," Mary Jane protested. She didn't understand, any more than George, Jr., did. "He needs a job, and that's a good one."

"A good job is a shore job, a job where you don't have to worry about getting drowned," Sylvia said. "If he'd gotten one of those, I'd stand up and cheer. This—" She shook her head. The kitchen spun slightly when she did. Yes, she was medicated, all right.

"He'll be fine." Mary Jane was fourteen. She also thought she was immortal, and everybody else, too. She hardly remembered her own father, and certainly didn't care to remember he'd died at sea. She went on, "Things are a lot safer than they used to be. The boats are better, the engines are better, and they just about all have wireless nowadays in case they run into trouble."

Every word of that was true. None of it did anything to reassure Sylvia, who'd seen too many misfortunes down by T Wharf. She said, "I want him to have a job where he doesn't need to worry about running into trouble."

"Where's he going to find one?" Mary Jane asked. "If he goes into building, somebody could drop a brick on his head. If he drives a truck, somebody could run into him. You want him to be a clerk in an insurance office, or something like that. But he'd be lousy at clerking, and he'd hate it, too."

Every word of *that* was true, too. Sylvia wished it weren't. Mary Jane was right. She did want George, Jr., in a white-collar job. But Mary Jane was also right that he wouldn't be good at one, and wouldn't like it. That didn't stop Sylvia from wishing he had one. She knew the sea too well ever to trust it.

* * *

When Jefferson Pinkard went down to the Empire of Mexico, he never dreamt he'd stay so long. He never dreamt the civil war would drag on so long. That, he realized now that he understood things here a little better, had been naive on his part. The Mexican civil war had started up not long after the Great War ended. The USA fed the rebels money and guns. The CSA sent money and guns and—unofficially, of course—combat veterans to prop up the imperialists.

Off in the distance, artillery rumbled. Jeff took a sip of strong, black coffee. The coffee had been improved—*corrected*, they said hereabouts—with a shot of strong rum. Alabama was officially dry. The Mexicans laughed at the very idea of prohibition. Some ways, they were pretty damn smart.

He finished the coffee as the artillery barrage went on. The front line ran quite a ways west of San Luis Potosí these days. Mexican-built barrels had driven back the rebels, and the damnyankees didn't seem to be helping *their* pet Mexicans build armored vehicles. Maybe they would one of these days, or maybe they'd just import some from the USA. If they did, a lot more greasers would end up dead, the front line would stabilize or start going back, and the civil war might last forever.

A Mexican soldier in the yellowish shade of butternut they wore down here politely knocked on Pinkard's open door. "Yeah?" Pinkard said, and then, "*Sí*, Mateo?"

"*Todo está listo*," Mateo said, and then, in English as rudimentary as Pinkard's Spanish, "Everyt'ing ready, Sergeant Jeff."

"All right, then." Pinkard heaved himself to his feet. He towered over Mateo, as he towered over almost everybody down here. Lieutenant Guitierrez—no, he was Captain Guitierrez these days—was an exception, but Jeff could have broken him over his knee like a stick.

He left the little wooden shack that served him as an office and strode out into sunlight bright and fierce enough to make what he'd got in Birmingham seem as nothing by comparison. Summer down here was really a son of a bitch. It was bad enough to make him understand just how the spirit of *mañana* had been born.

196

Standing out there in the broiling sun were several hundred rebel prisoners, drawn up in neat rows and columns. They all stiffened to attention when Pinkard came into sight. He nodded, and they relaxed—a little. Some of them wore uniforms of a darker shade than those of Maximilian III's soldiers. More, though, looked like peasants who'd chanced to end up in a place where they didn't want to be—which was exactly what they were.

Pinkard inspected them as if they were men he would have to send into battle, not enemies of whom he was in charge. While they stood out in the open, he strode through their barracks, making sure everything was shipshape and nobody was trying to tunnel out of the camp.

He wished he had a proper fence, not just barbed wire strung on poles, but he made the best of what there was. Guards on rickety towers at each corner of the square manned machine guns. Jeff waved to each of them in turn. "Everything good?" he asked, and then, in what passed for Spanish, *"Todo bueno?"*

He got answering grins and waves and nods. As far as the guards were concerned, everything was fine. They had easy duty, duty unlikely to get them shot, and they got paid for it—as often as anybody except Confederate mercenaries got paid. The Mexicans didn't stiff the men from the CSA the way they did their own people.

For a while, Jeff had wondered why the devil any Mexican would fight for Maximilian III. Then, from interrogating prisoners, he'd found out the rebels cheated their soldiers every bit as badly as the imperialists cheated theirs. Nobody down here had clean hands. Nobody even came close.

He went back up in front of the prisoners. "Dismissed!" he shouted. Mateo told them the same thing in Spanish. They all saluted. He thought they meant it, too. As long as they did what he told them to, he treated them fairly. Nobody'd ever treated a lot of them fairly before, and they responded to it even from the fellow in charge of a prison camp. If they got out of line, they were liable to earn a kick in the nuts. As far as Pinkard was concerned, that was fair, too.

As the prisoners went back to the barracks to get out of the ferocious sun, Mateo asked, "Sergeant Jeff, how you know so much about—this?" His—orderly, Pinkard supposed the word was—waved around at the camp. "In Confederate States, you *policía*—policeman?"

Jeff laughed like hell. "Me? A cop? Jesus God, no. I was a steelworker, a damn good steelworker, before I came down here."

Getting across what a steelworker was took a little while. When Mateo finally did figure it out, he gave Pinkard a peculiar look. "You do work like that, *mucho dinero,* eh? Why you leave?"

"On account of I couldn't stand it any more," Jeff answered. That plainly made no sense to the Mexican. Pinkard tried again: "On account of woman troubles." That wasn't the whole story, but it sure was a big part. If Emily hadn't decided she wasn't going to wait for him to come back from the war ... Well, he didn't know how things would have been, but he sure knew they would have been different.

"Ah." Mateo got that one right away. What man wouldn't have? *"Sí. Mujeres."* He rattled off something in Spanish, then made a stab at translating it: "No can live with, no can live without, neither."

"By God, buddy, you got that one right!" Pinkard burst out. Even now, when he thought about Emily ... He did his best *not* to think about Emily, but sometimes his best wasn't good enough.

"You no *policía*, how you know what to do with—?" Mateo waved again as he came back to what he really wanted to know.

Pinkard answered him with a shrug. "Just another job, God damn it. Somebody had to do it. Remember when we took all those prisoners after the barrels came up from Tampico?" He'd lost his orderly, and backtracked in clumsy, halting Spanish to let the other man catch up. When Mateo nodded, Jeff went on, "Like I say, somebody had to do it. Otherwise they probably all would've died. So I took charge of the poor sorry bastards—and I've been in charge of prisoners ever since."

He wasn't altogether sorry—far from it. The distant mutter of artillery reminded him why he wasn't sorry. If he weren't doing this, he'd have been up there at the front, and then some of those shells might have landed on him. He'd seen enough combat in the Great War to be glad he was part of an army, but not part of any immediate danger.

Mateo said, "You do good. Nobody never hear of nothing like how you do with prisoners. Everybody now try do like you. Even rebels now, they try do like you."

There was praise, if you liked. When the enemy imitated you, you had to be doing something right.

A couple of days later, Pinkard decided to do something right for himself. He grabbed a ride on a supply truck and went north to the village of Ahualulco, where Maximilian III's army had a supply dump that kept the prisoners eating. Ahualulco wasn't anything much. It wouldn't have been anything at all if two roads—well, two dirt tracks—hadn't crossed there.

Red-white-and-green flags fluttered everywhere. Both sides in the civil war flew those colors, which got as confusing as the Stars and Bars and the Stars and Stripes had during the Great War. For Maximilian's side, they were also the colors of Austria-Hungary, from which his ancestors had come. Pinkard was damned if he knew why the rebels also flew those colors, but he'd never been curious enough to find out.

The fighting was the biggest thing that had happened to Ahualulco since . . . maybe since forever. A couple of new cantinas had opened, and a whorehouse, and a field hospital. Jeff went into one of the cantinas—which had a picture of the Mexican emperor, cut from some magazine, tacked to the front door—and ordered a beer. Mexican beer was surprisingly good, even if they didn't believe in keeping it cold. He lit a cigarette, found a table, and settled down to enjoy himself.

He'd just started his second beer when the door flew open. In came a couple of big men talking English. One of them looked his way, waved, and called, "Freedom!"

"Freedom!" Jeff echoed. "Who the hell are you boys? Where y'all from?"

One of them, a blond, was named Pete Frazee. The other, who sported a fiery red mustache, called himself Charlie MacCaffrey. They sat down by him. Frazee got a beer. MacCaffrey ordered tequila. "How do you drink that stuff?" Pinkard asked him. "Tastes like cigar butts, you ask me."

"Yeah, but it'll get me drunk faster'n that horse piss you and Pete got," MacCaffrey answered. He knocked it back and waved for more.

He was from Jackson, Mississippi; Frazee from the country not far outside of Louisville. The Kentuckian said, "They told me I could've gone back after the war, but I was damned if I wanted to live in the United States. I spent three years tryin' to kill those damnyankees. Screw me if I wanted to be one myself."

"Oh, hell, yes," Pinkard said. "How'd you find out about the Party?"

"Heard one of their people talkin' on a street corner in Chattanooga, where I was at," Frazee answered with a reminiscent smile. "Soon as I did, I decided that was for me. Haven't looked back since." He nudged the fellow who'd come in with him. "How about you, Charlie?"

"I like bustin' heads," MacCaffrey said frankly. "Plenty of heads need bustin' in Mississippi, too. We got as many niggers as white folks, and some o' them bastards even got the vote after they went into the Army. I don't cotton to that—no way, nohow. Whigs and Rad Libs let 'em do it. Soon as I found me a party that didn't like it, I reckoned that was for me."

"How'd you come down here?" Jeff asked.

MacCaffrey made a face. "Ever since that stupid bastard plugged Wade Hampton V, we pulled in our horns like a goddamn snail. Wasn't hardly any fun any more. I still got more ass-kickin' in me than that. How about you?"

Jeff shrugged. "Didn't like what I was doin'. Didn't have nothin' holdin' me in Birmingham. I thought, *Why the hell not?*—and here I am."

"You're the fellow with the prisoners of war, ain't you?" Pete Frazee said suddenly. Pinkard nodded. So did Frazee, in a thoughtful way. He went on, "Heard about you. From what everybody says, you're doing a hell of a job."

"Thank you. Thank you kindly," Pinkard answered. He paused till the barmaid got him another beer, then chuckled and said, "Wasn't what I came down here to do, but it hasn't worked out too bad."

He spent most of the afternoon drinking with the other Party men and enjoying the chance to speak his own language. Then, despite a certain stagger, he made his way to the brothel and laid down enough silver for a quiet room and the company of a girl named Maria (not that half the women down here weren't named Maria), far and away the prettiest one in the place.

He'd drunk enough to have some trouble rising to the occasion. He'd paid enough to have her slide down the bed and start to help him with her mouth. He enjoyed it for perhaps half a minute. Then he remembered Emily's mouth on him after he'd found her with Bedford Cunningham, who had been his best friend. "No, goddammit," he growled, and pulled away.

"What?" Maria had no idea what the trouble was.

"No, I said." He scrambled onto her. She'd got him hard enough so he could manage. He did, and then got back into his clothes and left in a hurry.

Maria shook her head. *"Loco,"* she muttered, and tapped a finger against her temple.

Clarence Potter said, "My trouble is, I want to see the Freedom Party dead and buried, not just weak." He sipped at his whiskey in the Charleston saloon. "That makes me as much a fanatic as Jake Featherston, I suppose."

The Freedom Party was weak nowadays, and weaker in South Carolina than it had been before the previous year's Congressional election. Even so, in most saloons a comment like that would have been good for starting a fight. Not in the Crow's Nest, though, not on a Tuesday night. The Whig Party faithful met at the Odd Fellows' hall across the street, and then a lot of them were in the habit of coming over and hashing things out with the help of the lubricants the saloon provided.

Braxton Donovan was a prominent Charleston lawyer. He was also, at the moment, slightly—but only slightly—drunk. He said, "Only thing that'd put those know-nothing peckerheads into power is a calahamity—a calahamity, I tell you."

"A calamity, you mean?" Potter asked.

"That's what I said, isn't it?" Several of the chins beneath Donovan's neat gray goatee wobbled.

"As a matter of fact, no," Potter answered. Relentless precision had brought him into Confederate Army Intelligence, and later into investigative work.

"Well, it's what I meant—a calahamity is." The lawyer held up his glass. The colored bartender hastened to refill it. Braxton Donovan nodded regally. "Thank you kindly, Ptolemy."

"You're welcome, suh," Ptolemy said, professionally polite, professionally subservient.

"Tell me, Ptolemy," Donovan asked in his rolling baritone, "what is your view of the Freedom Party?" He might have been encouraging a friendly witness on the stand.

"Don't like 'em for hell, suh," Ptolemy said at once. "Somebody should ought to do somethin' about 'em, you wants to know what I thinks." He polished the top of the bar with a spotless white towel.

"This country is in a bad way when some not so small fraction of the electorate can't see what's obvious to a nigger bartender," Braxton Donovan said. He took a pull at his freshened drink. "Still and all, better a not so small fraction than a large fraction, as was so a few years back."

"Yes," Potter agreed. "And I believe Ptolemy here really does have no use for the Freedom Party—it's in his interest not to, after all, when you think about what Featherston has to say about blacks. But even so . . . Jeb Stuart III had a colored servant whose name, if I remember right, was also Ptolemy. Jake Featherston suspected the fellow was a Red—he was serving under Stuart in the First Richmond Howitzers. He told me about this servant not so long before the uprisings began."

"And so?" Donovan asked. "Your point is?"

"Jeb Stuart III pulled wires with his father to make sure

that Ptolemy didn't have any trouble." Clarence Potter finished his whiskey at a gulp. "And he *was* a Red, dammit, as became abundantly clear when the pot boiled over. Young Stuart died in combat—let himself be killed, they say, so he wouldn't have to face the music. His father's revenge was to make sure Featherston never rose above the rank of sergeant. Petty, I suppose, but understandable."

"Why are you telling me this?" the lawyer asked.

"A couple of reasons," Potter answered. "For one, we can trace the rise of the Freedom Party to such small things. And, for another, a white man's a fool if he takes a Negro's word at face value. Look what happened to Jeb Stuart III." He swung around on the stool so that he faced the bartender. "Ptolemy!"

"Yes, suh? 'Nother drink, suh?" the black man asked.

"In a minute," Potter said. "First, tell me something— what were you doing when the rebellion came in 1915?"

"Me, suh?" For all they showed, Ptolemy's eyes might have been cut from stone. "Nothin', suh. Stayin' home mindin' my business."

"Uh-*huh*." Potter knew what that meant. It meant the bartender was lying through his teeth. Every Negro in the CSA claimed to have stayed at home minding his own business during the Red rebellion. If all the blacks who said they had actually *had* stayed at home, there would have been no rebellion in the first place.

Ptolemy said, "Suh, it was a long time ago nowadays, an' it's all over an' done with. Ain't no way to change what happened. Onliest thing we can do is pick up the pieces an' go on."

"He's right," Braxton Donovan said. Potter found himself nodding. The Confederate States, and everybody in them, did have to do that. Saying it, though, was easier than doing it. Donovan took a half dollar out of his pocket and slid it across the bar to Ptolemy. "Here you are. Buy yourself a drink." A few hundred years before, kings had tossed out largess to peasants with that same sort of offhanded generosity.

"Thank you, suh." Ptolemy made the coin disappear. He did fix a drink for himself. By its pale amber color, it held a lot more water than whiskey. And the bartender nursed it, raising it to his lips every now and then but not doing much in the way of real drinking. Potter had known very few men who worked behind a bar and did much in the way of pouring down what they served. Too easy, he supposed, for a man who worked around whiskey all the time to come to like it too well.

Having been generous to one beneath him—or so he plainly felt—Braxton Donovan swung his attention back to Potter. "I have a question for you, sir," he said, "speaking of the Freedom Party."

"Ask it, then," Potter answered.

"I've heard you knew Roger Kimball while he was still alive," the lawyer said.

Clarence Potter nodded. "And so I did. That's the best time to get to know a man—while he's still alive, I mean."

"Indeed. And in fact." Donovan nodded grandly. "Now, sir, the question: while he was still alive, did Kimball ever hint to you that he'd torpedoed the USS *Ericsson* after we'd yielded to the damnyankees?"

"Never once, never in the slightest way," Potter replied at once. "We were acquaintances, you understand, not friends—he liked Jake Featherston as much as I loathe the man. But I would say he didn't tell his friends, either. He was, in my opinion, a first-class son of a bitch, but he knew how to keep a secret—by *keeping* it, at all times and everywhere. If his exec hadn't spilled the beans, I don't think anyone would ever have known."

"Poetic justice, what he got," Donovan said.

"Yes, I think so, too," Potter agreed. "If he hadn't come to a sudden demise, he would have been a sore spot between us and the USA, and we can't afford to give them excuses to kick us around. They're too liable to do it even without excuses, though Sinclair has taken a milder line than Teddy Roosevelt did."

"I quite agree," Donovan said. "I despise the Socialists and all they stand for—they set a bad example for our people, at the very least—but their foreign policy is . . . well, as you said, gentler than Roosevelt's."

"Now I have a question for you," Potter said. Braxton

Donovan looked cautious, but could hardly do anything but nod. Potter asked, "Why are you so interested in the late, unlamented Roger Kimball?"

"Idle curiosity," Donovan answered.

"Shit," Potter said crisply. All of a sudden, his metal-framed spectacles didn't make him seem mild and ineffectual any more. When he went on, "I deserve a straight answer," the implication was that he'd do something unpleasant if he didn't get one.

Braxton Donovan could have bought and sold him. Donovan owned enough property that the disastrous postwar inflation hadn't wiped him out. They both knew it. Most of the time, in the class-conscious Confederate States, it would have mattered a great deal. Now, somehow, it didn't. The lawyer flinched, muttered something under his breath, and gulped his drink. "Fill it up," he told the bartender.

"Yes, suh." Ptolemy did. Ice clinked as he built Donovan a fresh one.

The lawyer sipped from the new whiskey. Clarence Potter waited, patient and implacable as a father waiting up for a son out too late. At last, Donovan said, "You know Anne Colleton?"

"Personally? No," Potter said. "But I know *of* her. Who doesn't, in this state? What's she got to do with anything?"

"She and Kimball were . . . friends during the war, and for a while afterwards," Braxton Donovan answered, suggesting by the pause that they'd been more than friends. "Any dirt I can get on him will stick to her."

"Wait a minute." Potter held up a hand. "Wait just a minute. Didn't she help get the Yankee woman who punched Kimball's ticker for him out of jail and back to the USA?"

"Oh, yes." Donovan's silver pompadour was so securely in place, it didn't stir a hair as he nodded. "They broke up unpleasantly. I think it was over politics—he stayed in the Freedom Party, and she was one of the rats who left the sinking ship." His lip curled.

"Why tar her, then?" Potter asked. "If she's back to

being a Whig, don't you want her to keep on being one? If you drive her into Featherston's arms again, aren't you just asking for trouble? She's a high-powered woman, no two ways about it."

"That's the point," Donovan said. "She's talking like a Whig again, yes, but she's trying to pull us to the right till you can't tell us from the yahoos in white shirts and butternut pants who run around yelling, 'Freedom!' She wants to have another go at the United States—wants it so bad, she can taste it."

Potter pondered that. "We'd have to be damn lucky to win it. They beat us and they hurt us. And even if we do lick them, that just sets up *another* war ten, twenty, thirty years further down the line. I wish I could say something else—I fought those bastards from the very first day to the very last, and I'd've kept on fighting if we hadn't folded up. But come on, Donovan. A good big man won't always lick a good little one, but sure as hell that's the way to bet. And I don't think we can afford to lose again."

"I don't want to fight them again, either," Donovan said. "I fought plenty in the last war, too, and I am plumb satisfied. And I don't want her voice in the Whig Party."

"There may be something to that," Potter allowed. "On the other hand, there may not. You want to think twice about going after her. Maybe you want to think three times."

"I know what I'm doing." Braxton Donovan certainly sounded confident. Potter wondered if that was the whiskey talking. He also wondered how Donovan not only didn't fall over but kept on sounding coherent. The man had to have a sponge in place of a liver. Donovan went on, "She's not quite the force she used to be, anyhow, on account of she's ten years older than she used to be, same as the rest of us. But it hurts women more." He finished the latest drink. "One more of the same, Ptolemy."

"Comin' right up, suh," the Negro said. As he made the next whiskey, Potter studied him and, covertly, Donovan. He wondered if the lawyer really knew as much as he thought he did. Not too many people came away happy after they bumped up against Anne Colleton.

Which meant . . . Potter finished his own drink. He didn't ask for a fresh one, not right away. Instead, he did some quiet thinking. He came closer to agreeing with Donovan than with Anne Colleton. Nothing was stupider, though, than backing a loser, which he judged Donovan likely to be. *How much of a deal can I cut?* he wondered. *And should I?*

VII

As far as Cincinnatus Driver was concerned, the worst part of prison was getting used to it. After a while, Luther Bliss stopped interrogating him, which meant he didn't get beat up very much any more. Hardly anything happened to him any more, in fact. He sat in his cell with nothing to do, except for the one hour a week when he was led out to exercise, as a beast might have been.

Outside the gray stone walls of the prison, time was passing. What did Elizabeth think, back in Des Moines? What did Achilles think? How big was the boy these days? Cincinnatus struggled to remember his face. Did Amanda remember him at all? He was starting to doubt it.

Only the weather told him the season of the year. He never saw a newspaper, or anything else with print on it. He began to wonder if he still remembered how to read and write. That thought provoked him to bitter laughter. *Read and write? Hell, I'm startin' to wonder if I still recollect how to talk.* Days at a time would go by when he never said a word to anyone.

The guards did not encourage conversation, which would do for an understatement till a bigger one came along. When they gave orders, it was always, "Come here, nigger," "Go there, boy," or "Stand aside, nigger." They didn't want to hear Cincinnatus say, "Yes, suh." They just wanted him to do as he was told. He did it. He'd tried not doing it a couple of times. The results of that had proved more painful than they were worth.

He'd also tried protesting that he was a citizen of the United States, and nobody, not even Luther Bliss and the Kentucky State Police, had any business holding him like this. The results of *that* had proved even more painful than those of the other.

If I wasn't colored, they wouldn't be able to get away with it, no matter what they think I done. That had run through his mind more times than he could count. He did his best not to dwell on it. Its truth was all too obvious. He'd thought things would be better in the USA than they had been when Kentucky was part of the CSA. Maybe not.

But, in spite of all this, maybe. In the Confederate States, Negroes who made trouble often just stopped living. However much Luther Bliss wanted Cincinnatus on ice, he hadn't dug a hole and put his body in it. Sometimes Cincinnatus wondered why not.

On a hot, muggy afternoon in what he reckoned was the middle of summer, three guards came to his cell door. Two of them drew pistols and pointed them at him, while the third turned a key in the lock and opened the cell. Then that fellow jumped back and yanked his pistol from its holster, too. "Come along with us," one of the guards said.

"Where?" Cincinnatus' voice creaked with disuse, and with fear. This wasn't exercise time or mealtime. Maybe that hole in the ground waited for him after all.

"Don't give us no back talk, boy, or you'll be sorry for it," the guard snapped. "Get moving."

Cincinnatus did, thinking, *They can kill me here as easy as anywhere else, and then take my body wherever they need to.* He wanted to run. His legs had that light-as-a-feather feel panic could bring. He was sure he could outrun these three big-bellied white men. But he was also sure it would do him no good. Nobody outran a bullet.

They took him not to the room where they'd questioned him before but to an office in one of the prison's corner towers. He supposed it was the warden's office, but the man behind the desk was, inevitably, Luther Bliss. Bliss had light brown eyes, like a hound dog's. At the moment, those eyes were as sad as a hound dog's, too.

When Cincinnatus came in, the chief of the Kentucky State Police turned to the other man in the room, an older fellow who sat in a chair off to one side. "See, Mr. Darrow? Here he is, sound as a dollar."

"Whose dollars are you talking about, Bliss?" the old man—Darrow?—demanded. "The Confederates', after the war?"

Oh, sweet Jesus, Cincinnatus thought. *Bliss is going to lock him up and throw away the key.* But Bliss didn't do anything except drum his fingers on the desktop. If he was angry, he didn't show it past that—which made Cincinnatus take another long look at the man named Darrow.

He had to be close to seventy. His skin was grandfather-pink. His jowls sagged. He combed thinning iron-gray hair over the top of his head to make it cover as much ground as it could. But his gray-blue eyes were some of the sharpest—and some of the nastiest—Cincinnatus had ever seen.

After coughing a couple of times, he pulled his wallet from a vest pocket. He looked down at a photograph in it, then over to Cincinnatus. "You *are* Cincinnatus Driver," he said, sounding surprised. "I wouldn't've put it past this sneaky son of a bitch"—he pointed to Luther Bliss—"to try to sneak a ringer by me, but I guess he figured I'd spot it."

Again, the world didn't end. All Bliss said was, "I resent that, Mr. Darrow."

"Go right ahead," the other white man said cheerfully. "I intended that you should."

Plaintively, Cincinnatus said, "Will somebody please tell me what's going on?"

"My pleasure," said the old man with the ferocious eyes. "I'm Clarence Darrow. I'm a lawyer. I've got a writ of *habeas corpus* with your name on it. That means you get out of jail. If you've got any brains, it also means you get the hell out of Kentucky."

"My God." Cincinnatus understood the words, but he wasn't sure he believed them. He wasn't sure he dared believe them. He said, "I didn't think nobody could get me out of *here*."

"Sonny, there's something you have to understand: I'm a *good* lawyer." Darrow spoke with a calm certainty that compelled belief. "I'm a damn good lawyer, matter of fact. This petty tyrant here"—he pointed at Luther Bliss again, and again Bliss didn't rise to it—"kept thinking I wasn't, but he's not so smart as he thinks he is."

"I know who's my country's friend and who ain't," Bliss said. "What do I need to know besides that?"

"How to live by the rules you say you're protecting," Clarence Darrow answered. The head of the Kentucky State Police snapped his fingers to show how little he cared about them. Darrow had been blustery before. Now he got angry, really angry. "What's the point of having a country with laws if you get around 'em any time you happen not to care for 'em, eh? Answer me that."

But Luther Bliss was not an easy man to quell. "This here's Kentucky, Mr. Darrow. If we played by the rules all the time, the bastards who don't would get the jump on us pretty damn quick, and you can bet on that. Half the people in this state are Confederate diehards, and the other half are Reds."

He exaggerated. From what Cincinnatus remembered of the days before he'd moved north, he didn't exaggerate by much. Darrow said, "If nobody in this godforsaken place wants to live in the USA, why not give it back to the Confederates?"

Cincinnatus gaped—he'd never heard anyone except a diehard say such a thing. Mildly, Bliss replied, "You know, Mr. Darrow, advocating return to the CSA is against the law here."

"Wouldn't be surprised," Darrow said. "Wouldn't be one bit surprised. The law it's against is unconstitutional, of course, not that you care about the Constitution of the United States."

"Here's your nigger, Mr. Darrow." Bliss' air of calm frayed at last. "Take him and get the hell out of here. Or don't you think I could fix up a cell with your name on it right next to his?"

211

"I'm sure you could," Darrow said. "And I'm sure you could make it very unpleasant for me. But I'm sure of something else, too—I'm sure I could make it even more unpleasant for you if you did."

By the sour look on Luther Bliss' face, he was sure of the same thing. It didn't make him very happy. "Get out," he repeated.

"Come along, Mr. Driver," Clarence Darrow said. "Let's get you back to civilization, or what passes for it in the United States these days." He grunted with effort as he heaved himself to his feet. Cincinnatus needed a heartbeat to remember the surname belonged to him. He hadn't grown up with it, and people didn't use it very often. And nobody'd called him by it since he'd landed here. Dazedly, he followed the white lawyer.

Not till they got into the motorcar that had brought Darrow to the prison and the driver was taking them away did Cincinnatus turn to the lawyer and say, "God bless you, suh, for what you done there."

"I don't believe in God, any more than I believe in Mother Goose," Darrow said. "Foolish notion. But I do believe in justice, and you deserve that. Everyone deserves that."

Cincinnatus had known some Reds who said they didn't believe in God. With them, he'd always thought that was a pose, or that they substituted Marx for God. With Clarence Darrow, it was different. The man spoke as if he needed no substitute for the Deity. Cincinnatus sensed that, but couldn't fully fathom it. He said, "Well, God believes in you, whether you believe in Him or not."

Darrow gave him an odd look. "You've got grit, son, if you can joke after you get out of that place."

"I wasn't jokin', suh," Cincinnatus said. They eyed each other in perfect mutual incomprehension. Cincinnatus asked, "How'd you even know I was stuck there, suh, to come and get me out?"

"Your wife finally raised a stink that was big enough for me to notice it," Darrow answered. "It took her a while, because people in the USA don't want to notice a colored woman even when she's screaming her head off.

But she kept at it. Remarkable woman. Stubborn as a Missouri mule."

"Yes, suh," Cincinnatus said happily. "God bless Elizabeth, too." Clarence Darrow let out a long, rasping sigh. Cincinnatus took no notice of it. He went on, "But even if you knew I was in trouble, how'd you get Luther Bliss to turn loose o' me? That's one ornery man."

"That's one first-class son of a bitch, is what that is," Darrow said. "Even after I got the court order, he kept denying he'd ever heard of you. But I managed to persuade a judge otherwise—and here you are."

"Here I am," Cincinnatus agreed. Seeing farms and woods out the window, not stone and concrete and barbed wire, made him feel like a new man. But the new man had old problems. "What do I owe you, suh?" Lawyers didn't come cheap; he knew that. Even so . . . "Whatever it is, I pays it. May take me a while, you understand, but I pays it."

Darrow's grin displayed crooked, tobacco-stained teeth. "Your wife told me you'd say that. You don't owe me a dime—I did your case *pro bono publico*." He saw the Latin meant nothing to Cincinnatus, and added, "For the public good."

"That's mighty kind of you, suh, but it ain't right," Cincinnatus said. "I want to pay you back. I owe you."

"Your wife said you'd say that, too," Clarence Darrow told him. "But there's no need—I'll make more from publicity than you could pay. If you must, pay the favor forward—do something good for someone else. Bargain?"

"Yes, suh—so help me God," Cincinnatus said.

"More of that claptrap." Darrow sighed. "Well, never mind. I hope you know better than to stick your nose back into Kentucky again?"

"Long as my folks ain't poorly for true, sure," Cincinnatus answered. "That's what got me here before. I be more careful 'bout the message nowadays, but if I reckon it's so, what choice have I got *but* to come?"

Clarence Darrow gave him a long, measuring stare. The lawyer delivered his verdict in one word: "Fool."

* * *

213

Coal smoke pouring out the stack, the train hurried toward the Salt Lake City station. Sparks flew as the brakes ground its iron wheels against the iron rails that carried it. Colonel Abner Dowling would rather have been somewhere, anywhere, else than on the platform waiting for that train to pull in. By the expression on his mustachioed face, General Pershing felt the same way.

"No help for it, though," Dowling murmured, more than half to himself.

He hadn't been quiet enough. But Pershing only nodded and said, "He *has* earned the right to do as he pleases."

"I know that, sir," Dowling answered. "I just wish he would have pleased to do something—anything—else."

"Yes." Pershing nodded again. "There is that, isn't there?"

The train stopped right at the platform. Dowling had irrationally hoped against hope that it wouldn't, but would keep right on going. The leader of the military band gathered on the platform caught Pershing's eye. Pershing looked as if he wished the fellow hadn't. At last, reluctantly, he nodded. The band leader either didn't notice the reluctance or thought it wise to pretend he didn't. With a proud flourish, he began to wave his baton. The band struck up "The Stars and Stripes Forever."

No sooner had the vaunting music begun to blare forth than the door to one of the Pullman cars opened. Out came a bent ancient whose mustache and what Dowling could see of his hair—he always wore a hat, to keep the world from knowing he was bald—were a peroxided gold, defying time. A woman of about the same years followed him onto the platform.

"Well, Autie," she sniffed, "they are giving you a proper welcome, anyhow."

"What's that, Libbie?" The old man cupped a hand behind his ear.

"I said, they're giving you a proper welcome," she repeated, louder this time.

"Can't hear a thing over that music. At least they're giving me a proper welcome."

Colonel Dowling and General Pershing both stepped forward. They both saluted. They chorused, "Welcome to Utah, General Custer." Dowling was lying in his teeth. He would have bet Pershing was doing the same.

"Thank you. Thank you both," Custer said. He stiffly returned the salute, even though, having at last retired from the U.S. Army after more than sixty years of service, he wore a somber black suit and homburg. Three years before, he'd been as vigorous as a man in his eighties could be. Now . . . Dowling found himself surprised, dismayed, and surprised at being dismayed. He'd always thought—sometimes despairingly—that George Armstrong Custer was the one unchanging man on the face of the earth.

Here at last, he saw it wasn't so. The retired general was visibly slower, visibly more feeble. Some spark had gone out of him since his retirement, and he seemed to know it.

Libbie Custer, by contrast, remained as she always had. "Hello, Colonel Dowling," she said with a smile that showed white false teeth. "It's good to see you again. Now that Autie and I are civilians, may I call you Abner?"

"Of course," Dowling answered, though he'd always hated his Christian name.

Meanwhile, General Pershing was shaking hands with Custer and exchanging polite and, no doubt, insincere compliments. During the Great War, Pershing's command had been just to the east of Custer's. Pershing's Second Army had captured Louisville and generally pushed south faster than Custer's First—till Custer decided he knew more about barrels than anyone in the War Department . . . and, against all odds, turned out to be right. From things Pershing had said since Abner Dowling came to Utah, he still couldn't figure out how Custer had pulled that off.

At the time, Dowling had been sure Custer's lies to Philadelphia would get the general—and, not so incidentally, himself—court-martialed and sent to Leavenworth to do hard labor for the rest of their lives. Instead, his superior had ended up the USA's greatest military hero since George Washington, and Dowling, by reflected glory, had ended up a minor hero himself.

Custer said, "Are you keeping the Mormons here on a tight rein, General? I hope to heaven you are, because they *will* cause trouble if they get half a chance."

"Things have been tolerably quiet, anyway," Pershing answered. "They don't shoot at our men any more. Taking hostages worked pretty well for the Germans in Belgium, and for us in Canada and the CSA, and it works here, too. The Mormons may want us dead, but they don't want their friends and neighbors and sweethearts going up against a wall with a blindfold."

"And a cigarette," Custer added automatically, but he shook his head before anyone could correct him. "No, the Mormons don't even have that to console themselves. Poor devils. Nothing wrong with tobacco."

Libbie sniffed. Custer had been smoking and drinking and cursing ever since the disappointments of the Second Mexican War, and she still hated all three.

"It does work, cigarette or no," Pershing said. "We even quelled trouble with polygamists down in Teasdale by taking several hundred hostages and making it ever so clear we'd do what we had to do if trouble broke out."

Dowling wanted to wipe his forehead with the back of his hand and go, *Whew!* because of that. He didn't, but he wanted to. Instead, he said, "General, Mrs. Custer, your limousine is waiting just outside the station. If you'd be kind enough to come with me . . ."

They came. They didn't remark upon—perhaps they didn't notice—the sharpshooters on the roof of the station. More riflemen were posted in the buildings across the street. Custer had served as General Pope's right arm in the U.S. occupation of restive Utah during the Second Mexican War. Mormons had long memories, as everyone had found out in their uprising during the Great War. Someone might still want to take a potshot or two at Custer for what he'd done more than forty years before, no matter how many hostages' lives it cost his people.

The limousine carried more armor than an armored car. Even the windows were of glass allegedly bulletproof. That was one more thing Dowling didn't want to have to put to the test.

As they drove along the southern perimeter of Temple Square, Custer pointed to the ruins there and said, "That's a bully sight—their temples to their false gods pulled down around their ears. May they never rise again."

"Er, yes," Dowling answered, wondering when he'd last heard anyone—anyone but Custer, that is—say *bully*. Hardly at all since the Great War ended; he was sure of that. The old slang was dying out with the people who'd used it. Custer still lingered. Now, though, Dowling could see he wouldn't go on forever after all.

As old men will, Custer still dwelt on the past. "Do you know what my greatest regret is?" he asked.

"No, sir," Dowling said, as General Pershing shook his head.

"My greatest regret is that we didn't hang Abe Lincoln alongside the Mormon traitors he was consorting with," Custer said. "He deserved it just as much as they did, and if we'd stretched his skinny neck the Socialists never would have got off the ground—I'm sure of that."

"I suppose we'd have Republicans instead," Pershing said. "They'd be just about as bad, or I miss my guess." He was twenty years younger than Custer, which meant he'd been a young man the last time the Republican Party had amounted to anything much. It was a sad shadow of its former self, and had been ever since Abraham Lincoln took a large part of its membership left into the Socialist camp at the end of the Second Mexican War.

Custer sniffed and coughed and rolled his eyes. Plainly, he disagreed with General Pershing. For a wonder, though, he didn't come right out and say so. Abner Dowling scratched his head in bemusement. Had Custer learned tact, or some semblance of it, at the age of eighty-six? There might have been less likely things, but Dowling couldn't think of any offhand.

Odds were that Libbie had poked him in the ribs with her elbow when Dowling didn't notice. As the great man's longtime adjutant, Dowling had long since concluded Libbie Custer was the brains of the outfit. George put on a better show—Libbie, in public, was self-effacing as could be—but she was the one who thought straight.

Outside General Pershing's headquarters, guards meticulously checked the limousine, front to back, top to bottom. At last, one of them told the driver, "You're all right. Go on through."

"Thanks, Jonesy," the driver said, and put the motorcar back into gear.

"Still as bad as that?" Custer asked. "Will they blow us to kingdom come if we give them half a chance?"

"We hope not," Pershing said. "Still and all, we'd rather not find out."

"They don't love us, and that's a fact," Dowling added.

"Good," Custer said. "If they loved us, that would mean we were soft on them, and we'd better not be soft. If we let them up for even a minute, the Mormons will start conspiring with the limeys or the Rebs, same as they did in the last war and same as they did forty-odd years ago, too."

There was another obsolete word. Only men of Custer's generation still called the Confederates Rebels, and men of Custer's generation, these days, were thin on the ground. The armored limousine stopped once more, this time inside the secure compound. A company stood at stiff attention, awaiting Custer's inspection.

The retired general didn't notice them till a soldier held the door for him and he got out of the automobile. When he did, he tried to straighten up as he made his slow way over to them. He reminded Dowling of a fire horse put out to pasture that heard the alarm bell once more and wanted to pull the engine again. Around soldiers, he came alive.

Most of the men there in the courtyard were conscripts, too young to have served in the Great War. They still responded to Custer, though, grinning at his bad jokes and telling him their home towns when he asked.

In a low voice, General Pershing said, "He looks like he wishes he were still in uniform."

"I'm sure he does, sir," Dowling answered, also quietly. "The Socialists practically had to drag him out of it." He clicked his tongue between his teeth, remembering. "That was an ugly scene."

"Those people . . ." Pershing shook his head. "It's not for us to meddle in politics, and I know that's a good rule, but there are times when I'm tempted to say exactly what's on my mind."

"Yes, sir," Dowling said.

At the banquet that evening, Custer ate with good appetite and drank perhaps two glasses of white wine too many. Afterwards, Libbie told him, "Time to get to bed, Autie." She might have been talking to a child that had stayed up too late.

"In a moment, my dear," Custer answered. Before struggling to his feet once more, he turned to Dowling and said, "Do you know, Major, there are times since they took the uniform off me when I simply feel adrift on the seas of fate. Once upon a time, I mastered the helm. But no more, Major, no more. This is what the years have done."

Dowling couldn't blame Custer for forgetting his present rank and using the one he'd had when they served together during the war. "Yes, sir," he said, and then, "I'm sorry, sir." To his amazement, tears stung his eyes. Custer had lived too long, and knew it. Could any man suffer a worse fate? Dowling shook his head. He doubted it.

"God bless you, Major," Custer said. He let his wife, still competent as always, lead him out of the dining hall. One of those tears slid down Dowling's cheek. He would have been more embarrassed—he would have been mortified—if he hadn't seen that General Pershing's face was wet, too.

In a way, sitting in the Socialist Party offices in New York's Fourteenth Ward took Flora Blackford back to the days when she'd been Flora Hamburger. Waiting for the latest batch of election returns made her remember how nervous she'd been when her name first appeared on the ballot ten years before.

In another way, though, coming back reminded her how much things had changed. She didn't get back from Philadelphia all that often, even though the two cities were only a couple of hours apart by train. She didn't hear Yiddish spoken all that often any more, either; she had to stop and think and listen to understand. What had been her first language was now on the way to becoming foreign to her.

A telephone rang. Herman Bruck picked it up. He'd been sweet on Flora while she still lived in New York City, and maybe his smile had a wistful quality to it when he looked at her now. On the other hand, maybe it didn't. He had a four-year-old of his own, and a two-year-old, and a six-month-old besides. That was bound to be more than enough to keep anybody busy.

He scribbled something on a pad on his battered old desk. "Latest returns in our district—Hamburger, uh, Blackford, 9,791; Cantorowicz, 6,114." Cheers filled the office. The Democrat, Abraham Cantorowicz, wasn't quite a token candidate, but he hadn't had any great chance of winning, either. The Congressional district whose borders roughly corresponded to those of the Fourteenth Ward had been solidly Socialist since before the turn of the century.

On Flora's lap, Joshua Blackford began to fuss. He was sleepy. At not quite one, he was up well past his bedtime, and in a strange place besides. She was surprised he hadn't started making a racket before this.

The telephone rang again. Again, Herman Bruck picked it up. Then he laid his palm against the mouthpiece and said, "Flora, it's for you. It's Cantorowicz."

More cheers—everyone knew what that had to mean. Flora passed her son to her husband. "Here—mind him for a few minutes, please," she said.

Hosea Blackford took the toddler. "This is what the vice president is for," he said with a laugh. "He takes over so somebody else can go do something important."

That got two waves of laughter—one from those who followed it in English and another after it got translated into Yiddish. Flora made her way to the telephone. "This is Congresswoman Blackford," she said.

"And you'll have two more years of being a Congresswoman," Abraham Cantorowicz told her. "I don't see how I can catch you, and what's the point in waiting to make this call after the handwriting goes up on the

220

walls? Another election, another Democrat calling to concede. Congratulations."

"Thank you very much. That's gracious of you," Flora said. "You ran a strong campaign." He'd run as well as a Democrat in this district could.

"Someone had to be the sacrificial lamb—we weren't about to let you run unopposed," Cantorowicz answered. "We will keep fighting for this district, and we'll win one of these days."

"Not soon, I don't think," Flora answered.

"Maybe sooner than you think," her defeated opponent answered. "Will you run for reelection when your husband runs for president?"

Flora sent Hosea Blackford a look half startled, half thoughtful. She knew perfectly well he was thinking of running in 1928. Upton Sinclair almost certainly wouldn't seek a third term. The only president who'd ever run a third time was Theodore Roosevelt. He'd won the Great War, made himself twice a national hero—and lost anyhow. The United States weren't ready for one man ruling on and on.

"You aren't saying anything," Cantorowicz remarked.

"No, I'm not," Flora told him. "We still have a couple of years to worry about that."

"Maybe you should run anyway," the Democratic candidate said. "If he loses and you win, you'd still be able to support your family."

"I don't think we'd have to worry there," Flora answered coolly. She wasn't kidding. Hosea Blackford was a talented lawyer with years of government connections. He would have no trouble making his way even if—God forbid!—he lost the election. Flora wasn't sure she liked that in the abstract; whom a man knew shouldn't have mattered so much as what he knew. But that didn't change reality one bit.

When I first went into Congress, I would have tried to change reality. I did try to change reality, and I even had some luck, she thought. She took pride in being called the conscience of the House. But ten years there had taught her some things were unlikely to change in her lifetime, or her son's, or his son's, either, if he had a son.

Cantorowicz said, "Well, I hope you have to worry about it. But you don't want to listen to that right now. You want to celebrate, and you've earned the right. Good night."

"Good night," Flora told him. The line went dead. Silence had fallen in the Socialist Party office. Everyone was looking at her. She put the phone back on the hook and nodded. "He's conceded," she said.

Cheers and whoops shattered the silence. People came up and shook Flora's hand and thumped her on the back, as if she were a man. The racket woke up Joshua, who'd fallen asleep in Hosea's lap. The little boy started to cry. Hosea comforted him. Before long, he fell asleep again, his thumb in his mouth.

Someone knocked on the door. Eventually, one of the men in the office heard the noise and opened it. There stood Sheldon Fleischmann, who ran the butcher's shop downstairs. He looked a lot like his father, Max. The elder Fleischmann had quietly fallen over behind his counter one day, and never got up again. Like his father, Sheldon was a Democrat. Flora doubted he'd voted for her. Even so, he was carrying a tray of cold cuts, as Max had done more than once on election nights.

"You don't need to do that," Flora scolded him. "You're not even a Socialist."

"I try to be a good neighbor, though," Fleischmann answered. "That's more important than politics."

"If everyone thought that way, we'd hardly need politics," Hosea Blackford said.

His flat Great Plains accent stood out among the sharp, often Yiddish-flavored, New York voices in the office. Sheldon Fleischmann's gaze swung to him in momentary surprise. Then the butcher realized who he had to be. "You're right, Mr. Vice President," he said, giving Blackford a respectful nod. "But too many people don't."

"No, they don't," Blackford agreed. "I did say *if*."

"Yes, you did," Fleischmann allowed. "*Mazeltov*, Congresswoman." He chuckled. "I've been saying that so long, it starts to sound natural."

"And why shouldn't it?" Challenge rang from Flora's voice.

Had the butcher said something about women having no place in Congress, Flora would have exploded. She was ready to do it even now. But his answer was mild: "Only because there are a lot of men in Congress, ma'am, and just a couple of women. You do say what you're used to."

Flora couldn't very well argue there, however much she might have wanted to. She nodded. "All right," she said. "I suppose I'll let you get away with that."

By the relief on Sheldon Fleischmann's face, he felt as if he *had* got away with it. "*Mazeltov* again," he said, and went downstairs once more.

In the office, Herman Bruck was talking with Maria Tresca. Maria was one of the few Italians in the overwhelmingly Jewish Fourteenth Ward. She'd also been a thoroughgoing radical even before her sister was killed in the Remembrance Day riots of 1915. For as long as Flora could remember, Maria had stood foursquare for the proletariat and against the power of big capitalists. Now, though, she listened attentively as Bruck said, "Amalgamated Mills is a very solid firm. They make fine-quality goods, and I think their stock is going to go straight through the roof. I got fifteen shares when it was at thirty-two last month, and it's already gone up five and a half points."

When it came to cloth, he knew what he was talking about. He was a master tailor from a family of tailors, and always dressed as if he made five times as much as he really did. Flora wasn't much surprised when Maria Tresca gave back a serious nod. But she *was* surprised when strongly Socialist Maria offered a stock tip of her own: "I just bought five shares of Central Powers Steel in Toledo. They landed that new contract for the Great Lakes fleet, and they may split two for one soon."

"Central Powers Steel, eh?" Herman Bruck's round face grew alert. "I'll have to look into that."

"You're both buying shares in the stock market?" Flora knew she sounded amazed. She managed to keep from calling it speculating, though that was what it was.

Bruck looked faintly embarrassed, but he said, "I've made a lot of money the last year and a half—that's how long I've been in. And you only need to put up ten percent of the money when you buy on margin, so it's a lot cheaper than it seems."

"It's a lot cheaper as long as the market goes up," Flora said. "If it comes down, you need to pay more money or lose your shares."

"It's gone up for a long time now," Bruck replied. "I don't see why it should do anything else all of a sudden."

Flora wasn't sure how to answer that, or even if it had an answer. She turned to Maria Tresca. "*You're* putting money into Wall Street? You, of all people?"

"Yes, some," Maria answered defiantly. "If capitalism can make a secretary rich, let's see it happen. I hope it can. And if it can't"—she shrugged—"I'm not putting in more than I can afford to lose."

"Well, that's good," Flora said. "I can think of a lot of people who aren't being so careful, though."

"What we need is more regulation of the market, to keep cheats and swindlers from having their way with people," Maria Tresca said. "I don't know too much about what goes on in the stock market, but that looks pretty clear to me. Some of those people will yank the shirt off your back and then sell it to you."

Sadly, Flora answered, "I think you're right, but getting the legislation through Congress is a different story. The Democrats are against it, and so are the Republicans. And more than a few Socialists have made so much money in the market, they think it's the goose that lays golden eggs, too."

She looked over at her husband. He held their sleeping son, all his attention, for the time being, resting on the little boy. But Flora knew Hosea also had money invested in Wall Street. She didn't know exactly how much; he'd never talked much with her about that. Socialism in Dakota was altogether a milder thing, a more natively American thing, than it was here in New York City. What was shocking from Herman and Maria would have been nothing out of the ordinary for Hosea Blackford, though he and they belonged to the same party. He'd never cared to rub Flora's nose in the ideological differences between them.

But if even thoroughgoing Socialists were buying and selling stocks, where had those differences gone? *Would you use your own money to try to make a killing in the market?* Flora asked herself. She didn't think so, even now, but she admitted to herself that she wasn't sure.

Are you a capitalist? Do you want to be a capitalist? It was like asking herself if she wanted to become a Christian. *Very much like that,* she realized—Socialism was about as much an article of faith with her as was Judaism. And yet . . . *If I can provide for my family, why not?* But that was the question: could she? One thing she'd learned in school still seemed true—what went up had to come down. Herman Bruck didn't seem to believe that any more. For his sake, and the sake of many more like him, Flora hoped the rules had changed since she'd got out of Public School Number 130.

Rain pattered down on Hipolito Rodriguez's farm outside of Baroyeca. Here in the south of Sonora, winter rains were less common than those that came off the Gulf of California in the summertime. Rain at any season came seldom; were it not for the streams and ditches bringing water down from the mountains into the valley near whose edge Baroyeca sat, the town, the farms around it, and the silver mine close by couldn't have survived.

Chickens hopped in surprise when raindrops hit them. They pecked at the puffs of dust the raindrops kicked up. Maybe they thought those puffs were bugs. Rodriguez wasn't sure what, if anything, went through their minds. He could think along with the rest of the livestock; the mule, though a powerful animal, was as evil as any beast ever born. But trying to think like a hen was more trouble than it was worth. The pigs seemed brilliant next to hens.

Dark gray clouds rolled down from the northwest. The day was chilly, as chilly as it ever got near Baroyeca. Rodriguez was glad to stand close by the fire in the kitchen. His wife patted cornmeal into tortillas. Looking up from her work, Magdalena said, "Do you know what we need, Hipolito?"

"No. What?" Rodriguez answered.

"We need a *stove*," his wife said. Most of their conversation was in Spanish, but the key word came out in English. She went on, "A good iron stove would cook better than I can with an open fire. It would pay for itself, too, because it would save fuel. It would even keep the kitchen warm on days like this, because less heat would go up the chimney. And I think we can afford one."

"A stove?" Rodriguez also said it in English. He scratched his head. Magdalena had always cooked over an open fire. So had his mother. So had everyone, he supposed, for as long as his ancestors had lived in Baroyeca. But times weren't what they had been back in the old days. He knew that. Cautiously, he asked, "How much would a stove cost?"

"Twenty-seven dollars and sixty cents," Magdalena said without a moment's hesitation. "I saw just the one I want in the Henderson and Fisk catalogue." Henderson and Fisk was a leading Confederate mail-order house, and had been since before the Great War. Only after the currency stabilized again, though, had its catalogues started coming to places as remote from the concerns of most of the CSA as Baroyeca. Magdalena went on, "It's called the Southern Sunshine cook stove, and it will do everything I need." Again, the name of the stove came out in English.

"A stove," Rodriguez said musingly. "I'd bet a lot of women in Baroyeca itself don't cook on stoves." Changes filtered down to southern Sonora more slowly than almost anywhere else in the CSA, and the Confederate States had been founded on the principle that change was a bad idea.

"I'm sure you're right," his wife agreed. "But I don't care. We have the money. We even have the money for the stovepipe to take the smoke outside—another eighty-five cents."

If she said they had it, they had it. She kept track of finances with an eye that watched every penny. Even when the money went mad after the Great War, when a billion dollars had been nothing much, Magdalena had stretched things as far as they would go. The *patrón* had never had cause to complain about the Rodriguezes. The *patrón* . . . "Does Don Gustavo's wife cook on a stove?" Rodriguez asked.

Magdalena let out a dismissive snort. "Doña Elena doesn't cook at all. They have a cook of their own, as you know perfectly well." But it was a serious question. If the *patrón* didn't have an iron stove in his house, what would he think of a peasant family's getting one? Seeing the worry on Hipolito Rodriguez's face, Magdalena said, "Don't worry. I found out. Doña Elena's cook does use a stove."

"All right. Good. Very good." Rodriguez didn't try to hide his relief. Things weren't so rigid in the CSA as they were down in the Empire of Mexico, and they weren't so rigid now as they had been in his father's day, but he didn't want to offend Don Gustavo even so. *Better safe than sorry,* he told himself. To his wife, he said, "Next time I go to town, I'll send the order to Henderson and Fisk."

"Good, yes." Magdalena nodded. "And then the railroad will bring the crate, and then we will have a stove."

A hamlet like Baroyeca would never have had a railroad connection if not for the mine close by. In plenty of places in Sonora and Chihuahua, the last leg of the journey from merchandiser to customer would have been by rattling wagon (or possibly, these days, by rattling truck). But not here. The trains that took out precious metal could bring in a stove from Birmingham.

The mine also meant Baroyeca boasted a post office, a few doors down from *La Culebra Verde.* The Stars and Bars floated above the whitewashed adobe building. When Rodriguez went in, José Cordero, the postmaster, put aside the newspaper he'd been reading. He was a plump man with a small mustache and with his hair parted on the right and greased immovably into place. "And what can I do for you today?" he inquired. "Postage stamps?"

"No, *señor.* I have some," Rodriguez replied politely; by virtue of his office, the postmaster was a person of consequence. "I wish to purchase a postal money order, and to send the money to Henderson and Fisk." He spoke with a certain amount of pride. Not every farmer could scrape together the cash for such a purchase.

Cordero's answering nod was grave, for he recognized as much. He made a small ceremony of taking out the book of money orders. "What is the amount?"

"Thirty-one dollars and seventy-six cents," Rodriguez said; that included the stove, the stovepipe, and third-class freight. He set banknotes and coins on the counter till he had exactly the right amount.

The postmaster counted the money, then nodded again. "Yes, that is correct for the order itself," he said. He filled out the money order, then added, "You must also know, of course, there is a fee of thirty-two cents for the use of the order."

Rodriguez winced. He hadn't sent a money order in so long, he'd forgotten that one-percent fee. He fished in his pockets. He had some change lurking there; he'd intended to visit *La Culebra Verde* after sending away for the stove. He found a quarter and a dime. José Cordero solemnly gave him back three cents. He sighed. He couldn't buy a beer for that. Then he found another dime. He brightened. He could go to the cantina after all.

"How long will the stove take to come?" he asked.

"Ah, is that what you're getting? Good for you," the postmaster said. "How long?" He looked up at the ceiling as he made mental calculations. "My best guess would be three weeks or a month. You should light a candle for every day sooner than three weeks."

"*Gracias, señor,*" Rodriguez said. That was about what he'd thought. Now he could use Cordero's authority when he told Magdalena.

"*El gusto es mio,*" Cordero replied. Rodriguez didn't think the pleasure really was his, but he always spoke politely. He went on, "I hope your wife gets much use and much enjoyment from it. My own Ana has had a stove now for several years, and she would never go back to cooking over an open fire. The stove is much cleaner, too."

"I had not thought of that, but I'm sure it would be." Rodriguez hid a smile. He'd done a little bragging, and the postmaster had responded with some of his own. That was the way life worked.

"It is," Cordero said positively. "You've spent a lot of money, but you won't be sorry for it." He sounded as if he were giving a personal guarantee.

"Without doubt, you have reason." Rodriguez inked a pen, scrawled the name of the mail-order form on the envelope, put in the order form and the money order, and handed Cordero the envelope.

The postmaster looked embarrassed. "Personally, I would gladly send it for nothing. You understand, though, I cannot be my own man in this matter: I am but a servant of the Confederate government. I must ask you for five cents more for the stamp that shows you have paid me postage."

With a sigh, Rodriguez realized he hadn't brought a stamp of his own along. He passed Cordero the dime he'd found, but eight cents wouldn't let him go into the cantina. Before the war, beer had been five cents, but it was a dime nowadays. No help for it, though. He watched the postmaster put the envelope in the bin of mail that would leave Baroyeca. Once it was there, he left the post office.

Standing on the board sidewalk, he sighed again. No point in going into *La Culebra Verde* when he had no money to buy. He thought little of men who sat around in there hoping to cadge drinks from their more prosperous friends and neighbors. He didn't want to be one of those freeloaders himself. But he didn't want to turn around and head straight back to the farm, either. What point to that? He didn't escape from it often enough to care to go home as fast as he could.

What to do, then? He looked up and down Baroyeca's main street—*Calle de los Estados Confederados*—wondering which shops he could visit without drawing sneers from the proprietors. A man with eight cents in his pocket couldn't buy much. He jingled the coins. Because of the pennies, they did sound like more.

His eyes snapped back to a building at the far end of the street. It had stood empty since the weekly newspaper folded in the middle of the great inflation. Now, he saw, it was empty no more. A couple of bright new words were painted on the front window. From his angle, he couldn't make out what they were. He ambled toward the building, still jingling his few paltry coins.

Before long, he could read the words. He stopped in surprise and pleasure, a grin spreading over his face. FREEDOM! the window shouted, and below that, in slightly smaller letters, ¡LIBERTAD! As he got closer still, he could make out the much smaller words under the big ones: *Freedom Party Headquarters, Baroyeca, Sonora. Everyone Welcome.*

Everyone welcome? Hipolito Rodriguez's grin got wider. He stopped fooling with the coins and went in.

Inside, a blond man with his hair cut short like a soldier's clattered away at a typewriter. Rodriguez didn't scowl, but he felt like it. From what he'd seen in the Army, a lot of white Confederates looked down on Sonorans and Chihuahuans almost as much as they did on Negroes— unless the Sonorans and Chihuahuans had money, of course. He laughed a sour laugh. The eight cents in his pocket didn't qualify.

But this fellow startled him. *"Buenos días. Como está Usted?"* he said in pretty good Spanish. It plainly wasn't his first language, but he managed more than well enough. *"Me llamo* Robert Quinn," he went on, *"Represento el Partido de Libertad en Baroyeca. En qué puedo servirle?"*

"Hello, Mr. Quinn," Rodriguez said in English to the man who represented the Freedom Party in Baroyeca. "I do not know what you can do for me. I came in because I saw you were here and I wanted to find out why."

"Bueno. Excelente," Quinn continued in Spanish. *"Como se llama, señor?"*

Rodriguez gave his name. He added, "Why does the Freedom Party have an office here?" He couldn't imagine the Radical Liberals or the Whigs opening a headquarters in Baroyeca. The town simply wasn't big enough.

But Quinn said, *"Para ganar elecciones."*

"Having an office here will help you win elections?" Rodriguez returned to Spanish, since the Freedom Party man seemed comfortable in it. "How?"

"We did well here in 1925—we elected a Congressman from this district," Robert Quinn replied in the same language. "We intend to do better still this year. After all, in 1927 we will elect a president. With God's help—and some from the voters—it will be Jake Featherston."

"I have only eight cents right now," Rodriguez said, not mentioning the thirty-odd dollars he'd just sent to Birmingham. He kept quiet about that on purpose. Was this truly a party that might do a poor man some good? He'd find out. "With eight cents, how can I help you?"

Quinn didn't laugh at him or tell him to go away. Instead, seriously and soberly, he began to explain exactly what Rodriguez could do for the Freedom Party, and what the Party might do for him. He talked for about ten minutes. By the time he finished, Rodriguez was sure he would go on voting Freedom as long as he lived. That wasn't all he was sure of, either. He would go out and preach for the Party, too. He felt like one of the very first Christians in ancient days. He'd met a disciple, and now he was a disciple himself.

Colonel Irving Morrell hadn't heard the garrison in Kamloops, British Columbia, so animated, so excited, since he'd got there from Philadelphia more than a year before. He would have been happier, though, had something military sparked the excitement. But all the gossip centered on Chevrolet's proposed acquisition of the White Motor Company. White, as far as Morrell was concerned, made the best trucks in the world. No one seemed to care about that. What people were talking about was what the acquisition would do to the stock prices of the two companies.

By midafternoon, Morrell had had as much of that as he could take. "God forbid we should have to fight a war on a day when the market goes down," he said.

He was a colonel, which meant he outranked everyone who sat in the mess hall with him. At last, though, a captain named David Smith said, "Well, sir, you never can tell. It might make us meaner."

Silence fell. People waited to see how Morrell would take that. Ever since he'd come West from General Staff

231

headquarters, he'd made a name for himself as a man no one sensible would trifle with. But Smith's line was too good to make him angry. He grinned and said, "Here's hoping, anyhow."

The mess hall relaxed. He could almost feel the soft sighs of relief that came from just about everyone. In Philadelphia, a lot of soldiers had spent a lot of time laughing at him. The officers here took him seriously. His record was too good to ignore, and a colonel's eagles carried a lot more weight in Kamloops than they had back at General Staff headquarters. That wasn't why he'd been so eager to get out of Philadelphia; he'd never cared one way or the other about being a big fish in a small pond. All he wanted were a job he liked and the chance to do it without anybody looking over his shoulder. He hadn't had those in Philadelphia. He did here.

Captain Smith decided to push it a little, adding, "Besides, sir, we'll never get rich on Army pay. If we're going to, wouldn't you rather have us playing the market than knocking over a bank?"

That went too far. Morrell got to his feet. He carried his tray of dishes toward the waiting cooks. Over his shoulder, he answered, "If you want to get rich, you don't belong in the Army in the first place. And if you're not in the Army, I don't give a damn what you're doing. No one held a gun to your head to make you put on this uniform, Captain. If you want to resign your commission, I'll be glad to help you with the paperwork."

Smith turned very red. He said, "No, sir. I don't want to do that. I don't want to do that at all."

Morrell handed the tray to a man in an apron who'd drawn kitchen duty. Everyone eyed him, wondering how he would reply. He didn't want to get any deeper into the argument, so all he said was, "Remember why you did join, then, Captain."

As he left the hall, that silence returned. His leg twinged. It hadn't for a while. He'd been wounded when the Great War was young, and that was ... *Lord!* he thought in surprise. *That's heading toward thirteen years ago now. Where's the time gone?*

He took his thick wool overcoat from its hanger and wrapped it around himself. Kamloops lay where the north and south branches of the Thompson River came together, in a valley near the foot of the Canadian Rockies. Even in Philadelphia, Morrell would have been glad to have an overcoat on most February days. There were days—and more than a few of them—in Kamloops when he would have been glad to have two of them.

Cold slapped his face when he went outside. He shoved his hands into the overcoat's pockets to keep them from freezing. The rolling country around the town was in summer a near desert of tumbleweed and sagebrush. Snow painted it white at this season of the year, and white it would stay for another couple of months.

Morrell sighed. His breath smoked, as if he'd exhaled after a drag on a cigarette. The flat land would have been ideal for testing barrels. He'd said so, too, in the very first report he sent back to Philadelphia. He wondered if anybody had read that report, or even bothered to take it out of its envelope. He had his doubts. No one, certainly, had acted on the suggestion, or even acknowledged it.

So far as he knew, no one in the USA was testing barrels anywhere else, either. He kicked at the snow, which flew up from his boots. Down in the Empire of Mexico, the machines the Confederate-backed imperialists used were at least as good as the ones he'd been experimenting with back at Fort Leavenworth before budget cuts shut down the program. The rebels didn't have barrels that could match them, and the rebels, by now, had just about lost the civil war.

He kicked at the snow again. The Ottoman Turks weren't massacring Armenians these days the way they had a few years before, but American intervention had nothing to do with that. Kaiser Wilhelm—who wasn't good old Kaiser Bill any more—had ignored U.S. protests, and so had Abdul Majid, the Ottoman sultan. They'd figured the United States had more urgent things to worry about closer to home, and they'd been right.

They made us look like a bunch of chumps, is what they did, Morrell thought as he walked toward his office.

A horse-drawn garbage wagon rattled up the road toward him. He nodded to the men aboard it. The Canadian white wings pretended he didn't exist. They took money from the American occupiers, but that didn't mean they wanted anything else to do with them. Yes, the U.S. Army had snuffed out the latest uprising a couple of years before, but it didn't seem to matter. The Canucks were going to stay sullen for a long, long time to come.

How do we keep them from causing more trouble, next year or five years from now or fifteen years from now or fifty years from now? Morrell wondered. He wished he could talk to some German officers, even if things between the two greatest powers left in the world weren't so friendly as they had been up till the war ended. The Kaiser's men were occupying a hostile Belgium now, and they'd been occupying a hostile Alsace and Lorraine for more than fifty years. They had lots of practice at ruling territory that didn't want to be ruled.

Seldom had Morrell had a wish so promptly granted. When he got to the office building, his aide-de-camp, a lieutenant named Ike Horwitz, said, "Sir, there's a German officer waiting to see you. Said you saw action together during the war."

"Captain Guderian, by God!" Morrell exclaimed in delight. "He was an observer with my unit when we were fighting over by Banff, just a couple of hundred miles from here."

"Yes, sir," Horwitz said. "Only he's a lieutenant colonel now, if I remember German rank markings straight. Oh—and he's got an orderly with him, a sergeant."

Something in Horwitz's voice changed. Morrell needed a second to realize what it was. "You don't like the orderly?"

"No, sir," Horwitz said with more of that same stiffness.

"Why not?" Morrell asked curiously.

"He figured out I was a Jew," Horwitz answered. It probably hadn't taken much figuring; Morrell's aide-de-camp looked very Jewish indeed, with a nose of impressive proportions. "He didn't think I spoke any

German—and I don't, not really, but Yiddish is close enough to let me understand it when I hear it."

"Oh," Morrell said. "Well, to hell with him. Guderian's not like that, I can tell you for a fact. He doesn't care one way or the other."

Lieutenant Horwitz nodded. "He told his orderly to keep quiet and mind his own business. I just sat here and minded mine."

"Good for you, Ike."

"I wanted to punch the bastard right in the nose."

"Don't blame you a bit. But you didn't, and that makes you a good soldier."

Horwitz's snort said he would sooner have been a bad soldier. Morrell went into his office. Heinz Guderian bounded up from a chair to shake his hand. Sure enough, the energetic German had a single gold pip on each fancy shoulder strap—a lieutenant colonel's insignia. His orderly sprang to his feet, too, and gave Morrell a crisp salute. The fellow wore an Iron Cross, First Class. That gave Morrell pause; it hadn't been easy for a noncom to win that medal. Second Class, yes—First, no. The man might be a son of a bitch, but he'd done something special during the war.

He spoke in German: "Excuse me, sir, but I know no English."

"It's all right," Morrell replied in the same language. "I can get along in German." His voice hardened a little. "And so can my aide-de-camp."

Lieutenant Colonel Guderian grimaced. His orderly was unabashed. "So he knows what I think of his kind, does he? Well, too bad. The world would be a better place if we got rid of the lot of them."

"Nonsense," Morrell said sharply. He thought, *Damn fool sounds like Jake Featherston, except he's riding a different hobby horse.*

The sergeant might have replied, but Guderian held up a hand and said, "Enough." His orderly had discipline; he fumed, but he subsided. Then Guderian switched to English: "This is not why I came to talk to you, Colonel Morrell."

235

"Well, what can I do for you, then?" Morrell asked.

"I was wondering if you could arrange for me a tour of occupied western Canada," the German officer said. "We are interested in the methods you Americans use to control the lands you have won. . . . What is so funny, Colonel?"

"I'll tell you what's funny," Morrell answered when he got done laughing. "What's funny is, I was just wondering how you Germans held on to Belgium and Alsace-Lorraine. What we've been doing here hasn't worked out so well as we'd have liked. The Canadians still hate our guts. We smashed their last uprising, but they're liable to rebel again any old time. If you know a trick for keeping people quiet, I wouldn't mind learning it."

"What does he say, sir?" Guderian's orderly asked. With the air of a man humoring a subordinate who didn't really deserve it, Guderian translated. The sergeant made an almost operatic gesture of contempt. "It's simple," he declared. "Kill enough and you'll frighten the rest into giving in."

Guderian sighed. *"Später, später,"* he said, and turned back to Morrell. "That's the only answer he knows—kill everything in sight."

"You don't get any arguments that way, anyhow," Morrell observed.

"No, nor any chance to put things right later," the German said. "So you Americans have no sure answers for this, either, then?"

"I'm afraid not. I'll be glad to set up your tour for you, but I don't think you'll see anything very exciting," Morrell answered. *I'll make damn sure you don't see anything too very exciting, as a matter of fact,* he thought. *If you're looking for ideas from us, that means you need 'em badly. And if you don't get 'em, you'll have more trouble holding down your subjects if you ever wind up in a scrap with us.*

"Thank you. I should perhaps let you know certain American officers are in Belgium now, trying to learn from us." Guderian smiled and shrugged. "Between us, your country and mine share the problems of the strong, *nicht wahr?"*

"Yes," Morrell said. *And I bet our boys don't learn one damn thing from you, either, except where the officers' brothels are.* He wagged a finger at the German. "Nobody's looking at what you're doing in the east, in Poland and the Ukraine?"

Heinz Guderian shook his head. "No, Colonel, no one looks there—and it is as well that no one does, too." His eyes swung toward his tough-talking orderly. "In the east, *his* methods prevail. Poland pretends to be a kingdom. The Ukraine . . ." He shook his head. "After all, they're only Slavs." He might have been a Confederate saying, *After all, they're only niggers.* Morrell smiled with half his mouth. *Either way, God help the poor bastards on the receiving end.*

At seventeen, Mary McGregor had got used to being taller than her mother. Her father, after all, had been a big man. She remembered that very well, though these days she had trouble calling up the memory of just what his voice had sounded like.

She also remembered when her mother's hair had been the color of a bright new penny. Now she couldn't help noticing how much gray streaked that once-bright hair. She hadn't noticed it as it spread; one day, it seemed, that gray had simply appeared, as if by magic.

But magic is supposed to be good, Mary thought, looking out across the fields she and her mother and her sister and whatever hired man they got for the spring would be planting soon. Soon, but not yet: snow, a deeper blanket than usual, still covered those fields. Winter had been hard, even for Manitoba.

Mary clenched her fists so that her nails dug into her palms. This far north, the growing season was short enough anyhow. A late spring could make harvest touch-and-go before frosts came again in early fall. If they didn't get a good crop . . .

Well, so what? Mary thought, and went out to tend the horse and the cow and the rest of the livestock in the barn. *What if we've got no money and they throw us off the farm?* She knew the family had relatives back in Ontario;

237

her father had come west to Manitoba when he was a boy. But the McGregors weren't close to any of those kin. Mary'd never met a one of them. *Would they take us in?* Times were supposed to be even harder back there than they were here—not only had Ontario been fought over harder than Manitoba, the rebellion there had been worse.

We're on our own. Nobody cares whether we live or die. Mary shook her head. That wasn't true. The Americans hoped the McGregors died. They'd killed her brother, Alexander. They'd killed her father, too. Oh, yes, his own bomb, meant for General Custer, had been the actual means of his death, but he never would have become a bomber in the first place if the stinking Yanks hadn't decided Alexander was plotting against them and stood him against a wall.

Some of those dark thoughts faded away when Mary went into the barn. It was warmer in there, with the walls holding out the wind and holding in the animals' body warmth. Somebody from the city might have wrinkled his nose at the odor. Mary took it for granted; she'd smelled it all her life. And the work distracted her. She gave the horse and cow and sheep hay and put down corn for the chickens. Then she mucked out the stalls. The manure would go on the garden and on as much of the fields as it would cover.

She handled pitchfork and shovel with matter-of-fact skill. Her hands had thick bands of callus across the palms. Her nails were short and blunt and dirty. A dozen scars seamed her fingers and the backs of her hands—anyone who did a lot of work with sharp tools had accidents now and then. Every once in a while, she thought wistfully of a manicure, but how much good would it do? A day after she got it, she'd be back in the barn and out in the fields once more.

Hens squawked and tried to peck as she lifted them off their nests so she could gather eggs. One of them did more than try; the bird's beak drew blood. She gave it a baleful stare. "Chicken and dumplings," she whispered. "Fried chicken. Chicken soup." The bird looked back out of beady little eyes. It was too stupid to be afraid. It was only indignant at having its nest robbed—and, being a hen, would forget about that in short order.

Instead of taking the basket of eggs straight back to

the house, Mary sat down for a moment to rest. She leaned back against an old wagon wheel that had been sitting in the barn ever since she was a little girl. The iron tire on the wheel showed red streaks of rust. The wheel had a couple of broken spokes. Not for the first time, she wondered why her father had left it there instead of either repairing it or getting what use he could from the wood and the iron. Letting things lie idle wasn't like him.

She shrugged. She'd never get the chance to ask him now. If she ever needed anything that wheel could provide, she wouldn't hesitate to take it. Or, if she had to, she thought she could fix it. She hadn't tried her hand at carpentry till her father died. As with so much else, she'd had to learn the hard way—several of the scars on her hands came from slips. But she could do things nowadays that would have amazed her a few years before.

With a sigh, she climbed to her feet again, picked up the basket, and headed back to the farmhouse. She blinked in surprise when she saw a buggy by the house. People didn't visit the McGregors very often. She walked faster, curious to see who'd broken the unwritten rule.

A couple of Fords sped past on the road that led to Rosenfeld. One was painted green-gray, which meant it belonged to the U.S. Army. The other was the more usual black. All the same, odds were it had a Yank inside. Even now, almost ten years after the war ended, not many Canadians could afford a motorcar. *And most of the ones who can are a bunch of damned collaborators,* Mary thought.

She opened the kitchen door. Her mother sat at a table drinking tea with another woman of about her own age, who was saying, "I tell you, Maude, it's a disgrace. I'm sure she and that Yank—" She broke off and smiled. "Hello, Mary. How are you?"

"I'm fine, Mrs. Marble, thank you." Mary laughed at herself, thinking she should have recognized the buggy.

"Tell me more, Beth," her mother said. "You can be sure Mary won't let it get to the wrong ears."

"Well, I didn't expect she would," Beth Marble answered, sipping her tea. She was a couple of inches shorter than Mary's mother, with shoulder-length brown hair, blue eyes, rather flat features, and a habitual expression of good humor. After picking up a shortbread wafer from the plate on the table, she did go on with her story: one more tale of a Canadian girl who'd lost her virtue to a fast-talking American with a fancy motorcar and with money in his pocket.

Mary listened with only half an ear. She hardly knew this girl, who lived even farther from the McGregors than did the Marbles, and she'd been hearing such stories ever since the days of the Great War. Only the details varied. The American conquest of Canada continued on many different levels. Soldiers occupied the land. American men seduced Canadian women. Newspapers printed only what the conquerors wanted the conquered to read. Films pounded home the same messages, as she'd seen at the Bijou. So did the wireless, not that she'd ever heard it. Canadian schools taught the U.S. view of history—a pack of lies, as far as Mary was concerned. Her parents had pulled her and Julia out of school when the Yanks changed the curriculum. Most children, though, had kept on going, and the Americans had been in charge of such things for quite a while now. How long till a whole generation forgot what being Canadian meant?

Mary put the eggs she'd gathered on the counter. She went over to the table. "May I have a wafer, Mother?" she asked, and took one when Maude McGregor nodded.

"Such lovely manners," Beth Marble said, and beamed at Mary's mother. "Both your daughters are so sweet and charming, Maude."

Do you know me at all? Mary wondered as she nibbled at the shortbread. *I don't think so.* In her own mind, she was as much a fighter against the American occupation as her father had been, more of a fighter than her brother had been—even if the Yanks had murdered him for his opposition to their rule. Sweet? Charming? She felt like pouring a cup of tea and then spilling it on their visitor, even if Mrs. Marble had meant well, as she surely had.

As much to make a point as because she really wanted it, Mary took another shortbread wafer, this time without asking permission. Mrs. Marble, engrossed in another bit of gossip—she did like to talk—failed to notice. Mary's mother did, and wagged a finger at her. From behind Beth Marble's back, Mary stuck out her tongue.

Her mother raised her teacup to her mouth to hide a smile, but her eyes danced above it. Carrying that second piece of shortbread away as booty, Mary went into the parlor.

Two steps in were more than enough to show her she'd made a mistake. Her older sister sat on the rocking chair in there, and Beth Marble's son Kenneth on the sofa close by. More plainly than words, Julia's look said the two of them didn't want any company.

Face heating, Mary mumbled, "I . . . I guess I'll go upstairs now. Hello, Kenneth."

"Hello, Mary," Kenneth Marble answered politely, but he kept his eyes on Julia as he spoke. He'd been coming to call for most of a year now, sometimes with his mother, sometimes without. He was the first young man who'd come to call on Julia since Ted Culligan broke off their engagement after her father's death. There were times over the past few months when Julia had got all dreamy and absentminded. Mary didn't take that for a good sign.

Up the stairs she went, fast as her legs would carry her. When she turned around and looked back, Julia and Kenneth were leaning towards each other. She sighed. She didn't know what Julia saw in him. He was only an inch or two taller than she, and, to Mary's eyes, nothing much to look at. Some actress had got a reputation as the girl with *it*. In Julia's eyes, plainly, Kenneth Marble had *it*. Mary still found *it* more bewildering than exciting.

She flopped down on her bed and started reading a copy of *The Ladies' Home Journal* she'd got the last time she went into Rosenfeld. The magazine showed her a whole different world, and not just because it came from the USA. Skinny girls in short dresses strode city streets, rode in motorcars, listened to the wireless, lived in apartments, used electric lights and telephones, and did all sorts of other things Mary thought herself unlikely ever to do. Even more than what they did, that they took it so completely for granted was daunting.

If it weren't for the recipes and patterns the *Journal* included, Mary's mother probably wouldn't have let it come into the farmhouse. Nothing could have been better calculated to make someone on a farm discontented with her life. This issue even had a story about flying to California for a holiday. Flying! For pleasure! The only aeroplanes Mary had even seen were the fighting scouts and bombers that had buzzed above the farm during the Great War. She couldn't imagine wanting to get into one of those.

The *Journal* also had an article about a journey on an ocean liner. Mary couldn't decide whether she found stranger the idea of a liner or that of the ocean itself. She'd never seen it, and didn't expect she ever would. Before she could read much of the article, a commotion broke out downstairs: Julia and their mother and Beth Marble sounded even more excited than the hens had when Mary rifled their nests.

She flipped the magazine closed and hurried down to see what had happened. She found her older sister in tears, with their mother and Mrs. Marble both embracing her. Kenneth Marble stood off to one side, a sickly grin on his face. Mary stared at him. Had he tried to . . . ? With his own mother, and Julia's, in the next room? He couldn't have been that stupid. Could he?

Then Mary noticed both her mother and Beth Marble were crying and smiling at the same time. Maude McGregor said, "Kenneth just asked Julia to marry him, and she said yes."

"Oh." Mary couldn't have said anything more if she tried; she felt as if she'd been punched in the pit of the stomach. Even breathing was hard. The first thought that went through her mind was, *How will we do the work if Julia moves away?* Even with all three of them working flat out, it barely got done.

Despite her mother's smile, Maude McGregor looked worried, too. Mrs. Marble seemed oblivious to the glance that went between Mary and her mother. It wasn't *her* trouble, after all.

"This is the happiest day of my life," Julia said. Beth Marble burst into tears again. Mary congratulated her sister. *What a liar I am,* she thought.

VII

To Anne Colleton's ears, J.B.H. Norris' drawl sounded harsh and ignorant. But the Texas oil man had proved a sharp operator in spite of that backwoods accent. "Hope you'll see fit to invest in our operation here, ma'am," he said, tipping his hat to her. The Stetson, with its high crown and wide brim, also told her she wasn't in South Carolina any more.

She *was* near the banks of the Brazos River, northwest of Fort Worth. And she had questions that went beyond profit and loss. She pointed west. "That new Yankee state of Houston isn't very far away. What happens if there's another war? How are you going to keep U.S. soldiers and aeroplanes from wrecking everything you've got?"

"Ma'am, you'd do better asking Richmond about that than me," Norris answered. "If they hadn't given up so much last time, we wouldn't need to fret about it now."

"Yes, but they did, and so we do." Anne slapped at something. The mosquitoes were coming out early this afternoon. It wasn't quite so muggy as it would have been back home, but it would do.

J.B.H. Norris said, "Don't quite know what to tell you about that, except I don't think a war's coming any time soon."

"No," Anne said bleakly. "I don't, either. We're too weak."

"That's about the size of it," Norris agreed. "At least

President Mitchel has the sense to see it. That Featherston maniac would get us into a fight we can't hope to win."

"I used to like him better than I do now, but he hasn't got any real chance of getting elected, anyway," Anne said. "So I'm a Whig again. Some people don't much like that, but I've never much cared for what people like or don't like." She changed the subject, but only a little: "What do you think of the Supreme Court ruling that lets Mitchel run again?"

"Well, the Constitution says a president serves the six-year term he's elected for, and then he's done." Norris shrugged. "President Mitchel didn't run for the job—he got it when that Calkins bastard—pardon me, ma'am—killed President Hampton. So I suppose it's only fair to let him try and win it again on his own. And Calkins was one of those Freedom Party fools, so I'm not surprised the Supreme Court gave it to Featherston right between the eyes."

"Yes, that occurred to me, too. Featherston frightened people—powerful people—a few years ago. Now they're going to make him pay for it." Anne Colleton's smile had a certain predatory quality, enough so that J.B.H. Norris flinched when she turned it on him rather than the world at large. She went on, "I do thank you for showing me around. You've given me a lot to think about—more than I expected when I came out to Texas, in fact. I may well put some of my money here once I get home."

Norris beamed. "That'd be wonderful. We can use the capital, and I'm not lyin' when I tell you so." He scratched his cheek with his left hand. Only then did Anne notice his ring finger was just a stump. A war wound? Probably. A lot of men had such small mutilations. He added, "If you're heading back East, you'd better not waste a lot of time. From what the papers say, the flood in the Mississippi Valley just keeps gettin' worse and worse."

"I know." Anne had been reading the papers, too. Anger roiled her voice: "And it's hurt us so much worse than it hit the damnyankees. If they hadn't stolen Kentucky and that piece of Arkansas from us, it wouldn't have hurt them much at all. Cairo, Illinois, got flooded." She rolled her eyes. "Cairo, Illinois, never was any sort of a place to begin with. But we've had Memphis and Little Rock just drowned, and the levees in New Orleans were holding by this much"—she held thumb and forefinger close together—"when I went through Louisiana on my way here."

"May not be so easy gettin' back," Norris warned.

"Why not?" Anne said. "Most of the bridges over the Mississippi are still standing."

"Yes, ma'am." The oil man nodded again. "The bridges over the Mississippi are still good. They're the big, strong ones, and they were built to take whatever the river could throw at 'em. But what about the bridges *on the way to* the Mississippi? An awful lot of them'll go down, I bet. I may be wrong, but that's sure enough how it looks to me."

Anne muttered something under her breath. It wasn't quite far enough under, for J.B.H. Norris' gingery eyebrows leapt upwards. *He'll never think of me as a lady again,* Anne thought, and did her best not to giggle. *Well, fair enough, because I'm damn well not.* Worry wiped out the temptation to laugh. "You're dead right, Mr. Norris, and I wish I'd thought of that myself. Please take me back to my hotel. I can't afford to waste much time, can I?"

"No, I don't reckon you can," Norris said. "Wish I could see more of you, but I know how things are. Car's right over there." He pointed to a middle-aged Birmingham outside the shack that did duty for an office.

How does he mean that? Anne wondered. *Spend more time with me, or see me with my clothes off?* Ten years, even five years, before, she would have had no doubt. But she wasn't so young as she had been. *I'm just as picky as I ever was, though, maybe pickier. That's likely why I haven't got a husband yet. Nobody suits me. Maybe Tom was right. I've been on my own too long.*

The ride back to Fort Worth took close to three hours. A blowout halfway there didn't help. J.B.H. Norris fixed it with the aplomb of one who'd done it many times before—and what driver hadn't?—but it still cost a half hour Anne wished she could have got back. She checked out of the Dandridge as soon as Norris stopped the motorcar in front of the hotel. Then she hurled her luggage into a cab and made for the train station across town.

Before the war, she would have had a colored servant, or more than one, taking care of her. No more. And she didn't miss them, either. She'd discovered she was more efficient than anyone whose main aim was to do as little as possible. That had proved oddly liberating, where she would have expected losing servants to do just the opposite.

But the time lost to the blowout rose up to haunt her at the station. "Sorry, ma'am, but the eastbound express pulled out of here about twenty minutes ago," the clerk in the ticket window said. "Next one doesn't leave till ten tonight."

"Damnation," Anne said. "Can I take a local and connect with another express east of here sooner than that? I do want to beat the flood if I can; I have to get back to South Carolina."

"I understand, ma'am. Let's see what I can do." The clerk flipped through schedules so complex, God would have had trouble understanding them. People in line behind Anne surely fumed at the delay. She would have, had she been back there and not at the front. At last, with an unhappy half smile, he shook his head. "Sorry, ma'am, but no. And I've got to tell you, there's no Pullman berths left on the ten o'clock train. You'll have to take an ordinary seat. I'll refund the difference, of course."

"Damnation," Anne said again, this time with more feeling. She'd be a frazzled wreck by the time she finally got back to St. Matthews. But if she didn't leave as soon as she could, heaven only knew when she *would* get back. "Give me whatever you can, then."

"Sure will." The clerk handed her a ticket and several brown Confederate banknotes. "Your train will be leaving from Platform W. It's over that way." He pointed. "Follow the signs—they'll take you straight to it. Hope everything turns out all right for you."

"Thanks." Anne waved for a porter to handle her suitcases. The colored man put them on a wheeled cart and followed her to Platform W. She bought food there, and a cheap novel to while away the time till the train got in.

It was late. By then, Anne had stopped expecting anything else. It didn't arrive till half past one. She'd put the novel aside an hour earlier, and was trying without much luck to doze in a chair. The car to which she was assigned didn't even have compartments, only row after row of seats bolted to the floor. The man who sat down next to her was so fat, he encroached on her without meaning to. He hadn't had a bath any time recently. She gritted her teeth. Nothing she could do about it, though. As soon as the train pulled out of Fort Worth, the fat man threw back his head, fell asleep, and began snoring like a thunderstorm. That added insult to injury. Anne felt like jabbing him with a pin.

Unable to sleep herself, she stared glumly out the window at the night. Only blackness met her eye, blackness and an occasional handful of lights burning in the small towns at which the express didn't stop. She almost resented the lights, which put her in mind of fireflies. Blackness suited her mood much better.

The express did stop at Dallas. Anne understood the need, but hated the delay. The fat man beside her scarcely stirred. He didn't wake up. After what seemed forever but was by her watch forty-five minutes, the train rumbled east again. Presently, Anne had to use the toilet. She took more than a little pleasure in waking her seatmate to get by, though she sounded polite. By the time she returned, he was snoring again. She woke him once more. It did no good to speak of. He fell back to sleep, while she stayed awake.

Marshall was the next stop, near the Louisiana border. By the time the train left, the sky ahead was getting light. Morning had come by the time the express got into Shreveport, on the Red River. The Red was flooding, too, but not enough to delay the train any worse.

Monroe, Louisiana, on the Ouachita, was the next scheduled stop—by then, Anne had the schedule all but memorized. But the express didn't make it to Monroe. First, Anne saw tent cities on high ground, where people who'd escaped the floodwaters were staying till someone did something more for them. Then, as the ground got lower, mud and water covered more and more of it. The air was thick and humid and full of the stink of decay. At last, the train had to stop, for the simple reason that going forward would have meant going underwater. The tracks were laid on an embankment that raised them above the surrounding countryside, but that finally stopped helping.

"What do we do now?" Anne asked the conductor.

"Don't rightly know, ma'am," he answered. "I reckon we'll back up and try and find a way around—if there is one. Don't rightly know about that, either. Only other thing we can do is wait for the water to go down, and Lord only knows how long that'd take."

Trying to hold in her anger, she snapped, "Why didn't you find out in Shreveport that the way would be flooded?"

"On account of it wasn't when we left Shreveport," the conductor said. "Ma'am, this here is a . . . heck of a bad flood, worst anybody's seen since Hector was a pup. An' it just keeps gettin' worser an' worser."

He'd fought not to swear in her presence. Now she fought not to swear in his. After what seemed a very long time, the train shuddered into motion—backwards. It crawled that way till at last it came to a cross track. Anne felt like cheering when it started moving ahead once more.

But it didn't go far. Before long, the encroaching flood-waters blocked its path again. This time, Anne did curse, and didn't care who sent her shocked looks. By the time the train had made three or four false starts, everyone in the car was swearing. It didn't help.

Yet another tent city sprouted like a forest of giant toadstools outside the whistlestop hamlet of Anabell, Louisiana, where the express was balked again. "How are those people going to eat?" someone asked. "If trains have trouble getting through . . ."

It was a good question. It got an answer even as Anne watched. An aeroplane landed in a field only a couple of hundred yards from the train. The pilot started throwing out sacks of flour and flitches of bacon. A great light blazed

248

in Anne's mind. "Let me off the train!" she told the conductor. "This instant, do you hear me?"

"What about your luggage?" he asked, blinking.

"To hell with my luggage," she said. The conductor tapped the side of his head with his index finger, but did as she asked. She ran over to the aeroplane, waving and calling, "Can you fly me over the Mississippi and past the floods to where I can catch another train east?"

"Maybe I can, lady," the pilot answered, shifting a plug of tobacco in his cheek. "Why the devil should I?"

"I'll pay you three hundred dollars," she said. "Half now, half when we land."

That wad of tobacco shifted again. She wondered if he'd swallow it, but he didn't. "Lemme finish unloading," he said around it. "Then you got yourself a deal." Half an hour later, the biplane bumped across the soggy field and threw itself into the air. Anne Colleton whooped with delight. She'd never flown before, and wondered why not. Three hundred dollars was a small price to pay for this kind of fun—and for the money she hoped to make when she got home.

Floodlights glared into Jake Featherston's face, so that he couldn't see the crowd in the New Orleans auditorium. He didn't care; he'd made enough speeches so that he didn't need to see the people out there to know what they were thinking. "Good to be back here," he said. "This is the town where I was nominated six years ago. We did pretty good then, we did. And we'll do better this time, you just wait and see if we don't!"

"Freedom!" The roar came from over a thousand throats. Featherston grinned fiercely. That sound hit him harder than a big slug of hooch. Its absence was the one thing he hated most about making speeches on the wireless—it felt as if he were shouting at a bunch of deaf men, and he couldn't tell if he was getting through or not. *This* speech was going out over the wireless, too, and it would go complete with shouts of approval and excitement from the crowd.

This is the way it ought to be, he thought, and resumed:

"People say we're gonna have trouble electing me. People say that, but they don't always know what the devil they're talking about. And you tell me, friends—haven't the Confederate States got themselves enough trouble already?"

"Yes!" people shouted, and, "Hell, yes!" and, "You bet!" One woman cried, "Oh, Jake!" as if they were in bed together and he'd just given her the best time she'd ever had in her life.

His grin got wider. Maybe he'd have a flunky look for her after the speech was done. And maybe he wouldn't, too; he couldn't afford to get too much of a reputation as a tomcatting man, not when so many people who went to church every Sunday were likely to vote Freedom. He hated compromise, but that was one he'd had to make.

"Haven't we got ourselves enough trouble?" he said again. "Folks, I tell you, the Whigs have been carrying the ball too long. They've been carrying it too long, and now they've gone and dropped it." He slammed his fist down on the podium.

More applause from the crowd. Cries of, "Tell 'em, Jake!" and, "Give 'em hell!" rang out over the general din. They might have been listening to a preacher on the revival circuit, not an ordinary politician. Jake Featherston *wasn't* an ordinary politician, which was both his greatest weakness and his greatest strength.

"They've gone and dropped it," he repeated—again, as a preacher might have. "What else would you call it when here in the middle of July, a good month after the flood finally started going down, the Confederate States of America have still got more than half a million people—half a million, I tell you, and I'm not lying; it's what the Confederate Red Cross says—living in tents? If that's not a shame and a disgrace, you tell me what it is."

A lot of those people, maybe a majority, were colored cotton pickers who worked for white plantation owners in what differed from slavery in little more than name. More often than not, Jake would have gloated at their suffering. But if he could use them as a club with which to beat the present administration, he would.

He went on, "Up in the USA, there's not a soul still stuck in a tent. Oh, I know they didn't get hurt as bad as we did, but it makes a point. When the Yankees need to get things done, they up and do 'em. When we need to get things done, what happens?" He threw his arms wide in extravagant disgust. "Not a damn thing, that's what! I tell you, folks, you're just lucky New Orleans didn't go out to sea, on account of the government in Richmond wouldn't've done a thing—not a single, solitary thing—to stop it if it had."

That drew more applause: baying, angry applause. *They know I'm telling the truth,* he thought. Being a Whig meant doing as little as you could to get by.

The line wasn't in the text of his speech, but he used it, adding, "Folks say that works all right. Maybe it did, once upon a time. But this here ain't no fairy tale, and we haven't got no happy ending. People, we need a government in Richmond that'll stand up on its hind legs and *do* things.

"Who stumbled into the war? The Whigs! Who let the niggers stab us in the back without even knowing they were going to? The Whigs! Who went and *lost* the war? The Whigs!" Now the crowd shouted out the name of the CSA's longtime ruling party with him. He rolled on: "Who let the damnyankees steal Kentucky? The Whigs! Who let 'em steal Sequoyah? The Whigs! Who let 'em cut Texas in half? The Whigs! Who let 'em take northern Virginia away from us? The Whigs! I fought in the Army of Northern Virginia, and I'm proud of it, but the Yankees have taken the place away from us. And who let the Yankees tell us what we could do with our Army and Navy? Who left us too weak to fight back when those bastards started throwing their weight around? The Whigs again!"

He slammed his fist down on the podium. The crowd in the hall roared. They might have been so many coon dogs taking a scent. Featherston took a scent from them, too. If he didn't make a crowd hot and sweaty, he wasn't doing his job. His nose told him he was tonight.

"They've done everything they could to tear this country down," he went on. "Now they had their day

251

once. I give 'em that. Jeff Davis was a great president. Nobody can say different. So was Lee. So was Longstreet. But that was a long time ago. We had friends back then. Where are our friends now? The Frenchmen have the Kaiser on their back. England's trying to keep from starving every year. We're on our own, and the Whigs are too damn dumb to know it. God helps the people who help themselves. And as long as the Whigs hang on in Richmond, God better help us, 'cause we'll need it bad!"

That got him a laugh. He'd known it would. He understood that it should. But it wasn't funny to him. The contempt and hatred he felt for the Whigs—for all the Confederate elite, including the secondand thirdgeneration officers who'd done so much to lose the Great War—were big as the world. They hadn't given him a chance to show what he could do, no matter how right he'd been. In fact, they'd scorned him all the more *because* he'd been right.

Just see what I do if I win this election, you sons of bitches, he thought. *Just you see then.*

Meanwhile, he had this speech to finish: "If you want to go on the way the Confederate States have been going, you vote Whig," he thundered. "If you want your country to go straight down the toilet, that's the way to vote." He got another laugh there, an enormous one. He continued, "The Supreme Court says you can keep on having just what you've had—and aren't you lucky?" Their day would come, too. He'd promised himself that. "But if you want change, if you want strength, if you want pride—if you want to be able to look at yourselves in the mirror and look the USA straight in the eye, y'all vote . . ."

"Freedom!"

The shout from the crowd, more than a thousand voices speaking as one, made his ears ring. He threw up his hands. "That's right, folks. Thank you. And remember—no matter what else you do, *fight hard!*"

More applause shook the hall as he stepped away from the podium. The house lights came up, so he could see the people he'd been haranguing. He waved to them again. "Freedom! Freedom! Freedom!" they chanted, over and over again. The rhythmic cry rolled through him, rolled under him, and swept him along on its crest. He'd read somewhere that in the Sandwich Islands the natives rode waves lying or even standing up on flat boards. He supposed that was true. If it weren't true, who could make it up? He felt something like that now, buoyed up by the crowd's enthusiasm.

As he went offstage, the bodyguards and other men who'd come west from Virginia with him pumped his hand and told him what a great speech he'd given. "Thanks, boys," he said, and then, "For Christ's sake, somebody get me a drink!"

Louisiana had never surrendered to the siren song of prohibition. He could drink his whiskey here without shame or hypocrisy. It seared his throat and sent warmth exploding out from his middle. As soon as he emptied the glass, somebody got him a fresh one.

He sipped the second drink more slowly. *Got to keep my wits about me,* he thought. Not everybody was going to like the speech as well as his flunkies had.

No sooner had that thought crossed his mind than a tall, blond, handsome man in a suit that must have cost plenty came up and shook hands with him. "You gave 'em hell out there tonight, Jake," he said, a Texas twang in his voice.

"I thank you kindly, Willy," Featherston answered. Willy Knight had headed up the Redemption League, an outfit with goals much like those of the Freedom Party, till the bigger Party enfolded it. He wasn't the best number-two man around, mostly because he still had thoughts of being number one.

"Damn good speech," agreed Amos Mizell. He led the Tin Hats, the biggest Confederate veterans' organization. The Tin Hats weren't formally aligned with the Freedom Party, but they shared many of the same ideas.

"Thank you, too," Jake Featherston said. Mizell wore the ribbon for a Purple Heart on his shirt. "You were out there, same as me. You know how the Whigs sold us down the river. You know how they've been selling us down the river ever since."

"Sure do." Mizell nodded. "What Willy and I aren't so sure of, though, is whether you're the fellow who's going to kick 'em out on the street where they belong."

"No, huh?" Featherston looked from one of them to the other. "You boys felt like that, how come you didn't try and keep me from getting the nomination last month?" He wanted his enemies out there in the open where he could see them and smash them, not lurking in dead leaves like a couple of rattlesnakes.

"Wouldn't've been much point to that, on account of we'd've lost," Willy Knight said. "We'll see how you do come November, and we'll go from there. You really think you're going to win?"

Featherston made an impatient, scornful gesture. "That's to keep the troops happy, and you know it as well as I do. I'm hoping I finish ahead of the damn Rad Libs, and that we hold our ground in Congress. I think we can do that." He hoped the Freedom Party could do that. Before the great flood, he wouldn't even have bet on so much. But the flood had shown that the Whigs weren't so slick as they thought they were, and that they didn't respond well in emergencies. Some voters, at least, would see the light.

Knight and Mizell looked at each other. "All right, Jake," Knight said at last. "That sounds fair. If the Party does that well come fall, we'll keep on backing your play. But if we take another hammering, the way we did in the last couple of Congressional elections, everybody's gonna have to do a lot of thinking."

"I carried the Freedom Party on my back, God damn it," Jake growled.

"Nobody says you didn't, so keep your shirt on." Willy Knight was a bigger man than Featherston, but Jake, in a fury, was a match for anybody. Knight knew it, too. Still speaking placatingly, he went on, "Moses took the Hebrews out of Egypt, but he wasn't the one who got 'em into the Promised Land."

Amos Mizell nodded. "If the Party's vote slips again, the Tin Hats will have to think about getting what we want some other way."

Featherston had thought he wanted enemies openly declared. Now he had them, and wished he didn't. "And I suppose the two of you will try and screw me over so we don't get what I said we would."

They almost fell over themselves denying it. "As long as we do what you said we'd do, we're still in business," Knight said. "If we fall down now, who knows if there'll be any pieces worth picking up later on? We're still with you."

"You'd better be," Jake said. "Let's see what happens in November, then, and afterwards." Knight and Mizell both nodded. Featherston shook hands with each of them in turn. *And if you bastards think I'll let go without a fight even if things do go wrong, you're a hell of a lot dumber than I think you are.*

In the Terry, the colored district of Augusta, Georgia, Election Day meant next to nothing. Only a handful of Negro veterans of the Great War were registered to vote. To most people, it was just another Tuesday.

As usual, Erasmus was in his fish store and restaurant when Scipio walked in. Scipio got himself a cup of coffee to drink while sweeping up the place. His boss was setting newly bought fish on ice in the counter. Scipio said, "What you think? De Whigs gwine win again?"

"Dunno," Erasmus said with a shrug. "Them or the Rad Libs, don't matter one way or t'other. Long as it ain't that goddamn crazy man." He threw a crappie into place with more force than he usually used while handling fish. That Election Day meant next to nothing didn't mean it meant nothing at all.

"Dat Featherston buckra, he ain't gwine do nothin' much," Scipio said.

"Better not," Erasmus answered, and slammed down a gutted catfish. "That son of a bitch win, everything's even tougher for us niggers. And things is tough enough as they is."

Voice sly, Scipio said. "You ain't got it so bad. You owns your house free an' clear—"

"I ain't stupid," Erasmus said, and Scipio nodded. His

boss had been damn smart there. He'd paid off his mortgage just when inflation was starting to ravage the CSA, when he'd had a pretty easy time accumulating the money he needed but before Confederate dollars became nothing but a joke. The bankers had taken the money, even if they'd been unhappy about it. A few weeks later and they would have refused him. "I ain't stupid," he repeated. "I'm smart enough to know I ain't got it easy long as I's a nigger in the CSA."

He was right about that. Scipio didn't need to be a genius to understand as much. He said, "No, you ain't got it easy—I takes it back. But you has it worse—all us niggers has it worse—if dat Featherston, he win." Working for Anne Colleton had given him a feel for the way Confederate politics worked. Again, though, he didn't need to be a genius to find the truth in what he'd just said.

"Not so many parades with them goddamn white men in the white shirts an' the butternut pants yellin', 'Freedom!' this year," Erasmus observed. "They ain't been tryin' to bust up the other parties' meetin's, neither, like they done before. They walkin' sof' again."

"Don' want to remind nobody what that one buckra done," Scipio said. "But too many folks, dey recollects any which way."

"Hell, yes," Erasmus said. "Thing of it is, Freedom Party, they needs the white folks to be stupid, or else to *act* stupid on account of they scared. Now, Lord knows the white folks is stupid—"

"Do Jesus, yes!" Scipio said, as if responding to a preacher's sermon.

"But they ain't *that* stupid, not unless they's scared *bad*," Erasmus went on, as if he hadn't spoken. "Things ain't too bad for 'em right now—money's still worth somethin', most of 'em's got jobs—so they ain't gwine vote for no Jake Featherston, not this year they ain't. That's how I sees it, anyways."

"Way *I* sees it, you should oughta write fo' de newspapers," Scipio said, not intending it as any sort of flattery. On the contrary—he'd read plenty of editorials about what was likely to happen that didn't sum things up anywhere near so neatly as his illiterate but ever so shrewd boss had managed in a couple of sentences.

Erasmus lit a cigarette. He blew out a cloud of smoke, then said, "You bangin' your gums on all this politics so as you kin git out o' workin'—ain't that right, Xerxes?"

"Oh, yassuh, Marse Erasmus, suh." Scipio laid on his Low Country accent even thicker than usual. "Ah ain't nevah done one lick o' work, not since de day you hire me. Ah jus' eats yo' food an' drinks yo' coffee an' steals yo' smokes." He held out his hand, pale palm up, for a cigarette.

Laughing, Erasmus gave him one, then leaned close so Scipio could get a light from the one he already had in his mouth. He'd just taken his first drag of the morning and coughed a couple of times when the first customer of the day came in, calling for coffee and ham and eggs and, instead of grits, hash browns. Erasmus got busy at the stove. Scipio got busier doing everything else. They stayed busy all day long. When Scipio finally went home, Erasmus was still busy. Scipio sometimes wondered whether his boss ever went to bed.

And when Scipio got back to his roominghouse, he heard splashes and squeals from the bathroom at the end of the hall. He also heard Bathsheba's voice, rising in ever-growing exasperation and wrath. He smiled to himself. Antoinette was going on two years old now, and an ever-growing handful to bathe.

A few minutes later, Bathsheba carried the baby into the room. Antoinette, swaddled in a towel, saw Scipio and said, "Dada!" in delight. Scipio's wife looked wetter than the baby did. She also looked a lot less happy.

"What de matter, sweetheart?" Scipio asked. "Givin' 'Toinette a bath ain't dat hard. I even done it my ownself a time or two." He spoke as if that were some enormous accomplishment. In his mind, it was. He hadn't heard many fathers talk about giving their children even that much in the way of care.

But Bathsheba's baleful stare made him stop with his mouth half open. "The baby shit in the damn tub," she said bleakly.

"Oh," Scipio said. "Aw . . . golly." The first expression

257

of sympathy that came to mind wouldn't have been to Bathsheba's liking, not just then.

Instead of saying anything, Scipio went to a cupboard and pulled out a bottle of moonshine. Georgia was officially dry, but contraband liquor wasn't hard to come by. He poured his wife a stiff drink, and a smaller one for himself. Holding out the glass to Bathsheba, he said, "Here you is. Reckon you done earned dis here."

"Reckon I did." She poured down half of it. Then she puffed out her cheeks and exhaled violently. "Whew! Dat's nasty stuff." Scipio was inclined to agree. He'd always preferred rum even to good whiskey, and the murky yellowish fluid in his glass bore a closer relationship to paint thinner than it did to good whiskey.

Antoinette saw her parents drinking something, and naturally wanted some, too. Bathsheba fixed her a bottle. Then she started making supper. Since the room had only a hot plate for cooking, everything took a while. Scipio was glad for the chance to sit down and play with his little girl and talk with his wife and drink the moonshine and let it relax him.

"Buckra ladies I was cleanin' for, they all talkin' 'bout the election today," Bathsheba said. "Dunno why. They can't vote any more'n us black folks kin."

Bills allowing women's suffrage showed up in the Georgia Legislature almost every session. They got tabled or voted down with monotonous regularity. Even so, Scipio asked, "Who dey say dey husbands vote fo'?"

"Whigs, mostly." Bathsheba knew why he was worried, and added, "That Featherston fella, don't reckon he gwine go nowhere much."

"Do Jesus, hope you right," Scipio answered.

Bathsheba took lamb chops out of the pan and started frying potatoes in the grease they'd left behind. "Got me somethin' more important to tell you, anyways."

"What dat?" Scipio asked as he stuck a little bite of lamb in Antoinette's mouth. The baby made a face, but ate the morsel. Scipio gave her another one.

Bathsheba pointed at her. "Reckon she gwine have herself a little brother or sister come summertime."

"I was wonderin' about dat my ownself," Scipio said as he got up to give her a hug. "Didn't t'ink you monthlies, dey come." Her breasts had been tender lately, too, and she'd started falling asleep early in the evening.

As if to prove he was right, Bathsheba yawned. She laughed a moment later. "Better sleep now. When the new young 'un come, ain't never gwine sleep again."

"We gots to find a bigger place, too," Scipio said. The room they had was intended for one. It was tolerable for two, provided they got on well—which Scipio and Bathsheba certainly did. With three in it, there wasn't room to swing a cat. With four ... Scipio thought about that. With four people in this room, there wouldn't have been room to bring in a cat, let alone swing it.

"What you reckon Antoinette make o' the new baby?" Bathsheba asked.

"She ain't gwine like it," Scipio answered. "Young chillun, dey don' never like no new baby in de fambly. But she git over it. She have to. Dey allus does. Jus' sometimes take longer, is all."

Bathsheba nodded. "Reckon you's right." She yawned again. "I gots to get to sleep. Come here, 'Toinette. Time we both go to bed."

The baby didn't want to. She was convinced she'd miss something. Some evenings she was right, others wrong. Tonight, she fussed and fumed—and then got up the following morning not just ready but eager to play. Scipio was the one who, yawning, went out to face the day.

He paid his five cents for a copy of the *Constitutionalist* on his way to Erasmus' place. Newsboys shouted of Burton Mitchel's victory as president of the Confederate States. "President Mitchel reelected!" they yelled. A Confederate president wasn't supposed to get reelected, but the Supreme Court said this didn't count. No matter what the Supreme Court said, the newsboys knew what was what.

The Whigs had won easily this time, nothing like their razor-thin victory in 1921. The Freedom Party took Tennessee, Mississippi, and Texas, the Radical Liberals Arkansas and Chihuahua. Sonora still looked too close to call. Everywhere else, the people had voted Whig.

Scipio read that with more relief than he'd felt for a long time. Life in the CSA was hard enough for a black man any time. He imagined going to bed one morning and waking up to discover Jake Featherston was president. The mere idea chilled him worse than the cool November morning.

He methodically worked his way through the election stories below the headlines. The Freedom Party hadn't taken quite so many lumps as he would have liked to see. It had lost one Senator, but gained a pair of Congressmen— maybe three, because one of the races in Texas remained very tight.

"I may not be going to the Gray House next March," the *Constitutionalist* quoted Featherston as saying, "but we'll make ourselves heard in Congress, and in state houses all over the country. We aren't about to go away, no matter how much the Whigs wish we would. We're just reloading for the next round of the fight."

He'd lost. He hadn't come close to winning. But he still sounded confident right was on his side, and that he'd win one of these days. He reminded Scipio of nothing so much as Cassius and the other colored Reds who'd formed the ill-fated government of the Congaree Socialist Republic and dragged him into it. Their faith in the dialectic had kept them going through thick and thin. Jake Featherston sounded like a man with the same kind of faith.

He'd kill me if I could tell him so, Scipio thought. *The Reds would kill me, too—if they weren't already dead themselves.* No, neither side here would see its resemblance to the other. That didn't mean the resemblance wasn't there.

The Reds had proved wrong—dead wrong—about the dialectic. With any luck, the Freedom Party would prove just as wrong. That thought heartened Scipio. He tossed the *Constitutionalist* into a trash can and hurried to work. Erasmus would skin him if he was late.

The first time Sam Carsten had seen the *Remembrance*— going on ten years ago now, which struck him as very strange—he'd thought her the ugliest, funniest-looking ship in the U.S. Navy, or, for that matter, in anyone else's. She'd started out life intending to be a battle cruiser, but had had her design drastically revised while she was a-building. Back in those distant days not long after the Great War, nobody had seen a ship with a flight deck so she could launch and land aeroplanes.

Now, as Sam returned to the *Remembrance*, she still looked strange. He shook his head as the boat neared the carrier. No, that wasn't right. She looked strange all over again, but for different reasons this time. By now, the Navy had three aeroplane carriers that had been built for the purpose from the keel up. They were a lot more capable than the *Remembrance*, which looked like the hybrid she was.

She may not be pretty, but she gets the job done, he thought. The boat from the *O'Brien* came alongside. Sailors up on the *Remembrance* lowered a rope ladder. Carsten shouldered his duffel bag.

"Good luck, sir," one of the sailors said. "You're going from a little fish to a big one."

"Thanks, Fritz," Carsten answered. He grabbed the ladder and swarmed up it, as if boarding with intent to take the ship rather than to serve in her. He knew a lot of eyes were watching him. If he acted like a gouty old man on the way up from the boat, they'd treat him with less respect than if he did his best impression of a pirate.

As he scrambled up onto the *Remembrance*'s broad, flat deck, a sailor leaped forward and grabbed the canvas duffel bag. "Let me take that for you, sir," the fellow said. By his tone, Carsten had passed his first test.

A lieutenant commander strolled up at a more leisurely pace. Sam stiffened to attention and saluted. "Permission to come aboard, sir?" he said formally.

"Granted." The other officer returned his salute. Then he smiled. "My name is Watkins, Ensign. Michael Watkins. Do I understand this is your second tour aboard the *Remembrance*?"

"Pleased to meet you, sir. Yes, sir, I've spent some time on her before," Carsten answered. "But that was a while ago—I was just thinking about how long it seems—and I was only a petty officer in those days."

"Oh, really? I didn't know that." Watkins' voice gave no clue as to what he thought about it, either. "So you're a mustang, eh? Up through the hawse hole?"

Sam nodded. "That's me." Not a whole lot of men jumped from rating to officer. He supposed he should have been proud of himself. Hell, he *was* proud of himself, when he had time to think about it.

"I'm going to ask you one question, Carsten, and I hope you won't take it the wrong way," Lieutenant Commander Watkins said. Sam nodded. He had a pretty good idea what the question would be. And, sure enough, Watkins asked, "You do remember you *are* an officer now, I hope?"

Carsten nodded again. "I do my best, sir." He'd seen a couple of other mustangs—both of them men fifteen or twenty years older than he was—who'd been promoted during the war for bravery too conspicuous to ignore. Both of them acted as if they were still CPOs. He understood that—they'd got set in their ways long before their promotions—but he didn't try to imitate it.

He seemed to have satisfied Watkins. "Fair enough, Ensign," the *Remembrance*'s officer said. "I'll take you to your quarters. Dougherty, follow us."

"Aye aye, sir," said the sailor who had Sam's duffel bag. He was redheaded and freckled and very fair.

"Pharmacist's mate still carry plenty of zinc-oxide ointment and such?" Sam asked him.

Dougherty gauged his pale blond hair, blue eyes, and pink, pink skin. "Well, yes, sir," he answered. "Don't know how much you'll need it, though, in January off Baltimore." He jerked his chin toward the gray, cloudy sky.

"You never can tell. I'll burn damn near anywhere," Carsten said. The sailor smiled, Sam thought in sympathy. Dougherty certainly looked as if he too would burn under any light brighter than a kerosene lantern's.

Lieutenant Commander Watkins opened a steel door. "Here you are, Ensign," he said, flipping on a switch to turn on the lamp inside the cabin. As he stepped back to let Sam see in, he apologetically spread his hands and added, "Sorry it's so small, but it's what we've got."

"That's all right, sir," Sam said. "It's a lot more room than I had my last tour aboard her. They still triple-deck the bunks, don't they?" He waited for Watkins to nod, then went on, "And I served in one of the five-inch gun sponsons, so I didn't have any room there, either."

"Ah." Watkins started to nod and let that go, but then his gaze sharpened. "Were you aboard *Remembrance* when she took fire off Belfast?"

"I sure as hell was, sir," Carsten answered. "A shell killed two men in my crew. Only dumb luck none of the fragments got me."

"Well, well," Lieutenant Commander Watkins said. "I wonder if we have any men still aboard who served with you."

"Been five years, sir. I haven't seen any yet, not that that proves anything," Sam said. "I'd like to say hello if I do, but I don't suppose I could do much more than that, could I?"

"I wouldn't think so, Ensign," Watkins told him. "This is part of what I meant when I asked if you remembered you were an officer." Sam nodded; he'd figured that out for himself. Watkins stepped back. "I won't keep you any more—you'll want to get settled in, I'm sure. I hope to see you and talk with you more later on."

"Thank you, sir." Carsten saluted.

"My pleasure." Watkins returned the salute. "Come along, Dougherty," he said, and walked on down the corridor.

Sam closed and dogged the door to his cabin. He'd been telling the truth when he said it was spacious compared to his previous accommodations on the *Remembrance*. That didn't mean he had much room. If he stood with arms outstretched, he could touch the gray-painted metal walls with his fingertips. The cabin held a bunk, a steel chest of drawers bolted to the opposite wall, a steel desk, a chair, and a tiny washbasin with a steel mirror above it. All that left him just about enough room to put his feet down, provided he was careful doing it.

Stowing his worldly goods, such as they were, didn't take long. Then he went out on deck once more. The

O'Brien, having delivered him, steamed away, smoke pouring from her four stacks. The *Remembrance* pushed south through heavy seas. The rolling and pitching didn't bother Sam. He'd always had good sea legs and a calm stomach; his Achilles' heel was his pale skin.

Back toward the stern, a couple of mechanics worked on an aeroplane. The machine looked sleeker and more powerful than the modified Great War–vintage aeroplanes that had flown off the *Remembrance* during Carsten's last tour aboard her. *I'd better bone up on what the differences are,* he thought.

He didn't get to stand around watching for very long. A respectful petty officer soon came up to him and whisked him over to the office of a gray-haired commander named van der Waal. "What do you know about minimizing damage from torpedo hits?" the other officer demanded.

"Sir, I was aboard the *Dakota* when the Japs put a fish into her off the Sandwich Islands, but I didn't have anything to do with damage control there," Sam answered.

"All right, that's a little something, anyhow," van der Waal said. "You've experienced the problem firsthand, which is good. That's more than a lot of people can say. Does it interest you?"

"No, sir. Not a whole lot," Carsten said honestly. "I served a gun before I was an officer, and I'm interested in aeronautics, too. That's how I came aboard the *Remembrance* during my first tour here."

"Naval aeronautics is important. I'd have a hard time telling you anything different, wouldn't I, here on an aeroplane carrier?" Commander van der Waal's craggy face creased in unaccustomed places when he smiled. But he quickly turned serious again. "But so is damage control. The Japs aren't the only ones who've got submersibles, you know." He looked south and west, in the direction of the CSA.

"The Confederates aren't supposed to have 'em!" Sam blurted.

"I know that. And I know we send inspectors up and down their coast to make sure they don't," van der Waal told him. "But I'd bet they've got a few anyhow—and we haven't been inspecting as hard as we might have the past few years. The budget keeps going down, and President Sinclair wants to get along with everybody. And the British still have some boats, and the French might, and we know perfectly well that the Japanese do. And so does the German High Seas Fleet. And so, Ensign . . ."

"I see your point, sir," Sam said, knowing he couldn't very well say anything else. "If that's what you want me to do, I'll do it." He couldn't very well say anything but that, either. Then he dredged up a childhood expression: "But if I had my druthers, it's not what I'd do."

Van der Waal chuckled. "Haven't heard that one in a while. You gave up your druthers, you know, when you put on the uniform."

"Really, sir? I never would have noticed." Some men would have wound up in trouble after talking back to a superior officer that way. Carsten did have a knack for not getting people angry at him.

Commander van der Waal said, "Well, we'll see what happens. You'll start out in my shop, because I do need a man to back me up. If another opportunity comes along and you want to take it, I don't suppose I'd stand in your way. Fair enough?"

"More than fair enough, sir. It's damn white of you, matter of fact." Sam saluted. Most officers would have grabbed him and held on to him, and that would have been that. "Thank you very much!"

"I don't want a badly disaffected man serving under me. It's not good for me, it wouldn't be good for the officer in question, and it's not good for the ship." Van der Waal nodded briskly. "For now, you're dismissed."

Sam saluted again and went out on deck. He spied a knot of sailors at the starboard bow. They were all pointing in the direction van der Waal had—toward the Confederate States. Carsten looked that way himself. He had no trouble spotting the Confederate coast-defense ship steaming along between the *Remembrance* and the shore.

Like one of the U.S. Navy's so-called Great Lakes battleships, the Confederate warship was only about half the size of a real battlewagon. She'd carry a battleship's guns, but only half as many of them as, say, the *Dakota*. She wouldn't have the armor or the speed to take on a first-class battleship, either. And she and her three sisters were the biggest warships the C.S. Navy was allowed to have.

What does her skipper think, looking at the Remembrance? Carsten wondered. He could sink her if they fought gun to gun; the aeroplane carrier had nothing bigger than five-inchers aboard. But they wouldn't fight gun to gun, not unless something went horribly wrong. And how would that Confederate captain like to try shooting down aeroplanes that could drop bombs on his head or put torpedoes in the water running straight at his ship?

He wouldn't like it for hell, Sam thought. His grin stretched wide as the Atlantic. He liked the idea just fine himself.

Nellie Jacobs was keeping one eye on the coffeehouse and the other on Clara's arithmetic homework when Clara's half sister, Edna Grimes, burst into the place. That Clara was going on eight years old, and so old enough to have homework, surprised Nellie. That Edna should come bursting in astonished her.

Then Nellie got a look at her older daughter's face, and astonishment turned to alarm. "Good heavens, Edna! What's wrong?" she asked. "Are you all right? Are Merle and Armstrong?"

"Armstrong is a brat," Clara declared. Anything might have distracted her from the problems in her workbook. The mention of her nephew—who was only a couple of years younger than she was—more than sufficed.

Only a couple of customers were working on coffee and, in one case, a sandwich. Business would pick up after government offices closed in another forty-five minutes. Nellie hoped it would, anyhow. It had been a slow day—whenever snow fell in Washington, it tied the city in knots.

Nellie expected Edna to go into one of the back rooms before saying whatever was on her mind. That way, the men wouldn't be able to eavesdrop. But her daughter said,

"Oh, Ma, I don't know what to do! Merle's found out about Nick Kincaid!"

"Oh," Nellie said, and then, "Oh, Lordy."

"Who's Nick Kincaid, Edna?" Clara asked.

"He was a . . . a fellow I used to know, a soldier," Edna answered. "I was going to marry him, maybe, but he got killed in the war."

That told Clara enough to satisfy her. It didn't say everything there was to say on the subject, not by a long chalk. Edna had certainly been about to marry Lieutenant Nicholas H. Kincaid; she'd been walking down the aisle with him when U.S. artillery fire tore off his head. The other thing she'd neglected to tell her half sister was that Kincaid had been a soldier, all right, but one who fought for the Confederate States.

"Well, dear," Nellie said, as coolly as she could, "you knew this was liable to happen one of these days." She was, if anything, amazed it hadn't happened sooner.

Edna said, "When it didn't happen for so long, I reckoned it never would. And you know how Merle is, how he always put me on a pedestal."

Most men, Nellie was convinced, put women on pedestals so they could look up their skirts. But she found herself nodding. Merle Grimes was different—or had been different. He'd lost his first wife during the great influenza epidemic of 1918. Since meeting Edna and falling in love with her, he'd made as good a husband as any woman could want—better than Edna deserved, Nellie often thought.

Edna never would have gone up on that pedestal if Merle (who had a Purple Heart—a U.S. Purple Heart) had known everything—or even most things—about Nick Kincaid. What he would have thought had he known Kincaid had got Edna into bed . . . Nellie shied away from that. Sometimes the quiet ones were the worst when they did lose their tempers. Even finding out Edna's former fiancé had worn butternut and not green-gray was liable to be enough.

"What am I gonna *do*, Ma?" Edna wailed.

"How'd he find out?" Nellie asked.

"This fellow from the CSA came into his office for some kind of business or other." Now Edna had the sense to keep her voice down; one of the men drinking coffee had leaned forward to snoop a little too obviously. She went on, "They both wore Purple Heart ribbons, dammit—you know how the Confederates give 'em, too. And they got to talking soldier talk: where'd you fight, how'd you get hurt, that kind of thing."

"And?" Nellie asked.

"And one thing led to another, and they got to liking each other," Edna said. "And Merle said how he'd married a Washington gal, and that was the closest thing you could get to marrying a gal from the Confederate States. And the other fellow said that was funny, on account of his cousin had almost married this Washington gal who worked in a coffeehouse when he was here on occupation duty during the war."

"Uh-oh," Nellie said.

Edna nodded bitterly. "*Uh-oh* is right. Merle said his wife—me, I mean—was working in a coffeehouse when he met her, too. And they went and talked a little more, and they figured out they were both talking about the same gal. And I got this phone call from Merle, and I didn't like the way he sounded, not for beans I didn't, and so I left Armstrong with Mrs. Parker next door—he was playing with her boy Eddie anyways—and I came over here."

"All right, dear," Nellie said. "I may not be much, but I'm what you've always got, and that's for sure." Edna nodded, biting her lip and blinking back tears. There had been times when Nellie hoped she would never see her daughter again, not a few of them when Edna was fooling around with the late Confederate Lieutenant Kincaid. But Edna was what Nellie had, too, and always would be. It wasn't that she didn't love Clara, but her younger daughter often felt more like an afterthought or an accident than flesh of Nellie's flesh. Of course, Edna had been an accident, too, but that was a long time ago now.

"What am I gonna do, Ma?" Edna asked again.

"Just remember, sweetie, your husband ain't the only one in the family who's got himself a medal," Nellie said.

"He starts going on about you selling out your country, you hit him over the head with the Order of Remembrance. For heaven's sakes, Teddy Roosevelt put it on you his very own self."

"That's true." Edna brightened a little. "That *is* true." But then she turned pale. She pointed out through the big glass window in front. "Oh, Jesus, Ma, there he is."

"Nothing bad's going to happen," Nellie said, though she knew she couldn't be sure of any such thing. Edna's husband was a quiet fellow, yes, but. . . .

The bell above the door chimed cheerily as Merle Grimes walked into the coffeehouse. The rubber tip on his cane tapped against the linoleum floor. Behind the lenses of his spectacles, his eyes had a blind, stricken look, as if he'd had too much to drink, but Nellie didn't think he was drunk.

He nodded jerkily to her before swinging his gaze towards Edna. "When you weren't home, I figured I'd find you here," he said. She nodded, too. Grimes gestured with his cane. By the way he aimed it at Edna, Nellie thanked God it wasn't a Springfield. What came out of his mouth, though, was only one more word: "Why?"

Before Edna could say anything, Nellie told Clara, "Go upstairs. Go right now. This is grownup stuff." Clara didn't argue. Nellie's tone got through. Her younger daughter took her homework and all but fled.

"On account of if I told you I was . . . friendly with a Confederate soldier back in them days I thought I'd lose you, and I didn't want to lose you," Edna answered. "I didn't want to lose you on account of I love you. I always have. I always will."

It was, Nellie thought, about the best answer her daughter could have given. But when her son-in-law said, "You lied to me," Nellie knew it was liable not to be good enough. "You lied to me," Merle Grimes repeated. It might have been the very worst thing he could think of to say. "I thought I knew you, and everything I thought I knew . . . I didn't know."

One of the customers got up and left. A moment later, more reluctantly, so did the other one. Nellie went to the door behind him. She closed it in the face of a woman who started to come in. "Sorry—we're closed," she told the startled woman. She flipped the sign in the window to CLOSED, too. That was going to cost her money, but it couldn't be helped.

When she walked back behind the counter, Edna was saying, "—so sorry. But that was before I knew you, Merle, remember. I've never done nothing to make you sorry since, so help me God I haven't."

"I'd have believed you yesterday, because I'd've been sure you were telling me the truth," her husband said. "Now . . . How do I know it's not just another lie?"

"Edna wouldn't do nothing like that, Merle," Nellie said. "You think about that, you'll know it's true." She liked Merle Grimes enough to want to do everything she could to keep him in the family. Even if she had her problems with Edna, her son-in-law was the kind of man who tempted her to forget her low opinion of half the human race.

She didn't mollify him, though. The look he gave her was colder than the weather outside. "You must have known about this Kincaid fellow, Mother Jacobs—you couldn't very well not have. And you never said a word about him to me. So why should I believe you, either?"

"We said Edna had a fiancé during the war, and that he got killed," Nellie said. "Is that the truth or isn't it?"

"It's less than half the truth," Merle Grimes said stubbornly. "That's the best way I know how to lie—tell the part of the truth that goes your way, and leave out everything else."

He was right, of course. That was the best way Nellie knew how to lie, too. She said, "The man's dead, Merle. He's more than ten years dead now. You can just forget about him. Everybody else has."

Grimes shook his head. "That's not the point. What's more, you know it's not the point, Mother Jacobs. The point is that he was a . . . darned Confederate, and that Edna never told me about that. I've tried to take care of her and Armstrong. I've saved money. I've bought stocks. If she had told me, I don't know what I'd've done.

Washington was occupied, after all. Those things happened. But trying to sweep 'em under the rug afterwards . . ." He shook his head again. "No."

Nellie didn't like the grim finality in his voice. Tears trickled down Edna's face. *Sweet Jesus, she really thinks she's going to lose him right here and now,* Nellie thought, fighting against panic of her own. *She may be right, too.*

Before she or Edna could say anything, the bell over the door chimed again. In came Hal Jacobs. "I saw you put out the CLOSED sign from across the street," Nellie's husband said. "Why so early?"

"We're having a—a family discussion, that's why," Nellie answered.

"I've found out about Nicholas Kincaid, Father Jacobs," Merle Grimes said, sounding even harder than he had before. "I've found out *all* about him."

"Have you?" Hal whuffled out air through his gray mustache—almost entirely white now, in fact. "I doubt that. Yes, sir, I doubt it very much."

"What do you mean?" Grimes demanded. "I know he was a Confederate officer. I know he was going to marry Edna till he got killed. And I know she never told me what he was. What else do I need to know?"

As far as Nellie could see, that was plenty. But Hal Jacobs said, "The other thing you need to know is what Teddy Roosevelt knew, God rest his soul—Edna and Nellie were both spies during the war, working with me and Bill Reach, God rest his soul, too, for I'm sure he's dead." Nellie was even surer, but her secrets, unlike Edna's, were unlikely to come out. Her husband went on, "Whatever Edna told you—and whatever she didn't, too—she asked me about first, because of what we were doing. Do you understand what I'm saying?"

Behind his spectacles, Grimes' eyes widened. "I . . . think I may, sir," he answered. Unconsciously, he straightened towards, if not quite to, attention. But then his gaze swung back to Edna. "Don't you think almost marrying a Confederate went too far?"

Oh, she went further than that, Nellie thought. Wild horses wouldn't have dragged the words from her, though.

271

And Edna did a splendid job of picking up the cue Hal had given her. "I didn't almost marry him on account of I was a spy," she replied. "But Washington was occupied, like you said yourself. And Hal asked me not to talk about anything that went on that had to do with the coffeehouse and spying even a little bit, just to be on the safe side. So I didn't."

Hal had never asked her to do any such thing. He knew that, and so did Nellie, and so did Edna herself. But Merle Grimes didn't know it, and he was the one who counted here. "All right," he said after a long, long pause. "We'll let it go, then. God knows I do love you, Edna, and I want to be able to love you and trust you the rest of my days."

Edna did the smartest thing she could have: instead of saying even a word, she threw herself into Merle's arms. As the two of them embraced, Nellie caught Hal's eye. *Thank you,* she mouthed silently. Her husband gave a tiny nod and an even tinier shrug, as if to say it wasn't worth getting excited about. They'd been married for almost ten years. Till that moment, Nellie had never been sure she loved him. She was now.

Had Lucien Galtier not cut himself, he might not have found out for some little while that his life was about to change. It wasn't a bad wound, like the time when he'd laid his leg open with an axe. But he was sharpening a stake that would support some green beans when spring came, and the knife slipped, and he gashed himself between thumb and forefinger.

" *'Osti,*" he hissed. " *Calisse de tabernac.*" He put down the knife and the stake, pinched the lips of the wound shut, and went to the house to get a clean bandage. He hoped that would do the job, and that he wouldn't need stitches. If he did, though, he was reasonably sure he could get them for nothing. There were advantages to having a doctor for a son-in-law, even if Leonard O'Doull would tease him for being a clumsy old fool even as he sewed him up. Lucien hurried up the stairs, quietly wiped his boots on the thick, soft mat in front of the kitchen door, and went inside.

Marie was sitting at the kitchen table, one hand on her belly, tears running down her face.

"Marie?" Galtier whispered, his own cut forgotten. His right hand dropped to his side. Blood started dripping on the floor. "Qu'est-ce que tu as?"

"It's nothing," she said, springing to her feet with as much dismay and guilt as if he'd caught her in the arms of another man. "Nothing, I tell you. What have you done to yourself? You're bleeding!"

He grabbed a towel and wrapped it around his left hand. "This is truly nothing," he said. "A slip of the knife, that's all. But you . . ."

Marie might pause during her day's work for a cup of tea. Never, in all the years he'd known her, had she paused because she was in pain. That was literally true; she'd gone on working till ridiculously short stretches of time before she bore her children, and she'd got back to work after each birth much sooner than the midwife said she should. For her to hold herself like that and weep was . . . *The end of the world* was the first thing that occurred to him.

An instant later, he wished he'd thought of a different comparison.

"I think it could be that we both should see our *beau-fils*," he said.

Marie shook her head. "It's nothing," she insisted. "I'm just . . . tired, that's all."

Hearing her say that frightened him as badly as seeing her sit there crying. He knew she must have been tired at times through their close to thirty-five years of marriage. She was a farm wife, and she'd raised six children. But she'd never admitted it, not in all the time he'd known her, not till now.

"Here." He went to the closet and got her a coat. "Put this on, my dear. We are going into town, to talk with Leonard O'Doull."

"I don't need to see the doctor," Marie insisted. "And how can you drive the motorcar with your poor hand hurt?"

To keep her from going on about the hand, he let her bandage it, which she did with her usual quick competence.

As long as she was taking care of him, she seemed fine. But, once she'd done the job, she argued less than he'd expected when he draped the coat over her shoulders. "Come on," he said. "Our son-in-law will tell you why you are tired, and he will give you some pills to make you feel like a new woman."

"It could be that you are the one who feels like a new woman," his wife retorted. But, that gibe aside, she kept quiet. She let him lead her out to the Chevrolet and head for town. Her acquiescence worried him, too.

Leonard O'Doull's office was on Rue Frontenac, not far from the Église Saint-Patrice on Rue Lafontaine—the church over which Bishop Pascal no longer presided. Dr. O'Doull's office assistant exclaimed when she saw the bloody bandage on Lucien's hand. "He's vaccinating a little boy right now, *Monsieur* Galtier," she said. "As soon as he's done, he'll see you."

But Lucien shook his head again. "It's not me he needs to see. It's Marie."

That made the office assistant start to exclaim again. Just in time, she thought better of it. "Sit down, then," she said. "He'll see you both soon."

A howl from the part of the office out of sight of the waiting room told Galtier exactly when the vaccination was completed. A couple of minutes later, a city woman in a fashionably—even shockingly—short dress came out with her wailing toddler in tow. Normally, Lucien would have eyed her legs while she paid the assistant. That Marie was sitting beside him wouldn't have stopped him. That Marie was sitting beside him not feeling well did.

Their son-in-law stuck his head out into the waiting room as soon as the city woman and her son left. Like his assistant, he saw Lucien's bandage and wagged a finger. "What have you gone and done to yourself now?" he asked with mock severity. "Don't you think I get tired of patching you?"

Again, Galtier said, "I didn't come to see you on account of this scratch. Marie is not well."

"No?" Dr. O'Doull became very serious very fast. He almost bowed to his mother-in-law. "Come in, please, and

274

tell me about it." As Marie rose, O'Doull nodded, ever so slightly, to Lucien. "Why don't you wait here?"

"All right," Galtier said. He knew what that meant. His son-in-law would have to look at, perhaps even have to touch, parts of Marie only Lucien would normally look at and touch. He could do that much more freely if Lucien weren't in the room with the two of them. Galtier understood the necessity without liking it.

He buried his nose in a magazine from Montreal. All the articles seemed to talk about ways in which the Republic of Quebec could become more like the United States. Galtier was far from sure he wanted Quebec to become more like the USA. The people writing the magazine articles had no doubt that was what Quebec should do.

Every so often, he noticed he was reading the same sentence over and over. It wasn't because the sentences sounded so much alike, though they did. But he couldn't stop worrying about what was going on on the far side of that door.

After the longest half hour in Galtier's life, Marie came out again. Dr. O'Doull came out with her, saying, "Please sit here for a moment, if you would." She nodded and sat down beside Lucien. O'Doull continued, "*Mon beau-père*, I would speak with you for a few minutes. Come in, please."

"Very well." Galtier didn't want to get up. He wanted to stay there beside Marie. But he saw he had no choice. "Is everything as it should be?" he asked his son-in-law.

"Well, that is what I want to talk to you about," O'Doull answered.

Numbly, Galtier walked to the door. Dr. O'Doull stood aside to let him go through. Galtier had thought he was afraid before. Now his heart threatened to burst from his chest at every beat. O'Doull waved him into his own personal office. Lucien sat in the chair in front of the desk.

His son-in-law opened a desk drawer. To Galtier's surprise, he pulled out a pint bottle of whiskey. "Medicinal," O'Doull remarked as he yanked out the cork and took a swig. He held out the bottle to Galtier. "Here. Have some."

275

"Merci." Lucien drank, too. It wasn't very good whiskey, but it was plenty strong. He coughed once or twice as he set the bottle on the desk. O'Doull corked it. With a smile that might have come straight from the gallows, Galtier asked, "And now, *mon beau-fils,* have you a bullet for me to bite on?" He'd forgotten all about his cut hand.

And so had Leonard O'Doull, which was an even worse sign. "If I did, I'd give it to you," he said. "Your wife has a . . . a mass right here, in her belly." He put his hand on his own belly, on the spot that corresponded to the one Marie had been holding when Galtier had walked into their kitchen, a little more than an hour before.

"A mass," Galtier echoed. Dr. O'Doull nodded. He had surely used the mildest word he could find to give Lucien the news. Though Galtier hadn't had much schooling, he needed only a moment to figure out what the younger man was talking about. "A tumor, do you mean?"

"I'm afraid I do," his son-in-law answered, as gently as he could. "She should have an X ray. It is possible she should have a surgical operation."

"Possible? Only possible?" Lucien said. "What does this mean?"

"It depends on what the X ray shows," O'Doull answered. "She told me she first began feeling this pain a year and a half or two years ago, though it was less then. That means it could be—God forbid, but it could be—that there has been some . . . some spread of the mass. If the X ray shows there has . . . In that case, there would be less point to an operation."

In that case, an operation would do no good, because she would die anyway. Again, Lucien didn't need his son-in-law to explain that to him. He forced his mind away from it. "She had this pain for two years?"

"So she told me," Dr. O'Doull replied.

"And she said nothing? She did nothing? In the name of God, *why?*"

O'Doull sighed, uncorked the whiskey bottle once more, and took another drink. "I've seen this before among you Quebecois. Why? Maybe because you hope the pain will go away by itself and you won't need to go to the doctor. Maybe because you simply refuse to let pain get the better of you. And maybe because you're just too busy to get out of the house and into town to do what needs to be done."

Slowly, Galtier nodded. Any or all of those reasons could have fit Marie. He didn't think he had the nerve to ask her. Even if he did, he doubted he would get a straight answer. "Is it that you can take this X-ray picture?" he asked.

"No. I have no X-ray machine here," O'Doull answered. "She will have to go to Quebec City, to the capital. If she has the operation, she will have to have it there, too."

"All right. We will do that, then." Lucien didn't hesitate, even for a moment. He wondered how much the required treatment would cost. He wished he hadn't bought the Chevrolet. If he had to, though, he could sell it. Marie mattered more than money, and that was all there was to it. He did ask, "This operation, it will cure her?"

His son-in-law's shrug was more weary and worried than Gallic. "Without knowing what the X ray will show, without knowing what the surgeon will find, how can I answer that? Be fair to me, please."

"I'm sorry." Lucien bent his head and rubbed his eyes. "Let me ask you a different question, then. You have been a doctor for a good many years now. From what you see, from what you know, what do you think the chances are?"

Leonard O'Doull's lips skinned back from his teeth in what wasn't a smile. "I wish you hadn't asked me that, because now I have to answer it. From what I have seen, from what I know . . . I wish things were better, *mon beau-père*. That's all I can say. I wish things were better." He made a fist and brought it down on the desk.

"I will pray," Galtier said. Here lately he'd been thinking he'd got ahead of life. His laugh held only bitterness. No one ever got ahead of life, not for long, and life had just reminded him of it. *Why wasn't it me?* he wondered. *Dear God, why didn't You take me instead?* That question had no answer. It never would.

IX

Jonathan Moss nodded to the military judge in front of him. "Sir, no matter what the occupation codes say about collusion and incitement, my client is not guilty. The prosecutor hasn't introduced a single shred of evidence that Mr. Haynes either conspired against the United States, urged others to conspire or act against them, or, for that matter, acted against them himself in any way, shape, or form."

The judge, a grim-faced major named Daniel Royce, said, "Didn't you spend three years fighting against the Canucks?"

"Yes, sir, I did," Moss answered. "Right around here, as a matter of fact."

"I thought as much," Major Royce rumbled. "Why the devil are you defending them now, in that case?"

"To make sure they get a fair shake, sir," Moss said. "Plenty of people just want to jump on them with both feet now that they're down. This conspiracy charge against my client is a case in point. It's utterly groundless, as you can see."

"It is not!" yelped the military prosecutor, a captain surely too young to have fought in the Great War.

"Look at the evidence, sir, not the allegations, and you'll see for yourself," Moss told Major Royce. He hadn't lied to the judge. He did dislike seeing Americans swarming up into Ontario and ravaging the conquered province like so many locusts. But his reply hadn't been the whole truth, either. What would Royce have said had he answered, *Because I fell in love with a Canadian woman while my squadron's aerodrome was up by Arthur?* The major looked to have been a formidable football player in his younger days. He would have drop-kicked Moss clean out of his courtroom.

Scowling still, the military judge shuffled through the papers in front of him. He picked up one sheet and carefully read through it. Even from the back, Moss recognized it. It was a statement he'd got from his client's neighbors, saying they'd never seen anyone visit Haynes' house at a time when the prosecutor claimed he was shaping a plot there against the USA. His hopes leaped.

Bang! went Royce's gavel. Everyone in the courtroom who'd seen combat started; the sudden noise was too much like a gunshot for comfort. "I'm sorry, Captain, but I find myself agreeing with the defense attorney here," the military judge said. "I see no evidence of an offense against occupation regulations. Greed by people bringing the charges may be another matter. This case is dismissed. Keep your nose clean, Mr. Haynes, as you have been doing. You're a free man." The gavel banged again.

"Thank you very much, your Lordship." Paul Haynes sounded astonished that he wasn't heading for prison.

"I'm not a Lordship. You call me 'your Honor,' " Judge Royce said. "No more Lordships here, and a good thing, too, if you want to know what I think."

"Thank you, your Honor, then," Haynes said, not contradicting the military judge but not offering his own opinion, either. He turned to Jonathan Moss and stuck out his hand. "And thank *you* very much. I didn't think you could bring it off."

"You're not the only Canadian client I've had who's told me the same thing," Moss answered. "I'll tell you what I've told a lot of them—our courts *will* try you fairly if you give them half a chance."

"I wouldn't have believed it," Haynes said. "I thought they'd lock me up and throw away the key when they brought those treason charges against me."

In a low voice, Moss said, "You'd be smart to follow the judge's advice and not give them any excuse to charge you again. If you come before the court a second time, they're liable to think that where there's smoke, there's fire, even if they did let you off the hook once before." Listening to himself, he wondered how many clichés he could string together all at once.

"Wasn't any excuse to charge me this time," Paul Haynes grumbled. But then he nodded. "All right, Mr. Moss. I understand what you're telling me."

"Good," Moss said.

They left the courtroom together. Spring had been on the calendar for more than a month. Now, as April gave way to May, it was finally visible in Berlin, Ontario, too. The sky was blue, with only a few puffy white clouds drifting across it. The sun was, if not warm, at least tepid. It got up early and went to bed late. Trees were coming into new leaf. A robin chirped in one of them.

"You're a good fellow," Haynes said. He didn't even add *for a Yank*, as so many Canadians might have done. "I'll send you the rest of my fee soon as I can scrape the money together. You don't need to worry about that."

"I wasn't worried," Moss said, which was true. His Canadian clients reliably paid what they said they would when they said they'd do it. He wished the Americans he represented up here were as reliable.

Reporters were seldom allowed in military courts. Censorship still lay heavily on occupied Canada. Moss understood that without necessarily approving of it. Here in the street, a couple of newspapermen pounced on Paul Haynes. Moss slipped away before they could start grilling him, too. If they wanted him badly enough, they could run him down at his office. Meanwhile . . .

Meanwhile, he aimed to celebrate his victory in his own way. He got into his Bucephalus and pressed the starter button. The engine roared to life. A Bucephalus was a big, powerful motorcar. Owning one went a long way toward saying you were a big, powerful man. Owning a new one went a long way toward saying that, anyhow. Moss had owned this one when it was new. Here in the spring of 1928, it was anything but. One reason the engine roared was that it needed work he hadn't given it. The automobile's paint job and upholstery had seen better years. He had put new tires on it recently, but only because he'd got sick of patching the old ones when they blew out.

He put the car in gear and drove west out of Berlin. Roads were better than they had been when he first hung out his shingle in Ontario. The war, by now, had been over for ten and a half years. The roads the grinding conflict had cratered and pocked with shell holes were smooth once more—smoother than ever, in fact. Paving stretched for miles where only dirt had gone before.

About an hour after leaving Berlin, he drove through the much smaller town of Arthur, thirty miles to the west. Arthur hadn't bounced back from the war the way Berlin had. It lay off the beaten track. Few—hardly any—Americans came here with their money and their energy and their connections with the powers that be in the USA. But for a few more motorcars on the streets than would have been visible in 1914, time might have passed Arthur by.

A couple of people pointed to the Bucephalus as it rolled through town. Jonathan Moss saw one of them nod. They'd seen the motorcar before, many times. They had to know who he was. If a diehard wanted to take a shot at him . . . He shrugged. It hadn't happened yet. He wasn't going to start worrying about it now.

When he got to Laura Secord's farm, he found her where he'd expected to: out in the fields, plowing behind a horse about the size of a half-grown elephant. She must have seen his automobile pull in beside the farmhouse, but she didn't come in right away. The work came first. She'd stubbornly got a crop from the farm every year since the end of the war, and she didn't look like intending 1928 to be an exception.

Only after she'd done what she thought needed doing did she unhitch the enormous horse and lead him back toward the house and the barn. Moss got out of the Bucephalus and waved to her. She nodded back, sober as usual, but her gray eyes danced. "You got Paul Haynes off, didn't you?" she said.

"Sure did. Not just a reduced sentence, either: full acquittal," Moss said proudly. "Don't win one of those every day, not from Major Royce."

"That's . . . swell," she said. The hesitation probably meant she'd almost said *bully* instead; the old slang died hard, especially in out-of-the-way places like this. She led the immense horse into the barn. When she came out, she asked, "And how do you have in mind celebrating, eh, Yank?"

"I expect we'll think of something," he answered.

"What I'm thinking of first is a bath," she said.

Moss nodded. "Sure, sweetheart. I'll scrub your back, if you want me to."

"I'm sure you will," she told him. And, as a matter of fact, he did. One thing pleasantly led to another. After a while, they lay naked, side by side, on her bed. Lazy and sated, Moss lit a cigarette. He offered her the pack. She shook her head. That made other things jiggle, too. He watched with interested admiration. Though he didn't care to remember it, he was a little closer to forty than thirty these days; a second round wasn't so automatic as it had been a few years before. He thought he could rise to the occasion today, though. Laura Secord watched him watching her. "Did you enjoy your celebration?" she asked.

Had she smiled, that would have been different. As things were, her voice had an edge to it. "What's the matter, darling?" he asked, and reached out to toy with her left nipple.

She twisted away. "Why should anything be the matter?" she asked. "You come up here when it suits you, you . . . celebrate, and then you drive back down to Empire." She stubbornly kept using the name the Canadians had tried to hang on Berlin during the war, before the USA took it.

Although Jonathan Moss didn't have experience with a great many women, he knew trouble when he heard it. "Dammit, Laura, you'd better know by now that I don't come up here just to have a good time," he said.

"I know you didn't used to," she answered. "But things have been going on for a while now, and I do start to

282

wonder. Can you blame me? Will you still drive up here every couple of weeks in 1935, or will you have found someone younger and prettier and closer to Empire by then?"

"I'm not looking for anybody else," Moss said. "I love you, in case you hadn't noticed."

"Do you?" Laura Secord asked.

"Of course I do!" he said. She looked at him. She didn't say what she was obviously thinking: *in that case, what are you going to do about it?* The question was, if anything, more effective left hanging in the air. Jonathan Moss took a deep breath. His response looked pretty obvious, too. "Will you marry me?" he asked. "Will you sell this farm and come over to Berlin—you can even call it Empire if you want—and live with me for the rest of our lives?"

Her nod said that that *was* the right question, sure enough. But it wasn't a nod of acceptance. She asked a question of her own: "Why didn't you ask me that a long time ago, Jonathan?"

"Why? Because I know I'm nothing but a lousy American, and I figured you'd tell me no for sure. I'd sooner have gone on the way things were than have that happen. Hearing no to a question like that hurts worse than anything else I can think of."

"What if I said yes?" she asked quietly.

"I'd throw you into my motorcar, and we'd get back to Berlin in time to find a justice of the peace. If you think I'd let you have the chance to change your mind, you're nuts."

Laura Secord gave him the ghost of a smile. "It couldn't be quite that fast, I'm afraid. I'd have to make arrangements to sell the livestock or to have it taken care of before I leave the farm."

"*Are* you telling me yes?" Moss demanded. She nodded again. This time, she meant it the way he'd hoped she would. He let out a whoop that probably scared some of her feral farm cats out of a year's growth. Moss didn't care. And he did rise again, and they found the best way to inaugurate their engagement.

Afterwards, she said, "I was afraid you didn't want to buy a cow as long as milk was cheap."

"Moo, me?" he answered, and startled her again, this time into laughter. If that wasn't a good omen, he didn't know what would be.

George Enos, Jr., set cash on the kitchen table—more of it than Sylvia Enos had expected. "Here you go, Ma," her son said, his voice breaking with excitement. "We had us a he . . . heck of a run. Cod like you couldn't believe." He looked down at his hands, which had acquired the beginnings of the scabs and scars that always marked fishermen's fingers and palms. "I did more gutting than anybody could think of. And with the offal over the side, the birds that came, and the sharks—I never imagined anything like it."

"Your father used to talk the same way," Sylvia answered. She remembered him sitting up over a mug of coffee in the days when they were first married, telling her about what he'd done and what he'd seen and what it had felt like.

But this wasn't quite the same, after all. George Enos had done enough fishing by the time he married her that it had become routine, and wearying routine at that. George, Jr., didn't seem tired at all. Maybe that was because everything still seemed bright and new to him. Or maybe it was just because, at seventeen, he never got tired at all. His father certainly had, though, and he'd been only a few years older.

"How much is it, Ma?" Mary Jane asked, looking up from the onions she was chopping. She paused to rub her streaming eyes, then let out a yelp—she must have had onion juice on her fingers, and made things worse instead of better.

"Quite a bit," answered Sylvia, who'd been trained from childhood not to talk about money in any detail. "It will help a lot."

"That's good," Mary Jane said. "I'm going to look for a shopgirl job again tomorrow. I bet I find something, too. That one I had last summer was swell, but then you went and made me go back to school." She sent Sylvia as severe a look as a fifteen-year-old girl could give her mother.

Sylvia had no trouble withstanding it; she'd known far worse. "Summer work is one thing," she said. "School is something else. You need your schooling."

George, Jr., glanced at his sister. They both almost— but not quite; no, not quite—invisibly shook their heads. These days, they were old enough to team up on Sylvia, instead of fighting each other as they'd done for so long. Sylvia knew why George, Jr., sneered at school. He was making good money without it.

And Sylvia had a pretty good idea why Mary Jane didn't want to keep going. She was bound to be thinking something like, *Who cares whether I can divide fractions and diagram sentences? What difference will it make? I'm going to get married and have babies, and my husband will make money for me.*

"You never can tell," Sylvia said, half to herself, half to her daughter. "I thought George, Jr.'s, father was going to take care of things forever. But then the war came, and the Confederates captured him, and after that he joined the Navy, and he . . . he didn't come home. And I've had to run like crazy ever since, just trying to make ends meet. If I knew more about spelling and typing and arithmetic, I'd've had better jobs and made more money, and we'd've done better for ourselves. And if you think things like that can't happen to you and the people you love, Mary Jane, you're wrong. I wish you weren't, but you are. Because you never can tell."

By something surely not far from a miracle, she got through to her daughter. Instead of giving her a snippy answer, Mary Jane nodded and said, "I wish I could've known Pa better."

George, Jr., got up and set a hand on his younger sister's shoulder. "I wish I could have, too." His voice roughened. "But at least Ma paid back the stinking son of a bitch"—had he been out on the trawler instead of in his kitchen, he undoubtedly would have said something much hotter than that—"who sank the *Ericsson*. Everybody I sail with knows Ma's a hero."

285

Sylvia brushed that aside. "It won't get me any supper," she said, and stood up herself so she could start cooking. She hadn't felt heroic when she'd pumped a revolverful of bullets into Roger Kimball. She had trouble remembering now exactly how she had felt. Frightened and resigned was about as close as she could come to it. She hadn't thought she would ever see her children or Boston again.

But here she was, with all the same problems, all the same worries, she'd had before getting on the train for Charleston. Being a hero, she'd rapidly discovered, paid few bills. When she'd come home, she had got back the job she'd left so she could go to the Confederate States. She'd made a few speeches that brought in a little money. By now, though, she was old news. Even in this presidential election year, no one asked her to come out. Joe Kennedy, for instance, had used her and forgotten about her. Every once in a while, she wondered how many women he'd really, rather than metaphorically, seduced and abandoned. More than a few, or she missed her guess.

While washing dishes later that evening, Mary Jane asked, "Who are you going to vote for come November, Ma?"

Women's suffrage had finally come to Massachusetts— and to the rest of the holdout states in the USA—with the passage of the Nineteenth Amendment. These days, all the men who'd opposed it were busy explaining how they'd never really done any such thing, how they'd always looked out for the country's best interests, and as many other lies as they could find.

Most of those men were Democrats. Even so, Sylvia answered, "I'm going to vote for Governor Coolidge for president, because he's a Democrat and he'd be harder on the Confederates than Vice President Blackford. Coolidge fought in the war, too; he didn't stay back of the lines."

"Do you think Coolidge will win?" Mary Jane asked.

"I don't know," Sylvia said. "That's why they have the election—to find out who wins, I mean. Hardly anybody thought President Sinclair would beat Teddy Roosevelt in 1920, but he did."

"I was still little then," Mary Jane said thoughtfully, scrubbing at a frying pan with steel wool.

To Sylvia, Mary Jane was still little now, and would be the rest of her life. But she put that aside, and went back to the question her daughter had asked a little while before: "I do wish Governor Coolidge would be a little more . . . lively. People don't seem to get very excited about him, and that worries me. Blackford and his wife can really whip up the crowds. It matters a lot."

The following Sunday, someone knocked at the door to her flat. There stood her neighbor, Brigid Coneval. The Irishwoman said, "Blackford his own self will be after speaking on the Common today at half past two. Now that we can vote and all, I'm for hearing what he has to say for himself. Will you come with me, now?"

Sylvia found herself nodding. "I sure will," she said. "You're right—we ought to find out all we can about them."

"Indeed and we should," Brigid Coneval agreed. A war widow like Sylvia, she hadn't had an easy time of it since her husband was shot. She made ends meet by taking care of other people's children—though her own boys, by now, were also old enough to get jobs of their own and bring in a little money to help. Through everything, she'd kept an infectious grin. "And besides, it'll be fun. We can ride the subway over to the Common; there's a station close by there."

"Why not?" Sylvia didn't often do things on impulse, but this would be out of the ordinary, and it wouldn't cost anything except subway fare.

She didn't like the subway. It was even more crowded than trolley cars, and noisier, too. Between stations, the tunnel was black as coal. She kept wondering things like, *What would happen if this train broke down?* She knew she shouldn't. She knew that wasn't likely. But she couldn't help it.

The subway train got to the Common without incident. Sylvia and Brigid Coneval emerged from the bowels of the earth into bright sunshine. It glowed off the gilded dome of the State House, in front of which Vice President

Blackford would speak. "Let's get under one of the trees," Sylvia said, pointing. "We're early. There's still room under there. We can stay in the shade. It'll be cooler."

"Well, aren't you the clever one, now?" her friend said. They staked out their spot with no trouble at all.

They *were* early. The crowd hadn't really begun to fill the Boston Common. Most of the people there so soon were either Blackford's Socialist backers or the Democratic activists who would heckle the vice president when he spoke. The two groups jockeyed for position and traded insults, mostly good-natured. They'd squared off against each other many times before, and knew they'd often meet again after this afternoon.

One of the men carrying an 8 YEARS IS ENOUGH! sign was Joe Kennedy. Seeing him, Sylvia shrank back farther under the tree. She didn't want him to see her, even though she had every right to be here. But he did—she got the feeling he missed very little. He saw her, recognized her, and turned his back. She wanted to call out, *I'm going to vote for Coolidge!* She didn't. She could tell it would do no good.

A big black car pulled up by the platform. A tall, gray-haired man and a short woman, much younger than he, got out and went to the platform. "That's himself's wife," Brigid Coneval said. "A Congresswoman from New York City, she is, and a Christ-killing sheeny besides."

Sylvia didn't care much about Jews one way or the other. She said, "By all they say, she's done a good job in Congress. And look at her! She's been there since the war, and she doesn't look any older than we are."

"Foosh!" said Brigid, who seemed determined to stay unimpressed. "And what's her husband, then? Sure and he's a dirty old man, for I'd not care to hang since he's seen the sweet side of forty."

Flora Blackford stepped up to the microphone. The Democrats in the crowd immediately started to jeer. She made as if to urge them on, and then said, "Listen to them, comrades. They won't tell the truth themselves, and they don't want to let anyone else tell it, either. Is that fair? Is that honest? Is that what you want in the Powel House for the next four years?"

"No!" people shouted.

The Congresswoman from New York City made a short, strong speech, giving the Socialists credit for everything that had gone right the past eight years: the booming stock market, laws allowing strikes for higher wages, and on and on.

"What about the revolt in Canada? What about cutting off Confederate reparations?" the Democrats yelled. "What about the bank troubles in Europe?"

"Well, what about them?" Flora retorted, meeting the hecklers head on. "The Canadians lost. And we're at peace with the Confederate States, and getting along with them well enough. Isn't it about time this country was at peace with its neighbors? As for the banks in Europe, well, what can we do about them here?"

Most people cheered. The Democrats went right on heckling. Vice President Blackford himself stepped up to the microphone. "We've had eight good years!" he said. "Let's have four more. We've got prosperity. We've got peace. Give us a few more Socialists in the Senate and we'll have old-age insurance, too. If you want to go back to gearing up for a war every generation, vote for Governor Coolidge. He'll give you one. If you want to make sure your sons and husbands and brothers live to grow old, vote for me. It's that simple."

But it wasn't, not as far as Sylvia was concerned. She wanted the Confederate States punished for what they'd done to the *Ericsson*, not forgiven their reparations. Hosea Blackford might not want a war, but wouldn't the Confederates if they ever got strong again? "I'm glad we came," she told Brigid Coneval on their way back to the subway station. "Now I'm surer than ever I'll vote for Coolidge."

"Sure and you can't mean it!" Brigid exclaimed, and argued with her all the way home even though she'd mocked both Hosea Blackford and his wife. She didn't change Sylvia's mind, or even come close.

Over the supper table, Chester Martin grinned at his wife. "Election Day coming up," he said with a sly smile.

"And so?" Rita answered. But she smiled, too. "Plenty of worse ways to meet than at a polling place."

"I should say." Martin had met women at worse places—and that didn't even count the soldiers' brothels behind the front during the war, when you'd stand in line outside in the rain for a couple of minutes of what was much more catharsis than rapture. *At least I never got a dose of the clap,* he thought.

"Do you think Blackford can do it?" Rita asked.

"Hope so," Martin said. "I don't see why not. Everybody's making good money. Why should we change when things are going the way they're supposed to?" He spread his hands. "I still don't much like the Socialists' foreign policy—I'd take a stronger line than they do—but that's not enough reason to vote for the Great Stone Face."

Rita laughed at the nickname. "Coolidge doesn't have much to say for himself, does he?"

"I think there's a reason for that, too," Chester replied. "He's never done anything worth talking about."

"Massachusetts is prosperous," Rita said. "He takes credit for that."

After sarcastically clapping his hands a couple of times, Martin said, "He may take it, but who says he deserves it? The whole country's prosperous, and the Socialists deserve credit for *that*." He'd come late to the Socialists, but had what amounted to a convert's zeal. "Look where we were in 1920, before President Sinclair won, and look where we are now."

"You're preaching to the choir, you know," his wife told him with a smile. "I'm going to vote for Blackford, too."

"I know, but look." Chester felt expansive. He wanted to tell the whole world how well his party had run the country over the past eight years. Since the whole world wasn't sitting across the kitchen table from him and Rita was, she got to listen to him. He went on, "Look how high the stock market's risen. Who would have thought the proletariat could start owning the means of production by buying shares in the big companies? With buying on margin, though, it's awfully easy to do." He laughed. "If *we* can afford to do it, it must be easy to do."

Rita pointed to the newspaper, which lay on a chair. "The Wireless Corporation is splitting its stock again."

Martin nodded. "I saw that. I'm glad I got into Wireless somewhere close to the ground floor. I think it's going to be the big thing for years and years, and those four shares I managed to buy last summer are sixteen shares now. It's swell. Everything keeps going up and up and up. It's like coining money."

"Did you see that Congresswoman Blackford is coming to town Saturday?" Rita asked.

"No, I missed that," he answered. "Do you want to go see her?"

"Sure? Why not? It'll be fun," Rita said. "And besides, she shows what a woman can do when she puts her mind to it."

Although Chester wasn't sure he liked the sound of that, he said, "All right," anyhow, finding agreement the better part of valor. Then he added, "Did I ever tell you that I—"

"Met Flora Blackford when she was still Flora Hamburger?" Rita cut in. "Had her brother in your company during the war?" She shook her head. Her bobbed dark blond hair flipped back and forth. "No. You never, ever told me that. I've never heard it, not even once. Can't you tell?"

"I can tell you're giving me a hard time," he answered. She grinned. So did he.

Flora Blackford chose to speak near the Toledo city hall, in the shadow of the smaller copy of the great statue of Remembrance that stood on Bedloe Island in New York harbor. Chester found that interesting, even challenging. For more than a generation, remembrance had been the loudest drum the Democrats beat. For a nation twice defeated, twice humiliated, by the CSA and the Confederates' European allies, it was a drumbeat that had struck deep chords.

But now the Great War was eleven years past. The United States had won it. People still held Remembrance Day parades, but they didn't march with flags upside down any more. Having won, the United States were no longer in distress. And, ever since the Great War ended, the Democrats hadn't been able to find any other theme that resonated with the voters as remembrance had.

And now, here stood Flora Blackford under that great statue with the gleaming sword. By the way she stood there, she said Remembrance—and the Democrats—spoke to yesterday's worries, yesterday's needs. *I'm going to talk about what you need to hear today—and tomorrow,* she said without words, merely by standing there.

"We've come a long way the past eight years," she said, "but we've still got a long way to go. When President Sinclair was elected, you risked losing your job if you went out on strike. Some of you *had* lost your jobs. That can't happen any more, thanks to the laws we've passed."

Chester Martin pounded his palms together. He'd fought company goons, and he'd fought the police who served as the big capitalists' watchdogs and hunting hounds. Next to what he'd been through in the trenches, those brawls hadn't been anything much. And if you weren't willing to fight for what you wanted, did you really deserve to get it? He believed in the class struggle. He believed in it all the way down to his toes.

When the applause died down a little, Vice President Blackford's wife went on, "You know the Democrats never would have passed a bill like that, or like the one that gives workers the right to take leave without pay if there's a baby in the family or someone takes sick and then get their jobs back. They were in power from 1884 to 1920, and they still behave as though it's 1884."

That drew not only applause but whoops of laughter. It also fit in very well with what Chester had been thinking not long before. Flora Blackford continued, "And we tried to give you old-age insurance, too. We tried hard. But we couldn't quite manage that, because the Democrats had enough men in the Senate to tie up the bill with a filibuster. We've got to elect more Socialists. Friends, comrades, the presidency is important, but it's not enough, not by itself. We have to fight the forces of reaction wherever we find them. That's what the class struggle is all about."

It wasn't how Martin imagined the class struggle. He took the phrase literally. He'd broken enough heads in his time to have reason to take it literally. He'd taken his lumps, too; the real problem with the class struggle was that the capitalists and their lackeys fought back hard. But the idea of carrying the struggle even to the halls of Congress held a powerful appeal for him.

"We don't need the enormous Army and Navy we had before the Great War, the Army and Navy that ate up so much money and so much of our industry," Flora said. "We've won the war. Now we can enjoy what we won. Factories can make goods for people, not for killing. We can spend our wealth on what *we* need, not on battleships and machine guns and barrels. We've fought our neighbors too many times. We can work toward living at peace with them now."

That drew more loud cheers. Chester joined in them, but more than a little halfheartedly. This was the part of the Socialist platform that still graveled him. Still, Flora Blackford expressed it well. Maybe the 1920s were so prosperous because less money was going into weapons and fortifications and more into people's pockets. Maybe.

"Hosea Blackford will take us on toward the middle of the twentieth century," Flora declared. "Calvin Coolidge will drag us back into the nineteenth century. Which way do you want to go? The choice is yours—it's in the people's hands. I ask you not to turn your back on the future! I ask you to vote Socialist, to vote for Hosea Blackford for president and Hiram Johnson for vice president. Let Dakota and California show the rest of the country the way! Thank you!"

More applause—thunderous applause. Rita said, "I can't *wait* for November."

"Neither can I," Chester agreed. That was how a good stump speech was supposed to work. It made the faithful eager. Men and women pushed forward, trying to get a word with Flora Blackford now that she'd come down off the platform. "Come on," Martin told his wife, and did some pushing himself, wondering if the vice president's wife would remember him.

He didn't really expect her to, and she didn't, not when she looked at him. But when he shouted his name at her, she nodded. "You were David's sergeant," she said.

"That's right, ma'am." Chester grinned and nodded. "And this is my wife, Rita."

"Pleased to meet you." Flora clasped Rita's hand. "Will you vote for my husband on Election Day?"

"I sure will," Rita answered. "I was going to even before I heard you talk. But even if I'd been thinking about voting for the Democrats before, you would have made me change my mind."

"Thank you very much," Flora Blackford said. "He needs all the votes he can get, believe me. We can't take anything for granted. If we do, we're liable to lose."

"We'd better not," Chester Martin said. Before Vice President Blackford's wife could answer, a fresh surge of people from behind pushed Rita and him away from her. Again, that was no surprise; he felt lucky to have talked with her at all. Turning to Rita, he asked, "What do you think?"

"She's honest," Rita said at once. "If she is, it's a good bet her husband is, too. And she knew who you were as soon as you told her your name. That was something." She proudly took his arm. "You know important people."

He laughed. "Stick with me, kiddo, and I'll take you to the top."

Rita laughed, too, but only for a moment. Then she sobered. "You really do know important people, Chester. That might turn out to be important one of these days. You never can tell."

"Maybe." But Chester didn't believe it, not down deep. "I don't think Flora Blackford's the sort of person you can use to pull strings. She was in Congress, remember, when her brother got conscripted, and she didn't pull any for him. He could have had some soft, safe job behind the lines—typist or driver or something like that. He could have, but he didn't. He went into the fighting, and he got shot. If she didn't help David Hamburger, she's not likely to help me."

"That depends on what you'd need to ask her," Rita answered. "Like I said a minute ago, you never can tell."

Somebody stepped on Chester's foot, hard. "Ow!" he said. In the crowd, he couldn't even tell who'd done it. He pointed toward the trolley stop. "Let's get out of here and go home before we get trampled."

"Suits me," his wife said. "I'm glad we came, though. She made a good speech—and I found out what a special fellow I married."

Martin started to tell her he was just an ordinary guy. He started to, but he didn't. If Rita wanted to think he was a special fellow, he didn't mind a bit.

Flora Blackford had waited out six elections to the House of Representatives. She'd been nervous every single time, though her New York City district was solidly Socialist and she'd had easy races after the first one. Now, for the first time since 1914, she wasn't running for Congress—but she was more nervous than ever.

Worrying about her husband's race proved more wearing than worrying about her own ever had. She hadn't been this anxious in 1924; she was sure of that. In 1924, Hosea Blackford hadn't headed the ticket. It probably hadn't won or lost because of anything he did.

Things were different now. If they went as she hoped, her husband would become president of the United States next March. If they didn't . . . No, she wouldn't think about that.

Telegraph sets clicked in their apartments. Phones jangled. Off in one corner, an announcer on a wireless set spewed out results. Flora and Hosea got any news that came in as fast as they would have at Socialist Party headquarters in Philadelphia. But the same longstanding tradition that kept a presidential nominee away from the convention till he'd been declared the candidate bound a presidential hopeful to find out whether he'd won or lost away from the people who'd done the most to help him.

When Flora complained about that, her husband only shrugged. "It's one of the rules of the game," he said.

"One of the rules of the game used to be that the

Democrats won every four years," Flora answered. "We've changed that. Why not the other?"

Hosea Blackford looked surprised. "I just hadn't thought about it. I did this in 1920. The two of us did it in '24. Maybe we will change things . . . four years from now."

She gave him a kiss. "I like that. You're already starting to think about your second term, are you?"

"I'd better worry about the first one, don't you think?" he said.

The wireless announcer said, "In Massachusetts, Governor Coolidge continues to pull away. He also leads comfortably in Vermont and Tennessee, and early returns from Kentucky show him with a strong lead there."

"*Oy!*" Flora said in dismay.

Her husband took the news much more in stride than she did. "Massachusetts is Coolidge's home state," he said. "We've never done well anywhere in New England. And Kentucky is full of reactionaries. How could it be anything else, when it belonged to the Confederate States till the middle of the war? Wait till we start getting returns from the places where working people live, where they make things."

She nodded. She knew that as well as he did. Even so . . . "I don't like losing anywhere," she said.

Hosea Blackford smiled. "That's one of the reasons I'm so glad you're on my side."

A man at one of the telephones called out, "Your lead in New York City just went up another twenty thousand votes, Mr. Vice President!" Flora smiled too—then. She finally had something to smile about.

"Vice President Blackford's large lead in New York City looks likely to carry the state for him, in spite of Governor Coolidge's popularity in the upstate regions," the commentator on the wireless declared. "Pennsylvania will probably be a closer race. The Socialists are strong in Pittsburgh, but Philadelphia is still a Democratic bastion."

"We have to have New York," Flora murmured. "We have to." The state had the biggest bloc of electoral votes in the USA: one out of every seven. Pennsylvania came next, but far behind. The Democrats could count as well as the Socialists. They'd campaigned hard in New York. *Let them fall short.* In Flora's mind, it was more than half a prayer.

"New returns from Ohio," a telegrapher said. "You're up in Toledo, up in Cleveland, holding your own in Columbus, not doing so well in Cincinnati."

"About what we expected," Blackford said. "What do the overall figures in the state look like?"

"You're up by . . . let me see . . . seventeen thousand," the man answered after some quick work with pencil and paper.

"Not bad for this early in the night," Flora said.

"No, not bad," Hosea Blackford agreed. "Can't say much more than that without knowing just where all those votes are coming from. But I'd rather be ahead than behind." Flora nodded.

Little by little, returns began trickling in from farther west. Indiana had long been a Socialist stronghold; Senator Debs had twice lost to Teddy Roosevelt as the Socialist Party's standard-bearer. Hosea Blackford was well ahead there. Republicans remained strong in Illinois, Michigan, and Iowa—those three-cornered races wouldn't be settled till the wee small hours. Like Indiana, Wisconsin was solidly in the Socialist camp.

"We're doing fine," Flora said, and tried to make herself believe it.

"Maybe I'm glad I'm here after all," her husband said. "Looks like it's going to be a long night. This way, I can just go back into the bedroom and sleep whenever I feel like it. And there aren't any reporters yelling at me, either. I wouldn't be able to hear myself think over at Party head-quarters."

"I wish it didn't look like a long night," Flora said. "I wish we were sweeping the country, and we could declare victory as soon as the polls closed."

"Well, I wouldn't mind that myself." Hosea laughed. "The Democrats did it for one election after another. Maybe we will, too, somewhere down the line But we haven't got there yet. This one's going to be close."

Flora's fists tightened till her nails bit into the palms of her hands. It wasn't just that she wanted the Socialists to win Powel House and as many seats in the House and Senate as they could, though she did. She'd always wanted that, ever since becoming a Party activist before the Great War. But it felt secondary now. With her husband in the race, she wanted his triumph with an intensity that amazed her. A win tonight would cap a lifetime of service to the Socialist cause and to the country. Losing . . .

Again, she refused to think about losing.

Hosea Blackford didn't. "If I win, we stay in Philadelphia," he said. "If I lose, we go home. How would you like living way out West for a while?"

"It's beautiful country," Flora answered, and then said the best thing she could for it: "Joshua would like growing up there." Having said that, she went on, "It seems so . . . empty, though, to somebody who's used to New York City or Philadelphia."

She'd enjoyed spending holidays in Dakota with her husband. The wide open spaces awed her, for a while. But towns and trains and civilization in general seemed a distinct afterthought there. She didn't like that, not at all. To someone who'd grown up on the preposterously over-crowded Lower East Side, so many empty miles of prairie, relieved—if at all—only by a long line of telegraph poles shrinking toward an unbelievably distant horizon, felt more alarming than inspiring.

Someone slammed down a telephone and let out a string of curses that ignored her presence in the room. "Kansas is going for Coolidge, God damn it," he said.

That made Flora want to curse, too. Hosea Blackford took it in stride. "Confederate raiders hit Kansas hard during the war," he said. "They don't love Socialists there; they've been Democrats since the Second Mexican War."

"Well, they can *geh kak afen yam*," Flora said.

Her husband chuckled; he knew what that Yiddish unpleasantry meant. "There's no *yam* anywhere close to Kansas for them to *geh kak afen*," he pointed out.

"I don't care," Flora said. "They can do it anyway."

The new state of Houston, carved from the conquered

piece of Texas, went for Calvin Coolidge. So did Montana, which had been a Democratic stronghold ever since Theodore Roosevelt made a hero of himself there during the Second Mexican War. Flora began to worry in earnest. But a little past midnight, Pennsylvania, which had teetered for a long time, fell into her husband's camp—and Pennsylvania's electoral votes made up for a swarm of Montanas. New Jersey had also stayed close till then, and also ended up going Socialist.

"We may make it," Hosea Blackford said. "We just may."

By then, returns from the West were coming in. Colorado had a strong union tradition, and looked like going Socialist again. Idaho fell to Coolidge, and so did Nevada, but Blackford swept the West Coast, including populous California: Hiram Johnson had delivered his state.

Flora was yawning when one of the telephones rang a little past three in the morning. "Mr. Vice President," called the man who answered it, and then, in a different, awed, tone of voice, "Mr. President-elect, it's Governor Coolidge, calling from Massachusetts."

That woke Flora better than a big cup of black coffee could have done. She kissed her husband before he could go to the telephone. "Hello, Governor," he said when he picked up the instrument. "Thank you very much, sir. . . . That's very generous. . . . Yes, you did give me quite a scare, and I'm not ashamed to admit it. . . . What's that?" He had been smiling and cordial, but now his expression hardened. "I certainly hope you're wrong, Governor. I think you are. . . . Yes, time will tell. Thank you again. Good night." He hung up, perhaps more forcefully than he had to.

"What did he say that made you angry?" Flora asked.

"He said maybe he was lucky not to win," Hosea Blackford answered. "He said bull markets don't last forever, and this one's gone on so long and risen so high, the crash will be all the worse when it comes back to earth."

"God forbid!" Flora exclaimed.

"I think we've given God some help," Hosea said. "The business cycle's been rising steadily all through both of President Sinclair's terms. I don't see any reason why it shouldn't do the same for me. The Democrats may have enjoyed boom-and-bust capitalism before the war, but we've put that behind us now. We're prosperous, and we'll stay prosperous."

"*Alevai, omayn!*" Whenever Flora fell back into Yiddish these days, she spoke from heart and belly.

Hosea Blackford smiled. He understood that. "I really do think it'll be all right, Flora," he said gently. "Oh, there's more farm debt than I care to see out in the West, and the factories almost seem to be making things faster than people can buy them, but all that's just a drop in the bucket. We'll do fine."

"I'm not going to argue with you, not now—Mr. President." Flora kissed him again. The telegraphers and men at the phones all cheered.

"Not for another five months," Hosea reminded her. "Say that to me in front of President Sinclair and he'll arrest you for treason."

"Phooey," Flora said, which wasn't English or Yiddish, but was exactly what she meant.

Another telephone rang. "Mr. President-elect, it's the president."

This time, Flora didn't try to delay her husband when he went to the telephone. "Hello, Upton," he said. "Thank you so very much. . . . Yes, Cal threw in the towel a little while ago. He gave me some sour grapes, too, babbling about a crash. . . . Yes, of course it's idiocy. When in all the history of the country have things gone so well? And we have you to thank for it. I'll do my best to follow your footsteps. . . . Thanks again. Good-bye."

Flora went in and woke up Joshua. "Your father's going to be president," she told him.

"I want to go back to sleep," he said irritably—he wasn't quite three, and didn't care whether his father was president or a garbageman. Flora wanted to go to sleep, too. *Now I won't have to live in Dakota,* she thought. And if that wasn't reason enough, all by itself, to be glad Hosea had won, she couldn't imagine what would be.

* * *

The year had turned eight days before. Lucien Galtier didn't want to be standing out in the open, not with the weather down around zero and a raw wind blowing out of the northwest. Under his overcoat, his tight collar and black cravat felt as if they were choking him.

Charles and Georges stood beside him in the graveyard. His sons' faces were blank and bitter with grief. So, he suspected, was his own. His daughters—Nicole, Denise, Susanne, and Jeanne—could show their grief more openly, though that wind threatened to freeze the tears on their faces.

It also whipped at Father Guillaume's wool cassock. "Is everyone here?" he asked. Galtier nodded. Himself, his children, their spouses, his two grandchildren—and Charles' wife big with child, due almost any day—Marie's brother and sister and their spouses and children and grandchildren, some cousins, some friends. The priest raised his voice a little: "Let us pray."

Lucien bowed his head as Father Guillaume offered up sonorous Latin to the Lord. Absurdly, Galtier chose that moment to remember how strange the American priest who'd married Nicole and Leonard O'Doull had sounded while speaking Latin—he'd pronounced it differently from the way Quebecois clergymen did. But even they'd assured him it wasn't wrong, merely not the same.

After the Latin was done, Father Guillaume dropped back into French: "Marie Galtier no longer gives us the boon of her company on this earth. But she is at the right hand of the Father even as I speak these words, as she died in our true and holy Catholic faith. And she will live forever, for she was a good woman, as you show by coming here today to honor and commemorate her passing."

Nicole began to sob. Leonard O'Doull put his arm around her. Lucien wished someone would do the same for him. But he was a man. He had to bear this as a man did, as stoically as he could. His eyes slid to the black-draped coffin. He'd thought burying his parents was hard. And it had been. This, though, this felt ten times worse. That was his life going into the hole the gravediggers had hacked from the frozen ground. *How can I go on without*

Marie? he wondered. He couldn't imagine finding an answer.

"In a real way, too, Marie Galtier does still live here among us," the priest said. Lucien almost called him a liar and a fool, there in front of everyone. Before he could say the words, Father Guillaume went on, "She lives in our hearts, in our memories. Whenever we recall her kindness and her love, she lives again. And because she gave us so many reasons to do just that, she will live on for a very long time indeed, even if her years among us were fewer than we would have wished. Think of her often, and she will live for you again."

He turned toward the coffin, making the sign of the cross and praying once more in Latin. All the people standing there shivering as they listened to him crossed themselves, too. As Lucien did so, he felt a certain dull amazement. Father Guillaume had been right after all. Lucien could hear his wife's voice inside himself, could see her smile whenever he closed his eyes. A marvel, yes, but a painful marvel. Seeing her and hearing her that way only reminded him he wouldn't see her or hear her in the flesh any more. Helplessly, he began to cry.

"Here, Papa." Of all people, his foolish son Georges was the one who held him and gave him a handkerchief: Georges, whose always-smiling face was as twisted with sorrow as Lucien's had to be.

"Thank you, my son," Lucien whispered. He felt his eyelids trying to freeze together, and rubbed at them with the handkerchief.

Then he and his sons and Marie's brother and Dr. Leonard O'Doull lifted the coffin and set it in the grave. What struck Lucien was how little it weighed, which had little to do with six men lifting it. After Dr. O'Doull found the mass in Marie's belly, after the X ray and the operation that only confirmed the worst, the flesh had melted off her day by day, till she was little more than parchment skin wrapped around bones by the time the end finally, mercifully, came. Those were memories of his wife Galtier wished he wouldn't carry into the future with him. No matter what he wished, though, he would have them till his turn to lie in a coffin came. He made himself go over to the priest and say, "*Merci,* Father Guillaume."

The young priest nodded soberly. "You are welcome, and more than welcome. This is a cup I wish had passed from me, and one I wish had passed from your wife as well. I would have hoped she might enjoy many more happy years."

"Yes. I would have hoped for the same." Galtier looked up into the cloudy sky. More snow might start falling any time. "Better God should have taken me. Why did He take her and leave me all alone?" That thought had been with him since he first found out Marie was ill.

"He knows the answer to that, even if He does not give it to us to know," Father Guillaume said.

"Marie knows now, too," Lucien said. "If ever I see God face to face, I intend to ask Him about it, and His explanation had better be a good one." The priest coughed and turned red. Galtier went on, "And if I don't see Him face to face, if I meet the Devil instead, as could be, then I intend to find out from him."

Now Father Guillaume gravely shook his head. "Satan is the Father of Lies. Whatever he might tell you, you would not be able to believe it."

With Quebecois stubbornness, Lucien said, "I'll hear what he says, and then I'll make up my own mind."

Charles came up to him and asked, "Do you want me to drive you home, Papa?"

"Why would I?" Galtier asked in honest surprise.

"After this . . . I was not sure how you would be," his older son answered.

"I am not so very well," Galtier agreed. "But if I am not so very well after burying my wife, are you so very well after burying your mother? It could be you would make a worse menace on the road than I, *n'est-ce pas?*"

Charles looked surprised, but nodded. "Yes, it could be, I suppose." He turned away. "I should have known you were too stubborn to take help from anyone."

"When I need it, I take it," Lucien said. "When I don't, I don't. Don't be angry at me, son. I am not angry at you. And the two of us, we're not so very different, eh?"

He knew that was true. Charles took after him in more than looks. His older son also had a character much like his own. After a moment's thought, Charles gave him the same sort of grudging nod he would have used himself. "All right, Father. Yes, you're right—I can be a stiff-necked nuisance, too. I'll see you there, then?"

"Certainly," Galtier said. "Where else would I go, but to my own house?"

But when he got out of the Chevrolet close by the farmhouse on the land that had been in his family for almost 250 years, he wondered. He didn't want to go back into the house. Going in there had always—not literally always, but more than thirty years came close enough— meant going in to see Marie. Now she wasn't there. She never would be there, not any more. And remembering that she had been there, remembering the life together the two of them had built, the life now forever sundered, forever shattered, was like knives to Lucien. He had to gather himself before he could go inside.

Nicole and Leonard O'Doull were already there. So were Charles and his wife. One by one and in small groups, the rest of his children and his wife's relatives and his friends came in. There was plenty to drink and plenty to eat; the womenfolk in the family had been cooking since Marie died.

"Thank you all," Lucien said. "Thank you all very much for coming. Thank you for caring for Marie." His face twisted into a characteristically wry grin. "For I know you certainly would not have come for my sake."

"Certainly not, *mon beau-père*," Dr. O'Doull said. "We all hate you."

For a moment, Galtier took him seriously, being too emotionally battered to recognize irony. But then even he saw the smile on his son-in-law's face, and those on the faces of his other loved ones. He wanted to smile, too, but ended up weeping once more instead. He felt mortified all over again, and angrily turned away from Dr. O'Doull.

"It's all right," said the American who'd become part of his family. "No one thinks less of you for it. Here. Drink this." He gave Lucien a glass of applejack.

The homemade spirits went down Galtier's throat without his even noticing them. He had another glass, and another, all with scant effect. He felt too much already for applejack to make much difference. For the next half hour or so, he thanked everyone who'd come to his house to say good-bye to Marie.

"What will you do now, Papa?" Georges asked him. "Do you know yet?"

"What *can* I do?" Galtier answered. "I'll go on as best I can. If I don't feed the animals tomorrow, who will? If I don't take care of the farm, who will? The work doesn't do itself. You always thought it did, but it doesn't. Someone has to do it. If no one does it, it doesn't get done."

"But . . ." His younger son gestured. "How can you do all the farm work, and then do all the housework, too?"

"Electricity helps," Lucien said. "With electricity, everything is quicker and easier. And I was in the Army a long time ago. I know how to keep things tidy—unlike certain people I could name."

Georges didn't rise to that, which proved how solemn an occasion this was. He just asked, "And while you were in the Army, Papa, did they also teach you how to cook?"

"No, but then, who cares?" Galtier answered. "I am the only person I'll be cooking for. I won't starve to death. And if supper is particularly bad one night, I can always throw things at the clumsy fool who fixed it."

He made his son laugh at that, and thought he'd tricked Georges—maybe even tricked himself—into believing everything was, or at least soon would be, all right. A few minutes later, though, Georges sprawled in a chair, hands over his face, weeping with as much heartbreak as Lucien knew himself.

What will *I* do? Galtier wondered. For all his glib talk, he had no idea. At the moment, he didn't particularly want to go on living himself. Maybe that would change as time passed. He'd heard it did. He'd heard it, but didn't particularly believe it. *Why not me?* he wondered, as he had ever since he'd found Marie in the kitchen with tears running down her face.

He'd hoped Father Guillaume would have an answer

305

for that, but no such luck. It would have to wait till he saw God, as Marie was seeing God now. *If He doesn't have a good answer, I'll give Him a piece of my mind.*

Nicole came over to him. She looked achingly like her mother, though she was a few inches taller; Marie had been a little woman, not much over five feet. "She's gone, Papa," she said wonderingly. "I can't believe it, but she's gone."

"I know," Lucien said.

"I love you," his oldest daughter said.

He hadn't heard that from her for years. He suspected it meant, *I'm afraid I'll lose you, too.* "And I love you, my dear," he said, as if to reply, *I'm not going anywhere.* But that wasn't really for him to say. He looked up to, and past, the ceiling. *Don't You argue with me,* he told God, and dared hope God was listening.

"Another Inauguration Day," Nellie Jacobs said. "Dear God, where do the years go? First one I can recollect is President Blaine's, back in 1881. I was just a little girl then, of course."

"Well, I hope to heaven Hosea Blackford does a better job than James G. Blaine did," her husband answered.

"He'd better," Nellie exclaimed. "A few months after Blaine got elected, the Confederates were shelling Washington. I've been through that twice now. It had better not happen again, that's all I've got to say, because I don't think anybody could be lucky enough to live through it three times."

"I don't look for a war any time soon," Hal Jacobs said. "I don't see how we could have one. The Confederates aren't very strong, and we're prosperous. I still think the stock market is sound, even if the money trouble in Europe has set it hiccoughing."

"I'm glad it's hiccoughing," Nellie said. "It let us buy those shares of the Wireless Corporation for a lot less than they would have cost us a couple of months ago."

"Buy on the dips," Hal said wisely. "Buy on the dips, and you can't go wrong."

"That's what they say," Nellie agreed. "It's worked

out pretty well for us so far. I just wish we'd been able to start out when we were a lot younger."

Hal shrugged. "For one thing, we didn't have the money. For another, the market was a lot riskier in those days—it would crash every few years. And then the war came along, and we were too busy to worry about it for quite a while."

"Too busy? Well, yes, a little bit," Nellie said. Hal pinned his Distinguished Service Medal on the breast pocket of his black jacket. With his white shirt, black cravat, and black homburg, the medal's ribbon gave his outfit the only dash of color it had. Nellie nodded approval. "You look handsome," she told him, and he did indeed look as handsome as he could.

"Thank you, my dear." He always seemed to glow a little when she paid him a compliment. And he returned the favor: "You are as lovely as always."

"Oh, foosh." Nellie had heard too many compliments from men over the years to trust them or take them seriously. Men complimented women because they wanted something from them—most often one thing in particular. She put on her Order of Remembrance, then turned her back on her husband. "Fasten the ribbon at the back of my neck, would you, Hal?"

"Of course," he said, and did. Then he kissed the back of her neck, too. She'd more than half expected him to do that, and she let him get away with it. By his relieved expression, he'd wondered if she would.

"Are you ready, Clara?" she called.

"Yes, Ma," her daughter answered from the room across the hall. "Is it time to go?"

"Just about," Nellie said. "And don't forget your coat."

"Do I have to bring it?" Clara said. "It's not cold out."

She was right. The weather was springlike, even though spring still lay two and a half weeks away. But Nellie answered, "Yes, take it. I'm bringing one, too. You never can tell what it'll do." Clara grumbled, but she couldn't complain too hard, not if Nellie was also bringing a coat. And Nellie knew she was right. She also had an umbrella, though the sun shone brightly for now. No, you never could tell.

They walked toward the Mall, for the parade of bands and companies of soldiers and—since this was another Socialist administration—gangs of workers who would precede the new President Blackford's inaugural address. They had a spot picked out—right in front of the rebuilt National Museum of Remembrance, and not far from the platform where the new president would speak. Edna and Merle and Armstrong would meet them there if they could fight their way through the crowd.

They wiggled forward till they stood in the second row in front of the museum. Nellie could see the platform, which was already filling with dignitaries. "We made good time," she said.

"Yes, we did," Hal agreed. "We'll be able to see everything, and we won't have any trouble hearing the president talk."

Clara chose that moment to announce, "Mama, I have to go."

"You *always* have to go," Nellie said in no small exasperation. She sighed. "I'll take you into the museum. Hold our places, Hal. Do the best you can." Her husband nodded. She took Clara's hand. "Come along with me, young lady. Why didn't you go before we left? That's what I want to know."

"I did," Clara answered with a child's self-righteousness. "I have to go *again*."

The line for the women's powder room at the Museum of Remembrance was as long as Nellie had feared it would be. She and Clara needed twenty minutes to work their way to the front. By then, Clara was fidgeting enough to convince Nellie she hadn't said she needed to go just to be annoying.

Many more people had come to the Mall by the time Nellie and Clara emerged from the museum once more. Nellie had to do some elbowing, and stepped on a couple of feet that didn't get out of the way fast enough to suit her. "Watch where you're going, lady," an angry man said.

"I'm so sorry," Nellie answered, and stepped on him again, not in the least by accident.

Hal Jacobs wasn't a big man. Nellie began to wonder if she'd ever find him. She was starting to worry when Merle Grimes said, "Hello, Mother Jacobs." He and Edna and Armstrong stood with Hal.

"Hello, Merle," she said. "I'd've gone right past the lot of you if you hadn't spoken up, Lord help me if I wouldn't."

"We're all together now," Hal said. "That's the way things are supposed to be."

"That's right," Edna said, a little louder than she had to. She clung to Merle's hand. They both wore their decorations, too. From what Nellie could see, things between them weren't quite the same as they had been before Merle found out about Nicholas H. Kincaid. They were tolerable, and Edna didn't seem actively discontented, but they weren't so lovey-dovey as before. *Told you so, Edna,* Nellie said, but only to herself.

A band began to play. Nellie stopped worrying about her daughter and son-in-law—and even about her other daughter and her grandson, who got along no better than they ever did—and watched yet another inauguration, yet another passing of the torch from one president to another.

This year, the passing was odd, as outgoing President Sinclair was about fifteen years younger than incoming President Blackford. It was as if the USA were moving backwards in time, something the country didn't do very often. Chief Justice Holmes administered the oath to Hosea Blackford.

Voice aided by a microphone, Blackford repeated the words that made him president of the United States: "I do solemnly swear that I will faithfully execute the Office of President of the United States, and will to the best of my Ability, preserve, protect and defend the Constitution of the United States."

A sigh ran through the crowd. Nellie had heard that oath every four years since 1881—not counting 1916. It made official what had happened five months before. Now the country had a new president. *Now we see what happens next,* she thought, as if it were a new chapter in a novel. And so, in a way, it was.

The most immediate thing that happened next was Blackford's inaugural address. Nellie got a good look at him up there on the stand. Behind him, his wife, who was much younger than he, tried to keep a little boy younger than Armstrong quiet. *Robbing the cradle, Mr. President?* Nellie thought.

"I am pleased to tell you how well off our country is today, thanks to the inspired leadership given over the past eight years by my most distinguished predecessor, President Upton Sinclair." Hosea Blackford owned a ringing baritone. Nellie thought she remembered hearing he'd been a lawyer before going to Congress. He certainly had the voice for it. He led the applause for the president leaving office. Sinclair rose one last time from his seat behind the podium to acknowledge the cheers of the crowd.

As the new ex-president sat down again, Blackford went on, "We are at peace on our continent. We extend the hand of friendship to both the Confederate States and the Empire of Mexico. We share a common heritage with the CSA, and I am pleased to note that Confederate President Burton Mitchel, a civilized gentleman, shares this view. May we see no more war in North America, not ever again!"

Nellie clapped as loud as she could. If war came, it would surely come to Washington, would surely come down on her head. She wanted peace for her daughter, peace for her grandson. She'd seen too much of war ever to want to know it again.

"To the north, the Republic of Quebec is our staunch ally," Blackford declared. Even Nellie knew that meant the Quebecois would do as they were told. The president said, "English-speaking Canada continues to recover under our guidance." Even Nellie knew that meant the rest of the Canucks would damn well have to do as they were told. "And Utah, long turbulent, looks toward the day when it shall be a state like any other."

That drew scattered boos even from a mostly friendly crowd. Few people outside of Utah had much sympathy for the Mormons, not after two uprisings.

"Broad oceans protect us from foreign foes," President

Blackford said. "The Sandwich Islands serve as a bastion against the Empire of Japan, while the Atlantic shields us against Europe's unending turmoil and danger. And let me note that I am completely confident the panics of the past ten days in Vienna, in Rome, in Paris, and in London will not affect the Empire of Germany in any important way, and that they cannot possibly cross the Atlantic and endanger our own well-being."

Everyone applauded vigorously there. So far, the Berlin and New York exchanges had avoided most of the jitters afflicting the smaller European markets, though Richmond also seemed nervous. Beside Nellie, Hal murmured, "If we can ride it out for another week, we'll be fine. The Austro-Hungarians cause so much trouble. If they hadn't called for repayment of that Russian loan . . ."

"Hush," Nellie told him. "I want to hear the president."

Blackford seemed to have said everything he was going to say about foreign affairs. He switched to what he hoped to accomplish within the United States: "We want no man hungry. We want no one able-bodied without work. We want no capitalists exploiting the workers of our great land. We want justice for all, and we intend to get it. We will not let the aged, who have worked hard all their lives, be discarded like so many worn-out cogs in our industrial machine."

Nellie applauded that. She'd worked hard all her life, and looked forward to the day when she wouldn't have to any more. Old-age insurance sounded good to her—better than relying on whatever charity she might get from Merle and Edna, and perhaps from Clara and whomever she ended up marrying.

If Blackford can find a way for me to have enough to live on when I'm old, I'd vote Socialist forever—if I could vote at all. Women's suffrage was here, all over the USA— but not in Washington, D.C. Men were every bit as disenfranchised in the nation's legal capital. Now more than ever, that struck Nellie as monstrously unfair. Men had complained about it for as long as she could remember. It also affected her now, so she noticed it more. Hosea Blackford said not a word about votes for Washington.

X

Clarence Potter had to wait to see his broker. He spent the
time in Ulysses Dalby's waiting room drumming his fingers
on his thigh. To the outside world, he showed only impatience. He kept the fear and rage he felt bottled up inside.
No one would have known from his stolid, impassive face
the way his heart pounded or how cold and damp the
palms of his hands were.

At last, the broker's secretary said, "Mr. Dalby will
see you now, Mr. Potter."

"Thank you, Betty." Potter strode past her without
another word. She was a redhead whose generous contours
could usually be counted on to distract male investors from
their worries. Today, Potter was too worried to be distracted.

He closed the door behind him as he went into Ulysses
Dalby's office. The broker was a few years older than he:
a plump, gray-haired man with a jovial manner who wore
sharp suits. He extended a well-manicured hand with a
glittering pinkie ring for Potter to shake. "Good morning,
sir," he said, his Low Country accent sweet and syrupy.
"What can I do for you this fine day?"

"Get me out," Clarence Potter said.

Dalby raised an eyebrow. "I beg your pardon, sir?"

"Get me out," Potter repeated. "Sell every stock I have,
fast as you can do it, best price you can get, but sell.
Richmond and New York exchanges both. I'll be back for
the cash this afternoon."

"Mr. Potter, I hesitate to carry out an order like that," Dalby said. "Are you sure you've considered carefully?"

"Maybe you'll call me a fool a month from now," Potter answered. "If I'm wrong, I can buy back in. But I'll have something to buy back in with. My opinion is that there's a fire in the woods. If I don't get out now, it will burn me out."

"Panic selling, sir, will only make the fire worse," Dalby said.

"Sitting around while the woods burn won't do me any good," Potter said. "I'll take my chances on the other. What have you done with *your* portfolio, Mr. Dalby?"

"I've diversified as much as possible," Dalby replied.

"That's fancy talk. It means you're already out of the markets, doesn't it?" Potter asked. When the broker didn't answer right away, Potter nodded. "I thought so. I'm getting out while the getting is at least tolerable, if not good. Place those sell orders right this minute. I want to make sure you do it. I'll be back for my money this afternoon, mind you, and I expect to have it." He didn't quite say, *I know where you live, Dalby,* but it hung in the air.

Only after the broker made the necessary telephone calls did Clarence Potter leave his office. When he stepped back out onto the streets of Charleston, he still felt panic in the air. A newsboy shouted, "France leaves the gold standard!" Another one called, "London market plunges again! Big selloff in Richmond!" And yet another cried, "President Mitchel calls for calm! Confederate dollar still sound, he says!"

Potter hoped Burton Mitchel was right about that last. If the currency went out the window as it had right after the war, there'd be hell to pay, but no money for the Devil. *Will I have to buy gold?* Potter wondered. *Is there any gold to buy? I'll worry about that later. First things first. Banknotes. Nice brown banknotes. Let me get a good, fat wad of them and I can laugh at the world for a while.*

When he went back to Ulysses Dalby's office that afternoon, the newspaper hawkers were talking about the beating the Richmond exchange had taken, and about the one the New York exchange had taken, too. He set his teeth and hoped the broker hadn't decamped with his money.

Betty the decorative secretary led him into Dalby's office. Just seeing Dalby made him let out a sigh of relief. He let out another one when Dalby handed him a thick sheaf of brown banknotes. What he let out after counting the money was more on the order of a grunt of pain. "This is all?" he demanded.

"That's all, Mr. Potter. I tried to warn you: you don't get top dollar in a bear market," Ulysses Dalby said. "Here are the transaction records. I'm not cheating you."

"Well, maybe you don't," Potter said after carefully checking the records. He did his best to sound philosophical. "But I would have got a lot less if I'd waited till tomorrow or the day after or next week, wouldn't I?"

Dalby nodded. "I have to say you would have. I'm also going to ask you one thing more: in what bank do you intend to put your money now that you've got it?"

"Why, the First Secession Bank and Trust," Potter answered. "I've been doing business with them since I came down here after the war. You must know that. How come?"

"Mm . . . It may be nothing. You're a good judge of banks—I think the First Secession is a pretty solid outfit. It may come through all this just fine."

Clarence Potter stared at him. "It may, you say?" Dalby nodded again. Potter whistled softly. "You think it's going to be as bad as that? Banks going under, the way they did in '88 and '04?"

"Yes, it may be that bad," the broker answered after a little thought. "On the other hand, it may be a good deal worse." Potter started to laugh, thinking Dalby had made a grim sort of joke. But Dalby's face was serious, even somber. "I'm not kidding, Mr. Potter," he said. "I'm not kidding at all. In the last couple of panics, our markets took a beating, and so did Wall Street up in the USA, but the rest of the world went on about its business. It's not like that this time, sir. I wish to heaven it were. This time . . . It won't do much to Africa, I suppose, and maybe not to China, either—the heathen Chinese are already about as bad off as they can be. But I don't believe anyplace else will get off untouched."

Potter whistled again, an even lower, even more mournful note. He might have been tolling the passing of an era. *Maybe I am,* he thought. "My God," he said aloud. "And I thought I was a pessimist."

"I watched the ticker tape all day, Mr. Potter. I watched it get further and further behind the sales it was supposed to be listing," Dalby said. "When I saw you this morning, I still had some hope. I'd say it died about an hour and a half ago. Maybe I'm wrong. I hope I'm wrong. I hope so. But I don't think so, not any more."

He looked shellshocked. That was exactly how he looked, Potter realized. He'd been through too much, like men in the Army of Northern Virginia during the war. They'd got that stunned, beaten look on their faces, too. Half the time after that, they didn't care if they lived or died. Dalby didn't seem to, not right now.

Stowing your money in your mattress was a joke that went at least as far back as money and mattresses. Potter wondered which of those had come first. Joke or not, he did just that with the banknotes he'd got from Ulysses Dalby. The next morning, he closed out his account at the First Secession Bank and Trust. The lines at the bank weren't too bad. "I assure you, sir," said the young clerk who gave him his money, "we are perfectly sound."

"I believe you, son," Potter answered. "That's why I'm doing this now. Who knows how the devil you're going to be in a couple of weeks, though?"

The clerk didn't try to tell him everything would be fine. He found himself wishing the fellow would have.

He went to the Whig Party meeting the following Tuesday more out of morbid curiosity than for any other reason. The stock exchanges hadn't got any better. They'd kept right on sinking, Richmond faster than New York. Lines outside the banks were starting to get longer—and more anxious.

The meeting went very much as Potter expected—very much as he'd feared—it would. It put him in mind of a lot of maiden ladies talking—or rather, trying not to talk—about sex. The lawyers and businessmen circled the building crash like a man circling a rattlesnake in a small

315

room. They couldn't ignore it, but they didn't want to deal with it, either. They kept making noises about "changing conditions" and "uncertainty" and "a seeming slump in the business cycle."

Clarence Potter stuck up his hand. He needed a while to be recognized. He wasn't surprised; he'd expected they wouldn't want to notice him. He'd proved himself a gadfly, and they didn't like that. But he was, or could be, a patient gadfly. At last, the chairman had no choice but to turn his way and ask, "Yes, Mr. Potter?"

"Boys," Potter said, "the jig is up."

Bang! The chairman rapped loudly for order. "Have you anything more germane to say, Mr. Potter, or may we move on to the next order of business?"

"What *is* the next order of business in the middle of a crash?" Potter demanded. "Sending out for more strings so we can fiddle while the market burns?" *Bang!* went the gavel again. Potter ignored it. "Next Congressional elections are only a few months away," he said harshly. "If this is as bad as it looks, how do we intend to send one single solitary Whig incumbent back to Richmond for the new Congress? We'd better be thinking about that, eh, before we worry about anything else. And we'd better try to keep the country on its feet so it'll be in some sort of shape to want to vote for us. How are we supposed to go about that?"

Bang! Bang! Bang! "Mr. Potter, you are as thoroughly out of order as it is possible for one man to be," the chairman all but shouted.

"You're right," Potter agreed. "But the country is a lot further out of order than I can be, and so are the Whigs. I have one last question, gentlemen, and then I'm done: if this turns out to be as bad as it looks right now, how the hell do you propose to keep those Freedom Party yokels from trying to pick up the pieces?"

Bang! Bang! Bang! Bang! Bang! The gavel descended again and again, a veritable fusillade of banging. That succeeded in silencing Clarence Potter. But, he noticed, no one tried to answer his question. He'd expected nothing different, nothing better. He'd hoped for something better, but he knew too well the difference between hope and expectation. He walked out of the meeting gloomy, but he'd figured he would.

A couple of days later, after watching stocks tumble lower yet, after listening on the wireless to a speech by President Mitchel that was as full of misplaced optimism as any he'd ever heard, he decided to telephone Anne Colleton. He wasn't even sure she would remember him; a brief acquaintance in a political squabble a couple of years before didn't necessarily constitute an introduction.

But she said, "Oh, yes, Mr. Potter. I do appreciate the help you gave me against that fool of a Braxton Donovan. What's on your mind today?"

"I don't know, frankly," he answered. "The main reason I called was to see how you were doing. If anyone could land on her feet in this mess, you're the one."

"I'm not too bad," she said. "As soon as I saw which way the wind was blowing, I sold out as fast as I could. I got hurt. I didn't get wiped out. If I'd stayed in the market a little longer, I would have. How about you, Mr. Potter?"

"About the same," he told her. "I could have done better if I'd left a couple of days sooner, but I'm getting by for the time being. An awful lot of people aren't, though, and it may get worse before it gets better."

"I'm afraid you're right," Anne Colleton said. "Not many people can see that. In a way, it's good to know someone can."

"Belshazzar needed Daniel to read the writing on the wall," Potter said. "I hope someone can do the job for us."

"I wish there were no job to do," Anne answered.

"Well, so do I," he answered. "But I'm very much afraid this is only the beginning, and not just for the Confederate States. In a way, misery loves company. In another way, if everyone's in trouble, nobody can help anybody else get out of it."

Anne Colleton didn't say anything for perhaps half a minute. At last, she told him, "That makes good sense to me." Another pause. "You seem to make very good sense, Mr. Potter. Maybe we should talk some more if we get the chance."

And what am I letting myself in for if I say yes to that? Potter wondered. But the answer seemed obvious. Trouble. *Only question is, how much trouble?* He too paused, but not for long. "Maybe we should, Miss Colleton. Maybe we should."

When Chester Martin got off his shift at the Toledo steel mill, he went straight to the Socialist Party hall not far from the factory. He could have had himself a beer there, but opened a bottle of Nesbit's instead. He wanted to keep his wits about him.

Spotting Albert Bauer, he called, "What do you think of this management notion?"

"Cutting shifts from eight hours to six, you mean?" Bauer answered.

"Yeah, that's what I mean, all right, unless there's another brand-new management notion I haven't heard about yet," Chester said.

Bauer didn't look happy. "Way I see it, we've got two choices," he said. "We can say yes, and let 'em cut our pay by a quarter. Or we can say no, and have 'em fire one out of four of us." *He* was drinking a beer. He drained it, then added, "This is what you call being between the Devil and the deep blue sea."

"I don't trust those management bastards," Martin said. "Like as not, it's a trick to pump up their profits and hurt us at the same time. Instead of hiring goons and scabs, they play these games nowadays."

"I know." But Bauer looked mighty unhappy. "Hate to tell you, Chester, but I don't think so, not this time. I've seen the orders going through the pipeline. They've fallen right off a cliff. Nobody's buying steel, not to speak of. There's no point in making it if nobody's ordering. Less than no point, in fact—a big inventory just drives prices down when orders do start picking up. I don't think the bosses are playing games for the sake of playing games, not this time. I wish they were. I'd strike in a red-hot minute."

"Fine. Wonderful. But somebody'd better tell me how the hell I'm supposed to make ends meet on three-quarters of my proper pay."

"Well, that depends," Bauer said slowly. "Would you rather try to make ends meet on none of your proper pay? The company's trying hard not to get rid of people. I don't like the bosses, and I never will, but I have to give them credit for that."

Martin told him exactly where he'd like to give the bosses credit. Bauer laughed. Martin said, "It's not funny, dammit. If my wife didn't have work, we *wouldn't* make it on three-quarters of a paycheck. I'd sooner take my chances on getting the sack. If I did, I'd look for something else. And if I didn't, I'd be all right."

"So much for the solidarity of the proletariat," Bauer observed, and Martin felt himself flush. Bauer went on, "But if they didn't get you in the first round of firings, how do you know they wouldn't the next time? Because there will be a next time, Chester, sure as you're standing there."

"A next time." Martin scowled. "Hadn't thought of that. Bet you're right, though. Who would have thought a loan the Russians couldn't—or maybe wouldn't—pay back would cause all this trouble?"

"For want of a nail," Bauer said, and then sighed. "We're all going to be wanting nails before too long."

"Oh, yeah?" Chester said. "If we're all going to be wanting nails, how come they're cutting back on how much steel they're making?"

"Because whether we want them or not, we won't be able to afford them," Bauer answered.

"Of course we won't be able to afford them. They're cutting our hours."

Bauer's smile was full of anything but amusement. "Welcome to the vicious circle."

That circle was anything but welcome to Martin. He hung around the Party hall till he saw no one had any firm notion of how to respond to the bosses' proposal for cutting hours. No one could decide if it was good because it saved jobs or bad because it cut pay. Martin concluded the proposal would probably go forward. Strong opposition from the workers might have stopped it. If they couldn't decide whether it was good or bad, they would find out by experiment—on themselves.

He rode the trolley back to the flat he shared with Rita. His own mood was glum, or worse than glum. He'd told Albert Bauer the exact truth. If his hours and pay got cut to three-quarters of what he had now, the only thing that would keep him afloat was his wife's salary.

And Rita seemed anything but happy when he came through the door. After a perfunctory kiss, she said, "Orders have taken a real tumble since the market started going down. Nobody wants pipe any more—not new pipe, anyway."

It was spring, a bright spring, the weather full of new-puppy warmth and hope. Ice walked Chester Martin's back even so. He tried to remember when he'd known fear like this. The Roanoke front? He shook his head. That terror had been different, and far more immediate: fear of death and pain and mutilation. This was something else. Fear of loss, fear of hunger, fear of endless misery without escape. Fear of bills. Fear of moving back in with his mother and father—if this quiet, creeping horror didn't lay hold of them, too.

When Martin laughed, he might have been whistling while walking past a graveyard. "It was just a few weeks ago when we figured we could have any old thing we wanted," he said, and went on to tell Rita about the company's plan to cut everybody's hours.

She listened to that, her face getting longer and longer. "I know what I want," she said. "I want us to keep our jobs, that's what."

"Yeah," he said quietly. "That's about what it boils down to, isn't it?"

"It's hard times when your neighbor's out of work," Rita said. "It's the end of the world when you are."

"Maybe if the government really had seized the means of production this wouldn't have happened," Chester said, trying to make himself believe it. He couldn't. Shaking his head, he went on, "No, they couldn't've done it, I don't think. It would have meant real class war—and it might not have helped."

"What are we going to do?" Rita asked. "What *can* we do?"

"Hang on tight," he said. "We're still working. We're going to lose most of the stocks we bought, though. I hated answering the last margin call—felt like throwing money away. And we probably won't be able to afford to answer the next one."

"We've got each other. We're healthy." Rita sounded as if she was trying to reassure herself, and not having much luck.

"It can't get much worse," Chester said. "How could stocks go any lower than they have already? There's got to be a floor somewhere."

"Yes, but where?" Rita asked, and he had no answer. He felt less ashamed of that than he might have otherwise—for no one else in the USA—no one else in the whole world, by all the signs—had any answer to it, either. No, he wasn't ashamed, but that didn't mean he wasn't frightened.

He went to work day by day, having nothing else he could do. Before long, his shift did go from eight hours to six. His pay dropped by a quarter, too. He hated that, but he supposed he would have hated being without a paycheck even more. As long as Rita had a job, too, they got by.

The market continued to sink. Reading the papers, Martin took occasional consolation in noticing Richmond stocks had fallen even further than those on Wall Street. Did misery really love company? He didn't know about that, either. What he did know was that, every day, there seemed to be more misery to go around.

People started telling stories about brokers jumping off bridges and diving out of windows. Nobody could say whether those stories were true. People told them anyhow. One day in the middle of June, Wall Street stopped sinking. It dove. Maybe brokers didn't, but the market did. The wave of sell orders overwhelmed the ticker tape. It lagged ever further behind the tidal wave of disaster. The last few shares Chester had so proudly held on to went then, on what the papers called Swan-Dive Wednesday. By that time, he'd almost stopped caring. Not till almost four hours after the market closed did the chattering tape finally spit out the last of the day's losses.

When Thursday dawned, the market didn't open. An eerie calm prevailed at the steel mill. "Reminds me of the day after a big attack that didn't work," Martin said to Albert Bauer as they opened their lunch pails together.

Bauer had been at the front, too. He nodded. "Or maybe it did," he said, "only we were on the receiving end." He took a bite out of his cheese sandwich. He'd usually eaten bologna or pastrami before the market tumbled. So had Martin. His sandwich had cheese in it, too. Cheese was cheaper. Bauer went on, "President Blackford's got almost four years left in his term, but he's a lame duck already. Poor sorry son of a bitch."

"He's doing everything he can," Chester said. "I like what he said in the paper this morning. 'We have nowhere to go but up.' That's good. He means it, too—you can tell."

"Oh, yeah. I'm not arguing with you," Bauer answered. "But even if things do go up, what will people remember? They'll remember how far down we went, and who was in the Powel House when we did. Come 1932, he'll have Democrats lined up six deep to run against him."

Martin thought about that. It made altogether too much sense to be comfortable. "Well, the class struggle takes a step back," he said. "Or probably takes a step back. You never can tell, not for sure."

"Want to bet?" Bauer said. "I'm as good a Socialist as any man around, and I've got twenty bucks says there'll be a Democrat in Powel House after the '32 elections."

"You won't get my twenty," Martin said. "Wish I could, but Rita'd kill me—and I think I'd lose the dough. Times are tough enough without throwing it away."

"Of course, by the time '32 rolls around, I might have forgotten who I made the bet with," Bauer said.

"Fat chance," Martin answered. "It's not just that you wouldn't forget between now and then, Al. It's that you wouldn't let me forget."

"Who, me?" Bauer did his best to sound indignant. "Come on. Eat up. We've got to get back to it pretty goddamn quick."

"Right," Martin said tightly. The company was also

cracking down on people who violated its rules. He didn't want to end up on the street. Six hours' pay was better than none at all.

When he got home that night, he found Rita crumpled in tears on the sofa. "Oh, Lord!" he said. "What's the matter, sweetie?" He feared he knew the answer even without the question he had to ask.

And he was right. "They fired me," his wife answered. "They told me to clean out my desk and not come back tomorrow—they can't afford to keep me any more. I've been there seven years, and they threw me out like a piece of dirt. Where am I going to go? What am I going to do? What are *we* going to do?"

"I don't know," Chester said dazedly. "So help me God, I don't know." In a few weeks, they'd gone from having two paychecks to having three-quarters of one. That was bad enough—was worse than bad enough. But what was worse yet, what was really terrifying, was that, compared to an awful lot of people, they were still well off.

In the Terry, times hadn't been good since the last hectic days of the Great War. Back then, with every white man possible at the front, Augusta's Negroes had filled factory jobs galore. They'd made less money than the whites they were displacing, but even that added up to more money than they'd ever seen in their lives till that time. Then the whites, those who'd lived, came back, and the factory jobs dried up. People began living hand-to-mouth again.

Erasmus' place was a case in point. Scipio would have thought a fish market and café in a poor part of town immune from anything so remote as a stock-market panic. After all, the worst had happened in the Terry a dozen years earlier . . . hadn't it?

He would have thought that, but he would have been wrong. Erasmus' wrinkled face got longer with each passing day. His grizzled hair got grayer, too, or so it seemed to Scipio.

One morning, while Scipio washed the pile of breakfast dishes, Erasmus put his discontent into words: "They ain't comin' in."

"Ain't that bad, boss," Scipio said. "They ain't comin', where we get all these here dishes?"

"They ain't comin'," Erasmus repeated. " 'Fore all this panic happen, woulda been twice the dishes. Woulda been twice the money, too."

He was right, of course. Scipio's denial meant very little. Erasmus' place remained busy. It wasn't packed, not the way it had been before the market plunged. Scipio put the best face on things he could: "People's bein' careful wid dey money."

Erasmus shook his head. "A month ago, say, people was bein' careful with their money. Ain't like that no more. Now what it's like is, folks who come here, they ain't hardly got no money to be careful with."

"Lotta white folks outta work," Scipio admitted. "Bathsheba, she done lost fo', five cleanin' jobs las' few weeks. De buckra ain't got the money to give her."

"Here in the Terry, ain't many of us works for our ownselves," Erasmus said. "We mostly works for the buckra, almost like it was still slavery days. If the buckra outta work, we outta work, on account of they can't afford to pay us no more. How is I supposed to make money when there ain't no money to make?"

"Dunno," Scipio said. He waved. "Doin' pretty good so far."

"Ain't broke yet," Erasmus said. "Dunno why not, 'specially the way you eats." He wagged a finger at Scipio.

Had Scipio been white, he would have turned red. But taking meals at Erasmus' place was as much a part of what his boss paid him as the banknotes he got every Friday. It saved him money. The way things were going, the way Bathsheba's cleaning jobs were drying up, he needed to save all the money he could.

And Erasmus said not a word when he fixed himself a fried-egg sandwich and a big plate of grits for lunch. He'd just finished when the first lunch customer came in: a cleaning woman whose latest job had been close by the edge of the Terry. "Don't know how long I kin keep comin' here," she said as she took a bite out of a bacon-lettuce-and-tomato sandwich. "White folks is lettin' people go.

Ain't got no money their ownselves, sure ain't got none to spend on cleanin' their houses."

"I seen that, too," Scipio said. "My wife, she done los' half she people."

"World's a crazy place nowadays," the woman said. "Lady at the house I was at jus' now, her husband, he been a Whig forever, an' his daddy before him, an' *his* daddy before him. She say he talkin' 'bout votin' Freedom when the 'lections come round this fall. I didn't say nothin'. You don't like to tell the lady what's payin' you her husband ain't got no brains." She took another bite.

From his station in front of the stove, Erasmus said, "When the white folks see their money goin' away, some of 'em liable to do some crazy things."

"How many of 'em do dem crazy things?" Scipio wondered as he fetched the cleaning lady a cup of coffee. "We gwine have buckra in de streets yellin', 'Freedom!' again? Reckoned we was done wid dat."

"God do what He want to do, not what we wants Him to do," the cleaning woman said. "Thank you kindly, Xerxes," she added when Scipio set the coffee on the table.

"You's welcome," he answered absently.

How many whites were losing their jobs or losing money? He had no way of knowing, not for sure. More than a few, though; the stories in the *Constitutionalist* made that very clear. So did what was happening to the jobs of Negroes who depended on whites for work. How many of the whites who lost their jobs *would* start voting for Jake Featherston and his party?

Scipio had no way of knowing that, either, not for sure. But he'd just heard of one, and that was one more than he wanted to know about.

The cleaning lady gulped the coffee and got to her feet. She left money on the tabletop and hurried away. Over her shoulder, she said, "Can't be late gittin' back. Miz Hutton, I reckon she grab the first excuse she find to put me on the street. Don't aim to give her none." Out the door she went, in a hurry because her tip was small.

A man who sold secondhand furniture across the street came in for some fried catfish. As he ate, he remarked,

"Had me a couple-three buckra come in the last few days. Ain't seen none in a hell of a long time 'fore that."

"Buy anything?" Scipio asked.

"Sure enough did," the furniture dealer answered. "Sold me a couple beds and a good chest o' drawers."

"Good for you, Athenaeus," Erasmus said. " 'Bout time I hear of somebody doin' good right now."

"Fellas sellin' new furniture, they's the ones wouldn't be happy if they knowed," Athenaeus said. "White folks all say they look at the new stuff first, but they can't afford it, no way, nohow. So they come to me."

"Good to hear it," Scipio echoed; as Erasmus had said, any news of success was welcome. But Athenaeus wasn't wrong. What would the white furniture dealers whose goods hadn't sold think?

And it wasn't just what they would think. What would they do? What could any man do, when he stared at bills and had no money to pay them? Would they put on white shirts and butternut trousers and start shouting, "Freedom!" at the top of their lungs? If they did, could anybody blame them?

Scipio nodded. *I can blame them,* he thought, hearing inside himself the precise English he no longer dared speak loud. *I can blame them, for the Freedom Party will not make their troubles disappear, even if they think it will. And what the Freedom Party will do to me and mine if ever it should come to power . . .*

That fear had spread all through the colored communities of the CSA in the early 1920s, and then receded as the Party's fortunes ebbed. Now white men were seeing the Confederate States could still know hard times. What would that discovery, that rediscovery, mean for Negroes here? Scipio didn't know. He feared finding out. Try as he would, though, he saw no escape.

"What kin we do?" he said aloud, hoping one of the other men in the place would have a better idea than he did. "Can't go nowheres."

"Ain't noplace else wants us," Erasmus said. "Not the USA."

"That's for sure," Athenaeus agreed. "They don't like

the niggers they got. Ain't got very many, an' sure don't want no more."

"Stock market in de USA down de sewer, too," Scipio said. "They ain't got no money, no spirit, to help nobody else, not when they got trouble helpin' they ownselves."

"Good things they's down, too, you wants to know what I thinks," Athenaeus said. "If they was up, they be lordin' it over us. They do that, jus' git more buckra listenin' to Jake Featherston on the wireless and gittin' all hot and bothered afterwards."

For a long time before the world finally went mad in 1914, respect for each other's strength had kept the United States and Confederate States from going to war. Scipio had never imagined mutual weakness could do the same, but he couldn't deny Athenaeus had a point. It wasn't one he'd thought of, either.

"Empire of Mexico, mebbe," he said. But neither Erasmus nor Athenaeus paid much attention to that. Scipio couldn't take it seriously himself. To a Negro in eastern Georgia, the Empire of Mexico might as well have been on the dark side of the moon. Besides, what were the odds that Mexicans had any more use for Negroes than white men did?

Erasmus asked a more immediately relevant question: " 'Fore long, some black folks gwine start runnin' out o' money. What happen to 'em?"

"They git hungry," Athenaeus said.

"Church help some," Scipio said.

"Church be swamped," Erasmus said. Scipio nodded. By all the signs, that would come true, and soon. His boss went on, "Ain't no use waitin' fo' the gummint to do somethin'. Wait till Judgment Day, gummint won't do nothin' fo' no niggers."

" 'Fore long, some white folks starts runnin' out o' money and gettin' hungry, too," Athenaeus said. "Plenty po' buckra, they ain't hardly better off'n niggers. Gummint worry 'bout the buckra first, you wait an' see."

"What's a po' nigger gwine do?" Erasmus asked. "Starve?"

The word hung in the air. Scipio had known a lot of

hungry people; during the war, he'd been hungry himself after the Confederates destroyed the Congaree Socialist Republic. But there was a difference between being hungry and starving. He tried to imagine thousands, maybe tens of thousands, of Negroes (and whites, too) going without because they had no money with which to buy food.

Outside, the sun shone brightly. The day was hot and muggy. It would stay hot and muggy from now all the way till fall. Even so, Scipio felt a chill. This was liable to be a disaster of Biblical proportions.

"What kin we do?" Athenaeus asked mournfully. "What kin anybody do?"

"Pray," Erasmus answered. "God done made this happen. He kin make us come through it, too, so long as He take it in His mind He want to do dat."

"Amen," Athenaeus said. Scipio made himself nod. He didn't want to seem out of place—seeming out of place was one of his greatest fears, because it was deadly dangerous. But if God had really wanted to do something about this disaster, couldn't He have stopped it in the first place?

"More we pray, more He gonna know how much we loves Him," Erasmus said. Along with being a believer, though, he was a relentlessly practical man. He went on, " 'Course, we gots to work hard, too. God ain't never gonna pay no heed to nobody who don't work hard."

Scipio would have bet he'd say that. Erasmus not only believed in the virtues of hard work, he practiced what he preached. Scipio himself was sure it couldn't hurt. What he wasn't sure of was how much it could help.

Something was wrong in Salt Lake City. Colonel Abner Dowling shook his head. Something was always wrong in Salt Lake City. It wouldn't have been the place, or the sort of place, it was if something hadn't been wrong all the time. But something now was different. Anything different in Salt Lake City automatically roused Dowling's suspicions. As far as he could tell, *different* and *dangerous* were two sides of the same coin.

"I'll tell you what it is, sir," Captain Angelo Toricelli said.

"Go ahead, Angelo," Dowling urged. "Tell."

"Nobody's building anything, that's what," his adjutant said. "It's quieter than it ought to be."

Slowly, Dowling nodded. "You're right. I'll be damned if you're not right. It isn't on account of they've got everything rebuilt, either. Still plenty of wreckage lying around."

"Yes, sir," Captain Toricelli agreed. "But an awful lot of money that would have paid for more construction all of a sudden isn't there—it's gone."

Dowling nodded again. He gave Toricelli a sidelong glance. Fortunately, his adjutant didn't notice. The way the younger man watched every penny, he might have been a Jew, not an Italian. Dowling didn't want Toricelli to know he was thinking that. He didn't want to insult his adjutant. And everybody had to pay special attention to money these days, because it was so very thin on the ground.

With a sigh, Dowling said, "Not much we can do about it. At least we've got the Army paying our salaries."

"Yes, sir, and I'm damn glad of it, too," Toricelli answered. "I just got a letter from New York, from home. My brother-in-law's out of a job."

"What's he do?" Dowling asked.

"He reads X rays, sir—went to night school to learn the trade," Toricelli said, not without pride. "My sister and he've got five children, and another one on the way. I don't know what they'll do if he doesn't find something quick."

"I hope he does," Dowling said, on the whole sincerely. "Who would have thought the bottom could drop out of things so fast?"

"Nobody," Captain Toricelli answered. "But it has."

He was right about that, too. The Army censored Salt Lake City papers pretty hard. Pain came through their pages even so. Stories of half-done buildings abandoned, of banks going under, of people losing jobs, couldn't very well be prettied up. And the only way to leave those stories out of the newspapers would have been to have no papers at all.

Captain Toricelli touched a fat document on his desk. "Don't tell me what that is," Dowling said. "Let me guess: another normalization petition."

"Right the first time," his adjutant said.

"It's not as though I haven't seen enough of them," Dowling said. Every few months, the Mormons of Salt Lake City—and the occasional gentile, too—would circulate petitions asking that Utah finally be treated like any other state in the USA. Dowling had got a couple of dozen since coming to the state capital. With a sigh, he went on, "They still haven't figured out I'm not the one they ought to send these to, because I have no authority to grant them. They should go to General Pershing—he's supreme commander of the military district."

A thoroughly precise man, Toricelli said, "He hasn't got authority to grant them, either. Only the president and Congress can do that."

"What do you think the chances are?" Dowling asked.

"Better than decent, if the Mormons can keep their noses clean," Captain Toricelli answered. "The Socialists seem to want to do it."

"I know." Dowling packed a world of meaning into two words. "They think a zebra can change its stripes, the way the one in that Englishman's fable did. I think . . ." He shook his head. "What I think doesn't matter. I don't make policy. I just get stuck with carrying it out." He picked up the petition. It was a hefty one; it had to weigh a couple of pounds. "I'll take this to General Pershing's office, if you like."

"Oh, you don't need to do that, sir," Toricelli said. "It's not important. I can fetch it next time I go over there."

"I'm on my way," Dowling said. "Better Pershing's adjutant should have it on his desk than you on yours."

He caught Toricelli's eye. They shared a slightly conspiratorial chuckle. "Thank you very much, sir," the young captain said.

"You're welcome," Abner Dowling answered. "I've got to go over there and talk with the general about his scheme for mounting better guard on Temple Square. We need to do it; every broken rock from the Temple and the Tabernacle counts for a sacred relic with the more radical Mormons these days."

"Yes, sir," Toricelli said. "But there's a certain problem

in shooting anybody who bends to pick up a pebble in the square, too."

"A certain problem, yes," Dowling agreed. "And that's what I've got to talk to General Pershing about. How do we keep the Mormons from getting symbols of revolt without provoking them and ruining what ever bits of goodwill we've managed to build up since the war ended?"

"I'm sure I don't know, sir," his adjutant replied. "I hope you and the commanding general can find a way."

"So do I. Can't hope for much in the way of normalization if they're still picking up broken rocks and dreaming of treason." Dowling tucked the petition under his arm and strode down the hall to his superior's office. He took no small pleasure in dropping the document on Pershing's adjutant's desk, and in watching the papers already there jump as it thudded home.

"Thank you so much, sir," Pershing's adjutant, a major named Fred Corson, said with a sickly smile. "The general is waiting for you." He sounded reluctant to admit even that much to Dowling.

"Hello, Colonel," General Pershing said when Dowling walked in. A grin spread across his bulldog features. "Was that the thump of a normalization petition I heard just then?"

"It certainly was, sir," Dowling answered.

"Well, I'll forward it to Philadelphia," the commandant said. "That's my duty. And there that petition will sit till the end of time, along with all the others."

"Unless the Socialists decide to grant them all, that is," Dowling said.

"Yes. Unless. In that case, Colonel, you and I will both need new assignments, because normal states don't have soldiers occupying them. Part of me won't be sorry to get away." Pershing rose from behind his desk and went over to the window not far away. He looked at his fortified headquarters, and at Salt Lake City beyond. "Part of me, though, will regret leaving this state, because I'm convinced that, no matter what this administration may believe, Utah isn't ready for normalization. As a matter of fact, here we—"

331

Abner Dowling heard a distant *pop!* It might have been a motorcar backfiring, or a firecracker going off. It might have been, but it wasn't. At the same instant as he heard it, or perhaps even a split second before, the window in front of which General Pershing was standing shattered. Pershing made a surprised noise. That was the best way Dowling could have described it. It didn't hold much pain. Before Dowling fully realized what had happened, the military commandant of the state of Utah crumpled to the carpet in front of him.

"General Pershing?" Dowling whispered. He hurried over to the fallen man. He needed a moment to add two and two together. Only when he saw the neat hole and the spreading bloodstain in the middle of Pershing's chest did he fully understand what he was seeing. "General Pershing!" he said, sharply this time.

He grabbed for Pershing's wrist and felt for a pulse. He found none. Aside from that, the sudden sharp stink in the room told him what he needed to know. Pershing had fouled himself when the bullet struck home.

Thinking of a bullet made Dowling think of the man who'd fired it. He peered out through the shattered window. The U.S. perimeter around the headquarters ran out for several hundred yards. The gunman must have shot from well beyond it, which meant he had to be a brilliant sniper. In war-ravaged Utah, that was anything but impossible, as Colonel Dowling knew all too well.

Only while Dowling was shouting for Pershing's adjutant did he pause to wonder whether the sniper was still out there, peering through a telescope on his Springfield and waiting for another shot. He was, at the moment, too shocked, too stunned, to worry about it.

Major Corson hurried in. In his outer office, he hadn't even heard the gunshot. Dowling's shouts were what drew him. "Oh, Jesus Christ!" he said, which summed it up as well as anything. "Is he—?" He couldn't bring himself to say the word.

Dowling did: "He's dead, all right. He dropped down like somebody let all the air out of him. He was dead before he hit the rug—never knew what hit him."

Out on the perimeter, soldiers had started shouting and pointing. A couple of them started running. Dowling noted all that as if from a very great distance. In one sense, whether they caught the sniper mattered a great deal. In another sense, it hardly mattered at all. The damage was done, and more than done.

Pershing's adjutant saw the same thing. He got the truth into four words: "So much for normalization."

"Yeah," Dowling said. "We just went back to square one."

"Sir, you're senior officer in the state right now," Corson said. Dowling nodded; the city commandants in both Provo and Ogden were lieutenant colonels. Pershing's adjutant looked to him with desperate appeal in his eyes. "What are your orders?"

You're in charge of Utah. God help you, you poor, sorry bastard. Dowling tried to pull himself together. "Fetch a doctor. It won't do any good, but fetch him. Send men after that sniper." He feared that wouldn't do any good, either, but he had to try. "Call the president and the War Department, in that order. Let them know what's happened. After that, we close Salt Lake City down. We take hostages. We do whatever we have to do to let the Mormons know that if they want to play rough, we're going to play ten times rougher. Have you got that?"

"Yes, sir," Major Corson answered. He saluted and hurried away, leaving Dowling alone with General Pershing's body.

If the Mormons want to play rough, we'll play ten times rougher? Dear God in heaven, had he really said that? He nodded. He had. And, in saying it, he'd sounded a great deal like General George Armstrong Custer. He hadn't wanted to. He hadn't intended to. But he had, all the same. Custer had rubbed off on him after all. And if that wasn't a chilling thought . . .

If that wasn't a chilling thought, maybe it was a reminder that Custer, for all his enormous flaws—and nobody knew them better than Dowling; a general had no more secrets from his adjutant than a man from his valet—

had ended up the most successful soldier in the history of the United States.

I won't keep this command long, Dowling thought. *They'll bring in someone with stars on his shoulder straps as fast as they can.* Meanwhile, though, it was his. He had to do the best job he could while it remained his.

A doctor dashed into Pershing's office, little black bag in hand. "What do you need, Colonel?" he asked.

"Not me, Major," Dowling answered. "It's General Pershing who's dead." *Along with any hope for peace in Utah for God only knows how long.*

Jake Featherston strode through the streets of Richmond, his bodyguards surrounding him front and back, left and right. He moved swiftly and confidently, and with such abrupt decision that his turns would sometimes take even the alert guards by surprise, so they'd have to scramble to stay with him.

Richmond was not the city it had been before the war. By now, ten years after the Confederate States had yielded to the United States, almost all the damage from U.S. bombing aeroplanes had been repaired. Even so, something was missing from the city's heart. Before the Great War, everybody in Richmond had known the CSA sat on top of the world.

Nowadays ... Nowadays, Richmond felt poor and shabby. Everything looked gray. It all needed cleaning up, hosing down, painting. Nobody bothered to give it any such thing. And the people seemed as gray and grimy and defeated as the town in which they lived. Jake had thought the same thing even before the stock market submerged, but it was much more noticeable now.

He hurried past a man with shoulders slumped from lugging heavy sample cases to firms that weren't buying, that wouldn't have been buying if he'd been selling gold for the price of lead. That luckless drummer was a dead man walking—till he saw Jake. He straightened up. His eyes got back their spark. "Freedom, Mr. Featherston!" he called.

"Freedom to you, pal," Featherston answered. "Hang on. Just remember, we'll lick those bastards yet."

"How?" the man asked. "What can we do?"

"Same thing I've been saying all along," Jake told him. "First thing is, we've got to get rid of the stupid bastards who landed us in this mess in the first place. They aren't fit to carry guts to a bear, but they've been running this country—and running it straight into the ground—ever since the War of Secession. That means the politicians *and* the bonehead generals in the War Department."

"Sounds good to me. Sounds mighty damn good to me," the salesman said. "What else?"

"Got to pay back the niggers," Featherston said. "Got to get strong again, so we can look the USA in the eye again. Got to get strong, so we can spit in the USA's eye, too, if we ever have to. How do you like that?"

"Me? I like it fine," the man said. "You go on and give 'em hell."

"Just what I intend to give 'em. But I'll need your help, buddy. Remember, vote Freedom come November. We've got to get this country on its feet again. I've been saying that for years. Now maybe people will start paying attention to me." He walked on, leaving the drummer with a last, "Freedom!"

"Freedom!" the fellow echoed.

Back in the middle of the 1920s, that luckless drummer had probably been comfortable enough to vote Whig. Bad times made the Freedom Party grow. Featherston knew as much. He looked around. He'd seen plenty of bad times right after the war, when the money went down the toilet. This . . . This felt worse. This felt as if the Confederate States were closing down, one store, one factory, at a time, and might never open for business again.

"Freedom!" somebody else called—a woman, her voice high and shrill with worry.

"Freedom, dear," Jake told her. "Everything's going to be just fine." He waved and kept going.

During the war, he'd usually had a pretty good notion of whether the troops in front of him would succeed in an attack—or, later, if they would succeed in holding back the damnyankees when *they* attacked. Now, after years wandering in the wilderness, he felt things in his own country turning his way again.

Shame it took a panic and a crash to do it, he thought. *But that's the way it goes sometimes. If you don't grab with both hands when you get the chance, you deserve what ever happens to you.* He intended to grab what ever the times gave him. He'd had one chance, and seen it go glimmering. *God damn you to hell and gone, Grady Calkins.* That had been the first time. He'd wondered if he would ever see another. Now, here it was again, if he could make it so.

He and his escorting guards rounded a corner. One of them pointed up Grace Street toward Capitol Square. "Look at that, boss," he said. "Isn't it a shame and a disgrace?"

"It's a judgment on the damn Whigs, that's what it is," Jake answered.

Back just after the Great War ended, Capitol Square had been full of soldiers fresh out of the Army. They'd had nowhere to go and nothing to do, so they'd camped there, many of them still with their weapons—enough to make the police leery of trying to clear them out, anyhow, even though they'd rioted more than once.

Now tents and shanties sprouted in the square once more. Jake didn't know who all was in them. Some veterans, certainly. But some men who weren't, and a lot of women and kids, too. People who'd lost jobs and lost their homes or couldn't pay the rent on a flat any more . . . where else were they going to go?

Again, the police were going easy on them. Clearing them from the shantytown by force would have made dreadful headlines. Another guard said, "Those people shouldn't ought to be in a mess like that. Ain't their fault, not most of the time. But that ain't the only shantytown in the country, neither."

"Damn right it ain't, Joe," Featherston agreed. "There's one outside of every town in the CSA. And you're right—most of the people in 'em are decent, hardworking folks who're just down on their luck." He slapped Joe on the back, hard enough to stagger him. "And I'll be go to

336

hell if you didn't just give me next week's wireless talk on a silver platter."

By then, going into the studio was second nature for him. When the red light came on, he rasped out the greeting he'd been using for years: "This is Jake Featherston of the Freedom Party, and I'm here to tell you the truth."

Inside the glassed-in room next to the studio, the engineers nodded at him—everything was going the way it should. And his words were going out to far more people in the CSA than they had a few years before. A whole web of stations, a nationwide web, was getting this broadcast now. It went everywhere, from Richmond to Miami to deep in Sonora. And stations near the postwar, U.S.-imposed border beamed it up into Kentucky and Houston and Sequoyah.

"Truth is," Jake went on, "all across our country people are losing their jobs. Truth is, all across our country they're losing their homes. Truth is, all across our country they're trying to get by in shacks and tents a God-fearing *dog* wouldn't want to live in. And the truth is, my friends, *the Whig Party doesn't care.*"

He banged his fist down on the table, hard enough to make papers jump in front of him—but not hard enough to make them fall off or to tip over the microphone. He'd had practice with that thump. "So help me God, friends, that *is* the truth. I'm ashamed to say it about anybody in these Confederate States, but it is. What are the Whigs doing to help these folks get new jobs? Nothing! What are the Whigs doing to help 'em hang on to their houses? Nothing! What are the Whigs doing to keep 'em from starving? Nothing, one more time! 'That's not the government's job,' is what they say.

"Well, friends, I'm going to tell you something. The Whigs proved how useless they were two years ago, when the big floods came. Did they do anything much for the poor, suffering people in Tennessee and Arkansas and Mississippi and Louisiana? Did they? In a pig's ear they did. They patted 'em on the head and said, 'Sure wish you good luck. Y'all'll be just fine.' *Were* they just fine? You know better'n I do.

"I'll tell you something else, too. This here panic, this here crash, is dragging more people under than Mother Nature ever dreamt of doing. And that's happening all over the Confederate States, not just in the Mississippi Valley. God help us all, there's a shantytown in Capitol Square here in Richmond. The fat Whig Congressmen could look out their windows and see the poor hungry folks. They could, but they don't."

On and on he went, finishing, "Two years ago, the Supreme Court—the bought and paid-for Supreme Court—said Burton Mitchel could run for president again. Well, he did, and he got himself elected again, too. And now we're *all* paying for it.

"So if you want things to work again, if you want us to be strong again, if you want to tie a can to the Whigs' tail—and to the Supreme Court's tail, too—if you don't want to have to live in a shack like a nigger cotton-picker, vote Freedom in November. God bless you all, and thank you kindly!"

The lead engineer drew a finger across his throat. The red light in the studio went out. Jake Featherston leaned back in his chair, then gathered up his papers and left the small, soundproofed room.

Saul Goldman, the station managed, waited in the hallway. "That was a strong speech, Mr. Featherston, a very strong speech," he said.

"Let's hope it does some good," Jake answered.

"I've heard a lot of your speeches the past few years, Mr. Featherston," Goldman said. "I think this one will sway people, especially . . . with things the way they are."

"Yeah. Especially," Featherston said. "I think this one'll do some good, too. High time people got the wool pulled away from over their eyes. High time they see you don't have to be a Whig to run the country. High time they see we'd be better off with people who aren't afraid to get their hands dirty, who aren't afraid to pitch right in and do what needs doing. We've got to fix things. We can't go on like this."

"No." Goldman shook his head. "Times are very hard." He risked a smile at Jake. "You should be glad you have a job."

"I am," Jake said. "I've had a job ever since the war ended: to see the Confederate States back on top. It's taken me a long time to start doing that job. But I think my hour's coming round at last."

"I think you may be right," the station manager agreed. "If not now, when will it come?"

If not now, will it ever come? But Jake Featherston pushed that thought to the back of his mind, as he did whenever it cropped up. He couldn't afford to doubt, and so he didn't. "I'm going to tell you something, Mr. Goldman," he said. "This here station and the web you've set up have done the Freedom Party a hell of a lot of good. We don't forget our enemies. Everybody knows that. But we don't forget our friends, either. You'll see."

"Thank you," Goldman said. "That I should be your friend surprises me. We've had that talk before, a long time ago. But thank you. Thank you very much. It has passed over me."

"What's that?" Featherston asked. The Jew only shrugged and changed the subject. Jake didn't push it. He had other things to worry about. The world wasn't his, as he thought it should be. But now, at least, he had the hope it was going his way.

When Jefferson Pinkard opened his pay envelope at the Sloss Works, he discovered it contained a pink slip along with his salary. His curses were soft and bitter and heartfelt. "I should've stayed in Mexico, by God," he said. "If I'd known the company was going to treat me like a nigger, I would've."

The paymaster, a gray-haired man named Harvey Gordon, had known Pinkard since before the Great War. He shook his head. "You never should have gone to Mexico in the first place. You forfeited all the seniority you had. Now they're treating you like a new hire. I'm sorry as hell, Jeff, but them's the rules."

"Fuck the rules," Pinkard said. "How am I gonna *eat*?"

Gordon didn't answer that. It wasn't a question that had an answer, except maybe, *God knows*. If God did know, He hadn't bothered telling Jefferson Davis Pinkard.

"Get moving," the fellow in line behind him said. "Don't hold up the works."

"Fuck you, too," Jeff answered, hoping for a fight. He didn't get one, only a stony glare. Muttering under his breath, he strode out of the steel mill. *Won't be coming back, either,* he thought. *Ain't that a son of a bitch?*

He wondered where he would live, too. A fired man had two weeks to leave company housing. If he didn't go after that, they'd pitch his belongings out of his cottage and onto the sidewalk.

At least the yellow clapboard house he had now was a long way from the one he'd shared with Emily back in happier times. *How can I afford a new place if I just got fired?*

It was a good question. Again, he wished he had a good answer for it. He wished he had any answer at all. Inside the cottage, he had a cheap iron bed and a cheap iron stove, an icebox, a rickety table, and one chair. A furnished room would have had more in it. He didn't want to think about a room. Thinking about one reminded him he didn't know what he'd do when they threw him out of here.

He made a mess of bacon and eggs for supper. He'd had them for breakfast, too. He was no kind of cook. He never had been. He did a tolerable job on bacon and eggs most of the time. He'd started getting sick of them. But he did so few things well, he didn't have much choice.

When he went to bed that night, he set the alarm clock, forgetting he wouldn't need to get up the next morning. The clock was cheap, too. Its tinny jangle jolted him awake. He was dressed and eating breakfast—bacon and eggs yet again—before he realized he had nowhere to go.

"Shit," he said, without originality but with great feeling.

That morning was one of the strangest of his life. He sat on the one chair in the cottage and watched men streaming toward the Sloss Works, and others coming off the night shift. He could have been one of them. Up till the day before, he had been one of them. Now he felt as far apart from them as a prisoner of war did from his army. He didn't go to work there, not any more.

340

After a while, the two streams of men stopped. Everything grew quiet. Wives came out of the cottages to shop or gossip with the neighbors. Children headed for school. The ones too little to go to school played in front of their houses. All that had gone on for years while he worked at the steel mill, but he'd seen it only when he was too sick to go in. Now he felt fine (except for being sick of bacon and eggs), but he had nowhere to go.

He started to read a magazine, a pulp called *Aeroplane Adventures*. Some of the tales in it were set in the Great War, others afterwards. It was printed in Richmond; all the war stories had Confederate pilots gunning down Yankees, or Englishmen knocking German aeroplanes out of the sky. The later tales were set in the Confederate West or in odd corners of the world.

Aeroplane Adventures had sat on the kitchen table for more than a week without his looking at it. He'd been too tired to read when he came back from the Sloss Works. Now, with nothing else to do, he went through the magazine twice. A young Texan from a town called Cross Plains had written an exciting story about the air war over West Texas, where Jeff had served. The fellow had a few details wrong—he hadn't been old enough to see combat—but he could tell a tale. The other pieces were much less memorable.

Jeff started the magazine for a third time late that afternoon, but set it aside instead. He wished he had a wireless set, to make time pass more quickly. But then he brightened. "Freedom Party meeting tonight!" he said: the first words he'd spoken since the morning. As he'd forgotten to leave the alarm alone, he'd almost forgotten the weekly meeting.

When the time came, he put on a white shirt and butternut trousers and hurried to the trolley stop where he could ride into central Birmingham. Crickets chirped. Lightning bugs winked on and off, on and off. The trolley stop was crowded. Several men had on the same kind of outfit as Jeff. "Freedom!" one of them said.

"Freedom!" Jeff echoed. "When was the last time you went to a Party meeting, Clem?"

"Been four-five years," the other steelworker

answered. "I didn't reckon it was on the right track. Now I'm wondering if maybe I was wrong. Won't hurt none to come and find out."

"You stopped coming to meetings for a while, too, Jeff," another man said.

Pinkard shook his head. "Not me. Not like you mean, anyhow. I never walked away from the Party. What I did was, I went down to the Empire of Mexico."

"Oh," said the fellow who'd brought it up. He said not another word after that. Anybody who'd fought in Mexico took the Freedom Party and its business very seriously indeed. The trolley rolled up then, clanging its bell. The men bound for the Freedom Party meeting climbed aboard with everyone else at the stop. Pinkard threw a dime in the fare box. He hadn't worried about money since coming back from Mexico, not while he'd had work. But now, without it, those ten cents suddenly seemed to loom as large as ten dollars would have.

And here was the old livery stable again, the smell of horses fainter than ever but still there. Here were the old folding chairs, even more battered than they had been before he'd headed south. Here was the rostrum at one end of the hall, and the Stars and Bars and Confederate battle flag on the wall behind it. The two flags hadn't changed; they still carried the stars representing Kentucky and Sequoyah, though the states lay under U.S. occupation.

The meeting was crowded. That steelworker wasn't the only man returning after a long absence. And there were faces Jeff had never seen before, some of them belonging to men surely too young to have fought in the Great War. Jeff recognized the way those men bore themselves: stiff with a special, nervous sort of dignity. He carried himself the same way. It was the distinctive posture of men who'd lost their jobs but didn't want the world to know.

Somebody swigged from a bottle of homebrew. Pinkard grinned to see that. Some things hadn't changed. Alabama remained dry. But the police had never come around trying to enforce the temperance laws at a Party meeting. They had to know they would have had a fight on their hands if they'd been so rash.

He found a chair and sat down. He'd sat right about here, he remembered, when he'd got up and pushed past Grady Calkins on his way out of one meeting. People had still sat on hay bales in those days, not folding chairs. He cursed under his breath. Calkins, a Freedom Party man, had done more to hurt the Party by turning assassin than all its enemies put together.

Caleb Briggs stepped up onto the rostrum and took his place behind the podium. The dentist looked out over the crowd and called, "Freedom!"

"Freedom!" people shouted back.

Briggs cupped a hand behind one ear. "I can't hear you."

"Freedom!" This time, the yell shook the rafters.

"That's better." Briggs nodded. "Good to see some old familiar faces back with us again. Nice to know y'all have seen the light one more time. And you're welcome. We wish you'd've stayed with us all along, but it's good to have you back. And how many folks are here for the very first time?"

Several men raised their hands. Briggs nodded again. "Good to see new blood, too. We need you. We need everybody. For years and years now, we've been telling anyone who'd listen that the Confederate States were going over a cliff. Not enough people did listen, and over we went, dammit. Now we've got to get back up again, and we need help. We've got to fight for what we believe in. You new men, are you ready to do that?"

"Yes, sir!" the newcomers chorused. Jeff wondered whether they knew Briggs meant it literally. If they didn't, they'd find out.

Sure enough, the dentist said, "You'll have your chance, I promise you. We'll set this country to rights yet. Maybe people are starting to see what's wrong in Richmond. About time. And if we have to knock a few heads together, or more than a few, to get things going again, we'll do it, that's all. You can't make an omelette without breaking eggs."

"That's right," Pinkard said. "You bet that's right. If you aren't afraid to get blood on your clothes, you don't belong here. Remember, the stuff washes out with plenty of cold water."

"It sure does." Briggs turned his attention to Pinkard. "Did I hear right that the Sloss Works flung you out?"

"Yes, sir, you did." Jeff knew a certain amount of pride that the Birmingham head of the Freedom Party kept such close tabs on him. "You know of any other outfit that wants a man who's been on the casting floor since before the Great War, I'd be much obliged."

"Nooo," Briggs said slowly. "But don't I remember right that when you were down in Mexico, you were the fellow who ran a prisoners' camp for the rebels Maximilian's boys caught?"

"Yeah, that was me," Pinkard answered. "What about it?"

"I'll tell you what about it. I happen to know the Birmingham city jail's looking for an assistant jailer. If you want the job, fellow you ought to talk to is named Albert Sidney Griffith, over in city hall. He's a Party man, too. Let him know who you are and what you did down in Mexico. Tell him to give me a telephone call if he's got any questions. I'll set him straight."

"My Lord," Jeff whispered. He'd had hope machine-gunned with the pink slip in his pay envelope. Now, suddenly, it lived again. Tears stung his eyes. "God bless you, sir. Thank you. Thank you from the bottom of my heart."

Caleb Briggs waved that aside. "Don't you worry about it, Pinkard. Don't you worry one little bit. This here is the Freedom Party, remember. We aren't the Whigs or the Radical Liberals. We take care of our own. You've been a good Party man for a long time. We owe you for that, and we pay our debts. We pay 'em to our enemies, and we pay 'em to our friends."

"I'll see this Griffith fellow first thing in the morning," Jeff said. With the chance of work ahead of him, he felt like a new man. And the new man was every bit as loyal to the Freedom Party as the old one had been. "This is the best outfit in the *world*!" he exulted.

Briggs smiled and nodded. "Damn right it is."

XI

Hipolito Rodriguez had never thought about what a stock-market crash could do to the town of Baroyeca, and to the silver mine in the hills on which the town depended for its existence. Just because he hadn't thought about such things, though, didn't mean they weren't real. The mine shut down in September. A few days later, the railroad stopped coming into Baroyeca.

"A good thing we got the stove when we did," his wife said when he brought that news home. "It would take a lot longer to come here now."

"*Sí*, Magdalena," he said. "Everything will take a lot longer to come here now. The town is liable to dry up and blow away, and then what will become of the farms all around it?"

"We go on and do as we always did," Magdalena answered. "We stay on our land and mind our own business."

"But we can't make *everything* here," Rodriguez said. "If the general store closes, life will get very hard."

"How can the general store close?" Magdalena said. "Everyone around here goes to it. *Señor* Diaz is a rich man."

"How rich will he be if he has to ship everything into Baroyeca by wagon or by truck?" Rodriguez asked. "I don't know how much that costs, but I know it costs a lot more than the railroad."

"Now you worry me," Magdalena said. "I think you did that on purpose."

"As a matter of fact, yes," he replied. "I'm worried myself. I didn't want to be the only one."

"Oh." She'd been making tortillas. After rubbing cornmeal off her hands and onto her apron, she gave Hipolito Rodriguez a hug. "Who would have thought it could be this bad?"

"Who, indeed?" he answered. "Up till now, we complained that things that happened in Richmond didn't matter one way or the other here in Sonora, and that nobody back there cared about us." His laugh rang bitter. "Now things that happened in Richmond and in New York City matter very much here, and *Madre de Dios!* but I wish they didn't."

Magdalena nodded. "How do these things work out like this? You go to the meetings of the *Partido de la Libertad*—what do they say there? Do they know? Can they make it better?"

"What can they do now?" he asked in return. "The president is a Whig. Most of the Senators and Congressmen are Whigs. The Freedom Party can only protest what the Whigs do, and the Whigs don't do much. They don't seem to know what to do. They are fools." He'd always thought the Whigs were fools. Even before Sonora started electing men from the Freedom Party to Congress, the state had sent Radical Liberals off to Richmond.

"If the Freedom Party had power, what would it do?" Magdalena asked.

"Put people to work," Rodriguez answered at once. "Make sure they stayed at work. Make the country strong again. Tell the United States to leave us alone, and be strong enough to make sure the United States did it. Take back the states the USA stole from us in the war."

The only time he'd ever seen men from the United States was during his service in the Confederate Army during the Great War. The soldiers from the USA had done their best to kill him, and had come alarmingly close more than once. A lot of the west-Texas prairie where he'd fought was now included in the U.S. state of Houston. It was as

346

if the USA were mocking all his effort, all his courage—yes, and all his fear, too. Anything he could do to pay back the United States of America, he would do, and do gladly.

Nodding—she knew how he felt—Magdalena said, "These things sound wonderful. How will the Freedom Party make them happen?"

"Why . . ." He hesitated, then shrugged. "I don't know, not exactly," he admitted. "I don't think anyone knows. But I do know they will work hard and try everything. And I know they have no hope of helping the country if they aren't in power. The Whigs have made too many mistakes. It's time for them to go."

Robert Quinn, the Freedom Party organizer in Baroyeca, had said that very thing in his accented Spanish. Hipolito Rodriguez didn't mind that he spoke the language like a man whose first language was English. That Quinn spoke Spanish at all mattered to the farmer. It told him the Freedom Party was serious about winning followers in Baroyeca, in all of Sonora. The Whigs never had been. Even the Radical Liberals had worried about the big men, the rich men, first, and had expected them to bring the *campesinos* into line. It had worked for many years, too. But no more.

"When you vote Freedom, you know the Party cares," Rodriguez said. "Nobody else does, not like that."

"But the election is still more than a month away," Magdalena said. "What can the Party do in the meantime? What can anyone do if—the Blessed Virgin forbid it!—the general store closes its doors?" She crossed herself.

"I don't know," Rodriguez answered. "I don't think anyone knows."

"As long as we have enough water to keep the corn and beans growing and the livestock healthy, we can go on," his wife said. "Life may be hard, but life has been hard before. We will get through till it is better again."

"I hope so," Rodriguez said. He'd got used to being a fairly prosperous farmer—prosperous by the standards of southern Sonora, at any rate. He'd seen just enough of the rest of the Confederate States to have a suspicion bordering on certainty that prosperity here was something less than it might have been elsewhere in the country.

347

As a measure of that prosperity, Magdalena had a treadle-powered sewing machine. She'd bought it second-hand, from a woman in Baroyeca who'd got a better machine, but even secondhand it was a status symbol for a farmer's wife. It also let her get more work done faster than she could have managed without it. With six children to be clothed, that was no small matter.

A few days after Rodriguez came back from Baroyeca, the needle in the sewing machine broke. Like any farmer, he was a good handyman. Fixing anything that small and precisely made, though, was beyond him. "You have to go back into town," Magdalena told him. "I have half a dozen pairs of pants to make. You don't want the boys to run around naked, do you?"

"I'll go," he said. "Give me the broken needle, so I can be sure I'm getting the matching part. There are as many different kinds as there are different sewing machines, and you would have something to say to me if I brought back the wrong one, now wouldn't you?"

"Maybe not," his wife answered. "Maybe I'd just think you'd spent too much time in *La Culebra Verde* before you tried to buy the right one."

"I don't know what you're talking about," Rodriguez said with dignity. Magdalena laughed so raucously, she distracted Miguel and Jorge enough to make them stop wrestling for a little while.

With that laughter still ringing in his ears, Hipolito Rodriguez set out for Baroyeca the next morning. When he got there, he made sure he bought the sewing-machine needle first. Magdalena would never have let him live it down if, after all his care, he came back with the wrong one.

The general store remained open. Rodriguez was astonished to discover that a packet of three needles cost only eight cents. The machine, when Magdalena bought it, had come with the one that had just broken, and no others. "I expected they would be much more," he told Jaime Diaz as the proprietor took his money.

"Then I will gladly charge you twice as much," Diaz said. "One way or another, I have to make some money.

With the mine closed, I don't know how I'm going to do it. And the railroad, too! How will I get supplies?"

"I don't know," Rodriguez answered in a low voice. "My wife and I were talking about this. If you don't, how will Baroyeca go on?"

"I have no answers," the storekeeper said. "Every day, I keep hoping things will get better, and every day they get worse. Be thankful you live on a farm. It's not so bad for you. For anyone who has to get things from other places every day . . ." He shook his head.

"What can you do?" Rodriguez asked. "What can anyone do?"

"No one can do anything," Diaz replied. "No one can do anything to make things better, I mean. That's what makes this whole business so dreadful, my friend. The whole *world* is broken, and no one has the faintest idea how to fix it."

Hipolito Rodriguez hadn't thought of the collapse in those terms. He'd thought about what it meant to Baroyeca, to Sonora, and, to some degree, to the Confederate States. The world? That was too much for him to grasp. He said, "*Señor* Diaz, I know the man who can set things right."

"Who is that, then?" Diaz said. "In the name of God and the Blessed Virgin, tell me. If anyone can make the mine open and the train come back to Baroyeca, I will bless him with all my heart." In spite of his talk of the world, most of his thoughts stayed close to home, too. Such is life for most men.

"Jake Featherston of the Freedom Party, that's who," Rodriguez said. "They can make the country strong again, and if we are strong, how can we help being rich again, too?"

"Rich? I don't care about rich. All I care about is having the money to go on from day to day," the store-keeper said. He was polite enough to understate what he had and what he wanted. Rodriguez nodded, polite enough to accept the understatement for what it was. Diaz went on, "I don't know about the Freedom Party, either." He drummed his fingers on the countertop behind which he stood. "But the Whigs have no notion what to do. A blind man could see that. And the Radical Liberals"—he smiled a wry smile—"what have they ever been good for but making faces at the Whigs? So maybe, just maybe, you could be right."

"I think so," Rodriguez said. "When did you ever see the Whigs or even the Radical Liberals with a headquarters here in town? The Freedom Party has one. And Robert Quinn even learned Spanish to get us to join the Party. When have the others cared so much about us?"

"A point," Diaz admitted. "Quinn buys from me." Everyone who actually lived in town bought from him; what other choice did people have? Again, he was polite. He continued, "He always pays his bills on time, I will say, and he never treats me like a damn greaser." The rest of the conversation had been in Spanish. He used English for those two words.

Rodriguez nodded, a sour smile on his face. He'd also heard those English words, more often than he ever wanted to. He said, "You see? They speak English, but they don't look down their noses at Sonorans. If they can manage that, I think they can manage the whole country."

"I hadn't thought of it in that way," Diaz said. "Maybe you're right. It could be so."

"I really think it is," Rodriguez said. "Look at the mess the other parties have got us into. Doesn't the Freedom Party deserve the chance to get us out?" The storekeeper didn't say no. Rodriguez added the clincher: "And the election is coming up soon—only a little more than a month to go."

Anne Colleton drove a five-year-old Birmingham down toward Charleston. She'd finally sold the ancient Ford she'd acquired during the war after Confederate soldiers confiscated her Vauxhall. She knew she'd kept it longer than she should have, as a reminder of those grim times. But when she weighed sentiment against ever more cranky machinery, sentiment came off second best.

The Robert E. Lee Highway was better going than it had been in those days. It was paved all the way, where long stretches of it had been only rutted dirt. A lot more motorcars traveled up and down it, too. And nowadays, the bodies of hanged Negro Reds didn't dangle from trees by the side of the road. She'd seen plenty of them, coming back from Charleston to St. Matthews in 1915. She'd been going to see a lover then; she was going to see a lover now.

Back then, regardless of whether Roger Kimball had had a flat in Charleston rather than being on leave from the Navy, not even Anne, radical as she'd reckoned herself, would have dared park her motorcar in front of the building where he lived. That would have meant scandal. They'd always met in hotels: in Charleston, in Richmond, down in Georgia.

Times had changed. Much of what had been radical was now taken for granted. Anne didn't think twice about leaving the Birmingham in front of Clarence Potter's block of flats, or of knocking on his door. Inside, the clattering of a typewriter abruptly stopped. A man's voice kept on coming out of a wireless set.

Potter opened the door. He gave Anne a quick kiss and said, "Come in. Fix yourself a drink. I'm almost done with this damn report. Pretty soon, we'll find out how good the news is." By his tone, he didn't expect her to take *good* literally.

"A heavy turnout is expected in today's Congressional election," the reporter on the wireless said as Anne went into the kitchen to deal with whiskey and water and ice. "The Whigs remain confident of holding their strong position in the House despite the unfortunate state of the economy, and—"

The typewriter started clacking again just then, drowning out the rest. Clarence Potter was far and away the most unusual man Anne had ever met. He not only believed she could take care of herself, he encouraged her to do it. He'd never shown any interest what ever in running her life. A thoroughly competent man, he respected competence wherever he found it, and seemed happy he'd found it in her. Her whole life long, she'd fought against men who either tried to control her or simply assumed they would. Potter hadn't tried. Anne sometimes had trouble figuring out what to make of that.

Drink in hand, she came back into the front room. "Do you want me to fix one for you, too?" she asked. He didn't expect her to fix drinks. That, no doubt, was why she was willing to do it.

And he shook his head now. Lamplight glinted from the metal frames of his spectacles. "No, thanks. Not yet. Let me finish up here. I think I've figured out who's been lifting crates from Lucas Williamson's warehouse, and how he can keep it from happening again." Concentration on his face, he went back to typing.

"You did remember to vote, didn't you?" Anne asked.

He nodded. "Oh, yes. I'm not going to give the Freedom Party any help at all. The Whigs have done too much of that lately." He went back to typing, and might almost have forgotten Anne was in the room with him.

She listened to the wireless. The commentator kept on sounding optimistic about the Whigs' prospects. She hoped he was right. Like Clarence Potter, she hoped and believed two different things.

Ten minutes later, Potter took the sheet of paper out of the machine. "There," he said in his half-Yankee accent, laying it on a neat stack. "Another week's bills paid. Now I get to remember I'm a human being." He went back into the kitchen and fixed a whiskey for himself. Raising it in salute, he added, "It's damn good to see you, you know that? Always nice to have company on the deck as the ship goes down."

"It won't be as bad as that," Anne said.

"No, indeed. It'll probably be worse." Potter looked out the window. Twilight was setting in. "Polls'll close before long. Then we'll start getting returns, and then we'll know how big a mess we'll have for the next two years. To tell you the truth, I'd almost sooner not find out."

"Would you rather stay here and stay in bed, then?" Anne asked. "The election will be what it is, regardless of whether we go to Whig headquarters after supper."

Potter smiled but shook his head. "Plenty of time for

that afterwards. I have this restless itch to *know*, and it needs satisfying as much as any other urge."

"All right." And, to Anne's internal surprise, it *was* all right. She knew Clarence Potter was interested; she'd had plenty of very pleasant proofs of that. If he put business before pleasure . . . well, didn't she, too? *I'm keeping company with a grownup,* she thought. It was, in her experience, a novelty, but one she didn't mind.

When they went out for supper, she ordered a big plate of boiled shrimp. "They don't come fresh to St. Matthews," she said.

"No, I suppose not," Potter agreed. "When I first moved here, I remember thinking how wonderful all the seafood was." He'd chosen crab cakes for himself. "Now, unless people remind me about it the way you just did, I take it for granted. I shouldn't do that, should I?"

"No," Anne said. "The whole country's taken too many things for granted."

"We're liable to pay the price for it, too," he said. "That goes back a long way now, you know—starting when we took it for granted we'd win the Great War and be home to celebrate by the time the leaves turned red and gold."

The colored waiter brought their suppers. As Anne began to eat, she said, "I took that for granted, and I can't say otherwise. You didn't, did you?"

"No—but remember, I went to Yale. I was there for four Remembrance Days. I had a pretty fair notion of how desperately in earnest those people were. We figured we could whip them. They went out and made damn sure they could whip us." He took a bite of crab cake, nodded, and went on in meditative tones: "We've always figured we could whip the Freedom Party, too. But the damnyankees aren't the only people who are desperately in earnest. That's what worries me."

"We'll find out." Anne feared he might be right, but didn't want to think about it, not just then.

After they finished supper, they walked over to the Whig headquarters. It lay only three or four blocks away. Even in November, bugs still buzzed around street lamps.

Something—a bird? a bat?—swooped down, grabbed one of them out of the air, and vanished into darkness again.

When Anne and Clarence Potter came into the headquarters, they got their share, and more than their share, of suspicious looks. Anne had former Freedom Party ties that made people distrust her. Her companion didn't, but he did have the unfortunate habit of saying exactly what he thought, and that regardless of what the received wisdom was.

But then someone called out to them: "Have you heard the news?"

Potter shook his head. Anne said, "No, that's what we came here for. What's the latest?"

"Horatio Standifer out in North Carolina," the man replied. "In Congress since before the war, but a Freedom Party man just did him in."

"Oh, good God," Potter said. "If Standifer lost his seat, nobody's safe tonight. And if nobody's safe tonight, then God help the country tomorrow."

"What's the news here in South Carolina?" Anne asked.

"Not as bad as that," the Whig said. "We're going to lose the seat we picked up two years ago, and maybe one more besides."

Potter pointed at the blackboard on which new results were going up. "Maybe two more besides, looks like to me."

After a second look at the numbers, the other Whig scowled and nodded. "Maybe two more besides," he admitted, and went off as if Potter had some sort of contagious disease.

He does, Anne thought. *He tells the truth as he sees it, and he pulls no punches. Such men are dangerous.*

Returns from Georgia started coming, and then Tennessee and Alabama. The more of them there were, the longer the faces at Whig headquarters got. People started slipping over to the saloon across the street. Some of them came back. Others didn't—they stayed away and began the serious business of drowning their sorrows.

Clarence Potter didn't go. Each new seat lost to the

Freedom Party—and those came in one after another, with no possible room for doubt in most of them—brought not howls of dismay from him, but rather a bitter smile. He might have been telling the world, *I knew this was going to happen. Now here it is, and what are you going to do about it?* No one in the Whig headquarters seemed to have the slightest idea what to do about it . . . except for the men who headed across the street to get drunk.

As Anne watched the man she was with, so he watched her, too. After a while, he said, "It's probably not too late for you, you know."

"What do you mean?" she asked, though she had a pretty good idea.

And, sure enough, he said, "Your politics aren't that far from Jake Featherston's. If you want to, you can probably make your peace with him."

She wanted to haul off and slap him. She wanted to, but she couldn't, for the same thought had crossed her mind. He told her the truth as he saw it, too. Still, she said, "I don't know. I turned him down once when I asked for money, years ago. He doesn't forget things like that."

Potter laughed scornfully. "I'll tell you what he won't turn down. He won't turn down money if you give it to him now, that's what."

Anne wondered about that. She decided Potter was probably half right. Jake Featherston might take her money if she offered it to him again. But would he ever trust her, ever let her have any real influence? She had her doubts. Featherston struck her as a man whose memory for slights an elephant would envy.

Casually, Clarence Potter added, "If you do go back to him, we're through. I don't know how much that means to you. I hope it means something. Losing you would mean a lot to me. But I've known Featherston longer than any of the 'Freedom!'-shouting yahoos who go marching for him these days. We aren't on the same side, and we're never going to be."

"What if he gets elected president?" Anne asked.

A muscle jumped in his right cheek, perhaps an inch

below his eye. "No one ever went broke underestimating the stupidity of the Confederate people, but I still find that hard to imagine—even harder than it was in 1921, when he came so close. And 1933's still a long way away. Things are bound to look better by then." He paused and sighed. "And the way you asked that question makes me wonder if we aren't through anyhow."

"Up till now, you never put any conditions on me," Anne said. "I liked it that you never put any conditions on me."

"Up till now, I never imagined I needed to," he answered. "But I can't put up with the Freedom Party. I'm sorry, but I can't."

"Don't you want revenge on the USA?" she asked.

"I don't want anything that badly," Potter said.

Anne sighed. "Some things are worth any price." He shook his head. Now she sighed. "It's been fun, Clarence," she said. "But I'll do what I think I have to do, and not what anyone else tells me to. Not ever." *No wonder I never got married,* she thought. She walked out of the Whig headquarters and back toward her motorcar.

Kamloops, British Columbia, was a long way from Philadelphia, and a long way from the Confederate States, too. That didn't keep news from getting there about as fast as it got anywhere else, though, not in this age of telegraph clickers and wireless sets. Colonel Irving Morrell studied the Confederate election returns with a sort of horrified fascination.

"Sweet Jesus Christ!" he said, looking at the newspaper that had set them out in detail.

"Er—yes, sir," his aide-de-camp said, and chuckled.

"No offense, Lieutenant," Morrell said hastily. "Just a manner of speaking."

"Oh, yes, sir. I know that," Lieutenant Ike Horwitz answered. "You're not like that damn German sergeant who was tagging along with your buddy from the General Staff over there."

"I should hope not." Morrell set the paper on Horwitz's desk. "But look at this. For heaven's sake, *look* at this. The

Freedom Party went from—what?—nine Congressmen to twenty-nine. They won three governorships down there. They took control of four state legislatures, too, and that means they'll start electing Senators, because their state legislatures still choose 'em. They didn't switch to popular vote, the way we did."

"That's a big pickup, no doubt about it." Horwitz leaned forward to study the numbers. He looked up at Morrell. "I'm awful damn glad I'm a Jew in the USA, and not a *shvartzer* in the CSA."

"A what?" Morrell said, and then he nodded, making the connection from Yiddish to German. "Oh. Yeah. I bet you are."

"There's people here who don't like Jews—plenty who feel just like that stupid sergeant," Horwitz said. "But it isn't all *that* bad. Hell, even the president's wife's Jewish, not that I've got any use for her politics or his. If you're colored in the Confederate States, you've got to be shaking in your shoes—if they let you have any shoes."

He was right. Morrell hadn't even wondered what the Negroes in the CSA felt about the election returns he'd been dissecting. He rarely thought about Negroes. What white man in the USA did? Maybe Horwitz, being a Jew, was more likely to look at other people who had a hard time in their homeland.

"I'll tell you what," Morrell said. "Write me an appreciation of the Confederate Negroes' likely response to this. Do a good job on it and I'll forward it to Philadelphia, see if I can get you noticed."

"Thank you, sir. That's damn white of you," his aide-de-camp answered.

Morrell's own thoughts were on the more immediate. "Any time the Freedom vote goes up, that's trouble for us, because those bastards want another shot at the USA. And Featherston's boys haven't seen numbers like these since 1921. I hope to heaven the president sits up and takes notice."

"What do you think the odds are?" Lieutenant Horwitz asked.

"Do I look like a Socialist politician to you? I'd better

not, that's all I've got to say," Morrell replied. "They cut off Confederate reparations early, they haven't been checking about rearmament near as hard as they should have, they've cut *our* budget. . . ." He sighed. "They think everybody should just be friends. I wish that would work, I really do."

"People vote for it," Horwitz said. "Nobody wants to go through another war like the last one."

"No, of course not. But both sides have to want peace. You only need one to have a war. And the only thing worse than fighting a war like that is fighting it and losing. Ask the Confederates if you don't believe me."

"I don't need to ask anybody," Horwitz said. "I can see that for myself. Anyone with a brain in his head ought to be able to see that for himself. But what are we going to do?"

"That's the question, all right." Morrell drummed his fingers on the desktop. "I don't know. I just don't know. Half of those people who voted for Featherston's gang of goons probably don't hope for anything but jobs and three square meals a day if he calls the shots. They sure aren't getting 'em with the folks they've got running things now."

His aide-de-camp smiled unhappily. "And isn't that the sad and sorry truth, sir? When I joined the Army, I never thought I'd be glad to be in for the food and for the roof over my head. But that's how it looks nowadays. If I were a civilian, I'd probably be scuffling like everybody else."

"Good point." Morrell nodded. "We're insulated from that, anyhow, thank God."

"I suppose the Socialists *are* doing everything they can there," Ike Horwitz said grudgingly. "Feeding people who are out of work and giving some of 'em makework jobs— it's not great, God knows, but it's better than nothing, you know what I mean?"

"I guess so." Morrell sighed. "If you give a man something for nothing, though, will he want to stand up on his own two feet again when times get better, or will he keep wanting a handout for the rest of his life?"

"You ask me, sir, most people want to work if you

give 'em the chance," Horwitz answered. "Other thing is, if they do starve, talking about the rest of their lives starts looking pretty silly, doesn't it? And if they're afraid they're going to starve, then what happens? Then they start voting for somebody like Jake Featherston in the USA, right?"

"I suppose so," Morrell said again. Up till now, his politics had always been firmly Democratic; he'd never had to think about it. He still didn't, not really. But he'd never been a man to worry about subtleties, either, and now he wondered whether he'd made a mistake. "You're saying the Socialists are giving us a safety valve, aren't you?"

"I wouldn't have put it quite that way, but yes, sir, I guess I am," Lieutenant Horwitz answered. "If things blow up, what have we got? Trouble, nothing else but." Like any soldier—and like anyone else with an ounce of sense—he was convinced staying out of trouble was a good idea.

A couple of days later, Morrell went into the town of Kamloops to do some shopping—Christmas was coming, and he wanted to buy some things for Agnes and Mildred that he couldn't hope to find at the post exchange. The weather was crisp and chilly, the sun shining bright out of a blue, blue sky but not giving much in the way of warmth even so.

The reception he got in Kamloops gave little in the way of warmth, either. Here a dozen years after the end of the war, the Canucks cared for the green-gray uniforms their occupiers wore no more than they had after the USA finally battered them into submission. People on the streets turned their backs when Morrell walked by.

Most of them did, anyhow. He'd got used to that. What he hadn't got used to were the ragged-looking men who held out their hands and whined, "Spare change, pal?" And he especially hadn't got used to the respectable-looking men who held out their hands and said the same thing. One of them added, "Been a long time since my twin boys saw any meat on the table."

"Why don't you get a job, then?" Morrell asked.

"Why?" The man glared at him. "I'll tell you why, even though you're a damned fool to need telling. Because there damned well aren't any jobs to get, that's why.

Lumber companies aren't hiring—that's what I got fired from. Farms aren't taking on hired men, not when they can't sell half the sheep and cows and wheat they raise. Even here in town, only way you can keep your job is if you're somebody's brother—if you're just a brother-in-law, you're in trouble. *That's* why, you stinking Yank."

Well, I asked him, and he went and told me, Morrell thought. He dug in his pocket and gave the Canadian some coins. "Here, buddy. Good luck to you."

"I ought to spit in your eye," the hungry man told him. "Hell of it is, I can't. I've got to tip my hat"—he did—"and say, 'Thank you, sir,' on account of I need the money so goddamn bad."

Never in all his days had Morrell heard *Thank you, sir* sound so much like *Go to hell, you son of a bitch.*

And he discovered the problem that sprang from giving one beggar some money. As soon as he did, all the others became four times as obnoxious, swarming around him and cursing him as foully as they knew how when he pushed past without doing for them what he'd done for one of their fellows. Maybe they hoped they'd make him feel guilty. All they really did was make him mad.

He'd just shaken free of the crowd when a woman sidled up to him. Skirts were longer than they had been a couple of years before, and the day wasn't warm, but what she wore displayed a lot of her. "Want a good time, soldier?" she said. "Three dollars."

She was skinny. Like any town with soldiers in it, Kamloops had its share of easy women, but she didn't look as if she'd been part of their sorry sisterhood for very long. "What did you used to do?" Morrell asked quietly.

"What difference does it make?" she answered. "Whatever it was, I can't do it any more. Do you want to go someplace?"

"No, thanks," he answered. She cursed him, too, with a sort of dreary hopelessness that hit him harder than the anger the male beggars had shown.

Even the storekeepers' attitudes seemed different from the way they had before things went sour. He'd never seen men so glad to take money from him. When he remarked on that, the fellow who'd just sold him a doll for Mildred said, "You bet I'm glad. You're only the second customer I've had today. Anybody with any money at all looks good to me right now. How am I going to pay my bills if nobody buys anything from me? And if I can't pay my bills, what happens then? Do I end up out on the street? I sure hope not."

Later, another shopkeeper said, "Hate to tell you this, but Kamloops'd wither up and die if it wasn't for you Yank soldiers. They still pay you regular, so you still have money in your pockets. Damn few folks do, and you'd better believe that."

A third man was even blunter: "If things don't turn around pretty quick, what the hell's going to happen to us?"

Morrell had to run the gauntlet of beggars once more on the way back to the U.S. Army base. The men cursed him all over again, this time for spending money on himself and not on them. "How would you like it if you were hungry?" one of them called after him—a parting shot, as it were.

It was a good question. He had no good answer. Nobody wanted to be hungry. He remembered that skinny woman. Nobody wanted to have to choose between whoring and starving. But nobody seemed to have much of an idea how to make things better, either. Morrell hurried home, a troubled man.

Jonathan Moss was making a discovery as old as mankind: that not even getting exactly what you thought you'd always wanted guaranteed happiness. When he thought about it—which was as seldom as he could—he suspected Laura Moss, once Laura Secord, was making the same unpleasant discovery.

"I don't like the city," she said one morning over a cup of tea (Jonathan preferred coffee, which he brewed himself).

"I'm sorry," he answered, not altogether sincerely. "I don't know how I could practice law from a farm. . . ." He almost added *in the middle of nowhere*, but let that go at the last possible instant.

He might as well have said it. By her sour expression, Laura heard it even if it remained technically unspoken. "But everybody here loves the Yanks and knuckles under to them," she complained.

The first part of that wasn't even close to true, as she had to know. As for the second . . . "Whether you like it or not, dear, the United States won the war," Moss pointed out.

Laura's expression got unhappier yet. Out on her farm, and even in Arthur—which was far enough off the beaten path for the American occupiers to pay little attention to it—she'd had an easier time pretending that blunt truth wasn't real. Here in Berlin, she couldn't ignore it. U.S. military courts here tried cases under occupation law. Soldiers in green-gray uniforms were always on the streets. "Even the newspapers!" she burst out. "They spell *color* c-o-l-o-r and *labor* l-a-b-o-r, not c-o-l-o-u-r and l-a-b-o-u-r."

"That's how we spell them in the States," Moss said.

"But this isn't the States! It's the province of Ontario! Can't you leave even the King's English alone?"

He finished his coffee at a gulp. "The King doesn't run things around these parts any more. The United States do. Sweetheart, I know you don't like it, but that doesn't mean it isn't so." Carrying his cup over to the sink, he went on, "I'm going to the office. I'll see you tonight."

"All right." She sounded almost as relieved to have him out of the apartment as he was to go. With a sigh, she added, "I don't know what I'm going to do around here, though."

Back on her farm, finding ways to pass the time had never been a worry. Moss knew just enough of farm life to be sure of that. If you weren't busy every waking moment on a farm, you had to be neglecting something. It wasn't like that here in the city. To Moss, that was one of the advantages of getting off the farm. He wasn't sure Laura saw things the same way.

Before leaving, he put on his overcoat and a fur hat with ear flaps that tied under his chin. Berlin, Ontario, might be under U.S. occupation, but its winters remained thoroughly Canadian. Moss had grown up in Chicago.

He'd thought he knew everything there was to know about nasty winter weather. The war and coming back here afterwards to practice law had taught him otherwise.

Only after he was out the door and going down the stairs to his elderly Bucephalus did he realize he hadn't kissed Laura good-bye. He kept going. His sigh was more glum than bemused. For years, he hadn't been able to get the idea of her out of his mind. Then, when they finally did come together, their lovemaking had been the most spectacular he'd ever known.

And now they were married—and he forgot to kiss her good-bye. *So much for romance,* he thought unhappily. He got into the motorcar and turned the key, hoping the battery held enough charge to start the car. Someone down the street was cranking an old Ford. Most of the time, a self-starter was ever so much more convenient. In weather like this, though . . .

The Bucephalus' engine sputtered, coughed, and then came to noisy life. Moss let out a sigh of relief. The motorcar would get him to the office, which meant the odds were good it would get him home again, too. And then, once he got home, he would find out what new things Laura had found to complain about.

He put the Bucephalus in gear and pulled onto the street even though the engine hadn't had enough time to warm up. Only after the auto had started to roll did he wonder if he was running away from trouble. *Well, what if you are?* he asked himself. *It's not as if you won't go back to it tonight.*

Not many motorcars shared the streets with the Bucephalus. Considering the snow and the state of the machine's brakes, that might have been just as well. Moss saw one traffic accident, with steam pouring from a shattered radiator, and with two men in heavy coats standing there shouting at each other.

Moss thought fewer automobiles were on the streets than had been the winter before. He knew why, too: fewer people in Berlin had jobs to go to than had been so the winter before. That was true all over Canada, all over North America, all over the world. Everyone hated it, but no one seemed to have the faintest idea what to do about it.

Two words painted on the side of a building—YANKS OUT! Before long, somebody would come along and paint over them. The Canucks hadn't given up wanting their own country back. The United States remained determined they wouldn't get it. Since the USA had the muscle, the Canadians faced an uphill fight.

As Moss got out of the Bucephalus, a man in a ragged overcoat who needed a shave came up to him with a gloved hand out and said, "Can you give me just a little money, friend? I've been hungry a long time now."

"Here you are." Moss handed him a quarter. "Buy yourself something to eat."

The man took the coin. He went down the street muttering something about a damned cheapskate Yank. Jonathan Moss sighed. Try as you would, you couldn't win.

He had an electric hot plate in his office. As soon as he got in, he started perking more coffee. Not only would it help keep him awake, it would help keep him warm. Even before the coffee was ready, he got to work on the papers waiting for him on his desk.

He'd won his name among the Canadians of Berlin for keeping the U.S. occupiers off their backs as much as he could. That brought him a fair number of cases to be tried in military courts. It also brought him a lot of much more ordinary legal business. Most of his current case load involved bankruptcies.

So many of those were on his desk right now, in fact, that he thought of adding a slug of whiskey to the coffee he poured for himself. Maybe that would help him face the ruin of other men's hopes with something more like equanimity. *Or maybe it'll turn me into a drunk,* he thought, and left the whiskey bottle—it was only a pint— in his desk drawer.

How many of those bankruptcies would have happened if the Russians had managed to pay their loan to that Austro-Hungarian bank? Moss didn't know, not exactly. The only sure answer that occurred to him was, *a lot fewer*. Of course, he was lucky he was still in business himself. He'd sold out when the stock market started dropping like a rock, and had escaped before Swan-Dive Wednesday. The longer he'd stayed in, the worse he'd have got hurt.

By ten o'clock, he was starting to come up for air in his paperwork. That was when the door to his office opened and his first appointment of the day came in. "Good morning, Mr. Harrison," Moss said, getting up and leaning forward across the desk to shake hands. "What can I do for you today?"

"You can call me Edgar, for starters," Edgar Harrison answered. He was a short, thin, intense-looking man of about Moss' age. The top half of his left ear was missing: a war wound. Had the bullet that clipped him traveled a couple of inches to the right of its real course, he would have died before he hit the ground. As he sat down in the chair to which Moss waved him, he added, "It's not like we haven't worked together before."

"No, it's not," Moss agreed. Harrison sailed as close to the wind as he could when it came to urging more freedom for the conquered Canadian provinces. He'd spent time in jail not long after the Great War ended. Moss thought he'd been lucky not to get shot, though he'd never said that out loud. "Care for some coffee?" he asked, pointing to the pot on the hot plate.

Edgar Harrison shook his head. "Nasty stuff. Never could stand it. Don't know how you Yanks pour it down the way you do."

"We manage," Moss said dryly, and refilled his cup. "You've got something on your mind—I can tell by your lean and hungry look."

"Such men are dangerous," Harrison said with a laugh. "How would you like to mount a court challenge to the whole rationale for the U.S. occupation of Canada?"

"How would I like it?" Moss echoed. "Personally, I'd like it fine. I'll tell you straight out, though, you'll lose. Occupation law says the U.S. Army can do whatever it has to in occupied territory, and the Constitution doesn't apply here."

"I know that." The Canadian's face clouded. "I don't see how I could help knowing it. But that's what I want to challenge: the notion that your fancy, precious Constitution shouldn't apply in Canada. Don't we deserve the rule of law, same as you Yanks?"

"What you deserve and what you're going to get are two different things," Moss replied. "I'm sorry, Mr. Harrison—Edgar—but I can't help you make that case. I don't see any point to even trying to get a judge to hear it. The law here isn't any different from the law in Utah, and that's part of the USA."

"Yes, and you Yanks were right on the point of letting it go back to being a regular part of the USA, too," Harrison said.

"We *were*," Moss said. "Then that Mormon murdered General Pershing, and now it'll be another ten years before anybody so much as mentions making Utah a normal state again."

"Nobody's murdered a military governor here," Harrison said.

"That bomber tried, whatever his name was," Moss answered. "He tried twice, as a matter of fact. And there was the uprising a few years ago." He felt like fortifying this cup of coffee, too, but he wouldn't, not with Harrison watching. "I'm sorry. Whether you're right or wrong, you haven't got a Chinaman's chance of making an American court take you seriously."

Edgar Harrison's eyes were gray as ice—and, at the moment, every bit as cold. "What will your wife say, Mr. Moss"—he wouldn't use Jonathan's first name now—"when she finds out you don't want to help us toward our freedom?"

"I hope she'll say I'm the lawyer in the family, and I know what I'm doing," Moss answered. "That's what I hope. If she says anything else, well, that's between her and me, wouldn't you agree?"

"That depends," Harrison said. "Yes, indeed—that depends."

Moss looked at him. "Mr. Harrison, I think we're done here. Don't you?"

366

"Yes, I'm afraid we are," the Canadian replied. "I'm sorry you turned out to be just another goddamn Yank after all." He got to his feet. "Well, we have ways of dealing with that, too."

Stung by the injustice of Harrison's words, Moss exclaimed, "If it weren't for me, half the Canucks in this town would be in jail or dead." The other man paid no attention, but turned on his heel and walked out the door. Only after he was gone did Moss wonder if his words had been more than unjust. He wondered if they'd held a threat.

Cincinnatus Driver didn't like having to start over as he approached middle age. He'd spent the years since moving up to Des Moines getting his hauling business up to the point where it made a pretty good living for him and his family. He'd sold the beat-up old Duryea truck he'd driven to Des Moines from Covington, and bought himself a less beat-up, middle-aged White: a bigger, more powerful machine.

And then Luther Bliss had lured him back to Kentucky and thrown him into jail. Elizabeth had to sell the White to keep food on the table for his family and a roof over their heads. Cincinnatus had a little celebrity value when he got back. Thanks to that, he'd been able to get a new truck—well, actually, an old truck, a Ford that had seen a lot of better years—on credit. For a Negro, that was something not far from a miracle.

He'd kept up the payments, too. He'd never been afraid of work. If he had to get up before the sun rose and keep driving till long after it set, he would do it without a word of complaint. He had done it without a word of complaint.

And then the bottom fell out of the stock market. All of a sudden, fewer goods came into the railway yard. Fewer riverboats and barges tied up at the docks by the Des Moines River. But just as many hauling companies and independent drivers like Cincinnatus were fighting for less business.

One way to get it, of course, was to charge less for hauling. If, after that, you worked more hours still, you might make ends meet. You might—provided you didn't charge less than fuel and upkeep on your truck cost. Cincinnatus—and everybody else who drove a truck in Des Moines, and elsewhere in the country—collided head-on with that painful limitation.

"What am I supposed to do?" he asked Elizabeth one evening over supper. "What *can* I do? Can't charge less now. Don't make no money at all if I charge less."

"Don't make *any* money," Achilles said. After so long in Iowa, he'd lost a good part of the Kentucky Negro accent Cincinnatus still kept. And, having entered his teens, he was inclined to look on everything his father did with a critical eye. He went on, "I know you're not ignorant, Pa, but you sure do sound that way sometimes."

In another year or so, he probably would have come right out and called Cincinnatus ignorant. Cincinnatus knew it, too; he remembered the hell-raiser he'd been at Achilles' age. This was what boys did when they started turning into men. "I can't help it, son," Cincinnatus said now, as mildly as he could. "I talk the way I've always talked. Don't know no other—"

"Any other," Achilles broke in.

"—way to do it," Cincinnatus finished, as if his son hadn't spoken. "And I'm talkin' about important stuff with your ma, stuff we got to talk about. Maybe your English teacher don't like the way we do it"—this time, he quelled Achilles with a glance—"but we got to hash it out just the same."

"Your pa's right," Elizabeth said. "Things ain't easy." Her accent was thicker than her husband's, but Achilles held his peace. She went on, "I ain't been gettin' so much in the way of housekeeper's work lately, neither. Dunno what we gwine do. Like your pa say, dunno what we *kin* do."

"Government talks about them makework jobs for folks who can't get nothin' else," Cincinnatus said. Achilles stirred not once but a couple of times, but had the sense to keep his mouth shut. *Maybe he does want to live to grow up,* Cincinnatus thought. Aloud, he went on, "Trouble is, I don't want one o' them. All I want is to go on doin' what I been doin', go on doin' that and make a living at it."

Elizabeth nodded. "I know," she said. She didn't say she wanted to go on cleaning other people's houses, and Cincinnatus knew she didn't. What she did say made a painful amount of sense: "We got to get the money from somewheres, though."

"I know," Cincinnatus said glumly.

"I could look for something," Achilles said. "Plenty of people hire kids nowadays, because they can pay 'em less than grownups."

He was, of course, dead right. Cincinnatus shook his head even so. "Ain't gonna let you do that unless things get a lot worse'n they are now. First thing is, you wouldn't bring in much money, like you say. And second thing is, I want you to get all the education you can. Down the line, that'll do you more good than anything else I can think of. We ain't in the Confederate States no more. No law against you goin' out and gettin' any kind o' work you're smart enough to do. There's even colored lawyers and doctors in the USA."

So there were—a handful of each. Their clients were also colored, almost exclusively. Cincinnatus didn't dwell on that. He wanted his son ambitious, as he was. He'd done as well as he could himself to have the hauling business. Maybe, one of these days, Achilles would take over for him. But maybe, once the boy became a man, he would want something more—want it and be able to get it. So Cincinnatus hoped, anyway.

Amanda said, "Wish you was—wish you *were*—home more, Pa." She corrected herself before her older brother could do it for her.

"I wish I was, too, sweetheart," Cincinnatus answered. After getting out of jail, he'd had to get to know his little girl all over again. By the time he came home, she'd nearly forgotten him. And he'd found there was a great deal to like in her. She had an even sweeter nature than Elizabeth's, which was saying a lot. But wishes and the real world had only so much to do with each other. "I don't work, we don't eat. Simple as that. Wish it wasn't, but it is."

It had always been as simple as that. Now, though, a new and dreadful simplicity threatened the old: even if he worked as hard as he could, as hard as was humanly possible, they still might not eat. That terrified him.

Snow was falling when he got up the next morning. He fired up the truck and headed for the railroad yard even so. He intended to get there early. Some truckers would let snow make them late. They were the ones who'd get what was left after the more enterprising men won the good assignments—or maybe the latecomers would end up with nothing at all.

When Cincinnatus saw how few trains had come into the yard, he thanked heaven he'd come as fast as he could. He got a choice load, too: he filled the back of the old Ford with canned fish from Boston—the mackerel on the cans looked absurdly cheerful—and set out to deliver it to the several grocery stores run by a fellow named Claude Simmons.

Some of the grocery boys who helped him unload the fish were no older than Achilles. One or two of them looked younger than his son. Down in the CSA, even white kids would have pitched a fit about working alongside a colored man. Nobody here complained. The boys seemed as grateful to have work as Cincinnatus was himself.

At one of the stores, Simmons himself signed off on the paperwork. He nodded to Cincinnatus. "I've seen you delivering things here more than once, haven't I?" he asked.

"That's right, suh," Cincinnatus answered.

"You drive for yourself?"

"Yes, suh."

The grocery man studied him. "You do that just 'cause it's the way things worked out, or are you one of those people who can't stand taking orders from anybody? People like that, they start going crazy if they have to let somebody else tell 'em what to do, so they end up with a job where they work for themselves—either that or they really do go nuts. I've seen that happen a time or two."

With a shrug, Cincinnatus answered, "I don't reckon I'm like that. You ask somebody else, he might tell you different. But I think I just want to make a living, do the best I can for my family."

"You want a job with me?" Simmons asked. "Delivery

driver, twenty-two fifty a week. You won't get rich, but it's steady." He pointed to the clipboard in Cincinnatus' hand. "What you're doing there, you're liable to starve on."

That held the unpleasant ring of truth. Even so, Cincinnatus didn't need to think very long before he shook his head. "Thank you kindly, suh, but I got to tell you no."

"Do you?" Simmons scowled. Cincinnatus got the idea not many people—and especially not somebody like a colored truck driver—told him no. He went on, "You won't tell me you clear twenty-two fifty a whole lot of weeks these days."

"No, suh." Cincinnatus admitted what he could hardly deny. "But what happens if I take the job with you, and things get worse like they look like they're doin' and *then* you let me go? I'd've been drivin' one o' your trucks, right?—not my own. Probably sell that. Then I'd really have to start at the bottom. I done that before. Don't want to have to try and do it again."

"Have it your way," the grocery man said with a shrug. "Don't expect me to ask you twice, that's all."

"I don't, suh. Didn't expect you to ask me once. Right decent of you to do it."

Suddenly, Simmons seemed less a boss and more a worried human being: "Do you really think it'll get that much worse? How could it?"

"How? Dunno how, Mr. Simmons," Cincinnatus answered. "But you ever know times that weren't so bad, they couldn't get worse?"

That seemed to strike home. "Go on, get out of here," Claude Simmons said, his tone suddenly harsh. "Here's hoping you're wrong, but"—he lowered his voice—"I'm afraid you're liable to be right."

Over supper that night, Cincinnatus asked Elizabeth, "Did I do the right thing? Twenty-two fifty steady money, that ain't bad. Ain't great, but it ain't bad."

"You done just right." His wife spoke with great authority. "Couple-three months, he forget why he took you on and he let you go. What kind of mess we in then?

Way things is, leastways you know what you got to do to git by."

"I thought the same thing—the very same thing," Cincinnatus said. "We're in trouble now, but we'd be ruined if I took that job and I lost it. We'll go on the best way we know how, that's all."

"Can't get worse'n what it was when you was in jail," Elizabeth said.

"Hope to God it can't," Cincinnatus answered. He didn't know exactly how bad it had been for his family. But when he laughed, he didn't feel mirthful. "When I was in jail, I didn't have to worry none about where my next meal was comin' from. I knew I was gonna get fed. Wouldn't be much, an' it wouldn't be good, but I was gonna get fed."

He would have got beaten, too, but he didn't talk about that. It wasn't anything his family needed to know, and it wasn't relevant to the discussion. Elizabeth said, "One way or another, the Lord provide for us."

"That's right," Cincinnatus said. Clarence Darrow might not have believed in God, but he did. The confidence that God was keeping an eye on him even while he went through the worst of times in jail was hard to come by, but it had proved true. So he remained convinced, at any rate.

And, one day about six weeks later, when he went to the railroad yard to see what he could haul, he remarked to the conductor, "I ain't had nothin' for the Simmons stores in a while now."

The white man sent him an odd look. "You wouldn't want that assignment if I gave it to you, Cincinnatus," he answered. "Old man Simmons went bankrupt week before last. Didn't you know?"

"No," Cincinnatus said softly. "I missed that." He looked up toward the heavens. A drop of drizzle hit him in the eye, but he didn't care. "Thank you, Jesus," he whispered. He might not have much, but what he had, he would keep a while longer.

Sylvia Enos had always enjoyed books. Like anyone who'd

grown up in the days before wireless sets brought words and music straight into the home, she'd used books to while away a lot of empty hours in her life. That didn't mean she'd ever thought she would end up writing one herself.

Well, yes, she had a coauthor. He was a real writer. He told her to call him Ernie, so she did. He'd been shot up during the war; he'd served in Quebec, and had written a couple of novels about that. She'd even read one. But times were just as hard for writers these days as they were for everybody else. He'd got himself a thousand-dollar contract for *I Sank Roger Kimball*, by Sylvia Enos, as told to . . . and five hundred dollars of that went into his pocket and the other five hundred into Sylvia's, and five hundred dollars bought a hell of a lot of groceries, so Sylvia was writing a book.

"Tell me how it happened," Ernie would say, sitting in the chair in her front room, smoke curling up from his pipe as he took notes. "Tell me exactly how it happened. Make it very plain. Make it so plain anyone can follow."

"I'll try," Sylvia would say. "I'll do my best." She found herself echoing the direct way in which he spoke. "When I got on the train bound for Charleston, I thought—"

"Wait. Stop." Ernie held up a hand. He was a big man, burly like a prizefighter, and the scars above his eyebrows and on his cheeks argued he'd been in his share of scraps, whether in the ring or just in one saloon or another. "Don't tell me what you thought. Tell me what you did."

"Why don't you want to know what I thought?" Sylvia asked. "That's why I did what I did."

"Tell me what you did," Ernie insisted. "I'll write that. People will read it. Then they'll know what you did. And they'll know why, too."

Sylvia frowned. "Why will they know that?"

Ernie was a handsome man, but normally one with a slightly sullen expression. When he smiled, it was like the sun coming out. "Why? Because I'm good," he said.

That smile by itself was almost enough to lay Sylvia's doubts to rest. She'd had room in her life for precious few romantic thoughts since the *Ericsson* sank, but Ernie's smile coaxed some out from wherever they'd been hiding all these years. She knew that was foolishness and nothing else but. How could she help knowing it, when he was five or ten years younger than she was?

He listened. She didn't think she'd ever had anyone listen so closely to what she said. She knew George hadn't when he was still alive. She'd loved him, and she was sure he'd loved her, too. But he hadn't listened like that—nor, as she had to admit to herself, had she listened to him so. Paying such close attention hadn't occurred to either one of them.

Ernie not only listened, he took detailed notes. Sometimes he lugged a portable typewriter to her flat. The battered leather of its case said he'd lugged it to a lot of different places, most of them worse than Boston not far from the harbor. He typed in quick, short, savage bursts, pausing between them to stare at the ceiling and gnaw on the stem of his pipe.

In one of those pauses between bursts, Sylvia said, "The way the keys clatter, it sounds like a machine gun going off."

The pipe stopped twitching in his mouth. It swung toward her, as if it were a weapon itself. "No," he said, his voice suddenly harsh and flat. "You don't know what you're talking about. Thank God you don't know what you're talking about."

"I'm sorry," she whispered.

"I drove an ambulance," he said, at least as much to himself as to her. "Sometimes I was up near the front. Sometimes I had to fight myself. I know what machine guns sound like. Oh, yes. I know. But I was on the safe side of the St. Lawrence"—he laughed—"when I got shot. An aeroplane shot up a train full of soldiers. Poor, stupid bastards. They never even found out what it was about before they got shot." He shrugged. "Maybe that was what it was about, that and nothing more. I went to help them, to take them away. A hospital was close by. Another aeroplane came over. It shot up all of us. I got hit."

Ernie went back to typing then. The next time Sylvia

thought of making some unasked-for comment, she kept it to herself instead.

He delivered the finished manuscript on a day when winter finally seemed ready to give way to spring. Thrusting it at her, he said, "Here. Read this. It is supposed to be yours. You should know what is in it."

He flung himself down on the sofa, plainly intending to wait till she read it. It wasn't very thick. Sylvia sat down in the chair by the sofa and went through it. Even before she got halfway, she looked up at him and said, "I understand why I did what I did better now than I did when I did it."

She wondered if that made any sense at all. It must have, for he gave her a brusque nod. "I told you," he said. "I'm good."

"Yes." She nodded back. "You are." She went back to reading. When she looked up, another forty-five minutes had gone by and she was finished. "You make me sound better and smarter than I am."

That made him frown. "You should sound the way you are. How do I fix it?"

He was serious. Sylvia laughed and shook her head. "Don't. I like it." Ernie still looked discontented. She laughed again. "I like you, too." She'd never said that before.

"Thanks," he said, and put the manuscript back into a tidy pile and imprisoned it with rubber bands. "I enjoyed working with you. I think the book will be all right." By the way he sounded, the second was more important than the first.

Even so, when he headed for the door Sylvia planted herself in front of him, put her arms around him, and gave him a kiss. It was the first time she'd kissed a man, the first time she'd wanted to kiss a man, since she'd kissed George good-bye for the last time during the war.

Ernie kissed her back, too, hard enough to leave her lips feeling bruised. He squeezed her against him, then all at once shoved her away. "It's no good," he said. "It's no damn good at all."

"Why not?" Sylvia said. "It's been so long. . . ."

Knowing desire had been a delicious surprise. Knowing it, having it stirred, and now having it thwarted seemed more than she could bear.

"Why not, sweetheart? I'll tell you why not," the writer answered. "I got shot in Quebec. You know that. You don't know where. I got shot right *there*. Not enough left to do a woman any good. Not enough left to do me any good, either."

"Oh," Sylvia said. That didn't seem nearly strong enough. "Oh, *hell*."

He looked at her and nodded. "Why this is hell, nor am I out of it." The words weren't quite in his usual style. Maybe he was quoting from something, but Sylvia didn't recognize it. He bared his teeth in what seemed more snarl than smile. "I'm sorry, sweetheart."

"*You're* sorry?" Sylvia exclaimed. "You poor man!"

That was the wrong thing to say. She realized it as soon as the words were out of her mouth, which was, of course, too late. Ernie set his jaw and glared. No, he wasn't one to take pity—he'd despise it for weakness, maybe Sylvia's, more likely his own. "Shouldn't have messed with you," he said. "My own stupid fault. I forget every once in a while. Then it tries to wag. Like a goddamn boxer dog wagging his little docked tail. But a boxer can hump your leg. I can't even do that." He kissed her again, even harder and rougher than before. Then he walked straight out the door. Over his shoulder, he threw back a last handful of words: "Take care of yourself, kiddo."

The door slammed. Sylvia burst into tears. "Oh, *hell*," she said again. "Oh, hell. Oh, hell. Oh, hell." She was sure she would never see him again.

She was sure, but she was wrong. One day a couple of weeks later, he waved to her as she came out of her block of flats. She'd never known she could feel joy and fear in the same heartbeat. "Ernie!" she called. "What is it?"

"You have your money in a bank," he said. That wasn't at all what she'd expected. "Which bank is it?"

"Plymouth and Boston Bank and Trust," she answered automatically. "Why?"

"I thought I remembered that," Ernie said. "I saw the passbook on your coffee table. Take the money out. Take it all out. Take it out right away. The bank is going to fail. It will fail very soon."

Fear of a different sort shot through her. "God bless you," she whispered. "You're sure?"

"No, of course not," he snapped. "I came here because I was guessing. Why else would I come here?"

Sylvia flushed. "I was going somewhere else, but I'll head over there right now. Thank you, Ernie."

His face softened, just for a moment. "You're welcome. Writers find things out. I know someone who works for the bank. Who worked for the bank, I mean. He saw the writing on the wall. He quit. He said anywhere else in the world was better than to be there right now." He paused and nodded to Sylvia. "Nice to think I can do *something* for you, anyhow." Touching a finger to the brim of his sharp new fedora, Ernie hurried away. The crowd on the street swallowed him up.

Plymouth and Boston Bank and Trust was only a few blocks away: the main reason Sylvia banked there. She ran almost the whole way. The lines didn't stretch out the door, as she'd seen at other banks in trouble. But she felt panic in the air when she went inside. Everyone was speaking in the low near-whispers people used when they tried to show they weren't afraid. She filled out a withdrawal slip and worked her way to the front of the line.

How many lines have I stood in? How many hours of my life have I wasted in them? Too many—I know that.

At last she stood before a teller's cage, with its frosted glass and iron grillwork. The young man looked very unhappy when he saw the slip. "You want to close out your entire account?" he said in that soft, no-I'm-not-afraid voice.

"That's right," Sylvia answered firmly. "You *do* have the money to cover it?"

The teller flinched. "Yes, we do. We certainly do. Of course we do."

"Well, then, kindly give it to me," Sylvia said.

"Yes, ma'am. Please wait here. I'll be back with it." The teller disappeared into the bowels of the bank.

Before he returned, an older man stepped into the cage and said, "Ma'am, I want to personally assure you, the Plymouth and Boston Bank and Trust is sound."

"That's nice," Sylvia told him. "If it turns out you're right, maybe I'll put my money back in. If it turns out you're wrong, I'll have the money—if that teller ever gets back. How long is he going to take?"

He chose that moment to return. While the frowning older man looked on, he counted out bills and change for Sylvia. "Here you are, ma'am," he said. "Every penny that's owed you." He sounded as if he were doing her a favor by giving her back the money, and as if she hadn't done the bank a favor by depositing it there in the first place.

By the time she left, the lines did stretch out the door. "Did you get it?" someone called to her. She didn't answer; she didn't want to get mugged when people found out she was carrying cash. She just headed home, as fast as she could.

Plymouth and Boston Bank and Trust closed its doors for good the next day.

XII

Mary McGregor went about her chores with a certain somber joy. That had nothing to do with how hard things were on the Manitoba farm where she'd spent her whole life. It had a great deal to do with how hard the market crash had hit the United States. She hardly cared what happened to her, so long as the United States got hurt.

And, by all the signs, the occupiers did hurt. Fewer green-gray U.S. Army motorcars rattled along the road to Rosenfeld that ran past the edge of the farm. Fewer U.S. soldiers prowled the streets of the local market town. And the *Rosenfeld Register*, published these days by an upstart from Minnesota who used occupation propaganda as filler, kept on weeping about how hard a time people south of the border were having.

None of which made things on the farm any easier, only somewhat easier to bear. Things on the farm were desperately hard, and all the harder because Julia had married Kenneth Marble and gone off to live with him. She came back to visit fairly often, usually bringing Beth Marble, Kenneth's mother, with her, and Kenneth himself stopped by every so often for a burst of work for which a man's strength came in handy. Things weren't the same, though, and Mary and her own mother both knew it.

"One of these days before too long, you'll meet somebody, too," Maude McGregor said over supper after a long, wearing day out in the fields. "You'll meet somebody,

379

get married yourself, and move away. I'll probably have to sell this place and move in with you or Julia."

"I wouldn't do that!" Mary exclaimed.

Her mother smiled. "Of course you would. You should. That's the way the world works. Young folks do what they need to do, and older ones ride along with it as best they can. I don't see how we'd go on if things worked any different."

"It doesn't seem right. It *isn't* right," Mary said—she'd had that passionate certainty for as long as she'd been alive. After a moment, she went on, "If I ever marry anybody"—and the thought had crossed her mind more and more often since she'd passed her twentieth birthday—"he ought to come and live here and help us work this place. Then our children could go right on working it, years and years from now."

"The trouble with that, you know, is that Julia and Kenneth, and their children when they have them, have an interest in this land, too," her mother said.

"Julia doesn't seem very interested," Mary said. "She went off without so much as a backwards glance."

"Julia doesn't seem very interested *now*," her mother replied. "How she'll feel about things ten or twenty years from now—or how her husband and her children will feel—well, how can anybody know for sure?"

Thinking about what things might be like ten or twenty years from now still didn't seem natural to Mary. She tried to imagine herself at forty, but no picture formed in her mind. That lay too far in the future to mean anything to her now. She wondered if Julia still felt the same way. Maybe not—with a husband at hand, she had to be looking forward to having children.

How children were begotten was no mystery to Mary, as it could be no mystery to anyone who'd grown up on a farm. Why anyone would want to have anything to do with the process was a different question. To let a man do *that* with her, to her . . . She shook her head. The mere idea was repulsive. But people did it. That was what being married was about. She knew that, too. If people didn't do it, after a while there wouldn't be any more people.

Sometimes that didn't seem such a bad idea.

Her mother went on, "A couple of knotholes have popped out of the wood in the barn. I want you to nail wood over them when you get the chance, so the inside will stay warmer in winter. The sooner you do it, the sooner we don't have to worry about it any more."

"I'll take care of it," Mary promised. "I've noticed 'em, too, especially the one that came out right behind that old wagon wheel."

"Yes, that's the biggest one," Maude McGregor agreed. "A good patch there will keep a lot of warm air from leaking out when the weather turns cold again—and it will."

"I know," Mary said. No one who'd lived in Manitoba any time from September to April could help knowing.

When she went out to the barn the next morning, she took care of the livestock first. That *had* to be done, and done every day. As soon as she'd finished, she went over to her father's work bench. She cut a square off a flat board, then grabbed the wood, a hammer, and some nails and went to get at the knot that had turned into a knothole.

It was right behind that wagon wheel. She had to put down the tools and the patch to wrestle the wheel out of the way. "Miserable thing," she muttered, or perhaps something a little stronger than that. Why the devil hadn't her father got rid of it? Come to that, why hadn't she or her mother in the years since her father died? She had no good answer except that there had always been more important things to do.

Once she'd shifted the wheel, she picked up the square of wood and the hammer and nails and advanced on the knothole. As she took the next to last step, she frowned. It didn't sound right—she'd never known that reverberation anywhere else in the barn. It didn't feel quite right underfoot, either. Ground had no business giving slightly, as it did here. It almost felt as if . . .

Mary bent down to look more closely at where she'd been standing. It just looked like dirt, with straw scattered over it. But when she scraped at it with her hand, she didn't have to dig far at all before her fingers found a board—undoubtedly, the board she'd trodden on after moving the broken wagon wheel.

What's that doing there? she wondered. Almost of their own accord, her fingers kept searching till they found the edge of the board. She pulled up. Dirt slid from the board as she raised it.

Under it was a sharp-edged hollow dug into the soil. And in that hollow ... Mary's eyes got big and round. In that hollow rested sticks of dynamite and blasting caps and lengths of fuse and some highly specialized tools. "At last," she whispered. She'd finally found her father's bomb-making gear.

The first thing she imagined was going into Rosenfeld, as Arthur McGregor had done at the end of the Great War, and blowing as many Americans as she could sky-high. She didn't worry about getting caught. If it meant more revenge on the USA, she would gladly pay the price. The real problem was, she didn't know enough about explosives to make a bomb that had any real chance of doing what she wanted it to do.

I can learn, she thought. *It can't be too hard. I just have to be careful. I'm sure I can figure it out without killing myself while I'm doing it.*

"Thank you, Pa," Mary said. "I'm sorry you had to stop. I'm even sorrier you didn't get General Custer. But the fight's not done. The fight won't be done till Canada's free again."

She looked toward that old, broken wagon wheel. Suddenly, a wide smile flashed across her face. Now she understood why her father had never repaired it or got rid of it. It perfectly concealed his tools and explosives. Not one of the Yankee soldiers who'd searched this barn—and there had been a lot of them, for they'd suspected much more than they could ever prove—had thought to move it and see what lay underneath. She wouldn't have thought of it, either, if she hadn't had to shift the wheel for an altogether different reason.

She wondered if she could find anyone in the sputtering Canadian resistance movement who could teach her about making bombs. Then, almost as soon as the thought occurred to her, she shook her head. Her father had gone his own way in fighting the Americans, which meant no one had betrayed him. No one could betray him if no one knew what he was doing.

People told a bitter joke: *when three people sit down to conspire, one is a fool and the other two American spies.* That would have been funnier had it not held so painfully much truth. More than once, the *Rosenfeld Register* had exulted about plots that failed because one member or another gave them away to the Yankees.

Mary McGregor nodded to herself. *Whatever I do, I'll do it alone. That's how Pa did it. He'd still be blowing them up if he hadn't had bad luck. It's my turn now. I'll be as careful as he was, or even more so. Nobody will give me away, and I won't give myself away, either.*

Some people said even the big Canadian uprising of a few years before had been betrayed to the Americans before it broke out, that they'd been on the alert because of that. Mary had even heard some people with reputations as patriots had turned traitor because they'd fallen in love with invaders from the south.

She didn't want to believe that. She had trouble imagining any proper Canadian falling in love with a Yankee. The Americans had ravished the country. Wouldn't they be ravishing anyone in it who had anything to do with them? That was how it seemed to Mary. As far as she was concerned, nobody who'd betrayed the uprising deserved to live.

"Yes, that's what I'll do," she said, as if someone had suggested it to her. Getting rid of traitors was the best way she could think of to remind the whole country that going along with the occupation had a price.

She wanted to go out and start planting bombs that very morning. She knew some names. She was sure she could learn others without much trouble. But she checked herself. *You were going to be careful, remember?* After nodding, she patched the knothole that had led to her discovery. Then she carefully concealed the hole in the ground once more, replacing the board, covering it with dirt and straw, and putting the old wagon wheel back where it belonged. When she was done, she looked hard at the ground and did a little more smoothing. Satisfied at last, she nodded and went on to cover up the other knots that had come out of the planking.

"Took you long enough," her mother said when Mary came into the farmhouse. "I didn't think it was that hard a job."

"Sorry, Ma." Mary had known from the minute she lifted the edge of the board and saw what lay beneath it that she couldn't tell her mother about it. What would Maude McGregor do? Pitch a fit and tell her to leave the stuff alone. She was as sure of that as she was of her own name. She was also sure she wouldn't leave the stuff alone, no matter what her mother told her to do.

"Sorry?" Her mother shook her head. "Don't you think you have enough other things to take care of? What were you doing, playing with the chicks? You haven't done that since you were a little girl."

"I know, but I was looking at them, and they looked so cute—and they turn into stupid, boring old hens so fast. I wanted to have some fun with them while I could. They act so silly." Mary seized on the explanation with both hands. She didn't like to lie to her mother, but preferred that to telling the truth here.

"Can't afford to get sentimental about 'em," her mother said. "They'll go into the pot when they stop giving enough eggs to be worth their keep. Nothing like a good chicken stew on a cold winter night."

"I know that, too, Ma." Mary didn't want to say anything to stir her mother up or make her start asking questions. Agreeing with everything Maude McGregor said was also liable to make her mother wonder, but not in any dangerous way.

Or so Mary thought, till her mother asked, "Are you all right, dear?"

Mary thought that over. After a couple of seconds, she nodded. "I'm swell, Ma. I'm the best I've been for a long time, matter of fact." Her mother gave her a quizzical look, but not of the sort to make her worry. No, she didn't worry at all. Everything was going to be fine now. She could feel it.

The *Remembrance* sailed west through the Straits of Florida, out of Nassau in the Bahamas—the formerly British Bahamas, surrendered to the USA after the Great War—bound for Puerto Limón on the Caribbean coast of Costa Rica. The sun stood tropically high in the sky. The day was hot and bright and perfect . . . perfect, that is, for almost everybody aboard the aeroplane carrier except Sam Carsten.

No matter how hot and muggy it got, Sam had to keep his cap on and to jam it down as far down over his eyes as he could. A lot of officers went around in their shirtsleeves. He didn't; he left on his white summer jacket, to protect his arms as well as he could.

His ears, his nose (especially his nose), and the backs of his hands were snowy white with zinc-oxide ointment. Even so, every square inch of flesh he exposed to the sun was red and peeling or blistered. He hated weather like this, hated it where most men reveled in it.

Like most men, Commander Martin van der Waal tanned readily. Oh, he'd burn if he did something stupid, but even that would only last till he stayed out enough to get his hide acclimated to the sun. The torpedo-defense specialist looked at Sam with wry sympathy. "You'd sooner be patrolling somewhere between Greenland and Iceland, wouldn't you?" he said.

"Now that you mention it, sir—yes," Carsten answered.

"Sorry about that," van der Waal said. "They've got somebody else keeping an eye on the Royal Navy up there. We get to show the flag in what used to be a Confederate lake."

"Not *quite* enough little specks of land in the Florida Straits to let the CSA claim this as territorial water and make us go the long way round," Sam said.

"We would have had to before the war," his superior said. "The Confederates thought they were little tin gods then. Now . . . Now I don't care if they build themselves a bridge from Key West to Habana. We'll sail right under it, by God, and thumb our noses as we go by."

"Yeah." Carsten smiled and nodded, liking the picture.

Down at the *Remembrance*'s stern, a sailor spun an aeroplane's prop. The engine roared to noisy life. With a push from the steam catapult, the machine taxied along the carrier's flight deck, descended for a split second as it went off the end, and then gained altitude and buzzed away. Another followed, and another, and another.

Sam said, "Of course it'll be unofficial when they look over what the Confederates are up to in south Florida and Cuba." He winked. "Of course it will."

Commander van der Waal chuckled. "Yeah, and rain makes applesauce."

But two could play at that game. Before long, a biplane came down from Florida and began flying lazy circles above the *Remembrance*. Not caring for the company, the aeroplane carrier's commander ordered a couple of fighting scouts aloft to look over the newcomer and, if need be, to warn him off. Sam happened to be going by the wireless shack when one of the U.S. pilots said, "The Confederate says he's just a civilian. His machine's got *Confederate Citrus Company* painted on the side. He's out for a stroll, you might say."

What the officer inside the wireless center said meant, *Yeah, and rain makes applesauce,* but was a good deal more pungently phrased. The officer went on, "Tell the son of a bitch he can goddamn well go strolling somewhere else, or maybe he'll go swimming instead."

"Yes, sir," the pilot answered. Carsten lingered in the corridor to hear what happened next. After half a minute or so, the pilot came back on the air: "Sir, he says if we want an international incident from shooting down an unarmed civilian pilot in international waters, we can have one."

The officer in the wireless center expended more bad language. At last, he said, "I'd better talk to the old man about that one." He might have wanted to order the Confederate aeroplane knocked out of the sky, but he didn't have the nerve to do it without approval from on high. Carsten wouldn't have, either.

Maybe the skipper of the *Remembrance* used some blue language of his own. Whether he did or not, that CONFEDERATE CITRUS COMPANY aeroplane flew above the carrier for the next hour and a half. Nobody fired a shot at it. The pilot finally ran low on fuel or got bored or found some other reason to fly back off toward the north.

In the officers' galley at supper that evening, Sam said, "I bet they're developing that bastard's photographs right now."

"Probably," a lieutenant, junior grade, agreed. "Fat lot of good they can do with 'em, though. Maybe they've built a few submersibles without our noticing, and maybe than can keep 'em hidden from us, too—"

"Especially since the Socialists aren't spending the money on inspections that the Democrats did," a lieutenant commander put in.

"Yes, sir," the j.g. said. "But there's no way in hell they could build themselves an aeroplane carrier on the sly. That's too big a secret to keep. Besides, they haven't got the aeroplanes to put aboard it."

"We hope they don't," Sam said. "For all we know, they're all labeled *Confederate Citrus Company* right now."

That produced a few laughs and a few curses. The lieutenant commander said, "That machine had no guns. The pilots checked, first thing."

"Yes, sir," Sam said. "But how long would they need to convert the type to something they could use in combat?"

Nobody had anything resembling an answer for him. The lieutenant commander said, "That's something we ought to find out about. Maybe more of these fruit-company bastards will come look us over before too long. If they do, we'll look them over, too." He sighed. "I don't know how much good that will do us, not the way things are in Philadelphia these days, but we do have to make the effort."

By the next morning, though, they'd left the Straits and even Cuba behind. No more aeroplanes came out from the CSA to inspect them. Carsten was sure that didn't mean nobody was keeping an eye on them. Lots of little fishing boats, some Confederate, others Mexican, bobbed in the Gulf of Mexico. How many of them had wireless sets? How many of those sets were sending reports to, say, the Confederate Naval Academy at Mobile, or to New Orleans? He didn't know, but he had his suspicions.

He also had suspicions of another sort. Whenever he came up onto the flight deck, he kept staring out into the blue, blue waters of the Gulf. "What are you doing?" Commander van der Waal asked. "Looking for periscopes?"

"Yes, sir," Sam answered, altogether seriously.

Van der Waal stared. "Do you really think the Confederates would try to sink us?"

"No, sir," Sam said. "I think they'd have to be crazy to try that. But if they've got any submersibles, what better way to train their crews than by stalking a real, live aeroplane carrier?"

His superior pondered that, then nodded. "Good point, Carsten. Let's see what we can do about it. Maybe we ought to get some training in, too."

Before long, the *Remembrance* shut down her engines and drifted to a stop. Sam knew what that meant: she was giving her hydrophone operators the best chance she could to pick up the sounds of submarines moving on their electric engines somewhere under the sea.

What will we do if we hear one? Carsten wondered. The carrier couldn't start lobbing depth charges into the Gulf of Mexico. That would be an act of war, no less than if one of the hypothetical subs launched a torpedo at her. *We could report it to Philadelphia.* How much good would that do? Sam didn't know. But the Confederate States couldn't claim they had no submersibles if the *Remembrance* found one.

Or could they? Maybe they'd claim the boat belonged to the Empire of Mexico. Sam doubted the Mexicans could build such boats on their own, or man them if they did, but how could you know for sure? You couldn't. Subs under the sea were hard to find and even harder to

388

identify; they didn't come with license plates, the way motorcars did.

Nobody ever officially said whether the hydrophone operators found anything. Sam did get a letter of commendation in his service jacket for "enhancing the *Remembrance*'s readiness against surprise attack." He drew his own conclusions from that. He also kept his mouth shut about them. Sometimes advertising you'd done something smart was a good idea. Sometimes it was anything but.

When they neared the Central American coast, a tiny gunboat flying the blue-and-white Costa Rican flag came out of Puerto Limón to greet the *Remembrance*. An officer at the bow hailed her through a megaphone. He looked just the way Sam had thought a Costa Rican would look, and spoke English with a Spanish accent. The gunboat, which might have been a toy alongside the aeroplane carrier, got out of the way in a hurry so the elephantine ship could advance.

Puerto Limón itself turned out to be very different from what Carsten had expected. He'd come to ports in Latin America before. He'd figured the people here would be like the officer: swarthy, most of them of mixed white and Indian blood, and Spanish-speaking. Instead, most of them turned out to be Negroes, and they used more English than Spanish. In their mouths, the language had a lilt that put him in mind of what he'd heard in the Bahamas.

A long line of black men carrying huge bunches of bananas came up the pier next to the one where the *Remembrance* tied up. They vanished into the hold of a freighter flying the Confederate flag, then emerged to go back down the pier lugging crates: whatever that freighter had been carrying here to exchange for the golden fruit (actually, the bananas going aboard were green; Sam supposed they would ripen on the way up to the CSA).

White sailors aboard the freighter stared over at the aeroplane carrier. To Commander van der Waal, Carsten remarked, "I wonder how many of those bastards were in the C.S. Navy during the war."

"More than a few, or I miss my guess," the other

officer answered. "We've just given them some free intelligence." He shrugged. "That's the way it goes, sometimes."

The Costa Rican officer from the gunboat came aboard a few minutes later. His white uniform was more festooned with gold braid than that of the *Remembrance*'s skipper, but he introduced himself as Lieutenant Commander Garcia. That tickled Sam's funny bone. "I wonder what an *admiral* in the Costa Rican Navy looks like," he remarked.

"You probably can't see the cloth on his uniform at all, on account of the gold and the medals and such." Commander van der Waal's snicker had a nasty edge to it. "My little girl back in Providence likes to play dress-up the same way. Of course, she's got an excuse—she's only eight years old."

But Lieutenant Commander Garcia said all the right things: "We are pleased to see this great ship in our growing port. We hope it is a sign of friendship between your great republic and our own. Costa Rica and the United States have never been enemies. We do not believe we ever have to be."

Sam wondered whether the sailors aboard the Confederate freighter could hear Garcia's words, and how they liked them if they could. *Hope you don't like 'em for beans,* he thought.

When Abner Dowling went to the train station in Salt Lake City, a police officer patted him down before allowing him inside the building. Another cop, and a military policeman with him, went through Dowling's suitcase. "Sorry about this, sir," the MP said when he got to the bottom of Dowling's belongings. "I do apologize for the inconvenience."

"It's all right," Dowling answered. "Identity cards and uniforms can be faked—we've found that out the hard way. Now you know for a fact I won't be carrying contraband onto the train."

"Thank you for taking it so well, sir," the military policeman said.

"No point getting huffy about it," Dowling said. "You were going to search me any which way."

390

He was dead right about that. Everyone who left Utah was searched these days, whether at train stations or at checkpoints along the highways. Since assassinating General Pershing, Mormon diehards had set off bombs from San Francisco to Pittsburgh. They were suspected in a couple of murders of prominent men, too, and of bank robberies to finance their operations. And so . . .

And so lines into the railroad station were long and slow. Everyone was searched: men, women, children, even babies in flowing robes. At least once, somebody had tried to smuggle out explosives hidden under baby clothes. Dowling only hoped the diehards hadn't succeeded at that game before the U.S. occupiers got wise to it. Every suitcase got searched, too. Some, the ones suspected of false bottoms, also got X-rayed.

As Dowling took his seat in the fancy Pullman car, he marveled that any ordinary civilians at all got on in Utah. He muttered under his breath, a mutter uncomplimentary to the inhabitants of the state he helped rule. Utah had precious few ordinary civilians, and even fewer who were also Mormons. Up till General Pershing was killed, Dowling had dared believe otherwise. So had the administrators who'd been on the point of relaxing military occupation in Utah.

It could have become a state like any other, Dowling thought as the train began rolling east. *They could have rebuilt the Temple, if they'd wanted to. But some damnfool hotheads made sure that wouldn't happen. I hope they're pleased with themselves. Utah won't get out from under the U.S. Army's thumb for the next ten years now.*

He suspected the man who'd gunned down General Pershing—a man who'd never been caught—and his pals *were* pleased with themselves. Some people had a vested interest in trouble. If it looked as if calm threatened to break out, people like that would do anything they could to thwart it. And, as they'd shown, they could do plenty.

Colonel Dowling let out a loud, long sigh. He glanced toward the bed in his compartment. If he wanted to, he could take off his shoes—take off his uniform, for that matter—curl up there, and go to sleep. He didn't have to worry about Salt Lake City, or Utah as a whole, for the next several days.

Unless the Mormons have planted a bomb under the railroad tracks, he thought. He knew that wasn't likely. But he also knew it wasn't impossible.

He shook his head, angry at himself. *I said I wasn't going to worry about it, and what do I do? Start worrying, that's what.*

He looked out the window. An aeroplane flew past, also heading east but easily outpacing the train. It was one of those new three-motored machines that could carry freight or passengers. Suddenly, Dowling wondered what sort of precautions people were taking at landing fields. A bomb aboard an aeroplane would surely kill everybody on it. Muttering again, this time a sharp curse, he scribbled a note to himself. Maybe the Mormons hadn't thought of trying to bomb aeroplanes, the way they assuredly had thought of bombing trains. Maybe they wouldn't. But maybe they would, too. He wanted to stay one step ahead of them if he could.

When lunchtime came, he made his way back to the dining car. He was about to dig into a big plate of spare ribs when a clever-looking woman with reddish hair going gray came up to his table and said, "Mind if I join you, Colonel Dowling?"

"I suppose not." He frowned; she looked familiar, but he couldn't place the face. "You're . . ."

"Ophelia Clemens," she said crisply, holding out her hand man-fashion. "We met in Winnipeg, if you'll remember."

"Good God, yes!" Dowling exclaimed as he shook it. "I'm not likely to forget that!" She'd come to occupied Canada to interview General Custer, and she'd just escaped being blown to bits with him—and with Dowling—when Arthur McGregor planted a bomb in the steakhouse where Custer ate lunch. "How are you, Miss Clemens?"

"Tolerable well, thanks," the newspaperwoman answered. "Are you also heading to Washington for General Custer's funeral?"

Dowling nodded. "Yes, I am. I would have gone

anyway, but Mrs. Custer also sent me a telegram asking me to be there, which I thought was very kind and gracious of her."

"Do you have any comments on the general's passing?"

"It's the end of an era," Dowling said automatically. That he knew it was a cliché made it no less true. He went on, "He was an officer in the War of Secession. He was a hero in the Second Mexican War. He was a hero—probably *the* hero—of the Great War." *Even though he broke orders to do it. Even though he almost got himself court-martialed—and me with him.* "And he was a hero all over again, when he was coming home to retire, when he threw back the bomb that Canadian tossed at him." Every word of that was true, too. Dowling knew he would have died if General Custer hadn't stubbornly, irrationally—correctly—believed McGregor was the man who'd been out to kill him. He added, "He lived to ninety, too. That's a good run for anybody."

"It certainly is." Ophelia Clemens took out a notebook and scrawled in it. A waiter came by. She gave him her order, then turned back to Dowling. "May I ask you something, Colonel?"

"Go ahead," Dowling replied. "What kind of answer you get depends on what kind of question it is."

"It always does," she agreed. "Here's what I want to know: Teddy Roosevelt and George Custer always told different stories about what happened during the Second Mexican War. They're both dead now. You can't hurt either one of them with a straight answer. Do you know who had it right?"

"Do I know for a fact?" Abner Dowling remembered the quarrel he'd listened to in Nashville in 1917, right at the end of the Great War. Roosevelt and Custer had almost come to blows then, though one was in late middle years and the other already an old man. Dowling knew what his opinion was, but that wasn't what Miss Clemens had asked. "Ma'am, I wasn't there. I was a little boy during the Second Mexican War. Even if I had been there, odds are I wouldn't have heard exactly what orders were given, or by whom."

Ophelia Clemens gave him a sour nod. "I was afraid you were going to say that. I even talked to a couple of the surviving machine gunners—Gatling gunners, they called themselves—but they don't know or don't remember who did what when."

"We'll probably never know, not for certain," Dowling said.

"What do you think?" The newspaperwoman poised her pencil over the notebook, ready to take down whatever pearls of wisdom he gave her.

"Not for publication," he answered at once. The pencil withdrew. He still didn't say what he thought. Instead, he added, "Not even as 'a highly placed source' or anything like that."

The look she sent him this time was even more sour. "All right," she said at last. "You don't make things easy, do you?"

"Ma'am, Teddy Roosevelt and George Custer are dead, but you won't find a senior officer who doesn't have strong views about both of them," Dowling said.

Ophelia Clemens nodded again. That did seem to make sense to her. "I promise," she said solemnly. "And in case you're wondering, I don't break promises like that. If I did, no one would trust me when I made them."

Dowling believed her. She was, from everything he'd seen in Winnipeg and here on the train, a straight shooter. She probably had to be, to get ahead in a normally masculine business like reporting. He remembered she'd told him and Custer her father had been a newspaperman, too. Dowling said, "Strictly off the record, I'd bet on Teddy Roosevelt."

"I thought as much," she said. "Custer was nothing but a phony and a blowhard, wasn't he?"

"Strictly off the record," Dowling repeated, "he *was* a humbug and a blowhard. But if you say he was nothing but a humbug and a blowhard, you're wrong. He always went straight after what he wanted, and he went after it as hard as he could. When he was right—and he was, sometimes—that made him one of the most effective people the world has ever seen. The rest may be true, but don't forget that part of him."

Ophelia Clemens considered that. In the end, a little reluctantly, she nodded. "Yes, I suppose you have something. People need to judge a man by what he did, not just by the way he acted."

"Custer did a lot," Dowling said. "No two ways about that." He might have managed more, he might have managed better, if he hadn't become a self-parody in his later years. But what he *had* done would be remembered as long as the United States endured.

Dowling told Custer stories all the way from Salt Lake City to Washington, D.C., some on the record, some off. Ophelia Clemens wrote down what she could and either laughed or rolled her eyes at the rest. Dowling was sorry they went their separate ways after the train rolled into Union Station.

He paid his respects to Libbie Custer, who sat beside the general's body where it lay in state in the Capitol. "Hello, Colonel," Custer's widow said. "We had a fine run, Autie and I. I don't know what in heaven's name I'll do without him."

"I think you'll manage," Dowling said, on the whole truthfully. He'd always reckoned Mrs. Custer the brains of the outfit.

"I suppose I *could*," she said now. "But what's the point? I spent the past sixty-five years taking care of the general. Now that he's gone, what am I supposed to do with myself? I haven't much time left, either, you know."

With no answer for that—how could he contradict an obvious truth?—Dowling murmured, "I'm sorry," and made his escape.

He marched in the mourners' procession behind Custer's flag-draped coffin. The general's funeral was modeled on Teddy Roosevelt's; Dowling found it strangely fitting that the two men, longtime rivals in life, should be equals in death. The only difference he could see was that no foreign dignitaries came to say their farewells to General Custer.

A bespectacled man hoisted a boy onto his shoulders. In the funereal hush, his words carried: "Look, Armstrong. There goes the man you're named for."

Custer's final wishes—or maybe they were Libbie's wishes—were that his remains be buried at Arlington, across the Potomac from Washington in what was now West Virginia. He would spend eternity with Teddy Roosevelt, and Robert E. Lee, presumably, would spend it gnashing his teeth at having not one but two U.S. heroes take their final rest on his old estate.

"Well, to hell with Robert E. Lee," Dowling muttered, and he felt sure both Custer and Roosevelt would have agreed with him.

Flora Blackford had spent years speaking in front of crowds of workers. A women's club in Philadelphia wasn't the same thing. Speaking as First Lady in front of organizations like this wasn't even like speaking in the House of Representatives. There'd been plenty of cut-and-thrust in the House. Here, Flora had to be polite whether she wanted to or not.

"I'm sure you'll agree that we can return to prosperity, and that we *will* return to prosperity," she told the plump, prosperous women. Even if it was noncontroversial, it was also a campaign speech, with the 1930 Congressional election just around the corner. "The worst is over. From where we are now, we can only go up."

The women applauded. She'd told them what they wanted to hear, what they wanted to believe. She wanted to believe it herself. She'd wanted to believe it ever since the stock market crashed right after her husband became president. She'd wanted to, but believing got harder every day.

"We were the party of prosperity through the 1920s," she insisted. "We don't deserve to be labeled the party of depression."

Even though the women applauded again, Flora knew more than a little depression herself. Her husband had done what only twenty-nine men had done before him— he'd become president. And what had it got him? Only curses and the blame for the worst collapse the United States had known since the bad times after the Confederate States broke away in the War of Secession.

She got through the speech. She'd learned all about getting through speeches despite a heavy heart when she'd had to stand up in Congress after her brother David lost a leg in the Great War. She had to do a good job here. The coming election would be the first chance voters had to say anything about the Blackford administration and the Socialist Party since things went sour.

What would they say when they got the chance? Nothing good, she feared. The Socialists, naturally, had taken credit for everything that had gone right in their first two terms, Upton Sinclair's terms, in Powel House, regardless of whether they'd caused it. Political parties did that. How could they keep from getting the blame for everything that was going wrong now? The Democrats—even the remnants of the Republicans—were certainly doing their best to pin that blame on the party of Marx and Lincoln and Debs.

After the speech, after the coffee and cakes and polite talk that followed, she went back to the presidential residence. Traveling by chauffeured limousine to the Powel House struck her as expensive and wasteful, to say nothing of being the very opposite of egalitarian. But against entrenched presidential custom the Socialists had struggled in vain. The limousine waited for Flora outside the women's club—waited for her and whisked her away.

When she got back to Powel House, she found her husband studying a bill. "Is that the new relief authorization from Congress?" she asked.

Hosea Blackford nodded. "That's what it is," he said. "I'm going to sign it, too—even makework is better than no work at all, and no work at all is what too many people have these days. But it feels like putting a bandage on a man who's just been shot through the heart. How much good is it going to do?"

He'd been president for only a little more than a year and a half. The pressure of the job, though, had aged him more in that time than all the years he'd spent as vice president. His hair was thinner and grayer, his face more wrinkled and more weary-looking; his clothes hung on him like sacks, for he'd lost weight, too.

Would he look this way if things hadn't gone wrong? Flora wondered. Guilt gnawed at her. She'd encouraged Hosea to run for president. If she hadn't, the country would be blaming someone else for its troubles now. Shantytowns inhabited by men who'd lost their homes wouldn't be called Blackfordburghs. Comics wouldn't tell jokes about him on the vaudeville stage and over the wireless.

Then he said, "It's a good thing I've got this job instead of Calvin Coolidge. If he were sitting here, he'd veto this bill and all the others like it. Things would be a lot worse then—I'm sure of it. We have hungry people now—we'd have starving people then. The class struggle would go straight to the streets."

Tears stung her eyes. She said, "I was just thinking I never should have put you through all this."

"You didn't put me through it," he answered. "I did it myself. I wanted it, too, you know. And, in spite of everything, I think I'm a better man for the job than Coolidge would have been."

"The country doesn't deserve you," Flora said.

"Oh? Are you saying it does deserve Coolidge?" her husband asked with a wry grin. "I'm not sure even Massachusetts deserves him."

"That's not what I meant, and you know it," Flora said with some asperity.

"Maybe not, sweetheart, but it's what you said," Hosea Blackford answered. Even that wry grin had trouble staying on his face. "If only something we tried would do some real good for the country, so people would believe we had hope."

"Things would be a lot worse without the relief programs and the dole," Flora insisted. "We'd have men out selling apples on street corners to try to stay alive."

"We might as well, even now," her husband said. "I haven't seen the country so gloomy since . . . since before the Great War."

Flora knew what a hard time he had bringing that out. The Socialists still looked at the war in terms of the lives it had squandered, the lives it had wrecked, the ruin it had wrought. They didn't usually talk about the triumph it had been, as Democrats were in the habit of doing. But before the war, the USA, caught between the CSA and Canada, with England and France always ready to pounce, had a downtrodden feel. Enemies had ganged up on the United States twice. The fear those enemies might do it again had filled the country—and, perhaps, with reason.

No more. Now the United States had their place in the sun. No one had a bigger place, either. Only the Empire of Germany came close. The Kaiser's monarchy was a rival, yes, but not the deadly foes the Confederacy and her allies had seemed in the old days, the days before they were beaten at last.

And, from 1917 to 1929, under Theodore Roosevelt and then under Upton Sinclair, the United States had walked tall, had walked proud. After half a century of furtive skulking, the United States had strutted. But now this. Nobody in all the world was strutting these days. Everyone was trying to figure out how to fix what had gone wrong. No one, though, was having much luck.

"What *are* we going to do?" Flora asked.

"You mean, besides take a drubbing at the polls next Tuesday?" her husband asked in turn. "I don't know, dear. I really don't, and I wish to heaven I did. If I knew what to do, I'd be doing it. You can bet on that." He drummed his fingers on the desk. "Blackfordburghs." He spoke the word as if it were a curse. And so, in a way, it was: a curse on him, and a curse on the party he headed.

"Maybe it won't be so bad," Flora said. "People aren't stupid. The Democrats can't mystify everybody. What's happened the past year and a half isn't our fault, isn't *your* fault. It would have happened if Coolidge were president, too. It would be worse then—you said so yourself."

"That's logical. That's rational," Hosea Blackford said. "Politics, unfortunately, is neither. People won't think about what might have been. They'll think about what really happened. And they'll say, 'You were there. It damn well *is* your fault, and you've got to pay for it.'" He pointed to himself.

Flora wanted to tell him he was worrying about nothing. She couldn't. He was worrying about something all too real, and she knew it. She did walk over and give him a hug. "There," she said. "And Joshua loves you, too."

"That's all good," Blackford said. "That's all wonderful, as a matter of fact. In my personal life, I'm as happy and lucky as a man could be. But none of it will buy the Socialists a single extra vote when voting day rolls around."

He was right. Flora wished she could tell him he was wrong. He would only have laughed had she tried, though. He knew better. So did she.

Waiting for the election was like waiting for an old, sick loved one to die. Day followed day without much apparent change, but then, suddenly and somehow unexpectedly, the moment came at last. People went to the polls. Blackford's name wasn't on the ballot, but the election would be a judgment on him even so. He couldn't even vote for his party, nor could Flora; neither of them officially resided in Philadelphia.

Hosea Blackford could have gone over to Socialist Party headquarters to learn of voters' decision—or rather, decisions, for every race here, unlike in a presidential election, was individual, unique to its area. But he stayed in Powel House instead. Once more, custom triumphed.

Plenty of wireless sets and telegraph clickers brought in the news. And, from the very beginning, it was as bad as Flora and he had feared it would be. If anything, it was worse. Socialist after Socialist went down to defeat. Even the fellow who'd followed Flora to Congress in the Eleventh Ward in New York City found himself in deep trouble against a Democratic candidate of no particular luster.

"What are we going to do?" Flora wailed as the magnitude of the Socialist disaster grew plain.

"No. The question is, what will the new Congress do?" her husband said glumly. He answered his own question: "Odds are, the Democrats won't do much, and they won't let us do much, either. They think we've done too much already, and that we're part of the problem."

"They don't know what they're talking about," Flora snapped.

"Well, I happen to agree with you, you know," Hosea Blackford said. "The voters, unfortunately, look to have other ideas."

"How can they do this to us?" Flora didn't try to hide her bitterness.

"I'm sure the Democrats felt the same way ten years ago, when we first came to power," her husband said.

That struck her as cold consolation. "But we're right," she said. "They were wrong."

He managed another of those wry smiles. "Remember your dialectic: thesis, antithesis, synthesis. Now the antithesis gets its turn for a while, and we see what comes of that."

"Nothing good," Flora predicted darkly. The irony was that she'd always been a much more ideological Socialist than Hosea. His chiding her on basic Party doctrine stung, as he'd no doubt meant it to. She went on, "We have to keep them from doing nothing, the way you say they want to—and of course you're dead right about that. We have to. Maybe we can get a halfway worthwhile synthesis out of that."

"We're going to lose the House," Hosea said. "I don't think there's any doubt about it. The Senate . . . well, that depends on how some of the races in the Far West go. If we're lucky, there may be enough Socialists and Republicans to go with a handful of progressive Democrats and let us do some useful things. We'll see, that's all."

He sounded as if he looked forward to the challenge. That wasn't how Flora felt about it. As far as she was concerned, the faithless people had betrayed the Party. She'd always been on the barricades, throwing stones at the oppressors. Now, by their votes, the people thought the Socialists were *among* the oppressors. That hurt. It hurt a lot, and she knew she would be a long time getting over it.

Clarence Potter tried to remember the name of the Englishman who'd written a novel about a man who'd invented a machine that let him travel through time. He hadn't altogether liked the book—parts of it struck him as a Socialist tract about the divisions between capital and labor—but he couldn't deny that it had more than its share of arresting images. The mere idea of a time-traveling machine was one.

On New Year's Eve, 1930, as the year was poised to pass away and usher in 1931, Potter felt as if not just he but all of Charleston were caught in the grip of a time-traveling machine and hurled back almost a decade into the past. The Freedom Party had laid on an enormous rally to mark the changing of the year, and had succeeded, he feared, beyond its wildest dreams.

A strident sea of humanity filled Hampton Park to hear Jake Featherston, who'd come down from Richmond to speak. Dozens of searchlights stabbed up into the sky, creating columns of silvery radiance that seemed to transform the park into an enormous public building. Blocks of Freedom Party bully boys in their white shirts and butternut trousers, along with veterans from the Tin Hats—who wore uniforms even more closely resembling those of the Confederate Army—stood out amid the swarms of ordinary Charlestonians who'd come to the outskirts of the city.

More bully boys in white and butternut, these carrying long truncheons, formed a perimeter around the crowd. The searchlights spread just enough light around to let Potter see how very ready for a brawl they looked.

He touched Braxton Donovan's arm. "We can't try to break this up, not with the men we've got here," he said urgently. "They'll slaughter us."

Donovan grimaced, but then reluctantly nodded. "Just our luck," he said. "We try to take a leaf out of the Freedom Party's book, and it doesn't work." They'd brought along seventy-five, maybe even a hundred, stalwart young Whigs armed with a motley assortment of street-fighting weapons. The force would have been plenty to disrupt any ordinary Freedom Party gathering. Attacking this one ... Potter shook his head. He would sooner have sent infantrymen charging uphill against machine-gun nests and massed artillery.

Disgust in his voice, he said, "Featherston even has

the luck of the weather." A December night in Charleston could easily have been rainy, could have been freezing, could even have seen snow—though that was unlikely. But the thermometer stood in the upper forties, with a million stars in the sky trying to fight their way through the searchlight beams. The moon and, even lower in the east, Jupiter blazed bright.

"So what do we do now?" Donovan asked. "Just send the boys home? Go on home ourselves? That stinks, you want to know what I think."

"Getting massacred stinks worse," Potter answered. "You can go or stay, whichever you want. They can go or stay, whichever they want. Me, I'll hang around and hear what that Featherston bastard has to say."

"You thinking of going over to the Freedom Party?" Donovan asked. "You blocked me when I tried to read Anne Colleton out of the Whigs, and now she's back in bed with dear old Jake. Fat lot of good you did us."

"I was wrong," Potter said with a scowl. "You're lucky—you've never been wrong in all your born days, have you?" He still missed Anne. His mind kept exploring how things between them had soured, as a man's tongue will explore the empty socket that recently held a tooth.

Admitting he was wrong disconcerted Donovan. The lawyer probably didn't hear it happen often enough to know what to do when it did. "All right, all right," he said gruffly. "Let's forget about it, then."

"I wish I could," Potter said. The other Whig didn't know what to make of that, either. *Too bad,* Potter thought.

A white-shirted Freedom Party man came up to them. "You fellas want to move along now," he said, almost indulgently—he knew he had strength on his side.

Potter looked at him. "What we *want* to do is kick your damn teeth down your throat," he growled.

"Watch your mouth," the Freedom Party man said, indulgent no more. "We can squash y'all flat like a cockroach—and just what you deserve. If I give a yell—"

"If you give a yell, you're a dead man," Clarence Potter promised. "Your side might win the fight afterwards, but you won't be around to enjoy it. I promise."

The man in white shirt and butternut trousers scowled at him. He stared back, no expression at all on his face. The Freedom Party hooligan was the first to look away. A moment later, he spun and stalked off. "You told him," Braxton Donovan said, as if Potter and the Whigs had won some sort of victory.

"He's going to come back with enough men to squash us flat," Potter said. "Go on home, and take the boys with you. We'll get other chances. I'm going to hang around."

"You're crazy," Braxton Donovan declared.

"No, it's just that I was in intelligence during the war. I want to know what the enemy is up to," Potter replied with a shrug. "Or maybe I *am* crazy. You never can tell."

As the Whigs' outnumbered toughs headed away from Hampton Park and back toward downtown Charleston, Potter mingled with the Freedom Party men and women still streaming in to hear Featherston speak. That mingling came just in time, too. The fellow he'd faced down returned with a lot of men at his back. He looked around and laughed when he didn't see Potter or any of the other Whigs.

They were leaving anyway, you son of a bitch, Potter thought, *and now I've found my way inside.*

By their clothes, most of the men who wanted to hear Jake Featherston were farmers and laborers—most, but far from all. Potter saw druggists and shopkeepers and businessmen and even a few who looked like professional men. Not all the men were Great War veterans, either. More than Potter had expected looked too young to have fought in the war. That surprised and dismayed him. The women coming in—perhaps a third of the audience—likewise came from all social groups, with the emphasis on the lower middle class.

Potter pushed forward as far as he could. Even so, the rostrum from which Featherston would speak remained halfway across the park from him, and seemed tiny as a toy. Everyone exclaimed as searchlights, swinging toward the podium, picked out a face behind it. But that wasn't Jake Featherston's lean visage, which Potter knew all too well. Whoever that was, pinned in the glow of the bright lights, he'd never missed a meal and was nobody Potter recognized. Some of the people around Potter grumbled, too.

Then the plump stranger introduced himself as one of the new Freedom Party Congressmen South Carolina had sent up to Richmond in the election of 1929. That was plenty to win him a round of applause from the Party faithful. Clarence Potter had to join it to keep something dreadful from happening to him. He felt like washing his hands the first chance he got.

"And now," the Congressman boomed, "it gives me tremendous pleasure to have the privilege of presenting to you all the leader of our great Freedom Party, Mr. Jaaake *Featherston*!"

The roar of applause and cheers that went up stunned Potter's ears. He opened his mouth, but silently. He didn't have to shout, and keeping his mouth open helped protect his ears. Featherston, an old artilleryman, likely knew that trick himself.

Through the shouts and clapping from the crowd came disciplined yells from the men in white shirts and butternut trousers: "Freedom! Freedom! Freedom!" Little by little, more and more people joined that chant, so it began to drown out the noise all around: *"Freedom! Freedom! Freedom!"* The two-syllable word felt as heavy and regular as a heartbeat.

Jake Featherston let the chant build to a deafening crescendo, then raised both hands above his head. Still disciplined, the blocks of goons fell silent at once. Without their steadying influence, the cries faded away after perhaps fifteen seconds.

Into the ringing quiet that followed, Featherston said, "It's always good to come to Charleston, on account of this here is where the Confederate States of America were born." He couldn't miss getting applause with that line. He couldn't—and he didn't. Again, Clarence Potter had to clap along with everybody else to keep from standing out. He hated that, but saw no way around it.

Featherston went on, "They say showing's better than telling, and I guess they're right. We've been telling people what's wrong with the Confederate States for more than ten years now, and not enough folks wanted to listen. Now the Whigs have gone and shown we were right all along, and all of a sudden everybody's paying attention to us. I wish to heaven it didn't have to happen like this, I truly do, but here we are just the same."

To Clarence Potter, staunch Whig, it wasn't much of a joke, but people around him laughed. Featherston said, "I'm warning people right now, it's not a good idea to think about the Freedom Party like we're just another bunch of politicians."

Cries of, "No!" and, "Hell, no!" and, "Better not!" rang from the crowd. Featherston let them spread through Hampton Park, then raised his hands again. This time, silence fell at once.

Into it, he said, "We are the Confederacy's destiny. We are the Confederacy's future. We're giving our dear country a faith and a will again. We have to concentrate all our strength on action, revolutionary action. Because we're going that way, we're gathering into our ranks every last member of the Confederate people who still has energy and nerve—that's you, folks, and I'm glad of it!"

People were even more eager to applaud themselves than they were to applaud Jake Featherston. Again, Potter had to clap, too. As he did, he reluctantly nodded. *He's shrewder than he used to be,* he thought. *He doesn't just think of himself any more.* But that wasn't right. *No, he lets people think he's thinking about them. Inside, he's still the same cold-blooded snake he always was.*

"Burton Mitchel wants to cozy up to the United States. The USA saved his bacon once," Featherston shouted. "But the United States can't save his bacon this time around, on account of they haven't got any bacon of their own. And even if they did, do y'all want to be the USA's tagalong little brother from now till the end of time?"

Some people shouted, "No!" Others shouted things a good deal more incendiary. Potter would never have said anything like that where ladies might hear. But then, not ten feet away from him, a woman who looked like a schoolteacher yelled something that would have made a sergeant, a twenty-year veteran, blush.

"We've got us a duty: a duty to be strong," Jake Featherston declared. "We've got us a duty to stand up to the United States just as soon as we can. And to do that, we've got us a duty to put our own house in order. We've got us a duty to put people back to work. We've got us a duty to make sure they don't go hungry. We've got us a duty to keep the niggers in their place, and not to let them steal work from white folks. And we've got us a duty to remember what the Confederate States of America are all about. And folks, what we're about is—"

"*Freedom!*" The great roar staggered Potter.

"Y'all remember that," Featherston said. "Remember it every single day. When you see the liars and the cheats getting together, don't let 'em get away with it. Smash 'em up! How can you have freedom when the rich folks want to take it away from you?"

Does he see the irony there? Potter wondered. *Does he see it and not care, or does it go right by him?* As the crowd roared, as Jake Featherston wished them a happy New Year and exhorted them to vote for the Party in November, Potter wondered which of those possibilities frightened him worse.

When Jake Featherston came through South Carolina on his speaking tour, Anne Colleton tried to see him. She tried, and she failed. Featherston wouldn't talk to her; a flunky told her he wasn't available.

She fumed for days afterwards. She wasn't used to getting brushed off. Her habit, in fact, was to brush off others. Featherston annoyed her enough to make her wonder if she shouldn't stay a Whig after all. In the end, what made her decide she had to swallow her pride was the thought that staying a Whig meant admitting Clarence Potter had been right all along. If he had, why had she broken up with him over their political differences? Staying a Whig would mean swallowing her pride, too, and swallowing it in front of an old lover. She preferred making up with Jake Featherston to that.

After the papers announced Featherston's return to Richmond, she sent a telegram to Freedom Party headquarters: SHALL I COME NORTH TO TALK THINGS OVER?

The answer, at least, returned promptly: COME AHEAD. CONVINCE FERD KOENIG. THEN WE'LL SEE. FEATHERSTON.

Anne said something extremely unladylike as she crumpled up the telegram and threw it in the trash. Having to talk with anyone except Jake Featherston himself was galling. But Ferdinand Koenig wasn't a flunky, or not precisely a flunky. He'd been in the Freedom Party even longer than Featherston had, and had twice been his running mate on the Party ticket. The main difference between him and Jake was that he wasn't colorful.

And so, swallowing her pride again, Anne wired, ARRIVE NEXT TUESDAY. LOOKING FORWARD TO MEETING MR. KOENIG.

As she usually did when coming up to Richmond, she booked a room in Ford's Hotel, just north of Capitol Square. The room she got gave her a fine view of the square. In happier times, it would have been a peaceful, restful, patriotic view. She could have looked out on the grass and on the splendid statues of George Washington and Albert Sidney Johnston.

She could still see the statues. Tents and shanties swallowed almost all the winter-brown grass. Men walked aimlessly from one to another, some smoking, some sipping from whiskey bottles. Here and there, women hung out laundry on lines that ran from tents to trees. Children ran this way and that.

Columbia and Charleston had shantytowns, too. Even St. Matthews had a little one. But Anne had never seen any to match Richmond's. The capital of the Confederate States was a great city. When things went wrong, they went wrong more visibly here than anywhere else.

She asked the house detective, "How bad are things? Will my clothes and suitcases still be in my room when I get back?"

"Likely so, ma'am," he answered. "We work hard at keeping the trash out of the hotel. We had some trouble

408

with that when things first went sour, but we don't let it happen any more. It's just a matter of taking pains."

Giving pains, too, she thought. The house dick was about six feet three, with shoulders wide as a barn door. He wasn't visibly armed, but she was sure he had brass knucks or a blackjack stashed where he could get at them in a hurry. She wouldn't have wanted to run into him if he found her anywhere she wasn't supposed to be.

When she waited on the street for a taxi, though, beggars hurried across Capitol Street to try to pry money out of her. She knew that, if she gave anything to anybody, none of them would ever leave her at peace. Closing the motorcar door on them was a relief.

"Where to, ma'am?" the cabby asked.

"Freedom Party headquarters," Anne answered. She wondered if she would have to give him the address.

As things turned out, she didn't. The driver nodded. "Take you right over there. It ain't far at all. I'm thinking about voting that way myself come November, matter of fact."

Alert guards armed with bayoneted Tredegars stood outside the headquarters. They wore what was almost but not quite Confederate Army uniform. Their clothes weren't quite the same as what the Tin Hats put on. These men looked somehow more menacing than most members of the big veterans' outfit. Anne didn't know whether that was the cut of their uniforms or the expressions on their faces. *Some of each,* she thought.

"You're Mrs. Colleton, come to see Mr. Koenig?" one of them asked.

Anne shook her head. "I'm *Miss* Colleton, and you'd better remember it."

"Sorry," the disconcerted guard muttered, and passed her on into the building.

She had to ask two more people how to find Ferdinand Koenig's office, which struck her as inefficient. When at last she got there, a pretty secretary led her inside. Koenig looked like a man who'd done time in the trenches. He had fierce eyebrows, a jutting jaw, and a rumbling baritone voice. "Good to see you again, Miss Colleton," he said. "It's been a few years, hasn't it? Sit down. Make yourself at home. Tell me why you've decided the Freedom Party isn't such a bad thing after all."

He looked like a bruiser. He didn't sound like one, though. He'd been Jake Featherston's right-hand man for a long time now. That almost certainly meant he could think as well as break heads. Anne said, "When I left the Party, you were still tainted by what Grady Calkins did. Our politics have never been that far apart, whether I was formally with you or not."

"You're saying you're a fair-weather friend. You'll back us if we look like winners and dump us if we don't," Koenig said. "Question is, in that case, why should we want to have anything to do with you?"

"Because we're going the same way. Because I can help you get there. You'll know what I did in South Carolina. When I wasn't with you, I was trying to bring the Whigs more into line with what you've been saying all along."

Ferdinand Koenig paused to light a cigarette. After blowing out a cloud of smoke, he said, "And you were doing us a favor by this, you say?"

"No, I don't think so, and that isn't what I said," Anne answered. "But I think I was doing the country a favor. That's what this is really all about, isn't it?—what happens to the Confederate States, I mean."

Another cloud of smoke rose from Koenig. "That's . . . some of what this is about," he said at last. "The rest of it is, why should we trust you now? You walked away once, walked away and left us in the lurch. Who says you won't do it again?"

"No one at all, if I don't happen to like the way you're going," Anne said. "But as long as we're heading in the same direction, wouldn't you rather have me on your side than against you?"

"Maybe," he answered. "Maybe not, too." His eyes measured her. She didn't care for that gaze; Koenig might have been looking at her over the sights of a rifle. "You don't pull any punches, though, do you?"

"I try not to," Anne said. "Getting straight to the point saves time."

"Maybe," Koenig said again. He didn't say anything more till he'd finished the cigarette and stubbed it out in an brass ashtray made from the base of a shell casing. Then he went on, "You talk a good game, I will say that for you. I'm not going to tell you yes or no. I'm going to pass you on to the Sarge. He'll make up his mind, and we'll go on from there. How does that sound?"

"I came to Richmond to see him," Anne answered.

Ferdinand Koenig shook his head. "No, you *came* up here to see me, remember? Now you've passed the first test, so you *get* to see him. See the difference?"

"Yes," Anne said, though she'd always assumed she would pass it.

"Well, come on, then." Koenig heaved his bulk out of the chair. He led her down the hall, up a flight of stairs, along the corresponding hall on the next floor up, and into an office. The secretary there wasn't decorative; she was, in fact, severely plain. That probably meant she was very good at what she did. Koenig nodded to her. "Morning, Lulu. Here's Miss Colleton, to see the boss."

Lulu gave Anne the once-over. She sniffed, as if to say, *What can you do?* Anne bristled. The secretary took no notice of that at all. With a small sigh, she said, "Go right in, Miss Collins. He'll be expecting you." She wasn't the sort who'd get names wrong by accident. That meant she'd done it on purpose. Anne bristled all over again, and again got nothing resembling a rise from Lulu.

When she walked into Jake Featherston's office, the leader of the Freedom Party rose and leaned across the desk to shake her hand. He wasn't handsome. Still, those strong, bony features and the energy that sparked from him made mere handsomeness seem insipid. Anne had had that thought before. "Sit down," he said, waving her to a chair. "Sit down and tell me why I should pay any attention to you after you went and left us when we ne[ed]ed you bad."

He hadn't forgotten. Anne doubted he eve[r] anything that went against him. They weren't s[ ] there. She answered, "Two reasons: my mo[ ] brains."

411

He frowned. "If you had any brains, you never would've walked out on us in the first place."

"No." Anne shook her head. "I back winners. If you think you looked like a winner after Calkins killed President Hampton, you're not as smart as you think you are. But times are hard again, and in hard times the Freedom Party shines. So . . . here I am."

How many people gave him such straight talk? Not many, Anne suspected. What would he do when he heard it? Get angry? Yes, by the slow flush that mounted to his cheeks and by the way his eyes flashed. But he held it in, saying, "You're a cool one, aren't you? You're telling me straight out you'd walk away again if you saw us in trouble."

"No," Anne replied. "What I'm telling you is, this time I expect you to win."

"And you want to come along for the ride," Featherston said.

"Of course I do," Anne answered. "Sooner or later, we're going to have some things to say to the United States. If you don't think I want to be part of that, you don't know me at all. And I *can* help. At your rallies, you're still using tricks I figured out for you ten years ago, and you know it."

"You spent the last few years trying to teach the Whigs new tricks," he said.

"Yes, and they're old dogs—they couldn't learn them," Anne answered. "They've been in power too long. They can't learn anything any more. That's why they've got to go."

"They're dogs, all right, the sons of—" Featherston caught himself. "Well, I have plans for them, too. You'd best believe that. Way they've stomped on the people of the Confederate States . . . You're dead right they've got to go, Miss Colleton. And I aim to get rid of 'em."

Anne wondered how he meant that. Literally? She knew he was ruthless. Was he *that* ruthless? Maybe. She wouldn't have been astonished, but even the most ruthless man faced a formidable barrier of law. Anne nodded to herself. Here, that kind of barrier might not be bad at all.

412

"You come back in, you'll follow the Party line?" Jake Featherston asked.

You'll do as I say? was what he meant. Anne had never been one to do as anybody said. But if she said no, she'd have no place in the Freedom Party, not now, not ever. That was ever so clear. *This is why you came to Richmond,* she reminded herself. *Do you want to go home empty-handed?* Part of her said she did. She ignored it. Nodding to Featherston, she said, "Yes, I'll do that."

He didn't warn her—no, *You'd better,* or anything like that. "Good," he said. "We've got a deal." He didn't ask for her soul, either. But why would he? She'd just handed it to him.

XIII

The alarm clock jangled, bouncing Jefferson Pinkard out of bed at what he reckoned an ungodly early hour. His shift at the Birmingham jail started an hour and a half earlier than he'd gone to the Sloss Works. He yawned, lurched into the bathroom of his downtown flat—one more thing he was getting used to after so long in company housing—brushed his teeth, lathered his face and slid a straight razor over his cheeks, and then went into the kitchen and made coffee and the inevitable bacon and eggs on the fancy, newfangled gas-burning stove in there.

Thus fortified, he got out of his nightshirt and into the gray jailer's uniform he'd worn since Caleb Briggs found out the Sloss Works had given him the boot. He planted his wide-brimmed hat on his head at a jaunty angle and looked at himself in the mirror. His reflection happily nodded approval at him. "I'm hot stuff, no two ways about it," he said, and that reflection did not presume to disagree.

He put his nightstick on his belt and headed out the door. He'd toted longer, heavier bludgeons while breaking up Whig rallies with his Freedom Party pals, but he supposed he understood why jailers didn't usually carry guns. If something went wrong, that would give prisoners deadly weapons, which was the last thing anybody wanted.

People got out of his way when he walked down the street in that uniform. He liked that. He'd never had it happen before, except when he was in the company of a lot of his pals, all of them in white shirts and butternut pants, all of them ready—even eager—for trouble. Now he strode along by himself, but men and women still made way for him. He lit a cigarette and blew out a cheerful cloud of smoke.

Birmingham City Jail was a squat red-brick building that looked like a fortress. As far as Jeff was concerned, it looked just the way it was supposed to. He tipped his hat to a policeman in an almost identical uniform coming out. "Mornin', Howard," he said. "Freedom!"

"Mornin', Jeff. Same to you," the cop answered. A lot of policemen in Birmingham belonged to the Freedom Party. Pinkard had seen some of them at meetings. Since becoming a jailer, he'd found out that a good many who didn't go to meetings or knock heads were members just the same. Some policemen felt they shouldn't flaunt their politics. But that didn't mean they had none.

Inside the city jail, Jeff stuck his card in a time clock just like the one at the Sloss Works except for being painted gray rather than black. He stuck his head into the cramped little office where he had a battered desk. "Mornin', Billy," he said to his night-shift counterpart, who was writing a report at an equally beat-up desk. "What's new for me?"

"Not a whole hell of a lot," Billy Fraser answered. He was about Jeff's age, and like him a veteran—precious few white men of their generation in the CSA hadn't gone to the front. "A couple of niggers in for drunk and disorderly, and one burglar who was the easiest collar you'd ever want—dumb asshole fell out a second-story window making his getaway and broke his ankle. Yell he let out woke up the whole goddamn block. They were beating on him pretty good. He was probably glad when the cops pulled the citizens off him and hauled him away."

"Don't reckon we have to worry about him bustin' out for a while," Pinkard said with a chuckle.

"Hell, no," Fraser said. "Like I told you, a quiet night."

Jeff nodded. "Anything else I need to know?"

"Don't reckon so," the other man answered. He threw the report in his Out basket and got to his feet. "Gonna head on home and catch me some shuteye. See you tomorrow. Freedom!"

"Freedom!" Pinkard echoed. "Get some rest. I don't expect the bastards we've got locked up are going anywhere much."

"They better not," Billy Fraser said. "That'd leave us some pretty tall explaining to do." He grabbed his hat—the twin of Jeff's—from the rack, stuck it on his head, and went out whistling "The Pennsylvania Rag," a tune that had been popular during the early days of the Great War, back when the CSA had held a large part of Pennsylvania.

The first thing Jefferson Pinkard did then was look at the report Fraser had written. It was meant for the warden, not for him, but he didn't care about that. He'd discovered Billy sometimes wrote things down that he forgot to say, things Jeff needed to know. Nothing like that was in there today, but you never could tell. When you were dealing with prisoners, you couldn't be too careful, either. If his experience in the Empire of Mexico had taught him anything, that was it.

After Jeff put the report back where he'd got it, he ambled down to the kitchen and snagged himself a cup of coffee. He snagged a roll, too. One of the colored cooks clucked reproachfully at that, but he was grinning while he did it, a grin that showed several gold teeth. Jeff grinned back. He had no trouble with Negroes, as long as they remembered who the boss was.

After he did that, he prowled through the whole jail, peering into every cell to see who was where. He couldn't take the prisoners out of the cells and line them up for roll call, the way he had down in Mexico. He'd had all the room in the world down there: he'd built his prison camp on the loneliest stretch of ground he could find. Things were different in Birmingham, but he wanted to know as much about what was going on as he could.

"I ain't run away, jailer man," said a Negro named Ajax, who was doing a year for beating up another man whom he'd caught using loaded dice. The victim was also black. Had he been white, Ajax would have faced a lot more time behind bars. "I's still here. You don't got to check on me every mornin'."

"Morning I don't check on you is probably the morning you'll try some damnfool thing or other," Pinkard answered. "More I check, harder it is for me to get a nasty surprise."

Ajax reproachfully clicked his tongue between his teeth. "You ain't no fun a-tall," he said.

"You wanted fun, you shoulda thought twice about pounding on that other nigger," Jeff said.

"That cheatin' son of a bitch won ten dollars o' *my* money with them goddamn dice," Ajax exclaimed, nothing but indignation in his voice. "I see him when I gits out o' here, I kick his shiftless ass again, teach him not to try none o' that shit no more." If jail was supposed to rehabilitate, it wasn't working with the aggrieved Ajax.

But Jeff didn't think jail was supposed to rehabilitate. Like the other jailers he was getting to know, he thought it was supposed to keep people who belonged there inside till it was time to let them out again. He didn't worry his head about who belonged and who didn't, either. Figuring that out wasn't his job. As far as he was concerned, if somebody ended up in the Birmingham City Jail, he damn well belonged there.

By the time his rounds ended, the trusties were going through the corridors serving breakfast to the other prisoners. Jeff didn't like that, either. He thought using trusties begged for trouble, because they were so likely to be anything but. But the jail didn't have the money to hire enough guards to do everything inside that needed doing, and so trusties took care of a lot of work. He scowled at them as he headed back to his office. How much contraband did they smuggle in? They knew. Nobody else did.

He was halfway through a circuit of the jail before lunch when one of the corridor guards waved to him and called, "Hold on there. Warden wants to see you in his office right away."

"Does he?" Jeff said uselessly. The guard nodded, as if to affirm he hadn't been kidding. "What the hell does he think I did?" Pinkard muttered. The guard didn't hear

417

that. A prisoner did, and leered at Jeff. As far as the former steelworker knew, the boss wanted to see you only when you were in trouble. Still cursing under his breath, he walked to the warden's office.

Ewell McDonald had all to himself more space than Jeff and the other assistant jailers put together. He was a beefy man in his early sixties, with his silver hair greased down and with a bushy gray mustache he'd probably worn since it was dark and stylish back in the 1890s. He heaved himself out of his swivel chair and stuck out a well-manicured hand for Jeff to shake. "Sit down, Pinkard, sit down," he boomed, sounding more like a politician on the stump than anything else. "Sit down and make yourself comfortable."

"Uh, thank you kindly, sir," Jeff replied, wondering when and how and why McDonald was going to lower the boom on him. "What can I do for you?" *Might as well make it short and sweet,* he thought.

Instead of answering right away, McDonald reached into his desk and pulled out a bottle of whiskey. Pinkard's eyes widened slightly, or more than slightly. Alabama was a dry state, though there were ways around that. He knew as much. He didn't expect the warden of the Birmingham City Jail to know it, or at least to show he knew it to a man he was going to bawl out. But Ewell McDonald yanked out the cork, swigged, and then passed the bottle across the wide expanse of his desk to Jeff. "Here you go, Pinkard," he said. "Have a snort."

"Thank you kindly," Pinkard said again. He knew he sounded bewildered, but couldn't help it. After he drank, he whistled appreciatively. That was real whiskey, not something cooked up in a hurry over an illegal still. He hadn't drunk anything so tasty in quite a while. He passed the bottle back, more worried than ever. McDonald wouldn't waste that kind of whiskey on him if he were in only a little trouble.

But the warden beamed at him. "You know, Pinkard, when I hired you, I reckoned I was stuck with you on account of Freedom Party business," he said. "Happens sometimes; nothing you can do but make the best of it.

But I'll be goddamned if you ain't pulled your weight and then some. You weren't lyin' 'bout that prison-camp business down in Mexico, were you?"

"Lying, sir?" Pinkard shook his head. "Hell, no. I did all that stuff."

"I guess maybe you did," McDonald said. "I wouldn't have bet on it when I took you on, I'll tell you that. But you've worked out fine. Hell, son, you're doing better than some of the fellows who've been here ten years." He grabbed the whiskey bottle and tilted it back for another knock.

"Thank you very much, sir," Jeff said, more than a little dazedly. He'd thought the same thing himself, but he'd never dreamt the warden would come out and say so. "Thank you *very* much. I've learned a hell of a lot here, too. Down in Mexico, I was making it up as I went along. You-all really know what you're doing."

"Some of the time, maybe," McDonald said. "But I like the way you prowl the cells. I like that a lot. Nothing's going to happen unless you know about it first, is it?"

"Well, I hope not," Pinkard answered. "You can never be sure, but I hope not."

"Long as you *know* you can never be sure, you won't do too bad." The warden pushed the bottle across the desk again. "Go ahead. You've earned it."

"Don't mind if I do." As Ewell McDonald had, Jeff took a long pull at the bottle. Smooth fire ran down his throat. "Ahh! That's mighty fine," he said, and then laughed. "Prisoners'll smell it on my breath and say I've been drinking on the job."

McDonald laughed, too. "They don't like it, you tell 'em they can take it up with the warden." He corked the whiskey bottle and stuck it back in his drawer. "However you did it, I'm glad you found your way here. You're goddamn good at this business, you hear what I'm telling you?"

"Thanks," Jeff said once more. Yes, he did feel dazed, and not just on account of unaccustomed morning slugs of whiskey. How long had he been at the Sloss Works without ever hearing anybody tell him anything like that?

Too long, he thought as he got to his feet. *Much too damn long.*

In the summertime, heat and humidity could make Augusta close to unbearable, especially for Negroes in the crowded quarters of the Terry. When Scipio got the chance, he liked to bring his family up to Allen Park and relax in the fresh air under the shade of the trees that grew thickly there. He and Bathsheba and the children would lie on the grass on a Sunday afternoon and watch people with more energy—and, he was convinced, less sense—play volleyball or throw around a football.

Allen Park was in the white part of town, but close enough to the Terry that Negroes often used it. Scipio would gladly have gone to a park inside the Terry, but nobody'd bothered leaving any open space for a park there. He wasn't surprised. How could he have been, when he'd lived in the Confederate States all his life? Whites got whatever they needed and whatever they wanted. If anything happened to be left over after that, Negroes got it. If nothing happened to be left over, well, too bad.

That was how whites saw things, anyhow. And then they'd been shocked when blacks rose up against them in Red revolt during the Great War. Scipio had thought that a damnfool idea, because he'd been all too sure the revolts would fail—as they had. Nothing made the whites fight hard like seeing their privileges threatened. But fearing failure didn't mean Scipio hadn't understood the impulse to hit back as hard as his own people could.

One lazy July Sunday, after finishing a picnic lunch, Bathsheba pointed to a sheet of paper stuck to the trunk of an oak not far away. "What's that say, Xerxes?" she asked.

Scipio took his alias for granted. He also took being asked such questions for granted: Bathsheba couldn't read or write. "I goes and looks," he answered, climbing to his feet. Full of fried chicken and yams, he ambled slowly over to the tree, read the paper, and came back to sit down on the grass again.

"Well?" his wife asked.

"Well?" Antoinette echoed. She was six now, which astounded Scipio every time he thought about it. And Cassius—named, though Scipio had never said so, for the Red rebel in the swamps of the Congaree River—was already three, which astonished him even more.

But he shook his head. "Ain't so well," he said; the thick patois of the Congaree made him sound more ignorant than Bathsheba, whose accent was milder. "Big Freedom Party rally here two weeks from now."

The corners of Bathsheba's wide, generous mouth turned down. "You're right," she said. "That ain't so good. That ain't no good at all. Thought them people was all over and done with, but now they're back."

"Now they's back," Scipio echoed somberly. "Times is hard. De buckra, dey's scared. When dey's scared, dey starts yellin', 'Freedom!' "

"If they want it so bad, how come they don't want to let us have none?" Bathsheba asked.

"Dey does dat, who dey gots to t'ink day's better'n?" Scipio didn't hide his bitterness.

"Ought to tear that sheet o' paper down," Bathsheba said.

"Do Jesus, no!" Scipio exclaimed. "Anybody see me do dat, my life ain't worth a penny. An' dey's bound to be plenty more o' they papers. Don't put up no notice like dat in jus' de one place. Tearin' it down don't do no good."

She didn't argue with him, but she didn't look as if she agreed with him, either. When they walked back to their flat, Scipio saw more Freedom Party notices. He wondered how he'd missed them coming up to Allen Park. Maybe he hadn't wanted to see them, and so had turned his eye aside.

He'd expected to pay no attention to the rally. What else was a Negro supposed to do with anything pertaining to Confederate politics, especially with a part of Confederate politics of which he disapproved? But this rally, very much in the frightening Freedom Party style of ten years before, refused to let Augusta's Negroes ignore it. For one thing, it was enormous. Scipio didn't know exactly how many white men thronged to it, but he could hear great roars of, "Freedom!" coming from the park again and again, though it was blocks away from his family's apartment building.

"Why they yellin' like that, Pa?" Antoinette asked.

Scipio wished he knew what he was supposed to tell her. "On account o' dey don't like what de gummint doin'," he answered at last.

She could have left it there. Scipio wished she would have left it there. Instead, with a child's persistence, she asked the inevitable child's question: "Why?"

"They're some o' the buckra what have it in for black folks," Bathsheba said when Scipio hesitated. That satisfied their daughter. No Negro, no matter how young, could help knowing plenty of whites in the Confederate States had it in for blacks.

If any Negro from Augusta hadn't known it, the ralliers did their best to drive it home. They swarmed out of the park and into the Terry, shouting, "Freedom!" all the while. A few policemen came with the long, sinewy column, but more to observe it than to check it. Had the Freedom Party men turned on the police, they could have got rid of them in moments and then rampaged through the Terry altogether out of control.

They could have, but they didn't. Scipio didn't even think they beat anybody up. They just marched and yelled and marched and yelled. In a way, that was a relief. In another way, it left Scipio all the more terrified, not least because of the discipline it showed. It was sending a message: this is what our people do when we tell them to do this. If we tell them to do something else . . . Scipio shivered at what the Freedom Party might do then. And would that handful of policemen try to stop them? Could they if they tried? Neither struck him as likely.

He made a point of getting to Erasmus' fish store and restaurant early the next morning. He still didn't get there as early as his boss. "Mornin', Xerxes," Erasmus said when Scipio came through the door. "How you is?"

"I been better," Scipio answered. "Buckra march underneath my window yesterday. Don't like that none, not even a li'l bit."

422

Erasmus nodded gloomily. "They go past my front door, too," he said. "No, I don't like that none, neither. They scared. When they scared, they do somethin' stupid."

"Do somethin' big an' stupid," Scipio agreed. "Burn down de Terry, maybe. De *p*olice, dey don't stop 'em if dey tries."

"Reckon not," Erasmus agreed. "Reckon the *p*olice do try—they ain't all bad men. Reckon they try, but I don't reckon they kin do much, neither."

"Where dat leave we?" Scipio answered his own question: "In trouble, dat where."

Erasmus looked at him. "You's a black man in the CSA," he said. "You think you ain't been in trouble since the day you was born?"

"I was borned in slavery days, same as you," Scipio said. "I knows all about dat kind o' trouble. But de Freedom Party, dey worse'n usual."

He waited to see whether Erasmus would try to argue with him. If his boss did, he intended to argue right back. But Erasmus slowly nodded. "Reckon you's right. Didn't used to think so. I reckoned them crazy buckra'd find somethin' new to git all hot an' bothered about. They been around for more'n ten years now, though. Don't reckon they's goin' noplace."

"Wish they would—wish dey go far away an' never come back no more," Scipio said. "They gwine win plenty o' new seats in the 'lection come fall, too."

"God's will," Erasmus said. "We is a sinful lot, and the good Lord, He make us pay."

Before Scipio could think about it, he shook his head. "I don't care none how sinful we is," he said. "De Lord can't hate we enough to give we what de Freedom Party want to give we." Would he have had such thoughts before he got mixed up with the Red Negroes who'd led the uprising in 1915? He didn't know for certain, but had his doubts.

"The Lord do what He want to do, not what we wants Him to do," Erasmus said. "Blessed be the name o' the Lord."

"Lord help he what help hisself," Scipio replied. "De

Freedom Party git stronger, I reckon maybe niggers gots to help theyselves." Was he really saying that? After watching from the inside the destruction of the Congaree Socialist Republic, could he really be saying that? He could. He was.

"We rise up against the buckra again, we lose again. You knows it, too." Erasmus sounded very sure.

And Scipio *did* know it, too. Blacks in the CSA couldn't hope to beat whites. He'd thought as much before the rising of 1915, and he'd proved right. On the other hand . . . "De Freedom Party git stronger, we lose if we *don't* rise up, too."

Erasmus didn't answer him. Maybe that meant there *was* no answer. He hoped it didn't, but feared it did.

Three days later, he got an answer of sorts. After finishing at Erasmus', he went into the white part of Augusta to visit a couple of toy stores that had a better selection—and better prices—than any in the Terry. Coming home with something new and amusing—it didn't have to be very big or very fancy—was a good way to delight his children. Having been childless for so long, Scipio found he took enormous delight in making them happy now that he had them.

He found a doll for Antoinette, one that closed its eyes when it lay down. It was, of course, white, with golden hair and blue eyes. He'd never seen a doll with dark features like his own. He'd scarcely imagined there might be such a thing. Whites dominated the Confederate States in ways neither they nor the Negro minority quite understood.

No matter what this doll looked like, Scipio knew his little girl would enjoy it. He set money on the counter before asking the clerk for it. To that extent, he did understand how things worked in the CSA. But the clerk, once he had the price, was polite enough, saying, "Here you are. Have a good evening."

"Thank you, suh," Scipio answered. He started for the door, and had just set his hand on the knob when he heard a scuffle outside, and then a man's shout of pain.

From behind him, the clerk said, "Maybe you don't want to go out there right now. Freedom Party hasn't always been nice to colored folks they catch out in the evening."

Hasn't always been nice to seemed to translate into *is beating the stuffing out of*. Scipio's first emotion was raw fear. His next was shame that he couldn't help the luckless Negro the goons had found. He felt gratitude toward the clerk, gratitude mixed with resentment. "Ought to call the cops," he said: as close as he dared come to letting that resentment show.

"I've done it before," the man answered. "They don't usually come for a call like that. I'm sorry, but they don't."

Erasmus had insisted the Augusta police weren't all bad men. Maybe he was right. Scipio found it harder to believe now. He did nod to the clerk. "Thank you fo' tryin', suh," he said. Not all whites were bad. He was reasonably sure of that.

A little while after the sounds of violence ended, Scipio left the toy store and hurried back to the Terry. He got home safe. His daughter did love the doll. Everything should have been fine. And it would have been, if only he could have forgotten what had happened in the white part of town. As things were, he got very little sleep that night.

When the train pulled into Abilene, Texas, Jake Featherston knew he was in a different world from the one he'd left. The plains seemed to go on forever. Dust was in the air. This wasn't the narrow, confined landscape of Virginia. No wonder Texans had a reputation for thinking big.

But Texas itself wasn't so big as it had been. Not far west of Abilene, Texas abruptly stopped. What the damnyankees called the state of Houston began. That was why Jake had come all the way out here: to make a speech as close to what he still called occupied territory as he could.

The train stopped. His bodyguards got up, ready to precede him out onto the platform. Looking out there, one of them said, "It's all right. Willy Knight's there waitin' for us."

"Hell it's all right, Pete," another guard said. "What

if that Knight bastard's the one who wants to try and get rid o' the boss?"

Pete, an innocent soul, looked shocked. Jake wasn't. Willy Knight's Redemption League might have swallowed up the Freedom Party instead of the other way round. It hadn't, though, and Knight couldn't be happy that he wasn't the biggest fish in the pond, the way he'd dreamt of being. Still . . . "If he wants to put me six feet under, reckon he can do it," Featherston said. "This is his part of the country; he can hire more guns than I can bring along. But if you stick your head in the lion's mouth and get away with it, after that the lion knows who's number one. That's what we're gonna do here."

When Jake stepped out onto the platform, the band struck up a sprightly version of "Dixie." People cheered. Jake took off his hat and waved it. Willy Knight stepped forward to shake his hand. As the two Freedom Party leaders met, photographers took pictures. The flashes made Featherston's eyes water.

"Welcome to Texas, Jake—what's left of it," Knight said, a broad smile on his handsome face.

"Thank you kindly, my friend." Featherston lied through his teeth. "We'll see what we can do about getting back what the USA stole from us."

"How are you going to do that?" a reporter shouted. "The Yankees won't pay any attention to us."

"They don't have to pay any attention to the CSA, not as long as the Whigs hold on to Richmond," Jake answered. "The Whigs say we lost the war, and so we're stuck—stuck forever. And we are, too, long as we think that way. But even the Yankees knew better. After we whipped 'em, they set up Remembrance Day so they wouldn't forget what happened. The Whigs *want* to forget—they want to pretend all their mistakes never happened at all. And they want the country to forget. Me, I don't intend to."

"That's right." Willy Knight nodded vigorously. "That's just exactly right. Here in Texas, we live with that every day when we look west and see what the United States did to us."

426

The reporters scribbled. Jake sent Knight a sour look. The Texan wanted to be part of the story, too. *If you wanted to horn in on this, why'd you invite me out here to the middle of nowhere?* Featherston thought. But he knew the answer, knew it all too well. *Because you still want to be top dog, that's why, you son of a bitch.* Most ways, having ambitious men in the Party was wonderful. They worked hard, for their own good as well as its. But having them here meant Jake could never stop watching his back.

"I'm making my main speech at a park west of town, isn't that right?" he asked Knight, though he also knew that answer. "Almost within spitting range of what they call Houston. Spitting's not half what they deserve, either."

"Sure isn't," Knight said. "If the people in occupied Texas ever got the chance to vote, they'd come back to the Confederate States in a red-hot minute."

"Same with Kentucky," Featherston agreed. "Same with Sequoyah." He had mixed feelings about Sequoyah—it was, after all, full of redskins, and he had little more use for them than he had for niggers. (The USA had even less use for Indians; Sequoyah remained occupied territory, while Houston and Kentucky were full-fledged U.S. states.) But Sequoyah was also full of oil and gas, and cars and trucks and aeroplanes meant the Confederate States needed all the oil and gas they could lay their hands on. If the redskins came along, too, then they did, that was all. At least they'd been loyal during the war, unlike the blacks in the Confederacy.

"Take you to the hotel first, if that suits you," Knight said. "Give you a chance to freshen up, maybe rest a little bit, before you go out and give your speech. You aren't set to start till six, you know."

"Oh, yeah." Jake nodded as they left the platform together. "That way, it's eight o'clock back on the East Coast—a good time for folks on the wireless web to listen in." He laughed. "Who would've reckoned a few years back that we'd have to worry about such things? Times are changing—if we don't change with 'em, we're in trouble."

"That's what's wrong with the Whigs," Knight said. "They're a bunch of damn dinosaurs, is what they are."

Dinosaurs had been much in the news lately. A team of Japanese scientists in Mongolia had come back with not only spectacular skeletons but also some of the first dinosaur eggs ever seen. They'd sent some of their specimens to the Museum of Natural History in Richmond, where they'd drawn record crowds. Jake liked the phrase, too; it captured exactly what he felt about the Whigs.

He slapped Willy Knight on the back. "They sure are," he said. "You took the words right out of my mouth, matter of fact—I'm aiming to call 'em that very thing tonight." And so he was, even if he hadn't been a moment before.

"Good," Knight said, not suspecting Featherston was stealing his figure of speech.

Driving through Abilene was depressing. The town had flourished in the years just before the Great War and, like so much of the Confederacy, languished since. Timber buildings looked sun-blasted; brick ones looked old before their time. As he did all over the CSA, Jake saw men sleeping on park benches and in bushes, and others prowling the streets looking for food or work.

The hotel seemed as gloomy as the rest of the place. Ceiling fans spun lazily in the lobby, stirring the air without cooling it much. The carpet was shabby. The walls needed painting. The clerk behind the registration desk seemed pathetically glad to have anybody come in. "Welcome to Abilene, sir," he said as he gave Jake his key.

"Thanks," Jake replied, in lieu of what he really thought. "Freedom!"

"Uh, freedom," the clerk said, but not as if he were a Party man.

Since Featherston was due to speak at six, he and Willy Knight ate an early supper: enormous slabs of steak, a Texas specialty. Texas wasn't dry; they could drink beer without breaking the law. Knight swallowed a big piece of rare meat and then said, "God damn you, Jake. I thought you were buzzard bait, but you turned out to be right all along. Our time is coming."

"I always said so." Featherston cocked his head to one side. "You reckoned we were going down the drain, and you'd pick up the pieces."

The mixed metaphor didn't faze the former head of the Redemption League. "Damn right I did. This party was drying up and blowing away four years ago." He cut off another chunk of steak. By the way he did it, he would sooner have stuck the knife into Featherston. "Amos Mizell and I, we were ready to get on another horse. The Party did jussst well enough"—he stretched the word into a long hiss—"to keep us on board. But now—"

Jake finished for him: "Now we're back in business."

"We are." Knight nodded. "Hell with me if we're not. I'd take my hat off to you if I was wearing it. All through everything, you said this was going to happen one of these days. You said so, and you were right."

"You bet I was," Featherston said, adding, *You stinking bastard,* to himself. "Come November, we're going to pick up a hell of a lot more seats in the House. We'll pick up some in the Senate, too, from states where we got control of the legislature two years ago. And two years from now . . . Two years from now, by God . . ." Even in the dimly lit steakhouse, a feral glow shone in his eyes.

"Yeah." That same glow lit Willy Knight's face. He and Jake nodded to each other. Both men had been hungry, hungry in the spirit, for a long, long time, and at last they thought they could see satisfaction on the horizon.

Softly, Jake said, "If things go our way two years from now, I'm going to pay back every blue-blooded bastard and every nigger who ever did me wrong. And I'm going to put this poor, sorry country back on its feet again."

"Yeah," Knight said again. As with Featherston, he sounded more as if he looked forward to revenge than to rebuilding. He added, "We've got the United States to pay back, too."

"I haven't forgotten," Jake said. "Don't you worry about that, Willy. I haven't forgotten at all. That's why I came out here—to help everybody remember."

When he got to the park, it was filling up fast. Bare bulbs bathed the platform from which he would speak, though the sun hadn't set yet. As he walked up onto the platform and over to the microphone that would send his words across the CSA, a frightening, almost savage, roar went up from the crowd. He hoped the microphone would pick it up. He wanted people to get all hot and bothered when they heard him or thought about him.

"Hello, friends," he said at six on the dot. "I'm Jake Featherston, and I'm here to tell you the truth. The truth is, the United States are afraid of us. You look across what they call the border, you look into what they call Houston, and you'll know it's the truth. If they let people over there vote which country they wanted to belong to, they know what would happen. You know what would happen, too. Texas would be itself again. And so the Yankees don't let 'em vote."

Cheers in Abilene had that savage edge, too. Here not far from the border, people feared the United States, whether the United States feared them or not.

Jake went on, "The USA won't let people in Kentucky vote on that, either, or people in Sequoyah. They know where the people would go, and they don't aim to let 'em. Why? They're scared, that's why!"

He pointed east, a gesture full of contempt. "And do the Whigs way over there in Richmond, the Whigs who've been running this country ever since the War of Secession, do they do anything about it? Do they push the USA to let the folks in Houston—*Houston!*—and Kentucky and Sequoyah vote about who they want to belong to? Do they? *Do they? Noooo!*" He made the word a howl of rage. "They're nothing but a pack of dinosaurs, is what they are. And you know what you've got to do with dinosaurs, don't you? *Send 'em to the museum!*"

A vast roar went up. Featherston looked back at Willy Knight, standing there behind him. They grinned at each other. Knight was happy about his own cleverness, even though he thought Featherston had had the idea on his own, too. Jake was happy about how well the line had gone over. He knew he'd stolen it, knew and didn't care. The point was, it did what he wanted. And nobody else in the whole wide world knew, or cared, where he'd got it.

Little by little, Party men turned the roar into a chant: "Freedom! Freedom! Freedom!" The crowd followed along. The chant went on till Jake's head rang with it.

He raised his hands. Quiet slowly returned. Into it, he said, "Come November, you get your chance to send some more Whigs to the museum. I know you'll take care of it, friends. Folks who think they're smart used to say the Freedom Party was dead. We'll show 'em who's dead, see if we don't, and who needs burying, too. We're not dead, by God. We're just getting started!" Another roar went up, one that told him he'd found a brand-new slogan.

"Hasta luego," Hipolito Rodriguez told his wife. "I'm going into Baroyeca. I'll vote, and then I'm going to stay to see how the election turns out."

Magdalena wagged a finger at him. "And in between times you'll sit in *La Culebra Verde* and waste money on *cerveza.*"

"If a man can't have a beer or two with his friends, the world is in a sorry state indeed," Rodriguez said with dignity.

"A beer or two, or four, or six." Magdalena wagged that finger again, but indulgently. "Go on. Have a good time. I will say you've never been one to sit in the *cantina* all the time and come home drunk four days a week. *Libertad!*"

"Libertad!" Rodriguez echoed. He put a serape on over his shirt; the weather was about as chilly as it ever got around Baroyeca. He put on a wide-brimmed straw hat, too. It wasn't raining, but looked as if it might.

The polling place was in one room of the mayor's house. More often than not, Rodriguez still thought of the mayor as the *alcalde*; even though Sonora had belonged to the CSA longer than he'd been alive, the old Spanish forms died hard, especially here in the south.

He gave his name, signed on the appropriate line in the record book, and took his ballot into a voting booth. He voted for the Freedom Party candidates for Congress,

431

for his state legislature, and for governor of Sonora. When he'd finished, he folded the ballot, gave it to a waiting clerk, and watched till the man put it into a ballot box.

"*Señor* Rodriguez has voted," the clerk intoned, a formula as full of ritual as any in the Mass.

As Rodriguez left the mayor's office, Jaime Diaz came towards it. They exchanged greetings. From within, someone called out a warning: "No electioneering within a hundred feet of the polling place."

That too was ritual. Rodriguez snorted. "Election-eering!" he said. "All I want to do is say hello."

"I can't chat anyhow," Diaz said. "I've got Esteban back at the general store, and he can't count to eleven without looking at his toes, so I have to get back there as fast as I can."

"We'll talk some other time, then," Rodriguez said. "*Adios.*" He didn't say, *Libertad*. The fellow inside had warned him against electioneering.

When he wandered over to *La Culebra Verde*, he found it crowded. Many of the men sitting and drinking had worked in the silver mines that went belly-up soon after the stock market sank. These days, the miners didn't have much to do with their time but sit around and drink. Rodriguez wondered where some of them came up with the dimes they used to buy beer, but that wasn't his worry. A lot of the miners, he suspected, would spend money on *cerveza* before they spent it on their families. That wasn't the way he would have done it, but they wouldn't care.

Carlos Ruiz waved to him. He waved back, bought himself a bottle of beer, and joined his friend at a corner table. Ruiz was also a farmer. He might not have a lot of dimes—what farmer ever had a lot of money?—but he did still have some income. "Have you voted?" he asked as Rodriguez sat down across from him.

"Oh, yes. *Libertad!*" Rodriguez answered. He kept his voice down, though. Some people came into the *cantina* to brawl as well as to drink. Arguments over politics gave them a good excuse. Rodriguez had seen enough fighting during the Great War that he never wanted to see any more.

"Libertad!" Ruiz said, also quietly. "I think we are going to do very well this year."

"I hope so," Rodriguez said. "A pity, though, that it takes trouble to show people what they should have been doing all along."

His friend shrugged. "If you're fat and happy, do you want to change? Of course not. You keep on doing what you always did. After all, that's what made you fat and happy, *sí*? You need a jolt to want to change."

"Much truth in that," Rodriguez agreed. "But the whole country got a jolt in 1917. Too many people try to pretend it never happened. Ah, well—*así es la vida*." He shrugged, too, and took a pull at the beer.

The question that had occurred to Rodriguez was also on the minds of the out-of-work miners. One of them asked the man behind the bar for another beer, saying, "You know I'll pay you soon, Felipe."

Felipe shook his head. "*Lo siento,* Antonio, but if you pay me soon you'll get your beer soon, too—as soon as you pay me, as a matter of fact. I can't carry people, the way I could when times were better. I hardly make enough money to keep this place open as is."

Rodriguez had his doubts about that. If a *cantina* couldn't make money, what could? Probably nothing. After all, what did hard times do? They drove men to drink.

"My wife is going to get a job any day now," Antonio whined. "I'll have the money. By God, I will."

Women's jobs in Baroyeca were even harder to come by than those for men. There was, of course, one obvious exception. Somebody behind Antonio—Rodriguez couldn't see who—said, "She'll have a nice, comfortable time of it, too, working on her back."

Rodriguez didn't think the man who made the crack intended Antonio to recognize his voice, either. Coming from nowhere in particular, a gibe like that might be tolerated. But Antonio whirled, shouted, *"Chinga tu madre!"* and threw himself at another miner. They rolled on the floor, cursing and clawing and pounding at each other.

Felipe kept a club under the bar. Rodriguez had seen him take it out before, mostly to brandish it for effect.

He'd never seen a sawed-off shotgun come out from under there before. Men dove away from the two battling miners.

"Enough!" Felipe yelled. Antonio and his foe both froze. The bartender gestured with the shotgun. "Take it outside. Don't come back, either—and that goes for both of you. Out—or else I blow holes in you."

Out they went. Rodriguez realized he was holding his beer bottle by the neck, ready to use it as a club or break it against the table for a nastier weapon. He'd also scooted back his chair so he could dive under the table if he had to. Across from him, Ruiz was just as ready to fight or take cover. Very slowly and carefully, Rodriguez set down the bottle. "Some of the things we learned in the war don't want to go away," he remarked sadly.

"You're right," Ruiz said. "It's terrible that we should remember all the best ways to kill the other fellow and keep him from killing us."

As Felipe made the shotgun disappear, Rodriguez nodded. "Of course, most of the men who didn't learn those ways are dead now," he said. "And a lot of the ones who did learn are dead, too. A shell from the *yanquis* didn't care who it killed."

"Oh, yes." His friend nodded. "Oh, yes, indeed." Ruiz's face twisted, as at some memory that wouldn't go away. Rodriguez didn't ask him about it. He had memories of his own. Every once in a while—not so often as right after the war, when it would happen every week or two—he would wake up from a dream shuddering and drenched with sweat. Sometimes he would remember what he'd seen in his sleep. Sometimes the details would be gone, but the horror would remain. He didn't scream very often any more. That made him glad and Magdalena, no doubt, gladder.

Not wanting to think about such things, he got up, bought himself another beer, and got one for Carlos Ruiz as well.

"*Muchas gracias, amigo,*" Ruiz said when he brought it back.

"*De nada,*" Rodriguez answered. He sipped from the beer, then asked the bartender, "*Qué hora es?*"

434

Felipe wore a big brass pocket watch on a chain. It could have been a conductor's watch—a thought Rodriguez wished he wouldn't have had, since the railroad came to Baroyeca no more. The bartender made a small ceremony out of pulling it out and checking it. *"Son las cuatro y media,"* he answered, and made another ceremony of returning the watch to his pocket.

Half past four. Rodriguez nodded. *"Gracias,"* he said. Sure enough, by the lengthening shadows outside, the sun was getting low in the west.

Ruiz said, "Pretty soon we can go over to Freedom Party headquarters. The trains may stay away, but the telegraph still comes. We can find out what's happening in the elections, especially since the polls in the east of *los Estados Confederados* close earlier than they do here. Let me buy you a beer to pay you back for the one you so kindly got me, and then we'll see what we see, eh?"

Rodriguez was glad to let his friend buy him a beer. He was a little elevated—not drunk, but a little elevated—as he and Ruiz walked down the street to the shopfront that said FREEDOM! and ¡LIBERTAD!

A couple of men were already there. *"Hola, amigos,"* Robert Quinn said in his accented Spanish as Rodriguez and Ruiz came in. Three more men followed right behind them. Quinn went on, *"Libertad!* I wish we had a wireless set here. This town needs electricity, *por Dios."*

"If the mines had stayed open . . ." Rodriguez began, and then shrugged, as if to say, *What can anyone do?*

But Quinn didn't have that attitude. "Let the Party come into power, and we'll do something about the mines. We'll do something about all sorts of things. That's why you're here, right? You believe in doing things, not in sitting around and waiting for them to happen."

Is that why I'm here? Rodriguez wondered. He thought he was here mostly because he couldn't stand the United States and wanted revenge on them. But if that required doing other things, then it did, that was all.

A messenger from the telegraph office came in with a sheaf of flimsy yellow papers. *"Gracias,"* Quinn told him, and gave him a dime. He went through the telegrams in a hurry. Then he let out a banshee whoop of a sort Rodriguez hadn't heard since his days in the trenches. Some of the men there had called the battle cry a Rebel yell. "We're winning," Quinn said. "Virginia, North Carolina, South Carolina, Florida—wherever I have returns, we're picking up seats in Congress and in the state legislatures. And our men running for governor are ahead in South Carolina and Florida, and the race in Virginia is still very close. *Libertad!*"

"*Libertad!*" the Freedom Party men shouted. Rodriguez couldn't wait for results to start coming in from states closer to Sonora.

To while away the time, Quinn pulled a whiskey bottle out of a desk drawer. He took a pull himself, then passed it around. Rodriguez had always thought whiskey tasted nasty. He still did, but that didn't keep him from swigging when the bottle got to him. "Ahh!" he said. The stuff might taste bad, but he liked what it did.

More telegrams came in. So did more people. The Freedom Party didn't look as if it would win the governorship of Virginia after all, but it gained a Senator from Mississippi and another from Tennessee. Before long, it also picked up two more Congressmen in Alabama, a Senator from Arkansas, and several Congressmen from eastern Texas. "Will we have a majority?" Rodriguez asked. Even a few weeks before, the question would have seemed unimaginable. Now . . .

Now, to his disappointment, Robert Quinn shook his head. "No, I don't think so," he answered. "But we're still doing better than anybody thought we could." He pulled out a fresh bottle of whiskey and led the Party men in a new shout of, "*Libertad!*"

An hour or so later, returns from Chihuahua started arriving. The Freedom Party men in Baroyeca cheered: their candidate for governor there was well ahead of the Radical Liberal incumbent. And in Sonora itself, two more Congressional districts swung to the Party. As Rodriguez had known he would be, he was very late getting home that night. But he hadn't known—he'd had no idea—how happy he would be making that long walk in the dark.

Lucien Galtier parked his motorcar in front of the house where his daughter Nicole lived with Dr. Leonard O'Doull. Nicole opened the door at his knock and gave him a hug. "Hello, Papa," she said. "It's always good to see you."

"Is it?" Galtier said. "I don't want to make a nuisance of myself." Since Marie died, he'd started visiting his children as often as he could. For one thing, he was lonely. For another, he was sure he was the world's worst cook. Any evening where he didn't have to eat what he turned out was an evening gained.

Nicole made a face at him. "Don't be silly. You know you're welcome here."

As if to underscore that, little Lucien came running up shouting, *"Grandpère!"* When Galtier picked up his namesake, the boy threw his arms around his neck and gave him a big, sloppy kiss.

"You're growing up," Galtier told him. "You're heavier every time I try to lift you." He turned to his daughter. "It must be that you keep feeding him."

She snorted. "You sound like Georges. He must get his foolishness from you. Now come in, for heaven's sake. Sit down. Relax."

"This is a strange word for a farmer to hear." But Galtier wasn't sorry to sit down on the sofa. Leonard O'Doull walked in a moment later, with glasses of applejack and fine Habana cigars.

"I thank you very much," Galtier said, accepting the brandy and the tobacco. He raised his glass in salute. "To your good health!"

"And to yours," his son-in-law answered. They both drank, as did Nicole. The applejack went down soft and sweet as a first kiss. Little Lucien ran off to play. O'Doull asked, "And how are you, *mon beau-père?*"

Lucien shrugged. "As well as I can be, I suppose. It is not easy." That was as much as he would say. It would also do for an understatement till he found a bigger one, which might come along . . . oh, a hundred years from now.

Dr. O'Doull looked sly. "But of course you have all the pretty ladies for miles around looking in your direction now that, however unfortunately, you are a single man once more."

He probably meant it for a joke. In fact, Galtier was almost sure he meant it for a joke. But that didn't mean it held no truth. He'd been amazed how many widows and maiden ladies had come to call on him, to say how sorry they were that Marie was gone . . . and, sometimes quite openly, to size him up. He'd been even more amazed that a couple of farmers, both in the most casual, offhand way imaginable, had brought up their marriageable daughters with him. True, he wasn't an old man—he wouldn't see sixty for a few years yet—but what would he do with an eighteen- or twenty-year-old girl? Oh, there was one obvious answer, but he couldn't even do *that* so often as he had when he was younger. And, if he were to have a wife younger than his youngest daughter, wouldn't making love to her feel like molesting a child? Some men his age, no doubt, would have thought themselves lucky to get offers like those. He didn't.

Making a production out of lighting his cigar meant he didn't have to answer his son-in-law. Once he had it going, once he'd savored the fine, mild smoke, he asked, "And how is it with you here?"

"Not too bad," O'Doull answered. Nicole nodded. Galtier did, too, in approval. The American sounded more like a Quebecois with each passing year. It wasn't just his accent, though the years had also meant that Rivière-du-Loup supplanted Paris in his French. But Americans, from everything Galtier had seen, liked to brag. *Not too bad* was about as much as a man from this part of the world was ever likely to say. Dr. O'Doull went on, "I wish I could do more about influenza and rheumatic fever and a dozen other sicknesses, but I don't know of any other doctors anywhere else in the world who wouldn't say the same thing."

"Your glass is empty, Papa," Nicole said, and then did something to correct that.

"Pour me full of applejack, yes, and how will I go home?" Galtier asked, not that he didn't want the freshened glass. "The one advantage a horse has over an automobile is that the horse knows the way."

"You can sleep here. You know you're welcome," his daughter said.

He smiled. He did know that. He'd even done it once or twice, on nights when he'd been too drunk to find the door, let alone to fit the Chevrolet's key into the ignition. He might even have slept better here than at home, and that wasn't because he'd been drunk. Trying to sleep alone in a bed where he'd had Marie beside him for so long . . . He grimaced and took a quick nip from the brandy. No, that wasn't easy at all.

To keep from brooding about that empty bed back at the farmhouse, he asked his son-in-law, "What do you think of the state of the world?"

That was a question usually good for a long, fruitful discussion. Galtier got one this time, too, but not of the sort he'd expected. The corners of Dr. O'Doull's normally smiling mouth turned down. He said, "Right this minute, *mon beau-père,* I like the state of the world not at all."

"And why not?" Galtier leaned forward, ready to argue with what ever O'Doull said.

"Because I read the newspapers. Because I listen to what they say on the wireless," O'Doull replied. "How could anyone like it when the Freedom Party doubles its vote in the Confederate States? They hold more than a third of the seats in the Confederate Congress now, and heaven only knows what they'll do next."

With a shrug, Lucien said, "This, to me, is not so much of a much. The Confederate States are a long, long way from Rivière-du-Loup."

His son-in-law looked startled. "Yes, that's true," he said after a momentary hesitation. "I still think of myself as an American some ways, I suppose. I've been here more than fifteen years now, so it could be that I shouldn't, but I do."

"It is not so bad that you do," Galtier said. "A man should know where he springs from. If he does not know what he was, how can he know what he is?"

"You sound like a Quebecois, all right." Leonard O'Doull smiled.

"And why should I not?" Lucien replied. "By the good God, I know what *I* am. But tell me, *mon beau-fils,* why is this Freedom Party so bad for the United States?"

"Because it is the Confederate party for all those who don't want to live at peace with the United States," O'Doull replied. "If it comes to power, there will be trouble. Trouble is what its leader, this man Featherston, stands for."

"I see." Galtier rubbed his chin. "You say it is like the *Action Française* in France, then? Or that other party, the one whose name I always forget, in England?"

"The Silver Shirts." O'Doull nodded. "Yes, just like them." He cocked his head to one side, studying Galtier. "And what do you think of the *Action Française?*"

Lucien Galtier clicked his tongue between his teeth. "That is not an easy question for me to answer," he said slowly. As if to lubricate his wits, his son-in-law poured him more apple brandy. "Thank you," he murmured, and drank. The applejack might not have made him any smarter, but it tasted good. He went on, "I would not be sorry to see France strong again. She is the mother country, after all. And even if the Republic of Quebec is a friend of the United States, and so a friend of Germany, which is not a friend of France . . ." He could feel himself getting tangled up in his sentence, and blamed the applejack—certainly easier than blaming himself. He tried again: "Regardless of politics, I care about what happens in France, and I wish her well."

"Moi aussi," Nicole said softly.

Dr. O'Doull nodded. "All right. That's certainly fair enough. But let me ask you something else—do you think the *Action Française* will do well for France if they take power there? If France goes to war with Germany, for instance, do you think she can win?"

"My heart says yes. My head says no." Galtier let out a long, sad sigh. "I fear my head is right."

"I think so, too," his son-in-law agreed.

"But let me ask you something in return," Lucien said. "If the Confederate States were to go to war with the United States, do you think they could win?"

"Wouldn't be easy," O'Doull said. Then he shook his head. "No. They couldn't. Not a chance, not now."

"Well, then, why worry about this Freedom Party?" Lucien asked.

Before O'Doull answered, he poured his own glass of brandy full again. "Because I fear Featherston would start a war if he got the chance, regardless of whether he could win it or not. Because a war is a disaster whether you win or you lose—it's only a worse disaster if you lose. I'm a doctor; I ought to know. And because"—he took a long pull at the applejack—"who knows what might happen five years from now, or ten, or twenty?"

"Who knows, indeed?" Galtier wasn't thinking about countries growing stronger or weaker. He was remembering Marie, remembering her well, and then in pain, and then, so soon, gone forever. He gulped down his own glass of apple brandy, then reached for the bottle to fill it again.

Nicole reached out and set her hand on his own work-roughened one. Maybe she was remembering Marie, too. She said, "Hard times mean trouble, no matter where they land. And when they land everywhere . . ." She sighed, shook her head, and got to her feet. "I'm going to see how supper's doing."

By the odor of roast chicken floating out of the kitchen, supper was doing very well indeed. For a moment, Lucien kept thinking about his wife. Then he realized Nicole meant the hard times that made it easy for him to hire help with the planting and harvest; with so many out of work in Rivière-du-Loup, he could pick and choose his workers. Some of them had never done farm labor before, but they were pathetically grateful for a paying job of any sort, and often worked harder than more experienced men might have done.

To Leonard O'Doull, he said, "It seems to me, *mon beau-fils,* that you and I are lucky in what we do. People will always need something to eat, and, God knows, they will always fall sick. No matter what sort of troubles the world has, that will always be true. And so the two of us will always have work to keep us busy."

"No doubt you are right," Dr. O'Doull said. "I think

you are also lucky you own your farm free and clear and don't owe much on your machinery. There are too many stories these days of men losing their land because they cannot pay the mortgage, and of losing their tractors and such because they cannot keep up the payments."

"I've heard these stories, too." Lucien shivered, though the inside of his son-in-law's house was toasty warm. "To be robbed of one's patrimony . . . that would be a hard thing to bear."

"It *is* a hard thing to bear," O'Doull said. "That fellow in Dakota a couple of weeks ago who shot his wife and children, shot the sheriff and three of his deputies when they came to take him off the farm he'd lost, and then shot himself . . . Before all this started, who could have imagined such a thing?"

Galtier crossed himself. He'd seen that in the papers, too, and heard about it on the wireless, and he still wished he hadn't. "God have mercy on that poor man's soul," he said. "And on his family, and on the sheriff and his men. That farmer worked a great evil there."

He let it go at that. He'd told nothing but the truth. If he also said he understood how the desperate American had felt when he knew he must lose his patrimony, Nicole would understand if she was listening from the kitchen, but would Dr. Leonard O'Doull? Lucien doubted it, and so kept quiet.

Then Dr. O'Doull said, "Of all the sins in this world, which is more unforgivable than the sin of not having enough money? None I can think of." Galtier realized he'd underestimated his son-in-law.

"Well, well." Colonel Irving Morrell stared at the report on his desk. "Isn't that interesting?" He whistled tunelessly, then looked back at his aide-de-camp. "There's no doubt of this?"

"Doesn't seem to be, sir," answered Captain Ike Horwitz, who'd gone through the report before giving it to Morrell.

"It makes an unpleasant amount of sense," Morrell said, "especially from the Japs' point of view. I wonder

442

how long it's been going on." He flipped through the document till he found what he was looking for. "We never would have found out about it at all if that fellow in Vancouver hadn't had a traffic accident while his trunk was full of Japanese gold."

"Tokyo's denying everything, of course," Horwitz said.

"Of course." Morrell laced agreement with sarcasm. "But what makes more sense for Japan than keeping us busy with rebellion up here? The busier we are here, the less attention we'll pay to what goes on across the Pacific. Hell, we did the same thing during the war, when we helped the Irish rise up against England so the limeys would have more trouble getting help across the Atlantic from Canada."

"A lot of coastline in British Columbia," his aide-de-camp observed.

"Isn't there just?" Morrell said. "I wouldn't be surprised if the Japs are operating out of Russian Alaska, too. The Russians have to be afraid we'll take their icebox away from them one day."

"Why would anybody want it?" Horwitz asked.

"There's gold in the Yukon," Morrell answered. "Maybe there's gold in Alaska, too. Who knows? The Russians don't; that's for sure. They've never tried very hard to find out, or to do much else with the place."

"They tried to sell it to us after the War of Secession— I read that somewhere, a long time ago," his aide-de-camp said. "I forget what they wanted for it; seven million dollars is the number that sticks in my mind, but I wouldn't swear that's right. What ever it was, though, we turned them down because we didn't have the money."

"From what the old-timers say, we didn't have a pot to piss in after the War of Secession," Morrell said, and Horwitz nodded. Morrell went on, "But that's neither here nor there. The question is, what do we do—what can we do—about the damned Japanese?"

"At least now we know we've got to do something about them," Horwitz replied.

"Anybody with half an eye to see has known that since the Great War ended. No, since before it ended," Morrell said. "We didn't beat 'em; they fought us to a draw in the Pacific, and then they said, 'All right, that's enough. We'll have another go a few years from now.' And they're stronger than they used to be. They took Indochina away from the French and the Dutch East Indies away from Holland—oh, paid 'em a little something to salve their pride, but they would've gone to war if the frogs and the Dutchmen hadn't said yes, and everybody knows it."

"Who could have stopped them?" Horwitz said. "England before the war, yes—but not any more. She's got to be glad the Japs didn't take Hong Kong and Malaya and Singapore the same way and head for India. The Kaiser doesn't have the kind of Navy or the bases to let him fight the Japs in the Pacific. And *we'd* have to get past the Japanese Philippines to do anything. So . . ."

"Yeah. So," Morrell agreed sourly. "What they do six thousand miles away is one thing, though. What they do right here in our own back yard—that's a whole different kettle of fish. If they don't know as much, we'd better show 'em pretty damn quick." He'd been aggressive leading infantrymen. He'd been aggressive leading barrels. Now, with a vision that suddenly stretched to the Pacific a few hundred miles to the west, he wanted to be aggressive again.

"What have you got in mind, sir?" Horwitz asked.

"We ought to be flying patrols up and down the coastline," Morrell answered. "They couldn't sneak their spies ashore so easily then. And if they have a destroyer or something lying out to sea, we damn well ought to sink it."

"In international waters?"

"Hell, yes, in international waters, if they're using it as a base to subvert our hold on British Columbia. All we'd need is to spot a boat and the destroyer. That'd be all the excuse I needed, anyhow."

Horwitz frowned. "You might start a war that way."

"Better to start it when we want to than when they want to, wouldn't you say?" Morrell returned. "Sooner or later, we *will* be fighting 'em; you can see that coming like a rash. Why wait till they're ready for us?"

"I don't think President Blackford wants a war with Japan," his aide-de-camp said.

"I don't, either." But Morrell only shrugged. "But I also don't think Blackford has a Chinaman's chance of getting reelected this November. Come next March—"

Horwitz shook his head. "No, they've amended the Constitution, remember? The new president takes over on the first of February from now on. With trains and aeroplanes and the wireless, he doesn't need so long to get ready to do the job."

"That's right. I'd forgotten. Thanks. Come February first, then, we'll have a Democrat in the White House—or Powel House, take your pick—again. Maybe he'll have better sense. Here's hoping, anyhow." Morrell rubbed his chin. "It would be a funny kind of war, wouldn't it? Not much room for chaps like us: all ships and aeroplanes and maybe Marines."

"It would be good practice for a war with the Kaiser, if we ever had to fight one of those," Horwitz said.

"Yes, it would, wouldn't it?" Morrell grinned at his aide-de-camp. "There's another report for you, if you feel like writing it—tell the people back in the War Department what you just told me. Back it up with maps and force break-downs and distance charts and all the other little goodies you can think of."

Captain Horwitz's expression was less than overjoyed. "You've really got it in for me, don't you, sir?" he said, about half in jest.

And, about half in jest, Morrell nodded. "Damn right I do. I want to get you promoted again so I don't have to deal with you any more. If you don't want to be a major, don't write the report. I think the last one helped make you a captain."

"I'll write it," his aide-de-camp said. "Anything to escape you." They both grinned.

But Morrell wasn't grinning after Horwitz left his office. "The Japs!" he said softly. "*Son* of a bitch." As he'd told Horwitz, meddling in Canada did make good logical sense from their point of view. A USA distracted by troubles close to home would be less inclined to look or reach out across the Pacific. But now that Tokyo had got caught with its hand in the cookie jar, the United States would likely . . . do what?

Sure enough, that was what a popular wireless show called the ninety-nine dollar question. For the life of him, Morrell didn't know why that show didn't give winners a full hundred bucks, but it didn't. *He* took Japanese interference in British Columbia very seriously indeed. But how serious would it look to War Department functionaries back in Philadelphia? That wasn't so easy to see. He sometimes thought that, if it weren't for the Sandwich Islands the Navy had captured from the British at the start of the Great War, the War Department would have forgotten the Pacific Ocean and the West Coast existed.

Maybe this would make a useful wakeup call. Maybe it would remind those easterners that the United States did have two coastlines, and that they had unfriendly countries to the west as well as to the east. Maybe. He dared hope.

And maybe, just maybe, having an unfriendly power making a public nuisance of itself would remind even the Socialists of why the United States needed an Army and a Navy in the first place. They'd gone out of their way to conciliate the Confederates. (And the Confederates, to be sure, had gone out of their way to conciliate the USA. They were smart enough to remember they were weak, and not to get into trouble they couldn't get out of. They were under the Whigs, anyhow. The Freedom Party worried Morrell more than ever, not least because now it looked as if it might come to power one day.)

I wonder if I ought to write my own report. He laughed and shook his head. What point to that? He wouldn't have been posted to Kamloops if bureaucrats in Philadelphia were likely to pay attention to anything he said. For some people, a report from him might be an argument to do the opposite of what ever he suggested.

Besides, Horwitz might win promotion to major, in which case he *would* escape Morrell's perhaps stifling influence on his career. No report would get Morrell the brigadier general's stars he craved. Promotion during the war had been swift. Promotion after the war . . . Even men in good odor in Philadelphia languished. Promotion for someone who wasn't might never come.

And if you retire a colonel? Morrell shrugged. He'd done his part to win one war for his country. No one could take that away from him. If they wanted him to count jackrabbits and pine trees out here in Kamloops, he would do it till they wouldn't let him do it any more. *One of these days, they may decide they need someone who knows something about barrels again. You never can tell.*

He laughed a bitter laugh. He knew he did a good enough job here in Kamloops, but what he did had nothing to do with the specialized knowledge he'd acquired during the war. Any reasonably competent military bureaucrat could have taken his place and done about as well. That even applied to his proposed solution to Japanese meddling in British Columbia, though he might have wanted to push harder than most uniformed drones would.

He laughed again, this time with something approaching real amusement. Reasonably competent military bureaucrats shuddered at the prospect of ending up in a place like this. They intrigued and pulled wires to stay in Philadelphia, or to go on inspection tours of places like New Orleans. That meant Kamloops and other such garrisons in the middle of nowhere attracted drunks, fools, dullards . . . *and people like me,* Morrell thought.

When he went home after finishing the day's stint, he didn't walk. He couldn't, not when the last blizzard had left a foot and a half of snow on the ground, snow that piled into drifts higher than a man. Instead, he buckled on the pair of long wooden skis leaning against the wall of the entry hall.

Captain Horwitz came out while Morrell was making sure he'd got everything tight. His aide-de-camp shook his head. "You wouldn't get me on those things, sir."

"I know. I've tried," Morrell answered. "I keep telling you—you don't know what you're missing. It's the next best thing to flying with your own wings."

"I know what I'm missing," Horwitz said stubbornly. "A broken ankle, a broken leg, a dislocated knee, a broken arm, a broken neck . . . And if I go flying, I'll do it in an aeroplane, thanks."

"O ye of little faith." Holding both ski poles in one

hand, Morrell opened the door, then quickly closed it behind him.

Cold smote. He skied down the steps—there was enough snow on them to make it easy—and pushed off for home. Darkness had already fallen. He relished the wind in his face, the play of his muscles as he glided along over the smoothly undulating snow. A shimmer of motion in the sky caught his eye. He stopped, staring up in awe. White and golden and red, the northern lights danced overhead.

He didn't know how long he simply stood there staring. At last, he got moving again, though he kept looking up to the heavens. Warmth and home and family had their place, no doubt—he was always delighted to get back to Agnes and Mildred. But there were so many who, like Captain Horwitz, closed their souls to this chill magnificence.

"God, I'm sorry for them," he said, and skied on.

XIV

Another Friday. Another payday. It wouldn't be much of a check; Chester Martin knew as much. He'd been working six hours a day instead of eight for quite a while now, and not working at all on Saturdays. He should have enjoyed the extra time off. He would have enjoyed it a lot more if he'd had the money to do more things. As it was, fifty cents for a couple of cinema tickets once or twice a month made him and Rita worry. The evening out would mean beans for supper instead of liver and tripe—or, the way things were these days, it might mean potatoes and cabbage instead of beans.

I've still got a job, he thought as he inched toward the clerk who would give him his pay envelope. The clerk still had a job, too, and still had the faintly supercilious air he'd worn when times were good. *Petty-bourgeois bastard looking down his nose at the proletariat,* Martin thought sourly. *Do you really believe the bosses can't replace you, too?*

Later on, he remembered that that had gone through his mind just before he got to the clerk and gave him his name and pay number. The clerk checked him off a long, long list, handed him the envelope, and all of a sudden didn't seem so snotty any more. "Here you are, Martin," he said, as if speaking in a sickroom.

What's eating him? Chester wondered. He didn't open the envelope till he got to the front door of the steel mill.

A couple of galvanized iron trash cans stood there, to hold just such refuse. Martin pulled out the check and put it into the breast pocket of his overalls. He started to throw away the envelope when he noticed another piece of paper inside.

This one was pink.

Martin stood there staring at it, altogether unmoving, for at least half a minute. He'd known the same mix of numbness, disbelief, and swelling pain when he got wounded on the Roanoke front—never before, and surely never since.

He pulled out the second sheet of paper, hoping against hope it might be something else. It wasn't. Come Monday, he didn't have a job any more.

Other paydays, he'd seen stunned men holding pink slips here. You didn't say anything. You didn't look at them. Maybe that was cruel. Maybe it had a touch of, *There but for the grace of God go I.* But maybe it held a sort of rough kindness, too. If you didn't look at your fellow workers who all at once weren't working beside you, they could say anything, do anything, they chose, and not have to worry about losing face.

The only trouble with that was, Chester had no idea what to do with the license he had. What could he possibly say? Nothing would make any difference. He was gone, and the steel mill would go on without him.

At last, one thing did occur to him. "Fuck," he said softly. He tore up the pink slip, dropped the pieces into a trash can, and walked out. He might as well have torn himself up and thrown himself away instead. After all, what was he but a disposable proletarian the capitalists who ran the mill had just disposed of?

That thought made him look up the street toward the Socialist Party hall. He almost started over there. If anybody knew what to do, if anybody could help him, he'd find what he needed there. But he shook his head before taking his first step in that direction. The hall could wait. It was only a trolley ride away (but, with no money coming in, was it *only* a trolley ride?), and Rita deserved to know first.

When the trolley rattled past the statue of Remembrance across from the city hall, Martin had to look away. He'd remembered. He'd helped the United States get their honor back. He'd paid in blood and pain doing it, too. But now, it seemed, the whole world had forgotten him—him and how many hundreds of thousands, how many millions, of others just like him?

He almost missed his stop, and had to scramble off at the last minute. The motorman, who'd started rolling, sent him a sour look as he braked again. Most of the time, Martin would have apologized. Now he hardly even noticed. He trudged off toward his apartment building, his feet scuffing through snow.

A man in a ragged overcoat came toward him from an alley. "Spare change?" the fellow said, and coughed. He'd probably been hatchet-faced when he was eating well. Now a man could wound himself on the sharp angles of cheeks and nose and chin.

Martin had always given what he could, even though he hadn't had much. Tonight, he shook his head. "Sorry, buddy," he said. "I just lost my job, too."

"Just?" The hatchet-faced man's scorn said there were degrees in misery, too, degrees Martin hadn't yet imagined. "It's been two years for me. I used to have a house and a motorcar. Hell, I used to have a wife. Enjoy it. You're only a beginner." He tipped his battered hat and walked away.

Shivering from more than the cold, Martin hurried into his building. He half feared another beggar would find him before he got up the steps, but none did. *How long can we keep this place?* he wondered as he turned the key in the lock. *Is the next stop a Blackfordburgh?*

Rita came to the door and gave him a quick, wifely peck on the lips. "How did it . . . ?" she began. Her voice trailed away as she got a real look at his face. Slowly, the blood drained from hers. "Oh, no," she said. "You didn't . . ." She stopped again.

"I sure as hell did," Chester said. "Yes, I sure as hell did, and God only knows what happens now. Have we got anything to drink in this place?"

He knew they did. He took a bottle of bourbon—

KENTUCKY PRIDE, NOW MADE IN THE USA, it said—from a cupboard and poured himself a glass. Very much as an afterthought, he added a couple of ice cubes.

When he started to put the bottle away, Rita said, "Wait a minute." She made a drink for herself, too, though she added water as well as ice to the whiskey.

Martin raised his glass. "Cheers," he said—the very opposite of what he meant. He drank. A good many steelworkers celebrated payday by going out and getting drunk. He'd never fallen into that habit. Tonight, though, he felt like killing the bottle, and whatever other bottles they had in the place. *Why not?* he thought. *Why the hell not? It's not like I've got to get up in the morning. Who knows when I'll have to get up in the morning again?*

"What are we going to do?" Rita said in a thin, frightened voice.

"Maybe one of us'll find a job," Chester answered. He didn't mean that, either. He took another sip and shook his head. It wasn't so much that he didn't mean it as that he didn't believe it. Rita had been looking ever since she lost her job, and hadn't had any luck landing a new one. She hadn't just searched for typist positions, either. Nobody seemed to be hiring anyone, even as a waitress or a salesgirl.

As for him . . . He wanted to laugh, but he hurt too much inside. He wondered if he even ought to bother trying other steel mills. They were all laying people off, not hiring. He couldn't remember the last time he'd seen a new face on the foundry floor.

Rita said, "What do we do if . . . if we can't find a job? Neither one of us, I mean."

"Why do you think I'm drinking?" he said, which seemed as complete a reply as anything else. A couple of swallows of bourbon later, he added, "My pop's still working. We've got a place to stay, if we have to."

He couldn't imagine a worse humiliation than moving back in with his folks as he neared his own fortieth birthday—and bringing his wife with him. His father and mother would take them in. He was sure of that. But having to crawl back to them was the last thing he wanted.

He shook his head again. The *last* thing he wanted was to have nowhere at all to go, and to end up in a Blackfordburgh. Next to that, the prospect of trying to fit himself and Rita into the room that had been cramped for him alone didn't seem so bad.

Rita said, "Maybe you can find something in some other line: construction or something like that."

Even she sounded doubtful. Chester wanted to laugh again. Again, the pain was too much to let him. As gently as he could, he asked, "Hon, why would they want me when they've got real carpenters and whatnot coming out their ears?"

He didn't expect his wife to have an answer for him, but she did: "Why? I'll tell you why. Because you'd work cheaper."

"Oh." He winced. It wasn't because she was wrong. It was because she was right. *And so much for Socialist solidarity among workers,* he thought. If times got bad enough, if people got desperate enough, Socialist solidarity went straight out the window. A job now, no matter what the pay, counted for more than the damage taking that job did to labor's ability to get better wages later.

His glass was empty. He filled it again. Again, he started to put away the bottle. Again, Rita wouldn't let him. She poured herself another drink, too. After she'd taken a swallow, she said, "At least your father's still got work."

"Yeah," Chester said. Rita's father had worked in a cement plant for more than thirty years, except when he'd done his time in the Army during the Great War. That hadn't stopped him from losing his job a few months before. He hadn't been fired, or not exactly; the company had gone belly-up. He'd been able to land only odd jobs since, and worried about losing his house.

"How much exactly have we got in the bank?" Rita asked.

Their bank was still sound, where so many had gone under. If this mess had any sort of silver lining, that was it. "We can get by for a month or two, anyhow," Martin answered. "We'd be better off if we'd never bought any stocks at all, dammit."

"We were suckers," his wife said. "Lots of people were suckers."

"Don't I know it," he said bitterly. "Buy when the market was near the top, throw money away on margin calls when it went sour. And you're right, honey—we aren't the only ones."

"Election's coming up this year," she said. "I don't see how Hosea Blackford has a prayer of getting a second term."

"I almost went to the Socialist Party hall before I came home," Martin said. And then, proving the depths of his own despair, he asked, "Why the devil should anyone who's out of work vote Socialist, though?"

"It wasn't the Democrats who passed the relief bills," Rita said. "They voted against most of them."

"I know. But they say the crash never would have happened in the first place if they'd been running things." Martin sighed. "Maybe they're even right. Who knows?" Rita looked shocked. He held up a defensive hand. "I used to be a Democrat till after the war. My old man still is—you know that. I changed my mind when the bosses sicced the cops on us when we struck for higher wages. We needed worker solidarity then, and we needed the Socialists, too."

"We still do." Rita's family had always voted Socialist.

Chester wasn't so sure. Chester wasn't so sure of anything just then, except that the bourbon was hitting him hard. "They've had twelve years," he said. "Blackford's had his whole term to get us back on our feet, and he hasn't done it. Maybe the other side deserves a shot. How could it be worse?"

"You'd really vote for Calvin Coolidge?" his wife asked. The governor of Massachusetts again looked to be his party's likely candidate for president.

"Right now, I don't know what the hell I'd do," Martin answered. "All I know is, I wish I still had my job. I wish I did, but I don't. And God only knows what we're going to do on account of that." He waited to see if Rita would argue some more. He hoped she would—that might mean she'd seen a ray of hope he hadn't. But she said not a word.

* * *

Rounding the Horn in the USS *Remembrance* felt like old times to Sam Carsten. "I came the other way, from the Pacific to the Atlantic, in the *Dakota* during the war," he said as waves lifted and dropped the aeroplane carrier again and again.

"It's easier going that way," Lieutenant Commander Michael Watkins said. "The waves are coming with you instead of hitting you head-on."

"Yes, sir," Sam agreed. "I still don't know how they ever got around this place against the wind in sailing ships."

"It wasn't easy—I know that," Watkins said, snatching up his mug of coffee from the galley table as the *Remembrance* plunged into another trough. Sam did the same. The table was mounted on gimbals, but the pitching in the strait was more than it was designed to handle.

After another couple of rises and falls, Sam said, "I pity the poor fellows whose stomachs can't take this."

"That's no joke," Watkins said, and took another sip of coffee.

"I didn't think it was, sir," Carsten said. "Have you seen the sick-bay lists? It's a good thing we don't have to do any fighting in these latitudes, that's all I've got to say." He checked himself. "No, I take that back. Anybody else who tried to fight down here would have just as many seasick cases as we do."

"True enough." The other officer sent him a sly look. "But I'll bet you don't mind the weather a bit."

"Who, me?" Sam tried to look innocent. Lieutenant Commander Watkins snickered, so he couldn't have pulled it off. He went on, "Rounding the Horn in April—autumn down here, heading toward winter? No, sir, I don't mind it one little bit. It's the kind of weather I was made for. I can go on deck without smearing goop all over my face and my hands. I'm not burned. I'm not blistered. And we're heading for the Sandwich Islands. I'm going to toast up there. I've been there before, and I know I'll toast. So I'll enjoy this while it lasts."

He hadn't intended to get so worked up, but he didn't enjoy, never had enjoyed, owning a hide that scorched if the sun looked at it sideways. Watkins held up a hand.

"All right. I believe you. Do you think we're going to have to fight when we do get up there?"

"Me, sir?" Sam shrugged. "I'm no crystal-ball reader. No, we're talking about the Japs, so I guess I should say I'm no tea-leaf reader." Watkins made a face at him. He grinned, but then quickly became serious once more. "One thing I'll tell you, though, is that a scrap with them won't be any fun at all. I was aboard the *Dakota* when they suckered her out of Honolulu harbor and torpedoed her, and for the Battle of the Three Navies in the Pacific. They're tougher than most Americans think, and that's the truth."

"We can whip 'em." Lieutenant Commander Watkins sounded confident. "We can whip anybody, except maybe the High Seas Fleet—and the Kaiser's got more things on his plate than us right now. What do you know about these *Action Française* people?"

"Sir, when I was on the *O'Brien*, we put in at Brest. I went into town to have a few drinks and look around, and I saw an *Action Française* riot. What they remind me of most is the Freedom Party in the CSA. They remember how things were back before the war, and they want to turn back the clock so they're that way again."

"Good luck," Watkins said. "The Kaiser won't let them get away with that, and we won't let the damned Confederates get away with it, either. We'd better not, anyhow."

"Yes, sir," Carsten said. "But hard times mean parties like that get more votes, seems like. I don't know what anybody can do about it. I don't know if anybody can do anything."

He was sorry when the *Remembrance* rounded Cape Horn and made her way up the west coast of South America to Valparaiso, where she refueled. He'd been there briefly in the *Dakota* during the war. Chile was a staunch U.S. ally, not least because Argentina, her rival, had close ties to England and the other great alliance system. Argentina outweighed Chile, but the peace held because the Argentines didn't outweigh the United States and didn't want to give them any excuse to meddle in South American affairs.

Valparaiso had grown in the years since Sam was last there. He saw no signs of damage from the great earthquake of 1906. The weather was mild, which meant he got sunburned. Then the *Remembrance* started north and west again, toward the Sandwich Islands. He sighed, went to the pharmacist's mate, and drew himself yet another tube of zinc-oxide ointment.

"You don't happen to carry this stuff in five-gallon tubs, do you?" he asked, not altogether in jest.

"Sorry, no." Like most in his post, the pharmacist's mate had no sense of humor.

A few days out of Valparaiso, the *Remembrance* changed course, swinging more nearly toward the north. "Change of plan," Commander Martin van der Waal told Carsten. "Keep it under your hat for a bit, though, because the men won't like it. You can forget about Honolulu. No bright lights. No booze. No fast women, not any time soon. We're bound for patrol duty off the coast of British Columbia."

Sam had fond memories of some of the fast women in Honolulu. Even so, he said, "That's the best news I've had in months, sir. You ever eat one of those whole roasted pigs they cook in a pit in the Sandwich Islands? That's what I look like when I'm stationed there—cooked meat, nothing else but. The coast of British Columbia . . . That's not so bad." He'd sunburned in Seattle, too, but only a little.

Van der Waal looked him over, then nodded to himself. "No, you wouldn't be one to complain about going way north, would you? You've got your reasons."

"You bet I do, sir." Sam nodded. "But what's the scuttlebutt about the change in plans? What's going on off British Columbia?"

"We'll be flying combat air patrol, keeping an eye out for the Japs and giving 'em hell if we catch any of 'em in the neighborhood," Commander van der Waal replied. "I don't know this for a fact, but I hear they've been trying to stir up the Canucks, get 'em to rebel again."

"Bastards," Carsten said without much rancor. Having gone to Ireland during the Great War, he knew that was how you played the game. But, frowning, he asked, "Why us, sir? They've got to have other aeroplane carriers closer to Canada than we were when we set out. Why not use one of them? We're going the long way round, seems like."

"Yes, there are other carriers closer," van der Waal agreed. "They're purpose-built ships, not a converted battle cruiser like the *Remembrance*. They carry more aeroplanes than we do. And *they're* all going to the Sandwich Islands. So is a lot of the rest of the fleet—whatever we don't leave behind in the Atlantic to keep an eye on the Confederates and the limeys."

And the Germans, Sam thought. He lit a cigarette. "If they want the first team in Honolulu," he said slowly, "then they think there really might be trouble with the Japs."

"That's the way it looks to me, too," van der Waal said. "And that means we're going to have to pay special attention to torpedo-damage drills on our way north. Nobody knows what the Japs have operating off the Canadian coast. It may be nothing. It may be a destroyer or two. Or it may be more, including submersibles. And destroyers can launch torpedoes, too—that's their best hope against bigger ships, in fact."

"Yes, sir." Sam hoped he didn't sound too resigned. It wasn't that torpedo-damage control wasn't important. He knew it was. He'd seen how important it was aboard the *Dakota*. Important or not, though, it wasn't what he wanted to be doing. He'd come to the carrier hoping to work with aeroplanes or, that failing, to stay in gunnery, his specialty as a petty officer before he got promoted. Of course, what he wanted to do and what the Navy wanted him to do were two different beasts.

Van der Waal knew he was reluctant. He said, "This duty is vital to the ship's security, Ensign—vital, I tell you."

"Yes, sir," Carsten said again. "I know that, sir." He stifled a sigh. "I'll do what ever you need, sir."

"I'm sure you will. I appreciate it," van der Waal said. "You make a solid officer, Carsten, and I'm pleased to have you under me. If you'd gone to Annapolis instead of taking the mustang's route, I wouldn't be surprised if you'd made captain by now."

"Thank you very much, sir," Sam said. "I do appreciate that, believe you me I do." A lot of what he was doing these days amounted to showing people what he might have done if he'd had better chances when he was younger. He shrugged. Those were the breaks. He hadn't even thought about becoming an officer till years after the war. *But I passed my exams very first try,* he thought proudly. Some veteran CPOs had been trying for years, with no luck at all.

He went out on deck. This wasn't Cape Horn, not any more. The air was warm. The sea was blue and calm. The sun shone bright. Sam sighed. You couldn't have everything. He reached for the zinc-oxide ointment.

Berlin, Ontario, didn't boast a whole lot of fancy saloons. The best one, as far as Jonathan Moss was concerned, was the Pig and Whistle, not far from the courthouse. He found himself having a couple of drinks with Major Sam Lopat, the military prosecutor. They weren't sparring with each other in court today. They'd both ducked in to get warm; though the calendar declared it was April, a new blizzard had just left Berlin eight more inches of snow.

Hoisting a glass, Moss said, "Mud in your eye."

"Same to you," the U.S. officer said, and drank. "Of course, all the mud around here's frozen into a cheap grade of cement."

"Isn't that the sad and sorry truth?" Moss drank, too. "Nobody in his right mind would come here for the weather, that's for sure."

"Nope. Nobody in his right mind would come here at all." But then Lopat paused and shook his head. "I take that back, damned if I don't. You're here for a reason—you can't very well practice occupation law in the USA. Two reasons, matter of fact, because you married that Canadian gal, too."

"Yeah." Moss didn't mention that he'd gone into occupation law not least because even then he hadn't been able to get Laura Secord out of his mind.

Lopat's train of thought went down a different track, which was probably just as well. He said, "And everything's going to hell all over the world, but you're a civilian with a steady job. That's nothing to sneeze at, either, not these days it's not."

"Ain't it the truth?" Moss said, without grammar but with great sincerity. "I don't know when it's going to turn around. I don't know if it's ever going to turn around."

"Tell you one thing." The military prosecutor spoke with a glee unfueled as yet by whiskey. "Come November, old man Blackford can head back to Dakota, and nobody'll miss him a bit. And with a Democrat in Powel House, things here in Canada will tighten up—and about time, too. You see if they don't, Jonathan my boy."

"If they tighten up any more, you won't bother trying Canucks at all," Moss said. "You'll just give 'em a blindfold and a cigarette, the way it worked during the war."

"What a liar!" Lopat said. "Some of the fast ones you've pulled off in military court, and you're boo-hooing for the Canucks? Give me a break, for crying out loud!"

"Your trouble, Major, is that you think people spell *prosecute* and *convict* the same way," Moss said. "That's not how it works. Even in military court, a defendant's entitled to a fair shake."

"Most of the ones who come up before the court deserve to be shaken, all right," Lopat said. "One of these days, you're going to be sorry for getting so many of 'em off. You may be turning another Arthur McGregor loose on the world."

"McGregor never went to court," Moss snapped. "And there's not a lawyer in the world who doesn't have some clients he wishes he didn't. But what can you do, for Christ's sake? If you don't give everybody as good a defense as you can, everybody's rights go down the drain."

"Some people deserve to be locked up, and to have the jailer lose the key," Lopat insisted. "Or worse. How many people did McGregor end up killing? And a lot of 'em were just Canucks in the wrong place at the wrong time."

"McGregor deserved whatever happened to him—after

he had his day in court," Moss said. "Till you have a trial, you just don't know. You people have tried to railroad a few Canadians in your time, and don't try to tell me any different."

Lopat snorted. "You'd say that, wouldn't you? I've got news for you, though. Just because you say it doesn't make it so." He picked up his glass of whiskey, poured it down, and signaled for a refill.

"If you don't admit that . . ." Moss threw his hands in the air. Of course Sam Lopat wouldn't admit it. He was a lawyer, too. Expecting a lawyer to admit anything damaging to the point of view he was presenting was like wishing the Easter Bunny would hop across your lawn. You could do it, but it wouldn't do you any good, and you'd spend a long time waiting.

Lopat underscored the point, grinning and saying, "I don't admit one damn thing, Counselor. Not one damned thing."

Moss finished his own drink, then got to his feet. "Fine. Don't admit anything. I'm still going to whale the stuffing out of you when we go back to court tomorrow morning. For now, I'm heading home. See you in the morning." He plucked his hat off the rack, stuck it on his head, and strode out of the Pig and Whistle in more than a little annoyance. How could you have a civilized discussion with a man who wouldn't admit one damned thing and was proud of it?

That Lopat might think the same of him never crossed his mind.

His Bucephalus started reluctantly. He let out a sigh of relief when it did start. The battery was going, no doubt about it. Pretty soon he'd have to get a new one. Pretty soon he'd have to get a new, or at least a newer, auto, too. Too many things on the Bucephalus were breaking down. And the company had gone out of business in 1929, so parts were hard to come by and ever more expensive.

He parked it outside his block of flats and hoped it would fire up again in the morning. If it didn't . . . *If it doesn't, I'll walk in,* he thought, and reminded himself to set the alarm clock half an hour earlier than usual to give him time to walk if he had to.

461

His key turned in the lock. "I'm home!" he called as he stepped in the door. He wondered how glad Laura would be to see him. She'd been happy enough to marry him, but neither of them had been particularly happy since. Moss listened. Silence. "I'm home, honey," he said again, wondering what sort of trouble he was in.

But it turned out not to be *that* kind of silence. A moment later, noise came from the bathroom: the unmistakable sound of someone being sick. A moment after that, the water closet flushed.

Laura came out a minute or so afterwards. She looked distinctly green. "What happened, hon?" Moss asked. "Are you all right?"

"Better now," she said, and made a face, probably at the nasty taste in her mouth. "In about eight months, we'll know if it's a boy or a girl."

For a moment, that seemed a complete *non sequitur*. Then Moss' jaw dropped. "You mean we're—?"

She nodded. "Doesn't seem to be much room for doubt any more. I've missed a month, and I've got morning sickness, even if it isn't morning right now. We're going to have a baby, sure enough."

"That's . . . wonderful," Moss said. A good attorney was never supposed to be caught speechless. He went on, "But . . . how did it happen?"

His wife's mouth quirked in a wry grin. "Very much in the usual way, I'm sure. It hasn't happened any other way since the days of our Lord."

He made a face at her. "I didn't mean *that*. What I meant was, it's a surprise." He couldn't think of the last time he hadn't worn a safe when they made love.

"Those things aren't perfect," Laura said.

"Evidently not." Moss shrugged and laughed. "If it's a boy, we can call him Broken Rubber Moss. That has a ring to it, don't you think? Or how about Prophylactina for a girl?"

"What I think—" Laura Moss didn't, couldn't, go on. What ever she'd been about to say, a giggle swallowed it. She tried again: "What I think, Jonathan, is that you're dangerously insane."

He bowed. "Your servant, ma'am. You've known that for a long time, I'm sure."

"I certainly have." She nodded. "There I was, with this mad Yank who kept coming to the farm. I didn't want any mad Yanks coming to the farm."

"I should hope not," Moss said gravely. "You get into all sorts of trouble if you let those people anywhere near you. You might even end up married to one of them if you're not careful, and after that anything can happen. Obviously."

"Obviously," Laura echoed. She set one hand on her belly, though the pregnancy didn't show and wouldn't for months. "This was as much a surprise to me as it was to you, you know. I didn't much want a child. Now . . . Now we'll just have to make the best of it, won't we?"

"I don't know what else we can do." Moss kissed her on the cheek.

When he tried to kiss her on the mouth, too, she pulled away, saying, "You don't want to do that. I haven't properly cleaned my teeth yet."

"Oh." Jonathan nodded. "Well, why don't you, then?" While Laura went back to the bathroom, he hurried to the kitchen. The occasion really called for champagne, but they didn't have any. Whiskey over ice would do the job well enough. He had the drinks ready by the time Laura came out again.

She took one. They solemnly clinked glasses and drank. Then Moss did kiss her. Her mouth tasted of liquor and toothpaste. She said, "I hope this won't make me sick again." After seeming to listen to something internal, she shook her head in relief. "No, I think it will be all right." As if to prove it, she took another sip. "That's good."

"It is, isn't it?" Jonathan drank some more, too. He raised his glass. "Here's to us, and to . . . whom it may concern."

"That's pretty good. I like it a lot better than . . . what you said before." Laura wouldn't dignify it by repeating it.

"All right." Moss made his drink disappear in a hurry. Along with what he'd had at the Pig and Whistle, it left him owlishly serious. He took his wife's hands in his and said, "I do love you, you know. I always have."

"You always called it love, anyhow," she said. "I think for a long time it was just what any man feels when he's been away from women for too long."

Since she was bound to be right, he didn't dignify that with a direct reply. Instead, he said, "Well, you can't very well accuse me of that now." As if to prove as much, he kissed her again. His hands resting on the swell of her hips, he continued, "And, since you can't accuse me of that . . ." He kissed her once more, his lips hard against hers. One of his hands slid to her behind, to press her to him. Her own arms tightened around his back. As the kiss went on, she made a little wordless sound, almost a growl, in the back of her throat.

He lifted her off her feet. She let out a startled squawk: "Put me down! You'll hurt your back!" She had a reasonable chance of being right; she wasn't a small woman, and he was pushing forty. He ignored her all the same, carrying her off to the bedroom. "What *are* you doing?" she demanded.

"What do you think?" He set her on the bed and got down beside her. His hand slid under her skirt and up her thigh to the joining of her legs. He rubbed there. Her legs slid apart to make it easier for him. He hiked her skirt up and pulled her underpants down, then went back to what he'd been doing.

She laughed. "I think you're going to take advantage of me."

"Damn right I am." Jonathan unbuttoned his own fly. He was also going to take advantage of her being pregnant: if he didn't have to worry about putting on a rubber, he didn't intend to. He certainly liked it better without.

They both still wore most of their clothes when he went into her. She wasn't quite so wet as he would have wanted, but having to force his way in added to his excitement. She wrapped her legs around him and bucked hard. "Come on!" she said as he squeezed and fondled her breasts through the thin cotton fabric of her blouse. As she kindled, she said a good deal more than that. She was the very model of a lady ... except in the bedroom, when she was well and truly roused. Then anything could happen, and anything could come out of her mouth.

It hadn't lately. The two of them had started taking each other for granted since they'd got married. Today, though ... Today they thrashed on the bed and clawed at each other as they hadn't done since he would drive up to Arthur and they'd picnic and then fornicate at her farmhouse outside the little town.

His own building pleasure driving him on, Moss rammed at her, not caring in the heat of the moment if he hurt her a little, too. By the way Laura yowled, she didn't care, either. Suddenly, she arched her back, threw back her head, and let out a long, shuddering moan. At the same time, she squeezed him inside her, so tight that he couldn't help but erupt.

"You're rumpling me," Laura said a moment later, pushing at him.

He shook his head and replied with lawyerly precision: "No, sweetheart, I just rumpled you." She made a face when he gave her a kiss. He laughed, his weight still on her. "If I remember right, that has something to do with why we got married."

"You think so, do you?" She pushed at him again, harder this time. He flopped out of her, which reminded him that, despite the fierce lovemaking they'd just enjoyed, he didn't burn so hot as he had back in his twenties. Then he'd have been ready for a second round as soon as the first was over. Now ... Now he'd wait for tomorrow, or maybe the day after. Laura gave him another shove, and twisted under him, too. "Let me up. Let me set myself to rights."

"Oh, I suppose so," he said. But he couldn't keep wonder from his voice as he went on, "A baby. How about that?"

"Yes. How about that?" His wife's voice softened, too. "It isn't what I expected, but I'm glad it's happened."

"So am I." He wondered if he meant it. He decided he did. "About time we put down some roots here."

"*I've* already got roots here," Laura said pointedly.

She nodded, too, though. "It's about time we were a family."

"A baby," Moss said again. "I wonder what *he'll* see by the time he grows up." The baby would be his age in the early 1970s. What would the world be like then?

A creek ran through the farm on which Mary McGregor and her mother lived. Scrubby oaks and willows grew alongside it. They got some firewood there, which was all to the good. Ducks sometimes nested along it, too, which gave Mary practice with a shotgun and gave her mother and her a tasty dinner every so often. And she would pull trout out of it once in a while, though she seldom had the time to sit and fish.

The creek and the trees by it also came in handy in other ways. Mary lit a fuse and ducked down behind an oak to wait for the explosion. It came just when she thought it would—a harsh, flat *crack!* Mallards leaped into the air with a thunder of wings. A couple of crows in a willow flapped away, cawing in alarm. Moments later, quiet returned.

Mary stepped out from behind the tree trunk to see what the dynamite had done. She nodded to herself. The stump she'd blown up had landed in the creek, just as she'd thought it would. The hole in the ground it left was about the size she'd expected, too.

She hadn't done anything particularly useful—a stump here wasn't the nuisance it would have been out in the middle of a field. But she'd learned a little more about explosives and fuses, which was knowledge that wouldn't go to waste, either on the farm or. . . .

Or anywhere else, she thought. She was, after all, Arthur McGregor's daughter. She wondered what had gone through her father's mind while he waged his long one-man war against the Americans who occupied Canada. He'd never talked about it much—but then, he'd never been one to talk about anything much. What *had* he thought? Her guess was that he'd tried *not* to think about it except while he was actually busy at it. That would have made it harder for him to give himself away when the

466

Yanks came snooping around, which they had again and again.

Not thinking about it would also have made it easier for him to go on thinking of them as *the enemy*, as abstractions, not as human beings. Killing the enemy was what you did when you went to war. Blowing up men—people—who were just like you, who fell in love and drank beer and got sore backs and dug splinters out of their hands and played checkers . . . That was a different business. It had to be a different business. Mary couldn't see how anybody would want, or would even be able, to do that.

Had Major Hannebrink, the American officer who'd ordered her brother Alexander shot during the war, ever imagined him as a human being? Or had Alexander simply been *the enemy* to him? For a moment, Mary came close to understanding how the American could have done what he did, came close to understanding without hating.

For a moment, and for a moment only. She shoved that understanding away with all the force of the hate she'd nursed ever since the USA invaded her country in 1914. *She* saw Americans as *the enemy*, not as human beings at all. She saw them so, and intended to go right on seeing them so.

When she got back to the farmhouse, her mother sat at the kitchen table drinking a cup of tea. "I heard the boom," Maude McGregor said.

Mary nodded. "I took out a stump," she said. "I'm getting the hang of it, I think."

"Are you?" Her mother's voice held no expression what ever. "And what will you do with it once you've got it?"

"It'll come in handy around the farm, Ma," Mary answered. "You know it will."

"Yes—as long as you only use it around the farm," her mother said. "That's what worries me. I know you too well."

I don't know what you're talking about would have been a lie, an obvious lie. "I don't intend to use it anywhere else," Mary said. That was a lie, too, but maybe not so obvious. Maybe.

Maude McGregor looked at her for a long time. "I hope not," she said at last, and then, "Would you like a cup of tea?"

"Yes, please," Mary said. Her mother fixed her one. She added milk and sugar herself, and sat down to drink it across the table from her mother. Neither of them said another word till the tea was done—or, for that matter, for several hours afterwards. When they did start speaking to each other again, it was quietly, cautiously, as if they'd had a knockdown, drag-out fight that might pick up again if they weren't careful.

That's silly, Mary thought. *We didn't. Not even close. All we did was talk about that stump.* To her mother, that stump seemed plenty. And Mary herself wasn't inclined to change her mind. Maybe that was what worried her mother.

They were still wary around each other a few days later, when they had to go into Rosenfeld to shop. Mary remembered checkpoints outside of town, where the Americans would carefully examine wagons and goods for explosives before letting them go on. Not now. The Yanks seemed to think her countrymen weren't dangerous any more. One day, she hoped to show them they were wrong. That too, though, would have to wait for another day.

Many more motorcars were on the road now than had been there when Mary first started going into Rosenfeld. They whizzed past the wagon, one after another. Some of the drivers, angry because they had to slow down to keep from hitting it, honked as they went by.

"I wish I were a man," Mary said. "I'd tell them what I think of them."

Her mother nodded. "Yes, I'm sure you would," she said. It did not sound like praise. Mary muttered to herself, but didn't rise to it.

When they got into Rosenfeld, her mother tied the horse to a lamppost. "Hardly any hitching rails left," Mary said.

"I know." Maude McGregor nodded again. "Automobiles don't need them. You go to the post office and get some stamps. I'll be in Henry Gibbon's store."

"All right." Mary hesitated, then plunged: "Do you want to go to the cinema afterwards? We haven't been in an awfully long time."

"Maybe," her mother answered. "We'll see how much I have to spend at the general store, that's all."

Mary wished she could argue more, but knew she couldn't, not when the argument involved money. Even the half a dollar two tickets would cost was a lot, considering how little the farm brought in.

Wilfred Rokeby stood behind the counter at the post office, as he had for as long as Mary could remember. She noticed with surprise that he'd gone gray. When had that happened? It must have sneaked up when she wasn't looking. He still parted his hair in the middle and slicked it down with some old-fashioned, sweet-smelling oil whose spicy odor she indelibly associated with the post office.

Only one other customer was ahead of her: a young man close to her own age, who had a huge swarm of parcels. The postmaster had to weigh each one individually and calculate the proper postage for it, then stick on stamps and write down the sum so he could get a grand total when he finally finished.

Seeing Mary, the young man waved her forward. "If you want to take care of what you need, go ahead," he told her. "I'll be here for a while any which way."

She shook her head. "It's all right. You were here first. I can wait."

"Are you sure?" he asked.

"Positive," she said. "Where are you sending all those boxes, anyway?"

"Winnipeg. My brother just moved up there, and he figured out this was the cheapest way to get his stuff up there with him. Of course, that means *I* have to stand here and go through this, but why should Bob care?" He grinned.

To her surprise, Mary found herself grinning, too. "Brothers and sisters are like that," she said, speaking from experience. "You might as well be a pack mule, as far as they're concerned."

"That's right. That's *just* right." Bob's brother—Mary still had no better name for him—nodded enthusiastically.

"They always say they'll pay you back, and then they never do, or not enough." He paused to stoop and hand Wilfred Rokeby another package.

"Thank you, Mort," the postmaster said.

As if hearing his name reminded him Mary didn't know it, he said, "That's me—Mort Pomeroy, at your service." He touched the brim of his hat.

"Oh!" Mary said. She hadn't seen him before, or at least hadn't noticed him, but now she knew who his family was. "Your father runs the diner down the street from Gibbon's general store." With money so tight, she couldn't recall the last time she'd eaten there.

"That's me," he said again, and handed another package, a big, heavy one, to Rokeby. Then he turned back to her. "That's me, all right, but who are you?" He looked at her as if he were an explorer who'd just sighted a new and unimagined continent.

"I'm Mary McGregor." She waited.

"Oh," Mort Pomeroy said, in a tone very different from hers. He couldn't go on with something bright and chipper, as she had, something on the order of, *Your father blew up Yanks. Then he blew himself up, too.* He couldn't say anything like that, but his face told her he knew who her father was, sure enough. Who in and around Rosenfeld didn't know who Arthur McGregor was?

Too bad, she thought. *Now he won't want to have anything to do with me, and he seems nice.*

But, after giving Wilfred Rokeby yet another parcel—the next to last one—he managed to put the smile back on his face and say, "Well, that was a long time ago now, and it certainly didn't have anything to do with you."

He wasn't quite right. The only thing Mary regretted was that her father hadn't had more luck. But Pomeroy wouldn't know that, of course. And a lot of people in Rosenfeld still stared and pointed whenever she went by, and probably would for years to come. Someone trying to treat her kindly made a very pleasant novelty, especially when the someone in question was a good-looking young man. "Thank you," she whispered.

"For what?" He sounded honestly puzzled as he gave

the postmaster the last package. That made her like him more, not less.

Rokeby went to work with pencil and paper. "Comes to nine dollars and sixteen cents, all told," he said.

"For *postage*? Can you imagine that?" Mort Pomeroy said, genially astonished, as he paid Rokeby. "I'll take it out of Bob's hide—if he ever finds a job, I will."

"Times are hard," Mary agreed. "Let me have seventy-five cents' worth of stamps, Mr. Rokeby, if you would."

"I can do that," he said, and gave her twenty-five stamps—postage had recently gone up from two cents to three. He put the three quarters she handed him into his cash box. She sighed. The extra twenty-five cents she had to spend on stamps would have paid her way into the theater. Now the money was gone—and gone into the Americans' pockets. *One more reason to hate them,* she thought.

"Are you in town by yourself?" Pomeroy sounded hopeful.

"I have to meet my mother at the general store," Mary said with much more regret than she'd expected to feel.

His face fell. "Oh. Too bad." He hesitated, then asked, "If I was to come calling on you one day before too long, would that be all right? Maybe you'd like to see a moving-picture show with me?"

"Maybe I would." Mary realized she ought to say more than that. "Yes, I'm sure I would."

"Swell!" Now the grin came back enormously. "I've got an auto. Can I pick you up Saturday night? We'll go to a film, see what else there is to do after that—a dance at the church, or something."

"All . . . all right." Mary sounded dazed, even to herself. No one had ever shown this kind of interest in her. Her past left her damaged goods. That had always suited her fine—up till this minute. She was ever so glad Mort Pomeroy didn't seem to care who her father was or what he'd done. "Saturday night," she whispered, and hurried out of the post office. Pomeroy and Wilfred Rokeby both stared after her.

* * *

Cincinnatus Driver used a hand truck to haul crates of oatmeal boxes from his Ford to the market that had ordered them. "This here's the last load, Mr. Marlowe," he said, panting a little.

Oscar Marlowe nodded. "Yes, I've been keeping track of everything you've brought in," he answered. Cincinnatus believed him: the storekeeper was a thin, fussily precise man with a little hairline mustache so very narrow it might have been drawn on with a mascara pencil. He said, "I do appreciate how hard you've worked bringing it all in."

"It's my job, Mr. Marlowe," said Cincinnatus, who knew he would feel it in his back and shoulders tonight. Work that had seemed effortlessly easy in his twenties didn't now that he'd passed forty. He added, "Way things are these days, I got to do everything I can."

"Oh, yes." Marlowe nodded. He ran a pink tongue over that scrawny little excuse for a mustache. "I understand you completely—and agree with you completely, I might add. Even now, though, too many people don't seem to have figured that out. I'm always glad to see someone who has. Let me have your paperwork. The sooner I sign off, the sooner you can be on your way. I don't want to waste your time."

"Got it right here." Scipio handed him the clipboard.

"I expected you would." Marlowe scribbled his name on the forms, making sure he signed in all four necessary spaces. He and Cincinnatus leaned toward each other in mutual sympathy as he wrote. Their both being hardworking men counted for more than one's being white, the other black. The storekeeper said, "Here you are," and returned the clipboard to Cincinnatus.

"Thank you kindly, suh." Cincinnatus turned to leave.

He'd taken only a step or two before Marlowe said, "Here, wait a second." He went behind the counter where he kept his meat on ice, wrapped a package in butcher paper, and thrust it at Cincinnatus. "Take this home to your missus, why don't you? Marrow bones and a little meat—make you a good soup or a stew."

Cincinnatus wanted to say he couldn't possibly, but common sense won over pride. "Thank you kindly," he repeated, and touched the brim of his hap. "You didn't have to do nothin' like that, Mr. Marlowe."

"I didn't do it because I had to. I did it because I wanted to." The storekeeper sounded impatient. "If you work hard, you ought to know other people notice. And I do. I'm always glad to see you bringing me loads from the docks and the railroad yard."

"Much obliged." Cincinnatus touched his brim again, then took the package—it was nice and heavy—out to the truck and set it on the front seat beside him. He had one more delivery to make before he could go home with it.

His last stop wasn't at a grocery store, but at the offices of the *Des Moines Register and Remembrance*. The crates he unloaded there were large and heavy. "What is this thing?" he asked the man who took delivery.

"New typesetting machine," the fellow answered. "We'll get the paper out faster than ever."

"That's nice," Cincinnatus said obligingly.

"And we won't need so many compositors," the newspaperman added. Seeing that the word meant nothing to Cincinnatus, he chose a simpler one: "Typesetters."

"Oh." Cincinnatus hesitated, then asked, "What happens to the ones you don't need no—*any*—more? They lose their jobs?"

"That isn't settled yet." The newspaperman sounded uncomfortable now. He sounded so uncomfortable, Cincinnatus was sure he was lying. He went on, "Even if we do let some people go, we'll try to make sure they latch on somewhere else."

"Uh-*huh*," Cincinnatus said. How were they supposed to manage that, with jobs so hard to come by? He figured it for another lie, right up there with old favorites like *The check is in the mail*.

His skepticism must have shown in his voice; the man from the *Register and Remembrance* turned red. He said, "We'll try, goddammit. We will. What else can we do? We've got to save money wherever we can, because we sure as hell aren't making much."

For that, Cincinnatus had no good answer. He got his paperwork signed and went back to the truck. Outside the

Register and Remembrance building, a couple of men were hanging a banner over the doorway. WIN WITH COOLIDGE IN '32! it said, and then, in smaller letters, A RETURN TO PROSPERITY! The *Register and Remembrance* was the Democratic paper in Des Moines. Its Socialist counterpart, the *Workers' Gazette*, had its offices across the street and down the block. Even though this was a presidential-election year, the *Workers' Gazette* displayed no banners extolling the virtues of Hosea Blackford. The paper seemed to want to forget about him.

It was only May. There was, as yet, no guarantee Calvin Coolidge would be nominated for a second run at the Powel House. It certainly looked likely, though; no other Democratic hopeful roused much excitement. Cincinnatus snorted when that thought crossed his mind. Coolidge was about as exciting as a pitcher of warm spit. But everyone thought he could win when November rolled around. To the Democrats, locked out of Powel House the past twelve years, that was plenty to make the governor of Massachusetts seem exciting.

Nobody, by all the signs, thought President Blackford had much chance to win a second term. But the Socialists had made no move to dump him from their ticket. For one thing, not even they were radical enough to jettison a sitting president. For another, no one else from the Socialist Party looked like a winner this year, either. Blackford wouldn't run again, win or lose. If things went as they looked like going, he could perform one last duty for the Party by serving as sacrificial lamb. That way, defeat would taint no one else.

Cincinnatus shrugged. Whom the Socialists ran was all one to him. He intended to vote Democratic; the Democrats took a harder line about the Confederate States than the Socialists did. He couldn't imagine any Negro in the United States voting any other way—which didn't mean some wouldn't.

When he got back to the family apartment, Elizabeth greeted him with, "How did it go today?" *How much money did you make?* was what she meant, of course.

Some of the tension slid out of her face when he

answered, "Pretty well, thanks. How about you, sweet-heart?"

"Ordinary kind o' day," his wife said with a weary shrug. "Got me two dollars and a quarter. Every little bit helps, I reckon."

Achilles looked up from the kitchen table, where he was writing a high-school composition. He said, "Classes let out next month. Then I'll be able to look for work without you pitching fits, Dad."

He itched to do more than he was doing. Cincinnatus knew as much. He said, "Workin' summers is one thing. Workin' instead o' schoolin' is somethin' else. You're sixteen—you got two years to go 'fore you get your diploma. I want you to have it, by God. It's somethin' nobody can't never taken away from you."

By Achilles' expression, he'd made a mess of his grammar. But then, at sixteen (and where had the years since he was born gone?) Achilles wore that look of scorn around him a lot of the time. Cincinnatus remembered wearing it around his own father when he was that age. Boys turning into young men banged heads with their fathers. That was the way things worked.

"If we need the money—" Achilles began.

"We don't need it *that* bad," Cincinnatus said. "This is the rest of your life we're talkin' about, remember." To his relief, his son didn't choose to push it tonight. Cincinnatus knew he'd be smart not to push the boy too hard about staying in school. Achilles liked school, and did pretty well. But if his father urged him to stay in and do well, that might be enough to turn him against it.

Amanda came in and gave Cincinnatus a hug. She was still young enough to love without reservation. She said, "I got all my words right on my spelling test today."

"That's good, sweetheart. That's mighty fine," Cincinnatus said enthusiastically. "Can't hardly do no better than perfect."

"How can you do better than perfect at all?" Amanda asked.

"You can't. I was just jokin' a little," Cincinnatus answered.

"Oh." Amanda wrinkled her nose. "That's silly, Daddy." Her accent held even more Midwest, even less Kentucky, than Achilles'. She'd been born here, after all. Everyone she'd ever heard, except for her parents, had that harsh, precise way of talking, with sharp vowels and every letter of every word pronounced. It still sounded strange and ugly to Cincinnatus, although he'd been here for going on ten years (not counting time in Luther Bliss' jail).

A delicious odor reached Cincinnatus' nose. "What smells good?" he asked.

"I'm stewing giblets with potatoes and tomatoes and onions," Elizabeth answered. "Butcher shop had 'em cheap."

"Cheap?" Cincinnatus said, thumping himself on the forehead with the heel of his hand. He hurried down to the truck and returned with the butcher-paper package he'd left on the front seat. "Soup bones. Oscar Marlowe gave 'em to me for nothin'. Reckon I'd forget my head if it wasn't on tight."

"Soup bones? That's wonderful! I'll do 'em up tomorrow." Elizabeth hurried to put the package in the icebox.

"Giblets. Soup bones." Achilles made a face that looked remarkably like the one his little sister had just made. "Not many people eat that kind of stuff."

Cincinnatus had grown up eating chicken gizzards and beef tongues and lungs and other cuts richer people thought of as offal. He took them for granted, as he always had. When times here in Des Moines were good, Elizabeth hadn't bought them so often, so Achilles noticed them more now than he would have otherwise. But Cincinnatus wagged a finger at his son. "Happens that ain't so," he said. "Plenty of people who was eatin' roast beef's eatin' giblets now, and glad to have 'em. I ain't just talkin' 'bout colored folks, neither. It's the same way with whites. I seen enough to know that for a fact. Reckon it's the same with the Chinaman upstairs, too. When times are hard, you're smart to be glad o' what you've got, not sorry for what you ain't."

Achilles said, "Somebody at school told me Chinamen

cut up dogs and cats and use them for meat. Is that true, Dad?"

"I don't know," Cincinnatus answered. "I never heard it before, I'll tell you. Tell you somethin' else, too—don't you go asking the Changs about it, neither. They're nice folks, and I don't want you embarrassing 'em none, you hear?"

"I wouldn't do that!" Achilles sounded uncommonly sincere. A moment later, he explained why: "Grace Chang is in a couple of my classes. I think she's a cute girl."

That made Cincinnatus and Elizabeth exchange glances. Even if Cincinnatus had felt such a thing about a white woman in Kentucky, he never would have said so. But the Drivers weren't in Kentucky any more, and Grace wasn't white. What were the rules for Negroes and Chinese? Were there any?

Of course, just because Achilles thought Grace was cute, that didn't mean he was going to ask her to marry him, or even to ask her to go to a film with him. Just the same, a sensible father—a father who didn't want his boy beaten up or lynched—started worrying about these things as far ahead of time as he could. By Elizabeth's expression, she was worrying about them, too.

Before Cincinnatus could say anything about any of that, Achilles changed the subject: "Who are you going to vote for for president, Dad?"

"Whoever the Democrats run—looks like Coolidge now," Cincinnatus answered. Elizabeth nodded agreement. "Got to keep an eye on them Confederates." His wife nodded again.

Not Achilles. "If I could vote, I'd vote for the Socialists," he declared. "They don't care if you're black or white or yellow or red. They just want to know what you can do." And that declaration of political independence started a whole new argument, one that made Cincinnatus forget Grace Chang for the rest of the night.

"Pass the salt, Ma," Edna Grimes said, and Nellie Jacobs did. Her daughter sprinkled it on a drumstick. "This is awful good fried chicken." She took a big bite.

"Sure is, Mother Jacobs," Merle Grimes agreed. He turned to Edna. "You all right, honey? Everything staying down?"

Edna nodded. "Couldn't be better, Merle. Stomach isn't bothering me at all this time around." She yawned. "I still get sleepy a lot, though." She was three months pregnant; the baby would be born somewhere around New Year's Day, 1933. Suddenly, she pointed at her son. "For God's sake, Armstrong, I'm not too sleepy to miss you stuffing half a pound of mashed potatoes into your face all at once. Show some manners, or you'll find out you're not too big to paddle. Ten years old, and you eat like that? Jesus!"

"Sorry, Ma," Armstrong said, most indistinctly—maybe it hadn't been half a pound of mashed potatoes, but it hadn't missed by much. Across the table from him, Clara smirked. Aunt and nephew (which seemed silly, when only two years separated them) had never got along, not even when they were tiny.

Merle Grimes raised his glass of beer. "Here's hoping Cal sweeps the Socialists out of Powel House," he said. The Democrats wouldn't hold their convention for another month—they'd scheduled it for the Fourth of July—but Governor Coolidge's nomination now looked like a foregone conclusion.

"Amen," Nellie said, and drank. So did Edna. So did Hal Jacobs. Armstrong Grimes raised his glass of milk in imitation of the grownups. Clara made a face at him.

"That will be enough of that, young lady," Nellie said. Clara subsided. Armstrong laughed.

Edna said, "We're all Democrats, and it doesn't do us or Coolidge a bit of good. Hardly seems fair."

"It *isn't* fair," her husband said. "This is what we get for living in Washington, D.C. We're not a state, so we don't get to vote. Most of the government's been in Philadelphia for the past fifty years, but they can vote for president there and we still can't. There ought to be a law."

"It's been this way forever." Hal Jacobs paused to cough.

"You've lived here all your life," Merle said. "You're

used to not voting. I grew up in Ohio. I like having my voice count for something. Losing my vote was the hardest thing about coming to live here."

"A lot of places, Ma and me wouldn't have had a vote up till a few years ago anyway." Edna had to raise her voice, because Hal coughed again. "Summer cold?" she asked sympathetically.

He shrugged. "I do not know." He lit a cigarette, took a drag, and coughed yet again. "I am having trouble shaking it, though, what ever it is."

Merle lit up, too. He blew a smoke ring, which made Clara and Armstrong laugh. Despite what he was doing, he said, "Maybe you ought to cut back, Father Jacobs. I always cough worse if I smoke a lot while I've got a cold—I know that."

Hal blew a smoke ring, too. With another shrug, he said, "I have been smoking since before the Second Mexican War—more than fifty years now. Cutting back is not that . . . easy." The interruption was for more coughs yet.

Merle Grimes' laugh was rueful. "Oh, I know. I always feel like I've been steamrollered if I don't smoke my usual ration."

"You're cross as a bear, too," Edna said.

"Blow another smoke ring, Pa," Clara said. He needed two tries before he could; a cough in the middle ruined the first one.

"You *have* been coughing a lot lately," Nellie said. "Maybe you ought to see a doctor, get yourself looked at."

"What will he tell me, dear?" her husband replied, taking a last drag at the cigarette and then stubbing it out. "He will tell me I am not so young as I used to be. I already know this, thank you very much. I do not need to pay a doctor money to find out what I already know."

Even at the start of the Great War—*eighteen years ago now,* Nellie realized with no small surprise; where had the time gone?—Hal's hair and mustache had been gray, his face lined. He hadn't seemed to change much in all the time since. Now, though, Nellie tried to see him as if she were just meeting him. He was close to seventy, and looked every year of it. His skin sagged on his face. He was a sallow color he shouldn't have been.

She actually blinked, wondering if she was seeing things that weren't there. But she wasn't. She looked at her husband again. It wasn't just that the changes had sneaked up gradually and she hadn't noticed. She was sure it wasn't. They'd come on lately. She didn't care for any of the thoughts following from that.

"Hal," she said, "I think maybe you really ought to see a doctor."

"Nonsense," he told her, and sounded very firm. He seldom talked back to her; in that (as in most ways, she had to admit), he made a most satisfactory husband. She decided not to push it, especially not at the supper table. Maybe it was just a summer cold, and he would get better.

But he didn't. The cough went on. He lost more flesh, and he'd never had that much to spare. His appetite dwindled. A couple of times, Nellie started to tell him to go to a doctor's office. Each time, she held back. She didn't want to be a nag, especially where he'd dug in his heels.

Then, just before the Fourth of July, he had another coughing fit, and she saw red on his handkerchief. "That does it, Hal," she declared, trying her best not to show how alarmed she was. "You get yourself to the doctor right this minute, do you hear me?"

If he'd argued, she would have dragged him by the heels. But he didn't. He only sighed and nodded and said, "Yes, maybe you are right. All the pep has oozed right out of me the past few months, feels like."

He made the appointment. Nellie made sure he kept it. When he got back, she said, "Well? What did he tell you?"

"Nothing yet, not really," he answered. "He took an X ray of my chest. I have to go back in a couple of days, after he gets the photograph developed. He will not charge me anything extra for the second visit."

"He'd better not, not when it's his fault," Nellie said, and then, anxiously, "Do you want me to come along with you, dear?" She didn't use endearments with Hal very often; that she did now showed how worried she was.

"Thank you, Nellie. You are very sweet." He was, as usual, polite—almost courtly—but he shook his head without hesitation. "I hope I am by now a grown man. Whatever the news may be, you can trust me to bring it home to you."

"You know I trust you," Nellie said. And that was true. She could rely on him absolutely. That was the rock on which they'd built the past going on fifteen years. Some people had passion at the bottom of their marriage. Nellie was pretty sure Edna and Merle did—and yet that marriage had almost come apart when Merle found out the soldier Edna had nearly married before him wore C.S. butternut, not U.S. green-gray. Trust mattered in any marriage.

What if Hal knew I killed Bill Reach? Nellie shoved that question down, as she always did. *The only way two can keep a secret is if one of them is dead.* That fit her and Hal's former spy boss—her former client in her much, much younger days in the demimonde—to a T. Edna's secret had got out, as Nellie had thought it would sooner or later. She would take her own to the grave with her.

Considering Hal's cough, she wished she hadn't thought of it like that.

When the day for the new doctor's appointment came, he put a CLOSED sign in the window of the cobbler's shop where he'd worked so long and walked on over: it was only three or four blocks to the office. Across the street in the coffeehouse where *she'd* worked so long (though not as long as Hal), Nellie watched him go. Her eyes kept coming back to the CLOSED sign. She didn't like the look of it. And she kept missing customers' orders, either not hearing what they wanted or bringing them the wrong thing even though she'd written down the right one.

Hal came back about an hour and a quarter after he'd left. He took down the CLOSED sign and went back to work. Maybe that meant everything was fine. Maybe it just meant he had a lot to do. Nellie didn't think he would come across the street right away and tell her if the news was bad. He wasn't like that. And she couldn't go ask him right away, because she was busy herself. *If I keep making mistakes like I'm doing, though, I'll lose so many customers, I'll never be this busy again,* she thought.

At last, she had a moment when nobody was in the coffeehouse. She hung up her own CLOSED sign, waited for a break in the traffic, and crossed the street. The bell over Hal's door jingled. He looked up from a new heel he was putting on. Spitting a mouthful of brads into the palm of his hand, he said, "Hello, Nellie."

She couldn't tell anything from his face or voice. She had to ask it: "What did the doctor say? What did the X ray say?"

"I have something unusual." He laughed, as if proud of himself. "The doctor said he has only seen it a few times in all the years he has been practicing."

"What is it?" Nellie didn't scream at him. She never knew why or how she didn't, but she didn't. She waited, taut as a fiddle string.

"It is called carcinoma of the lungs." Hal pronounced the unfamiliar word with care. He pulled out his cigarettes and lit one.

When he offered the pack to Nellie, she shook her head. "Not now. What the devil does that mean, anyway?"

"Well, it is like a—a growth in there," he said.

"A growth? What kind of a growth? What can they do about it?" The questions flew quick and sharp, like machine-gun fire.

Hal sighed. "It is a cancer, Nellie. They can aim more X rays at it, the doctor said. That will slow it down for a while."

"Slow it down . . . for a while," Nellie echoed. Her husband nodded. She knew what that meant, knew what it had to mean, but grasped for a straw anyhow: "Can they stop it?"

"It is a cancer," he repeated. "We can hope for a miracle, but. . . ." A shrug. "Who knows why cancers happen? Just bad luck, the doctor said." He blew a smoke ring at the ceiling, as he had for Clara and Armstrong. Then, stubbing out the cigarette, he said, "I am not afraid of death, darling. I am afraid of dying, a little, because I do not think it will be easy, but I am not afraid of death. Death will bring me peace. The only thing I am sorry for is that it will take me away from you and Clara. I do not think many men have the last years of their lives be the happiest one, but I have. I feel like the luckiest man in the world, even now."

"Oh, Hal." Nellie hardly noticed the tears running down her face. "What are we going to do without you? What *can* we do without you? I love you. It took me a long time to figure that out—longer than it should have, you being the finest man I ever knew—but I do, and who knows? Maybe there'll be a miracle with the X rays." She grabbed for that straw again.

Hal's smile was gentle. "Yes, maybe there will," he said, meaning, *not a chance*. He brushed her lips with his. "With you and Clara, I have already had two miracles." Nellie shivered. She wasn't, couldn't be, ready for this. But who ever could? Ready or not, it always came.

XV

"Here you are, George," Sylvia Enos said, setting a plate of bacon and eggs in front of her son. When his fishing boat was in port, she liked to stuff him. She was convinced the cook on the *Whitecap* was trying to starve him. Logic told her that was silly, especially since he'd grown into a strapping man, almost six feet tall and broad as a bull through the shoulders. Logic, sometimes, had nothing to do with anything.

"Thanks, Ma." He slathered on salt and pepper and started to eat. With his mouth full, he went on, "You know what? When I went out to the Banks, I took along a copy of *I Sank Roger Kimball*. That's a good book—that's a really good book. You and that writer fellow did a . . . heck of a job." The brief pause there surely meant he was changing what he might have said on the deck of the *Whitecap*. Sylvia smiled. She'd raised him right. He didn't cuss in front of her—well, not much, anyhow.

"Thank you," she said now. "You ought to thank Ernie, too. He did the real work. And he's a brick, too—if it hadn't been for him, we'd've lost our money when the bank went under. He didn't have to come back and warn me about that, but he did."

She turned away so her son wouldn't see the look on her face. She didn't know what her expression was, exactly, but she did know it wasn't one she wanted George, Jr., seeing. She would have gone to bed with Ernie. She'd *wanted* to go to bed with him. *And a whole fat lot of good that did me,* she thought. *Just my damned luck, the first time I really want a man since George got killed, to fix on one who couldn't do me any good—or himself, either, poor fellow.*

George, Jr., got up and poured himself more coffee—and Sylvia, too, when she pushed her cup toward him. He added cream and sugar, sipped, and said, "There's a lot of stuff in there I never knew before."

"I'm not surprised," Sylvia answered. "That was nine years ago now. You were still a boy then."

"When you put me and Mary Jane on the train to Connecticut, did you really think you'd never see us again?"

"Yes, I thought that. It was the hardest thing about what I did," Sylvia said. "But no one was going to make that man pay for what he did to the *Ericsson* at the end of the war, and he deserved to."

"But you would have paid, too."

"I didn't even think about what would happen to me. When I found out he was running around loose, I didn't think about much of anything."

"That must have been . . . very strange," George, Jr., said. "A couple of fellows on the boat were in the Army during the war—they got conscripted before they could join the Navy, or else they weren't sailors yet: I don't know which. Where was I? Oh, yeah. Sometimes they tell stories. They talk about how they were going up against Confederate machine guns and they didn't think they'd come back alive. It must have been like that for you, too."

"Maybe." Sylvia wasn't so sure. If a man charged a machine gun, he had a chance of living—maybe not much of a chance, but a chance. Once she'd shot Roger Kimball, she was in the hands of the law, and she didn't think she had any chance of escape at all. She hadn't counted on having Confederate politics come to her rescue.

Her son said, "You have a book signing this morning?"

"That's right. Every time I sign one, that's fourteen and three-quarter cents in my pocket," Sylvia answered. She couldn't have figured that out herself from the murky language of the book contract she'd signed; Ernie had explained the way things worked.

"Call it fifteen cents." George, Jr.'s, face got a faraway look. He'd always been good in school. Sylvia wished he would have liked it more, would have got his high-school diploma instead of going to work on T Wharf. Years too late to worry about that, though. He went on, "If you sign twenty of them, then, that's three dollars. That's not a bad day's wage."

"I don't know if I'll sign that many of them," Sylvia said, "but they're buying the book—or I hope they are— from here to San Diego. We'll see what it does, that's all. The reviews have been pretty good." That was Ernie's doing, of course; the actual words on paper were his. *But the story's mine,* Sylvia reminded herself. *He couldn't have written it if not for me. My name deserves to be on the cover, too.*

"Might be just as well they took a while getting it into print," her son said. "With the Freedom Party coming up again in the CSA, people here are liable to be more interested in what happened to one of its bigwigs back then."

Sylvia blinked. That was true, and she hadn't thought of it herself. George, Jr., had a man's shrewdness. Well, fair enough—he *was* a man; he'd be old enough to vote in November. *Has it really been more than twenty-one years since he was born?* Sylvia didn't want to believe that, but couldn't very well help it.

The bookstore, Burke's, wasn't far from Faneuil Hall. No line stretched around the block waiting for her when she arrived. They did have a sign in the window saying she'd be there. That was good. She'd signed at two or three stores that hadn't let anyone know she'd be there. As a result, she hadn't signed much.

She took her place at a table near the door. The table held a dozen copies of *I Sank Roger Kimball* and a neat hand-lettered sign: MEET THE AUTHOR. A man in a suit that had seen better days came up to her and asked, "Excuse me, ma'am, but where's the bathroom?"

"I'm sorry. I don't work here," Sylvia said. She'd already seen people paid no attention to signs. The man muttered something and went away.

Another man came up. He took a book from the pile for her to sign. "I was in the Navy," he said. "You did everybody on the *Ericsson* a good turn."

"Thank you," Sylvia said.

A woman picked up a copy of the book. She said, "My brother would like this, and his birthday is coming up. Would you sign it 'To Pete,' please?"

" 'To Pete,' " Sylvia echoed, and wrote the man's name and hers on the title page. That was where Ernie had said the autograph was supposed to go. He knew such things, or Sylvia was willing to believe he did.

A plump woman in a flowered housedress approached. "Where are your cookbooks, dear?" she asked.

"I'm sorry. I don't work here," Sylvia said again. She held up a copy of *I Sank Roger Kimball*. "Would you like to buy *my* book? I'll be glad to sign it for you if you do." *Of course I will. It makes me money.*

The woman shook her head. "Not unless it's got good recipes for beans and cabbage in it." That, Sylvia couldn't claim. The other woman wandered off, in search of cookbooks.

Over the next two hours, four more people asked Sylvia questions whose answers only someone who worked at Burke's could have known. She sent them off to the clerk behind the cash register. She also did get another nine people to buy copies of the book, most by simply sitting there and having them come up, a couple by waving the book as they walked into the store. The first time she'd signed, she hadn't done that—she'd been too shy. But the manager of that bookstore gave her a tip she took to heart: "If you don't toot your own horn, lady, who's gonna do it for you?"

She was getting ready to go home when the bell over Burke's front door jangled again. In walked a lean Irishman with a lot of teeth. He tipped his fedora to her. "Good day to you, Mrs. Enos." Striding up to the table, he took a copy of her book and opened it to the title page. Most people, left to themselves, chose the half-title page or the blank sheet in front of it, but he knew the ropes. "If you'd be so kind . . . ?"

"Of course, Mr. Kennedy." She wrote, *For Joseph Kennedy—Best wishes, Sylvia Enos,* and gave the book back to him. *Another fourteen and three-quarter cents,* she thought, *but I didn't expect he'd want anything to do with me.*

Kennedy took the book over to the clerk, paid for it, and then came back to Sylvia's table. "I hope this means you've come to your senses, politically speaking," he remarked, though the way he looked at her didn't seem political at all.

She said, "I've always been a Democrat." That wasn't strictly true. She'd favored the Socialists till she saw Upton Sinclair do no more than protest to the Confederate States when it came out that Roger Kimball had torpedoed the USS *Ericsson* after the Confederates were supposed to have stopped fighting. But she'd voted Democratic for as long as she'd had the suffrage.

"You sometimes picked odd ways to show it." No, Kennedy hadn't forgotten seeing her at a Socialist rally on the Boston Common.

Knowing he hadn't forgotten, she asked him, "What do you want with me?"

The way his eyes flashed told her one thing he wanted. He knew she knew he was married; his wife had watched her children when she spoke at a Democratic function. He didn't care if she knew. He wanted what he wanted. But he made himself remember he wanted something else, too: "I hear you're doing well with your book. I look forward to reading it."

"Thank you," Sylvia Enos said.

Kennedy hefted his copy of *I Sank Roger Kimball.* "This has put you in the public eye, you know. We have a campaign to run, Mrs. Enos. Would you help Governor Coolidge—help the Democratic Party—take Powel House back from the Socialists? They were lucky at first, but what's happened to the country in President Blackford's term shows their true colors."

That wasn't even close to fair, and Sylvia knew it. But she'd already seen that political campaigns weren't designed to be fair. They were designed to convince, by whatever means possible. She said, "I'd like to help, Mr. Kennedy, but I don't know if I can. Times are hard."

"Don't you worry about that," Joseph Kennedy said. "Don't you worry about that a bit. We'll take care of you." That glint showed again in his eyes. "How does a hundred dollars a month sound, from now till the election? Plus expenses, of course."

For a moment, it sounded too good to be true. But then Sylvia remembered Ernie talking about his dicker with their publisher, and about first offers' being meant to snag people who didn't have the nerve the stand up for what they were really worth. Her spine stiffened. She said, "I'm sorry, Mr. Kennedy, but I've got so many things planned, that isn't really enough to pull me away."

Joseph Kennedy eyed her again, this time in a very different way. Plainly, he'd expected her not just to say yes but to swoon with gratitude. After a long moment, he nodded, perhaps seeing her for the first time as a person and not just as a tool or a nicely shaped piece of meat. "More to you than meets the eye, isn't there?" he said, more to himself than to her. He grew brisk. "Well, business is business, and you'll do us some good. How does two hundred a month sound, then?"

Sylvia didn't gasp, but she came close. The way things were, that was a lot of money. "And expenses? And full pay for November, too?" she asked.

Kennedy bared his teeth. "You sure you're not a sheeny, Mrs. Enos?" he said. She didn't answer. She just waited. He gave her a sour nod. "And expenses. And full pay for November, too," he promised, and stuck out his hand. "Bargain?"

She was oddly reluctant to touch him. She didn't see how she could avoid it, though. When they shook on the deal, his hand felt like . . . a hand. Somehow, she hadn't expected his flesh to seem so ordinary. "Bargain," she said. The wolf wouldn't come round her door again till the end of the year—longer, if she salted some money away, as she planned to. That made it a fine bargain indeed, as far as she was concerned.

* * *

Aeroplanes roared off the *Remembrance*'s flight deck, one after another. Even with a push from the catapult to speed them on their way, they almost dropped into the gray-green water of the northern Pacific till they gained altitude and buzzed away, some to the north, others to the south.

Sam Carsten scratched his nose. His fingertip came away white with zinc-oxide ointment. Even here, off the west coast of Canada, he needed shielding from the summer sun. But, though he might burn in these waters, he wouldn't scorch.

He turned to George Moerlein. Back when they were both petty officers, they'd bunked together. But Moerlein was even newer on the *Remembrance* than he was now, having rejoined her crew during a fueling stop in Seattle. Carsten said, "Feels good to see us in business again."

"Yeah—uh, yes, sir," Moerlein said. "Sorry, sir."

"Don't worry about it," Sam answered. His old bunkmate had forgotten for a moment he was an officer these days. He went on, "I'm just glad this ship isn't tied up at the Boston Navy Yard any more."

"Me, too, sir." Moerlein got it right this time. "That was what finally made me put in for a transfer—I wondered if she'd ever go to sea again. For a hell of a long time, sure didn't look like it." He pulled out a cigar, then sheepishly put it back in his pocket. The smoking lamp was out on the flight deck during takeoffs and landings, for excellent good reasons. The petty officer shook his head. "I've been away too damn long. I shouldn't even have started to do that."

"Well, you saved me the trouble of barking at you," Sam answered.

Moerlein gave him a wry grin, then said, "What the hell do we do if we catch the Japs with their finger in the cookie jar? They're in international waters, same as we are. What *can* we do?"

"Damned if I know," Carsten said. "But if they're sending people into Canada to try to get the Canucks to rise up against us, we can't let 'em get away with that, can we?"

"Beats me," Moerlein told him. "But if we do find 'em and we do clobber 'em, don't you figure it's about even money we're doing it on account of President Blackford needs votes and wants to look tough?"

Sam scowled. "I'd hate to think that." He drummed his fingers on his trouser leg. "Of course, just because I'd hate to think it doesn't mean it's wrong."

An hour later, another flight of aeroplanes took off from the *Remembrance*, while a flight that had gone out before landed on the deck. The carrier kept aeroplanes in the sky all the time. If the Japs really were trying to sneak something past her, they wouldn't have an easy time of it.

As far as Sam could prove, the *Remembrance* was just going through the motions. Her air patrols had spotted nothing out of the ordinary: fishing boats and merchantmen, none of them flying the Rising Sun. Whether they stumbled upon any actual Jap warships or not, though, the training the whole crew—and especially the pilots—got was priceless, as far as he was concerned. George Moerlein had it dead right: anything was better than sitting in the Navy Yard.

When klaxons started howling a couple of days later, Sam sprinted to his battle station figuring it was just another drill. He certainly hoped so; going to the bowels of the ship on antitorpedo duty wasn't, never had been, and never would be his favorite choice. By now, though, he'd spent more than twenty years in the Navy. He knew how things worked. The Navy did what it wanted, not what he wanted.

Commander van der Waal was down there ahead of him, at the head of a damage-control party. The other officer's face was thoroughly grim. "What's up, sir?" Sam panted. "They tell you anything?"

"Yes," van der Waal said. "Our aeroplanes spotted a high-powered motorboat pulling away from what looked like an ordinary freighter. Ordinary freighters don't carry speedboats, though."

"Son of a bitch," Sam said softly, and then, louder, "They sure don't. What flag is the freighter flying?"

"Argentine," van der Waal answered. "But the aeroplane

buzzed her at smokestack height, and the sailors don't look like they're from Argentina. She doesn't respond to wireless signals, either."

The throb of the *Remembrance*'s engine grew louder and deeper as the great ship picked up speed. "*Son* of a bitch," Sam said again. "What are we going to do about it?"

"Freighter's only about sixty miles north of us," van der Waal said. "Seems like we're going up for a look-see of our own."

"What about that speedboat?" Carsten asked.

"It won't outrun an aeroplane—probably a swarm of aeroplanes by now," Commander van der Waal said. "But if we find that freighter's full of Japs sailing under cover of a false flag . . . Well, I don't know what we'll do then."

"Argentine flag's handy for them—Argentina doesn't love us, either," Sam said. During the Great War, Argentina had fought Chile and Paraguay, both of them U.S. allies, because she'd been making money hand over fist sending grain and meat to Britain and France. Sam's old ship had been part of the American-Chilean fleet that sailed round the Horn to try to cut off that trade: not altogether successfully, not till the Empire of Brazil finally entered the war on the side of the USA and Germany, forcing Argentine and British ships out of her territorial waters.

"We may be only a couple of hours from war, Ensign," van der Waal said.

"Yes, sir," Sam answered. "Well, if we are, I hope we kick the Japs around the block, but good."

In fact, he wondered how much damage the USA and Japan could do to each other. An awful lot of ocean separated the two countries. The United States—the American Empire, counting Canada—had more resources. Could they bring them all to bear, though, with a long frontier facing a Confederacy that hated them and might be tempted to throw in with the Japs? Of course, the Japanese had to worry about the Russians sitting over their holdings in Manchuria.

After a while, a sailor brought word from the wireless room: "We've ordered them to stop for inspection,

492

and they say they don't have to, not in international waters. They sure as hell don't talk like Argentines."

Technically, whoever was aboard that freighter was right. Technically, a man who stepped out into the street with a traffic light was also right. If a truck ran the light and killed him, he ended up just as dead as if he'd been wrong. Another half an hour passed. Then one of the five-inch guns Sam knew so well bellowed.

"Shot across her bow," van der Waal said. Carsten nodded.

And then, quite suddenly, the *Remembrance*'s engines roared with emergency power. The great ship turned hard to port. Van der Waal and Carsten stared at each other. Sam said, "They must've—"

He got no further than that, because a torpedo slammed into the aeroplane carrier and knocked him off his feet. The lights flickered, but stayed on. "Starboard hit, felt like back toward the stern," van der Waal said. He was on his wallet. When he tried to get to his feet, he fell back with a groan and a curse. "I think the burst broke my ankle. I can't move on it. Are you sound, Carsten?"

Sam was already upright again. "Yes, sir."

"You're in charge of damage control, then," the other officer said, biting his lip against the pain. "I know it's not the job you wanted, but you've got to do it. We're taking on water, sure as hell."

"Yes, sir, I can feel it," Carsten agreed. Astonishing how small a list his sense of balance could detect. But this wasn't a time to marvel about such things, not if he wanted to have the chance to marvel later. He nodded to van der Waal. "I'll take care of it, sir, you bet. Come on, boys— let's get moving."

Even as he led the men of the damage-control party back toward the wound in the ship, he wondered if the next torpedo would slam into her amidships and flood the engine room. If she lost power, the lights and the pumps would fail, and then the *Remembrance* might well go down.

That damn Jap ship must've had a submersible tagging along, in case we found her, he thought unhappily. *And we're out here all by our lonesome, without any destroyers along. The Navy Department didn't really believe we'd come up with anything, so they decided to do this on the cheap. Now it's liable to kill us all.*

One of the sailors said, "Fuel storage for the aeroplanes is back here. We're lucky the gasoline didn't blow up and send us right to the moon."

"Gurk," Sam said. He hadn't thought of that.

All the watertight doors were closed. That was something. But how many doors, how many watertight compartments, had the blast shattered? That was what they had to find out. Whether the *Remembrance* lived or died would turn on the answer.

Water in the corridor told them they were nearing the hit. "Do we open that door, sir?" a sailor asked, pointing to the twisted portal, no longer tight, under which the seawater was leaking.

"You bet we do," Sam answered. "Likely men still alive on the other side. Now we fan out, too, cover as much ground as we can, start sealing off what we have to and getting out sailors. Let's go. This is what we've trained for, and it's what we've got to do." *I sound just like Commander van der Waal,* he thought. *Damned if he wasn't right all along, even if I didn't feel like admitting it.*

They found sailors closer to the damage who were already doing what they could to stem the tide of water pouring into the *Remembrance*: stuffing mattresses and whatever else they could find into sprung seams between doors and hatchways and such. Carsten took charge of them, too. He kicked aside a floating severed hand that still trailed blood.

Before long, he was sure the hit the aeroplane carrier had taken wouldn't sink her. Most of her compartments were holding against the flood. Both his sense of balance and a level he had with him insisted that her list had stabilized. Her pumps never faltered. Most important of all, the second torpedo, the one he'd dreaded so much, never came.

In spare moments, when he wasn't too busy sloshing

through seawater eventually up past his waist, he wondered why the Japanese submersible hadn't put another fish, or two or three more, into the *Remembrance*. Word eventually trickled down from above. "Sir, we sank the fucker," a messenger said. "She launched two at us. One missed. The other one nailed us. We had some aeroplanes with bombs underneath 'em in the air by then, to help sink the Jap freighter and the speedboat. One of 'em spotted the submersible as she launched, and he put a bomb right on the bastard's conning tower. That sub sank, and it ain't coming up again."

"Bully!" Every once in a while, especially when he didn't think, Sam still used the slang he'd grown up with. The messenger was a fresh-faced kid who'd surely been pissing in his diapers when the Great War started, and looked at him as if at the Pyramids of Egypt or any other antiquity. He didn't care. If the kid wanted to say *swell*, that was fine. Most of the time, Sam said *swell* himself. But *bully*, even if it did smack of the days before the war, said what he wanted to say, too. The United States had found themselves a new fight. They'd need the *Remembrance*. And Sam, old-fashioned or not, was glad not to be among its first casualties.

Headlines in the *Rosenfeld Register* shrieked of war: VICIOUS JAP ATTACK ON USS REMEMBRANCE! A subhead said, *Ship badly damaged but stays afloat!* Another headline warned, BEWARE THE YELLOW PERIL!

Mary McGregor had never seen a Japanese in her life. Except for pictures in books, she'd never seen a Negro, either. She imagined Japanese almost as yellow as sunflowers, with slit eyes set in their faces at a forty-five-degree angle. It wasn't a pretty picture. She didn't care. The Japs were fighting the United States. As far as she was concerned, nothing else mattered. If they were fighting the USA, she was all for them.

The Yellow Peril story in the *Register* warned anyone who spotted a Jap to report him at once to U.S. occupation authorities. She pointed that out to her mother. "Pretty funny, isn't it?" she said. "Can't you just see a Jap walking down the main street in Rosenfeld and stopping in at Gibbon's general store to buy a pickle and some thumbtacks?"

"That story must be going out all over Canada," her mother said. "Maybe there are places where you really might run into Japanese people—Vancouver, somewhere like that. I know they've got Chinamen in Vancouver. Why not Japs, too?"

"Maybe," Mary said. "That would make some sense—as much sense as the Yanks ever make, anyway. But why put that kind of notice in the *Register*? It's just stupid here, really, really stupid." She held up a hand before her mother could answer. "I know why. Some Yank in a swivel chair probably said, 'Stick this order in every paper in Canada, from British Columbia to Nova Scotia. And stick it in every paper in Newfoundland, too, while you're about it.' Who cares whether it makes sense if you're sitting in a swivel chair?"

Maude McGregor smiled. "You're probably right. The Americans do things like that. They like giving *big* orders, if you know what I mean. It's part of what makes them the kind of people they are."

Had Mary been a man among men and not a young woman talking with her mother, she would have expressed her detailed opinion about what sort of people Americans were. Her eyes must have sparked in a way that got her opinion across without words, for her mother's smile got wider. Then Maude McGregor said, "Next time you go to the cinema with Mort Pomeroy, make sure there aren't any Japs under the front seat in his motorcar."

"I'll do that," Mary said, laughing.

Her mother's smile changed. She said, "Your face just lit up. You think he's special, don't you?"

"Yes." Mary nodded without hesitation. "I've never felt like this about a boy before." She hadn't had much chance to feel anything special about boys up till now. Most of them stayed away from the McGregor house as if she had a dangerous disease. And, in occupied Canada, what disease could be more dangerous than not only

496

descending from someone who'd fought the Yanks to his last breath but also being proud of it?

"I'm glad he makes you happy," her mother said. "I hope he keeps making you happy for years and years, if that's what you both end up wanting."

"I think maybe it is," Mary said slowly, a certain wonder in her voice. "He hasn't asked me or anything, but I think I'll say yes if he does. The only thing I don't know about yet is how he feels about the USA."

"Would you let that stand between the two of you if you really love each other?" her mother asked.

"I don't think I could *really* love anybody who sucks up to the Americans," Mary answered. "I just couldn't stand it. So I'll have to find out about that. Then I'll make up my mind."

Maude McGregor sighed. "All right, dear. I'm not going to try to tell you any different. You're old enough to know your own mind. But I am going to tell you this: I'm afraid you won't have too many chances, so you'd be smart to think twice before you waste any of them."

"I never expected to have any," Mary said. "We'll see what happens, that's all. I'm going out to the barn now. I want to give the cow a bottle of that drench we got from the vet."

"I don't know how much good it will do," her mother said.

"Neither do I." Mary shrugged. "But it won't do any good if the cow doesn't drink it, so I'd better try."

The trick in getting medicine into a cow, she knew, was making sure she thrust the bottle almost down its throat. Otherwise, the drench would slop out the other side of the beast's mouth. It probably tasted nasty—it stank of ammonia, and she wouldn't have wanted to drink it herself. She poured it down the cow, though, and had the satisfaction of pulling the empty bottle from the beast's mouth and seeing only a few drops on the dirt and straw in the stall.

However satisfied Mary was, the cow was anything but. It drank from the trough, no doubt to get rid of the taste of the drench. Mary left the stall. She paused and sat down by the old wagon wheel. She hadn't given up. She didn't intend to give up. She still burned to pay back the Yanks—and the Canadians who collaborated with them.

"I'll take care of it, Father," she whispered. "Don't you worry about a thing. I'll take care of it."

And what would Mort Pomeroy think of that? He hadn't run away from her when he found out she was Arthur McGregor's daughter. That surely meant he had some interest in her—and that he liked the Yanks none too well. What else could it possibly mean?

Cold as Manitoba winter, she answered her silent rhetorical question. *It could mean he's head over heels for you and doesn't care about politics one way or the other—or, if he does care, he'll forget about that for the time being because he's head over heels for you.*

Or—colder yet—it could mean he's really a collaborator himself, but he's pretending not to be so he can trap you. Mary shook her head. It wasn't so much that she believed Mort incapable of such an outrage, though she did. It was much more that she didn't think the Yanks could be interested in her. Her father, after all, was almost nine years dead. She'd been a girl when he blew himself up. Since then, she hadn't done anything overt against the Americans. Oh, they were bound to know she didn't love them. But if they got rid of every Canadian who didn't love them, this would be a wide and ever so empty land.

She took her weekly bath earlier than usual that Saturday, and dressed in her best calico. Her mother smiled. "What time is Mort coming for you?" she asked.

"Between six and six-thirty," Mary answered. "Do I look all right?" She anxiously patted at her hair.

"You look wonderful," her mother answered. "I'm sure you'll have a good time. Talking pictures! Who would have thought of such a thing?"

Mary sniffed. "They've had them in the USA and the CSA for a couple of years now. We're only the poor relations. We have to wait our turn."

"That may be part of it, but Rosenfeld's not the big city, either," Maude McGregor said. "I'll bet they've had them in places like Winnipeg and Toronto for a while now."

With another sniff, Mary said, "Maybe." She didn't want to give the Americans the benefit of any doubt.

Mort Pomeroy pulled up in his Oldsmobile at six on the dot. Mary didn't, couldn't, hold his driving an American auto against him. After the U.S. conquest, the Canadian automobile industry no longer existed. "Hello, Mary," Mort said when she came to the door. "You look very pretty tonight. Hello, Mrs. McGregor," he added to her mother, who stood behind her.

"Hello, Mort," Maude McGregor answered gravely.

"Shall we go?" Mary didn't sound grave—she was eager.

"Have a nice time," her mother said. She didn't tack on, *Don't stay out too late,* as she had on Mort's first few visits to the farmhouse.

Riding in a motorcar was something Mary hadn't done very often before she got to know Mort Pomeroy, though she tried not to let on. It was ever so much faster and smoother than traveling by wagon. Almost before she knew it, they were back in Rosenfeld.

Mort laid down two quarters at the cinema as if he'd never had to worry about money in his life. That Mary doubted; his father might make a living from his diner, but nobody got rich running a business in Rosenfeld.

Inside the theater, he bought them a tub of popcorn and some sweet, fizzy stuff called Yankee Cola. The bubbles tickled as they went up Mary's nose. She laughed in spite of the fizzy water's name. Music blared from the screen as the newsreel started. Then there were pictures of a damaged warship that, with its flat deck and asymmetrical smokestack and superstructure, was as funny-looking as anything Mary had every imagined. "Jap treachery almost sank the USS *Remembrance,*" the announcer boomed, "but quick work by her damage-control team saved her."

On the screen, a very fair officer looked out at the audience. "We got her back to port," he said. "She'll be in action again before long, and then the enemy's going to pay."

Mary leaned toward Mort Pomeroy. "Too bad the Japs

didn't sink her," she whispered, and waited to see how he'd respond.

He nodded. He didn't make a fuss about it or get excited, but he nodded. Mary didn't think she could have stood it if he'd said he would rather see the USA win than Japan. As things were, she smiled and leaned her head on his shoulder in the dark theater and enjoyed the film. Sound did add to the story: more than it did to the newsreel, where most of it had been martial music and an announcer reading what would have been shown before in print on the screen. Hearing characters talk and sing made her feel as if she lived in New York City with them—and made her feel as if she wanted to, which was even more startling.

Afterwards, Mort drove her back toward the farmhouse. Voice elaborately casual, he said, "We could stop for a little while."

There were only the two of them, and the motorcar, and the vast Canadian prairie. Who would know if they did stop for a little while? No one at all. "Yes," Mary said, also casually, "we could."

He parked on the soft shoulder and turned off the engine and the headlights. It was very quiet and very dark. They slid towards each other on the front seat. His arms went around her. They kissed for a long time. He squeezed her breasts through the thin cotton fabric of her dress. The heat that filled her had nothing to do with the warm summer evening. But when he set a hand high on her thigh and tried to slide it higher yet, she twisted away. "I'm not *that* kind of girl, Mort," she said, and hoped her breathless voice didn't give away her lie.

Evidently not. He just nodded and said, "Kiss me again, then, sweetheart, and I'll take you home." She did, happily. He fired up the Oldsmobile's engine and put the auto in gear. Off toward the farm it went. Mary didn't know when she'd been so happy. Looking at Mort Pomeroy there beside her, she was almost sorry she wasn't that kind of girl.

"Occupation duty!" Colonel Abner Dowling made the

words into a curse. "My country's at war, and what do I get? *Occupation* duty. There's no justice in the world, none at all."

"As General Custer's adjutant, sir, you were right at the heart of things during the Great War," Captain Toricelli said.

"I wanted to be at the front, not at First Army headquarters," Dowling said. That was nothing but the truth. It wasn't the whole truth, of course. The whole truth was, he would have sold his soul for seventeen cents to escape the company of General Custer, provided the Devil or anyone else had offered him the spare change for it.

And yet Custer unquestionably was a hero, a hero many times over. How did that square with the other? Dowling cast a suspicious eye in the direction of Captain Toricelli. What did Toricelli think of *him*? Some things, perhaps, were better left unknown.

"If you must do occupation duty, sir," his adjutant persisted, "there are worse places than Salt Lake City. If the Mormons rise up again with all their might, they don't just tie down men we might use fighting the Japs—"

"Not likely they could," Dowling said. "Damned few battleships and cruisers and submersibles in the Great Salt Lake."

"Er—yes, sir," Captain Toricelli said. "But the railroads still run through Utah. An uprising could keep manufactured goods from getting to the West Coast and oil from getting to the East. That would make everything much harder."

"I should say it would," Dowling agreed. "And fighting Japan will be hard enough as is. The little yellow men have been getting ready for this ever since the Great War. And what have we been doing the past twelve years? Not enough, Captain. I'm very much afraid we haven't done enough."

"Do you know what worries me more than anything else, sir?" Toricelli said.

"Tell me, Captain," Dowling urged. "I can always use something new to worry about. I may not be able to find enough things on my own."

"Er—yes," Toricelli said again; Abner Dowling in a

sportive mood disconcerted him. Gathering himself, he went on, "I'm afraid President Blackford will pick up a lot of votes because we're at war."

"Oh." Dowling scowled. That made entirely too much sense for him to like it. "I do hope you're wrong. With luck, people will see a Democrat in Powel House is the best hope we have of winning this war. We've been in two with Republicans, and we lost both of those. And we're not off to a good start with a Socialist running one. I'll trade you—do you want to know what worries *me* more than anything else?"

"Tell me, sir," Angelo Toricelli replied. He didn't actually say he *wanted* to know, but he came close enough. He was an adjutant, after all; part of his job was listening to his superior.

Dowling knew more about that side of being an adjutant than he cared to. But the shoe was on the other foot now. He didn't have to listen to General Custer's maunderings any more. And he didn't intend to maunder here. He said, "I'm afraid the Japs will take the Sandwich Islands away from us, the way we took them away from England in 1914. That would be very bad. Without the Sandwich Islands, we'd be fighting this war out of San Diego and San Francisco and Seattle. The logistics couldn't get much worse than that."

"Well, no, sir," Captain Toricelli said. "But we caught the British by surprise when the Great War broke out. I can't imagine the Japanese pulling off a surprise attack against Pearl Harbor."

"I hope not, by God," Dowling said. "Still, who would have thought they could have pulled off a sneak attack on the *Remembrance*? That was a pretty slick piece of work."

"It cost them, too," his adjutant said. "They lost their freighter and their speedboat and their submersible."

"A good thing they did," Dowling said. "If that sub could have launched a second spread of torpedoes, we'd have lost our aeroplane carrier. By everything people say, we almost lost her anyhow." He shook his head. His jowls wobbled. "As far as you can in a situation like that, we got lucky."

Toricelli nodded. "And Canada's quiet—for the time being, anyhow. And President Mitchel's keeping the CSA quiet, too. He can't possibly strike at us—the Confederates are no more ready for a big war than we are: less, if anything. And the *Action Française* is busy puffing out its chest and making faces at the Kaiser. So it's just us and the Japs."

"And thousands of miles of water," Dowling added.

"Yes, sir—and several thousand miles of water," Captain Toricelli agreed.

Those thousands of miles of water, of course, were the main reason Abner Dowling would almost surely stay in Utah for as long as the war lasted. The United States had needed an enormous Army to take on the Confederate States along the land frontier the two American republics shared—had needed it, got it, and won with it. But what good was an enormous Army out in the Pacific, where most of the islands were small and where the only way to get to them was by ship? None Dowling could see.

He surged to his feet, saying, "I'm going to take a bit of a constitutional." Every doctor he'd ever seen told him he'd be better off if he lost weight. Trouble was, he had no great interest in losing it. He'd always been heavy. He felt good. And he liked nothing in the whole wide world better than eating.

By the time he got to the entrance to Army headquarters in Salt Lake City, a squad of armed guards waited to escort him on his stroll: his adjutant must have telephoned ahead. Dowling fumed a little; he didn't want to go for a walk surrounded by soldiers. But he could hardly claim he didn't need guards, not after he'd been in General Pershing's office when that still uncaught assassin gunned down the military governor of Utah.

If anybody in a third-story window had a rifle, or maybe just a grenade, all the guards wouldn't do him a hell of a lot of good. He knew that—knew it and refused to dwell on it. "Let's go, boys," he said.

"Yes, sir," they chorused. The privates among them were young men, conscripts. The sergeant who led the squad was in his thirties, a Great War veteran with ribbons for the Purple Heart and the Bronze Star among the fruit salad on his chest.

The wind blew out of the west. It tasted of alkali. Dowling thought tumbleweeds should have been blowing down dusty streets with a wind like that. The streets in Salt Lake City weren't dusty, though. They were well paved. Everything in the city—with the inevitable exception of the ruins of the Temple and Tabernacle—was shiny and new. Everything from before the Great War had been knocked flat during the Mormon uprising.

Sea gulls spiraled overhead. Seeing them always bemused Dowling. Staying within the borders of the United States, you couldn't get much farther from the sea than Salt Lake City. The gulls didn't care. They ate bugs and garbage and anything else they could scrounge. Farmers liked them. Dowling pulled down his hat, hoping the gulls wouldn't make any untoward bombing runs.

He strolled past the sandbagged perimeter around the headquarters. Soldiers in machine-gun nests saluted as he went by. He returned the salutes. Leaving headquarters wasn't so hard. To return, he knew he'd have to show his identification. The Mormons hadn't tried anything lately. That didn't mean they wouldn't.

People on the street looked like ... people. Women tugged at their skirts to keep them from flipping up in the breeze. Boys in short pants ran and shouted. A long line of men waited patiently in front of a soup kitchen. Dowling could have seen the like in any medium-sized city in the USA. And yet ...

Nobody said anything to him. He hadn't expected anyone would, not with soldiers tramping along beside him with bayonets glittering on their Springfields. No one even gave him a dirty look. But he still had the feeling of being in the middle of a deep freeze. The locals hated him, and they'd go right on hating him, too.

After a bit, he noticed one difference between Salt Lake City and other medium-sized towns in the USA. No election posters shouted from walls and fences. No billboards praised Hosea Blackford and Calvin Coolidge. Being under martial law, Utah didn't enjoy the franchise. Lawsuits to let the locals vote had gone all the way to the Supreme Court—and had been rejected every time. Ever since the War of Secession, the Supreme Court had taken a much friendlier line toward the federal government's authority than toward any competing principle.

And it's paid off, by God, Dowling thought. *We finally licked the damned Confederates. We're the strongest country in America. We're one of the two or three strongest countries in the world. We did what we had to do.*

He turned a corner . . . turned it and frowned. Half a dozen posters were plastered on a wall there: simple, wordless things showing a gold-and-black bee on a white background. The bee, symbol of industry, was also the symbol of Deseret, the name the Mormons had given to the would-be state the U.S. Army crushed.

Dowling turned to the sergeant who headed the bodyguards. "Note this address," he said. "If those posters aren't down tomorrow, we'll have to fine the property owner."

"Yes, sir," the sergeant said crisply.

Martial law meant no antigovernment propaganda. The Mormons and the government hadn't liked or trusted each other since the 1850s. They'd despised each other since the 1880s, and hated each other since 1915. That didn't look like changing any time soon. The government—and the Army—held the whip hand. If the posters didn't come down, the man on whose property they were displayed would be reckoned disloyal, and would have to pay for that disloyalty.

Of course he's disloyal, Dowling thought. *The only people in Utah who aren't disloyal are the ones who aren't Mormons—and we can't trust all of them, either. The Army didn't stop to ask a whole lot of questions about who was who back in 1915. We landed on everybody with both feet. So some of the gentiles haven't got any use for us, either. Well, too bad for them.*

As he walked down the block, he saw more bee posters. He nodded to the sergeant, who took down more addresses. One man was already out in front of his house with a bucket of hot water and a scraper, taking down the posters on his front fence. Dowling nodded to the noncom again, this time in a different way. That address didn't get taken.

But when Dowling asked the man scraping away at the posters if he knew who'd put them up, the fellow just shook his head. "Didn't see a thing," he answered.

He likely would have said the same thing if he'd given cups of coffee to the subversives who'd put the posters on his fence—not that pious Mormons would have either offered or accepted coffee. Even the locals who outwardly cooperated with U.S. authority weren't reliable, or anything close to it.

With a sigh, Abner Dowling went on his way. He wasn't in the front lines against the Japanese. He probably never would be. But whenever he went out into Salt Lake City, he got reminded he was at war.

"No, Mister—uh—Martin. Sorry, sir." The clerk in the hiring office shook her head. "We aren't looking for anyone right now. Good luck somewhere else."

"Thanks," Chester Martin said savagely. The clerk blushed and ran a sheet of paper into her typewriter so she wouldn't have to look at him.

Jamming the brim of his cloth cap down almost to his eyes, Martin stalked out of the office. He didn't even slam the door behind him. He might come back to this steel mill again, and he didn't want them remembering him the wrong way.

He wanted work. He wanted it so bad, he could taste it. But wanting and having weren't the same. Somewhere around one man in four in Toledo was out of a job. It was the same all over the country.

He hadn't really expected to find work here, but he had to keep going through the motions. He'd been to every steel mill in town at least four times, with never the trace of a nibble. He'd been other places, too. He'd been to every kind of outfit that might need a strong back and a set of muscles. He'd had just as much luck at the plate-glass and cut-glass works, at the docks, at the grain mills, and even at the clover-seed market as he had in his proper line of work. Zero equaled zero. He didn't remember much of what he'd learned in school, but that was pretty obvious.

A man in a colorless cloth cap shabbier than his own came up to him and held out a hand. Voice a sour whine, the man said, "Got a dime you can spare, pal?"

Chester shook his head. "I don't have a job, either."

The other man eyed him—here, plainly, was another fellow who'd lost his job early in the collapse. "You haven't been out of work all that long," he said. "You still think you'll get one pretty soon." The day was hot and muggy, but his laugh might have come from the middle of winter.

"I have to," Martin said simply.

"That's what I said," the other unemployed man replied. "That's just what I said. After a while, though, you find a Blackfordburgh isn't such a bad place. You just wait, buddy. You'll see." He tipped his shabby cap and walked on.

With a shudder as if a goose had walked over his grave, Martin went on his way, too. He and Rita were still hanging on to their apartment, thanks to money borrowed from his folks. But he didn't know how long his father and mother would be able to go on helping them. If his father lost *his* job . . . Chester didn't even want to think about that. How could he help it, though, with so many men pounding the pavement looking for work? *Guys just like me,* he thought as his own feet slapped up and down, up and down, on the sidewalk.

He had a long walk home. He didn't care. A long walk beat paying a nickel trolley fare. One of these days soon, though, he'd have to shell out some money to let the little old Armenian cobbler down the street repair his shoes. Walking wore on the soles as much as being out of work wore on the soul.

Somebody on a soapbox—actually, on what looked like a beer barrel—was making a speech under the statue of Remembrance across from city hall. A couple of dozen men and a handful of women listened impassively as the fellow bawled, "We've got to hang all the damn Reds! They aren't real Americans—they never have been! And the Democrats are just as bad. No, worse, by thunder!

507

They pretend they want us strong, but all they really aim to do is keep us weak! Half of 'em are in the Japs' pockets right this minute, so help me God they are!"

He paused for applause. He didn't get much. Chester Martin kept walking. He supposed it was inevitable that hard times would spawn reaction, but this fellow seemed no threat to imitate what the Freedom Party was doing in the CSA. *Just a noisy nut,* Chester thought. *It's not like we haven't got enough of those.*

VOTE SOCIALIST! posters a little farther on proclaimed. TOGETHER, WE HAVE POWER! they showed a brawny factory worker swinging a hammer under a bare electric bulb. Nowhere did they mention Hosea Blackford's name. It was as if they wanted to forget he was there while hoping he got reelected anyhow.

COOLIDGE! The Democrats' posters weren't shy about naming their man. HE'LL FIX THINGS! they promised, and showed the governor of Massachusetts as a confident-looking physician at the bedside of a wan U.S. eagle. That wasn't fair, but it was liable to be effective. And the Democrats seemed not only willing but proud to tell the world who their presidential candidate was. They even had his running mate, a native Iowan with slicked-down hair, at his side handing him a stethoscope.

Martin muttered under his breath. The depths to which the United States had fallen in the past three years and more truly made him wonder whether he'd done the right thing in turning Socialist after the Great War. It had seemed like a good idea at the time. He laughed, though it wasn't funny. For how many mistakes was that an excuse? About half the ones in the world, if he was any judge.

But it had. With the big capitalists clamping down tight on labor in the rough days right after the war, voting Socialist had seemed the only way to hold his own. And it had worked. For ten years and more, the country stayed prosperous. But when prosperity died, it died painfully.

Would the Democrats have let things get this bad? Chester pondered that as he tramped toward his apartment. He still had the letter Teddy Roosevelt had sent him after he was wounded. He'd met Roosevelt in the trenches during the war—had, in fact, jumped on the president and knocked him flat when the Confederates started shelling his position on the Roanoke front. Roosevelt hadn't forgotten him. TR's concern hadn't been based on class, as the Socialists' was. It had been personal. The Socialists sneered at such ties, saying they were like those of an old-time baron and his feudal retainers.

Maybe the Socialists were right. Chester had no reason to believe they were wrong. Right or wrong, though, they'd done none too well themselves. Maybe personal ties really did count for more than those of class.

"Damned if I know," Martin muttered. "Damned if I know anything any more, except that things are fouled up all to hell and gone."

A woman coming the other way gave him an odd look. She didn't say anything. She just kept walking. The way things were nowadays, plenty of people went around talking to themselves.

Martin opened the door to his apartment without having found any answers. He doubted anybody in the whole country had any answers. If anybody did have them, he would have been using them by now. Wouldn't he?

Rita's voice floated out of the kitchen: "Hello, honey. How did it go?"

"N.G.," Chester answered. The two slangy initials summed up the way things were in the USA these days. The United States were no good, no good at all. He went on, "They aren't hiring. Big surprise, huh?"

His wife came out of the kitchen, an apron around her waist. She gave him a hug and a kiss. "You've got to keep trying," she said. "We've both got to keep trying. Something's bound to turn up sooner or later."

"Yeah." Martin hoped his voice didn't sound too hollow. He remembered the fellow who'd tried to panhandle from him, the one who'd said he was living in the local Blackfordburgh. With a shiver, Martin made himself shove that thought down out of sight. He tried to sound bright and cheerful as he asked, "What smells good?" He meant that; something sure did. They hadn't had any meat for a few days, but the aroma said they would this evening.

"It's a beef heart." Rita did her best to sound bright and cheerful, too. "Mr. Gabrieli had 'em on special for practically nothing. I know they're tough, but if you stew 'em long enough they do get tender—well, more tender, anyhow. And I could afford it."

"All right," Chester said. "It *does* smell good." Since he'd lost his job, he'd found out about tripe and giblets and head cheese and other things he hadn't eaten before. Some of them turned out to be pretty good—giblets, for instance. He wouldn't get a taste for tripe if he lived to be a hundred. He ate it, because sometimes it was that or no meat at all. Sometimes—a lot of the time—it *was* no meat at all. Maybe the beef heart *would* prove tasty.

It proved . . . not too bad. No matter how long Rita cooked it, it remained chewy, with a faintly bitter taste. But it satisfied in ways cabbage and potatoes and noodles couldn't. "Here's hoping Mr. Gabrieli has it on special again before too long," Chester said. Rita nodded. Unspoken was the painful truth that, if even a cheap cut like beef heart wasn't on sale, they couldn't afford it.

When morning came, Martin went out looking for work again. He actually found some: hauling bricks from trucks to a construction site. It was harder work than any on a foundry floor, and didn't pay nearly so well. For a full day of it, he made two and a half dollars. But coming home with any money at all in his pocket felt wonderful—good enough to let him forget how weary he was.

And, when he set the coins and bills in front of his wife, she was delighted, too. "Will there be more tomorrow?" she asked hopefully.

"I don't know," he answered. "But you can bet I'm going to go back and find out."

He made sure he got to the construction site early. He didn't get there early enough, though. By the time he came up, a couple of hundred men already clamored for work. Toledo cops did their best to keep order. Chester had played football against one of the policemen. "How about a break, pal?" he said. "Let me slide up toward the front? I could really use the job."

The cop shook his head. "Can't do it," he said. "Everybody else here is hungry, too. Playing favorites'd be worth my neck."

He was probably right. That made Martin no less bitter. Knowing he had no chance for work there, he went off to look for it somewhere else. He had no luck, not even when he offered to help a truck driver bring crates of vegetables into a store for a quarter.

"No, thanks. I'll do it myself," the driver said. "If I give you a quarter, I lose money on the haulage." He stacked more crates—all of them with fancy labels glued to one side—on a dolly and wheeled them into the grocery. When he came out again, he said, "You that hungry?"

"Hell, yes," Martin said without hesitation. "I'd do damn near anything for a real job again."

"You ought to go to California, then," the driver said. "That's where this stuff comes from, and they grow so goddamn much out there, they're always looking for pickers and such. Weather's a damn sight better than it is here, too."

"Probably doesn't pay anything," Chester said. "If it sounds so good, why aren't you on your way yourself?"

"Believe me, buddy, I'm thinking about it," the truck driver said. "There are times when I don't want to see another snowflake as long as I live, you know what I mean?"

"Yeah," Martin admitted. "I do. But California? It's a hell of a long way, and who knows what things are really like out there?"

"Only one way to find out." The driver set more crates on the dolly. The spicy odors of oranges and lemons filled the air. They were, in their own way, better arguments than anything he could have said.

"California," Chester muttered as he went off to see what else he could scrounge in Toledo. Pickings were slim. Pickings, in fact, couldn't have been any slimmer. Would they be any better on the far side of the country? He shrugged. Maybe that was the wrong question. Maybe the right question was, how could they be worse?

Up till now, Flora Blackford had never been to the West Coast. When she got off the train in Los Angeles, she was surprised to find it was ninety degrees in the second week of October. She was even more surprised to discover that ninety-degree weather could be pleasant, not the humid hell it would have been in New York City or Philadelphia or Washington—or Dakota, for that matter.

She joined her husband on the platform at the station. President Blackford was smiling and shaking hands with well-wishers. "Four more years!" people chanted. Patriotic red-white-and-blue bunting was draped everywhere Socialist red bunting wasn't.

Vice President Hiram Johnson said, "Welcome to the Golden State, Mr. President. We're doing everything we can to make sure we deliver the goods three weeks from now."

"Thanks very much, Hiram," Hosea Blackford replied with a gracious smile. The two Socialist stalwarts stood side by side as photographers snapped pictures. Flora wondered what the captions to those pictures would say; the *Los Angeles Times* didn't love the Socialist Party.

"Your limousine is waiting, Mr. President—Mrs. Blackford." Johnson suddenly seemed to remember that Flora existed.

Escorted by police cars with wailing sirens, the limousine made its slow way from Remembrance Station to the Custer Hotel. The bright sunshine, the clear blue sky, and the palm trees made everything seem wonderful at first glance. The grinding despair of the business downturn might have been on the other side of the world, or at least on the other side of the United States.

It might have been, but it wasn't. Even in the couple of miles from the station to the hotel, Flora saw a soup kitchen, a bread line, and a lot of men in worn clothes aimlessly wandering the streets. Thanks to the mild weather, getting by without a roof over their heads was far easier in Los Angeles than in, say, Chicago.

Recognizing the president in the open motorcar, one of those men who looked to have nowhere to go shouted, "Coolidge!"

"Ignore him," Vice President Johnson said quickly.

"It's a free country," Blackford said with a smile. "He can speak up for whichever candidate he pleases. Certainly is a pretty day. I can see why so many people are coming here. We don't have Octobers like this in Dakota, believe you me we don't."

Another man, this one wearing a tweed jacket out at the elbows, pointed at the limousine and yelled, "Shame!"

This time, Hiram Johnson tried to pass off the heckling with an uneasy chuckle. Hosea Blackford said, "I have nothing to feel ashamed about. I've done everything I could from the moment this crisis began to try to repair it. I defy any citizen of either major party—or any Republican, either, for that matter—to show me anything I might have done and have not."

Flora reached out and set her hand on top of her husband's. She knew he was telling the truth. She also knew the toll the business collapse had taken on him. He'd aged cruelly in the three and a half years since taking the oath of office. She sometimes wished Coolidge had won the election in 1928. Then all of this would have come down on his head, and Hosea would have been spared the torment of fighting a disaster plainly too big for any one man to overcome.

At the Custer Hotel, a woman reporter called, "Why aren't we doing more in the war against the Japanese?"

"We're doing everything we can, Miss Clemens, I assure you," Blackford answered. "This is a war of maneuver, you must understand. It isn't a matter of huge masses slamming together, as the Great War was."

"Why weren't we ready to fight a war like that?" Ophelia Clemens persisted.

"We'll win it," he said. "That's what counts."

He and Flora managed to get to their suite without too many more questions. She tipped the swarthy porter—he spoke with a Spanish accent, and might have been born in the Empire of Mexico. As soon as the fellow left, Hosea

Blackford collapsed on the bed. "For the love of God, fix me a drink," he said.

"As soon as I find where they're hiding the liquor, I will," she said. "And I'm going to make myself one, too." She held up the whiskey bottle in triumph when she pulled it out of a cabinet. Her husband clapped his hands. The ice bucket was right out in plain sight. So were glasses. Whiskey over ice didn't take long.

"Thank you, dear." Hosea sat up and downed half his drink at a gulp. He let out a long, weary sigh, then spoke two words: "We're screwed."

"What?" Flora choked on her whiskey. She hoped she'd heard wrong. She hoped so, but she didn't think so. "What did you say?" she asked, on the off chance she really had been wrong.

"I said, we're screwed," the president of the United States replied. "Calvin Coolidge is going to mop the floor with me. Calvin goddamn Coolidge." He spoke in sour, disgusted wonder. "Half the time, no one's even sure if he has a pulse, and he's going to clean my clock. Isn't this a swell old world?" He finished the drink and held out the glass. "Make me another one, will you?"

"You've got a speech in a couple of hours, you know," Flora warned.

"Yes, and I'll be all right," her husband said. "Not that it would make a dime's worth of difference if I strode in there drunk as a lord. How could things be any worse than they are already?"

He'd never shown despair till that moment. He hadn't had much hope, but he'd always put the best face he could on it. No more. As Flora poured whiskey into the glass, she said, "You can still turn things around."

"Fat chance," he said. "I couldn't win this one if they caught Coolidge *in flagrante delicto* with a chorus girl. Probably not even if they caught him *in flagrante* with a chorus *boy*, for heaven's sake. Blackfordburghs." He spat the name out in disgust. "How can I win when my name's gone into the dictionary as the definition for everything that's wrong with the whole country?"

"It's not fair," Flora insisted. "It's not right." She

sipped her own drink. The whiskey burned on the way down, but not nearly so much as her husband's acceptance of defeat.

When she was a little girl, she'd watched her grandmother die. Everyone had known the old woman was going to go, but nobody'd said a word. Up till now, the Socialists' presidential campaign had been like that. In public, she supposed it still would be. But she could see her husband had told the truth, no matter how little she liked it.

Hosea Blackford said, "We knew it was going to happen if I couldn't turn things around. I did everything I knew how to do—everything Congress would let me do—and none of it worked. Now they're going to give the Democrats a chance." He took a big swig from the new drink. "Hell, if I'd lost my job and my house, I wouldn't vote Socialist, either."

"It'll only be worse under the Democrats," Flora said.

"But people don't know that. They don't believe it. They don't see how it *could* be worse. They only see that it's bad now, and that there was a Socialist administration while it got this way. I'm the scapegoat."

"You did everything you could do. You did everything anybody could do," Flora said. "If they don't see that, they're fools."

"It wasn't enough," her husband answered. "They don't have any trouble seeing that. And so—" He finished the drink at a gulp. "And so, sweetheart, I'm going to be a one-term president." He laughed. "In a way, it's liberating, you know what I mean? For the rest of the campaign I can say whatever I please. It won't make any difference anyhow."

Before very long, an aide knocked on the door and said, "We're ready to take you to your speaking engagement, Mr. President, ma'am."

"We're ready," Blackford declared. Flora anxiously studied him, but he looked and sounded fine as he went to the door. More than a little relieved, she followed him out to the limousine.

He spoke at the University of Southern California, just north of Agricultural Park. The USA had touted the park and the football stadium there as a venue for the 1928 Olympic Games, but had lost out to Kaiser Wilhelm's Berlin. People were talking about another bid in 1936, but the Confederates were also trumpeting the possibility of holding the Games in Richmond that year. The international decision would come in 1933.

President Blackford got a warm welcome on the university campus. The Socialist Party still attracted plenty of students, though Flora wondered how many of them were twenty-one. A handful of signs saying COOLIDGE! waved as the limousine went by. "Reactionaries," Flora muttered.

Friendly applause greeted the president when he strode into the lecture hall where he would speak. A young man did shout Coolidge's name, but guards hustled him from the hall. The Democrats didn't try in any organized way to disrupt Blackford's address. *They probably don't think they need to bother,* Flora thought bitterly. *They're probably right, too. My own husband doesn't think they need to bother, either.*

Behind the podium, Hosea Blackford waited for the applause to die away. "We've done a lot for the country the past twelve years," he said. "The Democrats will say we've done a lot *to* the country the past twelve years, but that's because they're part of the problem, not part of the solution. If they hadn't played obstructionist games in Congress, we've have an old-age pension in place today. We'd have stronger minimum-wage laws. We'd have stronger legal support for the proletariat against their fat-cat capitalist oppressors. We would, but we don't. The Democrats are glad we don't. We Socialists wish we did. That's the difference between the two parties, right there. It's as plain as the nose on your face. If you want the proletariat to advance, vote Socialist. If you don't, vote for Calvin Coolidge. It's really just as simple as that, friends."

He got another round of applause. Sitting in the front row, Flora clapped till her palms were sore. Not all the Coolidge backers had left the hall, though. Two or three of them raised a chant: "Bread lines! Blackfordburghs! Bread lines! Blackfordburghs!"

Hosea Blackford met that head on. "Yes, times are

hard," he said. "You know it, I know it, the whole country knows it. But answer me this: if my opponent had been elected in 1928, wouldn't we be talking about Coolidgevilles today? The Democrats would not have made things better. In my considered opinion, they would have made things worse."

"That's right!" Flora shouted. People in the hall gave her husband a warm hand. The only trouble was, making political speeches to an already friendly crowd was like preaching to the choir. These people (except for that handful of noisy Democrats) hadn't turned out to disagree with the president. And his words weren't likely to sway anybody who'd already decided to vote against him. Nothing was. Flora knew as much, even if she hated the knowledge.

Her husband pounded away at the Democrats, at Coolidge, at Coolidge's engineer of a running mate. He got round after round of applause. By the noise in the hall, he would have been swept back into office.

But then, just as Flora's spirits rose and even Hosea Blackford, buoyed by the reception, looked as if he too felt he wasn't just going through the motions, distant explosions made people sit up and look around and ask one another what the noise was. Then, suddenly, some of the explosions weren't so distant. They rattled the windows in the hall. Through them, Flora thought she heard aeroplane engines overhead.

She frowned. That was crazy, to say nothing of impossible . . . wasn't it? She looked up at her husband. No—she looked up at the president of the United States. "I don't know what's going on, my friends," he told the crowd, "but I think we ought to sit tight here till we find out."

He got his answer sooner than he expected. A man bleeding from a scalp wound burst into the hall and shouted, "The Japs! The goddamn Japs are bombing Los Angeles!" As if to underscore his words, a cannon somewhere in the distance began shooting at the aeroplanes. Flora wondered if it had any chance at all of bringing them down. She had her doubts.

The crowd, the crowd that had been so warm, so full of support, cried out in horror and dismay. A guard tapped Flora on the shoulder. "Come with me, ma'am," he said. "We're going to get the president and you out of here. If the roof comes down . . ."

Helplessly, she went with him. He and his comrades hustled the Blackfords into the limousine and drove off as fast as they could go. As they zoomed away from the University of Southern California, Flora saw fires flickering in front of the huts and tents of a huge Blackfordburgh in Agricultural Park. And she saw other fires burning farther away, fires Japanese bombs must have set. She put her face in her hands and began to cry. Now, for certain, there was no hope at all.

XVI

Colonel Irving Morrell kissed his wife good-bye and headed in to the U.S. Army base at Kamloops. "Election Day at last," he said. "It can't come any later than this, but it's finally here. November the eighth, 1932—time we throw the rascals out." He checked himself and sighed. "They aren't even rascals. I've met enough of them—I know they aren't. But they aren't what we need, either."

"I should say not!" Indignation filled Agnes' voice. "After what they let the . . . Japs do to Los Angeles . . ." By the pause there, she'd almost added some pungent modifier to the enemy's name.

"That was a nice piece of work. We haven't been so humiliated since the end of the Second Mexican War, more than fifty years ago now. It was just a pinprick, but what a pinprick!" Morrell reluctantly gave credit to a very sharp operation. "Two aeroplane carriers, a tanker to keep 'em fueled—and one great big embarrassment for the USA. They got away clean as a whistle, too, except for the one aeroplane we shot down and the two that collided with each other over the beach."

"Disgraceful." Agnes was, if anything, more militant than Morrell himself.

"Well, if President Blackford's goose wasn't cooked before L.A., Hirohito's boys put it in the oven and turned up the fire," he said.

"That's true." His wife brightened. "Maybe some good

will come of it after all, then. Calvin Coolidge wouldn't let himself get caught napping like that."

"I hope not," Morrell said, though he didn't know what the governor of Massachusetts could have ordered that President Blackford hadn't. He kissed Agnes again. As far as he was concerned, that was always worth doing. "I've got to go. I wish I could do something more useful than guarding a Canadian town that isn't likely to rise up, but that's what they say they need me for, so that's what I'll do."

"If they ordered you to do something else, you'd do that, too," Agnes said. "And you'd do a bang-up job at it, too, whatever it happened to be."

"Thanks, sweetie." Morrell would have been happy to stay there and listen to his wife say nice things about him. Instead, he left.

Snow had fallen the week before, but it was gone now. He couldn't ski to the office. Sentries came to attention and saluted as he went past. He returned the salutes with careful courtesy.

When he got in, his adjutant said, "Sir, you have a despatch from the War Department in Philadelphia—from the General Staff, no less."

"You're kidding," Morrell said. Captain Horwitz shook his head. So did Irving Morrell, in bemusement. "What the devil do they want with me? I thought they'd long since forgotten I even existed. I hoped they had, to tell you the truth."

"I just put it on your desk, sir," Horwitz replied. "It got here about fifteen minutes ago. If you like, you can probably catch up with the courier and ask him questions."

"Let's see what the order is first," Morrell said. "One way or another, it'll probably tell me everything I need to know."

He went into his office. As an afterthought, he closed the door behind him. That might miff his adjutant. If it did, too bad. He'd find a way to make amends later. Meanwhile, he wanted privacy. If the General Staff—specifically, if Lieutenant Colonel John Abell—was taking some more vengeance, he wanted to be able to pull himself together before he faced the world.

There lay the envelope, as Horwitz had said. Morrell approached it like a sapper approaching an unexploded bomb. It wouldn't blow up if he opened it. He had to remind himself of that, though, before he could make himself take the folded paper out of the envelope and read the typewritten order.

The more he read, the wider his eyes got. He sank down into his seat. The swivel chair creaked under his weight. When he'd neither come out nor said anything for several minutes, Captain Horwitz cautiously called, "Are you all right, sir?"

"Nine years," Morrell answered.

Horwitz opened the door. "Sir?"

"Nine years," Morrell repeated. He looked down at the order again. "Nine miserable, stinking years thrown away. Wasted. Wiped off the map. Gone."

He could have gone on cranking out synonyms for a long time, but his adjutant broke in: "I don't understand, sir."

Morrell blinked. It was all perfectly clear in his mind. He realized Horwitz hadn't read the order. Feeling foolish, he said, "They're sending me back to Fort Leavenworth, Captain."

"Oh?" For a second, that didn't register with Horwitz. But only for a moment—he was sharp as the business end of a bayonet. Then he leaned forward, like a hunting dog taking the scent. "To work on barrels, sir?"

"That's right. To work on barrels." Morrell didn't even try to hide his bitterness. "The very same project they took me off of—the very same project they closed down—almost nine years ago."

"Well . . ." His adjutant put the best face on it he could: "It's a good thing they are starting up again, wouldn't you say?"

That was true. Morrell couldn't begin to deny it. But he also couldn't help asking, "Where would we be if we hadn't stopped?"

Nine years before, they'd had a prototype of what a barrel should be. It was a machine much more agile, much less cumbersome, than the lumbering armored behemoths of the Great War. It carried its cannon in a turret that rotated 360 degrees, not in a mount with limited traverse at the front of the vehicle. It had a machine gun in the turret, too, and one at the bow, not half a dozen of them all around the machine. It took a crew of half a dozen, not a dozen and a half. It ran and shot rings around the old models.

But the prototype was powered by one truck engine. It could be, because it was made of thin mild steel, not armor plate. No one had wanted to spend the money to go any further with it. Manufacturing real barrels would undoubtedly reveal a host of flaws the prototype hadn't. For that matter, Morrell didn't even know if the prototype still existed. The way things were during the 1920s, it might have been cut up and sold for scrap metal. He wouldn't have been surprised.

Had the USA gone on building and developing barrels instead of letting them languish, it would have had the best machines in the world nowadays. As things were, the Confederates' Mexican stooges had built barrels at least as good as the prototype during the long civil war between Maximilian III and the U.S.-backed republican rebels. They hadn't only made prototypes, either. They'd had real fighting machines.

What they'd had, the CSA either had already or could have in short order. Morrell knew the same thing wasn't true—wasn't even close to true—in his own country. "Well," he said, "I've got a lot of work to do, don't I?"

"Yes, sir," Captain Horwitz said. "Congratulations, sir."

"Thanks, Ike." Morrell laughed, though it wasn't really funny. "I bet I know what finally got the Socialists off the dime."

"What's that, sir?" his adjutant asked.

"The Japs bombing Los Angeles—what else? And the sad part is, no matter what I do with barrels, even if I get it all done day after tomorrow, it won't matter much. How could it? Where are we going to use barrels fighting the Japanese?"

"Beats me, sir."

"Beats me, too." Morrell tapped the order with his fingernail. "I've got to let the base commandant know I've been transferred. And I've got to let my wife know."

"What will she think?" Horwitz asked.

"I hope she'll be pleased," Morrell answered. "We met in Leavenworth, Agnes and I. She was living in town, and I was stationed at the fort. I wonder how much it's changed since we left."

Captain Horwitz looked sly. "One thing, sir—you can leave your skis behind. No mountains in Kansas."

"Well, no," Irving Morrell agreed. "But I think I'll take 'em—they do get enough snow for cross-country skiing." He got to his feet, tucking the order into the breast pocket of his tunic. "And now I'd better tell Brigadier General Peterson he's going to have to live without me."

Brigadier General Lemuel Peterson was a lean, lantern-jawed New Englander. He said, "Congratulations, Colonel. I was wondering if you'd end up in command here when they sent me somewhere else. But you're the one who gets to go away instead, and you're actually going to do something useful."

"I hope so, anyhow," Morrell said. "If they give me twenty-nine cents for a budget and expect me to put barrels together out of railroad iron and paper clips, though . . ."

"You never can tell with those cheapskates in the War Department," Peterson said. If Morrell reported that to the powers that be, he might blight his superior's career. He intended no such thing—he agreed with Brigadier General Peterson. The commandant at Kamloops went on, "Maybe we'll see a little sense from now on, because it looks like the Democrats are going to win this election."

"Yes, sir." Colonel Morrell nodded. "Here's hoping, sir."

Lemuel Peterson could have used that against him—except few officers would have quarreled with the sentiments he expressed. "Why don't you go on home for the rest of the day?" Peterson said. "You're ordered out of here within a week—you'll be as busy as a one-armed paper hanger with hives. You should let your family know. What will your wife have to say?" As he had with his adjutant,

Morrell explained how he'd met Agnes in Kansas. Peterson nodded. "That's a point for you. Go on, then. Do you have a wireless set?"

"Yes, sir," Morrell answered. "One more thing to pack."

"True, but that's not what I was thinking of," Brigadier General Peterson said. "You can listen to election returns tonight."

"Oh." Morrell nodded. "Yes, sir. We will do that, I expect."

Agnes exclaimed in surprise when he showed up at the front door. She exclaimed in delight when he told her about the order. "I don't care about Kansas one way or the other," she said, "but this is wonderful. You'll be doing something important again, not just makework."

"I know." He kissed her. "That's what I'm really looking forward to." He kissed her again. "And I knew you'd understand."

"I've got a couple of steaks in the icebox, and some good Canadian beer, too." Agnes raised an eyebrow. "After that, who knows what might happen?"

"The wench grows bold." He patted her on the bottom. "Good. I like it."

What happened after dinner was that he played with Mildred on the living-room floor while the wireless blared out endless streams of numbers. Every so often, his little girl would complain because his mind wasn't fully on their game. "You're listening to that silly stuff," she said.

"You're right," he said. "I'm sorry." He was sorry to disrupt the game. He wasn't sorry, not in the least, about what he was hearing. What everyone had thought would happen was happening: Calvin Coolidge was trouncing Hosea Blackford. Even as he listened, Coolidge's lead in Ohio went up to a quarter of a million votes.

"And Coolidge is also ahead in Indiana, which last went Democratic in the election of 1908," the announcer said. Morrell clapped his hands in not quite childish glee. Mildred gave him a severe look a schoolmarm would have envied. He apologized again.

His daughter eventually went to bed. Morrell and

Agnes stayed up a while longer, to let her fall asleep and to hear some more returns. Coolidge kept capturing state after state. By the time they went to bed, too, they had a lot to celebrate—and they did.

Cincinnatus Driver knew a certain amount of local pride. "The new vice president, he was borned in Iowa," he said. "How 'bout that?"

His son sent him a jaundiced glance. "And he moved away as fast as he could go, too," Achilles retorted. "He moved as far as he could go, too—all the way out to California. What does that say about this place?"

"I don't know what it says, but I'll tell you what *I* say," Cincinnatus answered, giving back a jaundiced glance of his own: Achilles was getting altogether too mouthy these days. "What I say is, you can complain as much as you please, but you don't recollect enough about Kentucky to know when you's well off."

Elizabeth nodded. She used her fork to pull a clove out of her slice of beef tongue. "Your father, he right," she said, and took a bite.

At seventeen, Achilles was ready to lock horns with anybody over anything. "What do you two know about it?" he said. "Way you talk, it doesn't sound like you know anything." His own accent was ever more like a white Iowan's these days.

Cincinnatus said, "You're right." That startled Achilles; his father didn't say it very often. Cincinnatus went on, "You know *why* we talk like we do? You ever wonder 'bout that? Don't reckon so. It's on account of there weren't no schools for black folks there, on account of my ma and pa, and your mother's, too, they was slaves when they was little. Never had no chance to learn like you got here. I'm lucky I had my letters at all. You know that?"

"I better know it," Achilles said sullenly. "You go on about it all the time."

"Mebbe I do. But you better pay some attention, son. You go complainin' 'bout Iowa, you don't know when you's well off."

Achilles got up from the table even though he hadn't

finished supper. He stormed away. Amanda stared after him. She was still young enough to be convinced her parents had all the answers, not to be dedicated to proving they didn't. "Oh, my," she said softly.

"Mebbe you laid it on too thick," Elizabeth said.

"Mebbe I did," Cincinnatus answered with a shrug. "Mebbe—but I don't think so. He got to see he don't know everything there is to know jus' yet."

His wife smiled. "When you was his age, didn't you reckon you knowed everything, too, jus' like him?"

" 'Course I did," Cincinnatus said. "My pa thrashed it out o' me. I don't like hittin' a boy that size—he ain't far from a man, even if he ain't as close as he thinks. I don't like it . . . but if I got to, I got to." Deliberately, he made himself take a bite of tongue. He usually liked it; it had been a treat when he was growing up. But anger spoiled the flavor.

"You got his goat, but he got yours, too," Elizabeth said.

He started to deny it, then realized he couldn't. He let out a long sigh. "Yeah, he done did." He raised his voice: "Come on back an' eat your supper, Achilles. I won't talk no more 'bout politics if you don't." That was as far as he was willing to go.

From the long silence that followed, he wondered if it was far enough to satisfy his son. At last, though, Achilles said, "All right, Pa. That's fair enough." He returned to the table.

"Probably ain't even had time yet to get cold," Elizabeth said.

"No, Ma. It's fine." As if to prove as much, Achilles made tongue and potatoes and carrots disappear. "Mighty good," he said. "May I have some more, please?" He had manners when he remembered to use them.

"I'll get it for you," Elizabeth said. She turned to Cincinnatus as soon as she'd picked up Achilles' plate. "He sure do like his food."

"That's true." Cincinnatus wasn't sure it was a compliment, especially during hard times, but he could hardly deny it.

After supper, Achilles went off to do his homework. He'd never lost his liking for school. That pleased Cincinnatus—pleased him all the more because, even though Achilles seemed to want to disagree with everything he said, his son hadn't rejected the idea that education was a good thing.

The next morning, Cincinnatus scrambled into his Ford truck and hurried out to the railroad yards. He got there before the sun came up, but he wasn't the first man there looking for whatever hauling business he could get. These days, cargo wasn't always the only thing that traveled in boxcars. As a freight train pulled into the yard, a couple of men in tattered clothes leaped down even before it had completely stopped. They started running.

They didn't disappear quite fast enough. "Come back here, you sons of bitches!" a railway dick shouted. He had a nightstick and a .45 on his belt. Feet pounding on gravel, he lumbered after the fleeing freeloaders.

"Gotta be crazy to ride the rails like that," Cincinnatus said to the conductor with whom he was dickering over the price of hauling a load of office furniture to the State Capitol.

"Gotta be desperate, anyway," the conductor answered. "Why the hell anybody who was ridin' would want to get off in Des Moines . . ." He shrugged. "I don't know about crazy, but you sure gotta be stupid."

As he had with Achilles, Cincinnatus said, "This ain't a bad town, suh. Beats Covington, Kentucky, all hollow, and that's the truth."

"Well, sure, if that's what you're comparing it to," the other man said with a laugh. "But you run it up against Los Angeles or San Francisco or Portland or Seattle or Denver or Albuquerque or . . . You get the idea what I'm saying, buddy? I've seen all them places. I know what I'm talking about."

Cincinnatus knew his standards of comparison were limited. He was familiar with Des Moines, and with Covington, and with very little else. He knew Cincinnati a little, as it lay right across the Ohio from Covington. But San Francisco might have been on the far side of the moon, for all he knew of it. The newspaper had talked about building a bridge across the Golden Gate one day. That didn't mean much to Cincinnatus, either. He knew rivers, and bridges over rivers. The Pacific Ocean? He'd never even seen a lake—not a big one, anyhow.

He got back to the business at hand: "I may not know nothin' 'bout them places, Mistuh Gideon, but I knows haulin', and I knows I got to have another dollar to make this here trip worthwhile."

He ended up with another four bits. That was less than he'd hoped for, more than enough to make the journey worth his while. He stacked desks and swivel chairs and oak file cabinets in the back of the Ford till it wouldn't hold any more and the springs wouldn't bear much more. For good measure, he squeezed two more swivel chairs into the cabin with him.

The conductor nodded approval. "One thing I always got to give you, Cincinnatus—you work like a bastard."

"Thank you kindly." To Cincinnatus, that was high praise.

Getting to the Capitol took only a few minutes; it lay not far south of the railroad yards—like them, on the east side of the Des Moines River, across the river from Cincinnatus' apartment building. The gilded dome atop the ornate building was a landmark visible all over town. For that matter, since the Iowa countryside was so flat, the dome was visible from quite a ways outside of town, too.

Men in fancy suits, bright silk neckties, and expensive homburgs— legislators, lawyers, lobbyists—climbed the stairs to the Capitol's front entrance. Times might be hard, but men of that stripe seldom suffered. They were, of course, uniformly white. Cincinnatus, with his black skin, dungarees, wool sweater, and soft cloth cap, drove past the front entrance with hardly a glance. He pulled up at the freight entrance and backed his truck up to the loading dock.

A white man in an outfit almost identical to his own came over to the truck, clipboard in hand. "How you doin', Cincinnatus?" he said.

"Not too bad, Lou." Even after most of a decade in Des Moines, calling a white man by his first name still wasn't something Cincinnatus did casually. His upbringing in Confederate Kentucky ran deep. "How's yourself?"

"Damn cold weather makes my wound ache." Lou set a hand on his haunch. "If I'd known getting shot in the ass would stick with me so long, I wouldn't've left it up there for them Confederate sons of bitches to aim at. I'd've stuck my head up instead—ain't like I got the brains to worry about gettin' 'em blown out." He pointed to the truck. "So what the hell you got for us this time?"

"Office furniture," Cincinnatus told him.

" 'Bout time that shit started gettin' here," Lou declared. "All them fancy-pants bastards in there who waste our money been bellyachin' like you wouldn't believe about how their goddamn desk drawers squeak and they can't screw their secretaries on the old swivel chairs." Lou respected nothing and nobody, least of all the elected and appointed officials of the great state of Iowa.

Cincinnatus, on the whole a straitlaced man, hadn't thought about screwing in a chair, swivel or otherwise. Now that he did, he liked the idea—provided he and Elizabeth could both be home at the same time while their children weren't, which might not prove easy to arrange. He got out of the truck with a clipboard of his own. "I got papers for you to sign off on."

Lou laughed and flourished his clipboard, which made the papers on it flutter. "Listen, pal, this here is state business. I got more papers'n you do, and you can take that to the bank. Ain't nobody in the goddamn world got more papers'n you need to do state business, unless maybe it's them cocksuckers in Philly."

Again, Cincinnatus knew nothing about the habits, sexual or bureaucratic, of Philadelphians. From other trips to the State Capitol, he did know how many papers he'd have to sign before his delivery was official. "Let's get on with it," he said resignedly, and signed and signed and signed. Lou went through the relative handful of papers on Cincinnatus' clipboard in nothing flat.

Once Cincinnatus had got to the bottom of Lou's pile

of paperwork, he asked, "What do they *do* with all these here forms?"

"Let the mice chew 'em up—what the hell you think?" Lou answered. He raised his voice to a full-throated bellow: "Ivan! Paddy! Luigi! Get your asses over here, and get this crap outa my buddy's truck! You think he's got all day?" The workmen descended on the truck. Lou pulled a flask from his hip pocket—the opposite side from his war wound. "Want a snort?"

Iowa was a dry state that took being dry very, very seriously. That didn't stop liquor from getting made there or smuggled in. Cincinnatus' experience was that it did keep *good* liquor from entering the state. The nip he took from Lou's flask did nothing to change his mind. "Do Jesus!" he said when he recovered the power of speech. "Tastes like paint thinner an' possum piss."

"I'm gonna tell that to my brother-in-law," Lou said, laughing. "He cooked up the shit."

"He don't like you in particular, or he don't like nobody?" Cincinnatus asked, still trying to get his breath back. Lou laughed again, and aimed a lazy mock punch at him. As lazily, he ducked. He tried to imagine himself sassing a white man like that back in Kentucky—tried and felt himself failing.

Lou asked, "You got the whole kit and caboodle here, or is there more of this shit back on the train?"

"There's more, plenty more. Some o' them fellers should be bringin' it any time. Soon as you get me unloaded, I'm goin' back, see if I can get me another load."

"I'll give you another slug of this stuff when you get back." Lou patted the pocket with the flask.

"Damn good reason to stay away," Cincinnatus said. Lou laughed yet again, for all the world as if he'd been joking.

Jonathan Moss wasn't used to getting shaken awake at two in the morning. "Wuzzat?" he said muzzily. He wasn't used to waking up under any circumstances without a steaming cup of coffee or three at his elbow to make the transition easier.

Laura's voice, however, turned out to do the job well enough: "Jonathan, you'd better take me to the hospital now, because the pains are only four minutes apart, and they're getting stronger."

"Jesus!" Moss sat bolt upright. "Why didn't you tell me a while ago?"

His wife shrugged. "I've watched plenty of cows and sows and ewes give birth. I know what happens, as well as you can till it happens to you. I wasn't going anywhere much. Now I am—and so we'd better get moving."

"Right," he said. They'd packed a bag for her a couple of days earlier. He had clothes draped over the chair, ready to throw on. As he got out of bed, he gave her a kiss. "Congratulations, sweetheart. You're saving us some money."

"I'm not doing it on purpose, believe me," Laura said.

"I know." The lawyerly part of Moss' mind operated automatically. "But if Junior'd waited another week and a half, it would've been 1933, and then we couldn't write him off this year's taxes."

Having doffed her long wool nightgown, Laura was putting on a long wool maternity dress. A tent would have had no more material and been no less stylish. She draped a coat over the dress; it was snowing outside. "Somehow or other, taxes aren't my biggest worry right this minute," she said, her voice as chilly as the weather.

Moss lit a cigarette and patted her on the bottom. "Really, babe? Why is that, do you think?" She did her best to make her glare withering. He did his best not to wither.

Going downstairs was another adventure. He carried the case in one hand and held his wife's hand with the other. She had to pause on the stairs while a labor pain passed. He didn't want to think about what would happen if she fell. He didn't want to, and so he didn't. He did, however, let out a loud sigh of relief after they made it to the lobby, went down a few more stairs, and reached the sidewalk.

His breath would have smoked without the cigarette. When he inhaled, the air cut like knives. In conversational tones, Laura remarked, "The auto had better start, don't you think?"

"What, you don't want to hang around waiting for a cab?" Moss said, which earned him another glare. He opened the Bucephalus' door and carefully handed her in, then flung the overnight bag onto the back seat.

He slid behind the wheel and slammed his door shut. That got him out of the icy wind. When he turned the key, he uttered something between a prayer and a curse. Past two on a cold winter night ... *Would* the engine turn over?

The starter made a grinding noise. The engine didn't start. He tried again. Still no luck. "Come on, you goddamn fucking son of a bitch," he growled, wishing for a ground-crew man to spin the prop.

Laura looked down at her swollen stomach. "Don't listen to him," she advised the baby. "Hold your hands over your ears. He's just a barbarous Yank, and he doesn't know any better."

"I don't know any better than to keep driving this miserable old rattletrap," Moss said, and twisted the key once more, with savage force.

Grind ... Grind ... Grind ... He was about to throw up his hands in despair when the engine belched like a man after three quick beers. He came down hard on the gas, hoping, hoping. . . . Another belch, and then a full-throated roar. Steam and smoke poured from the tailpipe.

"There *is* a God!" Moss shouted.

"I should hope so," Laura said, "and I doubt He's very amused at what you said a minute ago."

"Too darn bad," Moss said; now that the Bucephalus had started, he was willing to make his language less incandescent. But he didn't back down: "I wasn't very amused with Him a few minutes ago, either."

"Jonathan, I think—" What ever his wife thought was lost as another labor pain seized her. When she could speak again, she said, "I think you'd better get me to the hospital as fast as you can."

"I will," he promised. "I want to make sure the engine warms up before I put it in gear, though. If it quits on me, that would be . . . not so good." Laura nodded. They might argue about a good many things, but she wasn't going to disagree with that.

Even though the streets of Berlin were almost deserted, he drove with great care. Skidding on snow would have been bad any time. Skidding on snow while his wife was in labor was one more thing he didn't care to contemplate.

Beside him, Laura let out a sharp hiss. She couldn't say anything more for most of a minute. At last, she managed, "I won't be sorry for the ether cone or whatever it is they give you to make the pain go away."

"We're almost there," he said. Nothing in Berlin was too far from anything else. He could have driven for quite a while longer in Chicago. Of course, Chicago also boasted more hospitals than Berlin's one.

As he took Laura toward the door, another auto pulled up behind his: a flivver even more spavined than his Bucephalus. The woman who got out was as extremely pregnant as Laura. Her husband said, "They can't pick two in the afternoon to do this, eh?"

"Doesn't seem that way," Moss agreed.

Nurses took the two women off to the maternity ward. Moss and the other man stayed behind to cope with the inevitable paperwork. After they'd dotted the last *i* and crossed the last *t*, another nurse guided them to the waiting room, which boasted a fine selection of magazines from 1931. Moss sat down on a chair, the other fellow on the leatherette sofa. They both reached for cigarettes, noticed the big, red NO SMOKING! FIRE HAZARD! signs at the same time, and put their packs away with identical sighs.

"Nothing to do but wait," the other man said. He was in his mid-twenties—too young to have fought in the Great War. More and more men these days were too young to have fought in the war. Moss felt time marching on him— felt it all the more acutely because so many of his contemporaries had gone off to fight but hadn't come home again.

Nodding now, he said, "I wonder how long it'll be."

"You never can tell," his companion said. "Our first one took forever, but the second one came pretty quick."

"This *is* our first one," Moss said.

"Congratulations," the other man said.

"Thanks." Moss yawned enormously. "I wish they had a coffeepot in here." Then he looked at the NO SMOKING! FIRE HAZARD! signs again. "Well, maybe not, not unless you want cold coffee."

"I wonder why it's a fire hazard," the Canadian said.

"Ether, maybe," Moss answered, remembering what Laura had said just before they got to the hospital. He sniffed. All he smelled was a hospital odor: strong soap, disinfectant, and a faintest hint of something nasty underneath.

They waited. Moss looked at the clock. The younger Canadian man did the same. After a while, he said, "You're a Yank, aren't you?"

"That's right," Jonathan admitted, wondering if he should have tried to lie. But his accent had probably given him away. American and Canadian intonations were close, but not identical.

Another pause. Then the Canadian asked, "Is your wife a Yank, too?"

Moss laughed. "No, she's about as Canadian as can be. Her first husband was a Canadian soldier, but he didn't come back from the war."

"Oh," the younger man said, and then shrugged. "None of my business, really."

Most Americans would have kept on peppering Moss with questions. Canadians usually showed more reserve, as this one had. Of course, some Canadians still wanted to throw all the Americans in their country back south of the border once more. Moss knew his own wife was one of them. If they hadn't been lovers, if she hadn't warned him of the rebellion a few years before, that might have been worse. He might have got caught in it, too, instead of coming through unscathed.

With another yawn, he picked up a magazine. The lead article wondered how many seats in the Confederate Congress the Freedom Party would gain in the 1931 elections. Not very many, the writer predicted. "Shows how much *you* know," Moss muttered, and closed the magazine in disgust.

He shut his eyes and tried to doze. He didn't think he had a prayer. He was worrying about what would happen in the delivery room, and the chair was stiff and uncomfortable. But the next time he looked at the clock, an hour and a half had gone by. He blinked in astonishment. His companion in the waiting room had slumped onto one arm of the sofa. He snored softly.

Daybreak came late, as it always did in Canadian winter. Moss wished for coffee again, and, when his stomach growled, for breakfast. The Canadian man slept on and on. Moss slipped out to use the men's room down the hall. He disturbed the other fellow not a bit.

A nurse came in at a little past ten. "Mr. Ferguson?" she said. Moss pointed at his sleeping comrade. "Mr. Ferguson?" she said again, louder this time. The Canadian man opened his eyes. He needed a moment to figure out where he was. As he straightened, the nurse said, "Congratulations, Mr. Ferguson. You have a baby boy, and your wife is fine."

"What'll you call him?" Moss asked, sticking out his hand.

Ferguson shook it. "Bruce," he answered, "after my wife's uncle." He asked the nurse, "Can I see Elspeth now? And the baby?"

"Just for a little while. Come with me," the nurse said.

As she turned to go, Jonathan asked her, "Excuse me, but how is Mrs. Moss doing?"

"She's getting there," the nurse answered. "Some time this afternoon for her, I expect."

"This afternoon?" Moss said in dismay. The nurse only nodded and led Mr. Ferguson out of the waiting room to see his wife and his son, who hadn't waited around before coming out to see the world.

It was half past four, as a matter of fact, with night falling fast and itchy stubble rasping on Moss' cheeks and chin, before another nurse came in and said, "Mr. Moss?"

"That's me." He jumped to his feet. "Is Laura all right?"

The nurse not only nodded, she cracked a smile; he'd thought that was against hospital regulations. "Yes, she's fine. You have a little girl. Not so little, in fact—eight pounds, two ounces."

"Dorothy," Moss whispered. A boy would have been Peter. "Can I see her, uh, them?"

"Come along," the nurse said. "Your wife is still woozy from the anesthetic."

Laura didn't just look woozy; she looked drunk out of her mind. "The peaches are spoiled," she announced, fixing Jonathan with a stare that said it was his fault.

"It's all right, honey," he said, and bent down and kissed her on her sweaty forehead. "Look—we've got a daughter!" The nurse holding the baby in a pink blanket lifted her up a little so both Mosses could get a look at her. She was about the size of a cat but much less finished-looking. Her skin was as thin and prone to crumple as finest parchment, and bright, bright pink. She screwed up her face. A thin, furious yowl burst from her lips.

"She's beautiful," Laura whispered.

At first, Jonathan Moss thought that was still the ether talking. Dorothy's head was a funny shape and much too big for her body, her skin was a weird color, she made her tiny, squashed features even stranger when she cried, and the noise that filled the maternity room put him in mind of a dog with its tail stuck in a door.

Those doubts lasted a good three or four seconds. Then he took another look at his new daughter. "You're right," he said, and he was whispering, too. "She *is* beautiful. She's the most beautiful baby in the world."

Five days into a new year. Nellie Jacobs couldn't make herself care. Her husband wouldn't see the end of 1933. Hal probably wouldn't see the end of January. He might not see the end of the week, and this was Thursday. He lay in the veterans' ward of Remembrance Hospital, not far from the White House. If it weren't for his Distinguished Service Medal, they wouldn't have admitted him, for he hadn't formally been a soldier. And if it weren't for the oxygen they gave him, he would have been dead weeks before. Nellie wasn't sure they were doing him any favors by keeping him alive. But they also gave him morphine, so he wasn't in much pain.

She got dressed and went downstairs and made breakfast for herself and Clara. She'd just sent her younger daughter off to school when her older one came in. "Hello, Edna," Nellie said. "Thank you very much." She didn't like being beholden to Edna—or to anyone else—but here she had no choice.

And Edna didn't say anything but, "It's all right, Ma. Go on down to the hospital. Spend all the time you can with him. I know there's not much left. I'll mind the shop for you. It ain't like I never done it before."

Nellie couldn't resist a jab: "No handsome Confederate officers coming in nowadays."

"That's all right, too," Edna answered. "I made my catch, and I'm glad I did." After a small hesitation, she went on, "I won't say I'm not glad to get out of the house every once in a while myself. No, I won't say that."

Balked because her daughter hadn't sniped back, Nellie set a hat on her head, picked up her handbag, and said, "I'll be back before you have to go take care of Armstrong."

"Sure, Ma." Edna nodded. "Be careful when you're going down to the trolley stop, though. It's cold out there, and the sidewalks are icy. You don't want to fall."

"I'm not an old lady yet," Nellie said sharply, though she was, when she stopped to think about it, closer to sixty than fifty. Shaking her head—she didn't like thinking about that—she hurried out of the coffeehouse. The bell over the door jingled behind her.

Her breath fogged out around her as she hurried up the street. A man in an ancient ragged Army greatcoat stepped out of a doorway and whined, "Got any spare change, lady?" Nellie walked past him as if he didn't exist. He didn't bother cursing her; he must have been ignored a thousand times before. He just shrank back into the doorway and waited for someone else to come along.

Three men and a woman were waiting for the trolley when Nellie got to the stop. "Any minute now," one of the men said. He carried a dinner pail, which probably meant he had a job.

"Thank you," Nellie said—not, *Good,* or anything of the sort. She would have given anything she had not to be making this trip, the one she'd made every day she could while Hal lay dying in the hospital. How much it tormented her measured how much she'd come to love him.

Sure enough, the trolley clanged up to the corner a couple of minutes later. Nellie threw her nickel in the fare box. The car was already crowded. A middle-aged man with a scar on his cheek stood up to offer her his seat. "Here you go, ma'am," he said.

"Thank you," Nellie said again, this time in real astonishment. She couldn't remember the last time that had happened. *Who would have thought any gentlemen were left in the world?* she thought, and then, *Who would have thought there were ever any gentlemen in the world?* Except for her husband, her son-in-law, and her grandson, she still had no use for the male half of the race—and she knew her grandson was an unruly brat, even if he was blood kin. *Well, Merle can always take Armstrong to the woodshed a little more often, that's all.*

Her stop was only a few minutes away from the coffee-house. "President-elect Coolidge in Washington to meet with Cabinet picks!" a newsboy shouted, waving a paper at Nellie. She shook her head and hurried on to Remembrance Hospital.

Built after the end of the war, the hospital was an immense, brutally modern building that resembled nothing so much as a great block of granite with windows. The stairs leading up to the front entrance were too wide for Nellie to take them in one step, too narrow for her to take them in two. The hitching strides she had to make annoyed her every morning. By the expressions some of the other people going up and down those steps wore, they didn't like them, either—or maybe they had other worries of their own, as Nellie did.

The only happy people she saw coming out of the place were a young couple, the man carrying a crying baby. *Maternity wards are different,* Nellie thought as she went past them. *I bet they're the only place in a hospital where people win instead of losing.*

538

She knew the way to the veterans' ward. By now, she'd come often enough to be a regular. A nurse in the corridor nodded to her as she walked past. A couple of the nurses had even dropped in at the coffeehouse when they came off their shifts.

Two long rows of metal-framed beds, facing each other, stretched the length of the ward. Hal lay in the sixth bed on the left-hand side as Nellie came in. Just beyond him lay a younger man, a fellow about forty, whose lungs were killing him faster than Hal's. He'd been gassed in Tennessee in 1917, and had been dying by inches ever since. Nellie had never seen anyone come to visit him. He nodded to her, his lips a little bluer than they had been the day before. Like Hal, he had a rubber attachment that fit over his nose to feed him oxygen.

"Hello, darling," Hal said, his voice rasping and weak. His lungs weren't all that was troubling him, not any more. The flesh had melted from his bones over the past few months. His skull seemed to push out through the skin of his face, as if to announce the death that lay not far ahead.

"How are you feeling?" As Nellie always did, she fought to hold worry and pain from her voice. Hal didn't need her reminders to know what was happening to him.

"How am I?" He wheezed laughter. "One day closer, that's all." He paused to fight a little more air into the lungs that didn't want to hold it any more. "We're always one day closer, but usually . . . usually we don't think about it. How's Clara?"

"She's fine," Nellie said. "I'll bring her Saturday. She wants to see you, but what with school and all now that New Year's is gone. . . ."

"School is important," Hal said. "What could be more important than school?" He stopped to gather breath again. "Maybe it's better . . . she doesn't see me . . . like this. Let her . . . remember me . . . like I was when I was stronger."

"Oh, Hal." Nellie had to turn away. She didn't want her husband to see the tears stinging her eyes. All she cared about was making sure he stayed as happy and comfortable as he could till the end finally came.

A man in the row of beds facing Hal's lit a cigarette. Hal said, "Do you know what I wish?" Nellie shook her head. He lifted a bony hand and pointed with a forefinger that still showed a yellowish stain. "I wish I had one of those, that's what. They won't let me smoke . . . on account of this oxygen gear. . . . Fire, you know."

"That's terrible." Nellie rose. "I'm going to see if I can't get 'em to change their minds." As far as she was concerned, cigarettes were more important for Hal than oxygen right now. The oxygen helped keep him alive, yes, but so what? Cigarettes would make him happy as he went, for he was going to go.

Out at the nursing station, a starched woman of about Edna's age, shook her head at Nellie. "I'm sorry, Mrs. Jacobs," she said, not sounding sorry in the least, "but I can't deviate from the attending physician's instructions." Nellie might have asked her to commit an unnatural act.

"Well, who is the attending physician, and where the devil do I find him?" Nellie asked.

"His name is Dr. Baumgartner, and his office is in room 127, near the front entrance," the nurse answered reluctantly. "I don't know if he's in. Even if he is, I don't think you can get him to change his mind."

"We'll see about *that*," Nellie snapped. She hurried off to room 127 with determined strides. Dr. Baumgartner was in, writing notes on one of his patients. He was in his late thirties, and wore the ribbon for a Purple Heart. Above his collar, the side of his neck was scarred. Nellie wondered how far down the scar ran and how bad it was. Shoving that aside, she told him what she wanted.

He heard her out, then shook his head. "I'm sorry, Mrs. Jacobs, but I don't see how I can do that. They don't call cigarettes coffin nails for nothing."

"What difference does that make?" Nellie asked bluntly. "He's dying anyhow."

"I know he is, ma'am," Baumgartner answered. "But my job is to keep him alive as long as I can and to keep him as comfortable as I can. That's what the oxygen is for."

"That's what the cigarettes are for," Nellie said: "the comfortable part, I mean."

Before Dr. Baumgartner could answer, an ambulance came clanging up to the front door of the hospital. The physician jumped to his feet and grabbed a black bag that sat on a corner of his desk. "You have to excuse me, ma'am," he said. "There might be something I can do to help there."

"We aren't done with this argument—not by a long shot we're not," Nellie said, and followed him as he hurried out of the office.

To her surprise, policemen rushed in through the entrance ahead of the men getting a stretcher out of the back of the ambulance. Some of them had drawn their pistols. Most people shrank away from them in alarm. Dr. Baumgartner eyed the pistols with the air of a man who'd known worse. "What the hell's going on?" he demanded.

"Come quick, Doc," one of the policemen told him. "Do what ever you can. He'd gotten out of the bathtub, they tell me, and he was shaving when he keeled over."

"Who's *he*?" Baumgartner asked. "And since when does an ambulance need a squad of motorcycle cops for escort?"

"Since it's got Calvin Coolidge in it, is since when," the policeman answered. "He keeled over, like I say, and nobody's been able to get a rise out of him since."

"Oh, dear God," Nellie said. Nobody paid any attention to her. The stretcher-bearers brought their burden into the hospital. Sure enough, the president-elect lay on the stretcher, his face pale and still.

Dr. Baumgartner knelt beside him. The doctor's hand found Coolidge's wrist. "He has no pulse," Baumgartner said. He peeled back an eyelid. "His pupil doesn't respond to light." He took his hand away from Coolidge's face. The president-elect stared up with one eye open, the other closed. Nellie could see what Dr. Baumgartner was going to say before he said it: "He's dead." Baumgartner's expression and voice were stunned.

"Can't you do anything for him, Doc?" a cop asked. "That's why we brung him here."

"You'd need the Lord. He can raise the dead. I can't," Dr. Baumgartner answered, still in that dazed voice. "If I'd been standing next to him the minute it happened, I don't think I could have done anything. Coronary thrombosis or a stroke, I'd say, although I can't begin to know which without an autopsy."

"Coro—what?" The policeman scratched his head. "What's that in English?"

"Heart attack," Baumgartner said patiently. "That'd be my guess. Without a postmortem, though, it's only a guess."

"What happens next?" Nellie asked. "He was president. I mean, he was going to be president. Now . . ." She looked down at the body, then quickly turned away. "Close his eye, please."

While Baumgartner did that, the policeman said, "Yeah, what the hell—'scuse me, lady—do we do now? We never had nothin' like this happen before. That damn Blackford—'scuse me again—better not get to be president on account of he finished second. That wouldn't be right, not after Cal here kicked his . . . tail."

"No, no, no. It doesn't work like that." Dr. Baumgartner shook his head. "The electoral college met yesterday, so the results are official. The vice president–elect becomes president-elect, and then he becomes president on the first of February."

"Well, that's a relief," the cop said. "Thanks, Doc."

And Nellie might have been the first one to taste the name and title the whole United States would know before the day was up: "President Herbert Hoover." She paused in thought, then slowly nodded and repeated the words. "President Herbert Hoover." She paused again. "I like the sound of it."

Along with her daughter, Mary Jane, Sylvia Enos crunched through snow to stand on the Boston Common and pay her last respects to Calvin Coolidge. George, Jr., would have come with them, too—Sylvia was sure of that—but his fishing boat was bringing in cod out on Georges Bank. For a moment, she wondered if he even knew. Then she

542

shook her head, feeling foolish. The *Whitecap* had a wireless set aboard, so he was bound to.

Like her and Mary Jane, most of the people in the square wore black. It seemed all the more somber against the snow. Up on a rickety wooden platform, a newsreel photographer swung his camera over the crowd.

"It doesn't seem fair," Sylvia said. "He wasn't an old man—he was only sixty." Mary Jane gave her an odd look. But then, Mary Jane was only twenty, and to twenty sixty was one with the Pyramids of Egypt. Sylvia knew better, and wished she didn't. She went on, "And it doesn't seem fair he died before he could be president, especially when we've been stuck with Socialists the past twelve years."

"Hoover is a Democrat, too," Mary Jane said. But then, before Sylvia could, she added, "But he's not from Massachusetts."

"He certainly isn't," Sylvia said. "Born in Iowa, then on to California . . ." She sighed. "He's from about as far from Massachusetts as he can be and stay in the USA."

"He's—" Mary Jane broke off as heads swung toward a string of black autos approaching the State House behind a phalanx of motorcycle policemen. "Here comes the funeral procession."

A hearse carrying Coolidge's mortal remains led the cortege. Behind it came an open limousine in which sat President-elect Hoover. Behind his autos were a stream of others, all full of dignitaries civilian and military. When the hearse halted, an honor guard of soldiers, sailors, and Marines lifted Coolidge's flag-draped casket from it and set the coffin on a temporary bier whose black cloth cover was half hidden by red-white-and-blue bunting.

"I wish Pa could have got a funeral," Mary Jane said suddenly. "Not a fancy one like this, but any kind of funeral at all."

"You were a little girl when the Confederates torpedoed his ship," Sylvia said. "And he was away at sea so much before that. Do you remember him at all?"

"Not very much," her daughter answered. "But I do remember one time when he was home on leave and he kept telling my brother and me to go to bed. I didn't much like that then, so I guess it stuck with me."

Sylvia's face heated despite the chilly weather. A sailor home on leave wanted his children to go to bed so he could, too—with his wife. Sylvia's own life had been empty that way since George was killed. She sighed, exhaling a cloud of fog. When she had wanted a man, poor Ernie hadn't been able to do anything about it. That seemed so horribly unfair, it made her want to cry from sheer frustration. She couldn't do that now. Instead, she lit a cigarette. It helped take the edge off what ever bothered her.

"Look." Mary Jane pointed. "Hoover's going to make a speech." Sure enough, the new president-elect get out of his limousine and, black top hat on his head, made his way towards a podium set up beside the catafalque on which Calvin Coolidge's remains rested.

Wires ran from the podium back into the State House. Microphones sprouted from it: one to amplify Hoover's words for the crowd actually there, the rest to send those words across the United States by wireless. An announcer (who also wore a somber black suit) waited behind the podium to introduce him. The man reached out and shook Hoover's hand. They spoke for a moment, too far away for the microphones to let anyone hear their words. Then the announcer stepped up to the podium and said, "Ladies and gentlemen, the new president-elect of the United States, Mr. Hoobert Heever."

Did I hear that? Sylvia wondered. Beside her, Mary Jane let out a small, startled giggle. Others rose from the crowd, too, so Sylvia supposed her ears hadn't tricked her after all.

If Herbert Hoover noticed his name being butchered, he gave no sign of it. He said, "Ladies and gentlemen, people of the United States, I would give anything I own not to stand here before you today in this capacity. I wish with all my heart that Governor Coolidge were still the president-elect, and that he, not I, would take the oath of office as president on February first of this year."

A polite round of applause followed. Sylvia joined it. She didn't see what else Hoover could say. With his round,

544

blunt-featured face and strong chin, he looked very determined—he put her in mind of a bulldog ready to sink its teeth into something and not let go no matter what.

He continued, "Since fate has thrust me into the highest office in the land, I pledge to you today that I will to the best of my ability continue the policies on which Governor Coolidge campaigned and which the American people overwhelmingly chose in the election two months ago. We shall go forward!"

More applause. Again, Sylvia clapped along with everybody else. Again, she didn't see how Hoover could say anything else, but he said what needed saying well.

"Ever since this crisis struck our country almost four years ago," he went on, "the Socialist administration has tried every quack nostrum under the sun to set things right, but not a single treatment has worked. To our sorrow, we have seen that only too clearly. Governor Coolidge campaigned on the Democrats' fundamental belief that business has seen altogether too much regulation these past twelve years and that, if left to itself, it would find its own way out of the mire in which it finds itself. I believe this with all my heart, and it will be the guiding principle of my administration."

Again, people clapped their hands. Again, Sylvia was one of those people. She had no great love of businesses; they'd treated her like dirt in the years after the war. But whatever the Socialists had done hadn't worked. The whole country could see that—the whole country had seen that. Maybe what Coolidge had proposed and what Hoover now promised would be better. Sylvia didn't see how it could be much worse.

Hoover plugged ahead with his speech: "We are currently engaged in an unfortunate war. By now, the Empire of Japan has plainly seen it cannot subvert the United States of America's hold on the territories we conquered at such cost during the Great War. Japan has also seen that we are ready to respond strongly to any challenge facing us. Any time the Japanese are ready to seek an honorable peace, I shall listen to their proposals with great attentiveness."

"What does that mean?" Mary Jane whispered.

"I don't know," Sylvia whispered back. The war had cost both sides some ships. After hitting Los Angeles, Japanese bombing aeroplanes had attacked the Sandwich Islands from carriers, but they were spotted on the way in, did little damage, and took losses from U.S. fighters based near Pearl Harbor. If neither side could hurt the other much, why go on fighting? Maybe Hoover hoped the Japs would figure that out for themselves.

The president-elect stuck out his formidable jaw. "Regardless of that, our first goal is restoring prosperity at home. Conditions are fundamentally sound. The fundamental strength of the nation's economy is unimpaired." Hoover shook his head; maybe he hadn't meant to use variants of the same word in back-to-back sentences. He gathered himself. "Thanks to the American system of rugged individualism, we shall certainly prevail over any and all obstacles.

"Governor Coolidge epitomized that system. I promise you here today that I shall do everything I can to walk in his footsteps. With God's help, we *will* triumph over adversity. And if it does not defeat us, it will make us stronger in the end. We are a great nation. The burden that has fallen on my shoulders leaves me awed and humbled. I know Governor Coolidge would have succeeded. All I can do is my best. With God's help again, that will suffice. Thank you, and may He bless the United States of America."

He stepped away from the podium and walked over to the catafalque. There, very solemnly, he took off his top hat and bowed to Coolidge's casket. The soldiers and sailors and Marines who'd borne the coffin from the hearse saluted. Hoover returned the salute; he'd done his two years as a conscript well before the turn of the century, and had been a major in engineering during the war.

The wireless announcer introduced the new governor of Massachusetts—and, incidentally, got his name right. More praise for Calvin Coolidge came forth, this time in the familiar accents of home, not Hoover's flat Midwestern speech. Sylvia listened with half an ear. Mary Jane began to fidget. When the lieutenant governor came to the podium and began saying everything for the third time, Sylvia asked, "Shall we go?" Her daughter nodded.

They began making their way toward the back edge of the crowd. It wasn't so hard as Sylvia had feared, not least because they weren't the only ones slipping away from the Boston Common. The newsreel photographer, up there on his platform, wasn't taking pictures of the crowd shrinking.

"Good day, Mrs. Enos." There stood Joe Kennedy, with his sharp-faced wife beside him. He wasn't going anywhere, not till the last speech was made. Even the way he stood was an effort to make Sylvia feel guilty about leaving.

It didn't work. He wasn't paying her now that the campaign was done. Behind them, the lieutenant governor's empty words kept blaring forth through the microphone. "Good day, Mr. Kennedy," she answered. "We've got to be getting home, and after a while everything sounds the same."

That made Rose Kennedy smile. When she did, her face lit up. She looked like a whole different person. Her husband, though, frowned. He didn't look like a different person; Sylvia had seem him frowning plenty of times. Voice stiff with disapproval, he said, "We should all take notice of the praise for Governor Coolidge. He would have made a fine president, and he would have done a lot of good for the state. Now . . ." He shrugged. "Now a lot of that will go somewhere else."

He thought like a politician. Sylvia didn't know why she was surprised. In fact, after she thought about it for a moment she wasn't surprised any more. She said, "If you'll excuse us—"

"Of course." Joe Kennedy was barely polite to her. His whole manner changed when his gaze swung to Mary Jane. "The last time I saw your daughter, Mrs. Enos, she was a little girl. She's not a little girl now."

"No, she's not," Sylvia said shortly. Kennedy was practically undressing Mary Jane with his eyes, there right in front of his wife. Didn't she notice? Didn't she care? Or had she seen it too many times before to make a fuss about it? If George had looked at another woman like that, Sylvia knew she wouldn't have kept quiet. She touched Mary Jane's arm. "Come on. We have to go."

"If there's ever anything I can do for either one of you charming ladies, don't be shy," Kennedy said.

Sylvia nodded. All she wanted to do was get away. As she and Mary Jane descended into the subway entrance, her daughter said, "He's an interesting man. I didn't think he would be, not from the way you talk about him."

"I'll tell you what he's interested in—he's interested in getting you someplace quiet and getting your knickers down," Sylvia said. "And I'll tell you something else, too: any man who'll run around *for* you will run around *on* you, any chance he gets."

Mary Jane laughed. "I wasn't going to do anything with him, Mother."

"I should hope not," Sylvia said. She and Mary Jane lined up to trade nickels for tokens for the ride back to the flat by T Wharf.

The red light in the studio went on. The engineer behind the glass pointed to Jake Featherston, as if to say he was on. He nodded and got down to business: "I'm Jake Featherston, and I'm here to tell you the truth."

All across the Confederate States, from the Atlantic to the Gulf of California, people would be leaning forward to listen to him. The wireless web knit the CSA together in a way nothing else ever had before. All the parties used the wireless these days, but he'd been doing it longer than anybody else, and he thought he did it better than anybody else. He wasn't the only one who thought so, either. By the way Whig newspapers flabbled about their party's ineffective speakers, they too knew he scored points every time he sat down in front of a microphone here.

"I'm here to tell you the truth," he repeated. "I've been trying to do that for a long time. Some of you kind folks out there didn't much want to believe me, on account of what I have to say isn't the sugar-coated pap you'll hear from the usual run of stuffed shirts in Richmond. No, it isn't sweet and it isn't pretty, but it's true.

"Up in the USA, they've got themselves a brand-new president—not the one they elected, but another Democrat just the same. Herbert Hoover." He spoke the name with sardonic relish. "He got famous up there for helping out in the big flood back in 1927. Of course, that hurt us a lot more than it did the Yankees. But even so, they voted for him up there because of the good he did. What did we do here, where it was so much worse? I'll tell you what. We voted for the people who let it louse up the country, that's what. And if that's not a judgment on us, I don't know what is. Before that, who ever had a platform that says, 'Throw the rascals *in*'?"

That made the engineer laugh, which convinced Jake it was a good line. The man was a staunch Whig. He was also a good engineer, and conscientious enough to make sure he gave his best to whoever was using the wireless. Featherston wished the Freedom Party attracted more men like that. *When we win, we will,* he thought, *and this time, by God, we're going to win.*

"They say the sky will fall if the Whigs lose an election," he went on aloud. "We've been our own country the past seventy years, and they've won every time. And I tell you something else, friends—we've paid for it. We've paid through the nose. What have they given us lately? A losing war. Two states stolen, and chunks carved out of three more. Money you took to the grocery store in a wheelbarrow. The worst flood since Noah's, with nobody doing much to clean up the mess. And now this here little— 'business turndown,' they call it." He snorted. "If business turned down any more, it'd turn dead. And they say everything'll be fine in the morning. But then the morning comes, and we're still in the middle of it.

"I say it's time to roll up our sleeves and get to work. I say it's time to build dams to keep the Mississippi from kicking us like that again. I say we can use the jobs building those dams'll give us, and I say we can use the electricity we'll get from 'em, too. I say it's time to stand on our own two feet in the world, and to weed out all the traitors who want to see us stay weak and worthless. And I say *seventy years is too long*. The Whigs have had their chance. They've

549

had it, and they fouled it up. I'm not telling you any secrets, friends. You know it, I know it, the whole country knows it. It's time to give somebody else the ball. Give it to the Freedom Party in November. Give it to us and watch us run. That's it for tonight." He had fifteen seconds left. "Remember, we won't let you down. The Whigs already have."

The engineer swiped a finger across his throat. The red light went out. By now, after going on ten years of sending his voice over the wireless web, Featherston could time a broadcast almost to the second. He gathered up his papers and left the studio. He'd be back in a week, pounding his message home. The country should have been ready to listen to him in 1927. He still thought it would have been if Grady Calkins hadn't murdered President Hampton.

"Son of a bitch had it coming," Jake muttered, but even he couldn't help adding, "Not like that, dammit."

Saul Goldman was waiting in the hallway, as usual. Featherston was glad he didn't seem to have heard those mutters. In the years since Jake started coming to the studio, the little Jew had put on weight, lost hair, and gone gray. Jake was glad time didn't show so much on his own rawboned frame and lean, harsh features. Goldman said, "Another fine broadcast, Mr. Featherston."

"Thank you kindly, Saul," Jake answered. "You've done the Party a lot of good, you know. When the day comes, you'll find we don't forget. We don't forget enemies, and we don't forget friends, either."

"That is not why I did it, you know," the wireless man said.

Jake slapped him on the back, hard enough to stagger him. "Yeah, I know, pal," he said. "You get extra points in my book for that. You don't lose any. When the time comes, how'd you like to be running all our broadcasts all over the country?"

"Do you mean all the broadcasts of the Freedom Party or all the broadcasts of the Confederate government?" Goldman asked.

"Six of one, half a dozen of the other," Jake replied.

"Before very long, we'll *be* the government, you know. And when we get our hands on it, we'll have a lot of cleaning up to do. We'll do it, too, by God."

Goldman didn't say anything. He didn't back the Freedom Party because he was wild for revenge against the USA, or because he wanted to punish the blacks who'd risen up and stabbed the Confederacy in the back. He was just relieved the Party kept quiet about Jews. Jake had never seen the need to get hot and bothered over Jews. There weren't enough of them in the CSA to matter. Negroes, now . . .

Saul Goldman had never hidden his reasons for riding along on the Freedom Party's coattails. Featherston gave him credit for that. The Jew said, "If the time comes, I'll do what I can for you."

"Swell!" Featherston staggered him again with another swat on the back. "You're a man of your word, Saul. I've seen that. And so am I. Wait till we win. Your telephone'll ring. Job'll pay good, too. You'll get rich." What more could a Jew want?

But all Goldman said was, "We'll worry about that when the time comes."

Shrugging, Jake went out to his automobile. The guards who accompanied him everywhere in public these days came to attention. His chauffeur bounced out of the motorcar and held the door open for him. Across the street, a man in an overcoat with a couple of missing buttons waved and yelled, "Freedom!"

"Freedom!" Jake called, and waved back. He ducked down into the Birmingham.

Virgil Joyner closed the door behind him and got back into the auto himself. As he settled in behind the wheel, he asked, "Straight back to Party headquarters, Sarge?"

"Yes," Jake said, and then, in the same breath, "No." He laughed at himself; he didn't usually change his mind like that. He went on, "Take me around Capitol Square first. I want to have a good, long look at the Mitcheltown there."

In the USA, they called shantytowns like this one Blackfordburghs. Featherston wondered if they would change the names of such places to Hoovervilles now that they had a new president. He doubted it. They'd been saying *Blackfordburgh* for almost four years. That was plenty of time for the word to grow roots. Here in the CSA, Burton Mitchel got the blame.

Well, by God, when I take over, nobody's going to call a shantytown Fort Featherston or any damn stupid thing like that, Jake thought. *Anybody tries it, he'll be sorry as long as he lives—and the son of a bitch won't live long.*

Joyner put the motorcar in gear. The guards piled into two more autos and followed. They didn't take any chances with Featherston's health. He wondered if the Party could win without him. Maybe—with times as hard as they were now, people were panting to throw the Whigs out on their ear. But he didn't want anybody to have to find out. He'd waited too long. Now his hour was come round at last. He intended to stay right here and enjoy it.

Huts and tents huddled in the shadows of the statues of George Washington and Albert Sidney Johnston. They would have lapped up against the Confederate Capitol, too, had a barbed-wire perimeter patrolled by soldiers not held them at bay. Men in wrinkled, colorless clothes smoked pipes and cigarettes. Women gossiped or hung up washing on lines that stretched from one makeshift dwelling place to another. Children scampered here and there. In a football game, a boy threw a forward pass. That was a Yankee innovation, but it had conquered the Confederate States.

Joyner ignored the football. "Shame and a disgrace when you've got to use wire to keep the people away from the politicians," he said. "I saw thinner belts than that when I was in the trenches."

"I know. I was thinking the same thing," Featherston said. "Well, we'll set that to rights, too. A little more than a year before the next Inauguration Day." The United States had moved up the date from March 4; the Confederate States, always more conservative, hadn't. Jake didn't care one way or the other. He had good guards. He figured he would last.

"Where now, Sarge?" the chauffeur asked him when they'd gone around the square.

"Now back to headquarters," Jake answered. "I hope Ferd's still there. I've got something I need to talk to him about." One of the reasons he hadn't wanted to go straight back was that he didn't want to talk with Ferdinand Koenig. He had to. He knew it. But he didn't want to. He'd known Koenig since 1917. The other man had backed every play he made, backed it to the hilt. Without Ferdinand Koenig, the Freedom Party probably would have been stillborn. This wasn't going to be easy.

Koenig was not only there, he was waiting in the entranceway when Featherston came in. "Good speech, Jake," he said. "It's getting ripe, isn't it? You can feel it there, ready for you to reach out and pick it."

"Yeah," Jake said. "Come on up to my office, will you? We need to chin for a few minutes."

"What's up?" Koenig sounded surprised and curious. Jake only went upstairs. He didn't want to do this in public. He didn't *want* to do it at all, but he saw the need, and need came first. Lulu still clattered away at a typewriter in the outer office. She looked surprised—and miffed—when Jake didn't explain anything to her. He knew he'd have to make it up to her later. That would be later. Now . . . Now he poured a shot for Koenig and another for himself. Ferd sipped the whiskey, lit a cigar, and asked his question again: "What's up?"

Give it to him straight, Jake thought. *Give it to him straight, then pick up the pieces.* "Made up my mind about something," he said. "When I run this summer, I'm going to put Willy Knight in the number-two slot to make sure we take Texas and some of the other states west of the Mississippi."

Ferdinand Koenig slowly turned red. "You goddamn son of a bitch," he said in a low, deadly voice. "So I'm not good enough for you all of a sudden? Is that it? I'll kick your stinking ass around the block. You don't think I can, let's go outside and find out."

"Easy, easy, easy." Featherston had known it would be bad. He hadn't known it would be this bad. He hurried on: "Vice president isn't worth a pitcher of warm spit anyhow. Let Willy-boy have it. He'll think it's great—till he figures out he hasn't really got anything. Give him the slot, if he wants it so bad. But I'll give you something that's really worth having."

"What is it?" Koenig's voice remained hard with suspicion.

"Well, now, I'll tell you." Featherston proceeded to do just that. He hadn't had such a tough audience since the early meeting that had left him master of the Party. And Ferd had been on his side then. Now he had to talk an old friend, an old comrade, around. At last, he asked, "Is it all right?"

Koenig stuck out his hand. "Yeah, Jake. It *is* all right. Don't worry about it." Featherston's clasp was full of relief.

XVII

"Here, Papa. Let me show you how it's done." Georges Galtier dug his pitchfork into a bale of hay and flung food to the livestock in the barn. When he got to the horse's stall, he said, "I don't know why you don't turn this miserable animal into glue and food for pampered poodles in Montreal."

"Tabernac!" Lucien Galtier said, and shook his head at his younger son. "I could never do that."

"What does he do but eat?" Georges persisted. "He doesn't take you into Rivière-du-Loup any more. He doesn't pull a plow. What good is he?"

"He listened to me. For years, he listened to me," Lucien answered. "Whenever I would hitch up the wagon, I would talk to him. He knows every thought I had."

"All the more reason to get rid of him," Georges said, absurd as usual. "Dead horses tell no tales." But even as he mocked the old beast, he gave it more hay than Lucien was in the habit of doing.

"With help like yours . . ." Lucien shook his head. "The trouble with you is, you think I can do nothing for myself any more."

"The trouble with *you* is, you think you can still do everything for yourself," Georges said.

"By the good God, I can!" Lucien said hotly. "I'm not sixty yet, and even sixty doesn't mean one foot in the grave." He grimaced, wishing he hadn't put it like that. Poor Marie had never seen sixty.

His son said, "Papa, you are a formidable man." Georges' praise alarmed him more than anything else he could think of. The younger Galtier continued, "Even so, will you tell me you are as formidable as you were when you were my age? Will you say that?"

"Well . . . no." Lucien wanted to say yes, but it would have been a lie. He knew it as well as Georges did—better. His joints were stiff, he got tired more easily than he had, his wind wasn't what it had been. . . .

"Even for a young man, farm work isn't easy," Georges said. "I ought to know. There are times when I wish I were still in my twenties."

Twenties! Lucien laughed at that. For him, the twenties seemed as long gone as Caesar's conquest of Gaul. He wished he were in his forties. That would no doubt have horrified Georges, who had yet to see them. Lucien said, "Thanks to you and your brother and my sons-in-law, I do not have to do everything by myself. I am not ready to walk away from the farm. Did you think I would?"

"No, not really," Georges replied. "But one day, you know, it could be that you might need to. If you think about it now, you will be readier when the time comes."

"Mauvais tabernac!" Lucien said, which summed up what he thought about that. *" 'Osti!"* he added for good measure. "I will worry about such things when the time comes, and not until then. Meanwhile, let's get this work done here—or would you rather stand around and gab? You always were a lazy one."

"Nonsense," Georges said with dignity. "I am merely . . . efficient."

"You are the most efficient I have ever seen at getting out of work," Lucien said. But, between them, they quickly finished off the rest of what needed doing.

Cold smote when they left the barn. As always, the land around Rivière-du-Loup laughed at the calendar, which insisted spring was only a couple of weeks away. Snow blanketed the ground. More danced in the air. Lucien took it altogether for granted—and then, all at once, he didn't. How would one explain something so curious to someone from, say, the Confederate state of Cuba, or the

U.S. state of California, or someplace else where it didn't snow? It wasn't like rain, which simply fell, splat. It fluttered on the breeze, it swirled, it twisted. Would a stranger who didn't know about it take your word when you described it?

"I wouldn't believe it myself," Lucien muttered, stamping up the stairs toward the kitchen door.

Georges, on his heels, asked, "Wouldn't believe what?"

"I wouldn't believe what a nosy son I have." Lucien opened the door. "But come in anyhow, and I'll see what I can find for you to eat. I know you'll waste away if I don't." Charles, his older son, was small and lean like him and Marie. Georges, somehow, had grown up a great strapping man, most of a head taller than Lucien and broad through the shoulders. His appetite—all his appetites—seemed in proportion.

He sighed as he followed Lucien out of the snow. "Every time I come in here, I keep thinking—I keep hoping—I'll see *chère Maman* at the stove, baking something good."

"I know." Lucien sighed, too. "I feel the same. But it will not happen, not this side of heaven—which means a couple of sinners like us had better mend our ways."

"This is a better reason to be good than most others I can think of," Georges said. "And what do we have?"

"Cold chicken in the icebox," Lucien answered. "Bread on the counter there—all the ladies for miles around give me bread, for they know I am no baker—and a good jug of applejack in the pantry. Even for a walking steam shovel like you, it should be enough, *n'est-ce pas?*"

"Steam shovel? I believe I've been insulted," Georges said. "Do you know, Papa, I permit only two people in all the world to insult me—you and Sophie."

"You do not need to permit your wife to insult you," Lucien said, pouring two glasses of applejack. "It will happen whether you permit it or not—of this you may be sure." He handed one glass to his younger son, then raised the other. "Your good health."

"And yours." Georges knocked back the drink. "Whew!" He whistled respectfully. "A good thing I didn't

557

have a cigarette in my mouth, or I think my lungs would have caught fire. That's strong stuff."

Lucien sipped. The applejack, like most of what he drank, didn't conform to the Republic of Quebec's tedious rules about licenses and taxes. A nearby farmer cooked it up from the harvest of his orchard. As a result, quality varied widely from one batch to the next: As Georges had said, this jug was on the potent side.

"Here," Lucien said. "Slice the bread and get some butter for it. I'll cut up the chicken. If you want it hot, I can build up the fire in the stove."

"Don't bother," Georges told him. "If the stove were electric like everything else here, so it was easy . . . But now, cold is fine."

"All right. Cold it will be, then." As Lucien got out the chicken and a knife, he felt Marie's ghost hovering there. He could almost hear her telling him he was making a clumsy botch of things, that he didn't keep the kitchen clean enough to suit her. No matter what he did, he knew he couldn't hope to match her standards. He tried as hard as he could, though. He wanted her to know he was making the effort.

Georges sighed as he dug in. "I ate a lot of suppers in this house," he said. "No matter where I live, this will always be what I think of as home."

"It is your patrimony," Lucien said simply.

"It is where I grew up," Georges said, which wasn't quite the same thing but wasn't far removed from it, either. He sighed again. "It was another time."

"When you were a boy, it was another country," Lucien said.

"I don't think about Canada much any more," Georges said. "Considering what's happened to the rest of it, we're lucky to be where we are."

"Yes. Considering." Lucien Galtier could hardly disagree with that. He poured himself some more apple brandy. "You were young when the change happened— not so hard for you to get used to it. I was a grown man. There were times when I felt torn in two, especially when the Americans treated us so badly in the first part of their occupation. I did all the small things a man can do to resist—all the small things, but none of the large. I had not the courage for that, not with six children, and four of them girls."

"And now you have an American son-in-law, and a half-American grandson," Georges said. "And what do you think of that?"

"Leonard O'Doull is a fine man. Even you will not deny he is a fine man," Lucien said, and Georges didn't. Lucien went on, "And the boy who bears my name . . . He is as fine a boy as a grandfather could want. I wish he had brothers and sisters, but that is in the hands of *le bon Dieu*."

He suspected it was in Dr. O'Doull's hands at least as much as in God's. Contraception was of course illegal in staunchly Catholic, staunchly conservative Quebec. If anyone could get around such laws, though, a doctor could. And his son-in-law, while a good Catholic, was also a man who thought his own thoughts. A priest probably would not hear everything he might have to confess.

"Well, Charles has three, Susanne has three, Denise has four, my Sophie's expecting her third, and even Jeanne is going to have her second in a few weeks," Georges said. "Lucien may lack for brothers and sisters, but he doesn't lack for cousins."

"This is good. This is all good," Galtier said. Repeating himself—was the applejack hitting so hard? Was he getting old, so he couldn't hold his liquor? Or was he getting old, so he talked too much whether he was drunk or not? He was getting old. However much he'd been at pains to deny it to Georges, he knew better than to deny it to himself.

Georges said, "Sure enough, we Galtiers will end up taking over Quebec before we're through."

"And why not?" Lucien said. "After all, someone has to. And if we don't, it's liable to be people like Bishop Pascal's—excuse me, Pascal Talon's—twins."

His son laughed. "Not all children can have such a distinguished father."

"He was always out for whatever he could get. Always," Lucien said. "He served God so he could help himself. He served the Americans so he could help himself. And if the Americans had lost, if the English-speaking Canadians and the British had won instead, he would have wormed his way back into their good graces, too."

"He certainly wormed his way into his lady friend's good graces," Georges said. "Twins!"

"That's what I said at the time," Lucien agreed. "A priest—even a bishop—is also a man. This is true, beyond a doubt. But twins are excessive."

"Excessive. There's a good word." Georges nodded. This time, he was the one who filled the glasses with apple brandy. "Tell me, Papa—do you not think it is also excessive to begin sending our young men from Quebec to help the Americans hold down the parts of Canada they occupy?"

"They have asked us to do this for a long time," Galtier said slowly. "Up till now, we have always managed to get around it."

"Now they say that, because they are fighting this war with Japan, they need our help more than ever," Georges said. "I don't see how we can get around it any more. So what do you think?"

"What I always thought. When the Americans recognized the Republic of Quebec, they didn't do it for us Quebecois. They did it for themselves. They are the big brother, the rich brother; we are the little brother, the poor relation, and we have to do what they say. That is how they see it, anyhow."

"How do *you* see it?"

Before answering, Lucien drained the glass Georges had poured for him. "How do I see? Blurrily . . . But that is not what you asked. The United States *are* very large. They *are* very rich. They *are* the ones who made us a country they say is free. But if we truly *are* free, we can tell them no if we like."

"And suppose they don't like it after that?"

"Will they go to war with us because they don't like it? I have my doubts. Whether our politicians in Quebec City have the wit to see this . . . *Malheureusement*, that is another question. We will probably end up doing what the

560

Americans want without even thinking about whether we should. What do *you* think?"

"I think you're right. I think it's too bad. And I think nobody cares what either one of us thinks," Georges answered.

Lucien reached for the jug of applejack. "I think that calls for another drink," he said.

Clarence Potter smelled trouble as soon as he walked into Whig headquarters in Charleston. The first thing he did was go over to a neat rank of bottles set against one wall and pour himself a whiskey. Thus armed, he buttonholed Braxton Donovan, who, by his red face, had started drinking quite a while before. Donovan was typical of the men in the hall: more than one whiskey, which he held well, made him look as if he'd been hit in the head with a club. A speechless lawyer was a novelty Potter had thought he would relish, but he turned out to be wrong.

"God damn it, snap out of this funk," Potter said crisply.

"Why?" Donovan answered, breathing whiskey fumes into his face. "I don't even know why I'm going through the motions. It's only March, but you can already see how the Freedom Party is going to kick our ass come November. What's the use of pretending anything different?"

"Of course those know-nothing bastards will win—if nobody stands up and tries to stop 'em," Potter said. "That's what we're here for, isn't it?"

"What can we do? What can anybody do?" Donovan said. "Who's going to vote for us, with one white man in four out of work? Christ, if I'd lost my job I wouldn't vote Whig, either."

"Yes, I believe that." Withering scorn filled Potter's voice. "You'd be out there yelling, 'Freedom!' and wondering how to spell it."

The lawyer glared. "Fuck you, Clarence."

Potter beamed. "Now you're talking!" Donovan stared at him. He nodded emphatically and repeated himself: "Now you're talking, I say. If you can get pissed off about me, you can get pissed off about the Freedom Party, too. And you'd better—if you don't, the Confederate States are going right down the drain."

But Braxton Donovan, no matter how angry at Potter he might be, couldn't or wouldn't turn that anger where it might do some good. He said, "I can deal with you. How are we supposed to deal with Featherston? Grady Calkins' way?"

"If you want to know the truth, I've heard ideas I liked less," Potter answered. "The Freedom Party without Jake Featherston is like a locomotive without a boiler. Odds are it wouldn't go anywhere, and it wouldn't take the country with it."

"Fine sort of republic you want," Donovan said. "Anybody disagrees with you, off with his head."

"Oh, rubbish," Potter said. "I've got no quarrel with the Radical Liberals. I think they're wrong, but the world wouldn't end if they got elected. And you know why, too: they play by the same rules we do. But the only thing the Freedom Party cares about when it comes to the republic is using the rules to take it over. If Featherston wins the election, look out."

"What can he do?" Donovan asked. "We've got the Constitution. If he does get in, he has to play by the rules, too."

He had a point—of sorts. It was enough of a point to make Potter draw back from more direct argument. He said, "I hope you're right," and let it go at that.

"Of course I am," Donovan said, which made Potter regret being conciliatory. The lawyer fixed himself another drink, then added, "The regular meeting's going to start in a few minutes. If you intend to fortify yourself before it does, you'd better do it now."

"God forbid I should face it sober." Potter built himself a tall one.

After the minutes and other routine business, the meeting might have been a reaction against the Freedom Party. People talked about more effective campaigning on the wireless. They talked about recruiting tough young men to protect Whig street rallies and even to try to break up the Freedom Party's. They talked about getting the Whig message out to disaffected voters.

That made Potter raise a hand. With the look of a man doing something against his better judgment, Robert E. Washburn recognized him. "Mr. Chairman, what *is* our message?" Potter asked. " 'Sorry you're out of work, and we'll see if we can do better next time'? That didn't do the Socialists up in the USA much good."

Bang! went the gavel. "Mr. Potter, you are out of order—again," Washburn said.

"Not me—I'm fine," Potter insisted. "The country's out of order. We're supposed to be trying to make it better."

"I was under the impression that was what we were doing," the chairman said. "Forgive me if I'm wrong."

"What's our message?" Potter asked for the second time. "Why should anybody vote for us? If you ask me, the only chance we've got is to make Jake Featherston look like a dangerous lunatic. That shouldn't be too hard, because the son of a bitch really *is* a dangerous lunatic. But we aren't working hard enough to make him out to be one."

Bang! went the gavel again. "I repeat, you're out of order, Mr. Potter."

"Hang on." That was Braxton Donovan. "Clarence has a point, by God. We can't campaign on what we did this past presidential term, that's for damn sure. And if we can't make ourselves look good, we'd better try to make the Freedom Party look bad. Otherwise, we are stone, cold dead."

"I'll be damned," Clarence Potter muttered. Somebody had listened to him. He wasn't used to that. Even the clients who paid him pretty decent money to find out this, that, or the other thing often ignored what he learned when it didn't gibe with what they thought they already knew.

Donovan went on, "We ought to pass that notion on to the national party in Richmond. They may not have thought of it for themselves." He made a sour face. "Who knows how well they're thinking up there these days?"

Reluctantly, Washburn nodded. "Let it be noted in the minutes," he said. He was a good man. He'd been a good man for a long time—he had to be seventy, near enough. Potter wondered if the Freedom Party had any city chairmen that old. He would have bet money against it.

As far as he was concerned, nothing else of any importance happened during the meeting. Since he hadn't expected anything at all important to happen, he left feeling ahead of the game: not easy, not for anyone who cared about the Whig Party in 1933. Maybe, just maybe, the Whigs could keep Jake Featherston out of power one more time by making him look like a raving maniac. Potter felt like Horatius at the bridge, doing everything he could to keep the enemy from breaking into the city.

He started back toward his neat little flat. Behind him, Donovan called, "Wait a second, Potter. I had an idea."

Clarence stopped. "Congratulations."

"Smarty-britches. Your pa should have walloped you more when you were little." But the lawyer spoke without heat. He went on, "You ever see Anne Colleton these days?"

"No," Potter said shortly. That he didn't still pained him. They'd got on very well; in a lot of ways, they were two of a kind. But they hadn't come close to seeing eye to eye about politics, and they both took politics too seriously to let them stay together. *So much for bedfellows, strange or otherwise,* he thought.

"Maybe you ought to try again," Donovan said. "If you can convince her that Featherston needs a straitjacket and a rubber room, you'll hurt the Freedom Party."

"I would," Potter said, "but I don't think she's likely to pay any attention to me."

"What have you got to lose?" Donovan asked. "If you haven't got the price of a long-distance telephone call, I can pay for it." He reached for his hip pocket.

"I've got it, I've got it." Potter waved for him to stop, and he did. *What have you got to lose?* It was a good question. How would he be worse off if Anne hung up on him or told him to go peddle his papers? Oh, his self-respect would take a beating, but that didn't have anything to do with the Whigs and their hopes, such as those were.

564

He nodded to Braxton Donovan. "All right, I'll take a shot at it. Don't say I never did the Party a good turn."

"Heaven forbid such a thought from ever crossing my mind." Donovan sounded pious as a preacher. Such fine phrases meant exactly nothing, as Potter knew perfectly well. Maybe Donovan would remember them, maybe he wouldn't. Potter also knew which way he would guess.

Being in the line of work he was, he had a telephone back at his flat. As he took the mouthpiece off the hook, a black excitement filled him. "Operator, I'd like to make a long-distance call, please," he said, and gave the telephone number he'd never scratched out of his address book.

"One moment, sir, while I place the call," the operator replied. "And whom shall I say is the calling party?" Potter gave her his name. The call took longer than the promised moment to complete. He listened to clicks and pops on the line and a couple of faint, almost unintelligible, conversations between operators.

Then a telephone rang. He heard that quite plainly. "Hello?" There was Anne Colleton's voice, almost as clear as if she were down the block instead of halfway across the state. Telephones had come a long way since the Great War. The operator announced the long-distance call and gave her Potter's name. "Yes, I'll speak to him," Anne said at once, and then, "How are you, Clarence? What's this all about?"

"I'm fine," he answered. "How have you been? Haven't talked to you in a while."

"No—you chose your party, and I chose mine," Anne said. "When November rolls around, we'll see who chose better."

Clarence knew then his call was hopeless. He went ahead anyway: "That's what I wanted to talk to you about. You've met Jake Featherston. You must know as well as I do, he's got a few screws loose up there. Lord knows we're sinners here in the CSA, Anne, but do we really deserve Jake for president? What ever we may have done to make God angry at us, it's not *that* bad."

Anne laughed. "What does he say that's wrong? That

we need to get back on our feet? We do. That the niggers rose up and stabbed us in the back? They did. That the War Department didn't know what was going on till way too late? It didn't. That we ought to stand up to the United States? We should. If any of that's crazy, then I'm crazy, too."

"Wherever you want to go, there are lots of ways to get there," Potter said stubbornly. As long as they were talking, he'd give it his best try even if he was sure it wasn't good enough. "Featherston's going over the rocks and through the swamp. You ask me, he's more likely to put us on our backs than on our feet."

"I didn't ask you, Clarence," Anne said. "You made this call."

"I'm trying to tell you the man's dangerous."

"I know he is—to everybody who wants to keep us down."

"No, to us," Potter insisted. "Is he going to pay the niggers back or scare them into another uprising? Wasn't one bad enough?"

"If they try it twice, they'll never try it three times." Anne sounded almost as if she looked forward to crushing another Negro revolt.

Even so, Potter went on, "If he cleans out the War Department, who goes in instead? His drinking buddies? Will they be any better?"

"How could they be any worse?" Anne returned.

"I don't know. I don't want to find out, either. And do you really want us to fight the United States again and lose?"

"No. I want us to fight those goddamn sons of bitches again and *win*," Anne said. "And so does Jake Featherston, and I think we will."

"How?" Potter demanded. "Think straight, Anne. I know you can if you want to. They're bigger than we are. They're stronger than we are. They would be even if they hadn't stolen two of our states and pieces of others. Whatever we *want* to do to them—and I don't love them, either; believe me, I don't—what chance have we got to actually *do* it?"

"We haven't got any chance if we don't try," Anne said. "Good-bye, Clarence." She hung up. Potter wondered if he ought to call her again and try to make her see reason. Slowly, he shook his head. She wouldn't do it. That seemed only too plain. With a soft curse, he set the mouthpiece back in its cradle.

Like most Confederate veterans, Jefferson Pinkard belonged to the Tin Hats. They weren't nearly so important in his life as the Freedom Party. He paid his dues every year, and that was about it. Still, when Amos Mizell, the longtime head of the Tin Hats, came to Birmingham to make a speech on a bright spring Sunday, Jeff went over to Avondale Park to hear what he had to say.

Taking the trolley to the east side of town, just past the Sloss Works, made him mutter to himself. He hadn't gone that way very often since losing his job at the steel mill. Even the air here tasted different: full of sulfur and iron. The first good lungful made him cough. The second one made him smile. He'd lived with that taste, that smell, for most of his adult life. He hadn't even known he missed it till he found it again.

He wore a clean white shirt and butternut trousers, the not-quite-uniform of the Freedom Party. Most of the people on the trolley car were men about his age, and many of them had on the same kind of outfit he did. He didn't see anybody with a bludgeon. This wasn't supposed to be that kind of meeting. You could belong to the Tin Hats without being a Freedom Party man, and some people did.

When the trolley stopped at the Sloss Works, half a dozen more men got on. He recognized two or three of them. They nodded to one another. "Good to see you," one of them said. "How are you doing?"

"Not too bad, Tony," Pinkard answered. "No, not too bad. Party found me a job after I got canned, so I'm eating. And things look mighty good when the election rolls around."

"Sure do," Tony said. "About time, too."

The trolley stopped, brakes screeching. The motorman

clanged his bell. "Avondale Park!" he said loudly. By the time men finished getting off the car, it was almost empty.

Under that warm, hopeful sun, Jeff walked toward the rostrum from which Amos Mizell would speak. Confederate flags and Tin Hat banners fluttered in the breeze. Here and there in the swelling crowd, men waved Freedom Party flags: the Confederate battle flag with colors reversed, red St. Andrew's cross on blue. Those, though, were unofficial.

Or were they? Up there on the rostrum, chatting with Mizell, stood Caleb Briggs, the head of the Freedom Party in Birmingham. The leader of the Tin Hats leaned closer to hear what Briggs had to say. Even nowadays, Briggs couldn't talk above a rasping whisper; the damnyankees had gassed him during the Great War.

Somebody yelled, "Freedom!" In an instant, the cry was deafening. Jefferson Pinkard shouted it out at the top of his lungs. The Freedom Party was the most important thing in his life these days. If it weren't for the Party, he hardly would have had a life.

Caleb Briggs grinned out at the crowd. His teeth were white and straight. A good thing, too—he was a dentist by trade. If he'd had a couple of missing choppers, he wouldn't have made much of an advertisement for his own work. He waved. The cries of, "Freedom!" redoubled.

Amos Mizell grinned and waved, too. A few people started singing "The Bonnie Blue Flag," the song the Tin Hats had taken for their own. Only a few, though—"The Bonnie Blue Flag" was hard to make out among the shouts of, "Freedom!" Mizell's grin slipped, although he kept waving. As at the rally, so across the CSA: these days, the Freedom Party spoke with a louder voice than the Tin Hats. That hadn't always been so. Had things gone a little differently, Mizell might have been standing in Jake Featherston's shoes. He had to be thinking about what might have been.

Then Caleb Briggs stepped up to the microphone. In his ruined voice, he said, "This is a Tin Hats rally, boys, not one of ours," and he started singing "The Bonnie Blue Flag." That tipped the balance. Following his lead, the Freedom Party men in the crowd sang the Tin Hats' anthem. Amos Mizell tipped his hat to Briggs. He still didn't look perfectly happy, though. The men weren't singing "The Bonnie Blue Flag" because they'd thought of it themselves, but because a Freedom Party big wig had asked them to. That had to sting.

Jeff pushed and elbowed his way toward the front of the crowd, trying to get as close to the platform as he could. A lot of other determined men were doing the same thing. He didn't get quite so close as he would have liked. Still, he was taller than most, and he could see well enough.

When the loud chorus of "The Bonnie Blue Flag" ended, Caleb Briggs walked up to the microphone again. He raised both hands in the air, asking for quiet. Little by little, he got it. "Let's give a big hello to a man who's done a lot for the cause of freedom in the Confederate States," he said, and paused to draw in a wheezing breath. He sounded as if he'd smoked a hundred packs of cigarettes all at once. "Friends, here's Mr. Amos Mizell."

Mizell towered over Briggs. He held up both hands, too. He was missing his left little finger—one more man who'd spilled his blood for the Confederate States. The fat cats had got the CSA into the war, Pinkard thought, and then they'd sat back in Richmond, miles away from the trenches, and let other people do the fighting. Well, their time was coming. His smile had nothing to do with mirth. Yes, their time was coming fast.

"We've been through it," Mizell said. "We've all been through it, and we wonder why the devil we went. By the time we were done, the Confederate States were worse off than when we started, and that's not how things were supposed to work. We were patriots. They told us we were going to teach the damnyankees another lesson. And then what happened?

"I'll tell you what, my friends. *They left us in the lurch.* We had to stand up to gas before we could give it back. We had to face barrels before we had any barrels of our own. We were fighting the USA, but we had to fight our own civil war, too, on account of they were asleep at the switch and didn't know the niggers were going to rise up and kick us in the . . . the slats. I see some ladies here."

The veterans who made up most of the audience snickered. They knew what Mizell would have said if he were, say, sitting in a saloon with a whiskey in his hand. The few women surely knew, too, but he *hadn't* said it, so their honor was satisfied.

He went on, "And then, after we did everything we could do, we lost anyway. I don't reckon we would have if the niggers had stayed and done their work, but we did. And what about the folks who sent us out to die? They kept on getting rich. They let the money go down the drain, but you didn't see them missing any meals."

"That's right," Jeff growled, and his was far from the only angry, baying voice in the crowd. He turned to a man beside him and said, "We should have strung those bastards up a long time ago."

"Oh, hell, yes," the other man said, as if the idea that anyone could disagree was unimaginable. He slammed a hand against the side of his thigh. "*Hell,* yes."

Mizell was continuing, "—no chance the Whigs will fix their own house. They've been in power too long. All they know about is hanging on to what they've already got. And the Radical Liberals?" He made a scornful gesture. "Losers. They've always been losers. They'll never be anything but losers. No. If we're going to set our own house in order, what we need is . . ." His voice trailed away. He waited expectantly.

He didn't have to wait long. The cry of, *"Freedom!"* roared from almost every throat. After that first great yell, it settled down into a steady chant: "Freedom! Freedom! Freedom!" Pinkard shouted it along with all the others, his fist pumping the air.

Amos Mizell raised his hands once more. Slowly, reluctantly, silence came. Mizell said, "That's right, friends. The Tin Hats know what this country needs. We need a new broom, a broom that will sweep all the old fools out of Richmond. We reckon the Freedom Party is the right one for the job. That's why I want all the Tin Hats in the country, regardless of whether they're registered in the Freedom Party or not, to vote for Jake Featherston. I tell you, we need to do everything we can to make that man president of the Confederate States of America. We'll throw everything we've got behind him, on account of he'll make this a country we can be proud to live in again."

He paused. "Freedom! Freedom! Freedom!" The chant rang out again. And then, a little at a time, another chant began to supplant it: "Featherston! Featherston! Featherston!" The heavy, thudding stress on the last syllable was almost hypnotic.

"Featherston! Featherston! Featherston!" Jefferson Pinkard shouted it, too. He'd been a Freedom Party man ever since the first time he heard Jake Featherston speak, not long after the war ended. He'd come this far with Jake; he wanted to go further. And now it looked as if he could, as if the whole CSA could.

As he looked around the crowd, he saw knots of men in white and butternut from whom the chant of, "Featherston!" came loudest. He smiled to himself. No, Caleb Briggs didn't miss a trick. He must have given some of the boys special instructions. The only thing that surprised Pinkard was that the local Party boss hadn't recruited *him* to help change the chant. He shrugged. Briggs did as Briggs pleased.

"Featherston! Featherston!" Mizell seemed startled to hear the Freedom Party leader's name. The cry of, "Freedom!" he'd undoubtedly expected. This? No.

Well, too bad, Jeff thought. *You back the Freedom Party, you've got to back Jake Featherston, too. No way around that, even if you wish there were.*

By his manner up there on the rostrum, maybe the head of the Tin Hats wished exactly that. No matter how he wished things had turned out, his outfit was in second place, not first. Hearing Jake's name roared in his face at his own rally had to show him he would never run first.

Caleb Briggs stepped up to the microphone. It helped his harsh near-whisper carry: "We're all in this together, friends: Freedom Party, Tin Hats, the Redemption League out West, all the people who see what's wrong and who've got what it takes to stand up and fix it. When Jake Featherston wins this fall, we all win—every single one of us, and every single group. That's what we've got to take away from this rally today. Just like we were in the trenches, we're all in this together. Only difference is, this time, by God, we're going to *win*!"

No chant rose this time, just a great roar of agreement. Jeff pumped his fist in the air again, and his was far from the only one raised high. Up on the rostrum, Briggs put a hand on Amos Mizell's shoulder. He was smaller than the man who led the Tin Hats, but still somehow had the air of a father consoling a son.

After a moment, Mizell straightened—almost to attention, as if he were back in the Army again. He went to the microphone and said, "Dr. Briggs is right. When Jake Featherston's president, we all win. And we *will* win come November!"

He got his own round of applause then. Somebody in the crowd started singing "Dixie." Maybe it was one of the men with instructions from Briggs, maybe someone who'd had a good idea on his own. Either way, in the blink of an eye everyone sang it. Along with the rest of the men and women in Avondale Park, Pinkard bawled out the words. Tears stung his eyes. *This* was what mattered, this feeling of being part of something bigger, more important, than himself.

When the last raucous chorus ended, Briggs went over to the microphone. "Remember this, folks," he said. "Remember it good. What we've got here today, the whole country gets when we win."

Only a smattering of applause answered him. No more than a handful of people understood what he was talking about. But Jefferson Pinkard was one of those few. He beat his palms together till they were red and sore. That was what he wanted—the whole country like a Freedom Party rally. What could be better? Nothing he could think of.

The way things looked, the whole country wouldn't be able to think of anything better, either. That seemed very fine indeed to Jeff.

Something tickled Anne Colleton's memory when she checked into the Excelsior Hotel in Charleston. It tickled harder when she got into her room. The tickling wasn't of the pleasant sort. After she looked around the room, she realized why. Roger Kimball had tried to rape her here, almost ten years ago now. She'd given him a knee between his legs, aimed a pistol at him, and sent him on his way. In short order, he was dead, shot by that woman from Boston.

Anne sighed. Kimball had been loyal to Jake Featherston come hell or high water. Anne was loyal to nobody but herself, not like that. She'd thought Featherston was a loser, and she'd broken her ties to the Freedom Party. That was the biggest reason she and Roger had broken up, the biggest reason she hadn't given herself to him, the biggest reason he'd tried to take her by force.

And now here she was, back in Charleston, back in the Freedom Party. She tasted the irony there. Had Roger been right all along? Anne shook her head. She didn't care to admit that, even to herself. After she'd walked away from Featherston, the country had changed. That was what had brought her back.

Still, she granted herself the luxury of another sigh. It *was* too bad. She'd never found anybody who could match Roger Kimball in bed.

A glance in the mirror on the dresser told her she probably never would. A good start on a double chin, lines on her face no powder could hide, the harshness of dye to hold gray at bay . . . She wasn't a young beauty any more. Now she had to get her way with brains, which wasn't so easy and took longer.

"What can't be cured . . ." she said, and deliberately turned away from the mirror. The only alternative to getting older was *not* getting older. The Yankees had gassed her younger brother, Jacob. They'd gassed him, and the Negroes on the Marshlands plantation had murdered him in the uprising of 1915. He'd never had a chance. She'd taken some revenge on them after the war. More still waited. She'd never disagreed with the Freedom Party about that.

She unpacked her own suitcase. Once upon a time, she'd have had a colored maid to do it for her. The last one she'd had came much too close to murdering *her* in the long aftermath of the uprising. No more.

Once everything was put away, she went downstairs. A man sitting on an overstuffed chair in the lobby, a chair whose upholstery had seen better days, got to his feet and took off his hat. "Evening, Miss Colleton!" he said. "Freedom!"

"Good evening, Mr. Henderson," Anne answered. A beat slower than she should have, she added, "Freedom!" herself. The Party greeting still struck her as foolish. But she'd made the bargain, and she had to go through with it.

"Hope you had a pleasant drive down," James Henderson said. He held out his hand. She briskly shook it. His eyes widened slightly. He hadn't expected so firm a grip. He was a few years younger than Anne—*everyone is a few years younger than I am these days,* she thought unhappily—lean as a lath, with a face so bony, it might have come off the label of an iodine bottle. He wore the ribbon for the Purple Heart on his lapel.

"It was all right," Anne said. "Some people drive for the sport of it. I drive to get where I'm going."

"Sensible," Henderson said. Men said that to her a lot these days, as they'd once said, *Beautiful.* She missed the other. This would have to do. Beauty didn't last. Brains did. She'd realized that a long time ago. She'd had brains even then, though men had done their best not to notice. Henderson went on, "Shall we eat some supper? We can talk then, and figure out where to go from there."

"All right," Anne said. Not so many years earlier, he would have wanted to go back to her room and take her to bed. Now he probably didn't. That made doing business simpler. Most of the time, she appreciated it because it did. Every once in a while, she found herself pining for days gone by.

"Hotel restaurant suit you, or would you rather go somewhere else?" Henderson was doing his best to be polite. A fair number of Freedom Party men either didn't bother or didn't know how.

574

"The hotel restaurant is fine," she answered.

She ordered crab cakes; she took advantage of Charleston seafood whenever she came down to the coast. Henderson chose fried chicken. They both ordered cocktails. The colored waiter who took their orders went back to the kitchen without writing them down; odds were he couldn't write. James Henderson's eyes followed him. "Wonder where he was in 1915, and what he did."

"He looks too young to have done anything much," Anne said. "Of course, you never can tell."

"Sure can't." Henderson scowled. He needed a visible effort to draw himself back to the business at hand. "Let's talk about Congress and the Legislature."

"Right," Anne said briskly. Henderson might be skinny enough to dive through a soda straw without hitting the sides, but he came to the point. She liked that. She went on, "We can figure that Jake Featherston is probably going to win this state."

"Doesn't mean we won't campaign for him here," Henderson said.

"No, of course not," Anne agreed. "We don't want any nasty surprises. But the rest of the ticket has to run well, too. Freedom Party Congressmen will help Jake get his laws through. The state legislators need to back us, too—and they're the ones who choose C.S. Senators. We're still weak in the Senate, because we didn't start getting a lot of people elected to state legislatures till 1929."

James Henderson nodded. He began to say something more, but the waiter came back with drinks, and then with dinner. The fellow started to give Anne the chicken; she pointed to her companion to show where it should go. "Sorry, ma'am," the colored man said. He set things right, then withdrew.

Henderson looked around to make sure he was out of earshot before resuming. "Can't trust 'em," the Freedom Party man said. Anne couldn't quarrel with him there. Henderson continued, "Anything they hear, the Rad Libs know tomorrow and the Whigs the day after."

Anne wasn't so sure about that, but didn't care to argue with it, either. All she said was, "They know they have to try to stop us any way they can. They know, but I don't think they can do it."

"Have to make sure they don't. We have to make sure any way we need to." Henderson let her draw her own pictures.

She had no trouble doing just that. "We don't want to go too far," she said. "If we do, it'll only hurt us, cost us votes. The average law-abiding Confederate has to think we're the right answer, not the wrong one. We've shot ourselves in the foot before when we pushed too hard. We need to pick our spots."

The skeletal man across the table from her nodded. "See who's really dangerous," he said, and bared a lot of teeth in a grin. "Won't be so dangerous once we run over 'em with barrels a few times."

Anne thought that was a figure of speech. She wasn't quite sure, though, and didn't care to ask. Theoretically, the armistice with the USA banned barrels from the CSA. The government had never admitted to having any—nor could it, without risking Yankee wrath. If a couple of them should suddenly clatter down a street with Freedom Party men inside . . . If that happened, Anne wouldn't have been astonished.

She said, "Looks to me like we're thinking along the same lines, Mr. Henderson . . . Do you want to get some more chicken?" He'd reduced half a bird to bones in nothing flat.

"Don't mind if I do." Henderson waved for the waiter. As the Negro took the request back to the kitchen, Henderson gave a half apologetic smile. "Always been scrawny, no matter how much I eat."

"I wish I could say that." Corsets had been out of fashion for a good many years now, but Anne was tempted to get back into one to help her remind the world she did still have a waist. She wished she could wear a corset under her jaw, too, to fight the sagging flesh there. In fact, there were such things, intended to be put on at night. Three different doctors, though, had assured her they did no good.

The waiter returned with another whole chicken leg.

Henderson devoured it. He patted his pale lips with his napkin. "Hit the spot."

"Good." Even if she envied him at the same time, Anne couldn't help liking a man who put away his food like that. She went on, "We have to hit the spot in November, too. We *have* to. If we lose this time, I don't think we'll ever get another chance."

After Grady Calkins assassinated President Hampton, after the Confederate currency stabilized when the USA eased back on reparations, the Freedom Party had sunk like a stone, and had stayed down though almost all the 1920s. If it failed again, she was sure it wouldn't revive. She couldn't stand the idea of trying to make peace with the Whigs once more. This run had to reach the top.

"Don't you worry about that, ma'am," James Henderson said. "Jake Featherston, he isn't about to lose." So, four hundred years before, a Spanish soldier seeing the might and wealth of the Inca Empire might have spoken of Pizarro. The Spaniard would have been right. Anne thought the Freedom Party man was, too, even if that *ma'am* rankled. Henderson wasn't so very much younger than she was.

She said, "It's not just Jake, remember. We want to grab with both hands."

"Think you're right," Henderson said. "Legislators, Congressmen—every place where we can win, we'll fight like the devil."

"That's right. Mayors and county commissioners and sheriffs, too. Some of those people can appoint judges, and the more judges on our side, the better. Same with sheriffs. A lot of them—and city policemen, too—have been on our side for a long time."

"Better be," Henderson said, nodding. The waiter came up with a coffeepot. After he'd filled cups for Anne and Henderson, he retreated once more. Henderson waited, poured in lots of cream and sugar, tasted, added more sugar yet, and then continued, "By the time we're done, we'll have this state sewed up tight, you bet."

"Oh, yes," Anne said softly. "And not just South

Carolina, either. By the time we're done, we'll have the whole country sewn up tight."

"That's the idea," Henderson said.

Anne wondered if Jake Featherston had thought he could come within arm's reach of ruling the Confederate States when he first joined the Freedom Party. What would he say if she asked him? And would what he said be true? Would he really recall here in 1933 what he'd thought and hoped and dreamt back in 1917? Even if he did, would he admit it? She had her doubts.

The waiter returned again. "Dessert, folks? Apple pie is mighty fine today, or we've got cherry or lemon meringue or pecan, too."

"Apple," Henderson said at once. "Slap some ice cream on top, too."

"Yes, suh." The waiter looked to Anne. "Anything for you, ma'am?"

She shook her head. "I couldn't possibly."

James Henderson could, and did. He had a second cup of coffee to go with the pie à la mode, too, and doctored it as thoroughly as he had the first. With a sigh of regret, he pushed away the empty plate. "Yeah, that hit the spot."

"If we do as well in November as you did at the supper table here, the Whigs are in even more trouble than I thought," Anne said.

He grinned. "We'll clean 'em up and wash 'em down the drain. Just what they've got coming." Anne nodded. She felt victory in the air, too.

When Scipio walked into Erasmus' fish store and café, he knew right away something was wrong. His boss looked like a man whose best friend had just died. Without preamble, Erasmus said, "I gwine shut her down, Xerxes."

"Do Jesus!" Scipio said. He'd spent a lot of time here; he'd thought the place would go on forever—or at least as long as Erasmus did, which had looked as if it might be the same thing. "Why for you do dat?" he demanded.

"You recollect how once upon a time them Freedom Party bastards come by here?" Erasmus said. "They was gonna take money from me so nothin' happen to the store."

578

"I recollects, uh-huh," Scipio said. "Then the Freedom Party go down de drain, an' dey don't come back no mo'."

"They's back." All of a sudden, Erasmus looked old. He looked beaten. And he looked afraid. "Can't rightly tell if they's the same bastards as all them years ago, but they's the same *kind* o' bastards, an' that's what counts. They say I don't pay 'em what they want, I git bad luck like you don't believe. I ain't no fool, Xerxes. You don't got to draw me no pictures. I know what that means."

"How much they want?" Scipio asked.

"Too much," his boss answered. "Too damn much. Cut my profit down to nothin'. Down to less'n nothin'. I try an' tell 'em that. Way they look at me, it's *That's your worry, nigger. We don't care, long as we gits ours.* So I's shuttin' down, like I say. Sell this place, live off what I gits. I'm an old man now. Reckon the money'll last me."

"This here's blackmail," Scipio said. "You ought to go to the *police.*"

Erasmus shook his head. "Ain't no use. It's like it was back the las' time. Some o' these fuckers, they *is* the *police.*"

Scipio had never heard the older man use an obscenity like that. "Got to be somebody kin he'p you."

"If I was white . . ." But Erasmus shook his head. "Mebbe even that don't do no good, not now. These Freedom Party buckra, it's like they got everything goin' their way, and nobody else got the nerve to stand up to 'em. They win the 'lection, they's top dogs for six years, an' everybody reckon they gwine win."

"I knows it. I's scared, and dat de trut'," Scipio said. "What kin a nigger do? Can't do nothin'. Can't even vote. Can't run, neither—ain't nowhere to run to. USA don't want nothin' to do wid we. An' if we fights—"

"We loses," Erasmus finished for him. "Dumb Reds done showed dat durin' the war. Never shoulda riz up then, on account of they shoulda knowed they lose."

I thought the same thing. I told Cassius the same thing. He wouldn't listen to me. He was sure the revolution would carry everything before it. He was sure, and he was wrong, and now he's dead. Scipio couldn't say a word of that. He had a new name here. He had a new life here. Remembering things he'd done long ago, in another state and in another state of mind ... What point to it? None he could see, especially since time-yellowed, creased wanted posters still proclaimed his other self fugitive from what South Carolina called justice.

Erasmus went on, "Sorry I got to let you go like this here. I know it ain't right. Times is hard, an' you gots young 'uns. But I can't help it, Xerxes. Can't stay in business no more. You hook on somewheres else, mebbe."

"Mebbe." Scipio didn't really believe it. How many places were hiring waiters? Even asking the question of himself made him want to laugh.

But it wasn't funny. It was anything but funny, as a matter of fact. Bathsheba's housekeeping work brought in some money, but not enough. He would have to find something to do, and find it fast.

I could be the best butler Augusta, Georgia's, ever seen. If he'd passed muster for Anne Colleton, he could pass muster here. True, he had no references, but he was good enough to show what he could do even without them. And rich people always had money. People like that were always looking for good help. When he opened his mouth and showed he could talk like an educated white man ...

He shook his head and shivered, as if coming down with the influenza. *When I show that, I put a noose around my neck.* He knew what a good servant he made. If he started playing the butler again, word would spread among the rich whites of Augusta. *Old So-and-So's got himself a crackerjack new nigger, best damn butler you ever saw.* Word wouldn't spread only in Augusta, either. St. Matthews, South Carolina, wasn't that far away. Anne Colleton would hear before too long. And when she did, he was dead.

She'd gone back to helping the Freedom Party. He'd seen that in the newspapers. She wouldn't have forgotten him. So far as he knew, she hadn't tried very hard to find him after he'd escaped South Carolina for Georgia. But if he did anything to bring himself to her notice, he deserved to die for stupidity's sake.

Erasmus reached into the cash box and took out two

brown twenty-dollar banknotes. He thrust them at Scipio. "Here you is," he said. "Wish it could be more, but I druther give it to you than to them Freedom Party trash."

Pride told Scipio to refuse. He had no room in his life for pride. "Thank you kindly," he said, and took the money. "God bless you."

"He done bless me plenty," Erasmus said. "Hope He watch out for you, too."

Someone else had pressed money on Scipio when he lost a job waiting tables. He snapped his fingers. "Reckon I go see me Mistuh John Oglethorpe. Anybody in this here town got work, reckon he know 'bout it."

"Good idea." Erasmus nodded. "Not all white folks is Freedom Party bastards."

These days, Scipio ventured out of the Terry only with trepidation. He didn't like the way white men looked at him when he walked along the streets outside the colored district. They looked at him the way they had to look at possums and squirrels and raccoons when they hunted for the pot.

Freedom Party posters and banners and emblems were everywhere. He saw several white men with little enamel-work Freedom Party pins—those reversed-color Confederate battle flags—on their lapels. More than anybody else, they glared at him as if he had no right to exist. He kept his eyes down on the sidewalk. Giving back look for look was the worst thing he could do. If one of those pin-wearing fellows decided he was an uppity nigger, he might not get back to the Terry alive.

When he walked into Oglethorpe's restaurant, Aurelius was taking care of the breakfast crowd. Whites sat on one side of the room, Negroes on the other. They'd always done that. It wasn't law, but it was unbreakable custom. Scipio perched at a small table. Aurelius nodded when he recognized him.

"Ain't seen you in a long time," he said. "What kin I git you?"

"Bacon and eggs over easy and grits and a cup o' coffee," Scipio answered. "I see Mistuh Oglethorpe when things slows down?"

"I tell him you's here," Aurelius said. "How come you ain't at Erasmus' place?"

"He shuttin' down," Scipio said, and the other man's eyes widened in astonishment. In a voice not much above a whisper, Scipio explained, "They wants too much money for he to stay open." He didn't explain who *they* were. Aurelius would know.

"Hey, Aurelius!" a white man called. "I need some more coffee over here."

"Comin', Mr. Benson." Aurelius hurried off to take care of the customer, and then another one, and then another one after that.

He didn't get back to Scipio's table till he set plate and coffee cup in front of him. "Thank you kindly," Scipio said, and dug in. John Oglethorpe was in no way a fancy cook, but few of his kind could match him. The breakfast was easily as good as any Erasmus made: high praise indeed. Scipio hadn't eaten grits in his days as Anne Colleton's privileged servant; he'd thought of them as field-hands' food. He'd remade their acquaintance since, and found he liked them.

With Aurelius filling his cup every time it got low, he hung around in the restaurant till the rush thinned out. John Oglethorpe emerged from the kitchen then. His hair had gone gray and pulled back at the temples. He wore thick bifocals he hadn't had before, and was thinner and more stooped than Scipio remembered.

"What's this nonsense I hear about Erasmus goin' out of business?" he demanded. "He can't do that. He's been cooking even longer than I have."

"No mo'," Scipio said. "Freedom Party fellas, they wants too much money from he."

"Oh. Those people." The white man's voice went flat and hard. "I've always been a Whig, and so was my pappy, and so was *his* pappy—well, he was a Democrat before the War of Secession, but that doesn't count. Some people, though—some people think yelling something loud enough makes it so."

"Free*dom*!" Aurelius didn't yell it, but the scorn in his voice ran deep.

Scipio blinked. The cook and the waiter had worked together for God only knew how many years. Even so . . . As far as Scipio could remember, this was the first time— outside the brief, chaotic madness of the Congaree Socialist Republic—he'd ever heard a Negro mock a Confederate political party where a white could hear.

"Yellin' ain't all them Freedom Party fellas does," Scipio said. "Erasmus reckon somethin' bad happen to he if he don't pay, so he done quit."

"That's a shame and a disgrace," Oglethorpe said. "That is nothing but a shame and a disgrace. This town needs hardworking folks like Erasmus a hell of a lot more than it needs blowhards like those Freedom Party yahoos."

Did he know *Gulliver's Travels*? Or was he using the word as a general term of contempt? Scipio didn't see how he could ask. That might involve trying to explain how *he* knew *Gulliver's Travels*. He kept trying to bury his past, but it lived on inside him.

All he said was, "Yes, suh." And then he got down to the business that had brought him out of the Terry: "Mistuh Oglethorpe, I gots me a family to feed. I been workin' fo' Erasmus a good long time now. Ain't like you an' Aurelius, but a long time. You know somebody lookin' for a waiter? I does janitor work, too, an' I cooks some. Ain't as good as you an' Erasmus, but I ain't bad, neither."

Oglethorpe frowned. "I was afraid you were gonna ask me that. Why else would you come up here?" Scipio's face heated. The restaurant owner only shrugged. "I don't mind. If you know somebody, you better ask him. Only trouble is, I can't think of anyone who's short of help right now. What about you, Aurelius? You know the Terry a damn sight better than I do."

"I ought to, boss, don't you reckon?" But Aurelius' smile didn't stick on his face. "No, I don't know nobody, neither. Wish to heaven I did."

"*Damn.*" Scipio spoke quietly, but with great feeling.

"May not be so bad," Oglethorpe said. "This isn't like some businesses—slots do open up now and again. You pound the pavement—you'll find something. You can use my name, too. Don't reckon you'll need to, though. You tell people you worked for Erasmus all these years, they'll know you're the straight goods."

"Hope so. Do Jesus, I hope so." Scipio drummed his fingers on the tabletop. "Hope somethin' come up pretty damn quick. Don't wanna end up in no Mitcheltown."

As soon as he said the word, he wished he hadn't. It wasn't that he didn't feel that fear. He did. But the shanty-towns named after the Confederate president were a judgment on the Whigs. Calling them by that name—even thinking of them by that name—only helped the Freedom Party. Trouble was, everyone in the Confederate States called them Mitcheltowns, just as they were Blackfordburghs in the United States. Whoever chanced to be in power when the disaster struck got the blame.

"Good luck, Xerxes," John Oglethorpe said. "Wish to God I could do something more for you."

"Thank you kindly, suh," Scipio answered. "I thanks you very kindly. An' I wishes you could, too."

As Hipolito Rodriguez had seen when he went up north to fight in Texas, spring could be a wonderful time of year, a time when the land renewed itself after the chill and gloom of winter. It wasn't like that in Sonora. Here, it was the time when the rains petered out. The weather got warmer, yes, but it had never really turned cold. He'd seen snow in the trenches of Texas. The memory still appalled him.

He eyed the streams coming down from the mountains. If they dried up, his crops would dry up with them. They seemed all right. He worried anyhow. He'd never known a farmer who didn't worry. Even the white men beside whom he'd fought had worried about what was happening to their farms while they went to war.

He'd plowed. He'd planted his corn and beans and squashes. Now he and the rest of his family watched them grow—and weeded to make sure they *would* grow. Work on a farm was never done. Even so, he sent his children into Baroyeca for schooling as often as they could go. He wanted them to have a chance at a life that wasn't work, work, work every minute of every day. He didn't know how much of a chance they would have, but any chance was better than none.

Teachers taught in English, of course. Rodriguez worried about that only every now and again—would the children forget their heritage? More often, he thought it good that they learn as much of the dominant language of the CSA as they could.

Magdalena knew very little English. With his wife, Rodriguez stuck to Spanish. Because of that, his sons and daughters—especially his sons—thought he understood less English than he really did. They started using it among themselves to say things they didn't want him to follow.

"Silly old fool," Miguel called him one day, smiling as if it were a compliment.

Rodriguez boxed his son's ears. He smiled, too, though he doubted whether Miguel appreciated it. "Silly young fool," he said, also in English.

After that, his children were a lot more careful when they had something to say either to him or about him. He went on about his business, more amused than otherwise. Life taught all sorts of lessons, and only some of them came from school.

No matter how tired he was at the end of a day, he tried to go into Baroyeca one evening a week for the Freedom Party meeting. Magdalena had given up complaining about that when she saw he came back neither drunk nor smelling of a *puta*'s cheap perfume.

As far as Rodriguez was concerned, the scent of victory in the air was headier than liquor, sweeter than the dubious charms of Baroyeca's handful of women of easy virtue. (With the closing of the silver mines, a lot of the whores had moved to other towns, towns where they hoped to do better for themselves. The business collapse had had all sorts of unexpected, unfortunate consequences.)

Robert Quinn did his best to fan that scent all over the countryside. Baroyeca still had no electricity. Quinn couldn't call people together to listen to Jake Featherston's weekly speeches on the wireless. He did the next best thing: he got the text of the speeches by telegram and translated them into Spanish himself. Even though it wasn't his native tongue, he spoke well, and plainly believed every word he said.

Those speeches gave Hipolito Rodriguez a window on a wider world, a world beyond Baroyeca. After one of them, he said, "*Señor* Quinn, you are a traveled man. Is it true what *Señor* Featherston says, that these politicians in Richmond are nothing but criminals?"

"If Jake Featherston says it, you can take it to the bank," Quinn answered—he would sometimes translate English idioms literally into Spanish. Considering the sad state of banking in the CSA these days, this one lost something in the translation. Even so, Rodriguez understood it. Quinn went on, "How can you trust the Party if you don't trust what Jake Featherston says? You can't. It's as simple as that. You *do* trust the Party, don't you?"

"Of course I do," Rodriguez answered quickly; he knew a dangerous question when he heard one. That didn't mean he wasn't telling the truth, though. "Without the Party, what would we be?"

"Bad off, that's what," Quinn replied. "But as long as we follow what Jake says, we'll be fine. He's the leader. He knows what's what. All we have to do is back him up. That's our job. *Comprende?*"

"*Sí, señor,*" Rodriguez said as the other men at the meeting nodded.

"*Bueno.*" Quinn grinned. "If Jake was wrong, he couldn't have come as far as he has, now could he? He couldn't see what all was wrong with *los Estados Confederados*, either, eh? We've got a lot of work to do to win this election, and we'll have even more to do *after* we win it."

Carlos Ruiz asked a question that had also been in Rodriguez's mind: "After *Señor* Featherston wins the election, what will the Confederate States be like?"

"That's easy, Carlos," Robert Quinn answered. "That's real easy, to tell you the truth. Once Jake Featherston gets to be president, we will fix everything that's wrong with the Confederate States of America. Everything, by God. And once we fix everything that's wrong inside the country, then we start thinking about getting even with *los Estados Unidos*, too. How does that sound?"

"I like it," Ruiz said simply. Rodriguez nodded. So did the rest of the local men at the Freedom Party headquarters. How could anyone not like such a program? The United States were a long way off, yes, but they deserved vengeance. The room was full of veterans. They'd all fought the USA during the war.

Someone behind Rodriguez said, "I don't want to go back into the Army, but I will if I have to." That drew more nods. To his own surprise, Rodriguez found himself contributing one. He'd had all the war he wanted, and then some. But if it was a matter of turning the tables on the USA, he knew he would redon the color the Confederates called butternut.

"You are all good, patriotic men. I knew you were," Quinn said in his deliberate Spanish. "But I have a question for you. I know your *patrón* is not such a big man as he was in your grandfather's day. How many of you, though, have a *patrón* who tries to keep you from voting for the Freedom Party?"

Two or three men raised their hands. Carlos Ruiz was one of them. He said, "Don Joaquin says the Freedom Party is nothing but a pack of *bandidos*, and must be stopped."

"Does he? Well, well, well." Robert Quinn grinned again, a grin that was all sharp teeth. "We have a saying in English: who will bell the cat? Does Don Joaquin think he can put the bell on the *Partido de la Libertad*?"

"I don't know what you mean, *Señor* Quinn," Ruiz answered. "He thinks he can tell people how to vote. Of that I am certain."

"And you do not think he ought to?" Quinn asked. Ruiz shook his head. The local Freedom Party leader said, "Perhaps he should change his mind."

"Don Joaquin is a stubborn man," Ruiz warned. Quinn showed his teeth again, but didn't say a word, not then.

As the meeting was breaking up, he asked Ruiz and Rodriguez and three or four other men to stay behind. "It would be a shame if anything happened to Don Joaquin's barn," he remarked. "It would be an even bigger shame if anything happened to his house."

"He has guards," Carlos said. "They carry pistols."

Quinn opened a closet. Inside were neatly stacked Tredegar rifles. "Do you think the guards would listen to reason?" he asked. "If they decide not to listen to reason, do you think you could persuade them?"

The locals looked at one another. No, a *patrón* wasn't what his grandfather had been. Still, the idea of attacking his grounds, of attacking his buildings, hadn't crossed their minds up till now. "If we do this," Hipolito Rodriguez said slowly, "we have to win, and *Señor* Featherston has to win in November. If either of those things fails, we are dead men. You understand this, I hope."

"Oh, yes." Quinn nodded. "This is not the Army. This is not even the way it is in some of the other Confederate states. I am not going to give you orders. But if you want to teach this fellow a lesson, I can help you." He pointed to the Tredegars. "The question is, how badly do you want to be free?"

A few nights later, Rodriguez slid quietly through the darkness, a military rifle in his hands. He hadn't carried a Tredegar since 1917, but the weight felt familiar. So did the crouch in which he moved.

A dog barked. Somebody called, "Who's there?" Silence, except for the barking. A moment later, a yelp punctuated it, along with the sound of a kick. "Stupid dog," Don Joaquin's sentry muttered. Rodriguez waited. One of his friends was going forward.

The brief sound of a scuffle. No shouts—only bodies thrashing. A fresh voice called, "Come on." The Freedom Party men hurried past a body.

There stood Don Joaquin's house. The grandee had only two sons and a daughter, but his dwelling was four or five times the size of Hipolito Rodriguez's. And the stable and barn not far away were even bigger. How much livestock did he have? How much did any one man need? A guard paced around the barn. He paced, yes, but he wasn't looking for trouble. It found him all the same. Silent as a serpent, a raider sneaked up behind him and clapped a hand over his mouth. He let out only a brief, horrified gurgle as the knife went home.

When the raider let the body sag to the ground, another man ran forward with gasoline. He splashed it on the wooden doors and the wall of the barn, then stepped back, lit a cigarette, and flipped it into the pool of gas that had run down from the doors. Yet another Freedom Party man gave the stables the same treatment.

Flames leaped and roared. Through their growing din, Rodriguez heard horses and mules and cattle and sheep neighing and braying and bellowing in terror. He also heard Don Joaquín's guards shouting in alarm. Their booted feet pounded on gravel and dirt as they ran to see what they could do.

He'd been waiting for that, waiting behind a boulder that gave him splendid cover. Almost of itself, the Tredegar leaped to his shoulder. He hadn't fired one in a long time, but he still knew what to do. The range was ridiculously short, and the flames lit up his targets for him. *If only things were so easy during the Great War,* he thought, and squeezed the trigger.

One of the targets fell. He tried to think of them like that, as he had during the war. He wasn't the only Freedom Party man shooting. Another guard toppled, and another, and another. The guards had fought against the USA, too. They dove for whatever hiding places they could find, and started shooting back. The cracks of their pistols seemed feeble beside the Tredegars' roars. But, when one of their bullets pinged off the stone behind which Rodriguez crouched, he reminded himself any gun could kill.

"Away!" Carlos Ruiz called. No shouts of *Freedom!* here. Don Joaquín might suspect who'd done this, but what could he do, what would he dare do, without proof? He had to know the raiders could as easily have burned his house, with him and his family in it.

Rodriguez slipped back to another sheltering boulder, and then to one behind that. Then he was far enough from the blazing buildings to stop worrying about the flames giving him away. Before too long, people would be scouring the countryside, looking for him and his friends. He intended to be back in bed by then. Magdalena and his children would say he'd been there all night. And Don Joaquin would know better than to tell people with guns of their own how to vote.

XVIII

Spring in Dakota was a riot of burgeoning green and of glorious birdsong. It was one of the most beautiful things Flora Blackford had ever seen. She would have given a great deal not to be seeing it now. If Hosea had won the election . . . But he hadn't. He'd got trounced. How badly he'd got trounced still ate at Flora.

The shock of President-elect Coolidge's death, less than a month before he was to take office, had jolted her no less than the rest of the American political world. After that, though, the pain returned. Her husband had to go down to Washington to hand over the reins of power to a man who hadn't even beaten him in November—one more humiliation piled on all the rest.

As soon as Herbert Hoover took the oath of office, the Blackfords had gone on what the papers called an extended holiday. The papers, for once, were polite. Hosea Blackford had gone back to his home state to lick his wounds, and taken his family with him.

Flora turned away from the farm window that showed Great Plains spring to such good advantage. "When do you think we should go back East?" she asked.

Her husband set down his coffee cup. He managed a crooked smile. "Are the wide open spaces starting to get on your nerves?"

"Yes!" Flora's vehemence startled even her. Hosea had put it better than she'd managed to, even in her own mind.

"I grew up in New York City, remember, on the Lower East Side. Even Philadelphia seems roomy."

"I'm so sorry for you." Hosea Blackford sighed. "And I'm sorry, but I really don't feel like going back yet. People here leave me alone. Nobody in Philadelphia or Washington leaves you alone. I think it's against the law there."

"But the country's in trouble. We need to do something," Flora said.

He sighed again. "I spent the last four years doing everything I knew how to do. None of it seemed to help much. I'm willing to let someone else worry about it for a while—especially since the people have shown they aren't willing to let me worry about it any more."

He sounded tired. Worse, he sounded old. Flora had seen how cruelly he'd aged in four hard years in Powel House. He was, she reminded herself, past his seventieth birthday. When they'd married, his being close to twice her age hadn't bothered her. It still didn't, not in most ways. But this loss of vigor, of resiliency, troubled her. She was sure that when she'd first come to know him, when she'd first fallen in love with him, he would have bounced back stronger and faster.

On the other hand, nobody who'd spent three years in the trenches during the Great War came out afterwards the same man he'd been when he went in. Hosea had spent four years in the presidential trenches, and he'd lost the war. She didn't suppose expecting him to stay unchanged was fair.

"When we do go back," she said, "I wonder if I ought to take a flat in the Fourteenth Ward."

"Aha!" her husband said, and smiled. "Something makes me think you want to go back to Congress."

"I'm thinking about it," Flora said. "I don't like seeing my old district in the hands of a Democrat. I don't like seeing a lot of our districts in the hands of Democrats."

"Neither do I." Hosea Blackford's smile was sour. "I don't think any of our candidates will ask me to hit the campaign trail for them next year, though. They'd probably want me on the stump for their opponents instead."

"It's not that bad," Flora insisted.

"No—odds are it's worse," Hosea answered. "I can't think of anything less welcome in a political party than a president who's just lost an election. After a while, I'll get to be an elder statesman, but right now I'm nothing but a nuisance." With a mournful shake of the head, he added, "By the the time I get to be an elder statesman, I'll probably be so elder, I'm dead."

"God forbid!" Flora exclaimed. No one in her family, no one among the immigrant Jews of the Lower East Side, spoke of death straight on like that. Words had power; to speak of something was to help bring it into being. The rational part of her mind knew that was nonsense, but the rational part of her mind went only so deep. Down underneath it, superstition still flourished.

"It's true," her husband said. "We both know it's true, even if you don't want to talk about it. I don't need to take out pencil and paper to know how old I am. I get reminded whenever I look in the mirror. I'd like to stay around long enough to see Joshua grow up, but how likely is that? I've already beaten the odds by lasting as long as I have."

"That's nothing but—" Flora began.

"The truth," Hosea finished for her. "You know it as well as I do, too. And if you don't, ask the next insurance salesman you happen to run into. He'll tell you what the actuarial tables say."

Flora wanted to tell him that was nonsense. She couldn't, and she knew it. The best she could do was change the subject: "Let's talk about something else."

"Fine." Now her husband's grin showed real amusement. "Do you think this new professional football federation's going to last?"

That wasn't what she'd had in mind. "I don't care," she said tartly. "What I think is, it's disgraceful to pay men so much to run around with a football when so many people can't find work at all. Talk about a waste of money!"

"It's an amusement, the same as an orchestra is an amusement," her husband said. "Nothing wrong with them. We need them. Especially in hard times, we need them."

"An orchestra is worthwhile," Flora said. "A football game?" She shook her head.

"A lot more people go to watch the Philadelphia Barrels than to the Philadelphia Symphony," Hosea said.

Since that was true, Flora could only stick out her chin and say, "Even so."

"Amusement is where you find it," Hosea said. "I'm not going to be elitist and look down my nose at anything."

To a good Socialist, *elitist* was a dirty word. Flora tried to turn it back on her husband: "When the top football players make more than the president of the United States—and some of them do—they're the elitists."

"They asked one of them about that two or three years ago. Did you happen to see what he said?" Hosea Blackford asked. Flora shook her head. She paid as little attention to sports as she could. One of her husband's eyebrows rose. "What he told the reporter was, 'I had a better year than he did.' All things considered, how could anyone tell Mr. Gehrig he was wrong?"

"A *choleriyeh* on Mr. Gehrig!" Flora said furiously. "Nothing that happened was your fault."

That eyebrow lifted again. "The Party told that to the voters. We told them and told them and told them. And Herbert Hoover is president of the United States today, and here I am in Dakota. If you're there, it's your fault."

"It isn't fair," Flora said.

Hosea laughed out loud, which only made her angrier. "Joshua might try to use an argument like that, but you shouldn't," he said. "It's the way politics works. 'What have you done for me lately?' is the question voters always ask—and maybe it's the question they *should* always ask. Teddy Roosevelt won the Great War. They didn't give him a third term, though, because of all the strikes and unrest that came afterwards. That's how Upton got to be president—and how I got to be vice president, if you remember."

"I'm not likely to forget," she answered. "I was so proud of you. And I'm still proud of you, and I still think you ought to be president, not that . . . that *lump* of a Hoover."

"As a matter of fact, I agree with you. I think you're sweet, too," he added. "Unfortunately, fifty-seven percent of the voters in the United States had a different opinion, and theirs counts for more than ours." He sighed. "It was even worse in the Electoral College, of course."

"Not right," Flora muttered.

"What's not right, Mama?" That was Joshua, still in his flannel pajamas. He was yawning. From somewhere on one side of the family or the other, he'd found a taste for sleeping late. On the Lower East Side—or, for that matter, on a Dakota farm—he would have had to get up early whether he wanted to or not. As the son of a man first vice president and then president, he could usually sleep as late as he wanted to. *Privilege is everywhere,* Flora thought.

But she had to answer him: "It's not right that your father lost the election."

"Oh." Joshua tried to frown, but a yawn ruined it. "Why not? The other guys got more votes, didn't they?"

Hosea laughed. "That's it in a nutshell, Josh. The other guys got more votes."

Josh. Flora didn't like the one-syllable abridgment of a perfectly good name. Joshua Blackford was rolling, majestic. Josh Blackford sounded like someone who wore overalls and a straw hat. *And if that's elitist, too bad,* she thought. Hosea didn't see the problem.

"The point is, the other guys"—she used her son's phrase as if it had quotation marks around it—"shouldn't have got more votes."

Joshua muttered something under his breath. Flora thought she heard, "Stinking Japs." Without a doubt, the Japanese bombing of Los Angeles had been the last straw—or rather, the last nail in the coffin. If Joshua wanted to think his father would have won without that, he could. Flora wanted to think the very same thing. The only problem was, she knew better. Looking at the last nail in the coffin meant ignoring all the others, and there were a lot of them.

"You'll win again in four years, though, won't you, Father?" Joshua had a boy's boundless confidence in his father. He also had a boy's strange notions about the way time worked.

Neither of his parents said anything. Hosea Blackford would be too old to nominate in 1936, even if he'd never lost an election in his life. Since he'd lost the way he had, the Socialists would be trying their best to forget he'd ever existed.

"Won't you?" Joshua asked again.

"I like to think I would win against Mr. Hoover," Hosea said slowly. "He doesn't seem to me as if he's moving things in the right direction. But I don't know if I would want to run again, and I don't know if the Socialist Party would nominate me if I did. We would have to see how things look in 1936 before we could know."

Flora added, "The next election for president is almost four years from now. That's a long time."

"Especially in politics," her husband added.

Joshua nodded. He'd just turned seven; to him, four years were a very long time indeed. He said, "*I* think you still ought to be president."

"Thank you, son," Hosea Blackford said.

"I think the very same thing," Flora said, and ruffled Joshua's hair. He was dark like her, but otherwise looked more like his father, with a long face, prominent cheekbones, and a straight, pointed nose. He also had more of his father's temperament: he was steadier than Flora, and not given to sudden enthusiasms that took control of him for days or weeks at a time.

"Who do the Socialists have that could be any better than you, Dad?" he asked. He couldn't imagine anyone better. Flora ruffled his hair again. Neither could she. But she knew the practical politicians in the Socialist Party would have a different opinion—and Hosea really would be too old to run again in 1936. He probably would have been too old to run in 1932 if he hadn't been the incumbent.

"One way or another, everything will work out fine," she said. Joshua believed her. He was still only a little boy.

* * *

The *Remembrance* steamed west across the Pacific, accompanied by three destroyers, a light cruiser, a heavy cruiser, and two battleships. Sam Carsten wished one of the battlewagons would have been the *Dakota*, but no such luck. His old ship was off doing something else; he had no idea what.

Repairs in Seattle had been as quick as the Navy yard there could make them. He did his best not to worry about that. Back during the Great War, the *Dakota* had been hastily repaired after battle damage—and her steering had never been reliable again. Her steering probably still wasn't reliable. So far as Sam knew, the Japanese torpedo hadn't damaged the *Remembrance*'s steering—but what *had* it damaged that hasty repairs might not discover? He hoped he—and the ship—wouldn't find out the hard way.

Commander van der Waal wasn't aboard. Broken ankles healed at their own pace; you couldn't hurry them. A new damage-control officer, a lieutenant commander named Hiram Pottinger, was nominally in charge of antitorpedo work. But Pottinger's previous service had been in cruisers. Sam knew the *Remembrance* backwards and forwards and inside out—literally inside out, after the torpedo hit off the Canadian coast. Most of the burden fell on his shoulders.

He'd led the sailors in the damage-control parties when things looked black. That had earned him respect he could have got no other way. It had also earned him thin new gold stripes on his cuffs; he'd been promoted to lieutenant, junior grade, for what he'd done. Glad as he was of the promotion, he could have done without some of the respect. He feared he would end up trapped in an assignment he'd never wanted.

Martin van der Waal had always insisted it was an important assignment. Even had Sam been inclined to argue, the experience of getting torpedoed would have changed his mind. But he agreed with his injured superior. Important, antitorpedo work definitely was. That still didn't mean he cared to make a career of it.

He spent as much time as he could on deck. That meant more tinfoil tubes of zinc-oxide ointment, but he did it anyhow. Watching aeroplanes take off and land never failed to fascinate him. He got plenty of chances to watch, for the *Remembrance* flew a continuous air patrol. The Japanese Navy had ships out here, too, and who found whom first would have a lot to do with how any fight turned out. The way the arrester hook caught the cables stretched across the deck and brought a landing aeroplane to an abrupt halt still fascinated him.

One perfect morning, he was taking the air on the flight deck after breakfast when alarms began to sound. Klaxons hooting in his ears, he ran for his battle station, wishing it weren't deep in the bowels of the aeroplane carrier. He wanted to be able to see what was going on. As usual, the Navy cared not at all for what he wanted.

"What's the word, sir?" he panted as he came up to Lieutenant Commander Pottinger.

"Nothing good," his superior answered. "One of our machines spotted a whole flight of aeroplanes with meatballs on their wings heading this way."

"There's no Jap base within a couple of thousand miles of where we're at," Sam said. The light went on in his head before Pottinger needed to enlighten him: "We've found a Japanese aeroplane carrier or two."

The other damage-control officer shook his head. "Not quite. Their aeroplanes have found us, but we haven't found them yet."

"Heading back along their bearing would be a pretty good bet," Carsten said.

Lieutenant Commander Pottinger nodded. He was a tall, lean man with a weathered face, hollow cheeks, a long, narrow jaw, and a pointed nose. He looked like a New Englander, but had a Midwestern accent. "I expect you're right," he said. "This is liable to be a damn funny kind of naval battle, you know? We're not even in sight of the enemy's fleet, but our aeroplanes are going to slug it out with his."

As if to underline his words, one machine after another roared into the sky, the noise of the straining engines loud even several decks below the one from which the aeroplanes were taking off. "Long-range artillery, that's what they've turned into," Sam said. "They can hit when our battleships can't."

Pottinger nodded again. "That's right. Battleships are probably obsolete, though plenty of men will try and run you out of the Navy if you say so out loud." He made a disdainful noise. "Plenty of men likely tried to run people out of the Navy if they spoke up for steam engines and ironclads, too."

"I wouldn't be surprised." Sam had known more than a few officers who never stopped pining for the good old days.

Something burst in the water not far from the *Remembrance*. He felt the carrier heel into the sharpest turn she could make, and then, a moment later, into another one in the opposite direction. More bombs burst around her.

Hiram Pottinger might have been talking things over back on shore, for all the excitement he showed. "Zigzags," he said approvingly. "That's what you do against submersibles, and that's what you do against aeroplanes, too."

"Well, yes, sir," Carsten said. "That's what you do, and then you hope like hell it works. You get hit by a bomb, that could put a little crimp in your morning." He did his best to imitate his superior's nonchalance.

One-pounders and other antiaircraft guns on the deck started banging away at the attacking aeroplanes. So did the five-inch guns in the sponsons under the flight deck. The noise was terrific. They could reach a lot farther than the smaller weapons, but couldn't fire nearly so fast.

"I wonder what's going on up there," Sam said. "I wonder how nasty it is."

"It's no walk in the park," Pottinger said.

"I didn't figure it was, sir," Sam said, a little reproachfully. He'd seen plenty of nasty action—it didn't come much nastier than what he'd been through in the Battle of the Three Navies. A moment later, he realized Pottinger, if he'd ever been in a battle before, had probably gone through it down here.

Maybe this was harder. Carsten wouldn't have believed

it beforehand, but it might have been true. When he was fighting a gun, he had some idea, even if only a small one, of what was going on. Here . . . Here it might have been happening in a distant room. The only difference was, what happened in that distant room might kill him.

Later, he wished he hadn't had that thought at that moment. The *Remembrance* shuddered when a bomb burst on her flight deck. Lieutenant Commander Pottinger said, "Oh, shit," which summed up Sam's feelings perfectly. Then Pottinger added, "Well, time for us to go to work."

"Yes, sir," Carsten agreed.

That was how he got up to the flight deck in the midst of combat. He wanted to be there, but not under those circumstances. The flight crew were already doing what they had to do: manhandling steel plates across the hole the bomb had torn in the deck and doing everything they could to flatten out the torn lips of steel.

"Well done," Pottinger shouted. "We have to be able to land aeroplanes and get them in the air again."

"Yes, sir," Sam said again. His boss might be new to carrier duty, but he'd just proved he understood the essence of it. Sam went on, "They could have done a lot worse if they'd fused the bomb differently."

"What do you mean?" Lieutenant Commander Pottinger asked.

"If they'd given it an armor-piercing tip and a delayed fuse, it would have gone through before it blew up," Sam answered. "Then we'd really be in the soup."

"Urk," Pottinger said, which again matched Sam's thought.

Sam said, "They're like us: they're still learning what all they can do with aeroplanes and carriers, too."

An aeroplane with the red Rising Sun of Japan painted on wings and fuselage roared overhead, machine guns in the wings blazing. The engine was even louder than the guns; the fighter couldn't have been more than fifty feet above the deck. Bullets struck sparks from the new steel plates. Others smacked flesh with wet thuds. Men shrieked or crumpled silently. Streams of tracers from the *Remembrance*'s antiaircraft guns converged on the Japanese machine. For a dreadful moment, Sam thought it would get away in spite of all the gunfire. But then flames and smoke licked back from the engine cowling toward the cockpit. The fighter slammed into the sea.

"Scratch one fucker!" Sam shouted exultantly.

A sailor next to him was down and groaning, clutching his leg. Red spread over his trousers. "It hurts!" he groaned. "It hurts bad!"

"George!" Sam's exultation turned to dismay in the space of a heartbeat. He'd known George Moerlein ever since first coming aboard the *Remembrance*. Seeing him down with a nasty wound made Sam's stomach turn over. By the way the petty officer was bleeding, he needed help right away. Sam tore off his belt and wrapped it around Moerlein's thigh above the bullet wound, tight as he could. "Give me a hand over here!" he yelled.

"Let's get him down to sick bay, sir," a sailor said. He helped Carsten haul George Moerlein up. Moerlein moaned and then, mercifully, passed out. As they hauled the petty officer towards a passageway, another Japanese fighter strafed the *Remembrance*. Bullets cracked past Sam and clattered off the flight deck. He breathed a sigh of relief when he had steel between him and the deadly chaos overhead.

As soon as he saw a sailor, though, he said, "take over for me. Get this man below. I've go topside." He hurried back up to put his life on again, though he did his best not to think of it

Off to starboard, one of the American deste on fire from bow to stern and sinking fast. Bothese in life jackets bobbed around her. Even as S shiv- the destroyer rolled over and went to the bo waters, the bottom was a long, long way d the Re-ered at how far down it was.

A bomb burst in the sea not f the others on *membrance*, drenching Carsten and m guided an aero-deck. Even so, a sailor with wigwag sig led it. Its prop plane to a landing. Maintenance m ht deck it rolled, started spinning again. Down the p into the air again. bumping over the hasty repairs, an

"Didn't think we could do that," Sam said to Lieutenant Commander Pottinger.

"He must have been flying on fumes, or he never would have tried coming in," Pottinger agreed. "Lucky the Japs have let up a little."

"I wonder what we're doing to them," Sam said. "Worse than this, I hope. We'd better be, by God."

"Yes, we'd better be. But how can we know?" Pottinger said. "They're over the horizon. The only ones who have any real idea how the fight's going are our pilots."

"No, sir—not even them," Sam said. His superior raised an eyebrow. He explained: "They don't know what the Jap pilots are doing to us, just like the Japs can't be sure what we're doing to them. Maybe the fellows in the wireless shacks—ours and theirs—have the big picture. Maybe nobody does. Wouldn't that be a hell of a thing?"

Lieutenant Commander Pottinger laughed. "We won't know who won till day after tomorrow, when we read it in the newspapers."

"Yeah." It wasn't exactly funny, but Carsten laughed, too. "As long as we live through it, we've come out all right." A Japanese aeroplane and an American machine both splashed into the Pacific within a quarter of a mile of the *Remembrance*. Sam hoped *somebody* would live through the fight.

The *Kansas City Star* was the daily published closest to Leavenworth that was actually worth reading. Irving Morrell had discovered that during his last stay in Kansas. Of course, the wireless supplemented the paper. Back when wireless had only started passing from Morse code could Even now, the newspaper gave him a far more picture than the quick reports on the wireless

battle, "think anybody knows who won this stupid sea fight "he said two days after reports about the "I really don't the Sandwich Islands started coming in. whole Jap fleet you look at our claims, we sank the theirs, they did it didn't take a scratch. If you look at us."

His wife shrugged and poured him another cup of coffee. "My bet is, both sides are lying as hard as they can."

"My bet is, you're right," Morrell answered. "I suppose we'll sort it out in time for Mildred's children to study about it in school."

Hearing her name made his daughter look up from her scrambled eggs. "Study what in school?" she asked.

"A big naval battle in the Pacific," her father said.

She rolled her eyes. "For heaven's sake, who cares?"

Agnes laughed. "If everybody felt that way, we wouldn't have to fight any more wars. That wouldn't be so bad, would it?"

"That would be wonderful," Morrell said with the deep conviction of a man who'd seen—who'd taken part in—the worst man could do to his fellow man. He gulped the scalding coffee. "That would be wonderful, but it's not going to happen any time soon, no matter how much I wish it would. Speaking of which, I'm off to the Barrel Works."

"All right, dear." Agnes got up, too, and came over to give him a kiss. "I'll see you when you get back. Some more things should be out of boxes by then."

"Good." Morrell was convinced he could no more escape from boxes than a bug could get out of a spiderweb. He wondered how many times he'd moved in the course of his military career. He didn't try to count them all up. That way lay madness.

Barbed wire enclosed a field in which sat the experimental barrel he'd been working with ten years earlier. The machine hadn't been in the field all those years; it would have been a rusted, useless hulk if it had. Even though the Socialists had stopped work on new barrels for so long, the Army had carefully greased this one and stored it in a garage, in case it was ever wanted again. Morrell gave the General Staff—not his favorite outfit—reluctant credit for that. He didn't know what he would have done if he'd had to start altogether from scratch.

Sentries at the gate saluted. "Good morning, Colonel," they chorused.

"Morning, boys." Morrell pointed into the field. "Who's working on the barrel?"

"Sergeant Pound, sir," one of the sentries answered.

"I might have known." Morrell opened the gate and went inside. One of the sentries closed it after him. As he hurried toward the barrel, he called, "You're up early today, Sergeant."

"Oh, hello, sir." Sergeant Michael Pound was a broad-shouldered, muscular man with close-cropped brown hair and a neat mustache showing the first silver threads. "The carburetor still isn't what it ought to be, you know."

"I'm not surprised, seeing how long the whole vehicle's been sitting there doing nothing," Morrell answered. "How are you going to get it clean?"

Sergeant Pound held up a coffee can. "There's this new solvent called carbon tetrachloride. It gets grease off of anything," he said enthusiastically. He was wild for any new invention; that was what had drawn him into barrels in the first place. "It's wonderful stuff—nonflammable, a really excellent cleaner. Only one drawback." He plopped the carburetor into the can.

"What's that?" Morrell asked, as he was surely supposed to.

"If you use it indoors, it's liable to asphyxiate you," Pound replied. "Some people are fools, of course. Congressmen get excited about that sort of thing. They want to ban the stuff. If you ask me, anyone who's dumb enough not to read the label deserves whatever happens to him." He had no patience with incompetent people, no doubt because he was so all-around competent himself.

Morrell slapped him on the back. "It's damn good to see you again, Sergeant, to hell with me if it's not."

"Thank you very much, sir," Michael Pound replied. "I felt I was wasting my time these past few years in the artillery. Of course, the Army would have thrown me out on my ear if I'd tried to stay in barrels, but the men in charge of things aren't exactly the smartest ones we've got, are they?"

"I believe I'll plead the Fifth on that one," Morrell

604

said, laughing. "Do you think you could do a better job of it?"

"Sir, I'm sure I could." Pound wasn't joking. Because he did so many things well, he thought he could do anything. Sometimes he turned out to be right. Sometimes he was disastrously wrong. Occasional disasters did nothing to damage his self-confidence.

"How *did* you put up with going back to the artillery after the Barrel Works closed down?" Morrell asked.

"Well, for one thing, sir, like I said, if I hadn't they would have found something else even worse for me to do—or they would have thrown me out altogether, and that wouldn't have been good, not when the collapse came," Pound said. "And besides, I always thought the politicians would eventually come to their senses. I just never imagined they'd take so long."

"Who did?" Morrell said. He'd asked for Sergeant Pound by name when he came back to Leavenworth. The man was worth his weight in gold—which, considering his massive frame, was no mean statement. If he occasionally suffered delusions of omnipotence . . . well, nobody was perfect.

"Knaves. Fools and knaves," he said now: one of his favorite phrases.

"You'd better be careful," Morrell warned him. "You're starting to sound like you belong in the Freedom Party."

"Oh, no, sir. I didn't say they were a pack of traitors who need to be lined up against a wall and shot." Pound had no trouble imitating the Freedom Party's impassioned rhetoric. He added, "Besides, that Featherston is a dangerous lunatic. If he gets elected this fall, he's liable to show just how dangerous he is."

"I wish I could tell you you were wrong," Morrell said.

"He's liable to prove as troublesome to us as those *Action Française* people are to the Kaiser," Pound said. "What can you do about a government that hates you if a majority voted it into office?"

"Get ready to fight," Morrell answered. "That's what we're doing here."

"How soon before we have a real barrel with specifications based on the experimental model here?" Sergeant Pound asked, taking the carburetor out of the carbon tetrachloride and setting it down on a rag.

"They're saying six or eight months in Pontiac," Morrell replied. "That's what they're saying, but I'll believe it when I see it. Bet on a year, maybe longer."

"Disgraceful," Pound said. "So much time not even frittered away—*thrown* away, for heaven's sake." He rubbed the carburetor with the rag, then passed it to Morrell. "This thing is better, though. I think it's really clean now, clean enough to work the way it's supposed to."

"I hope you're right," Morrell said. "Put it back in the engine, Sergeant. We'll gas up the beast and see if it runs."

"Right, sir." Pound opened the louvers on the engine compartment—one improvement over Great War barrels the experimental model did boast was a separate engine compartment, which drastically reduced noise and noxious fumes for the crew. As Pound turned a wrench, he went on, "You know, we really ought to have a diesel engine in here, not one fueled by gasoline. A fire starts, gasoline goes up like a bomb. Diesel fuel just burns quietly. The men in the fighting compartment have a much better chance to get away."

"That's a good idea," Morrell said. Pound was full of ideas, good, bad, and indifferent. "Model after next, we ought to think about incorporating it." He pulled a notebook from his breast pocket and scribbled a few lines so the idea wouldn't be lost.

"Why waste time, sir?" Sergeant Pound asked. "Why not put it right into the model they're working on now? That way, we'd have it."

"We'd have it—eventually," Morrell answered. "How many plans would they have to change to put a new engine in that compartment? How many dies and stamps and castings would they have to revise? I don't know the exact number, but it's bound to be a big one."

"We ought to do this right," Pound insisted.

"We will—eventually." Morrell used that word again. "Right now, that we're doing it at all is miracle enough, if you ask me. Just remember, I was in Kamloops a few weeks ago, and you were an artilleryman. Let's get something finished, and then we can set about improving it."

"Everything ought to be right the first time," Pound muttered.

"Not everything is. That's why they put erasers on pencils," Morrell said. "Or are you one of those people who fill out crossword puzzles in ink?" He was fond of those puzzles himself. Their popularity had exploded since the collapse. They gave people something interesting to do, and you could buy a book of them for a dime.

Michael Pound looked puzzled. "Of course, sir. Doesn't everybody?" He sounded altogether innocent. Was that sarcasm, or did he really believe people were so generally capable? Morrell suspected he did. Like most men, he judged others by his own standards, and those standards were pretty high. After bending to get a better look at the connection he was making, he said, "I've got a question for you, sir."

"Go ahead," Morrell told him.

"Where do you suppose we could be if we hadn't spent all this time lying fallow, and how big a price will we pay because we did?"

"We'd be a lot further along than we are now, and we'll have to find out. There. Aren't I profound?"

"That's hardly the word I'd use, sir," Michael Pound replied.

He didn't say what word he *would* use, which might have been just as well. Morrell said, "Shall we see if this miserable thing actually runs now?"

"It had better," Pound said.

He was properly a gunner by trade, but he could drive. He slid down through the turret—an innovation when the experimental model was new, but a commonplace in barrel design nowadays—and into the driver's seat at the left front of the vehicle, next to the bow machine gun. When he stabbed the starter button, the engine wasted no time roaring to life.

"You see, sir?" he said in his best *I-told-you-so* tones.

"I see," Morrell answered. "All right, shut it down for now. We're not ready to go anywhere, not with a two-man crew."

"We could if we were at war," Pound said.

"We could if we were but we aren't so we won't." Morrell had to listen to himself to make sure that came out right. "Actually, we *are* at war, but barrels won't do much against the Japs. Now we have to revive some more of the old machines, to have opponents to practice against." He wished real barrels, modern barrels, would be so easy to face.

These days, nobody around Baroyeca was likely to tell anybody how to vote. Hipolito Rodriguez hadn't been sure things would work out that way, but they had. The unfortunate accidents that happened to Don Joaquin's barn and stable—to say nothing of the even more unfortunate accidents that happened to Don Joaquin's guards—had quickly persuaded the prominent men in this part of Sonora not to push too hard against the Freedom Party.

"You understand what it is," Robert Quinn said at a Freedom Party meeting a couple of weeks after those unfortunate things happened. "It has been a very long time since anyone told a *patrón*, 'No, *señor*, you may not do this.' They needed a lesson. Now they have had one. I do not think they will need any more."

"What could we have done if they had come after us with everything they have?" Rodriguez asked.

Quinn looked steadily back at him. "It is like this. The rich men around Baroyeca have so much. The Freedom Party has *so* much." He held his hands first close together, then wide apart. "If you put them in a fight, who do you think is going to win?"

"But suppose they talked to the governor," Rodriguez said stubbornly. "Suppose they said, 'Call out the state militia. We have to put down these Freedom Party men with guns.' "

"*Muy bien*—suppose they did that." The Freedom Party organizer sounded agreeable. "Suppose they did exactly that.

How many *soldados* in this state, *Señor* Rodriguez, do you suppose are Freedom Party men?"

"Ahh," Rodriguez said, and his voice was just one in a small, delighted chorus of oohs and ahhs that filled Freedom Party headquarters. He went on, "You mean they cannot trust their own soldiers?"

"Did I say that?" Quinn shook his head. "I did not say that. Would I say anything that would go against the state government? Of course not."

"Of course not," Carlos Ruiz agreed in sly tones. "We don't want to go against the state government. We want to take it over."

"Ahh," Hipolito Rodriguez said again. He found winning a national election easier to imagine than toppling the state government. Richmond was far away, and wouldn't matter so immediately. A Freedom Party administration in Hermosillo would send shock waves rippling through Sonora.

Of course, a Freedom Party defeat in November would send shock waves of a different sort rippling through the state. Quinn said, "Remember, we have to win, or the lesson Don Joaquin learned goes for nothing."

He didn't say who had taught Carlos Ruiz's *patrón* that lesson. He certainly didn't say the men who'd taught that lesson had got their rifles and ammunition from him. Some things were better unadmitted.

Quietly Hipolito Rodriguez said, "That lesson had better not go for nothing, whether we win or lose. If they push us too hard, we can still fight."

"You are a brave man, a bold man," Quinn said. "You are the sort of man we want, the sort of man we need, in the Freedom Party."

Rodriguez shrugged. "If a *patrón* wants to stay a Radical Liberal, that is all right with me. I used to be a Radical Liberal myself. I changed my mind. They have no business telling me I may not change my mind. I would never try to tell them any such thing."

"Yes. You have reason. That is how it should be," Ruiz said. Several other men nodded.

But Robert Quinn said, "Once we win, well, other

parties will just have to get used to that. The difference between the Freedom Party and the other parties in the Confederate States is that we have reason and they do not. If they are wrong, why should we let them pretend they are right?"

"They are political parties, too," Ruiz said. "One of these days, they will win an election."

"I do not think so," Quinn said. "I do not think one of them will win an election for a very, very long time once we take over."

"What do you mean?" Ruiz asked. "Sometimes you win, sometimes you lose. That is how politics works."

"Not always," Rodriguez said. "How many times in a row have Whigs been presidents of the Confederate States? Every single time, that's how many. If the Freedom Party is good enough to win, it will win just as many elections. That's what you meant, isn't it, *Señor* Quinn?"

"Sure it is, *Señor* Rodriguez," Quinn said easily, with a small laugh. "That is exactly what I meant."

Rodriguez wondered why he laughed. Because he hadn't meant exactly that? If he hadn't, what had he meant? What could he have meant? Rodriguez shrugged. Whatever it was, he didn't think he needed to worry about it very much.

Someone asked, "*Señor* Quinn, how do we make certain the Freedom Party wins in Sonora this November?"

"That is a good question. That is a very good question." Now Robert Quinn sounded not only serious but altogether sincere. "We ourselves here can only make sure we win in Baroyeca." He waited for nods to show everyone understood that, then went on, "We have to do a few things. We have to let people know what the Party will do for them once it wins. We have to let them know what it will do for the country once it wins. We have to show them the other parties cannot do the things they promise, and that most of what they promise is not good anyway. And we have to do everything we can to keep them from having the chance to tell their lies."

Hipolito Rodriguez understood all of that but the last. "What do you mean, *Señor* Quinn?" he asked. "How do we keep them from doing that?"

"However we have to," the Freedom Party man said bluntly. "However we need to. Don Joaquin had a sad accident, *verdad*?" Again, he waited for nods. Again, he got them. Everybody here knew what kind of accident Don Joaquin had had. Nobody much felt like talking about details—better safe than sorry. Quinn continued, "When they come here to make speeches and stir up their followers, we do not let them. We shout, we heckle, we make enough of a disturbance to keep them from talking to an audience. If they cannot talk, they cannot get their message out, eh?"

"*Sí, señor.*" Several men said it together. Rodriguez wasn't one of them, but he nodded. If the Freedom Party got to talk and no one else did, that was surely a large advantage. But . . .

He held up his hand. Quinn pointed his way. "*Señor*, how do we keep them from talking on the wireless?" he inquired.

"Ah, *Señor* Rodriguez, you do ask interesting questions." As always, Quinn was scrupulously polite. He treated the men who'd joined the Freedom Party as if they were dons. Most white men thought of Sonorans and Chihuahuans as nothing but greasers. If Quinn did, he kept it to himself. That was another reason his following grew and grew. He continued, "We cannot stop that, not altogether—not yet. But it does not matter so much here in Sonora, because fewer places here have electricity than is true in most of the Confederate States."

Carlos Ruiz clicked his tongue between his teeth. "That is not fair. That is not right."

"I agree with you, *Señor* Ruiz," Quinn said. "It is one of the things the Freedom Party will fix once we have power. But, whether we like it or not, it is true, and we have to take it into account." He paused and looked around the room. "Are there any more questions? No? All right, then. This meeting is adjourned."

Rodriguez was the first one to start out of the Freedom Party headquarters. From across the street, a shot rang out. Whoever held that gun didn't really know what to do with it. The bullet cracked past Rodriguez's head and thudded into the planking of the building behind him. Automatic reflex made him throw himself flat. Another bullet sang through the air where he'd stood a moment before. Glass shattered. Chunks rained down on him.

He rolled back into the building. "Blow out the lamps!" he cried. The headquarters plunged into darkness.

"Here." Someone pressed a Tredegar into his hands. "If they want to play such games . . ."

He crawled up to the shot-out window. One of the men who'd fired at him was running across the street, straight toward the headquarters, a lighted kerosene lantern in hand. That made the fellow an even easier target than he would have been otherwise. He wanted to fight fire with fire, did he? The rifle leaped to Rodriguez's shoulder. He squeezed the trigger. The man with the lantern shrieked, whirled, and crumpled, clutching his belly. The lantern fell on his chest. Burning kerosene poured out and made him into a torch.

Never shoot twice in a row from the same place unless the cover is very good—one more lesson Rodriguez had absorbed during the Great War. Staying low, he wriggled over to the other side of the window. Another Tredegar banged, this one at the back of Party headquarters. No cry of anguish from outside, but a triumphant yell from inside the building: Robert Quinn shouting, in English, "Take that, you fucking son of a bitch!" For good measure, he added, *"Chinga tu madre!"*

Bang! Bang! Bang! Somebody emptied a pistol into the headquarters as fast as he could shoot. Behind Rodriguez, a man yowled. At least one of those bullets had struck home. Rodriguez fired at the muzzle flashes. He worked the bolt, fired again, and then rolled away from that spot. He didn't know whether he'd hit the enemy, but no more shooting came from that direction, so he hoped he had.

Running feet in the street, these from the direction of the *alcalde's* house. A sharp cry of *"Vámonos!"* came from behind Freedom Party headquarters. Rodriguez heard more running feet, these running away. Quinn's Tredegar barked again. The Freedom Party leader whooped again, the high, shrill cry English-speaking Confederates called the Rebel yell.

"*Madre de Dios.*" An officer of the *guardia civil*—a policeman, in other words—stared at the burning corpse in the middle of the street. He crossed himself, not bothering to take the heavy pistol from his hand first. Then, pulling himself together, he strode up to Freedom Party headquarters. In a loud voice, he demanded, "What happened here?"

"I will handle this," Robert Quinn declared. To the policeman, he said, "They tried to murder us. They tried to burn down our building and roast us inside of it. They wounded one of our men—I do not know how badly poor Carlos is hurt. All we did was defend ourselves."

"Some defense," the officer muttered. "If you'd done any more defending, nothing would be left of Baroyeca. Come out here now, with your hands up, all of you." He sounded nervous, as well he might have. If the Freedom Party men felt like fighting instead of obeying, the *alcalde*—the mayor—probably didn't have enough force to make them follow orders.

But Quinn said, "We are law-abiding citizens. The Freedom Party is the party of law and order. And I told you, we have a wounded man. We will come out." In a low voice, he added, "Hip, stay behind and cover us in case this *pendejo* is not to be trusted."

"*Sí, señor,*" Rodriguez whispered. The other Freedom Party men strode past him and out into the street. Carlos Ruiz walked unsteadily, his right hand pressed tight to his left shoulder.

A couple of more men from the *guardia civil* came up. They spoke with Quinn and the rest of the Freedom Party men in low voices, then led them away. Nobody made any move to shoot anyone, not now. Hipolito Rodriguez set down his Tredegar. As quietly as he could, he crawled to the back door and left. No one waited for him there—no one living, anyhow. Two bodies lay in the alley behind the headquarters. Magdalena wouldn't be happy with him. He was happy just to be breathing. He expected he could deal with his wife. She argued much less than a bullet.

*   *   *

Early summer in Nashville made a good practice ground for hell. Of course, that was true through most of the Confederate States. Jake Featherston had brought the Freedom Party nominating convention to the capital of Tennessee for a couple of reasons. Moving it off the Atlantic coast reminded people the Party was a national outfit. And looking just a little north into stolen Kentucky reminded them what was at stake.

Flash bulbs popped when Jake got off the train from Richmond. Purple and iridescent green spots danced before his eyes. Supporters on the platform shouted, "Freedom! Freedom! Freedom!" Others called his name, again and again: "Feather*ston*! Feather*ston*! Feather*ston*!" The two cries merged and blended in his ears. Together, they felt sweeter than wine, stronger than whiskey. Despite those spots before his eyes, he waved to the crowd.

Despite those shouts, his bodyguards formed up around him, protecting his flesh with their own. One bastard with a rifle had gunned down a Confederate president and sent the Freedom Party on a ten-year journey through hell. Another one now could wreck things again. If they put Willy Knight in the top spot instead of number two, could the Party win in November? *Probably,* Jake thought. *This year, probably.* But it wouldn't be the same. He was sure of that. Willy Knight had a handsome face and handled himself pretty well on the stump. Jake . . . Jake had plans.

Maybe, just maybe, Knight had plans, too. Maybe, just maybe, those plans involved a hero's funeral for Jake Featherston. That was another reason the bodyguards in their almost-Confederate uniforms didn't leave an assassin a clear shot.

"What will you do if you're elected, Mr. Featherston?" a reporter shouted through the din.

"Put this country back on its feet," Jake answered, as he had so many times before. "Settle accounts with everybody who's done us wrong."

"Who would that be?" the eager beaver asked.

"You know who. You know what we stand for. Traitors better run for the hills. Niggers better behave

614

themselves. The Confederate States have been too soft for too long. We won't be soft any more."

"Would you—?" The reporter never got to finish the question. The phalanx of guards, with Featherston at its core, pushed off the platform and through the station towards a waiting limousine. Freedom Party men and women waving Confederate and Party flags surrounded them, hands reaching between the bodyguards to touch Jake, if only for an instant. He shook some of them. When he squeezed one woman's soft, plump fingers, she moaned as if she were coming right where she stood. He almost laughed out loud. He'd seen that before, and heard it, too.

The limousine took him to the Heritage Hotel. The lobby was full of painted scenes of Confederate victory in the War of Secession and the Second Mexican War; a plaque said they came from the brush of Gilbert Gaul. There were no scenes from the Great War, perhaps because Gaul died in 1919, but more likely because there were no victories to record.

The Hermitage Hotel had come through the war without much damage. Most of Nashville hadn't been so lucky when Custer's First Army seized it from the Confederate defenders in 1917. The Memorial Auditorium, across the street from the hotel, was a postwar building. What ever had stood there before wasn't standing when the damnyankees grudgingly gave the land south of the Cumberland back to the CSA in exchange for the bit of Kentucky they hadn't overrun. Jake reluctantly acknowledged that that was smart—with all of Kentucky in U.S. hands, no Confederate Senators and Representatives from the rump of the state could fulminate in Congress about how it needed to be redeemed.

His suite looked out at the Memorial Auditorium. Confederate flags and Freedom Party banners flew above it. Inside, delegates would be going through the motions of a political convention. Going through the motions was all they'd be doing. Unlike Whig and Radical Liberal conventions, this one was sewn up tight as a drum.

And I know who did the sewing. Featherston peered into a mirror with a gilt frame of rococo extravagance.

His lean, leathery features suddenly lit up in a grin. "Me," he said aloud, and pointed at his own reflection.

He'd just fixed himself a drink when someone knocked on the door. He had guards in the hallway. They wouldn't let anyone dangerous past. He opened the door without hesitation. There stood Ferdinand Koenig, who'd come west from Richmond with him. "Come on in, Ferd," he said.

"Willy here yet?" Koenig asked as he stepped into the suite.

Featherston shook his head. But then another door down the hall opened. Out stepped Knight, dapper in a gray pinstriped suit with sword-sharp lapels. He waved and walked down the hall toward the two longtime Freedom Party men. "Pat him down, boss?" one of the guards asked out of the side of his mouth.

"No, it's all right," Jake whispered back. "Nothing to worry about." The guard looked dubious. So did Koenig. They both played it Jake's way, though. *Everybody plays it my way from now on,* he thought, and smiled. *Everybody.*

Maybe Willy Knight thought the smile was meant for him. He grinned back and stuck out his hand. Jake took it. The clasp turned into a quiet trial of strength. Knight was a little taller and a lot wider through the shoulders, but Featherston's rawboned frame carried more muscle than it seemed to. When the two men let go, Knight was the one who opened and closed his hand several times to ease the pain and bring it back to life.

"Come on in," Jake said genially. "Have a drink."

"Don't have to ask me twice." In spite of the hand that was surely throbbing, Willy Knight managed another grin. "You barely have to ask me once."

They all went into Jake's hotel room. He closed the door behind them. The guards looked even less happy. He still wasn't worried. Knight wouldn't plug him himself. That wouldn't just take Jake off the ticket—it would take him off, too. He didn't want that. He wanted to be number one, but he'd settle for number two.

Jake made himself another drink. Ferdinand Koenig

and Willy Knight fixed whiskeys for themselves, too. He raised his glass in salute first to Knight, then to Koenig. "Mr. Vice President," he said. "Mr. Attorney General."

"Mr. President," the other two men said together. All three drank.

"It's going our way," Featherston said. "We've got what it takes, and the country finally knows it. What we have to do now is make sure the Rad Libs and especially the Whigs are whipped dogs long before November rolls around. I like what's happening down in Sonora—somebody hits you in the cheek, hit him back so goddamn hard, you knock his head off."

Koenig chuckled. "That's not quite what Jesus said."

"Yeah, and look what happened to him," Jake answered.

"Maybe we don't want to come on *too* strong," Willy Knight said. "We've spent the last ten years trying to live down that Grady Calkins son of a bitch."

"But now we've done it," Featherston said. "I want people to know—they'll be sorry if they even think about going the wrong way. We backed down ten years ago. We had to. We don't have to any more. We're going to win in November. You can take it to the bank. But even if we don't, by God, we're going into Richmond anyways."

Knight's bright blue eyes widened. "That's treason!" he said, and finished his drink with a gulp.

"It's only treason if you don't bring it off," Jake said calmly. "If we have to grab it, we'll win. We're getting things ready, all nice and quiet-like. Like I told you, I don't reckon we'll need it."

"We'd better not," Willy Knight said, still jolted. "Christ, you're talking civil war."

"Jeff Davis wasn't afraid of it. We shouldn't be, either," Jake answered. "I keep telling you and telling you, this is just in case. You've got to cover everybody who can carry the ball, and that's what I intend to do."

He almost hoped he would have to try to seize power by force. Storming the War Department would be as sweet as marching into Philadelphia would have been during the Great War.

"Once we're in, however we're in, we'll make everything legal," Koenig said. "If you're in, you make the rules, and that's just what we'll do."

Knight managed a sheepish smile, as if realizing he'd shown weakness. "You don't think small, do you, Jake?"

"Never have. Never will," Featherston replied. "As long as you can imagine something, you can make it real. That's what the Freedom Party's all about. We know the Confederate States can be great again. We know we can pay back all the bastards who held us while the damnyankees sucker-punched us. We can do it, and we're gonna do it. Right?"

"Right!" Willy Knight said. Jake was watching him. He seemed as hearty as he should have. Maybe he'd just had cold feet for a moment. Featherston shrugged. How much did it really matter? As vice president, all Willy'd do was make speeches, and Jake intended to make sure of what was in them before they came out of the handsome puppet's mouth. Knight still hadn't figured out he'd been condemned to oblivion. That only proved he wasn't so smart as he thought he was.

Jake and Ferdinand Koenig looked at each other. Koenig nodded, ever so slightly. The more he'd thought about it, the more he'd liked escaping the worthless number-two slot and being promised one where he could actually do things. Featherston had plans for the attorney general's office. *Once I'm elected . . .*

Three days later, he took another step toward the Gray House in Richmond. When he strode up onto the speakers' platform at the Memorial Auditorium to accept the Freedom Party nomination, the roar from the assembled delegates left his ears as stunned and battered as any artillery barrage ever had. The klieg lights blazing on him put the sun to shame. A thicket of microphones in front of him amplified his voice for the delegates, for people listening on the wireless web, and for the newsreels that would soon show his image all over the Confederate States.

"Hello, friends," Jake said to all the millions who would see and listen to him. "You know me. You know

618

what I stand for. I've been up here in front of you before. I'm Jake Featherston, and I'm here to tell you—"

"*The truth!*" the Freedom Party men bellowed.

Featherston nodded. "That's right. I'm here to tell you the truth. I've been doing that for a long time now. I think you're finally ready to listen. The truth is, this country needs to put people—white people, decent people—back to work, and we will. The truth is, this country needs to put the niggers who stabbed us in the back in their place, and we will. The truth is, Kentucky and Sequoyah and that joke the USA calls Houston still belong to the Confederate States. We ought to get 'em back—and we will."

He had to stop then; the applause was too loud and too long to let him continue. When at last it ebbed, he went on, "The truth is, the Whigs have had seventy years to run this country, and they've run it into the ground. Somebody else needs to do it, and do it right—*and we will.*" Another great roar. He held up his hands. Silence fell, completely and at once. Into it, he said, "If you like the way things have gone the past few years, vote Whig. But if you want to tell those people what you really think of 'em, vote—"

"*Freedom!*" That cry outdid all that had gone before. And then the delegates began to chant, "Feather*ston*! Feather*ston*! Feather*ston*!" Jake stood tall on the platform, waving to the crowd, waving to the country, glorying in what he had and reaching out for what he wanted.

Bouncing around South Carolina, from Charleston to Columbia to Greenville and to the smaller towns in between, Anne Colleton felt more than a little like a table-tennis ball. When she got out of her Birmingham in St. Matthews, her brother greeted her with, "Hello. Didn't I know you once upon a time?"

"Funny, Tom," she answered, meaning anything but. "Very funny. For God's sake, fix me a drink." Her own flat looked unfamiliar to her. Maybe her brother hadn't been joking after all.

He mixed whiskey and a little water for her and

plopped in a couple of ice cubes. After he'd made himself a drink, too, he said, "Well, you've got Jake Featherston, and it looks like he's going to win. Are you happy?"

"You bet I am." She would have said more, but a long pull at the whiskey came first. "Thank you. That's a life-saver."

"I ought to go places with a little cask around my neck, like those St. Bernard dogs in the Alps," Tom Colleton said.

"I'd be glad to see you, that's for sure." Anne took another sip. "Yes, I'm happy. I've waited for this day ever since the end of the war, even though I didn't know what I was waiting for at first."

"You walked away from Featherston once," Tom said.

"I made a mistake," Anne said. "Aren't you glad you never made a mistake in all your born days?"

"Now that you mention it, yes." Tom was irrepress-ible. Anne snorted. Her brother went on, "I'll tell you one mistake I didn't make: once I got out of politics, I didn't get back in."

"You wouldn't have talked that way before you got married," Anne said. *It made you soft,* was what she meant. To anyone else, she would have said that, said it without a moment's hesitation. With Tom, she hesitated.

He understood what she meant whether she said it or not. With a shrug, he answered, "Maybe you wouldn't talk the way you talk if you had. Nothing to cure the fire in your belly like a little boy."

"Maybe," Anne said tonelessly. Some small part of her wished she had settled down with Roger Kimball or Clarence Potter or that Texas oil man or one of her other lovers. A husband, a child to carry on after her . . . Those weren't the worst things in the world. But they weren't for her, and never would be. "I'm on my own, Tom. Too late to change it now."

Her brother eyed her. "And heaven help anybody who gets in your way?" he said.

Anne nodded. "Of course."

"What happens if Featherston decides you're in his way?"

She wished he hadn't asked that particular question. For a long time, she'd been a big fish in the small pond of South Carolina politics, and not the smallest fish in the much bigger pond of Confederate politics. Going from the Whigs to the Freedom Party, back to the Whigs and now back to Freedom had cut her influence down to size. So had getting older, as she was all too ruefully aware.

What if Jake Featherston decided she was in the way? What if *President* Jake Featherston decided she was in the way? She saw only one answer, and gave it to her brother: "In that case, I'd better move, don't you think?"

"You say that? You?" Tom looked and sounded as if he couldn't believe his ears. "You don't move for anybody."

"If it's a question of move or get squashed, I'll move," Anne said. "And Jake has more clout than I do. Jake has more clout than anybody does." She spoke with a certain somber pride. She might have been saying, *Yeah, I got licked, but the fellow who licked me was the toughest one of the bunch*. She shook her head. Might have? No. She *was* saying exactly that.

Tom shook his head, too, in wonder. "What's going to happen to the country, if a fellow who can make *you* pull in your horns starts running things?"

"We'll all go in the same direction, and it'll be the right direction," Anne said. "We've owed a lot of debts for a long time. Don't you want to pay them back? I know I do."

"Well, yes, but not if I have to go bust to do it."

"We won't," Anne said positively. "He'll do what needs doing, instead of fumbling around the way Burton Mitchel has ever since things went sour."

"Maybe. I hope so," her brother said. "Hell, I'll probably even vote for him myself. But that's all I intend to do. You can go running around the state if you want to. Me, I'll stay home and tend my garden."

Had he read *Candide*? She doubted it; she couldn't imagine a book that seemed less her brother's cup of tea. She said, "The whole Confederacy is my garden."

"You're welcome to it," Tom replied. "It's too big for me to get my arms around. South Carolina's too big. I think even St. Matthews is too big, but I can try that. My wife and my little baby boy, now—*that* I understand just fine."

He'd gone into the war a captain, and a boy himself. He'd come out a lieutenant-colonel, and a man. Now he was a family man, but that seemed a pulling-in, not a growing-out. It made Anne sad. "You've got a lot of time left," she said. "I hope you do, anyway. You can do whatever you want with it. What I'm going to do with mine is, I'm going to put this country back on its feet."

"I hope so." Tom got up and kissed her on the cheek. "What I'm going to do is, I'm going home to my family. Take care of yourself, Sis. I worry about you." He went out the door, taking her chance for the last word with him.

I'm going home to my family. Ever since they'd lost their parents when they were small, *she'd* been his family, she and their brother Jacob, who was dead. He didn't think that way any more. He didn't care about the country any more, either. Anne made herself another whiskey. Tom might have his wife and a little boy. She had a cause, and a cause on its way to victory.

She slept in her own bed that night. She couldn't remember the last time she'd slept there. It had been weeks, she knew. Her own mattress felt as unfamiliar as any of the hotel beds where she'd lain down lately.

When morning came, she was on her way again, driving down to Charleston. Featherston was coming into town in a couple of days for a rally that should finish sewing up South Carolina for the Freedom Party. She hurled herself into the work of making sure everything went off the way it was supposed to. Things were more complicated than they had been when she first started planning rallies. Making sure the wireless web and the newsreels were taken care of kept her busy up until an hour and a half before Featherston's speech began. Saul Goldman did a lot of work with them—more than she did, in fact. She wondered if the head of the Freedom Party knew just what a smart little Jew he had running that part of his operation.

"Hello, there," Featherston said, coming up behind

her as she peered out from the wings to make sure the lighting arrangements were the way she wanted them.

She jumped. She wasn't the sort of person who jumped when someone came up behind her, but Jake Featherston wasn't the ordinary sort of person coming up behind her. "Oh. Hello." She hated herself for how callow she sounded. No one had any business making her feel so unsure, so . . . *weak* was the only word that seemed to fit. No one had any business doing it, but Jake did.

He eyed the hall with the knowing gaze of a man who'd given speeches in a lot of different places. "Good to have you back in the Party," he said, his attention returning to her. "I wasn't even close to sure it would be, in spite of the pretty speeches you made me. But it is. You've given me a lot of help here, and I do appreciate it."

"Happy to do anything I can," Anne said: a great thumping lie. She knew she was doing things *for* Featherston, doing them as a subordinate. She wasn't used to being a subordinate, wasn't used to it and despised it. Once, she and Roger Kimball had thought they would guide Jake Featherston to power and then enjoy it themselves, with him in the role of puppet. The only small consolation she had was that they weren't the only ones who'd underestimated him. At one time or another, almost everybody in the CSA had underestimated Featherston.

He said, "There's a lot of people I owe, and I'm going to pay every single one of them back. But you, you owe me—you owe me plenty for walking out on me when I really needed a hand."

He hadn't forgotten. He never forgot a slight, no matter how small. Anne knew as much. And hers hadn't been small, not at all. She said, "I know. I'm trying to pay you back." Her gesture encompassed the hall where he'd speak.

The answer seemed to catch him by surprise. Slowly, thoughtfully, he nodded. "Well, you're doing better than a lot of folks I can think of," he said.

"Good." Anne didn't like the way he looked at her. He'd been an artilleryman during the war, not a sniper, but he eyed her as she thought a sniper would: all cold, deadly concentration. She was used to intimidating, not being intimidated. Being on the receiving end of a glance like that chilled her.

But Featherston sounded warm and lively when he went into his speech. "I never had a fancy name," he declared. "I was only one more Confederate soldier, with a stamped tin identity disk around my neck. But every great idea draws men to it. Every idea steps out before the nation. It has to win from the nation the fighters it needs, so one day it's strong enough to turn the course of destiny. Our day is here!"

The hall erupted. Anne found herself clapping as hard as anyone else in the building. When she listened to Jake on the stump, she always believed what he said while he was saying it. She might not believe it later, when she thought about it, but at the time.... She shivered, though she also went on clapping. She hadn't met many people who frightened her. He did.

He thundered on: "Lots of people in the Confederate States think the Freedom Party can't do the job if we get in. They're fooling themselves! Today our movement can't be destroyed. It's here. People have to reckon with it, whether they like it or not. We recognize three principles—responsibility, command, and obedience. We've built a party—a party of millions, mind—based on one thing: achievement. And if you don't like it, we say, 'We'll fight today! We'll fight tomorrow! And if you don't fancy our rally today, we'll hold another one next week, even bigger!' "

He slammed his fist down on the podium. More applause interrupted him. Anne looked down at her carefully tended, carefully manicured hands. Her palms were red and sore. She'd broken a nail without even noticing.

"I'm not just here to ask you for your vote, or to ask you to do this or that for the Party," Featherston said. "I'm here to tell you the truth, and what I aim to do. What I've got to give is the only thing that can pull our country back on its feet again. If all you Confederates had the same faith in your country that our Freedom Party stalwarts do, we wouldn't be in the mess we're in. We *will* pull ourselves together. We're on the way, and I know you'll help."

I'm already helping, Anne thought proudly. Not being in charge didn't bother her so much any more—not as long as she was listening to Jake, anyhow.

XIX

In an odd way, Colonel Abner Dowling was glad to have something to worry about that didn't involve keeping the Mormons in Salt Lake City from erupting. The desultory war with Japan hadn't done the job. He'd wanted to go fight, and the War Department hadn't let him. That brought nothing but frustration.

Looking with alarm at events south of the border, though, did a fine job of distracting him. He rounded on his adjutant one morning, growling, "What the devil are we going to do if that Featherston maniac really does get elected in the CSA come November?"

"I don't know, sir," Captain Toricelli answered. "What *can* we do if he wins the election? We can't very well tell the Confederates to go back and vote again."

"No, but I wish we could," Dowling said. "That man is nothing but trouble waiting to happen. He wants another go at us. He hardly even bothers hiding it any more."

"I don't see how we can stop a politician from making speeches, sir," Angelo Toricelli said. "If he gets to be president and then starts building up the C.S. Army and violating the terms of the armistice the Confederates signed, we can do something about him. Till then . . ." He shrugged.

"But *will* President Hoover do anything?" Dowling said. "He certainly hasn't done much since he landed in Powel House six months ago."

Toricelli gave him a sly smile. "Would you rather we still had President Blackford?"

"Good God, no!" Dowling exclaimed; he'd always been a solid Democrat. "But I would like to see Hoover doing a little more. If things are any better than they were when Blackford went home to Dakota, I haven't seen it."

"It won't happen overnight, sir." His adjutant was a Democrat, too. Most officers were.

"Obviously," Dowling said. "I do wish it would show some signs of happening at all, though."

"The whole world has troubles," Toricelli said, and Dowling nodded, for that was obviously true.

"Utah probably has more troubles than the rest of the world." Abner Dowling corrected himself: "Utah certainly has worse troubles than the rest of the world. Maybe that's why we're not seeing things looking better here." He spoke as if trying to convince himself, hoping he could convince himself. But he remained incompletely convinced. He said, "If more people here had jobs, we wouldn't need to worry . . . quite . . . so much about this place going up in smoke."

"Yes, sir," Captain Toricelli agreed; his adjutant was nothing if not polite. But Toricelli was also stubborn. He went on, "If you know how to arrange that, sir, you should have run for president last year."

General Custer had always claimed he'd had a shot at the presidency in 1884. There were any number of ways in which Dowling didn't want to imitate the officer under whom he'd served for so long. He couldn't imagine any job he wanted less than that of the president, especially in these thankless times.

And yet . . . He snapped his fingers. "You know, Captain, we could put a lot of people to work if we cleared Temple Square of the rubble that's been sitting there for almost twenty years now."

Toricelli frowned. "Yes, sir, we *could*. But isn't the point of keeping the rubble there to remind the Mormons we gave them a licking? There's not going to be a new Temple in Salt Lake City, any more than there's going to be one in Jerusalem."

Dowling muttered under his breath. Not only was

Captain Toricelli polite and stubborn, he was also smart. But Dowling still liked the idea, or part of it. "All right, suppose we cordon off the part of the square that held the Temple and get rid of the rest of the rubbish?" he said. "The Tabernacle and the other buildings weren't holy ground."

He waited, wondering what his adjutant would make of that. Toricelli spent close to a minute thinking it over. Then he said, "Shall I draft a telegram for you to send to the War Department?"

"Yes, Captain, if you'd be so kind." Dowling beamed. He suspected Captain Toricelli made a tougher audience than any he'd face back in Philadelphia.

The wire went out two days later. The afternoon it did, Dowling got a wire from the War Department: WINNING HEARTS AND MINDS IN UTAH DESIRABLE. YOUR IDEA FORWARDED TO SECRETARY OF WAR FOR APPROVAL. The printed signature on the sheet of yellow paper belonged to Lieutenant General Sam Sturgis, chief of the General Staff.

He heard from the Secretary of War the next day. PRESIDENT HOOVER PERSONALLY CONTROLS ALL DECISIONS ON UTAH, the wire said. I HAVE PASSED THIS PROPOSAL TO HIM RECOMMENDING APPROVAL, WHICH IS EXPECTED. Dowling understood that this Cabinet official, a distant relative of the last Democratic president before Hoover, remained in the service of his country despite being confined to a wheelchair by some rare, debilitating disease.

Though Captain Toricelli already knew what was in the telegram, Dowling set it on his desk anyhow. "If the chief of the General Staff says yes, and if the Secretary of War says yes, how can the president say no?" he exulted.

"I don't know, sir," his adjutant replied. "I hope we don't find out."

But they did. The very next day, the telephone in Dowling's office rang. He picked it up. "Abner Dowling speaking."

"Colonel Dowling, this is Herbert Hoover." And it was. Dowling had heard his voice on the wireless and in newsreels too many times to have any doubt.

He stiffened to attention in his chair. "It's a privilege to speak with you, sir."

"Maybe you won't think so when I'm done," the president said. "Your proposal for makework for the people of Utah is *not* to go forward. Do you understand me?"

"It is not to go forward," Dowling repeated. "I hear you, and I will obey, of course, but I have to say I do not understand."

"We have had too much of Socialist-style, individualism-sapping false nostrums the past twelve years," Hoover said. "Paternalism and state socialism have done a great deal of harm to the country. They stifle initiative. They cramp and cripple the mental and spiritual energies of the people. And I will not have them under my administration."

Well, that's that, Dowling thought. But he couldn't help asking, "Sir, don't you think Utah is a special case?"

"Every case has partisans who insist it is special," Hoover answered. "I recognize none of them. I believe none of them. The same principles must apply throughout the United States."

Quickly, Dowling said, "I meant no harm, Mr. President." He'd never heard Hoover sound so vehement, not in any of his speeches. He hadn't imagined the new president *could* sound so vehement.

"I believe you, Colonel. I am not angry at you," President Hoover said, which made Dowling feel a little— though only a little—better. Hoover went on, "I'm sure the Socialists meant no harm, either. But you know which road is paved with good intentions."

"Yes, sir," Dowling said.

"All right, then," the president said. "We'll say no more about it. But my decision is final. I do not want this issue raised again."

"Yes, sir," Dowling repeated.

"Good." Hoover hung up.

Dowling emerged from his office feeling like a man who'd survived a bomb going off much too close. Thanks to the Confederates during the war and that damned Canuck afterwards, he knew more about bombs going off too close than he'd ever wanted to learn. What he felt must not have shown on his face, though, for Captain Toricelli said, "I heard you talking to the president, sir. May we go ahead?"

His voice said he was confident of the answer. Well, Abner Dowling had been confident of the answer, too. Much good his confidence had done him. He shook his head. His jowls wobbled back and forth. "No, Captain. In fact, we're ordered *not* to go ahead, and so we won't."

Toricelli gaped. "But . . . why, sir?"

"The president feels the scheme smacks of socialism. He says we've had enough government programs trying to get us over the hump, and he doesn't want another one."

"But . . ." his adjutant said again.

"He's the president. What he says goes," Dowling said. "And he and Coolidge did campaign against government interference, and they did get elected. If I look at it that way, maybe I'm not so surprised."

"But . . ." Toricelli said once more. After a moment, he gathered himself and managed something else: "We're not competing against any private firm clearing Temple Square. There *is* no private firm clearing Temple Square."

"If you care to call Powel House, Captain, go right ahead," Dowling said. "As for me, I'm sure I know what the president wants done and what he doesn't. And he doesn't want us giving the Mormons even a dime to haul rocks out of Temple Square."

"A few days ago, we were saying he didn't seem to want to do much of anything," his adjutant observed. "Don't you think this goes too far, though?"

"What I think is, he's the president of the United States. If you set my opinion next to his, I know whose comes out on top. We've been ordered not to proceed. That being so, we won't proceed."

"I can't argue with you there, sir," Toricelli said.

"Good," Dowling said. "I'm glad. For your sake, I'm glad. It's a free country. You can disagree with the president. Nobody will say a word. But when he gives an order, we follow it."

"Of course, sir," Captain Toricelli replied, as any officer in the Army would have done.

A few days later, Dowling received Heber Young in his office. Young, a handsome man in his early thirties, was a grandson of Brigham Young. Given the number of wives and children Brigham had had, that was hardly a unique distinction in Utah these days. This particular Young came as close to being an official leader as the Mormons had. Since, under martial law, the Church of Jesus Christ of Latter-Day Saints was proscribed, he couldn't be very official. But he wasn't exactly unofficial, either.

"What can I do for you, Mr. Young?" Dowling asked after greetings that were what diplomats called "correct": polite and chilly.

"People here need work, Colonel," Heber Young replied.

"People all over the country need work, sir," Dowling said.

"Will you tell me the problem is not worse here?" Young asked.

"If it is, whose fault is that?" Dowling said. "I was with General Pershing when a Mormon fanatic murdered him—a Mormon fanatic we've never caught, for other Mormon fanatics have sheltered him for all the years since."

"I don't know how you can say that, Colonel, when the U.S. government insists again and again that there is no such thing as the Mormon Church in Utah these days." Young spoke with surprisingly mild irony.

It was still enough to raise a flush on Dowling's plump cheeks. "Funny, Mr. Young. Very funny. Come to the point, if you'd be so kind."

"All right. I will." Young looked serious to the point of solemnity. "We could use—we desperately need—a public-works program to give men jobs, help them support their families, and, most important of all, give them hope."

Dowling sighed. "As it happens, I have discussed that very notion with President Hoover in the past few days. He opposes such programs not only here but anywhere in the USA. Don't expect them. Don't hope for them. You will be disappointed."

Heber Young proved he could quote the Old Testament as well as the Book of Mormon, murmuring, " 'Mene, mene, tekel upharsin. Thou art weighed in the balance, and art found wanting.' As God said to Belshazzar, so I say to Hoover." And he walked out of Abner Dowling's office without a backward glance.

Scipio hadn't got so dressed up since his days as Anne Colleton's butler. The Huntsman's Lodge was as fine a restaurant as Augusta boasted, and expected its waiters to look the part. (It paid no better than any other restaurant, and worse than some. It expected the men who served food to make most of their money from tips. The customers tipped no better there than anywhere else. One reason they'd got rich enough to afford to eat at the Huntsman's Lodge was their reluctance to part unnecessarily with even a penny.)

Walking to the restaurant in boiled shirt, black tie, and tails was torture for Scipio in the sodden heat of late August. If he hadn't needed work of any sort so badly . . . But he did, and he was glad to have any at all. So many men in Augusta, Negro and white, didn't.

Walking to the Huntsman's Lodge in formal attire was, or could be, torture in more ways than one. It exposed him to the wit, such as that was, of the white citizens of Augusta. He could usually see trouble coming before it struck. That did him no good what ever, of course.

"Looky what we got here!" a fellow in straw hat and bib overalls whooped, pointing at Scipio. "We got us a nigger all tricked out like a penguin! Ain't that somethin'?"

Other whites coming down Marbury Street smiled. One or two laughed. Three or four stopped to see what would happen next. Scipio hoped nothing would happen next. Sometimes one joke was enough to get the meanness out of a white man's system. Smiling what was probably a sickly smile, Scipio tried to walk on by.

As he came closer to the man in overalls, he saw a Freedom Party pin glittering on one overalls strap. His heart sank. That was likely to mean worse trouble than he would have got from somebody else. And, sure as hell, the white man stepped into his path and said, "What the hell's a nigger doin' dressed up like he's King Shit?"

When Scipio tried to walk around him, the man blocked his way again. He had to answer. He did, as meekly as he could: "I's a waiter, suh. I gots to wear dis git-up."

He should have known—he *had* known—nothing he said would do him any good. Scowling, the white man demanded, "How come you got a job when I ain't, God damn you? Where's the justice in that?" Scipio tried to escape with a shrug. It didn't work. The man shouted, "Answer me, you goddamn motherfucking son of a bitch!"

Because I have a brain, and you haven't. Because my mouth isn't hooked up to the toilet. Because I've had more baths this week than you have this year. If Scipio said any of that, he was a dead man. He looked down at the sidewalk, the picture of a submissive Negro. Softly, he said, "Suh, I been waitin' table forty year now. I's right good at it." *What are you good at, besides causing trouble? Not much, I'll bet.* One more thing he dared not say.

"You know how many white folks is hungry, and you're marchin' off to work in your goddamn fancy penguin suit?" the man in overalls snarled. "I ought to kick your black ass around the block a few times, teach you respect for your betters."

He drew back his foot as if to do just that. All Scipio could do was take it or try to run. He intended to run— he didn't want his outfit damaged. Getting it repaired or, worse, having to buy a new one would cost him money he didn't have. But then one of the other white men said, "Hell, let him go. Ain't his fault he has to dress up like a damn fool to go to work."

"Thank you, suh," Scipio whispered. "I thanks you from de bottom of my heart."

The white man with the Freedom Party pin glanced around at the little crowd. Most people nodded at what the other fellow had said. Scowling, the Freedom Party man said, "All right. All right for now, goddammit. But when Jake Featherston gets elected, we'll put every damn nigger in his place, not just the ones in the fancy suits." He strutted down the street as if he were a mover and shaker, not a man with no more than a fifty-fifty chance of being able to write his own name.

"Thank you," Scipio said once more.

"I didn't do it for you," said the man who'd urged he be left alone. "I did it on account of I purely can't stand the Freedom Party." He laughed bitterly. "And I wonder how long I'll be allowed to say that in public if Featherston *does* win."

Somebody's not blind, anyhow, Scipio thought as he hurried up the street toward the Huntsman's Lodge. *But if Featherston wins, this fellow can change his mind. He can say he was for the Freedom Party all along, and he'll get on fine. I'm black. I didn't choose that, and I can't change it.*

As far as he could see, he had no choices at all if the Freedom Party won.

Getting to the restaurant was a relief. For one thing, he did make it on time. If he got in trouble for any reason, he could be back pounding the pavement looking for work. He knew that all too well—how could he help knowing? For another, the rhythms and rituals of work kept him too busy to worry . . . much.

He was obsequious to the prosperous white men and their sleek female companions who dined at the Lodge, but that bothered him much less than having to be obsequious to whites on the street. A white waiter in New York City would act subservient on the job. Acting subservient was part of a waiter's job—which went a long way towards explaining why there were so few white waiters in the Confederate States, where whites thought subservience the province of blacks alone. But that waiter in New York City became his customers' equal as soon as he left his job. Scipio didn't, and never would.

A portly, middle-aged man eating pheasant looked up from his meal and said, "Don't I know you from somewhere?"

With a small thrill of horror, Scipio realized the man had danced attendance upon Anne Colleton at Marshlands before the war. Had his own past come back to haunt him after all these years? He shook his head and put on his thickest accent to answer, "Ah don' reckon so, suh."

The customer shrugged. "You must be right. The boy I knew spoke better than I do myself."

Boy. Even then, Scipio had been in his thirties. Whites in the CSA refused to take Negroes seriously. He supposed that was why the Red uprising during the war had got as far as it had. Not even clever whites like Miss Anne had imagined Negroes could conceive of grievances serious enough to make them take up arms for redress.

All that went through his head in a flash. To reassure the white man—he was Tony Somebody, and Anne Colleton had thought him a pompous ass—he said, "Ah talks lahk I talks, suh. Dis heah de onliest way Ah knows how." He wondered if he *could* speak like an educated white man any more. Or would that dialect of English have disappeared from his tongue like a foreign language seldom used?

"All right. Never mind," the customer said, and went back to his pheasant. When he walked out, he left a fifty-cent tip, as if to apologize for bothering Scipio. *Noblesse oblige,* Scipio thought, and made the silver coin disappear. These days, there were men desperate enough to kill for half a dollar.

It was after ten when the Huntsman's Lodge closed. Scipio worried less about being on the street in black tie and tails than he had during the day. Fewer whites would be out there to see him than during the day—and, with Augusta's bad street lighting, whoever was there wouldn't be able to get that good a look at him anyhow.

But as soon as he opened the door, he closed it again in a hurry and ducked back into the restaurant. "What's the matter with you, Xerxes?" demanded his manager, a skinny, energetic young white man named Jerry Dover. "Go on home. Get the hell out of here."

"Marse Jerry, I reckons I waits a while," Scipio answered. "Dem Freedom Party white folks"—he almost said *buckra,* but caught himself before using that word in front of a white—"is marchin' down de street. Don't want them seein' me, you don't mind too much."

He had no idea what Dover's politics were. Talking politics with a white man could only be futile and dangerous. But whatever else Dover might have been, he was no fool. The other three colored waiters in the place showed no eagerness to leave. "All right," the manager said. "Don't worry about it. Stay as long as you need to. Sooner or later, those folks out there'll be done, and then y'all can go on about your business."

But, staring out through the small panes of glass set into the door of the Huntsman's Lodge at eye level, Scipio wondered if Jerry Dover knew what he was talking about. Block after well-organized block of men and women—mostly men—paraded past on Marbury Street. Some carried Confederate flags. Some carried Freedom Party flags. Some carried torches, to make the rest easier to see and the gathering as a whole more impressive.

A lot of the men marched in step. Most of the ones who did wore the white shirts and butternut trousers of Freedom Party stalwarts. Some few of the disciplined marchers, though, were in what was almost but not quite Confederate uniform. They carried Tredegars whose bayonets gleamed bloody in the torchlight.

"Feather*ston*! Feather*ston*! Feather*ston*!" The endless chant came close to making Scipio long for the old cry of, *Freedom!* That had been a frustrated shout, the cry of men who didn't fully understand what they wanted or how to go about getting it. This . . . This promised trouble right around the corner, and said just what kind of trouble it was, too.

And the parade went on and on and on. Scipio wouldn't have believed that Augusta held so many people, let alone that it held so many Freedom Party backers. Jake Featherston wasn't in town. Neither was Willy Knight. These people had nothing special to lure them out of their houses. But they came. Maybe that was the scariest thing of all.

At last, after half an hour, the procession ended. Jerry Dover hadn't gone outside, either. He had pushed Scipio and the other blacks out of the way a few times to look at things for himself. "Well, well, well," he said when it was over and the raucous cries of *Featherston!* at last ebbed away. "I always wondered, but now I know. Those bastards really *are* crazy."

Scipio and the other waiters exchanged glances. Dover didn't need to say that. What white man in the CSA needed to make Negroes like him? The question was so ridiculous, it might not even have occurred to Scipio without the goad of something as massive as the Freedom Party procession.

The sheer scope of it got through to Dover, too. He spoke again: "Crazy or not, though, there's a hell of a lot of 'em, ain't there? Don't see how they're going to lose the election. Wish to God I did." He made pushing motions at the waiters. "They're gone. You can disappear, too."

Searchlights blazed from Allen Park, not far off to the west. With the door open, the rhythmic shouting of Jake Featherston's name grew louder and more frightening. Scipio scuttled back toward the Terry, a black dust mote adrift on that dreadful sea of sound.

Jefferson Pinkard came to the Freedom Party meeting in his jailer's uniform. No time to go back to his apartment and put on the usual white shirt and butternut trousers, not if he wanted to be sure of having a place to sit down when he got to the old livery stable. Party meetings had never been so crowded. He saw faces he hadn't seen for years, and he saw plenty of faces he'd never seen before—more at every meeting, it seemed.

Now people want to hop on the train—when it looks like it's just about to get to the station, he thought, eyeing with no small scorn the strangers who suddenly called themselves Freedom Party men. He'd been with the Party train every inch of the way, through ups and downs and derailments. Hell, he'd been at the Alabama State Fairgrounds out at the west end of town when Grady Calkins murdered President Hampton. He hadn't given up even then, even when things looked blackest.

He sent the Johnny-come-latelies another sour stare. Would they have stuck with Jake Featherston when the going got rough? Not likely, not most of them. They were here because they wanted to ride a winner's coattails, not because they *believed.* You could use people like that, but could you ever really trust them? He had his doubts.

Caleb Briggs strode briskly up onto the rostrum. He had a microphone up there these days, to help his gas-ruined voice fill the meeting hall despite the buzz from the big crowd. In the row behind Pinkard, a man who'd been in the party for a while explained to a couple of new fish who Briggs was. Jeff muttered something incredulous under his breath. Didn't they know *anything*? Evidently not.

Behind the dentist who headed up the Freedom Party in Birmingham stood Confederate and Party flags. He crisply saluted each of them in turn, then stepped up to that microphone and said, "Freedom!"

"*Freedom!*" The roar from the crowd made Pinkard's head spin. The new Party men were good for something, anyhow—they had big mouths.

Briggs' smile showed white teeth. "Good to see y'all here," he rasped, "old friends and new." A few of the long-time Freedom Party men, Jeff among them, laughed softly. Caleb knew what was what, same as anybody else who'd seen the light a while ago. Smiling still, Briggs went on, "A month to go, boys, and then we get to the Promised Land. We've been in the wilderness a long time now, but we're almost there."

Pinkard whooped. "Freedom!" he shouted, as if he were a Negro responding to a preacher's sermon. He wasn't the only one, either. Far from it.

But when Briggs held up a hand, silence fell, just like that. By God, the Freedom Party had discipline. "The one thing we've got to do now," he said, and paused to draw more air into his ravaged lungs, "is make sure we don't stumble and fall. We've come too far for that. This time, we *win*."

More shouts of, "Freedom!" rang out. So did a chorus of, "Feather*ston*!" Pinkard tried to imagine waking up the morning after Election Day and finding out Jake Featherston had lost again. He didn't think the Party could survive it. He wasn't sure he could.

"We've got to make *sure* we win," Briggs went on. "We've been doing plenty, but we've got to do more. Just for instance, Hugo Black is coming to town Saturday."

A low murmur ran through the crowd. The Whig vice-presidential candidate was good on the stump—not so good as Featherston or Willy Knight, not as far as Pinkard was concerned, but still a formidable speaker.

Caleb Briggs grinned a sly, conspiratorial grin. "I'm sure we'll give him a nice, warm Birmingham welcome when he pays us a call." He waited for the grins and sniggers to stop, then held up a hand. "It may not be so easy. The Whigs aren't ashamed to steal our tricks. They'll have their own tough boys at Black's rally, you can bet on that."

"We'll lick 'em!" Jeff roared, before anybody else could. Somebody behind him clapped him on the back.

"We'd better lick 'em," Briggs said. "We need to make damn sure we do. I want a show of hands for volunteers."

Every man in the place raised his hand. Some men held up both hands at once to look more prominent. Pinkard thought about doing that, but didn't. One hand was plenty. He didn't need to show off.

Up on the platform, Caleb Briggs grinned. "I knew I could count on you. Be here Saturday at half past twelve. Black's speaking at two. He reckons he is, anyways."

Half past twelve was a good time to gather. The men who still worked Saturday mornings would have time to put in their half days. A lot of businesses had cut back to five days a week. Men who worked for them wouldn't have any problems showing up, either. And, of course, the men who were out of work could come whenever the Party needed them, as long as they could scrape up trolley fare.

Jeff was scheduled to work all day that Saturday. He traded shifts with another jailer, a man who despised politics of all sorts almost as much as he despised prisoners of all sorts. He got to Freedom Party headquarters fifteen minutes early. His shirt was so white, it gleamed like polished marble. His pants were the exact color of the uniform he'd worn during the war. He'd put on a pair of steel-toed shoes he hadn't worn since leaving the Sloss Works. They weren't a required part of a stalwart's outfit, but they let him kick like a mule.

Across the street from the headquarters, a couple of Whigs were arguing with a gray-clad policeman. "They're preparing for a riot in there!" one of them said loudly. "You've got to do something to stop them."

The cop shrugged broad shoulders. "I can't arrest anybody till he commits a crime," he said. "It's still a free country, you know." As the Whigs started to expostulate, he smiled and sank his barb: "Freedom!"

They jerked as if stung. The loud one cried, "Why, you miserable, stinking—"

"Shut up, buddy, or I'll run you in." The policeman set a hand on his nightstick.

"I thought you couldn't arrest anyone till he committed a crime."

"Disturbing the peace is a crime."

"What do you think the Freedom Party's going to do?" the Whig demanded.

"That's a political demonstration. That's different."

Into the old livery stable Pinkard went. When he came out again, a stout bludgeon in his hand, the Whigs were still yelling at the cop. They withdrew—hell, they ran for their lives—as soon as the Freedom Party started coming out. Jeers chased them down the street.

The day Grady Calkins killed Wade Hampton V, Tredegar-carrying state militiamen had held the stalwarts away from the president of the CSA. Nobody had called out the militia this time—so Caleb Briggs insisted. Back in the early 1920s, people had thought they could suppress the Freedom Party. The governor of Alabama wouldn't dare try it now. The legislature might not impeach him, convict him, and throw him out on his ear if he did. On the other hand, it might.

Down the street toward the park marched the Freedom Party stalwarts, several hundred strong. People on the sidewalk either cheered or had the sense to keep their mouths shut. People in autos drove away in a hurry. The ones who didn't got their windscreens and windows smashed. Pinkard supposed, if the Whigs had been ruthless enough, they could have sent cars smashing through the ranks of Freedom Party men. Featherston's followers would have done it to the Whigs in a minute if they thought it would help. The Whigs didn't try it.

Jeff was up in the fifth or sixth row of marchers. The leaders let out whoops when they turned the last corner and saw Ingram Park, near city hall, dead ahead. Shouts followed the whoops a heartbeat later, as the Whig stalwarts charged them. The Whigs aimed to fight in the narrow confines of the street and not let the Freedom Party men into the park at all.

That probably means we have got more men than they do, Jeff thought. Then the first Whig swung a club at him, and he stopped thinking. He blocked the blow and aimed one of his own at the Whig's head. They stood there smashing at each other for a few seconds. Then someone tripped the Whig. Jeff hit him in the face with his bludgeon, kicked him in the ribs with those steel-toed shoes, and strode forward, looking for a new foe.

He and another man in white shirt and butternut trousers teamed up on a Whig. They both stomped the fellow once he was down. Shouting "Freedom!" they pressed forward, shoulder to shoulder. "Freedom!" Jeff yelled again. "Featherston and freedom!"

"Longstreet!" the Whigs yelled back. "Longstreet and liberty!" Samuel Longstreet, a grandson of the famous James, was a Senator from Virginia. He wasn't bad on the stump, either. "Longstreet and Black!" a rash Whig shouted.

That gave the Freedom Party men an opening. "Longstreet the nigger-lover!" they yelled, and pushed forward harder than ever.

Pinkard's left arm ached where a club had got home. Another one had laid his forehead open above his left eyebrow. He kept shaking his head like a restive horse, trying to keep the blood out of his eyes. Step by bitter step, the Freedom Party men forced the Whigs back toward the end of the street. If they broke out into the crowd, they'd win the day, rampaging through the crowd and wrecking Hugo Black's rally.

A pistol barked. Jeff saw the muzzle flash rather than hearing the report; that was lost in the din of battle. The Freedom Party man next to him grunted and clutched his belly and folded up like a concertina.

As soon as the first shot was fired, pistols came out

on both sides. Freedom Party men and Whigs blazed away at one another from point-blank range. The Whigs had fired first—Pinkard thought they had, anyhow—but the Freedom Party men had more firepower and more determination, or maybe just more combat experience. They kept going forward, smashing down or shooting the last few Whigs who stood against them.

"Freedom!" Pinkard bawled as he ran across the grass toward the people who'd thought they were going to hear the Whig vice-presidential candidate speak. "Freedom!" his fellow stalwarts howled at his side and behind him. This had to be what a breakthrough felt like, what the damnyankees had known when they smashed the Confederate lines in Tennessee and Virginia during the war.

He whooped with delight when more Freedom Party men burst out from another street and charged the assembled Whigs. Then the stalwarts were in among the crowd, some clubbing, some kicking, some shooting. A few of the men in the crowd tried to fight back. Most of the tough ones, though, had tried to hold the Freedom Party men out and were already down.

From the podium, Hugo Black cried out, "This is madness!"

He was right, not that it did him any good. Madness it was, madness engulfing his party, madness engulfing his country. After the third bullet cracked past him, after the Birmingham police did nothing to slow down the Freedom Party stalwarts, he leaped down and made his escape.

Pinkard's club broke when he hit a rich-looking man in the head. The Whig's skull broke, too; Jeff could feel it. He waded on through the fray with fists and heavy shoes. "Freedom!" he yelled exultantly. "Featherston and freedom!"

Whig headquarters in Charleston a week before the election reminded Clarence Potter of Army of Northern Virginia headquarters a week before the Confederate States had asked the United States for an armistice. He was among the walking wounded: two fingers of his left hand were splinted, he sported a shiner and wore a new pair of glasses he couldn't afford, and he was all over bruises. And, all things considered, he was one of the lucky ones.

Braxton Donovan had a bandage wrapped around his head. He'd needed an X ray to make sure he didn't have a fractured skull. His nod held a graveyard quality. "Almost over now," he said.

"Everything's almost over now," Potter said gloomily. "We showed those bastards we could fight, too, by God."

The lawyer nodded, then grimaced and reached into his jacket pocket for a vial of pills. He washed down two of them with a sip from his drink. "Wonderful stuff, codeine," he remarked. "It's especially good with whiskey. Doesn't quite make the headache go away, but it sure makes you stop caring. Yeah, we showed the yahoos we could fight, too. Fat lot of good it's done us. How many dead?"

"A couple of dozen here in Charleston." Even before Potter went into intelligence, he'd always had figures at his fingertips. "Over a hundred in the state. All over the country? Who knows? More than a thousand, or I miss my guess. Close to fifty men killed in that one shootout in Birmingham all by itself. Hugo Black is lucky to be alive, if you want to call it luck."

"Ha. Funny." Donovan drained the whiskey. He scowled. "I hope those pills hurry up. My head feels like it wants to fall off. If that bastard had hit me just a little harder, you'd be counting one more dead man here."

"I know." Potter held up his left hand. "I got these broken keeping another one of those stinking stalwarts from caving in my skull. We have made them pay, though. Even if they do win, they know they've been in a brawl."

"If they win, it doesn't matter," Braxton Donovan said. "Do you know what I wish?"

"Hell, yes, I know what you wish. You wish the same thing I do," Potter said. "You wish the Radical Liberals would drop out of the race and throw whatever weight they've got left behind Longstreet and Black. And you know what?"

"What?"

For once, Potter let a full, rich drawl come into his

voice as he answered, "It ain't a-gonna happen, that's what."

"It should, by God," Donovan said. "The Rad Libs have just as much to lose if Jake Featherston wins as we do."

"You know that, and I know that, but Hull and Long don't know that," Clarence Potter said. "All they know is, we've been kicking their tails every six years as long as there've been Confederate States of America. If we were in hell—"

"What do you mean, 'if'?" Donovan said. "With Jake Featherston president . . ."

"If we were in hell and screaming for water, they'd throw us a big jar of gasoline to drink." Potter was damned if he'd let the lawyer step on a good line.

"What are we going to do?" Braxton Donovan said. "What *can* we do? Only thing left is to go down swinging."

"Far as I'm concerned, we battle 'em all the way up till next Tuesday," Potter replied. "The more Congressmen and legislators we elect, the more trouble Featherston and his goons will have getting their laws through. And the bastard can't run again in 1939, so this too shall pass."

"Like a kidney stone," Donovan said morosely. By the way he set one hand on the small of his back for a moment, he spoke from experience. But then he managed a smile and gently touched his bandaged head. "Codeine *is* starting to work."

"Good," Potter said. People were setting down drinks and taking seats on the folding chairs at the front of the hall. "Looks like the meeting's going to come to order. Let's see how exciting it is, shall we?"

It was about as bad as he'd expected. The speakers insisted on staying optimistic long after the time for optimism had passed. When Potter heard, "Sam Longstreet will make a *great* president of the Confederate States!" for the fourth time, he stopped listening. He didn't think Longstreet was a bad man at all—on the contrary. But as long as the Whigs kept running sons and grandsons and great-grandsons of the men who'd won the War of Secession, they gave Jake Featherston an easy target.

He thought about getting to his feet and saying so. In the end, he didn't. Time enough for that at the postmortem; the death wasn't official yet. The meeting was less quarrelsome than a lot he'd been to. He doubted he was the only one saving recriminations for after the election.

Quarrels did go on, though, through the streets of Charleston and across the Confederate States. Potter did his share. He didn't need his left hand to swing a blackjack. He dented a couple of Freedom Party crania—and had his new pair of spectacles broken. Only afterwards did he realize he hadn't had to wear them into the brawl. Hindsight was twenty-twenty. He, unfortunately, wasn't, and now he had to pay twice for the privilege of seeing straight. He was pretty sure the stalwarts he'd clobbered couldn't see straight now, either. That was something.

Tuesday, November 7, 1933, dawned chilly and drizzly. Polls opened at eight in the morning. Jamming a broad-brimmed fedora down low on his forehead to keep water out of his eyes, Potter made his myopic way to the polling place around the corner from his apartment building. Election officials had chalked on the sidewalk a hundred-foot semicircle with the polling place as its center. Inside that circle, electioneering was forbidden. Outside it, Freedom Party men chanted Jake Featherston's name.

Potter smiled at them. "Go ahead, boys. Make yourselves as obnoxious as you can. The more votes you cost your man, the better."

As he walked into the charmed circle, one of the men in white and butternut asked, "Who's that smart-mouthed son of a bitch?"

"Name's Potter," another answered. "Lives around the block. You don't need to write him down. He's already on the list."

Already on the list, am I? Potter thought. *An honor I could do without.* Behind him, the Freedom Party men resumed their chant. *Where are our men, shouting for Longstreet and Black?* he wondered. He knew the Whigs had men outside some polling places. Not this one. The business collapse wasn't the only reason the Freedom Party looked like winning today. How-ever much Potter hated to admit it, even to himself, the opposition was better organized than his own party. He would have bet every Freedom Party man—and woman, in states where women could vote—would get to the polls today. He wished he could have made the same bet about Whig backers. How many of them would sit on their hands? Too many. Any at all would be too many.

He cast his own ballot, then walked back the way he'd come. He didn't think the Freedom Party men would set on him so close to the polling place, where people could see them for what they were. They didn't . . . quite. They shouted, "Nigger-lover!" and, "You'll get yours!" at him, but they didn't try to give it to him. He was almost disappointed. For this trip, he had a pistol in his pocket, not a blackjack.

Having voted, he went to work. It was less than interesting today: a husband wanted evidence his wife was cheating, but the wife, busy with shopping and the couple's two small children, gave none. Potter thought the husband was inventing things to worry about, but he kept his opinions to himself. For one thing, clients seldom paid attention to opinions contradicting their own. For another, the man paid well. If he wanted to throw away his money . . . well, it was a free country, wasn't it?

It is till that Featherston bastard takes over, Potter thought.

On the trolley ride back to his flat after knocking off for the day, he passed another polling place. Police cars were parked in front of it. Blood stained the sidewalk and nearby walls. Freedom Party men waving their reversed-color Confederate battle flags still stood on the street. "Feather*ston*! Feather*ston*!" Even through the trolley's closed windows, the chant lacerated Clarence Potter's ears. The police didn't try to run the stalwarts off. If Whigs had been here, they were no longer. This skirmish belonged to the Freedom Party.

After pan-frying a pork chop and some potatoes and washing them down with a stiff whiskey, Potter went over to Whig headquarters to hear . . . whatever he heard. Dance music blared from the wireless sets: the polls hadn't closed yet. He pulled out his pocket watch. It was a little past seven-thirty—less than half an hour to go.

That gave him plenty of time for another drink, or two, or three. He nodded to Braxton Donovan, who also had a whiskey in his hand, and said, "The condemned man drank a hearty meal."

"Funny," the lawyer said. "Funny like a crutch."

"Oh, I didn't mean you," Potter said. "If you think I meant you, I apologize. I meant the country. Before they execute a man, they give him a blindfold and a cigarette. What do we do when the Confederate States of America go up against the wall?"

Donovan studied him. "I don't think I've ever heard you say you were sorry before. You must mean it. You don't waste time being polite."

I try not to waste time at all, Potter thought. But he had nothing to do but stand there banging his gums till clocks in Charleston started striking eight. "All along the eastern seaboard of the Confederate States, the polls have closed," an announcer on the wireless declared. "We'll bring you the latest results from the presidential, Congressional, state, and local elections—but first, a word from our sponsor." A chorus of young women started singing about the wonders of a soap made from pure palm oil. Potter wondered what could be going through their minds as they trilled the inane lyrics. Probably something like, *We're getting paid.* Times were hard indeed.

Then the numbers started coming in. Somebody posted each new installment on a big blackboard at the front of the room. That meant the Whigs could go on chattering and still keep up. As soon as Clarence Potter saw the early results from North Carolina, he knew what kind of night it would be. North Carolina was a solid, sensible, foursquare Whig state. The collapse hadn't hit it so hard as a lot of other places.

Jake Featherston led there. He led by more every time the fellow at the board erased old numbers and put up new ones. And he had coattails. Freedom Party Congressional candidates were winning in districts where they'd never come close before. And it looked as bad everywhere else.

Braxton Donovan stared owlishly at the returns. He fixed himself another drink, then came back to stand by Potter and stare some more. He didn't say anything for a long, long time. At last, he did: "Jesus Christ. It's like watching a train wreck, isn't it?"

Potter shook his head. "No, Braxton. It's like being *in* a train wreck." Donovan thought that over, then slowly nodded.

And it got no better, not from a Whig point of view, as the polls closed in states farther west. Back in 1921, Tennessee had decided the election when it finally went Whig. This year, it went for Featherston and the Freedom Party. So did Mississippi and Alabama. Potter hadn't expected anything different there, but he would have loved to be proved wrong. The Whigs led in Arkansas, but Arkansas wasn't big enough to matter.

"My God," somebody behind Potter said. "What *is* the world coming to?"

He didn't need to ask the question, not when he could see the answer. Jake Featherston was going to be president. He would have a majority—a big majority—in the House. The Senate, whose members were chosen by state legislatures rather than popular vote, wasn't so obvious. Even so, it all added up to the same thing: after seventy years in the saddle, the Whigs were going into the minority.

"The minority?" the man in back of Potter said when he spoke that thought aloud. "That's crazy." He still seemed unbelieving.

"If you don't get it, think like a nigger," Potter said. "It'll come to you then, believe me."

Along with news of a corruption scandal in the Iowa legislature, newsboys in Des Moines shouted about Jake Featherston's victory down in the Confederate States. More of them yelled about the scandal, which was right there in town. The election news hit Cincinnatus Driver a lot harder. He got out of his truck on the way to the railroad yards and bought a paper, something he hardly ever did:

getting there a minute late might cost him a good cargo. But today he spread the *Register and Remembrance* on the seat beside him and read a paragraph or two whenever he had to stop.

He was still shaking his head when he got out of the Ford at the yards and started dickering with a conductor over a load of beds and dressers and nightstands. "What's the big deal?" asked the conductor, a white man too young to have fought in the Great War. "Who cares what happens down in the Confederate States?"

"I cares." Cincinnatus knew that was bad grammar even without Achilles telling him so. "I grew up in Kentucky when it was part of the CSA. Glad it ain't no more. I got out of there once the USA took it over. This here's a better place if you're colored."

The conductor was not only white, he was a blond who couldn't have got any whiter if somebody'd thrown him into a tub of bleach. He said, "I don't know nothin' about that. All I know is, you may be colored, but you haggle like a damn kike."

If he'd been talking about Cincinnatus to a Jew, he probably would have called him a damn nigger. Cincinnatus took such names in stride; he'd heard them all, especially the one applying to his own race, too often to get excited about them. He said, "I tell you, Mr. Andersen, I don't reckon it's against the law to try an' git me enough money to make the job worth my while. I ain't no charity."

"Well, I'm a penny-pinching squarehead myself, and I won't tell you anything different," Andersen said. Cincinnatus liked him better after that; if he could insult himself as casually as he insulted everybody else, odds were none of those insults meant much.

Cincinnatus got fairly close to the price he wanted for hauling the load of bedroom furniture, too. He drove it over to a furniture store on Woodland Street on the west side of town, only a little north of the bend of the Raccoon River. After growing up by the bank of the Ohio, Cincinnatus didn't think either the Raccoon or the Des Moines was anything special.

Olaf Thorstein, who ran the furniture store, was even paler than Andersen. Cincinnatus had trouble believing anybody this side of a ghost could be. Thorstein was a tall, thin man of stern rectitude, the sort who would skin you in a deal if he could but would walk across town in the snow to give back a penny—or a hundred-dollar bill— you accidentally left in his store. With a similar streak in his own character, Cincinnatus had no trouble getting along with him.

Thorstein said, "Way you talk, you used to live in the Confederate States." He was not far from Cincinnatus' age, which meant he'd likely fought in the Great War.

"Yes, suh, that's a fact." Cincinnatus nodded. "Came to Des Moines ten years ago. Ain't been sorry, neither. This here's a lot better'n Kentucky." He remembered Luther Bliss and shivered in spite of himself.

"Well, what do you think of what's going on down there now?" the white man asked.

"Don't reckon you'll hear no black man sayin' nothin' good about the Freedom Party," Cincinnatus answered. "What do *you* think, Mr. Thorstein?" A surprising—or maybe a depressing—number of whites weren't the least bit shy about saying what they thought of people who didn't look like them. Had the USA had more Negroes, it probably would have had something like the Freedom Party, too.

"Me? I don't know much. I have not been there, except in the Army," Thorstein said, confirming Cincinnatus' guess. The furniture-seller went on, "I tell you this, though: I think that man Featherston will bring trouble. He lies. How can you trust a man who lies? You cannot. And any man who comes on the wireless and says, 'I am going to tell you the truth'—well, what else can he be except a liar?" Behind bifocals, his ice-blue eyes flashed. Plainly, he was condemning Jake Featherston to some chilly hell.

Cincinnatus wished getting rid of the man were that simple. But he nodded to Thorstein. Hating dishonesty of any sort, the Swede might also hate injustice of any sort. "I got me no quarrel with any o' that," Cincinnatus said.

"How could anyone quarrel with it?" Olaf Thorstein

sounded genuinely bewildered. "Is it not as plain as the nose on a man's face? And yet how could the people in the Confederate States have voted for the man if they saw it? They must not have seen it. This I do not understand."

"Sometimes folk don't want to see," Cincinnatus said. "I reckon that had a lot to do with it."

"But why would anyone blind himself on purpose?" Thorstein asked, seeming more bewildered still.

Cincinnatus had asked himself the same question, more than once. He said, "Seems to me they got a choice. They can look square in the mirror and see how ugly they are, or they can be blind. Looks like they done picked what they aim to do."

"Uh-*huh*." Olaf Thorstein chewed on that. At last, he asked, "And what would a Freedom Party man say about what you just said?"

"Oh, that one's easy." Cincinnatus laughed. "Reckon he'd say I was an uppity nigger, a crazy nigger. Reckon he'd be right. When I used to live in the CSA, I wouldn't never've said nothin' like that. Colored fella livin' in the CSA got to be crazy to talk that way. But I been in the USA since 1914 now. This ain't no great place for black folks—don't reckon there's anywhere that's a great place for black folks—but you take it all in all an' it's a lot better than the Confederate States ever was. I got me a chance here—not a good one, maybe, but a chance. Down there?" He shook his head. "No way, nohow, not before the Freedom Party, an' not now, neither."

Again, Thorstein thought before he spoke. "I have never heard a Negro talk so freely of these things," he said, and then shrugged. "How many Negroes are there in Des Moines for me to talk to?"

"Not many. We're thin on the ground here. We're thin on the ground all over the USA," Cincinnatus said. *And maybe that's why things are a little easier for us here,* he thought. *White folks in the USA don't like us much, but they ain't afraid of us like in the Confederate States. Not enough of us here to be afraid of.*

"I hope I have not delayed you too much," the furniture-store owner said. "I know you need as much work as you can get. Who does not, the way things are these days?"

"It's all right, Mr. Thorstein. Don't you worry about it none," Cincinnatus said, for Thorstein really did sound concerned. "When I seen in the paper that that Featherston fella won, I was so upset, I didn't know what to do. Times gonna be hard for colored folks down in the CSA—gonna be real hard. Glad I got me a chance to talk about it some."

He was less glad when he got back to the railroad yard just in time to see another driver go off with a choice load that might have been his had he returned five minutes earlier. But he got a load for himself half an hour after that, when a train full of canned salmon from the Northwest puffed to a stop. Several groceries were waiting for their fish, and he took them a lot of it.

He was tired but happy—he'd made good money that day—when he got back to his apartment building and parked the truck in front of it. Joey Chang, the Chinaman who lived upstairs, was checking his mailbox when Cincinnatus walked into the lobby. "Hello," Cincinnatus said, affably enough. He got on well with Chang, who brewed good beer in a dry state.

"Hello," Chang answered, his English flavored with an accent unlike any other Cincinnatus had heard. "We talk a few minutes?"

"Sure," Cincinnatus said in some surprise. "What's on your mind?"

"Your son Achilles ask my daughter Grace to go to the cinema with him," Chang replied. "What you think of this?"

"*Did* he?" Cincinnatus said, and the other man solemnly nodded. Achilles had said he thought Grace Chang was cute. As Olaf Thorstein had remarked, there weren't that many Negroes in Des Moines. If Achilles found somebody he might like who wasn't a Negro . . . Well, if he did, what then? "What do *you* think of that, Mr. Chang?" Cincinnatus asked.

"Don't know what to think," Chang said, which struck Cincinnatus as basically honest. He went on, "Your Achilles good boy. I don't say he not good boy, you understand? But he not Chinese."

Cincinnatus nodded. He had similar reservations about Grace. He asked, "What's your daughter think?"

"She is modern. She wants to be modern." Mr. Chang made it sound like a curse. "She says, what difference it make? But it makes a difference, oh yes."

"Sure does," Cincinnatus said. The laundryman gave him a surprised look. Perhaps Chang hadn't thought a Negro might mind if his son wanted to take a Chinese girl to the cinema. After scratching his head, Cincinnatus went on, "Maybe we just ought to let 'em go out and not say anything about it. Going to the moving pictures together ain't like gettin' married. And if we tell 'em no, that'll only make 'em want to do it more to rile us up. Leastways, Achilles is like that. Dunno 'bout your Grace."

"Her, too," Chang said morosely. "The more I do not like, the more she does. Modern." He made the word sound even worse than he had before. Now he screwed up his face. "Yes, maybe we do this. I talk to my wife, see what she say." By his tone, whatever Mrs. Chang decided would prevail.

"Fair enough," Cincinnatus said. "I'll talk to Elizabeth, too—and to Achilles."

His wife wasn't home yet. Neither was his son. After graduating from high school, Achilles was doing odd jobs and looking—along with so many others—for something more permanent. He got home before Elizabeth did, and set two dollars on the kitchen table, where Amanda sat doing homework. He *was* a good kid; he brought his pay home every day he worked.

As casually as Cincinnatus could, he said, "Hear you're goin' to the pictures with Grace Chang." Amanda dropped her pencil.

Achilles glared defiance. "That's right. What about it? I think some of the money I make ought to be mine to have some fun with. Don't you?"

Having fun with the money wasn't the point. Having fun with Grace Chang was. But all Cincinnatus said was,

"Reckon I do. It's all right with me. Just wish I'd've heard about it from you and not from Grace's pa."

Set for a fight, Achilles didn't seem to know what to do when he didn't get one. "Oh," he said, and left his mouth hanging open. After a long moment, he added, "I figured you'd have a fit." Another pause, even longer. "Maybe I was wrong."

"Maybe you was," Cincinnatus agreed. "No matter what you think, son, I ain't quite one o' them dinosaur things. Not *quite*." He waited out one more pause. At last, Achilles nodded. His agreement made Cincinnatus feel he'd done a few things right after all.

Thanksgiving was supposed to be one of the happiest days of the year. When Chester Martin and Rita went to his parents' apartment for dinner, that was in the back of his mind. In the front of his mind was the chance to stuff himself till he was about ready to burst at the seams. The money his father had given him let his wife and him keep their own apartment and keep eating. It didn't let them keep eating well. He was sick of cabbage and potatoes and boiled noodles and day-old brown bread.

"Turkey," he said dreamily as he and Rita got off the trolley and walked toward the block of flats where he'd lived so long. The weather was sunny but crisp—a perfect late November afternoon. "*Roast* turkey. Stuffing with giblet gravy." He'd eaten a lot of giblets since losing his job, but they *belonged* in gravy. "Mashed potatoes. Sweet potatoes. Rolls and butter. Pumpkin pie. Apple pie, too. Whipped cream."

"Stop it, Chester," Rita said. "I'm going to drool on my shoes." A motorcar went by. Somebody inside waved. The Chevrolet parked in front of the apartment building. "There's your sister and her husband and little Pete."

"I see 'em." Chester waved back. His brother-in-law, Otis Blake, worked in a plate-glass plant and still had a job. He'd never given Chester a hard time about losing his. He couldn't very well, not when his own brother was out of work.

"Uncle Chester! Aunt Rita!" Pete Blake, who was five,

hit Chester in the knees with a tackle harder than a good many he'd met on the gridiron.

"Careful there, tiger." Martin ruffled his hair. "You almost knocked me on my can. You gonna be a tough guy when you grow up?"

"Tough guy!" Pete yelled. Then he gave Rita a kiss. Either he wasn't so tough yet, or he knew a pretty girl when he saw one.

Chester hugged Sue and shook hands with her husband. Otis Blake had his blond hair permanently parted in the middle by a scar from a scalp wound during the war. An inch lower and he wouldn't have been standing there. "How are you?" he asked now.

With a shrug, Martin answered, "I'm still here. They haven't knocked me out yet."

"Good," Blake said. "That's good."

"Come on. Let's go up to the place," Sue said. She turned to Pete. "You want to see Gramps and Grandma, don't you?"

"Gramps! Grandma!" Pete was enthusiastic about everything. Chances were he'd never heard of a business collapse. If he had, it meant nothing to him. Chester wished he could say the same.

Wonderful smells filled his nose as soon as he walked through the door. When he saw his mother's face a moment later, he knew something was wrong no matter how good the odors wafting out of the kitchen were. She looked as if she'd been wounded and didn't want to admit it even to herself. After the hugs, after the kisses, Martin asked, "What is it, Ma? And don't tell me it's nothing, on account of I know that's not so."

Sue and Otis exchanged glances. Whatever it was, they already knew. Louisa Martin spoke in a low voice, as if in a sickroom: "Your father's been laid off."

Five words. Five words that changed—ruined—not just one life but at least two, maybe four. "Oh," Chester said, a soft, pained exhalation—he might have been punched in the stomach. Rita's lips skinned back from her teeth. Like her mother-in-law, she was trying to find out how much it hurt.

Laid off. It hurt bad. Martin didn't need to find out how much. What, after all, was the difference between bad and worse? Not enough to matter.

A toilet flushed. Out came Stephen Douglas Martin, rubbing his hands together. One look at Chester's face told him everything he needed to know. "So you heard already, did you?"

"Yeah," Chester said harshly. "I heard. What are you going to *do*, Pa?"

"Darn good question," his father replied. "Wish I had a darn good answer to go with it. Almost forty years at that place, and then—" He snapped his fingers. "I'm scrap metal. That's what I am now, scrap metal. Yesterday was my last day. But I tell you one thing: I'm going to have the best darn Thanksgiving anybody ever had, and you can take that to the bank." If Louisa and Sue and Rita hadn't been there, and especially if Pete hadn't, he might have expressed himself more pungently.

"This is a fancy spread." Chester wouldn't say any more than that. Lurking behind the bland statement was a not-so-bland worry. *If you're out of work, how can you afford it?*

Casually, Louisa Martin said, "Otis and Sue gave us a little help. Not much, just a little." Chester nodded. Otis was still working. The older Martins must have told him so they could make sure they got whatever help they needed for a proper holiday dinner.

Knowing what Chester knew took some of the enjoyment away from the feast: it seemed too much like sharing a condemned man's last meal. But that didn't stop him from eating till he was groaningly full. When would his next chance to gorge himself on meat come? He had no idea. Like a savage in the jungle, he made the most of the chance he did have.

About ten o'clock, Pete started getting sleepy and fussy. Sue and Otis took their son and some leftovers and headed back to their place. Chester had waited for that; he needed to speak to his parents without his sister and brother-in-law listening. He started, "Pa, the bosses had no business—"

"No business?" Stephen Douglas Martin said. "Ha!

Business is all they had, the . . . so-and-so's." Yes, he had trouble swearing in front of women.

"What I meant was, we'll figure out something now that . . ." Chester's voice trailed away. He thought his father would know what he meant any which way. Now that the elder Martins had no money coming in, how could they afford to give anyone else a hand? They had to worry about keeping their own place.

"Yes, we'll manage. One way or another, we'll manage," Rita said. She had the same stubborn pride as anyone born a Martin.

Stephen Douglas Martin said, "I hear you two were talking about California."

"Yes, that's true," Chester said. "There's no work in Toledo, or none to speak of. If you have a job, you're all right. If you lose one, though, you haven't got a prayer of finding anything new."

"Thanks so much," his father said. "That's just what I wanted to hear."

"I'm sorry, Pa. I'm sorry as . . . the devil. But that doesn't mean I wasn't telling the truth."

"I know," his father said. "I sure wish it did, though."

"What about California?" Rita kept her mind on business.

"I'll tell you what," Chester's father said. "Louisa and I have some money set aside. They aren't going to throw us in the poorhouse right away, so you don't need to worry your heads about that. I know this is a hard place to find work, on account of you've both done everything you could, but you haven't had any luck. If I stake you two train tickets out West and enough money to keep you going a couple of months . . . well, what do you think about that?"

"We'll pay you back," Chester said without even looking at Rita. "As soon as one of us gets something, we'll pay you back, a little bit at a time till it's all done."

"You don't need to say that, Chester," his father said with a small smile. "If I wasn't sure of it, you think I'd offer?"

"I don't know," Chester answered. "Depends on how bad you and Ma want to get rid of us, I guess."

"Chester!" his mother said reproachfully.

"California." Rita murmured the word. "Things are supposed to be good there, or as good as they are anywhere. They've got the farms, and they've got the moving pictures, and they've got all the people building houses for the people moving there for the other things."

"And the weather," Chester said. "If we go to Los Angeles, we can kiss snow good-bye. I wouldn't miss it a bit, and that's the truth."

"You ready to tear everything up by the roots?" Stephen Douglas Martin asked. "If you do this, I can't give you much more help till I'm back on my own feet." *If I ever am* hung unspoken in the air. He went on, "Don't want you winding up in a Blackfordburgh out there, even if you did vote for the fellow."

"I voted for Coolidge and Hoover this time around," Chester said. Rita made a face at him. He made a face right back, and went on, "I held my nose, but I did it. But I don't think Hoover's exactly a ball of fire."

"He's a ball of . . ." Now Rita seemed hampered in her choice of language. "*I* didn't vote for Coolidge," she added.

"He's had most of a year to make things better. He hasn't done it," Louisa Martin said. "He hasn't done much of anything, not as far as I can see."

"President Blackford did everything under the sun for four years in a row," Stephen Douglas Martin said. "He didn't make things better, either." Chester's father was a rock-ribbed—Chester sometimes thought a rock-headed—Democrat. He continued, "Look how the war with the Japs is winding down now."

"Neither side ever wanted to fight that one all out, though," Chester said. "That's why it's winding down. It's not anything special Hoover's done."

"They haven't dropped any bombs on his head, the way they did on Blackford's," his father retorted. He wagged a finger at Chester. "Still want to go to Los Angeles after that?"

"Yes!" This time, Rita spoke up before Chester could. She sounded even hungrier for California than he was.

"Thank you, Pa, from the bottom of my heart," Chester said.

"If you get work, I may come out there myself," his father said. "Anybody who thinks I'd miss snow is crazy."

"California," Rita said again, as if she expected to pan for gold and pull nuggets the size of eggs from a clear, cold mountain stream.

"California," Chester echoed, as if he expected to go to Los Angeles and wind up a motion-picture leading man the day after he got there. He went on, "There are people who hop a freight for a chance like this." He had, every now and then, thought of being one of them. "I *will* pay you back, Pa. So help me God, I will."

"I told you once, I wouldn't stake you if I didn't think you were good for it," Stephen Douglas Martin answered. "Only thing I worry about is how many people will be going out there, looking for whatever they can find."

"At least there are things to find in California," Chester said. "This town is dying on its feet. I've lived here all my life, except for when I was in the Army, but I won't be sorry to say good-bye." He laughed. Sorry? He hadn't been so glad since the day the guns stopped and he realized he'd made it through the Great War alive.

XX

At three in the morning on an early December day when the sun wouldn't be up for hours and hours in Berlin, Ontario, Jonathan Moss thought wistfully of California or the Sandwich Islands or Florida or some other place with a halfway civilized climate. It was snowing outside. It had been snowing for a month. It would go on snowing till April, maybe May. He twisted in bed, trying to go back to sleep. *Trust me to move out of Chicago for a place with worse weather,* he thought. Most of the time, such musings carried wry amusement. Every so often, as tonight, they felt too much like kidding on the square.

"There," Laura said from the other bedroom. "Isn't that better?"

"Mama," Dorothy said. At not quite a year, she could say a couple of dozen words. That made her advanced for her age. She wasn't nearly advanced enough to keep from needing her diaper changed, though.

"Now lie down and go back to sleep," Laura said. The crib creaked as she put the baby back into it.

"Mama!" Dorothy wailed as her mother left her bedroom and came back to the one she shared with Jonathan. That desperate appeal failing, Dorothy started crying and screaming and making as much racket as she could.

All the books said you were supposed to let children cry themselves out when you put them to bed. After a while, they would get used to the idea that they could settle down by themselves. What the books didn't say was how you were supposed to keep from going crazy while the baby had conniptions. Earplugs might have helped, except that Jonathan had never found any good enough to keep out the noise.

His wife lay down beside him. "What are we going to do?" she said.

"How is she going to learn to go to sleep by herself if you go in there and pick her up?" he asked.

"How are we ever going to go to sleep if she screams her head off for the next two hours?" Laura returned.

Jonathan didn't have a good answer for that, because it had happened. It had happened more than once, as a matter of fact. The books said it wasn't supposed to. Dorothy hadn't read the books. She wasn't advanced enough to know how to read, either.

The next-door neighbors pounded on the wall, which meant the baby's racket had woken them up. "That does it," Laura said, and got out of bed. "I don't care what the books say. I don't want the Boardmans hating us. I'm going to rock her."

"All right." Moss didn't want to argue. He wanted to go back to sleep. And he did, as soon as the screaming stopped.

When the alarm went off a few hours later, Moss thought it was Dorothy crying again. "Turn it off, for Christ's sake!" Laura snarled. Muzzily, he did. His wife started snoring again before he left the room. He made his own coffee in the kitchen, and scrambled some eggs to go with it. Then he put on his overcoat and went downstairs to see if the Bucephalus would start.

It did. A new battery helped. As he piloted the auto to the office, he imagined he was piloting one of the fighting scouts he'd flown during the war. Aeroplanes were faster these days. One-deckers were replacing two-deckers—but then, he'd flown a one-decker, a U.S. copy of the German Fokker, through a long stretch of the war. He figured he could do it again if he ever had to.

An old Ford ran a red light and shot across his path.

That was moronic any time, and all the more so with snow on the ground, when stopping was as much a matter of luck as anything else. Fortunately for Moss and the other guy, the Bucephalus *did* stop. Even so, he wished its headlights were twin machine guns. Then he could have given the fool in the Ford just what he deserved.

That was funny, in a way. He chuckled about it till he got to the office. But the world didn't feel so comfortable as it had a couple of years before. The sputtering war with Japan was only one sign of that. With the *Action Française* in the saddle in France, with Charles XI on the throne there and sounding fiercer every day, with the Mosley thugs a noisy minority in the British Parliament, both the German Empire and the United States, he thought, had reason to worry.

And with the Freedom Party set to take over the Confederate States, the USA had another reason to be anxious, one much closer to home. "Idiots," Moss muttered, cautiously applying the brakes at another light. "How *could* they have voted for that crazy blowhard?"

Actually, he knew how, or thought he did. The Confederates didn't just want to put their own house in order. Like the French, they wanted revenge for what had happened to them during the Great War. Of course, the French had friends. Little by little, Russia was shaking off the trauma of the war and the endless Red uprising afterwards—an uprising that made the Red revolt in the CSA seem a walk in the park by comparison. And England wanted another crack at Kaiser Bill . . . and, no doubt, at the United States as well.

A patrol of men wearing green-gray and carrying Springfields tramped past Moss' building as he parked the Bucephalus. That reminded him he was in a land—not a country any more—that also despised his nation. His very shingle reminded him of the same thing. JONATHAN MOSS, it said. OCCUPATION LAW.

He got out of the auto. He was laughing again as he went into the office, not that it was any too funny. Not a day went by when his marriage didn't remind him he was in a land that despised his nation.

At least we're occupying a place without all that many people, he thought. *The Germans would have needed to put half their men in France to keep an eye on all the frogs who hate them.* That was probably why they'd let the *Action Française* get off the ground: till too late, they hadn't seen it as a real threat. *And now King Charles is talking about rearming. I'm sure the Kaiser loves that. But would he start another war to stop it? He's an old man now.*

President-elect Featherston also made loud noises about rearming. Moss wished he hadn't remembered that, not least since no one in the USA seemed much inclined to stop him.

Moss turned the key in his door, turned on the lamp in his office, and turned the knob on the steam radiator to make the place feel as if it was at least a little south of the Arctic Circle. That done, he plugged in the hot plate and got a pot of coffee perking. It would be black, oily sludge by this afternoon. He knew that. He knew he'd go on drinking it anyway, too.

A letter from a military prosecutor lay on his desk. He'd left it there when he went home the morning before. Major Lopat's secretary had neatly typed, *We are not obligated to turn over this evidence to you prior to its production in court. Rules of discovery applicable in civilian cases do not apply here, as you are doubtless perfectly well aware. If I can be of further assistance to you, do not hesitate to call on me.* Then Lopat had signed it—in red ink, for good measure.

"Well, screw you, Sam," Moss muttered. What the military prosecutor didn't know was that he already had back-channels photostats of the documents in question. They'd come in the same mail delivery as the snotty letter.

He was gloating about the surprise he had planned for the prosecutor when the telephone rang. He was his own secretary. Picking up the telephone, he said, "Jonathan Moss."

A man's voice on the other end of the line: "You're the Yank barrister, aren't you?"

"That's right," Moss answered. "Who are you? What can I do for you?"

"If I was you, I wouldn't start my motorcar no more," the voice said. A click followed. The line went dead.

Moss looked out the window. There sat the Bucephalus, right where he'd left it. Had someone done something to it there on the street, brazen as could be? Or was somebody just trying to rattle his cage?

That wasn't the biggest question, he realized. The biggest question was, did he feel like finding out the hard way?

He didn't. He called the local garrison and reported what had just happened. The sergeant with whom he spoke knew who he was. The noncom thought the call highly amusing. "You're worth more to the Canucks than a dozen of their own kind," he said. "They ought to give you a medal, not blow you up."

"Funny. Ha, ha," Moss said. "Will you send your bomb squad out to go over my auto?"

"Yes," the sergeant answered. "I'll do that. The squad may take a while to get there, though. Yours is the fifth call we've had this morning."

"A hoaxer, then," Moss said. "He must want to make people run around in circles and waste time."

"We thought so, too," the sergeant told him. "The first two times we sent out the bomb squad, nothing. The third time, there was a bomb. They're still playing with it. If you hear a bang and your windows rattle, you can bet the squad will be late to your place." He laughed again.

Moss remembered such humor from his own days in the Army. It had seemed funny then. It didn't now—not to him, anyhow. The sergeant enjoyed it. "You ought to be trying to find out who your practical joker is," Moss said. "We could have another Arthur McGregor on our hands."

"Don't worry about it, Mr. Moss," the sergeant said. "When we do catch this son of a bitch, whoever he turns out to be, you can get him off the hook. So long. The bomb squad will be along sooner or later." He hung up.

That shows what my own people think of me, Moss thought unhappily. *I'm not doing anything against the law—I'm working strictly within it. This is the thanks I get.*

He wondered whether the bomb squad would show up at all, or whether he would get to find out if his car was wired by going out to it and turning the key. He heard no sudden and dreadful boom, though he worked with his ears peeled all day. Toward evening, a squad of men whose heavy armor made them look like a cross between modern soldiers and medieval knights showed up and went over his car. After twenty minutes or so, one of them waddled into the building.

By the time he got to Moss' door, he was sweating despite the chilly weather. How much did that protective clothing weigh? If a bomb went off, how much good would it do? Even had Moss intended to ask those questions aloud, he didn't get the chance. The man from the bomb squad asked if he was Jonathan Moss. When he nodded, the fellow said, "No bomb. Just that asshole running us from pillar to post." Without waiting for an answer, he waddled away.

"Thanks," Moss called after him. He raised a gauntleted hand and kept on walking.

Who would want to blow me up, or at least to scare me spitless? Moss wondered. The U.S. sergeant was right. He had done a lot of good for the Canucks. They shouldn't have wanted to hurt him. They should have wanted to coat him in bulletproof glass.

Do they hate me just because I'm a Yank? He shook his head in slow wonder. Who could be that stupid?

Mary Pomeroy. Mary Pomeroy. Mary Pomeroy. No matter how often she wrote her new name, trying to get used to it, she still thought of herself as Mary McGregor. She'd been married only a couple of months. The change in her name sometimes seemed the smallest of the changes that had swept over her. She'd known they would be there when she said yes after Mort got down on one knee in front of her. She'd known they would be there, but she hadn't had any idea how overwhelming they would prove.

How could living in Rosenfeld, for instance, be so very different from living on a farm not *that* far outside of

665

town? So she'd asked herself before going from the farmhouse where she'd spent her whole life to rooms across the street from the diner where her new husband worked with his father. So she'd asked herself, and she'd found out.

Electricity, for instance. She'd never had it at the farm, so she'd never known what she was missing. Now she felt as if she'd spent her life in the Dark Ages. That was literally true; kerosene lamps didn't come close to matching light bulbs for brilliance or convenience. But there was so much more. A refrigerator beat an icebox all hollow. A vacuum cleaner was ever so much easier to use and more effective than a carpet sweeper. An electric toaster knocked the stuffing out of the wire grid that went over the fire. An electric alarm clock didn't stop running if she forgot to wind it.

An electric phonograph also didn't run down, unlike the windup machine the McGregors had had on the farm. And a wireless set—a wedding present from Mort's father—offered a window on the world Mary had never imagined. Music, dramas, comedies—all in the apartment, all at the twist of a dial? If that wasn't a miracle, what was? She had to keep reminding herself the news that came from the machine on the hour was only what the Yanks wanted her to hear.

The apartment had a telephone, too. That didn't impress Mary so much. None of the few people who might have wanted to call her had telephones of their own, so they couldn't. Whenever it rang, it was for Mort. She suspected that would change as time went by. The Pomeroys were still a very new couple. Bit by bit, they would fit themselves into Rosenfeld's jigsaw puzzle of class and sociability.

That thought had hardly crossed her mind before the other half of the Pomeroys came out of the bedroom pulling his overcoat tight around himself. "I'm off to the diner," he said, and paused to give Mary a kiss.

"Oh, Mort," she said. Her arms tightened around him. The kiss took longer and got hotter than he'd probably expected. He didn't seem disappointed, though, when they finally broke apart.

"I'll see you tonight," he said huskily.

Mary nodded. Some of the other things that went with marriage and a move to town were even more startling, even more exciting, than electricity. Although if it wasn't electricity that set her pulse racing now, what was it? She knew what it was, all right. "Tonight," she said.

Mort looked as if he had to remind himself he was supposed to go out the door, down the stairs, and across the street to the diner. Mary watched him from the window. He hurried across when no motorcars were coming in either direction. Snow flew up from his overshoes as he crossed the street. Rosenfeld would have a white Christmas in a couple of weeks. More snow started falling even as Mary watched.

Mort opened the front door to the diner, ducked inside, and closed it after him. With a regretful sigh, Mary turned away. *What shall I do with the rest of my day?* she wondered. Oh, she had work to do keeping the place clean and getting supper ready for tonight. But that was work for a few hours, not work that would devour a day. She had no livestock to look after but a cat, and Mouser, like any of his kind, looked after himself perfectly well.

Mary laughed. "I never thought I would miss shoveling manure," she said. It wasn't that she missed it, exactly, but she didn't have certainty in her routine any more.

Once she was done with what she had to do, she could go out and explore Rosenfeld. She'd done that a lot after coming back from her honeymoon at the Canadian side of Niagara Falls. She hadn't wanted to set foot in New York, and Mort hadn't argued with her. She didn't go out into Rosenfeld so often as she had on first coming home. She hadn't needed long to figure out there was only so much to see and do here. Compared to a farm, Rosenfeld was a metropolis. Compared to a real metropolis, Rosenfeld . . . might as well have been a farm.

When she finished her chores today, she sat down and turned on the wireless. The tubes inside glowed to life. She waited for sound to start coming out of the machine. *This is what it's for,* she realized. *It fills up the spaces when you're not working.* She hadn't had to worry about many spaces like that on the farm, for she was almost always working or eating or sleeping. But town life was different.

She could make herself a cup of tea, sit down in a rocking chair and read a book or a magazine, and listen to the wireless, and nobody would call her lazy or worthless. And she wasn't, either; she'd done everything that needed doing except for making supper, and that could—should—wait till the afternoon.

The book she had was called *I Sank Roger Kimball*. She didn't remember Kimball's death; she'd been a lot younger then, and the Confederate States had seemed farther away than the mountains of the moon. Come to that, they still did. Her honeymoon train ride was the first time she'd ever left Manitoba, and even then she'd gone only one province away.

But Sylvia Enos' travels weren't what leaped out of the sparsely written book at her. The American woman's revenge was. She'd found out what had happened to her husband, and she'd paid back the man who did it. Her government had seemed powerless to do any such thing, but she'd pulled it off. Not only that, she'd got off scot free—and people all across the United States acclaimed her as a heroine.

Part of Mary applauded that. But it infuriated more of her. This Enos woman had struck back for her country, and politicians in the USA praised her to the sky. Mary's own father had struck back at the USA for Canada, and he'd been hounded and hunted and ended up dying fighting the Americans. They'd murdered her brother, Alexander, who'd also been a patriot: murdered him under the disguise of law. Where was the justice in that?

And I haven't done anything—not a single, solitary thing—to pay the Yanks back for what they did to Alexander and to my pa. Shame burned Mary's cheeks. Her father's bomb-making tools remained hidden in the barn back at the farm. *How am I supposed to bring them here? One day I'll have the chance, I suppose, but it hasn't happened yet. How old will I have to be before I can do something?* To twenty-three, even twenty-five looked far away.

She went through *I Sank Roger Kimball* at a feverish pace. *She did it*, she thought again and again. *She did it, and she got away with it.*

I haven't done anything. When will I do something? Will I ever do anything? She went to the window and looked outside. As if on cue, a green-gray U.S. Army truck rolled slowly up the street. The Americans had been in Rosenfeld for going on twenty years now. The most she'd ever done to them was flatten a Model T's tires with a nail, and she'd been a little girl then.

Most Canadians, these days, found it easier just to . . . get along with the Yanks. Even people who'd called themselves patriots during and after the war were in bed with the Americans these days, sometimes literally. She despised them even more than she despised the Yanks. Americans were wrong, but at least they served their own country. What could you say about a Canadian who did the bidding of the United States? Mary didn't know any words vile enough for such people.

She'd had thoughts like that before, had them and done nothing about them. But *I Sank Roger Kimball* fired her all over again. Her father hadn't feared to pay the price. Did she?

She shook her head. It wasn't that. Life had got in the way. She'd never expected to fall in love, to get married, to leave the farm. She didn't see how anyone could do that sort of thing and keep fighting the Americans.

That was all right—as long as she eventually got on with the war. As far as she was concerned, it hadn't ended in 1917. It would never end till the Yanks left Canada and her country got its freedom back.

She salted and peppered a pork roast and put it in the oven with dried apples—the potatoes could wait till later. Buying meat at the butcher's shop instead of doing the slaughtering herself was one more thing she'd had to get used to. It was much more convenient, even if she couldn't always get the cuts exactly the way she wanted them.

Mort came home carrying a copy of the *Rosenfeld Register*. "Here's something funny from Ontario," he said, pointing to a story on an inside page. "Somebody threatened to bomb an American barrister's auto in Berlin."

"Just threatened?" Mary said. "Shame he didn't do it."

Mort Pomeroy nodded. He didn't love the Yanks, either; Mary couldn't have loved him if he had. But then he said, "He's not an ordinary barrister, though. Have you heard of Jonathan Moss? He defends Canadians in trouble with the occupation government, and he gets a lot of them off."

"No, I hadn't heard of him," Mary said. "Why does he do that, if he's an American? He must have some kind of angle."

"I don't think so," her husband said. "He *is* married to the woman whose maiden name was Laura Secord, but he was doing the same thing before he married her. And she wouldn't have anything to do with the ordinary run of Yank, would she?"

Mary didn't want to argue with Mort, even about something like this—which proved she was a newlywed, and very much in love. "I wouldn't think so," she said, and then, "Supper should be ready. Let me go make sure."

"Smells good," Mort said, and Mary smiled.

But she wasn't smiling on the inside. She remembered Laura Secord's name from the failed Canadian uprising of the mid-1920s. Wasn't the woman supposed to have warned her American lover about it? And wasn't it likely that that lover was this Moss fellow?

If that was so, the fellow who'd threatened to bomb the motorcar really should have done it, but with Moss' wife in the machine. Mary remembered her scorn—no, her hatred—for collaborating Canadians when the rebellion fizzled. She'd vowed revenge on them then. She'd vowed, and then she'd ignored her vow.

She took the pork roast out of the oven. Savory steam filled the kitchen. Mort exclaimed again. Mary hardly heard him. As she plunged her carving knife deep into the roast, she knew what she had to do.

"And I will," she murmured.

"Will what?" Mort asked.

"Get some butter for the potatoes," Mary answered smoothly. She took the butter out of the refrigerator. She'd bought it. She hadn't had to churn it: one more change from farm to town. But that wasn't what she'd meant. No, that wasn't what she'd meant at all.

When the door to your flat opens at three in the morning and you wake up at the noise and you smile and murmur, "Oh, thank God," odds are you are a fisherman's relative. Raising her voice slightly from that relieved murmur, Sylvia Enos called, "Is that you, George?"

"It's me, Ma," he answered, also in a soft voice: Mary Jane lay sleeping in the bedroom she now shared with her mother. "I'm sorry I woke you up."

"Don't worry about it. I'm glad you're here," Sylvia said. Mary Jane muttered, rolled over, and started to snore again. Sylvia went on, "Four days after New Year's and I've got my Christmas present. What time did your boat get in?"

"Last night, about five," George, Jr., said.

"What?" Sylvia couldn't believe her ears. She jumped out of bed and angrily hurried to her son. She wanted to shake him, but he was too big to shake. "And what were you doing between then and now? Drinking away your pay with a pack of worthless sailormen, I'll bet—that or worse." She sniffed, but she didn't smell beer or whiskey on her son's breath. She didn't smell cheap perfume, either, so maybe he hadn't been doing worse.

"Ma, I'm not drunk," George, Jr., said, and Sylvia had to nod, for she could tell that was true. He went on, "I didn't do . . . anything else, either. Not like that. Not what you meant."

Reluctantly, Sylvia nodded again. She didn't think he would lie to her straight out. "What *did* you do, then?" she asked. "Why didn't you come home?"

George, Jr., took a deep breath. "Ma, I didn't come home because I paid a call on Constance McGillicuddy and her folks. I asked her to marry me, Ma, and she said yes."

"Oh." The word took all the breath out of Sylvia. She stared up at her tall, broad-shouldered son in the gloom inside the flat. To her, he would always be a little boy. "Oh," Sylvia said again. Yes, she'd had to inhale first. Little boys didn't give her news like that.

"I love Connie, Ma," her son said. "She loves me, too. We'll be happy together. And she's got a waitressing job that looks like it's good and steady. We'll be able to make it, with a little luck."

In times like these, how much luck was out there? Sylvia didn't know. Times were hard when you had to worry about what your wife-to-be could bring in. She did know that. But George, Jr., was sensible enough to make the calculation instead of ignoring it. *I did something right,* Sylvia told herself.

Aloud, she said, "I haven't even met this girl, or her family. What do they do?"

She could barely make out her son's smile in the darkness. "Her father's a fisherman—what else? He knew Pa a little. I don't think they ever sailed together, though. He was in a destroyer during the war, too. He even got torpedoed, but he made it to a boat and got picked up."

"He didn't get torpedoed after the damn war was over." Sylvia's voice stayed soft, but she could hear the savagery in it. Even after more than sixteen years, what Roger Kimball had done still felt filthy to her. She remembered the weight of the pistol in her hand, remembered the way it had bucked when she pulled the trigger, remembered the deafening report, remembered Kimball falling with a look of absurd surprise on his face and blood spreading over the front of his shirt. *If I had it to do over again, would I?* she wondered.

She didn't wonder long. *Hell, yes! I'd do it in a red-hot minute!*

Coming back to here and now took a distinct effort of will. "McGillicuddy," she said. "She'll be Irish, then. Catholic."

"Does it bother you?" her son asked. "It doesn't bother me a bit, honest to God it doesn't." He laughed at his own choice of words.

Sylvia had to think about how much it bothered her. Some, yes, but how much? It wasn't as if she went to church every Sunday herself. She'd known plenty of Catholics who were perfectly nice, perfectly good people. How much did it really matter if her grandchildren grew up as mackerel-snappers? Less than she'd expected it to before she looked things over inside herself. "I guess it's all right," she said, and then nodded, firming up her acquiescence. "Yes, it *is* all right."

"That's taken care of, then," George, Jr., said. "They don't mind too much that I'm not." That side of the coin hadn't occurred to Sylvia. Her son went on, "It's the United States. Who you are counts for more than who your folks were. President Blackford's wife was Jewish, and nobody made a big fuss about that."

"I suppose," Sylvia said. "I'm still glad he lost. The Socialists just don't know what to do about the Confederate States."

"With this new Freedom Party taking over, who does?" George, Jr., said.

"I know." Sylvia hesitated, then went on, "That Roger Kimball was a grand high panjandrum in the Freedom Party. If he hadn't been, I never would have found out about him. That's the kind of people that party draws, and it's the best reason I can think of to figure they're up to no good."

"We licked the CSA once," her son said. "If we ever have to, we can lick 'em again."

He remembered only the last war. Unlike people born in the nineteenth century, he didn't think of the repeated humiliations the United States had suffered at the hands of the Confederacy, Britain, and France before the Great War. And, though his own father was part of the cost of licking the Confederate States, he didn't think about that, either.

Well, why would he? went through Sylvia's mind. *He hardly remembers his father. How do you miss what you didn't even know you had?*

She stood on tiptoe to kiss George, Jr., on the cheek. "Go to bed now. It's late. It's so late, it's getting early." He laughed at that, though Sylvia knew perfectly well what she'd meant. She went on, "I'm happy for you."

"Connie's the most wonderful girl in the world." He spoke with absolute conviction.

Did she already let him into her bed, to make him that happy? Sylvia shrugged. It hardly mattered, not if they were getting married soon. The worst that could happen was a baby, and most people looked the other way if a first baby came seven or eight months after the wedding instead of the usual nine. "All right, son. Sleep tight tonight, and we'll talk more in the morning."

In the morning, though, George, Jr., was still asleep when Mary Jane's alarm clock went off. He didn't wake up, either; in fact, his breathing didn't even change. Mary Jane got dressed while Sylvia made coffee for both of them. Her daughter had landed a typist's job. Neither of them knew how long it would last. They both knew she couldn't afford to be late. She'd got the job when the girl who had it before was late three times in two weeks.

Along with the coffee and eggs over hard, Sylvia gave Mary Jane the news. "That's wonderful!" Mary Jane squealed. She hugged Sylvia. "Wonderful!"

"Have you met the girl?" Sylvia asked. "I haven't."

"Once," her daughter answered. "We were at a dance together. We'd come separately, but we were both there at the same time. She's blond—green eyes. Pretty enough, I guess." Mary Jane shrugged, as if to say what men saw in women was largely a closed book to her.

It was to Sylvia, too, but she said, "George certainly seems to think so. Do you care that she's Catholic?"

"Not me," Mary Jane said at once. "As long as she gets along with George, that's what matters."

"That's what I think, too. We're going to have to meet her and her folks, you know. I wonder what they'll be like." Sylvia sighed. "I wonder if they have a telephone. If they do, I could go to a booth and call them up and arrange it. But Lord only knows how many McGillicuddys there are in Boston."

"If they have a telephone, George will know the number." Mary Jane was bound to be right about that. She gulped down the last of the coffee, rose from the table, and put on hat and overcoat against the cold, nasty weather outside. She hurried to the door, then turned back. "I'll see you tonight. Gotta run now, or I'll miss the trolley."

Sylvia had been laid off from a job in a canning plant not long before, just as she had after the Great War ended. She wasn't hurting yet, not with Mary Jane working and with the money she'd made in the 1932 presidential campaign, some of which she still had. Not going out to look for work one morning didn't worry her.

George, Jr., emerged from bed, still yawning, a little before nine. "They want to meet you, too, Ma, and Mary Jane," he said when Sylvia asked him about the McGillicuddys. "They haven't got a telephone, though. I'll set it up when I see Connie."

Sylvia and Mary Jane went to the McGillicuddys' house—it was a house, not a flat—near T Wharf two days later, on Sunday afternoon. Constance's father, Patrick, was a redhead, going gray; her mother, Margaret, had hair whose defiant gold had to come from a dye bottle. George, Jr.'s, intended also had three strapping brothers and a kid sister who couldn't have been much above ten. A big black dog named Nemo barked and wagged his tail and generally considered the house to be his, with the McGillicuddys tolerated guests whose purpose in life was to keep him full of horsemeat.

"You've got a fine boy there," Patrick McGillicuddy said, squeezing Sylvia's hand as she stood in the front hall. "We're glad to have him in the family." He didn't particularly talk like an Irishman. Looking Mary Jane up and down, he went on, "And I think Connor and Larry and Paul will be glad to have his sister in the family." His sons grinned.

"I'm glad to have her in the family, too," said Constance's sister, whose name was Liz.

"Good for you, dear," her father said, "but I don't think you're glad the way your brothers are." The young men's grins grew wider. Liz look confused. Whatever the McGillicuddys were going to tell her about the birds and bees, they didn't seem to have told her yet.

The way Connie looked at George, Jr., and the way she clung to him whenever she got the chance, told Sylvia everything she needed to know on that score. Her eyes met Margaret McGillicuddy's. The two women shared a moment of perfect understanding. *Enjoy it while it lasts,* their faces both said, *because it doesn't usually last long.*

"One of these days, I'm going to read your book," Patrick McGillicuddy told Sylvia. She nodded politely; she'd heard that a good many times. He went on, "You made a lot of people proud when you went down to the CSA and did what you did. Could have been me you were paying that sub skipper back for, easy as not."

She could tell he spoke from the heart. "Thank you," she said. "That means a lot to me, especially since George tells me you were in the Navy, too."

"Only luck I'm still here." He suddenly seemed to remember he had a drink in his hand. Raising it, he said, "And we've got luck right here in the room with us. To Connie and George!" He drank. So did Sylvia. So did everyone else.

Another lonely winter night. Lucien Galtier took some fried chicken off the stove. He would never make a good cook, but he'd got to the point where he didn't mind eating what he made. After he finished supper, he washed dishes and tidied up as meticulously as he could. Marie would have expected it of him, and he didn't want to let her down. It wasn't as good a job as she would have done, but he hoped she would give him credit for making the effort.

After he put the last plate in the drainer—no matter what his wife had done, he couldn't make himself waste time drying dishes—he left the kitchen and went out to the parlor: the living room, people were calling it these days. He turned on the wireless and waited for sound to start coming out of it.

As music began to play, Lucien tapped the cabinet. "This is a marvelous machine," he said, talking to himself as he often did while alone. "It makes me feel I have company, even when I have none."

The music stopped. The people on the wireless began to try to sell him laundry soap. He listened to the pitch with half an ear while he lit a cigarette. Not all the company was welcome. Another little skit proclaimed the virtues of a brand of tobacco different from the one he smoked. He shrugged and took another puff.

More music came out of the speaker—a concertina solo. He grinned. "Welcome to *Voyageurs*," the announcer said. Lucien settled down to listen. All of Quebec settled down to listen at half past seven on Monday, Wednesday, and Friday nights. The comedy about fur traders and Indians was the most popular show in the country.

One of the Indians started complaining the *voyageur* had cheated him. That was a running gag on the show— in fact, the Indian got the better of the *voyageur* every time. He also spoke French not like an Indian but like a Jewish peddler, which made things funnier and made them funny in a different way.

As usual, everything turned out all right—and turned out absurd—within the appointed half hour. After the show was done, Lucien turned to a station that played music, poured himself some apple brandy, and settled down with a French translation of an American story: a woman who'd gone down into the Confederate States to avenge her husband.

It was a strange kind of French, extraordinarily terse and to the point. He wondered if the English was the same. Then he wondered if he could make enough sense out of written English to find out. He doubted it.

"But I can ask my son-in-law," he said. He had to remind himself Dr. Leonard O'Doull was a born anglophone. Whenever the two of them talked together, they spoke French. O'Doull sounded more like a Quebecois every year, too, losing bit by bit the Parisian accent with which he'd originally learned his second language.

At about a quarter to nine, someone knocked on the door. Wondering who could be mad enough to pay him a call at this hour, Lucien put down the book and went to find out. It wasn't snowing at the moment, but it had been and it would be, and it probably was below zero outside.

When he opened the door, his younger son waited there. "Oh, hello, Georges," Lucien said. "I might have known it would be you. What are you doing here so late?"

"Well, you wouldn't expect me to leave my house before *Voyageurs* was done, would you?" Georges asked reasonably. He stepped into the farmhouse where he'd been born and grown up. Lucien closed the door behind him to stop letting out precious heat. He went on, "I am not a rich man, to have a wireless set in my automobile. I am lucky to have an automobile."

"I've got the applejack out, to settle me before I go to bed," Lucien said. "Would you like some?"

"Yes, thank you, *mon père*. It will warm me up after the chilly drive over, the motorcar also lacking a heater. Ah, *merci*." Georges accepted the glass and took a cautious sip—with bootleg applejack, you never knew what you were getting till you got it. He nodded. "This is a good batch. Strong enough to feel, but not strong enough to burn off the roof of your mouth."

"Yes, I thought the same," Lucien agreed. "Is that why you came over—to drink my brandy, I mean?"

"As good a reason as any, eh? And better than most, I think." Georges looked around. He lit a cigarette, then sighed and shook his head. "Whenever I come here, I keep expecting *chère Maman* to come out of the kitchen and say hello."

That made Lucien pour his own glass full again. "Whenever I come in the house, son, I expect the same thing. But what I expect and what I get"—he sighed—"they are not the same."

"*Calisse*," Georges said—almost more of an invocation of the holiness of the chalice than the usual Quebecois curse. He saw the book Lucien had been reading. "I went through that. A brave woman."

"I remember something about it in the papers when it happened," Lucien said. "Not much, though, and of course there was no wireless then. Strange how we've come to take it for granted in just a few years' time."

"My next-door neighbor visited me last fall," Georges said. "It was a Wednesday night, and he listened to *Voyageurs*. He had no electricity on his farm till then, did Philippe, though he does well for himself. He never saw the need. A week after that, he went out and got it so he could have a wireless set for himself. A wireless show decided him."

"I believe you," Lucien said. "Is this why you came, then? You wanted to tell me about your neighbor and the wireless and electricity?"

"I came because I wanted to visit my father," Georges replied. "Sour as you are, it could be that you find this hard to believe. If so . . . well, too bad. My neighbor Philippe cannot visit his father, for he has no father to visit. I am lucky, and I take advantage of my luck." He hefted his glass. "And if I get a knock of applejack in the side, this is not so bad, either."

Lucien looked down into the pale yellow liquid filling his own glass. Slowly, he said, "I am going to tell you something I thought I would never say to you in all my days. You are a scamp, you know, and a rogue, and a fellow who gets away with everything he possibly can and then with one thing more."

"You never thought you would say this to me?" Georges raised an eyebrow and made a comical face. "*Mon cher papa,* you have been telling me this ever since I could stand up, and probably before that, too."

"Yes, before that, too," the elder Galtier agreed. "But that is not what I intended to say. What I intended to say is, you are a good son, Georges. It pains me to say it, and it must pain you to hear it, but there it is. You *are* a good son."

Georges didn't say anything for close to a minute. When he did speak, his words were slow and thoughtful: "This means a very great deal to me, *mon père.*" He paused again, then went on, "What it means is, you are obviously senile, and suffering from softening of the brain. I am sure my esteemed brother-in-law, Dr. O'Doull, would have a fancier name for it, but that is what it is."

"Thank you," Lucien said, and sounded enough as if he meant it to make his younger son give him a puzzled look. He explained: "Thank you for showing me you really are the ungrateful wretch I thought you were, and not the caring fellow I believed I saw before. I don't recognize him, and wouldn't know what to do with him if I saw him again."

"Oh, good." Georges' voice held nothing but relief. "Now we are insulting each other again. I know how to do this. I know why I should, too. We understand each other this way. The other?" He shook his head. "What could we do if we talked to each other like that all the time?"

Lucien thought it over. "Lord knows."

His son got up and poured their glasses full of apple-jack again. "We can always get drunk. We know how to do that, too. How much work have you got in the morning?"

"The usual." Lucien shrugged. "How much have *you* got?"

"The usual." Georges shrugged, too. "But I have help, and you don't."

With another shrug, Lucien said, "It's winter. I have to feed the animals and muck out. Past that, things can wait. It's not like plowing or harvest time. If you want to get drunk, we can get drunk. Too bad Charles and Leonard are not here to do it with us."

"Winter does not make the brilliant and talented Dr. O'Doull's work lighter, as it does ours," Georges said. "If anything, it makes his work worse."

"We'll just have to drink by ourselves, then," Lucien said. "What shall we drink to?"

"How about drinking to being a small country where not much happens?" his son suggested. "The way the world seems to be going these days, we may be luckier than we know."

"I confess, I pay less attention to the world now than I did when we were part of Canada," Lucien Galtier said. "In those days, we had to worry about the United States, because the United States used to worry about us. Now the United States don't care much about us one way or the other."

"We don't bother them any more. We *can't* bother them any more," Georges replied. He paused, sipped, and then asked, "What do you think of *Action Française*?"

"It is good to see France feeling strong again. What ever else we are, we are still French, eh?" Lucien said, and his son nodded. He continued, "But to be strong, France has to get ready for war. I do not think this is good, not since I have seen war with my own eyes."

"Most Frenchmen have also seen war with their own eyes," his son said. "Those who have will not be eager to fight again, even if England goes the same way as France, which seems more likely every day."

"An eighteen-year-old in France will no more remember the Great War than an eighteen-year-old here," Lucien replied. "It is 1934 now. Come this summer, the war will have been over for seventeen years." He sipped at his applejack, wondering how that was possible.

But then Georges said, "Half a lifetime for me—oh, not exactly, but close enough. That truly seems unbelievable, but it is so. All the time of my manhood, I have lived since the war in the Republic of Quebec."

"So you have." Lucien also had trouble believing that, though it too was so. To keep from thinking about the passage of the years, he thought some more about how things were across the ocean. "England," he said musingly. "I don't love England—what Quebecois who grew up in Canada before the turn of the century could? But I don't hate her, either, not quite."

"Why not?" Georges asked. "I know plenty of men your age who do."

"Because I always feel that, bad as she was, she could have been much worse," Lucien replied after some thought. "She could have been like the Belgians in Africa, and made her name a stench among the nations. She didn't, and so I give her . . . some . . . credit."

"Ah, but would you rather be on her side or on the side of the United States?" Georges asked slyly.

"I would rather be on the side of Quebec, and of Quebec alone," Lucien said. But his son hadn't give him that choice, and he knew it.

For some reason Nellie Jacobs couldn't fathom, her coffee-house was full of men from the Confederate States one chilly February afternoon. Three or four of them had served in Washington during the war. By the cheerful way they reminisced, the CSA might have won the fight instead of losing it.

The fellow who'd led them here was a genial, middle-aged man named Robert E. Kent. He'd not only been in Washington, but insisted he'd been a regular at the coffee-house. Nellie didn't remember him; she did her best not to remember men. But he remembered her and her doings altogether too well. "What ever happened to that pretty daughter of yours?" he asked. "You know, the one who was going to marry our officer."

"After the war, she married a U.S. veteran," Nellie said coolly. "Their son, Armstrong, will be twelve this year. They've got a little girl, too." Kent was named for a C.S. hero, her own grandson for one from the USA. She used Custer's middle name as a weapon against the genial Confederate.

Another man from south of the border said, "I saw a girl, maybe thirteen or fourteen, in here a while ago. Is that your daughter's daughter?"

"No," Nellie said. "Clara's *my* daughter. I married Hal Jacobs, who ran the cobbler's shop across the street. He died last year." She looked down at the counter as she said that. It still hurt. A young Italian fellow had bought the cobbler's shop. He looked to be running it into the ground. Watching that hurt, too.

"Sorry to hear it, ma'am," Robert E. Kent said politely. "He fixed my boots once or twice. He was right good at it."

He gave Hal the sort of impersonal praise he might have given a whore who'd pleased him. Maybe thinking of that particular comparison was what made Nellie ask, "Do you know what else he was good at?"

"No, ma'am," Kent said. Confederates *were* polite, sometimes even when Nellie wished they weren't.

She said, "He was good at finding out what you people were up to, that's what. He was a big part of the U.S. spy ring in Washington during the war—and so was I."

That proud announcement spawned a considerable silence from the Confederates. At last, Kent said, "Well, ma'am, you helped your country, same as we helped ours."

He was, to Nellie's way of thinking, too polite by half. She'd hoped to get a bigger rise out of him and his countrymen. What good was gloating if the people you were gloating over refused to acknowledge you were gloating? To cover her feelings, she poured herself a cup of coffee.

One of the other Confederates said, "Ma'am, your country won the last war, no doubt about it. That's one for you, and we can't deny it." His compatriots nodded. He went on, "You've got to remember, though, when Jake Featherston gets to be president of the CSA in a couple of weeks . . . well, tomorrow belongs to us."

Almost all of the Confederates, Robert E. Kent among them, nodded again. One man looked sour as vinegar. Nellie would have bet he hadn't voted for Featherston. The others, though . . . The others looked as if they were talking not about ordinary earthly politics, but about the Second Coming. Kent said, "He'll put us back on our feet, by heaven."

"And he'll put the niggers in their place," another man said. "If there's anything worse than an uppity nigger, I don't know what it is."

Still more nods. Nellie had the feeling she ought to listen carefully, then take what she heard across the street to Hal, just as she had during the Great War. But Hal wasn't there, never would be there any more. The Italian fellow who had the place now would think she was crazy if she burst in and started babbling about what the Confederates were saying in her coffeehouse. He might be right, too.

"You Yankees waited a long time before you finally whipped us," Robert E. Kent said. "You needed to build yourselves up, and you went and did it. Now we're the ones who have to do that."

"Why?" Nellie asked, as if she were still a spy trying to ease important information out of people and not simply a proprietor trying to get her customers to hang around and order more coffee and sandwiches. "What difference does it make? If we're going to stay at peace, who cares whether one side's built up and the other one isn't?"

Kent said, "Ma'am, I think there's two different kinds

of peace. One's where this fellow's strong and that fellow's weak, and when *this* fellow says, 'This is how we'll do things,' they do 'em that way, on account of *that* fellow's got no choice. That there is what we've got nowadays. The other kind is where both fellows are strong, and neither one pushes the other one around because he knows he'll get pushed back. That there is what Jake Featherston is after, and I reckon he can get it."

They all nodded again. Even the one who plainly hated Featherston and the Freedom Party nodded. Nellie wondered what that meant. Probably that he might not have much use for the president-elect of the CSA, but that he despised the United States still more. Nellie had never known any Confederates who had much use for the USA, not even when they came up here to do business.

"Let me have another cup of coffee, ma'am, if you'd be so kind," Robert E. Kent said, "and if you could get me a ham and cheese sandwich to go with it, that'd be good." Three or four of the others ordered more food and drink, too. They had plenty of money—U.S. coins and greenbacks, not the scrip and brown Confederate banknotes they'd used during the war. Nellie was glad to take it from them, and they tipped generously. All in all, it was the best business day she'd had in weeks.

Even so, she wasn't sorry when they finally left. She wanted Confederates to know their country was weaker than the United States. She wanted them afraid of the USA. When she found them cocky instead, she worried. She'd seen the CSA bombard Washington in the Second Mexican War as a child and in the Great War when she was in the prime of life. She didn't want it to happen again when she was an old woman.

Edna came by at closing time, as she often did now that Hal was dead. "How are you, Ma?" she said. "How was your day?"

"Fair. No, better than fair," Nellie answered, and told her about the Confederates.

Her daughter sighed, probably thinking of Confederate Lieutenant Nicholas H. Kincaid and what might have been. *Another world,* Nellie thought, and laughed a little. If she was going to think of other worlds, why not one where the United States won the War of Secession and there never was any such thing as the Confederate States of America? With Virginia still in the USA, Washington wouldn't have been shelled. It would still be the capital in more than name, too. And who would ever have heard of Jake Featherston? Nobody at all, odds were.

"What are you smiling about?" Edna asked. When Nellie told her, she said, "Wouldn't that be something? You ought to write a book, Ma, like that gal from Boston did—you know, the one who shot the Confederate submersible skipper. You could get rich."

"Maybe I could get rich—if I could write a book. And if pigs could fly, we'd all carry umbrellas," Nellie said.

"You wouldn't have to do it all by your lonesome," Edna said. "That other gal had somebody else, a real writer, do most of the work. You could split the money and still have plenty."

"I haven't got enough ideas for a book," Nellie said firmly. "The only other thing I'm sure of is that we wouldn't have had this stinking collapse if we were one big country, and anybody can see that. It's not worth writing about."

"I suppose." Her daughter didn't want to give up the idea. "I know what you could do, then. Write about your life story. That's exciting enough for anybody, what with the spy stuff during the war and the ... the other stuff back before the turn of the century."

By *the other stuff*, of course, she meant Nellie's time in the demimonde. "I don't want to write about that!" Nellie exclaimed. "I wish to heaven none of that ever happened. I spent all these years getting to be halfway respectable, and now you want me to write about . . . that? Forget it, Edna."

"Too bad," Edna said. "It'd be exciting. People'd pay money to read about it."

"It wasn't exciting. It was just nasty." Nellie couldn't imagine how anybody who'd actually been in the demi-monde could think it was exciting. She hadn't come close to warming up to a man more than a couple of times in all the years since she'd left. And how much would people want to read about *that*?

She expected Edna to go on harping about it. Her daughter refused to believe how foul it had been, how foul it had made Nellie feel after a man put gold on the dresser, got undressed, and then did what he wanted—and had her do what he wanted. But Edna didn't nag, or not exactly. Instead, she said, "You remember that Bill Reach, the fellow who Hal said ran the whole spy show?"

The fellow who made me out to be a whore in front of a coffeehouse full of Confederates, Nellie thought grimly. "I remember him," she said, and not another word.

"I wonder what ever happened to him," Edna said. "If you know that, you could stick it in the book, too."

I know what happened to him. I killed the drunken son of a bitch when he tried to rape me. She almost told that to Edna, just to shut her daughter up. How much could it matter now that Hal, who'd idolized Bill Reach for no good reason Nellie could ever see, was dead? But she swallowed the words. She'd promised herself she would take that secret to her own grave, and she aimed to do it.

"If I had to guess," she said after an all but imperceptible pause, "he got killed when the United States bombarded Washington before they took it back. An awful lot of people did."

"No story in that, though," Edna said.

"I don't care," Nellie said. "That's what I'm telling you. There *was* no story."

"Ma, you're a stick."

"Well, maybe I am. I don't care. I worked too hard for too long to tell a bunch of fancy lies now that I'm on the edge of turning into an old lady. What would Hal say if I did?"

"Tell the truth, then," Edna said.

"I have been telling the truth," Nellie lied.

Her daughter threw her hands in the air. "What am I supposed to do with you, Ma?" she said, half affectionate, half exasperated.

"You could just leave me alone. That's what you told me and told me, and then I finally went and did it." Nellie

686

came as close as she ever had to admitting she might have meddled too much and too long in Edna's life. "Now maybe I get to tell you the same thing."

"Why do you think I'll listen any better than you ever did?" Edna asked. Nellie had no answer to that, and not having one frightened her. A child outgrew a parent's efforts at care, but a parent wasn't likely to outgrow a child's.

March 4, 1934, was a Sunday. Church bells rang in Richmond. Some of them summoned the faithful to worship. Others, later, proclaimed the imminent inauguration of a new president of the Confederate States of America.

At Freedom Party headquarters, Lulu fussed over Jake Featherston, fiddling with his collar as if she were his mother and not his secretary. He put up with it for as long as he could. Then he stepped away and said, "I'm fine. You don't need to fool with it any more."

"I want it to be perfect," Lulu said, for about the fifth time that day.

"Come two o'clock this afternoon, the chief justice of the Supreme Court is going to swear me in," Jake said. "Nothing in the world—in the *world*, you hear me?—could be more perfect than that." He shook his head. "No, I take it back. Burton Mitchel, that . . . so-and-so"—he was careful of his language around Lulu—"has to stand there and watch me do it and shake my hand before I do it— and afterwards, too. That's even better than all the rest."

"I mean, I want you to *look* perfect." His longtime secretary had said that five or six times, too.

"I'm fine," Jake answered. And he was fine, too, as far as he was concerned. No clawhammer coat for him, no white tie and stiff-fronted white shirt, no top hat. The butternut outfit he had on was almost identical to what he'd worn during the three years of the war. He even had three stripes on his sleeve, though these were also of butternut, not artilleryman's red. The War Department had left him a sergeant, had it? Well, all right. Now the whole country had a sergeant heading it up. He wasn't ashamed of that. He was proud of it, by God.

Willy Knight strode into his office. The vice president–elect also wore a quasi-uniform, one a good deal fancier than Featherston's. Some European armies had a grade one step up from general. They usually called it field marshal. Had the CSA used that rank, the men who held it would have worn uniforms a hell of a lot like Knight's.

"Whoa!" Jake shielded his eyes against the glare of gold lace and brass buttons. "You look like the nigger doorman at an expensive hotel, you know that?"

"Go to hell," Knight said, and grinned enormously. He stuck out his hand. Featherston shook it. No furtive trial of strength today. For once, they both had all the strength they needed. "We did it!" Knight's grin got wider. Jake hadn't thought it could. "We really did it!"

"You bet we did," Featherston said, "and this is only the first day. What you got to remember, Willy, is that getting here's just the start. Now we've got to do what we set out to do with the Party—"

"And with the Redemption League," Willy Knight added.

"Yeah—and with the Redemption League," Jake allowed generously. "We're in. We keep going right on forward." That was where he had the edge on Knight and everybody else. He kept thinking about the next step, the step to take after the one he was on now. He looked at his pocket watch. "Where's Ferd?"

"I'm here." Ferdinand Koenig stepped into the office. He wore a plain business suit that seemed all the plainer next to the uniforms.

"Then let's get on with it," Jake said.

They went downstairs. Two identical limousines waited there. Featherston and Koenig got into one, Knight into the other. As they drove the short distance to Capitol Square, they traded places in the motorcade several times. An assassin wouldn't have an easy time figuring out who was who, not in the welter of escorting motorcycle cops and government bodyguards and Freedom Party bodyguards—who regarded one another like two rival packs of mean dogs. That instant rivalry suited Jake fine; the more everybody stayed on his toes, the better.

At his request, the platform where he would take the oath of office had gone up on the south side of the square, near the statue of Albert Sidney Johnston and near Bank Street. Congressmen and Freedom Party bigwigs and other important people packed the platform and nearby wooden bleachers. Party stalwarts in white and butternut and Party guards in not-quite-Confederate uniform kept order in the square. Featherston hadn't requested that. He'd insisted on it.

Among the important people on the platform and in the bleachers were a dozen or so men, most of them elderly, in perfectly genuine Confederate uniforms: the highest-ranking officers from the War Department. Jake chuckled as the limousine stopped near the platform. He pointed to the generals. "I hope those bastards are shaking in their boots."

"If they're not, they're even dumber than you always said they were," Koenig answered.

Jake got out of the motorcar. The stalwarts sprang to attention. The guards presented arms. "Freedom!" they shouted as one. Congressmen who weren't Party members—a minority, now—flinched. They'd never watched Party rallies up close. They'd stayed away on purpose, in fact. They had some lessons to learn, and Featherston looked forward to teaching them.

His boots thumped on the wooden stairs as he ascended to the platform, Knight and Koenig trailing him. Waiting to greet him were President Burton Mitchel and Chief Justice James McReynolds. Mitchel extended his hand. Featherston shook it. They'd had the four months since the election to get to know each other as Mitchel prepared to leave office and Featherston to take over. Getting to know each other hadn't meant getting to like each other; on the contrary.

"May I give you one last bit of advice?" Mitchel asked formally.

With newsreel cameras turning, Jake couldn't say no without looking ungracious. "Go ahead," he answered.

Mitchel looked weary unto death. He'd become president after a Freedom Party man murdered his predecessor.

Now he handed his office over to the head of the Freedom Party. *And how do you feel about that, Burton old boy?* Jake wondered. The outgoing president said, "I believe, Mr. President-elect, that you and your followers will find it has been easier to criticize than it will be to govern."

"Do you?" Jake said. Mitchel nodded stiffly. For the benefit of the cameras, Featherston smiled and clapped him on the back. "Well, Mr. President," he went on quietly, smiling still, "I reckon some folks'll believe anything, won't they?"

He stood well away from the microphones. He didn't think they would pick that up. If by some mischance they did . . . Well, that bit of film could always end up on the cutting-room floor. Burton Mitchel winced as if bayoneted. Willy Knight laughed.

Chief Justice McReynolds was a handsome man with a long face, a jutting chin, and white hair that had receded just enough to give him a high, high forehead. He had frowned when Jake delivered his cut, but made himself rally. "Are you ready to take the oath, Mr. President-elect?"

Jake looked out over Capitol Square, over the crowd filling it (after the local Mitcheltown had been bulldozed to let a crowd fill it), and the throngs of people on the sidewalks of Bank Street. "Am I ready?" he echoed. "You bet I'm ready."

"Very well, sir. Raise your right hand and repeat after me. . . ."

"I, Jake Featherston . . . do solemnly swear . . . that I will faithfully execute . . . the office of President . . . of the Confederate States, and will . . . to the best of my ability . . . preserve, protect, and defend . . . the Constitution thereof."

There. It was official. When Featherston lowered his hand, he did so as president of the Confederate States of America. Chief Justice McReynolds shook hands with him. "Congratulations, Mr. President," he said. "I am the first one to have the privilege of addressing you thus."

"You sure are," Jake agreed. He even smiled. *But if you think I've forgotten your Supreme Court let this Mitchel bastard run again in 1927, you'd better think again. I haven't forgotten one goddamn thing, not me. And I know how to settle your hash when the time comes. You may not think so, you fancy-pants son of a bitch, but I do.*

The time hadn't come yet, though. For now, he had to show everybody what a smooth fellow he was. He shook hands with Burton Mitchel again, then stepped to the microphones. "Friends, I'm Jake Featherston, and I'm *still* here to tell you the truth."

"Feather*ston*! Feather*ston*! Feather*ston*!" The rhythmic chant from the crowd in Capitol Square and across the street rolled over him. He drank it in. He liked his whiskey as well as the next fellow, but the intoxication of a crowd took him higher and didn't leave him with a headache the next morning.

He held up his hands. Not everybody who was cheering had Party discipline; the noise took longer than it should have to die away. When it did, he went on, "The truth is, we're going to make this country work again, and we're going to make it work better than it ever did before. We're going to dam the big rivers and keep them from flooding the way they did seven years ago. We're going to use the electricity from the dams for people's houses—the houses of honest people, working people, white people—and for factories that will make all the things we need, and make 'em cheap enough so folks can afford 'em."

More applause. Again, it faded more slowly than it might have. Once it did, he continued, "And it's high time we show the USA that the Confederate States are a country that works, too. It's time we stand up straight again and look the United States in the eye and say, 'We've got a few things to talk about.' We haven't been able to do that yet, even though the war's been over for a long time. We haven't been strong enough. We will be, though."

This time, the rapturous shouts from the crowd were the older Party cry: "Freedom! Freedom! Freedom!" They were deeper and fiercer than those that had gone before, with more men and fewer women joining in. Even the generals in their gleaming uniforms looked intrigued. *What's this, boys? You think I'll put my toys in your hands?*

691

In the quiet of his own mind, Jake laughed out loud. *You're fools, too. You're worse fools than that stinking McReynolds, only you're too dumb to know it.*

He kept the inaugural address short and sweet. That was best for the wireless web and for the crowd there in person. After the speech came the parade, for the crowd and for the newsreel cameras. An Army marching band began it. Behind the band strutted a crack regiment in dress uniform.

And behind that one regiment came formation after formation of Freedom Party men from every state in the CSA: stalwarts in white shirts and butternut trousers, smaller units of guards in those almost military uniforms. Some bands of stalwarts simply marched. Some carried truncheons. Like the Army regiment, the Freedom Party guards carried rifles, and they plainly knew what to do with them.

"Look at the generals," Jake whispered to Ferdinand Koenig. "Now they're seeing what we've got, and and they want it for themselves."

Scorn filled Koenig's voice: "Not likely."

"Oh, hell no," Featherston said. "All that there"—he pointed to the parade—"that's ours. *We* made it, and *we'll* use it. I know just how, too. By God, you'd better believe I do."